THE GREAT NOVELS AND SHORT STORIES OF

Somerset Maugham

W. Somerset Maugham
Introduction by Nick Lyons

Skyhorse Publishing
A Herman Graf Book

Skyhorse Publishing books may be purchased in bulk at special discounts for sales promotion, corporate gifts, fund-raising, or educational purposes. Special editions can also be created to specifications. For details, contact the Special Sales Department, Skyhorse Publishing, 307 West 36th Street, 11th Floor, New York, NY 10018 or info@skyhorsepublishing.com.

Skyhorse® and Skyhorse Publishing® are registered trademarks of Skyhorse Publishing, Inc.®, a Delaware corporation.

Visit our website at www.skyhorsepublishing.com.

10 9 8 7 6 5 4 3 2

Library of Congress Cataloging-in-Publication Data is available on file.

ISBN: 978-1-62873-784-4

Printed in the United States of America

Contents

Introduction

<hr />

W. SOMERSET MAUGHAM (1874–1965) is one of the most readable of all twentieth-century authors. Late in life he viewed himself as sitting "in the very first row of the second-raters," and his work, for all of its immense popularity, has been scored by many literary critics for blandness of style, flatness of characters. But he is much more than that. Popular he was and surely remains, and the simple reason for this has always been the genuine interest and pleasure a huge number of readers have always taken in his work. This ample collection of three early novels and five short stories (his favorite form) is bound to be widely enjoyed.

   Liza of Lambeth, his first novel and probably the one drawn most closely from his life experiences as a medical student and fledgling doctor, is still striking in its cold-eyed depiction of poverty, illness, and despair. It was greatly popular when it was first published in Maugham's early twenties and remains stark and blistering today in its realistic depiction of the tense, tragic life of a young woman in a London slum. *The Magician*, with its nasty depictions of contemporary writers like Hugh Walpole, a close friend of Maugham's, followed ten years later, in 1908, and by the time *Of Human Bondage* was published in 1915, Maugham was one of the most popular writers in the world. He had become a playwright, too, and at that time had four plays on the London stage simultaneously—though his plays, except in clever cinematic adaptations like *Being Julia*, are rarely seen today.

   The Moon and Sixpence, roughly taking the bolder frame of Paul Gauguin's life, remakes the French artist as a contemporary Englishman and uses Maugham himself as narrator—a role he felt comfortable using and makes excellent use of again in *The Razor's Edge* and other works. Charles Strickland, a British stockbroker, abandons his wife and children, and goes to Paris where he plunges fully into the life of a painter. He is monotonic in his commitment to his painting, indifferent to the lives of others, often brutally cold and cruel. And then, like Gauguin, he leaves the West and takes up life in Tahiti. Throughout, Maugham's voice is patient and curious and nonjudgmental, and he serves as foil for the moral, social, and even aesthetic extravagances of Strickland's life, making them more believable.

The Trembling of a Leaf, Maugham's second collection of stories, grew from his travels and fascination with the South Sea islands. It was published in 1921, two years after *The Moon and Sixpence*, which looked so closely at Strickland's removal from Western life to a totally different life on a Pacific island. You'll find five of the best stories from that collection here: "Red," "Mackintosh," "The Pool," about a couple that return from the islands to live in Scotland; "The Fall of Edward Barnard," who has left life in the West for a new life with the islanders; and the enduring classic, "Rain." All contain contrasts of the presumably simpler life of the islanders with life in the West.

"Rain" depicts a particularly tenacious missionary who passionately proselytizes Sadie Thompson, trying to redeem her from her life as a prostitute. Sadie's position is simple. "Why couldn't you leave me be?" she asks. "I wasn't doin' you no harm." But he persists and persists and finally his efforts lead to raw tragedy. The story has been a perennial favorite—first as the story, then as a popular play by Maugham, and then as a spate of successful movies with Gloria Swanson, Joan Crawford, and even Rita Hayworth. It presumably earned its author, in all its forms, more than a million dollars.

This collection offers an excellent sampling of Maugham's work, with its clear prose, shrewd plotting, and story-telling strengths. They reveal most of his seminal themes—his dislike of hypocrisy, hokum of all kinds, cruelty, and the many ironies of life, and also some of his own cold cynicism. Chiefly, though, these novels and stories are wonderfully readable, memorable, and enormously engaging.

—Nick Lyons

SHORT STORIES

Mackintosh

⊗⊗⊗

HE SPLASHED ABOUT for a few minutes in the sea; it was too shallow to swim in and for fear of sharks he could not go out of his depth; then he got out and went into the bath-house for a shower. The coldness of the fresh water was grateful after the heavy stickiness of the salt Pacific, so warm, though it was only just after seven, that to bathe in it did not brace you but rather increased your languor; and when he had dried himself, slipping into a bath-gown, he called out to the Chinese cook that he would be ready for breakfast in five minutes. He walked barefoot across the patch of coarse grass which Walker, the administrator, proudly thought was a lawn, to his own quarters and dressed. This did not take long, for he put on nothing but a shirt and a pair of duck trousers and then went over to his chief's house on the other side of the compound. The two men had their meals together, but the Chinese cook told him that Walker had set out on horseback at five and would not be back for another hour.

Mackintosh had slept badly and he looked with distaste at the paw-paw and the eggs and bacon which were set before him. The mosquitoes had been maddening that night; they flew about the net under which he slept in such numbers that their humming, pitiless and menacing, had the effect of a note, infinitely drawn out, played on a distant organ, and whenever he dozed off he awoke with a start in the belief that one had found its way inside his curtains. It was so hot that he lay naked. He turned from side to side. And gradually the dull roar of the breakers on the reef, so unceasing and so regular that generally you did not hear it, grew distinct on his consciousness, its rhythm hammered on his tired nerves and he held himself with clenched hands in the effort to bear it. The thought that nothing could stop that sound, for it would continue to all eternity, was almost impossible to bear, and, as though his strength were a match for the ruthless forces of nature, he had an insane impulse to do some violent thing. He felt he must cling to his self-control or he would go mad. And now, looking out of the window at the lagoon and the strip of foam which marked the reef, he shuddered with hatred of the brilliant scene. The cloudless sky was like an inverted bowl that hemmed it in. He lit his pipe and turned over the pile of Auckland papers that had come over from Apia a few days before. The newest of them was three weeks old. They gave an impression of incredible dullness.

Then he went into the office. It was a large, bare room with two desks in it and a bench along one side. A number of natives were seated on this, and a couple of women. They gossiped while they waited for the administrator, and when Mackintosh came in they greeted him.

"Talofa li."

He returned their greeting and sat down at his desk. He began to write, working on a report which the governor of Samoa had been clamouring for and which Walker, with his usual dilatoriness, had neglected to prepare. Mackintosh as he made his notes reflected vindictively that Walker was late with his report because he was so illiterate that he had an invincible distaste for anything to do with pens and paper; and now when it was at last ready, concise and neatly official, he would accept his subordinate's work without a word of appreciation, with a sneer rather or a gibe, and send it on to his own superior as though it were his own composition. He could not have written a word of it. Mackintosh thought with rage that if his chief pencilled in some insertion it would be childish in expression and faulty in language. If he remonstrated or sought to put his meaning into an intelligible phrase, Walker would fly into a passion and cry:

"What the hell do I care about grammar? That's what I want to say and that's how I want to say it."

At last Walker came in. The natives surrounded him as he entered, trying to get his immediate attention, but he turned on them roughly and told them to sit down and hold their tongues. He threatened that if they were not quiet he would have them all turned out and see none of them that day. He nodded to Mackintosh.

"Hulloa, Mac; up at last? I don't know how you can waste the best part of the day in bed. You ought to have been up before dawn like me. Lazy beggar."

He threw himself heavily into his chair and wiped his face with a large bandana.

"By heaven, I've got a thirst."

He turned to the policeman who stood at the door, a picturesque figure in his white jacket and lava-lava, the loin cloth of the Samoan, and told him to bring kava. The kava bowl stood on the floor in the corner of the room, and the policeman filled a half coconut shell and brought it to Walker. He poured a few drops on the ground, murmured the customary words to the company, and drank with relish. Then he told the policeman to serve the waiting natives, and the shell was handed to each one in order of birth or importance and emptied with the same ceremonies.

Then he set about the day's work. He was a little man, considerably less than of middle height, and enormously stout; he had a large, fleshy face, clean-shaven, with the cheeks hanging on each side in great dew-laps, and three vast chins; his small features were all dissolved in fat; and, but for a crescent of white hair at the back of his head, he was completely bald. He reminded you of Mr Pickwick. He was grotesque, a figure of fun, and yet, strangely enough, not without dignity. His blue eyes, behind large gold-rimmed spectacles, were shrewd and vivacious, and there was a great deal of determination in his face. He was sixty, but his native vitality triumphed over advancing years. Notwithstanding his corpulence his movements were quick, and he walked with a heavy, resolute tread as though he sought to impress his weight upon the earth. He spoke in a loud, gruff voice.

It was two years now since Mackintosh had been appointed Walker's assistant. Walker, who had been for a quarter of a century administrator of Talua, one of the larger islands in the Samoan group, was a man known in person or by report through the length and breadth of the South Seas; and it was with lively curiosity that Mackintosh looked forward to his first meeting with him. For one reason or anoth-

er he stayed a couple of weeks at Apia before he took up his post and
both at Chaplin's hotel and at the English club he heard innumerable
stories about the administrator. He thought now with irony of his
interest in them. Since then he had heard them a hundred times from
Walker himself. Walker knew that he was a character, and, proud of
his reputation, deliberately acted up to it. He was jealous of his "legend" and anxious that you should know the exact details of any of the
celebrated stories that were told of him. He was ludicrously angry with
anyone who had told them to the stranger incorrectly.

There was a rough cordiality about Walker which Mackintosh
at first found not unattractive, and Walker, glad to have a listener to
whom all he said was fresh, gave of his best. He was good-humoured,
hearty, and considerate. To Mackintosh, who had lived the sheltered
life of a government official in London till at the age of thirty-four an
attack of pneumonia, leaving him with the threat of tuberculosis, had
forced him to seek a post in the Pacific, Walker's existence seemed
extraordinarily romantic. The adventure with which he started on his
conquest of circumstance was typical of the man. He ran away to sea
when he was fifteen and for over a year was employed in shovelling
coal on a collier. He was an undersized boy and both men and mates
were kind to him, but the captain for some reason conceived a savage
dislike of him. He used the lad cruelly so that, beaten and kicked, he
often could not sleep for the pain that racked his limbs. He loathed
the captain with all his soul. Then he was given a tip for some race and
managed to borrow twenty-five pounds from a friend he had picked
up in Belfast. He put it on the horse, an outsider, at long odds. He had
no means of repaying the money if he lost, but it never occurred to
him that he could lose. He felt himself in luck. The horse won and he
found himself with something over a thousand pounds in hard cash.
Now his chance had come. He found out who was the best solicitor
in the town—the collier lay then somewhere on the Irish coast—went
to him, and, telling him that he heard the ship was for sale, asked him
to arrange the purchase for him. The solicitor was amused at his small
client, he was only sixteen and did not look so old, and, moved perhaps
by sympathy, promised not only to arrange the matter for him but to
see that he made a good bargain. After a little while Walker found

himself the owner of the ship. He went back to her and had what he described as the most glorious moment of his life when he gave the skipper notice and told him that he must get off his ship in half an hour. He made the mate captain and sailed on the collier for another nine months, at the end of which he sold her at a profit.

He came out to the islands at the age of twenty-six as a planter. He was one of the few white men settled in Talua at the time of the German occupation and had then already some influence with the natives. The Germans made him administrator, a position which he occupied for twenty years, and when the island was seized by the British he was confirmed in his post. He ruled the island despotically, but with complete success. The prestige of this success was another reason for the interest that Mackintosh took in him.

But the two men were not made to get on. Mackintosh was an ugly man, with ungainly gestures, a tall thin fellow, with a narrow chest and bowed shoulders. He had sallow, sunken cheeks, and his eyes were large and sombre. He was a great reader, and when his books arrived and were unpacked Walker came over to his quarters and looked at them. Then he turned to Mackintosh with a coarse laugh.

"What in Hell have you brought all this muck for?" he asked.

Mackintosh flushed darkly.

"I'm sorry you think it muck. I brought my books because I want to read them."

"When you said you'd got a lot of books coming I thought there'd be something for me to read. Haven't you got any detective stories?"

"Detective stories don't interest me."

"You're a damned fool then."

"I'm content that you should think so."

Every mail brought Walker a mass of periodical literature, papers from New Zealand and magazines from America, and it exasperated him that Mackintosh showed his contempt for these ephemeral publications. He had no patience with the books that absorbed Mackintosh's leisure and thought it only a pose that he read Gibbon's Decline and Fall or Burton's Anatomy of Melancholy. And since he had never learned to put any restraint on his tongue, he expressed his opinion of his assistant freely. Mackintosh began to see the real man, and under the boisterous good-humour he discerned a vulgar cunning which was hateful; he was vain and domineering, and it was strange that he had notwithstanding a shyness which made him dislike people who were not quite of his kidney. He judged others, naïvely, by their language, and if it was free from the oaths and the obscenity which made up the greater part of his own conversation, he looked upon them with suspicion. In the evening the two men played piquet. He played badly but vaingloriously, crowing over his opponent when he won and losing his temper when he lost. On rare occasions a couple of planters or traders would drive over to play bridge, and then Walker showed himself in what Mackintosh considered a characteristic light. He played regardless of his partner, calling up in his desire to play the hand, and argued interminably, beating down opposition by the loudness of his voice. He constantly revoked, and when he did so said with an ingratiating whine: "Oh, you wouldn't count it against an old man who can hardly see." Did he know that his opponents thought it as well to keep on the right side of him and hesitated to insist on the rigour of the game? Mackintosh watched him with an icy contempt. When the game was over, while they smoked their pipes and drank whisky, they would begin telling stories. Walker told with gusto the story of his marriage. He had got so drunk at the wedding feast that the bride had fled and he had never seen her since. He had had numberless adventures, commonplace and sordid, with the women of the island and he described them with a pride in his own prowess which was an offence to Mackintosh's fastidious ears. He was a gross, sensual old man. He thought Mackintosh a poor fellow because he would not share his promiscuous amours and remained sober when the company was drunk.

He despised him also for the orderliness with which he did his official work. Mackintosh liked to do everything just so. His desk was always tidy, his papers were always neatly docketed, he could put his hand on any document that was needed, and he had at his fingers' ends all the regulations that were required for the business of their administration.

"Fudge, fudge," said Walker. "I've run this island for twenty years without red tape, and I don't want it now."

"Does it make it any easier for you that when you want a letter you have to hunt half an hour for it?" answered Mackintosh.

"You're nothing but a damned official. But you're not a bad fellow; when you've been out here a year or two you'll be all right. What's wrong about you is that you won't drink. You wouldn't be a bad sort if you got soused once a week."

The curious thing was that Walker remained perfectly unconscious of the dislike for him which every month increased in the breast of his subordinate. Although he laughed at him, as he grew accustomed to him, he began almost to like him. He had a certain tolerance for the peculiarities of others, and he accepted Mackintosh as a queer fish. Perhaps he liked him, unconsciously, because he could chaff him. His humour consisted of coarse banter and he wanted a butt. Mackintosh's exactness, his morality, his sobriety, were all fruitful subjects; his Scot's name gave an opportunity for the usual jokes about Scotland; he enjoyed himself thoroughly when two or three men were there and he could make them all laugh at the expense of Mackintosh. He would say ridiculous things about him to the natives, and Mackintosh, his knowledge of Samoan still imperfect, would see their unrestrained mirth when Walker had made an obscene reference to him. He smiled good-humouredly.

"I'll say this for you, Mac," Walker would say in his gruff loud voice, "you can take a joke."

"Was it a joke?" smiled Mackintosh. "I didn't know."

"Scots wha hae!" shouted Walker, with a bellow of laughter. "There's only one way to make a Scotchman see a joke and that's by a surgical operation."

Walker little knew that there was nothing Mackintosh could stand less than chaff. He would wake in the night, the breathless night of the rainy season, and brood sullenly over the gibe that Walker had uttered carelessly days before. It rankled. His heart swelled with rage, and he pictured to himself ways in which he might get even with the bully. He had tried answering him, but Walker had a gift of repartee, coarse and obvious, which gave him an advantage. The dullness of his intellect made him impervious to a delicate shaft. His self-satisfaction made it impossible to wound him. His loud voice, his bellow of laughter, were weapons against which Mackintosh had nothing to counter, and he learned that the wisest thing was never to betray his irritation. He learned to control himself. But his hatred grew till it was a monomania. He watched Walker with an insane vigilance. He fed his own self-esteem by every instance of meanness on Walker's part, by every exhibition of childish vanity, of cunning and of vulgarity. Walker ate greedily, noisily, filthily, and Mackintosh watched him with satisfaction. He took note of the foolish things he said and of his mistakes in grammar. He knew that Walker held him in small esteem, and he found a bitter satisfaction in his chief's opinion of him; it increased his own contempt for the narrow, complacent old man. And it gave him a singular pleasure to know that Walker was entirely unconscious of the hatred he felt for him. He was a fool who liked popularity, and he blandly fancied that everyone admired him. Once Mackintosh had overheard Walker speaking of him.

"He'll be all right when I've licked him into shape," he said. "He's a good dog and he loves his master."

Mackintosh silently, without a movement of his long, sallow face, laughed long and heartily.

But his hatred was not blind; on the contrary, it was peculiarly clear-sighted, and he judged Walker's capabilities with precision. He ruled his small kingdom with efficiency. He was just and honest. With opportunities to make money he was a poorer man than when he was first appointed to his post, and his only support for his old age was the pension which he expected when at last he retired from official life. His pride was that with an assistant and a half-caste clerk he was able to administer the island more competently than Upolu, the island of which Apia is the chief town, was administered with its army of functionaries. He had a few native policemen to sustain his authority, but he made no use of them. He governed by bluff and his Irish humour.

"They insisted on building a jail for me," he said. "What the devil do I want a jail for? I'm not going to put the natives in prison. If they do wrong I know how to deal with them."

One of his quarrels with the higher authorities at Apia was that he claimed entire jurisdiction over the natives of his island. Whatever their crimes he would not give them up to courts competent to deal with them, and several times an angry correspondence had passed between him and the Governor at Upolu. For he looked upon the natives as his children. And that was the amazing thing about this coarse, vulgar, selfish man; he loved the island on which he had lived so long with passion, and he had for the natives a strange rough tenderness which was quite wonderful.

He loved to ride about the island on his old grey mare and he was never tired of its beauty. Sauntering along the grassy roads among the coconut trees he would stop every now and then to admire the loveliness of the scene. Now and then he would come upon a native village and stop while the head man brought him a bowl of kava. He would look at the little group of bell-shaped huts with their high thatched roofs, like beehives, and a smile would spread over his fat face. His eyes rested happily on the spreading green of the bread-fruit trees.

"By George, it's like the garden of Eden."

Sometimes his rides took him along the coast and through the trees he had a glimpse of the wide sea, empty, with never a sail to disturb the loneliness; sometimes he climbed a hill so that a great stretch of country, with little villages nestling among the tall trees, was spread out before him like the kingdom of the world, and he would sit there for an hour in an ecstasy of delight. But he had no words to express his feelings and to relieve them would utter an obscene jest; it was as though his emotion was so violent that he needed vulgarity to break the tension.

Mackintosh observed this sentiment with an icy disdain. Walker had always been a heavy drinker, he was proud of his capacity to see men half his age under the table when he spent a night in Apia, and he had the sentimentality of the toper. He could cry over the stories he read in his magazines and yet would refuse a loan to some trader in difficulties whom he had known for twenty years. He was close with his money. Once Mackintosh said to him:

"No one could accuse you of giving money away."

He took it as a compliment. His enthusiasm for nature was but the drivelling sensibility of the drunkard. Nor had Mackintosh any sympathy for his chief's feelings towards the natives. He loved them because they were in his power, as a selfish man loves his dog, and his mentality was on a level with theirs. Their humour was obscene and he was never at a loss for the lewd remark. He understood them and they understood him. He was proud of his influence over them. He looked upon them as his children and he mixed himself in all their affairs. But he was very jealous of his authority; if he ruled them with a rod of iron, brooking no contradiction, he would not suffer any of the white men on the island to take advantage of them. He watched the missionaries suspiciously and, if they did anything of which he disapproved, was able to make life so unendurable to them that if he could not get them removed they were glad to go of their own accord. His power over the natives was so great that on his word they would refuse labour and food to their pastor. On the other hand he showed the traders no favour. He took care that they should not cheat the natives; he saw that they got a fair reward for their work and their copra and that the traders made no extravagant profit on the wares they sold them. He was merciless to a bargain that he thought unfair. Sometimes the traders would complain at Apia that they did not get fair opportunities. They suffered for it. Walker then hesitated at no calumny, at no outrageous lie, to get even with them, and they found that if they wanted not only to live at peace, but to exist at all, they had to accept the situation on his own terms. More than once the store of a trader obnoxious to him had been burned down, and there was only the appositeness of the event to show that the administrator had instigated it. Once a Swedish half-caste, ruined by the burning, had gone to him and roundly accused him of arson. Walker laughed in his face.

"You dirty dog. Your mother was a native and you try to cheat the natives. If your rotten old store is burned down it's a judgment of Providence; that's what it is, a judgment of Providence. Get out."

And as the man was hustled out by two native policemen the administrator laughed fatly.

"A judgment of Providence."

And now Mackintosh watched him enter upon the day's work. He began with the sick, for Walker added doctoring to his other activities, and he had a small room behind the office full of drugs. An elderly man came forward, a man with a crop of curly grey hair, in a blue lava-lava, elaborately tatooed, with the skin of his body wrinkled like a wine-skin.

"What have you come for?" Walker asked him abruptly.

In a whining voice the man said that he could not eat without vomiting and that he had pains here and pains there.

"Go to the missionaries," said Walker. "You know that I only cure children."

"I have been to the missionaries and they do me no good."

"Then go home and prepare yourself to die. Have you lived so long and still want to go on living? You're a fool."

The man broke into querulous expostulation, but Walker, pointing to a woman with a sick child in her arms, told her to bring it to his desk. He asked her questions and looked at the child.

"I will give you medicine," he said. He turned to the half-caste clerk. "Go into the dispensary and bring me some calomel pills."

He made the child swallow one there and then and gave another to the mother.

"Take the child away and keep it warm. To-morrow it will be dead or better."

He leaned back in his chair and lit his pipe.

"Wonderful stuff, calomel. I've saved more lives with it than all the hospital doctors at Apia put together."

Walker was very proud of his skill, and with the dogmatism of ignorance had no patience with the members of the medical profession.

"The sort of case I like," he said, "is the one that all the doctors have given up as hopeless. When the doctors have said they can't cure you, I say to them, 'come to me.' Did I ever tell you about the fellow who had a cancer?"

"Frequently," said Mackintosh.

"I got him right in three months."

"You've never told me about the people you haven't cured."

He finished this part of the work and went on to the rest. It was a queer medley. There was a woman who could not get on with her husband and a man who complained that his wife had run away from him.

"Lucky dog," said Walker. "Most men wish their wives would too."

There was a long complicated quarrel about the ownership of a few yards of land. There was a dispute about the sharing out of a catch of fish. There was a complaint against a white trader because he had given short measure. Walker listened attentively to every case, made up his mind quickly, and gave his decision. Then he would listen to nothing more; if the complainant went on he was hustled out of the office by a policeman. Mackintosh listened to it all with sullen irritation. On the whole, perhaps, it might be admitted that rough justice was done, but it exasperated the assistant that his chief trusted his instinct rather than the evidence. He would not listen to reason. He browbeat the witnesses and when they did not see what he wished them to called them thieves and liars.

He left to the last a group of men who were sitting in the corner of the room. He had deliberately ignored them. The party consisted of an old chief, a tall, dignified man with short, white hair, in a new lava-lava, bearing a huge fly wisp as a badge of office, his son, and half a dozen of the important men of the village. Walker had had a feud with them and had beaten them. As was characteristic of him he meant now to rub in his victory, and because he had them down to profit by their helplessness. The facts were peculiar. Walker had a passion for building roads. When he had come to Talua there were but a few tracks here and there, but in course of time he had cut roads through the country, joining the villages together, and it was to this that a great part of the island's prosperity was due. Whereas in the old days it had been impossible to get the produce of the land, copra chiefly, down to the coast where it could be put on schooners or motor launches and so taken to Apia, now transport was easy and simple. His ambition was to make a road right round the island and a great part of it was already built.

"In two years I shall have done it, and then I can die or they can fire me, I don't care."

His roads were the joy of his heart and he made excursions constantly to see that they were kept in order. They were simple enough, wide tracks, grass covered, cut through the scrub or through the plantations; but trees had to be rooted out, rocks dug up or blasted, and here and there levelling had been necessary. He was proud that he had surmounted by his own skill such difficulties as they presented. He rejoiced in his disposition of them so that they were not only convenient, but showed off the beauties of the island which his soul loved. When he spoke of his roads he was almost a poet. They meandered through those lovely scenes, and Walker had taken care that here and there they should run in a straight line, giving you a green vista through the tall trees, and here and there should turn and curve so that the heart was rested by the diversity. It was amazing that this coarse and sensual man should exercise so subtle an ingenuity to get the effects which his fancy suggested to him. He had used in making his roads all the fantastic skill of a Japanese gardener. He received a grant from headquarters for the work but took a curious pride in using but a small part of it, and the year before had spent only a hundred pounds of the thousand assigned to him.

"What do they want money for?" he boomed. "They'll only spend it on all kinds of muck they don't want; what the missionaries leave them, that is to say."

For no particular reason, except perhaps pride in the economy of his administration and the desire to contrast his efficiency with the wasteful methods of the authorities at Apia, he got the natives to do the work he wanted for wages that were almost nominal. It was owing to this that he had lately had difficulty with the village whose chief men now were come to see him. The chief's son had been in Upolu for a year and on coming back had told his people of the large sums that were paid at Apia for the public works. In long, idle talks he had inflamed their hearts with the desire for gain. He held out to them visions of vast wealth and they thought of the whisky they could buy—it was dear, since there was a law that it must not be sold to natives, and so it cost them double what the white man had to pay for it—they thought of the great sandal-wood boxes in which they kept their treasures, and the scented soap and potted salmon, the luxuries for which the Kanaka will sell his soul; so that when the administrator sent for them and told them he wanted a road made from their village to a certain point along the coast and offered them twenty pounds, they asked him a hundred. The chief's son was called Manuma. He was a tall, handsome fellow, copper-coloured, with his fuzzy hair dyed red with lime, a wreath of red berries round his neck, and behind his ear a flower like a scarlet flame against his brown face. The upper part of his body was naked, but to show that he was no longer a savage, since he had lived in Apia, he wore a pair of dungarees instead of a lava-lava. He told them that if they held together the administrator would be obliged to accept their terms. His heart was set on building the road and when he found they would not work for less he would give them what they asked. But they must not move; whatever he said they must not abate their claim; they had asked a hundred and that they must keep to. When they mentioned the figure, Walker burst into a shout of his long, deep-voiced laughter. He told them not to make fools of themselves, but to set about the work at once. Because he was in a good humour that day he promised to give them a feast when the road was finished. But when he found that no attempt was made to start work, he went to the village and asked the men what silly game they were playing. Manuma had coached them well. They were quite calm, they did not attempt to argue—and argument is a passion with the Kanaka—they merely shrugged their shoulders: they would do it for a hundred pounds, and if he would not give them that they would do no work. He could please himself. They did not care. Then Walker flew into a passion. He was ugly then. His short fat neck swelled ominously, his red face grew purple, he foamed at the mouth. He set upon the natives with invective. He knew well how to wound and how to humiliate. He was terrifying. The older men grew pale and uneasy. They hesitated. If it had not been for Manuma, with his knowledge of the great world, and their dread of his ridicule, they would have yielded. It was Manuma who answered Walker.

"Pay us a hundred pounds and we will work."

Walker, shaking his fist at him, called him every name he could think of. He riddled him with scorn. Manuma sat still and smiled. There may have been more bravado than confidence in his smile, but he had to make a good show before the others. He repeated his words.

"Pay us a hundred pounds and we will work."

They thought that Walker would spring on him. It would not have been the first time that he had thrashed a native with his own hands; they knew his strength, and though Walker was three times the age of the young man and six inches shorter they did not doubt that he was more than a match for Manuma. No one had ever thought of resisting the savage onslaught of the administrator. But Walker said nothing. He chuckled.

"I am not going to waste my time with a pack of fools," he said. "Talk it over again. You know what I have offered. If you do not start in a week, take care."

He turned round and walked out of the chief's hut. He untied his old mare and it was typical of the relations between him and the natives that one of the elder men hung on to the off stirrup while Walker from a convenient boulder hoisted himself heavily into the saddle.

That same night when Walker according to his habit was strolling along the road that ran past his house, he heard something whizz past him and with a thud strike a tree. Something had been thrown at him. He ducked instinctively. With a shout, "Who's that"? he ran towards the place from which the missile had come and he heard the sound of a man escaping through the bush. He knew it was hopeless to pursue in the darkness, and besides he was soon out of breath, so he stopped and made his way back to the road. He looked about for what had been thrown, but could find nothing. It was quite dark. He went quickly back to the house and called Mackintosh and the Chinese boy.

"One of those devils has thrown something at me. Come along and let's find out what it was."

He told the boy to bring a lantern and the three of them made their way back to the place. They hunted about the ground, but could not find what they sought. Suddenly the boy gave a guttural cry. They turned to look. He held up the lantern, and there, sinister in the light that cut the surrounding darkness, was a long knife sticking into the trunk of a coconut tree. It had been thrown with such force that it required quite an effort to pull it out.

"By George, if he hadn't missed me I'd have been in a nice state."

Walker handled the knife. It was one of those knives, made in imitation of the sailor knives brought to the islands a hundred years before by the first white men, used to divide the coconuts in two so that the copra might be dried. It was a murderous weapon, and the blade, twelve inches long, was very sharp. Walker chuckled softly.

"The devil, the impudent devil."

He had no doubt it was Manuma who had flung the knife. He had escaped death by three inches. He was not angry. On the contrary, he was in high spirits; the adventure exhilarated him, and when they got back to the house, calling for drinks, he rubbed his hands gleefully.

"I'll make them pay for this!"

His little eyes twinkled. He blew himself out like a turkey-cock, and for the second time within half an hour insisted on telling Mackintosh every detail of the affair. Then he asked him to play piquet, and while they played he boasted of his intentions. Mackintosh listened with tightened lips.

"But why should you grind them down like this?" he asked. "Twenty pounds is precious little for the work you want them to do."

"They ought to be precious thankful I give them anything."

"Hang it all, it's not your own money. The government allots you a reasonable sum. They won't complain if you spend it."

"They're a bunch of fools at Apia."

Mackintosh saw that Walker's motive was merely vanity. He shrugged his shoulders.

"It won't do you much good to score off the fellows at Apia at the cost of your life."

"Bless you, they wouldn't hurt me, these people. They couldn't do without me. They worship me. Manuma is a fool. He only threw that knife to frighten me."

The next day Walker rode over again to the village. It was called Matautu. He did not get off his horse. When he reached the chief's house he saw that the men were sitting round the floor in a circle, talking, and he guessed they were discussing again the question of the road. The Samoan huts are formed in this way: Trunks of slender trees are placed in a circle at intervals of perhaps five or six feet; a tall tree is set in the middle and from this downwards slopes the thatched roof. Venetian blinds of coconut leaves can be pulled down at night or when it is raining. Ordinarily the hut is open all round so that the breeze can blow through freely. Walker rode to the edge of the hut and called out to the chief.

"Oh, there, Tangatu, your son left his knife in a tree last night. I have brought it back to you."

He flung it down on the ground in the midst of the circle, and with a low burst of laughter ambled off.

On Monday he went out to see if they had started work. There was no sign of it. He rode through the village. The inhabitants were about their ordinary avocations. Some were weaving mats of the pandanus leaf, one old man was busy with a kava bowl, the children were playing, the women went about their household chores. Walker, a smile on his lips, came to the chief's house.

"Talofa-li," said the chief.

"Talofa," answered Walker.

Manuma was making a net. He sat with a cigarette between his lips and looked up at Walker with a smile of triumph.

"You have decided that you will not make the road?"

The chief answered.

"Not unless you pay us one hundred pounds."

"You will regret it." He turned to Manuma. "And you, my lad, I shouldn't wonder if your back was very sore before you're much older."

He rode away chuckling. He left the natives vaguely uneasy. They feared the fat sinful old man, and neither the missionaries' abuse of him nor the scorn which Manuma had learnt in Apia made them forget that he had a devilish cunning and that no man had ever braved him without in the long run suffering for it. They found out within twenty-four hours what scheme he had devised. It was characteristic. For next morning a great band of men, women, and children came into the village and the chief men said that they had made a bargain with Walker to build the road. He had offered them twenty pounds and they had accepted. Now the cunning lay in this, that the Polynesians have rules of hospitality which have all the force of laws; an etiquette of absolute rigidity made it necessary for the people of the village not only to give lodging to the strangers, but to provide them with food and drink as long as they wished to stay. The inhabitants of Matautu were outwitted. Every morning the workers went out in a joyous band, cut down trees, blasted rocks, levelled here and there and then in the evening tramped back again, and ate and drank, ate heartily, danced, sang hymns, and enjoyed life. For them it was a picnic. But soon their hosts began to wear long faces; the strangers had enormous appetites, and the plantains and the bread-fruit vanished before their rapacity; the alligator-pear trees, whose fruit sent to Apia might sell for good money, were stripped bare. Ruin stared them in the face. And then they found that the strangers were working very slowly. Had they received a hint from Walker that they might take their time? At this rate by the time the road was finished there would not be a scrap of food in the village. And worse than this, they were a laughing-stock; when one or other of them went to some distant hamlet on an errand he found that the story had got there before him, and he was met with derisive laughter. There is nothing the Kanaka can endure less than ridicule. It was not long before much angry talk passed among the sufferers. Manuma was no longer a hero; he had to put up with a good deal of plain speaking, and one day what Walker had suggested came to pass: a heated argument turned into a quarrel and half a dozen of the young men set upon the chief's son and gave him such a beating that for a week he lay bruised and sore on the pandanus mats. He turned from side to side and could find no ease. Every day or two the administrator rode over on his old mare and watched the progress of the road. He was not a man to resist the temptation of taunting the fallen foe, and he missed no opportunity to rub into the shamed inhabitants of Matautu the bitterness of their humiliation. He broke their spirit. And one morning, putting their pride in their pockets, a figure of speech, since pockets they had not, they all set out with the strangers and started working on the road. It was urgent to get it done quickly if they wanted to save any food at all, and the whole village joined in. But they worked silently, with rage and mortification in their hearts, and even the children toiled in silence. The women wept as they carried away bundles of brushwood. When Walker saw them he laughed so much that he almost rolled out of his saddle. The news spread quickly and tickled the people of the island to death. This was the greatest joke of all, the crowning triumph of that cunning old white man whom no Kanaka had ever been able to circumvent; and they came from distant villages, with their wives and children, to look at the foolish folk who had refused twenty pounds to make the road and now were forced to work for nothing. But the harder they worked the more easily went the guests. Why should they hurry, when they were getting good food for nothing and the longer they took about the job the better the joke became? At last the wretched villagers could stand it no longer, and they were come this morning to beg the administrator to send the strangers back to their own homes. If he would do this they promised to finish the road themselves for nothing. For him it was a victory complete and unqualified. They were humbled. A look of arrogant complacence spread over his large, naked face, and he seemed to swell in his chair like a great bullfrog. There was something sinister in his appearance, so that Mackintosh shivered with disgust. Then in his booming tones he began to speak.

"Is it for my good that I make the road? What benefit do you think I get out of it? It is for you, so that you can walk in comfort and carry your copra in comfort. I offered to pay you for your work, though it was for your own sake the work was done. I offered to pay you generously. Now you must pay. I will send the people of Manua back to their homes if you will finish the road and pay the twenty pounds that I have to pay them."

There was an outcry. They sought to reason with him. They told him they had not the money. But to everything they said he replied with brutal gibes. Then the clock struck.

"Dinner time," he said. "Turn them all out."

He raised himself heavily from his chair and walked out of the room. When Mackintosh followed him he found him already seated at table, a napkin tied round his neck, holding his knife and fork in readiness for the meal the Chinese cook was about to bring. He was in high spirits.

"I did 'em down fine," he said, as Mackintosh sat down. "I shan't have much trouble with the roads after this."

"I suppose you were joking," said Mackintosh icily.

"What do you mean by that?"

"You're not really going to make them pay twenty pounds?"

"You bet your life I am."

"I'm not sure you've got any right to."

"Ain't you? I guess I've got the right to do any damned thing I like on this island."

"I think you've bullied them quite enough."

Walker laughed fatly. He did not care what Mackintosh thought.

"When I want your opinion I'll ask for it." Mackintosh grew very white. He knew by bitter experience that he could do nothing but keep silence, and the violent effort at self-control made him sick and faint. He could not eat the food that was before him and with disgust he watched Walker shovel meat into his vast mouth. He was a dirty feeder, and to sit at table with him needed a strong stomach. Mackintosh shuddered. A tremendous desire seized him to humiliate that gross and cruel man; he would give anything in the world to see him in the dust, suffering as much as he had made others suffer. He had never loathed the bully with such loathing as now.

The day wore on. Mackintosh tried to sleep after dinner, but the passion in his heart prevented him; he tried to read, but the letters swam before his eyes. The sun beat down pitilessly, and he longed for rain; but he knew that rain would bring no coolness; it would only make it hotter and more steamy. He was a native of Aberdeen and his heart yearned suddenly for the icy winds that whistled through the granite streets of that city. Here he was a prisoner, imprisoned not only by that placid sea, but by his hatred for that horrible old man. He pressed his hands to his aching head. He would like to kill him. But he pulled himself together. He must do something to distract his mind, and since he could not read he thought he would set his private papers in order. It was a job which he had long meant to do and which he had constantly put off. He unlocked the drawer of his desk and took out a handful of letters. He caught sight of his revolver. An impulse, no sooner realised than set aside, to put a bullet through his head and so escape from the intolerable bondage of life flashed through his mind. He noticed that in the damp air the revolver was slightly rusted, and he got an oil rag and began to clean it. It was while he was thus occupied that he grew aware of someone slinking round the door. He looked up and called:

"Who is there?"

There was a moment's pause, then Manuma showed himself.

"What do you want?"

The chief's son stood for a moment, sullen and silent, and when he spoke it was with a strangled voice.

"We can't pay twenty pounds. We haven't the money."

"What am I to do?" said Mackintosh. "You heard what Mr Walker said."

Manuma began to plead, half in Samoan and half in English. It was a sing-song whine, with the quavering intonations of a beggar, and it filled Mackintosh with disgust. It outraged him that the man should let himself be so crushed. He was a pitiful object.

"I can do nothing," said Mackintosh irritably. "You know that Mr Walker is master here."

Manuma was silent again. He still stood in the doorway.

"I am sick," he said at last. "Give me some medicine."

"What is the matter with you?"

"I do not know. I am sick. I have pains in my body."

"Don't stand there," said Mackintosh sharply. "Come in and let me look at you."

Manuma entered the little room and stood before the desk.

"I have pains here and here."

He put his hands to his loins and his face assumed an expression of pain. Suddenly Mackintosh grew conscious that the boy's eyes were resting on the revolver which he had laid on the desk when Manuma appeared in the doorway. There was a silence between the two which to Mackintosh was endless. He seemed to read the thoughts which were in the Kanaka's mind. His heart beat violently. And then he felt as though something possessed him so that he acted under the compulsion of a foreign will. Himself did not make the movements of his body, but a power that was strange to him. His throat was suddenly dry, and he put his hand to it mechanically in order to help his speech. He was impelled to avoid Manuma's eyes.

"Just wait here," he said, his voice sounded as though someone had seized him by the windpipe, "and I'll fetch you something from the dispensary."

He got up. Was it his fancy that he staggered a little? Manuma stood silently, and though he kept his eyes averted, Mackintosh knew that he was looking dully out of the door. It was this other person that possessed him that drove him out of the room, but it was himself that took a handful of muddled papers and threw them on the revolver in order to hide it from view. He went to the dispensary. He got a pill and poured out some blue draught into a small bottle, and then came out into the compound. He did not want to go back into his own bungalow, so he called to Manuma.

"Come here."

He gave him the drugs and instructions how to take them. He did not know what it was that made it impossible for him to look at the Kanaka. While he was speaking to him he kept his eyes on his shoulder. Manuma took the medicine and slunk out of the gate.

Mackintosh went into the dining-room and turned over once more the old newspapers. But he could not read them. The house was very still. Walker was upstairs in his room asleep, the Chinese cook was busy in the kitchen, the two policemen were out fishing. The silence that seemed to brood over the house was unearthly, and there hammered in Mackintosh's head the question whether the revolver still lay where he had placed it. He could not bring himself to look. The uncertainty was horrible, but the certainty would be more horrible still. He sweated. At last he could stand the silence no longer, and he made up his mind to go down the road to the trader's, a man named Jervis, who had a store about a mile away. He was a half-caste, but even that amount of white blood made him possible to talk to. He wanted to get away from his bungalow, with the desk littered with untidy papers, and underneath them something, or nothing. He walked along the road. As he passed the fine hut of a chief a greeting was called out to him. Then he came to the store. Behind the counter sat the trader's daughter, a swarthy broad-featured girl in a pink blouse and a white drill skirt. Jervis hoped he would marry her. He had money, and he had told Mackintosh that his daughter's husband would be well-to-do. She flushed a little when she saw Mackintosh.

"Father's just unpacking some cases that have come in this morning. I'll tell him you're here."

He sat down and the girl went out behind the shop. In a moment her mother waddled in, a huge old woman, a chiefess, who owned much land in her own right; and gave him her hand. Her monstrous obesity was an offence, but she managed to convey an impression of dignity. She was cordial without obsequiousness; affable, but conscious of her station.

"You're quite a stranger, Mr Mackintosh. Teresa was saying only this morning: 'Why, we never see Mr Mackintosh now.'"

He shuddered a little as he thought of himself as that old native's son-in-law. It was notorious that she ruled her husband, notwithstanding his white blood, with a firm hand. Hers was the authority and hers the business head. She might be no more than Mrs Jervis to the white people, but her father had been a chief of the blood royal, and his father and his father's father had ruled as kings. The trader came in, small beside his imposing wife, a dark man with a black beard going grey, in ducks, with handsome eyes and flashing teeth. He was very British, and his conversation was slangy, but you felt he spoke English as a foreign tongue; with his family he used the language of his native mother. He was a servile man, cringing and obsequious.

"Ah, Mr Mackintosh, this is a joyful surprise. Get the whisky, Teresa; Mr Mackintosh will have a gargle with us."

He gave all the latest news of Apia, watching his guest's eyes the while, so that he might know the welcome thing to say.

"And how is Walker? We've not seen him just lately. Mrs Jervis is going to send him a sucking-pig one day this week."

"I saw him riding home this morning," said Teresa.

"Here's how," said Jervis, holding up his whisky.

Mackintosh drank. The two women sat and looked at him, Mrs Jervis in her black Mother Hubbard, placid and haughty, and Teresa, anxious to smile whenever she caught his eye, while the trader gossiped insufferably.

"They were saying in Apia it was about time Walker retired. He ain't so young as he was. Things have changed since he first come to the islands and he ain't changed with them."

"He'll go too far," said the old chiefess. "The natives aren't satisfied."

"That was a good joke about the road,"laughed the trader. "When I told them about it in Apia they fair split their sides with laughing. Good old Walker."

Mackintosh looked at him savagely. What did he mean by talking of him in that fashion? To a half-caste trader he was Mr Walker. It was on his tongue to utter a harsh rebuke for the impertinence. He did not know what held him back.

"When he goes I hope you'll take his place, Mr Mackintosh," said Jervis. "We all like you on the island. You understand the natives. They're educated now, they must be treated differently to the old days. It wants an educated man to be administrator now. Walker was only a trader same as I am."

Teresa's eyes glistened.

"When the time comes if there's anything anyone can do here, you bet your bottom dollar we'll do it. I'd get all the chiefs to go over to Apia and make a petition."

Mackintosh felt horribly sick. It had not struck him that if anything happened to Walker it might be he who would succeed him. It was true that no one in his official position knew the island so well. He got up suddenly and scarcely taking his leave walked back to the compound. And now he went straight to his room. He took a quick look at his desk. He rummaged among the papers.

The revolver was not there.

His heart thumped violently against his ribs. He looked for the revolver everywhere. He hunted in the chairs and in the drawers. He looked desperately, and all the time he knew he would not find it. Suddenly he heard Walker's gruff, hearty voice.

"What the devil are you up to, Mac?"

He started. Walker was standing in the doorway and instinctively he turned round to hide what lay upon his desk.

"Tidying up?" quizzed Walker. "I've told 'em to put the grey in the trap. I'm going down to Tafoni to bathe. You'd better come along."

"All right," said Mackintosh.

So long as he was with Walker nothing could happen. The place they were bound for was about three miles away, and there was a fresh-water pool, separated by a thin barrier of rock from the sea, which the administrator had blasted out for the natives to bathe in. He had done this at spots round the island, wherever there was a spring; and the fresh water, compared with the sticky warmth of the sea, was cool and invigorating. They drove along the silent grassy road, splashing now and then through fords, where the sea had forced its way in, past a couple of native villages, the bell-shaped huts spaced out roomily and the white chapel in the middle, and at the third village they got out of the trap, tied up the horse, and walked down to the pool. They were accompanied by four or five girls and a dozen children. Soon they were all splashing about, shouting and laughing, while Walker, in a lava-lava, swam to and fro like an unwieldy porpoise. He made lewd jokes with the girls, and they amused themselves by diving under him and wriggling away when he tried to catch them. When he was tired he lay down on a rock, while the girls and children surrounded him; it was a happy family; and the old man, huge, with his crescent of white hair and his shining bald crown, looked like some old sea god. Once Mackintosh caught a queer soft look in his eyes.

"They're dear children," he said. "They look upon me as their father."

And then without a pause he turned to one of the girls and made an obscene remark which sent them all into fits of laughter. Mackintosh started to dress. With his thin legs and thin arms he made a grotesque figure, a sinister Don Quixote, and Walker began to make coarse jokes about him. They were acknowledged with little smothered laughs. Mackintosh struggled with his shirt. He knew he looked absurd, but he hated being laughed at. He stood silent and glowering.

"If you want to get back in time for dinner you ought to come soon."

"You're not a bad fellow, Mac. Only you're a fool. When you're doing one thing you always want to do another. That's not the way to live."

But all the same he raised himself slowly to his feet and began to put on his clothes. They sauntered back to the village, drank a bowl of kava with the chief, and then, after a joyful farewell from all the lazy villagers, drove home.

After dinner, according to his habit, Walker, lighting his cigar, prepared to go for a stroll. Mackintosh was suddenly seized with fear.

"Don't you think it's rather unwise to go out at night by yourself just now?"

Walker stared at him with his round blue eyes.

"What the devil do you mean?"

"Remember the knife the other night. You've got those fellows' backs up."

"Pooh! They wouldn't dare."

"Someone dared before."

"That was only a bluff. They wouldn't hurt me. They look upon me as a father. They know that whatever I do is for their own good."

Mackintosh watched him with contempt in his heart. The man's self-complacency outraged him, and yet something, he knew not what, made him insist.

"Remember what happened this morning. It wouldn't hurt you to stay at home just to-night. I'll play piquet with you."

"I'll play piquet with you when I come back. The Kanaka isn't born yet who can make me alter my plans."

"You'd better let me come with you."

"You stay where you are."

Mackintosh shrugged his shoulders. He had given the man full warning. If he did not heed it that was his own lookout. Walker put on his hat and went out. Mackintosh began to read; but then he thought of something; perhaps it would be as well to have his own whereabouts quite clear. He crossed over to the kitchen and, inventing some pretext, talked for a few minutes with the cook. Then he got out the gramophone and put a record on it, but while it ground out its melancholy tune, some comic song of a London music-hall, his ear was strained for a sound away there in the night. At his elbow the record reeled out its loudness, the words were raucous, but notwithstanding he seemed to be surrounded by an unearthly silence. He heard the dull roar of the breakers against the reef. He heard the breeze sigh, far up, in the leaves of the coconut trees. How long would it be? It was awful.

He heard a hoarse laugh.

"Wonders will never cease. It's not often you play yourself a tune, Mac."

Walker stood at the window, red-faced, bluff and jovial.

"Well, you see I'm alive and kicking. What were you playing for?" Walker came in.

"Nerves a bit dicky, eh? Playing a tune to keep your pecker up?"

"I was playing your requiem."

"What the devil's that?"

"'Alf o' bitter an' a pint of stout.'"

"A rattling good song too. I don't mind how often I hear it. Now I'm ready to take your money off you at piquet."

They played and Walker bullied his way to victory, bluffing his opponent, chaffing him, jeering at his mistakes, up to every dodge, browbeating him, exulting. Presently Mackintosh recovered his coolness, and standing outside himself, as it were, he was able to take a detached pleasure in watching the overbearing old man and in his own cold reserve. Somewhere Manuma sat quietly and awaited his opportunity.

Walker won game after game and pocketed his winnings at the end of the evening in high good humour.

"You'll have to grow a little bit older before you stand much chance against me, Mac. The fact is I have a natural gift for cards."

"I don't know that there's much gift about it when I happen to deal you fourteen aces."

"Good cards come to good players," retorted Walker. "I'd have won if I'd had your hands."

He went on to tell long stories of the various occasions on which he had played cards with notorious sharpers and to their consternation had taken all their money from them. He boasted. He praised himself. And Mackintosh listened with absorption. He wanted now to feed his hatred; and everything Walker said, every gesture, made him more detestable. At last Walker got up.

"Well, I'm going to turn in," he said with a loud yawn. "I've got a long day to-morrow."

"What are you going to do?"

"I'm driving over to the other side of the island. I'll start at five, but I don't expect I shall get back to dinner till late."

They generally dined at seven.

"We'd better make it half past seven then."

"I guess it would be as well."

Mackintosh watched him knock the ashes out of his pipe. His vitality was rude and exuberant. It was strange to think that death hung over him. A faint smile flickered in Mackintosh's cold, gloomy eyes.

"Would you like me to come with you?"

"What in God's name should I want that for? I'm using the mare and she'll have enough to do to carry me; she don't want to drag you over thirty miles of road."

"Perhaps you don't quite realise what the feeling is at Matautu. I think it would be safer if I came with you."

Walker burst into contemptuous laughter.

"You'd be a fine lot of use in a scrap. I'm not a great hand at getting the wind up."

Now the smile passed from Mackintosh's eyes to his lips. It distorted them painfully.

"Quem deus vult perdere prius dementat."

"What the hell is that?" said Walker.

"Latin," answered Mackintosh as he went out.

And now he chuckled. His mood had changed. He had done all he could and the matter was in the hands of fate. He slept more soundly than he had done for weeks. When he awoke next morning he went out. After a good night he found a pleasant exhilaration in the freshness of the early air. The sea was a more vivid blue, the sky more brilliant, than on most days, the trade wind was fresh, and there was a ripple on the lagoon as the breeze brushed over it like velvet brushed the wrong way. He felt himself stronger and younger. He entered upon the day's work with zest. After luncheon he slept again, and as evening drew on he had the bay saddled and sauntered through the bush. He seemed to see it all with new eyes. He felt more normal. The extraordinary thing was that he was able to put Walker out of his mind altogether. So far as he was concerned he might never have existed.

He returned late, hot after his ride, and bathed again. Then he sat on the verandah, smoking his pipe, and looked at the day declining over the lagoon. In the sunset the lagoon, rosy and purple and green, was very beautiful. He felt at peace with the world and with himself. When the cook came out to say that dinner was ready and to ask whether he should wait, Mackintosh smiled at him with friendly eyes. He looked at his watch.

"It's half-past seven. Better not wait. One can't tell when the boss'll be back."

The boy nodded, and in a moment Mackintosh saw him carry across the yard a bowl of steaming soup. He got up lazily, went into the dining-room, and ate his dinner. Had it happened? The uncertainty was amusing and Mackintosh chuckled in the silence. The food did not seem so monotonous as usual, and even though there was Hamburger steak, the cook's invariable dish when his poor invention failed him, it tasted by some miracle succulent and spiced. After dinner he strolled over lazily to his bungalow to get a book. He liked the intense stillness, and now that the night had fallen the stars were blazing in the sky. He shouted for a lamp and in a moment the Chink pattered over on his bare feet, piercing the darkness with a ray of light. He put the lamp on the desk and noiselessly slipped out of the room. Mackintosh stood rooted to the floor, for there, half hidden by untidy papers, was his revolver. His heart throbbed painfully, and he broke into a sweat. It was done then.

He took up the revolver with a shaking hand. Four of the chambers were empty. He paused a moment and looked suspiciously out into the night, but there was no one there. He quickly slipped four cartridges into the empty chambers and locked the revolver in his drawer.

He sat down to wait.

An hour passed, a second hour passed. There was nothing. He sat at his desk as though he were writing, but he neither wrote nor read. He merely listened. He strained his ears for a sound travelling from a far distance. At last he heard hesitating footsteps and knew it was the Chinese cook.

"Ah-Sung," he called.

The boy came to the door.

"Boss velly late," he said. "Dinner no good."

Mackintosh stared at him, wondering whether he knew what had happened, and whether, when he knew, he would realise on what terms he and Walker had been. He went about his work, sleek, silent, and smiling, and who could tell his thoughts?

"I expect he's had dinner on the way, but you must keep the soup hot at all events."

The words were hardly out of his mouth when the silence was suddenly broken into by a confusion, cries, and a rapid patter of naked feet. A number of natives ran into the compound, men and women and children; they crowded round Mackintosh and they all talked at once. They were unintelligible. They were excited and frightened and some of them were crying. Mackintosh pushed his way through them and went to the gateway. Though he had scarcely understood what they said he knew quite well what had happened. And as he reached the gate the dog-cart arrived. The old mare was being led by a tall Kanaka, and in the dog-cart crouched two men, trying to hold Walker up. A little crowd of natives surrounded it.

The mare was led into the yard and the natives surged in after it. Mackintosh shouted to them to stand back and the two policemen, sprang suddenly from God knows where, pushed them violently aside. By now he had managed to understand that some lads who had been fishing, on their way back to their village had come across the cart on the home side of the ford. The mare was nuzzling about the herbage and in the darkness they could just see the great white bulk of the old man sunk between the seat and the dashboard. At first they thought he was drunk and they peered in, grinning, but then they heard him groan, and guessed that something was amiss. They ran to the village and called for help. It was when they returned, accompanied by half a hundred people, that they discovered Walker had been shot.

With a sudden thrill of horror Mackintosh asked himself whether he was already dead. The first thing at all events was to get him out of the cart, and that, owing to Walker's corpulence, was a difficult job.

It took four strong men to lift him. They jolted him and he uttered a dull groan. He was still alive. At last they carried him into the house, up the stairs, and placed him on his bed. Then Mackintosh was able to see him, for in the yard, lit only by half a dozen hurricane lamps, everything had been obscured. Walker's white ducks were stained with blood, and the men who had carried him wiped their hands, red and sticky, on their lava-lavas. Mackintosh held up the lamp. He had not expected the old man to be so pale. His eyes were closed. He was breathing still, his pulse could be just felt, but it was obvious that he was dying. Mackintosh had not bargained for the shock of horror that convulsed him. He saw that the native clerk was there, and in a voice hoarse with fear told him to go into the dispensary and get what was necessary for a hypodermic injection. One of the policemen had brought up the whisky, and Mackintosh forced a little into the old man's mouth. The room was crowded with natives. They sat about the floor, speechless now and terrified, and every now and then one wailed aloud. It was very hot, but Mackintosh felt cold, his hands and his feet were like ice, and he had to make a violent effort not to tremble in all his limbs. He did not know what to do. He did not know if Walker was bleeding still, and if he was, how he could stop the bleeding.

The clerk brought the hypodermic needle.

"You give it to him," said Mackintosh. "You're more used to that sort of thing than I am."

His head ached horribly. It felt as though all sorts of little savage things were beating inside it, trying to get out. They watched for the effect of the injection. Presently Walker opened his eyes slowly. He did not seem to know where he was.

"Keep quiet," said Mackintosh. "You're at home. You're quite safe."

Walker's lips outlined a shadowy smile.

"They've got me," he whispered.

"I'll get Jervis to send his motor-boat to Apia at once. We'll get a doctor out by to-morrow afternoon."

There was a long pause before the old man answered,

"I shall be dead by then."

A ghastly expression passed over Mackintosh's pale face. He

forced himself to laugh.

"What rot! You keep quiet and you'll be as right as rain."

"Give me a drink," said Walker. "A stiff one."

With shaking hand Mackintosh poured out whisky and water, half and half, and held the glass while Walker drank greedily. It seemed to restore him. He gave a long sigh and a little colour came into his great fleshy face. Mackintosh felt extraordinarily helpless. He stood and stared at the old man.

"If you'll tell me what to do I'll do it," he said.

"There's nothing to do. Just leave me alone. I'm done for."

He looked dreadfully pitiful as he lay on the great bed, a huge, bloated, old man; but so wan, so weak, it was heart-rending. As he rested, his mind seemed to grow clearer.

"You were right, Mac," he said presently. "You warned me."

"I wish to God I'd come with you."

"You're a good chap, Mac, only you don't drink."

There was another long silence, and it was clear that Walker was sinking. There was an internal hæmorrhage and even Mackintosh in his ignorance could not fail to see that his chief had but an hour or two to live. He stood by the side of the bed stock still. For half an hour perhaps Walker lay with his eyes closed, then he opened them.

"They'll give you my job," he said, slowly. "Last time I was in Apia I told them you were all right. Finish my road. I want to think that'll be done. All round the island."

"I don't want your job. You'll get all right."

Walker shook his head wearily.

"I've had my day. Treat them fairly, that's the great thing. They're children. You must always remember that. You must be firm with them, but you must be kind. And you must be just. I've never made a bob out of them. I haven't saved a hundred pounds in twenty years. The road's the great thing. Get the road finished."

Something very like a sob was wrung from Mackintosh.

"You're a good fellow, Mac. I always liked you."

He closed his eyes, and Mackintosh thought that he would never open them again. His mouth was so dry that he had to get himself something to drink. The Chinese cook silently put a chair for him.

He sat down by the side of the bed and waited. He did not know how long a time passed. The night was endless. Suddenly one of the men sitting there broke into uncontrollable sobbing, loudly, like a child, and Mackintosh grew aware that the room was crowded by this time with natives. They sat all over the floor on their haunches, men and women, staring at the bed.

"What are all these people doing here?" said Mackintosh. "They've got no right. Turn them out, turn them out, all of them."

His words seemed to rouse Walker, for he opened his eyes once more, and now they were all misty. He wanted to speak, but he was so weak that Mackintosh had to strain his ears to catch what he said.

"Let them stay. They're my children. They ought to be here."

Mackintosh turned to the natives.

"Stay where you are. He wants you. But be silent."

A faint smile came over the old man's white face.

"Come nearer," he said.

Mackintosh bent over him. His eyes were closed and the words he said were like a wind sighing through the fronds of the coconut trees.

"Give me another drink. I've got something to say."

This time Mackintosh gave him his whisky neat. Walker collected his strength in a final effort of will.

"Don't make a fuss about this. In 'ninety-five when there were troubles white men were killed, and the fleet came and shelled the villages. A lot of people were killed who'd had nothing to do with it. They're damned fools at Apia. If they make a fuss they'll only punish the wrong people. I don't want anyone punished."

He paused for a while to rest.

"You must say it was an accident. No one's to blame. Promise me that."

"I'll do anything you like," whispered Mackintosh.

"Good chap. One of the best. They're children. I'm their father. A father don't let his children get into trouble if he can help it."

A ghost of a chuckle came out of his throat. It was astonishingly weird and ghastly.

"You're a religious chap, Mac. What's that about forgiving them? You know."

For a while Mackintosh did not answer. His lips trembled.

"Forgive them, for they know not what they do?"

"That's right. Forgive them. I've loved them, you know, always loved them."

He sighed. His lips faintly moved, and now Mackintosh had to put his ears quite close to them in order to hear.

"Hold my hand," he said.

Mackintosh gave a gasp. His heart seemed wrenched. He took the old man's hand, so cold and weak, a coarse, rough hand, and held it in his own. And thus he sat until he nearly started out of his seat, for the silence was suddenly broken by a long rattle. It was terrible and unearthly. Walker was dead. Then the natives broke out with loud cries. The tears ran down their faces, and they beat their breasts.

Mackintosh disengaged his hand from the dead man's, and staggering like one drunk with sleep he went out of the room. He went to the locked drawer in his writing-desk and took out the revolver. He walked down to the sea and walked into the lagoon; he waded out cautiously, so that he should not trip against a coral rock, till the water came to his arm-pits. Then he put a bullet through his head.

An hour later half a dozen slim brown sharks were splashing and struggling at the spot where he fell.

Rain

~~~~~

IT WAS NEARLY bed-time and when they awoke next morning land would be in sight. Dr Macphail lit his pipe and, leaning over the rail, searched the heavens for the Southern Cross. After two years at the front and a wound that had taken longer to heal than it should, he was glad to settle down quietly at Apia for twelve months at least, and he felt already better for the journey. Since some of the passengers were leaving the ship next day at Pago-Pago they had had a little dance that evening and in his ears hammered still the harsh notes of the mechanical piano. But the deck was quiet at last. A little way off he saw his wife in a long chair talking with the Davidsons, and he strolled over to her. When he sat down under the light and took off his hat you saw that he had very red hair, with a bald patch on the crown, and the red, freckled skin which accompanies red hair; he was a man of forty, thin, with a pinched face, precise and rather pedantic; and he spoke with a Scots accent in a very low, quiet voice.

Between the Macphails and the Davidsons, who were missionaries, there had arisen the intimacy of shipboard, which is due to propinquity rather than to any community of taste. Their chief tie was the disapproval they shared of the men who spent their days and nights in the smoking-room playing poker or bridge and drinking. Mrs Macphail was not a little flattered to think that she and her husband were the only people on board with whom the Davidsons were willing to associate, and even the doctor, shy but no fool, half unconsciously acknowledged the compliment. It was only because he was of an argumentative mind that in their cabin at night he permitted himself to carp.

"Mrs Davidson was saying she didn't know how they'd have got through the journey if it hadn't been for us," said Mrs Macphail, as she neatly brushed out her transformation. "She said we were really the only people on the ship they cared to know."

"I shouldn't have thought a missionary was such a big bug that he could afford to put on frills."

"It's not frills. I quite understand what she means. It wouldn't have been very nice for the Davidsons to have to mix with all that rough lot in the smoking-room."

"The founder of their religion wasn't so exclusive," said Dr Macphail with a chuckle.

"I've asked you over and over again not to joke about religion," answered his wife. "I shouldn't like to have a nature like yours, Alec. You never look for the best in people."

He gave her a sidelong glance with his pale, blue eyes, but did not reply. After many years of married life he had learned that it was more conducive to peace to leave his wife with the last word. He was undressed before she was, and climbing into the upper bunk he settled down to read himself to sleep.

When he came on deck next morning they were close to land. He looked at it with greedy eyes. There was a thin strip of silver beach rising quickly to hills covered to the top with luxuriant vegetation. The coconut trees, thick and green, came nearly to the water's edge, and among them you saw the grass houses of the Samoans; and here and there, gleaming white, a little church. Mrs Davidson came and stood beside him. She was dressed in black and wore round her neck a gold chain, from which dangled a small cross. She was a little woman, with brown, dull hair very elaborately arranged, and she had prominent blue eyes behind invisible pince-nez. Her face was long, like a sheep's, but she gave no impression of foolishness, rather of extreme alertness; she had the quick movements of a bird. The most remarkable thing about her was her voice, high, metallic, and without inflection; it fell on the ear with a hard monotony, irritating to the nerves like the pitiless clamour of the pneumatic drill.

"This must seem like home to you," said Dr Macphail, with his thin, difficult smile.

"Ours are low islands, you know, not like these. Coral. These are volcanic. We've got another ten days' journey to reach them."

"In these parts that's almost like being in the next street at home," said Dr Macphail facetiously.

"Well, that's rather an exaggerated way of putting it, but one does look at distances differently in the South Seas. So far you're right."

Dr Macphail sighed faintly.

"I'm glad we're not stationed here," she went on. "They say this is a terribly difficult place to work in. The steamers' touching makes the people unsettled; and then there's the naval station; that's bad for the natives. In our district we don't have difficulties like that to contend with. There are one or two traders, of course, but we take care to make them behave, and if they don't we make the place so hot for them they're glad to go."

Fixing the glasses on her nose she looked at the green island with a ruthless stare.

"It's almost a hopeless task for the missionaries here. I can never be sufficiently thankful to God that we are at least spared that."

Davidson's district consisted of a group of islands to the North of Samoa; they were widely separated and he had frequently to go long distances by canoe. At these times his wife remained at their head-quarters and managed the mission. Dr Macphail felt his heart sink when he considered the efficiency with which she certainly managed it. She spoke of the depravity of the natives in a voice which nothing could hush, but with a vehemently unctuous horror. Her sense of delicacy was singular. Early in their acquaintance she had said to him:

"You know, their marriage customs when we first settled in the islands were so shocking that I couldn't possibly describe them to you. But I'll tell Mrs Macphail and she'll tell you."

Then he had seen his wife and Mrs Davidson, their deck-chairs close together, in earnest conversation for about two hours. As he walked past them backwards and forwards for the sake of exercise, he had heard Mrs Davidson's agitated whisper, like the distant flow of a mountain torrent, and he saw by his wife's open mouth and pale face that she was enjoying an alarming experience. At night in their cabin she repeated to him with bated breath all she had heard.

"Well, what did I say to you?" cried Mrs Davidson, exultant, next morning. "Did you ever hear anything more dreadful? You don't wonder that I couldn't tell you myself, do you? Even though you are a doctor."

Mrs Davidson scanned his face. She had a dramatic eagerness to see that she had achieved the desired effect.

"Can you wonder that when we first went there our hearts sank? You'll hardly believe me when I tell you it was impossible to find a single good girl in any of the villages."

She used the word good in a severely technical manner.

"Mr Davidson and I talked it over, and we made up our minds the first thing to do was to put down the dancing. The natives were crazy about dancing."

"I was not averse to it myself when I was a young man," said Dr Macphail.

"I guessed as much when I heard you ask Mrs Macphail to have a turn with you last night. I don't think there's any real harm if a man dances with his wife, but I was relieved that she wouldn't. Under the circumstances I thought it better that we should keep ourselves to ourselves."

"Under what circumstances?"

Mrs Davidson gave him a quick look through her pince-nez, but did not answer his question.

"But among white people it's not quite the same," she went on, "though I must say I agree with Mr Davidson, who says he can't understand how a husband can stand by and see his wife in another man's arms, and as far as I'm concerned I've never danced a step since I married. But the native dancing is quite another matter. It's not only immoral in itself, but it distinctly leads to immorality. However, I'm thankful to God that we stamped it out, and I don't think I'm wrong in saying that no one has danced in our district for eight years."

But now they came to the mouth of the harbour and Mrs Macphail joined them. The ship turned sharply and steamed slowly in. It was a great land-locked harbour big enough to hold a fleet of battleships; and all around it rose, high and steep, the green hills. Near the entrance, getting such breeze as blew from the sea, stood the governor's house in a garden. The Stars and Stripes dangled languidly from a flagstaff. They passed two or three trim bungalows, and a tennis court, and then they came to the quay with its warehouses. Mrs Davidson pointed out the schooner, moored two or three hundred yards from the side, which was to take them to Apia. There was a crowd of eager, noisy, and good-humoured natives come from all parts of the island, some from curiosity, others to barter with the travellers on their way to Sydney; and they brought pineapples and huge bunches of bananas, tapa cloths, necklaces of shells or sharks' teeth, kava-bowls, and models of war canoes. American sailors, neat and trim, clean-shaven and frank of face, sauntered among them, and there was a little group of officials. While their luggage was being landed the Macphails and Mrs Davidson watched the crowd. Dr Macphail looked at the yaws from which most of the children and the young boys seemed to suffer, disfiguring sores like torpid ulcers, and his professional eyes glistened when he saw for the first time in his experience cases of elephantiasis, men going about with a huge, heavy arm or dragging along a grossly disfigured leg. Men and women wore the lava-lava.

"It's a very indecent costume," said Mrs Davidson. "Mr Davidson thinks it should be prohibited by law. How can you expect people to be moral when they wear nothing but a strip of red cotton round their loins?"

"It's suitable enough to the climate," said the doctor, wiping the sweat off his head.

Now that they were on land the heat, though it was so early in the morning, was already oppressive. Closed in by its hills, not a breath of air came in to Pago-Pago.

"In our islands," Mrs Davidson went on in her high-pitched tones, "we've practically eradicated the lava-lava. A few old men still continue to wear it, but that's all. The women have all taken to the Mother Hubbard, and the men wear trousers and singlets. At the very beginning of our stay Mr Davidson said in one of his reports: the inhabitants of these islands will never be thoroughly Christianised till every boy of more than ten years is made to wear a pair of trousers."

But Mrs Davidson had given two or three of her birdlike glances at heavy grey clouds that came floating over the mouth of the harbour. A few drops began to fall.

"We'd better take shelter," she said.

They made their way with all the crowd to a great shed of corrugated iron, and the rain began to fall in torrents. They stood there for some time and then were joined by Mr Davidson. He had been polite enough to the Macphails during the journey, but he had not his wife's sociability, and had spent much of his time reading. He was a silent, rather sullen man, and you felt that his affability was a duty that he imposed upon himself Christianly; he was by nature reserved and even morose. His appearance was singular. He was very tall and thin, with long limbs loosely jointed; hollow cheeks and curiously high cheek-bones; he had so cadaverous an air that it surprised you to notice how full and sensual were his lips. He wore his hair very long. His dark eyes, set deep in their sockets, were large and tragic; and his hands with their big, long fingers, were finely shaped; they gave him a look of great strength. But the most striking thing about him was the feeling he gave you of suppressed fire. It was impressive and vaguely troubling. He was not a man with whom any intimacy was possible.

He brought now unwelcome news. There was an epidemic of measles, a serious and often fatal disease among the Kanakas, on the island, and a case had developed among the crew of the schooner which was to take them on their journey. The sick man had been brought ashore and put in hospital on the quarantine station, but telegraphic instructions had been sent from Apia to say that the schooner would not be allowed to enter the harbour till it was certain no other member of the crew was affected.

"It means we shall have to stay here for ten days at least."

"But I'm urgently needed at Apia," said Dr Macphail.

"That can't be helped. If no more cases develop on board, the schooner will be allowed to sail with white passengers, but all native traffic is prohibited for three months."

"Is there a hotel here?" asked Mrs Macphail.

Davidson gave a low chuckle.

"There's not."

"What shall we do then?"

"I've been talking to the governor. There's a trader along the front who has rooms that he rents, and my proposition is that as soon as the rain lets up we should go along there and see what we can do. Don't expect comfort. You've just got to be thankful if we get a bed to sleep on and a roof over our heads."

But the rain showed no sign of stopping, and at length with umbrellas and waterproofs they set out. There was no town, but merely a group of official buildings, a store or two, and at the back, among the coconut trees and plantains, a few native dwellings. The house they sought was about five minutes' walk from the wharf. It was a frame house of two storeys, with broad verandahs on both floors and a roof of corrugated iron. The owner was a half-caste named Horn, with a native wife surrounded by little brown children, and on the ground-floor he had a store where he sold canned goods and cottons. The rooms he showed them were almost bare of furniture. In the Macphails' there was nothing but a poor, worn bed with a ragged mosquito net, a rickety chair, and a washstand. They looked round with dismay. The rain poured down without ceasing.

"I'm not going to unpack more than we actually need," said Mrs Macphail.

Mrs Davidson came into the room as she was unlocking a portmanteau. She was very brisk and alert. The cheerless surroundings had no effect on her.

"If you'll take my advice you'll get a needle and cotton and start right in to mend the mosquito net," she said, "or you'll not be able to get a wink of sleep to-night."

"Will they be very bad?" asked Dr Macphail.

"This is the season for them. When you're asked to a party at Government House at Apia you'll notice that all the ladies are given a pillow-slip to put their—their lower extremities in."

"I wish the rain would stop for a moment," said Mrs Macphail. "I could try to make the place comfortable with more heart if the sun were shining."

"Oh, if you wait for that, you'll wait a long time. Pago-Pago is about the rainiest place in the Pacific. You see, the hills, and that bay, they attract the water, and one expects rain at this time of year anyway."

She looked from Macphail to his wife, standing helplessly in different parts of the room, like lost souls, and she pursed her lips. She saw that she must take them in hand. Feckless people like that made her impatient, but her hands itched to put everything in the order which came so naturally to her.

"Here, you give me a needle and cotton and I'll mend that net of yours, while you go on with your unpacking. Dinner's at one. Dr Macphail, you'd better go down to the wharf and see that your heavy luggage has been put in a dry place. You know what these natives are, they're quite capable of storing it where the rain will beat in on it all the time."

The doctor put on his waterproof again and went downstairs. At the door Mr Horn was standing in conversation with the quartermaster of the ship they had just arrived in and a second-class passenger whom Dr Macphail had seen several times on board. The quartermaster, a little, shrivelled man, extremely dirty, nodded to him as he passed.

"This is a bad job about the measles, doc," he said. "I see you've fixed yourself up already."

Dr Macphail thought he was rather familiar, but he was a timid man and he did not take offence easily.

"Yes, we've got a room upstairs."

"Miss Thompson was sailing with you to Apia, so I've brought her along here."

The quartermaster pointed with his thumb to the woman standing by his side. She was twenty-seven perhaps, plump, and in a coarse fashion pretty. She wore a white dress and a large white hat. Her fat calves in white cotton stockings bulged over the tops of long white boots in glacé kid. She gave Macphail an ingratiating smile.

"The feller's tryin' to soak me a dollar and a half a day for the meanest sized room," she said in a hoarse voice.

"I tell you she's a friend of mine, Jo," said the quartermaster. "She can't pay more than a dollar, and you've sure got to take her for that."

The trader was fat and smooth and quietly smiling.

"Well, if you put it like that, Mr Swan, I'll see what I can do about it. I'll talk to Mrs Horn and if we think we can make a reduction we will."

"Don't try to pull that stuff with me," said Miss Thompson. "We'll settle this right now. You get a dollar a day for the room and not one bean more."

Dr Macphail smiled. He admired the effrontery with which she bargained. He was the sort of man who always paid what he was asked. He preferred to be over-charged than to haggle. The trader sighed.

"Well, to oblige Mr Swan I'll take it."

"That's the goods," said Miss Thompson. "Come right in and have a shot of hooch. I've got some real good rye in that grip if you'll bring it along, Mr Swan. You come along too, doctor."

"Oh, I don't think I will, thank you," he answered. "I'm just going down to see that our luggage is all right."

He stepped out into the rain. It swept in from the opening of the harbour in sheets and the opposite shore was all blurred. He passed two or three natives clad in nothing but the lava-lava, with huge um-brellas over them. They walked finely, with leisurely movements, very upright; and they smiled and greeted him in a strange tongue as they went by.

It was nearly dinner-time when he got back, and their meal was laid in the trader's parlour. It was a room designed not to live in but for purposes of prestige, and it had a musty, melancholy air. A suite of stamped plush was arranged neatly round the walls, and from the middle of the ceiling, protected from the flies by yellow tissue paper, hung a gilt chandelier. Davidson did not come.

"I know he went to call on the governor," said Mrs Davidson, "and I guess he's kept him to dinner."

A little native girl brought them a dish of Hamburger steak, and after a while the trader came up to see that they had everything they wanted.

"I see we have a fellow lodger, Mr Horn," said Dr Macphail.

"She's taken a room, that's all," answered the trader. "She's getting her own board."

He looked at the two ladies with an obsequious air.

"I put her downstairs so she shouldn't be in the way. She won't be any trouble to you."

"Is it someone who was on the boat?" asked Mrs Macphail.

"Yes, ma'am, she was in the second cabin. She was going to Apia. She has a position as cashier waiting for her."

"Oh!"

When the trader was gone Macphail said:

"I shouldn't think she'd find it exactly cheerful having her meals in her room."

"If she was in the second cabin I guess she'd rather," answered Mrs Davidson. "I don't exactly know who it can be."

"I happened to be there when the quartermaster brought her along. Her name's Thompson."

"It's not the woman who was dancing with the quartermaster last night?" asked Mrs Davidson.

"That's who it must be," said Mrs Macphail. "I wondered at the time what she was. She looked rather fast to me."

"Not good style at all," said Mrs Davidson.

They began to talk of other things, and after dinner, tired with their early rise, they separated and slept. When they awoke, though the sky was still grey and the clouds hung low, it was not raining and they went for a walk on the high road which the Americans had built along the bay.

On their return they found that Davidson had just come in.

"We may be here for a fortnight," he said irritably. "I've argued it out with the governor, but he says there is nothing to be done."

"Mr Davidson's just longing to get back to his work," said his wife, with an anxious glance at him.

"We've been away for a year," he said, walking up and down the verandah. "The mission has been in charge of native missionaries and I'm terribly nervous that they've let things slide. They're good men, I'm not saying a word against them, God-fearing, devout, and truly Christian men—their Christianity would put many so-called Christians at home to the blush—but they're pitifully lacking in energy. They can make a stand once, they can make a stand twice, but they can't make a stand all the time. If you leave a mission in charge of a native missionary, no matter how trustworthy he seems, in course of time you'll find he's let abuses creep in."

Mr Davidson stood still. With his tall, spare form, and his great eyes flashing out of his pale face, he was an impressive figure. His sincerity was obvious in the fire of his gestures and in his deep, ringing voice.

"I expect to have my work cut out for me. I shall act and I shall act promptly. If the tree is rotten it shall be cut down and cast into the flames."

And in the evening after the high tea which was their last meal, while they sat in the stiff parlour, the ladies working and Dr Macphail smoking his pipe, the missionary told them of his work in the islands.

"When we went there they had no sense of sin at all," he said. "They broke the commandments one after the other and never knew they were doing wrong. And I think that was the most difficult part of my work, to instil into the natives the sense of sin."

The Macphails knew already that Davidson had worked in the Solomons for five years before he met his wife. She had been a missionary in China, and they had become acquainted in Boston, where they were both spending part of their leave to attend a missionary congress. On their marriage they had been appointed to the islands in which they had laboured ever since.

In the course of all the conversations they had had with Mr Davidson one thing had shone out clearly and that was the man's unflinching courage. He was a medical missionary, and he was liable to be called at any time to one or other of the islands in the group. Even the whaleboat is not so very safe a conveyance in the stormy Pacific of the wet season, but often he would be sent for in a canoe, and then the danger was great. In cases of illness or accident he never hesitated. A dozen times he had spent the whole night baling for his life, and more than once Mrs Davidson had given him up for lost.

"I'd beg him not to go sometimes," she said, "or at least to wait till the weather was more settled, but he'd never listen. He's obstinate, and when he's once made up his mind, nothing can move him."

"How can I ask the natives to put their trust in the Lord if I am afraid to do so myself?" cried Davidson. "And I'm not, I'm not. They know that if they send for me in their trouble I'll come if it's humanly possible. And do you think the Lord is going to abandon me when I am on his business? The wind blows at his bidding and the waves toss and rage at his word."

Dr Macphail was a timid man. He had never been able to get used to the hurtling of the shells over the trenches, and when he was operating in an advanced dressing-station the sweat poured from his brow and dimmed his spectacles in the effort he made to control his unsteady hand. He shuddered' a little as he looked at the missionary.

"I wish I could say that I've never been afraid," he said.

"I wish you could say that you believed in God," retorted the other.

But for some reason, that evening the missionary's thoughts travelled back to the early days he and his wife had spent on the islands.

"Sometimes Mrs Davidson and I would look at one another and the tears would stream down our cheeks. We worked without ceasing, day and night, and we seemed to make no progress. I don't know what I should have done without her then. When I felt my heart sink, when I was very near despair, she gave me courage and hope."

Mrs Davidson looked down at her work, and a slight colour rose to her thin cheeks. Her hands trembled a little. She did not trust herself to speak.

"We had no one to help us. We were alone, thousands of miles from any of our own people, surrounded by darkness. When I was broken and weary she would put her work aside and take the Bible and read to me till peace came and settled upon me like sleep upon the eyelids of a child, and when at last she closed the book she'd say: 'We'll save them in spite of themselves.' And I felt strong again in the Lord, and I answered: 'Yes, with God's help I'll save them. I must save them.'"

He came over to the table and stood in front of it as though it were a lectern.

"You see, they were so naturally depraved that they couldn't be brought to see their wickedness. We had to make sins out of what they thought were natural actions. We had to make it a sin, not only to commit adultery and to lie and thieve, but to expose their bodies, and to dance and not to come to church. I made it a sin for a girl to show her bosom and a sin for a man not to wear trousers."

"How?" asked Dr Macphail, not without surprise.

"I instituted fines. Obviously the only way to make people realise that an action is sinful is to punish them if they commit it. I fined them if they didn't come to church, and I fined them if they danced. I fined them if they were improperly dressed. I had a tariff, and every sin had to be paid for either in money or work. And at last I made them understand."

"But did they never refuse to pay?"

"How could they?" asked the missionary.

"It would be a brave man who tried to stand up against Mr Davidson," said his wife, tightening her lips.

Dr Macphail looked at Davidson with troubled eyes. What he heard shocked him, but he hesitated to express his disapproval.

"You must remember that in the last resort I could expel them from their church membership."

"Did they mind that?"

Davidson smiled a little and gently rubbed his hands.

"They couldn't sell their copra. When the men fished they got no share of the catch. It meant something very like starvation. Yes, they minded quite a lot."

"Tell him about Fred Ohlson," said Mrs Davidson.

The missionary fixed his fiery eyes on Dr Macphail.

"Fred Ohlson was a Danish trader who had been in the islands a good many years. He was a pretty rich man as traders go and he wasn't very pleased when we came. You see, he'd had things very much his own way. He paid the natives what he liked for their copra, and he paid in goods and whiskey. He had a native wife, but he was flagrantly unfaithful to her. He was a drunkard. I gave him a chance to mend his ways, but he wouldn't take it. He laughed at me."

Davidson's voice fell to a deep bass as he said the last words, and he was silent for a minute or two. The silence was heavy with menace.

"In two years he was a ruined man. He'd lost everything he'd saved in a quarter of a century. I broke him, and at last he was forced to come to me like a beggar and beseech me to give him a passage back to Sydney."

"I wish you could have seen him when he came to see Mr Davidson," said the missionary's wife. "He had been a fine, powerful man, with a lot of fat on him, and he had a great big voice, but now he was half the size, and he was shaking all over. He'd suddenly become an old man."

With abstracted gaze Davidson looked out into the night. The rain was falling again.

Suddenly from below came a sound, and Davidson turned and looked questioningly at his wife. It was the sound of a gramophone, harsh and loud, wheezing out a syncopated tune.

"What's that?" he asked.

Mrs Davidson fixed her pince-nez more firmly on her nose.

"One of the second-class passengers has a room in the house. I guess it comes from there."

They listened in silence, and presently they heard the sound of dancing. Then the music stopped, and they heard the popping of corks and voices raised in animated conversation.

"I daresay she's giving a farewell party to her friends on board," said Dr Macphail. "The ship sails at twelve, doesn't it?"

Davidson made no remark, but he looked at his watch.

"Are you ready?" he asked his wife.

She got up and folded her work.

"Yes, I guess I am," she answered.

"It's early to go to bed yet, isn't it?" said the doctor.

"We have a good deal of reading to do," explained Mrs Davidson. "Wherever we are, we read a chapter of the Bible before retiring for the night and we study it with the commentaries, you know, and discuss it thoroughly. It's a wonderful training for the mind."

The two couples bade one another good night. Dr and Mrs Macphail were left alone. For two or three minutes they did not speak.

"I think I'll go and fetch the cards," the doctor said at last.

Mrs Macphail looked at him doubtfully. Her conversation with the Davidsons had left her a little uneasy, but she did not like to say that she thought they had better not play cards when the Davidsons might come in at any moment. Dr Macphail brought them and she watched him, though with a vague sense of guilt, while he laid out his patience. Below the sound of revelry continued.

It was fine enough next day, and the Macphails, condemned to spend a fortnight of idleness at Pago-Pago, set about making the best of things. They went down to the quay and got out of their boxes a number of books. The doctor called on the chief surgeon of the naval hospital and went round the beds with him. They left cards on the governor. They passed Miss Thompson on the road. The doctor took off his hat, and she gave him a "Good morning, doc.," in a loud, cheerful voice. She was dressed as on the day before, in a white frock, and her shiny white boots with their high heels, her fat legs bulging over the tops of them, were strange things on that exotic scene.

"I don't think she's very suitably dressed, I must say," said Mrs Macphail. "She looks extremely common to me."

When they got back to their house, she was on the verandah playing with one of the trader's dark children.

"Say a word to her," Dr Macphail whispered to his wife. "She's all alone here, and it seems rather unkind to ignore her."

Mrs Macphail was shy, but she was in the habit of doing what her husband bade her.

"I think we're fellow lodgers here," she said, rather foolishly.

"Terrible, ain't it, bein' cooped up in a one-horse burg like this?" answered Miss Thompson. "And they tell me I'm lucky to have gotten a room. I don't see myself livin' in a native house, and that's what some have to do. I don't know why they don't have a hotel."

They exchanged a few more words. Miss Thompson, loud-voiced and garrulous, was evidently quite willing to gossip, but Mrs Macphail had a poor stock of small talk and presently she said:

"Well, I think we must go upstairs."

In the evening when they sat down to their high-tea Davidson on coming in said:

"I see that woman downstairs has a couple of sailors sitting there. I wonder how she's gotten acquainted with them."

"She can't be very particular," said Mrs Davidson.

They were all rather tired after the idle, aimless day.

"If there's going to be a fortnight of this I don't know what we shall feel like at the end of it," said Dr Macphail.

"The only thing to do is to portion out the day to different activities," answered the missionary. "I shall set aside a certain number of hours to study and a certain number to exercise, rain or fine—in the wet season you can't afford to pay any attention to the rain—and a certain number to recreation."

Dr Macphail looked at his companion with misgiving. Davidson's programme oppressed him. They were eating Hamburger steak again. It seemed the only dish the cook knew how to make. Then below the gramophone began. Davidson started nervously when he heard it, but said nothing. Men's voices floated up. Miss Thompson's guests were joining in a well-known song and presently they heard her voice too, hoarse and loud. There was a good deal of shouting and laughing. The four people upstairs, trying to make conversation, listened despite themselves to the clink of glasses and the scrape of chairs. More people had evidently come. Miss Thompson was giving a party.

"I wonder how she gets them all in," said Mrs Macphail, suddenly breaking into a medical conversation between the missionary and her husband.

It showed whither her thoughts were wandering. The twitch of Davidson's face proved that, though he spoke of scientific things, his mind was busy in the same direction. Suddenly, while the doctor was giving some experience of practice on the Flanders front, rather prosily, he sprang to his feet with a cry.

"What's the matter, Alfred?" asked Mrs Davidson.

"Of course! It never occurred to me. She's out of Iwelei."

"She can't be."

"She came on board at Honolulu. It's obvious. And she's carrying on her trade here. Here."

He uttered the last word with a passion of indignation.

"What's Iwelei?" asked Mrs Macphail.

He turned his gloomy eyes on her and his voice trembled with horror.

"The plague spot of Honolulu. The Red Light district. It was a blot on our civilisation."

Iwelei was on the edge of the city. You went down side streets by the harbour, in the darkness, across a rickety bridge, till you came to a deserted road, all ruts and holes, and then suddenly you came out into the light. There was parking room for motors on each side of the road, and there were saloons, tawdry and bright, each one noisy with its mechanical piano, and there were barbers' shops and tobacconists. There was a stir in the air and a sense of expectant gaiety. You turned down a narrow alley, either to the right or to the left, for the road divided Iwelei into two parts, and you found yourself in the district. There were rows of little bungalows, trim and neatly painted in green, and the pathway between them was broad and straight. It was laid out like a garden-city. In its respectable regularity, its order and spruceness, it gave an impression of sardonic horror; for never can the search for love have been so systematised and ordered. The pathways were lit by a rare lamp, but they would have been dark except for the lights that came from the open windows of the bungalows. Men wandered about, looking at the women who sat at their windows, reading or sewing, for the most part taking no notice of the passers-by; and like the women they were of all nationalities. There were Americans, sailors from the ships in port, enlisted men off the gunboats, sombrely drunk, and soldiers from the regiments, white and black, quartered on the island; there were Japanese, walking in twos and threes; Hawaiians, Chinese in long robes, and Filipinos in preposterous hats. They were silent and as it were oppressed. Desire is sad.

"It was the most crying scandal of the Pacific," exclaimed Davidson vehemently. "The missionaries had been agitating against it for years, and at last the local press took it up. The police refused to stir. You know their argument. They say that vice is inevitable and consequently the best thing is to localise and control it. The truth is, they were paid. Paid. They were paid by the saloon-keepers, paid by the bullies, paid by the women themselves. At last they were forced to move."

"I read about it in the papers that came on board in Honolulu," said Dr Macphail.

"Iwelei, with its sin and shame, ceased to exist on the very day we arrived. The whole population was brought before the justices. I don't know why I didn't understand at once what that woman was."

"Now you come to speak of it," said Mrs Macphail, "I remember seeing her come on board only a few minutes before the boat sailed. I remember thinking at the time she was cutting it rather fine."

"How dare she come here!" cried Davidson indignantly. "I'm not going to allow it."

He strode towards the door.

"What are you going to do?" asked Macphail.

"What do you expect me to do? I'm going to stop it. I'm not going to have this house turned into—into...."

He sought for a word that should not offend the ladies' ears. His eyes were flashing and his pale face was paler still in his emotion.

"It sounds as though there were three or four men down there," said the doctor. "Don't you think it's rather rash to go in just now?"

The missionary gave him a contemptuous look and without a word flung out of the room.

"You know Mr Davidson very little if you think the fear of personal danger can stop him in the performance of his duty," said his wife.

She sat with her hands nervously clasped, a spot of colour on her high cheek bones, listening to what was about to happen below. They all listened. They heard him clatter down the wooden stairs and throw open the door. The singing stopped suddenly, but the gramophone continued to bray out its vulgar tune. They heard Davidson's voice and then the noise of something heavy falling. The music stopped. He had hurled the gramophone on the floor. Then again they heard Davidson's voice, they could not make out the words, then Miss Thompson's, loud and shrill, then a confused clamour as though several people were shouting together at the top of their lungs. Mrs Davidson gave a little gasp, and she clenched her hands more tightly. Dr Macphail looked uncertainly from her to his wife. He did not want to go down, but he wondered if they expected him to. Then there was something that sounded like a scuffle. The noise now was more distinct. It might be that Davidson was being thrown out of the room. The door was slammed. There was a moment's silence and they heard Davidson come up the stairs again. He went to his room.

"I think I'll go to him," said Mrs Davidson.

She got up and went out.

"If you want me, just call," said Mrs Macphail, and then when the other was gone: "I hope he isn't hurt."

"Why couldn't he mind his own business?" said Dr Macphail.

They sat in silence for a minute or two and then they both started, for the gramophone began to play once more, defiantly, and mocking voices shouted hoarsely the words of an obscene song.

Next day Mrs Davidson was pale and tired. She complained of headache, and she looked old and wizened. She told Mrs Macphail that the missionary had not slept at all; he had passed the night in a state of frightful agitation and at five had got up and gone out. A glass of beer had been thrown over him and his clothes were stained and stinking. But a sombre fire glowed in Mrs Davidson's eyes when she spoke of Miss Thompson.

"She'll bitterly rue the day when she flouted Mr Davidson," she said. "Mr Davidson has a wonderful heart and no one who is in trouble has ever gone to him without being comforted, but he has no mercy for sin, and when his righteous wrath is excited he's terrible."

"Why, what will he do?" asked Mrs Macphail.

"I don't know, but I wouldn't stand in that creature's shoes for anything in the world."

Mrs Macphail shuddered. There was something positively alarming in the triumphant assurance of the little woman's manner. They were going out together that morning, and they went down the stairs side by side. Miss Thompson's door was open, and they saw her in a bedraggled dressing-gown, cooking something in a chafing-dish.

"Good morning," she called. "Is Mr Davidson better this morning?"

They passed her in silence, with their noses in the air, as if she did not exist. They flushed, however, when she burst into a shout of derisive laughter. Mrs Davidson turned on her suddenly.

"Don't you dare to speak to me," she screamed. "If you insult me I shall have you turned out of here."

"Say, did I ask Mr Davidson to visit with me?"

"Don't answer her," whispered Mrs Macphail hurriedly.

They walked on till they were out of earshot.

"She's brazen, brazen," burst from Mrs Davidson.

Her anger almost suffocated her.

And on their way home they met her strolling towards the quay. She had all her finery on. Her great white hat with its vulgar, showy flowers was an affront. She called out cheerily to them as she went by, and a couple of American sailors who were standing there grinned as the ladies set their faces to an icy stare. They got in just before the rain began to fall again.

"I guess she'll get her fine clothes spoilt," said Mrs Davidson with a bitter sneer.

Davidson did not come in till they were half way through dinner. He was wet through, but he would not change. He sat, morose and silent, refusing to eat more than a mouthful, and he stared at the slanting rain. When Mrs Davidson told him of their two encounters with Miss Thompson he did not answer. His deepening frown alone showed that he had heard.

"Don't you think we ought to make Mr Horn turn her out of here?" asked Mrs Davidson. "We can't allow her to insult us."

"There doesn't seem to be any other place for her to go," said Macphail.

"She can live with one of the natives."

"In weather like this a native hut must be a rather uncomfortable place to live in."

"I lived in one for years," said the missionary.

When the little native girl brought in the fried bananas which formed the sweet they had every day, Davidson turned to her.

"Ask Miss Thompson when it would be convenient for me to see her," he said.

The girl nodded shyly and went out.

"What do you want to see her for, Alfred?" asked his wife.

"It's my duty to see her. I won't act till I've given her every chance."

"You don't know what she is. She'll insult you."

"Let her insult me. Let her spit on me. She has an immortal soul, and I must do all that is in my power to save it."

Mrs Davidson's ears rang still with the harlot's mocking laughter.

"She's gone too far."

"Too far for the mercy of God?" His eyes lit up suddenly and his voice grew mellow and soft. "Never. The sinner may be deeper in sin than the depth of hell itself, but the love of the Lord Jesus can reach him still."

The girl came back with the message.

"Miss Thompson's compliments and as long as Rev. Davidson don't come in business hours she'll be glad to see him any time."

The party received it in stony silence, and Dr Macphail quickly effaced from his lips the smile which had come upon them. He knew his wife would be vexed with him if he found Miss Thompson's effrontery amusing.

They finished the meal in silence. When it was over the two ladies got up and took their work, Mrs Macphail was making another of the innumerable comforters which she had turned out since the beginning of the war, and the doctor lit his pipe. But Davidson remained in his chair and with abstracted eyes stared at the table. At last he got up and without a word went out of the room. They heard him go down and they heard Miss Thompson's defiant "Come in" when he knocked at the door. He remained with her for an hour. And Dr Macphail watched the rain. It was beginning to get on his nerves. It was not like our soft English rain that drops gently on the earth; it was unmerciful and somehow terrible; you felt in it the malignancy of the primitive powers of nature. It did not pour, it flowed. It was like a deluge from heaven, and it rattled on the roof of corrugated iron with a steady persistence that was maddening. It seemed to have a fury of its own. And sometimes you felt that you must scream if it did not stop, and then suddenly you felt powerless, as though your bones had suddenly become soft; and you were miserable and hopeless.

Macphail turned his head when the missionary came back. The two women looked up.

"I've given her every chance. I have exhorted her to repent. She is an evil woman."

He paused, and Dr Macphail saw his eyes darken and his pale face grow hard and stern.

"Now I shall take the whips with which the Lord Jesus drove the usurers and the money changers out of the Temple of the Most

High."

He walked up and down the room. His mouth was close set, and his black brows were frowning.

"If she fled to the uttermost parts of the earth I should pursue her."

With a sudden movement he turned round and strode out of the room. They heard him go downstairs again.

"What is he going to do?" asked Mrs Macphail.

"I don't know." Mrs Davidson took off her pince-nez and wiped them. "When he is on the Lord's work I never ask him questions."

She sighed a little.

"What is the matter?"

"He'll wear himself out. He doesn't know what it is to spare himself."

Dr Macphail learnt the first results of the missionary's activity from the half-caste trader in whose house they lodged. He stopped the doctor when he passed the store and came out to speak to him on the stoop. His fat face was worried.

"The Rev. Davidson has been at me for letting Miss Thompson have a room here," he said, "but I didn't know what she was when I rented it to her. When people come and ask if I can rent them a room all I want to know is if they've the money to pay for it. And she paid me for hers a week in advance."

Dr Macphail did not want to commit himself.

"When all's said and done it's your house. We're very much obliged to you for taking us in at all."

Horn looked at him doubtfully. He was not certain yet how definitely Macphail stood on the missionary's side.

"The missionaries are in with one another," he said, hesitatingly. "If they get it in for a trader he may just as well shut up his store and quit."

"Did he want you to turn her out?"

"No, he said so long as she behaved herself he couldn't ask me to do that. He said he wanted to be just to me. I promised she shouldn't have no more visitors. I've just been and told her."

"How did she take it?"

"She gave me Hell."

The trader squirmed in his old ducks. He had found Miss Thompson a rough customer.

"Oh, well, I daresay she'll get out. I don't suppose she wants to stay here if she can't have anyone in."

"There's nowhere she can go, only a native house, and no native'll take her now, not now that the missionaries have got their knife in her."

Dr Macphail looked at the falling rain.

"Well, I don't suppose it's any good waiting for it to clear up."

In the evening when they sat in the parlour Davidson talked to them of his early days at college. He had had no means and had worked his way through by doing odd jobs during the vacations. There was silence downstairs. Miss Thompson was sitting in her little room alone. But suddenly the gramophone began to play. She had set it on in defiance, to cheat her loneliness, but there was no one to sing, and it had a melancholy note. It was like a cry for help. Davidson took no notice. He was in the middle of a long anecdote and without change of expression went on. The gramophone continued. Miss Thompson put on one reel after another. It looked as though the silence of the night were getting on her nerves. It was breathless and sultry. When the Macphails went to bed they could not sleep. They lay side by side with their eyes wide open, listening to the cruel singing of the mosquitoes outside their curtain.

"What's that?" whispered Mrs Macphail at last.

They heard a voice, Davidson's voice, through the wooden partition. It went on with a monotonous, earnest insistence. He was praying aloud. He was praying for the soul of Miss Thompson.

Two or three days went by. Now when they passed Miss Thompson on the road she did not greet them with ironic cordiality or smile; she passed with her nose in the air, a sulky look on her painted face, frowning, as though she did not see them. The trader told Macphail that she had tried to get lodging elsewhere, but had failed. In the evening she played through the various reels of her gramophone, but the pretence of mirth was obvious now. The ragtime had a cracked, heart-broken rhythm as though it were a one-step of despair. When she began to play on Sunday Davidson sent Horn to beg her to stop at once since it was the Lord's day. The reel was taken off and the house was silent except for the steady pattering of the rain on the iron roof.

"I think she's getting a bit worked up," said the trader next day to Macphail. "She don't know what Mr Davidson's up to and it makes her scared."

Macphail had caught a glimpse of her that morning and it struck him that her arrogant expression had changed. There was in her face a hunted look. The half-caste gave him a sidelong glance.

"I suppose you don't know what Mr Davidson is doing about it?" he hazarded.

"No, I don't."

It was singular that Horn should ask him that question, for he also had the idea that the missionary was mysteriously at work. He had an impression that he was weaving a net around the woman, carefully, systematically, and suddenly, when everything was ready would pull the strings tight.

"He told me to tell her," said the trader, "that if at any time she wanted him she only had to send and he'd come."

"What did she say when you told her that?"

"She didn't say nothing. I didn't stop. I just said what he said I was to and then I beat it. I thought she might be going to start weepin'."

"I have no doubt the loneliness is getting on her nerves," said the doctor. "And the rain—that's enough to make anyone jumpy," he continued irritably. "Doesn't it ever stop in this confounded place?"

"It goes on pretty steady in the rainy season. We have three hundred inches in the year. You see, it's the shape of the bay. It seems to attract the rain from all over the Pacific."

"Damn the shape of the bay," said the doctor.

He scratched his mosquito bites. He felt very short-tempered. When the rain stopped and the sun shone, it was like a hothouse, seething, humid, sultry, breathless, and you had a strange feeling that everything was growing with a savage violence. The natives, blithe and childlike by reputation, seemed then, with their tattooing and their dyed hair, to have something sinister in their appearance; and when they pattered along at your heels with their naked feet you looked back instinctively. You felt they might at any moment come behind you swiftly and thrust a long knife between your shoulder blades. You could not tell what dark thoughts lurked behind their wide-set eyes. They had a little the look of ancient Egyptians painted on a temple wall, and there was about them the terror of what is immeasurably old.

The missionary came and went. He was busy, but the Macphails did not know what he was doing. Horn told the doctor that he saw the governor every day, and once Davidson mentioned him.

"He looks as if he had plenty of determination," he said, "but when you come down to brass tacks he has no backbone."

"I suppose that means he won't do exactly what you want," suggested the doctor facetiously.

The missionary did not smile.

"I want him to do what's right. It shouldn't be necessary to persuade a man to do that."

"But there may be differences of opinion about what is right."

"If a man had a gangrenous foot would you have patience with anyone who hesitated to amputate it?"

"Gangrene is a matter of fact."

"And Evil?"

What Davidson had done soon appeared. The four of them had just finished their midday meal, and they had not yet separated for the siesta which the heat imposed on the ladies and on the doctor. Davidson had little patience with the slothful habit. The door was suddenly flung open and Miss Thompson came in. She looked round the room and then went up to Davidson.

"You low-down skunk, what have you been saying about me to the governor?"

She was spluttering with rage. There was a moment's pause. Then the missionary drew forward a chair.

"Won't you be seated, Miss Thompson? I've been hoping to have another talk with you."

"You poor low-life bastard."

She burst into a torrent of insult, foul and insolent. Davidson kept his grave eyes on her.

"I'm indifferent to the abuse you think fit to heap on me, Miss Thompson," he said, "but I must beg you to remember that ladies are present."

Tears by now were struggling with her anger. Her face was red and swollen as though she were choking.

"What has happened?" asked Dr Macphail.

"A feller's just been in here and he says I gotter beat it on the next boat."

Was there a gleam in the missionary's eyes? His face remained impassive.

"You could hardly expect the governor to let you stay here under the circumstances."

"You done it," she shrieked. "You can't kid me. You done it."

"I don't want to deceive you. I urged the governor to take the only possible step consistent with his obligations."

"Why couldn't you leave me be? I wasn't doin' you no harm."

"You may be sure that if you had I should be the last man to resent it."

"Do you think I want to stay on in this poor imitation of a burg? I don't look no busher, do I?"

"In that case I don't see what cause of complaint you have," he answered.

She gave an inarticulate cry of rage and flung out of the room. There was a short silence.

"It's a relief to know that the governor has acted at last," said Davidson finally. "He's a weak man and he shilly-shallied. He said she was only here for a fortnight anyway, and if she went on to Apia that was under British jurisdiction and had nothing to do with him."

The missionary sprang to his feet and strode across the room.

"It's terrible the way the men who are in authority seek to evade their responsibility. They speak as though evil that was out of sight ceased to be evil. The very existence of that woman is a scandal and it does not help matters to shift it to another of the islands. In the end I had to speak straight from the shoulder."

Davidson's brow lowered, and he protruded his firm chin. He

looked fierce and determined.

"What do you mean by that?"

"Our mission is not entirely without influence at Washington. I pointed out to the governor that it wouldn't do him any good if there was a complaint about the way he managed things here."

"When has she got to go?" asked the doctor, after a pause.

"The San Francisco boat is due here from Sydney next Tuesday. She's to sail on that."

That was in five days' time. It was next day, when he was coming back from the hospital where for want of something better to do Macphail spent most of his mornings, that the half-caste stopped him as he was going upstairs.

"Excuse me, Dr Macphail, Miss Thompson's sick. Will you have a look at her."

"Certainly."

Horn led him to her room. She was sitting in a chair idly, neither reading nor sewing, staring in front of her. She wore her white dress and the large hat with the flowers on it. Macphail noticed that her skin was yellow and muddy under her powder, and her eyes were heavy.

"I'm sorry to hear you're not well," he said.

"Oh, I ain't sick really. I just said that, because I just had to see you. I've got to clear on a boat that's going to 'Frisco."

She looked at him and he saw that her eyes were suddenly startled. She opened and clenched her hands spasmodically. The trader stood at the door, listening.

"So I understand," said the doctor.

She gave a little gulp.

"I guess it ain't very convenient for me to go to 'Frisco just now. I went to see the governor yesterday afternoon, but I couldn't get to him. I saw the secretary, and he told me I'd got to take that boat and that was all there was to it. I just had to see the governor, so I waited outside his house this morning, and when he come out I spoke to him. He didn't want to speak to me, I'll say, but I wouldn't let him shake me off, and at last he said he hadn't no objection to my staying here till the next boat to Sydney if the Rev. Davidson will stand for it."

She stopped and looked at Dr Macphail anxiously.

"I don't know exactly what I can do," he said.

"Well, I thought maybe you wouldn't mind asking him. I swear to God I won't start anything here if he'll just only let me stay. I won't go out of the house if that'll suit him. It's no more'n a fortnight."

"I'll ask him."

"He won't stand for it," said Horn. "He'll have you out on Tuesday, so you may as well make up your mind to it."

"Tell him I can get work in Sydney, straight stuff, I mean. 'Tain't asking very much."

"I'll do what I can."

"And come and tell me right away, will you? I can't set down to a thing till I get the dope one way or the other."

It was not an errand that much pleased the doctor, and, characteristically perhaps, he went about it indirectly. He told his wife what Miss Thompson had said to him and asked her to speak to Mrs Davidson. The missionary's attitude seemed rather arbitrary and it could do no harm if the girl were allowed to stay in Pago-Pago another fortnight. But he was not prepared for the result of his diplomacy. The missionary came to him straightway.

"Mrs Davidson tells me that Thompson has been speaking to you."

Dr Macphail, thus directly tackled, had the shy man's resentment at being forced out into the open. He felt his temper rising, and he flushed.

"I don't see that it can make any difference if she goes to Sydney rather than to San Francisco, and so long as she promises to behave while she's here it's dashed hard to persecute her."

The missionary fixed him with his stern eyes.

"Why is she unwilling to go back to San Francisco?"

"I didn't enquire," answered the doctor with some asperity. "And I think one does better to mind one's own business."

Perhaps it was not a very tactful answer.

"The governor has ordered her to be deported by the first boat that leaves the island. He's only done his duty and I will not interfere.

Her presence is a peril here."

"I think you're very harsh and tyrannical."

The two ladies looked up at the doctor with some alarm, but they need not have feared a quarrel, for the missionary smiled gently.

"I'm terribly sorry you should think that of me, Dr Macphail. Believe me, my heart bleeds for that unfortunate woman, but I'm only trying to do my duty."

The doctor made no answer. He looked out of the window sullenly. For once it was not raining and across the bay you saw nestling among the trees the huts of a native village.

"I think I'll take advantage of the rain stopping to go out," he said.

"Please don't bear me malice because I can't accede to your wish," said Davidson, with a melancholy smile. "I respect you very much, doctor, and I should be sorry if you thought ill of me."

"I have no doubt you have a sufficiently good opinion of yourself to bear mine with equanimity," he retorted.

"That's one on me," chuckled Davidson.

When Dr Macphail, vexed with himself because he had been uncivil to no purpose, went downstairs, Miss Thompson was waiting for him with her door ajar.

"Well," she said, "have you spoken to him?"

"Yes, I'm sorry, he won't do anything," he answered, not looking at her in his embarrassment.

But then he gave her a quick glance, for a sob broke from her. He saw that her face was white with fear. It gave him a shock of dismay. And suddenly he had an idea.

"But don't give up hope yet. I think it's a shame the way they're treating you and I'm going to see the governor myself."

"Now?"

He nodded. Her face brightened.

"Say, that's real good of you. I'm sure he'll let me stay if you speak for me. I just won't do a thing I didn't ought all the time I'm here."

Dr Macphail hardly knew why he had made up his mind to appeal to the governor. He was perfectly indifferent to Miss Thompson's affairs, but the missionary had irritated him, and with him temper was a smouldering thing. He found the governor at home. He was a large, handsome man, a sailor, with a grey toothbrush moustache; and he wore a spotless uniform of white drill.

"I've come to see you about a woman who's lodging in the same house as we are," he said. "Her name's Thompson."

"I guess I've heard nearly enough about her, Dr Macphail," said the governor, smiling. "I've given her the order to get out next Tuesday and that's all I can do."

"I wanted to ask you if you couldn't stretch a point and let her stay here till the boat comes in from San Francisco so that she can go to Sydney. I will guarantee her good behaviour."

The governor continued to smile, but his eyes grew small and serious.

"I'd be very glad to oblige you, Dr Macphail, but I've given the order and it must stand."

The doctor put the case as reasonably as he could, but now the governor ceased to smile at all. He listened sullenly, with averted gaze. Macphail saw that he was making no impression.

"I'm sorry to cause any lady inconvenience, but she'll have to sail on Tuesday and that's all there is to it."

"But what difference can it make?"

"Pardon me, doctor, but I don't feel called upon to explain my official actions except to the proper authorities."

Macphail looked at him shrewdly. He remembered Davidson's hint that he had used threats, and in the governor's attitude he read a singular embarrassment.

"Davidson's a damned busybody," he said hotly.

"Between ourselves, Dr Macphail, I don't say that I have formed a very favourable opinion of Mr Davidson, but I am bound to confess that he was within his rights in pointing out to me the danger that the presence of a woman of Miss Thompson's character was to a place like this where a number of enlisted men are stationed among a native population."

He got up and Dr Macphail was obliged to do so too.

"I must ask you to excuse me. I have an engagement. Please give my respects to Mrs Macphail."

The doctor left him crest-fallen. He knew that Miss Thompson would be waiting for him, and unwilling to tell her himself that he had failed, he went into the house by the back door and sneaked up the stairs as though he had something to hide.

At supper he was silent and ill-at-ease, but the missionary was jovial and animated. Dr Macphail thought his eyes rested on him now and then with triumphant good-humour. It struck him suddenly that Davidson knew of his visit to the governor and of its ill success. But how on earth could he have heard of it? There was something sinister about the power of that man. After supper he saw Horn on the verandah and, as though to have a casual word with him, went out.

"She wants to know if you've seen the governor," the trader whispered.

"Yes. He wouldn't do anything. I'm awfully sorry, I can't do anything more."

"I knew he wouldn't. They daren't go against the missionaries."

"What are you talking about?" said Davidson affably, coming out to join them.

"I was just saying there was no chance of your getting over to Apia for at least another week," said the trader glibly.

He left them, and the two men returned into the parlour. Mr Davidson devoted one hour after each meal to recreation. Presently a timid knock was heard at the door.

"Come in," said Mrs Davidson, in her sharp voice.

The door was not opened. She got up and opened it. They saw Miss Thompson standing at the threshold. But the change in her appearance was extraordinary. This was no longer the flaunting hussy who had jeered at them in the road, but a broken, frightened woman. Her hair, as a rule so elaborately arranged, was tumbling untidily over her neck. She wore bedroom slippers and a skirt and blouse. They were unfresh and bedraggled. She stood at the door with the tears streaming down her face and did not dare to enter.

"What do you want?" said Mrs Davidson harshly.

"May I speak to Mr Davidson?" she said in a choking voice.

The missionary rose and went towards her.

"Come right in, Miss Thompson," he said in cordial tones. "What can I do for you?"

She entered the room.

"Say, I'm sorry for what I said to you the other day an' for—for everythin' else. I guess I was a bit lit up. I beg pardon."

"Oh, it was nothing. I guess my back's broad enough to bear a few hard words."

She stepped towards him with a movement that was horribly cringing.

"You've got me beat. I'm all in. You won't make me go back to 'Frisco?"

His genial manner vanished and his voice grew on a sudden hard and stern.

"Why don't you want to go back there?"

She cowered before him.

"I guess my people live there. I don't want them to see me like this. I'll go anywhere else you say."

"Why don't you want to go back to San Francisco?"

"I've told you."

He leaned forward, staring at her, and his great, shining eyes seemed to try to bore into her soul. He gave a sudden gasp.

"The penitentiary."

She screamed, and then she fell at his feet, clasping his legs.

"Don't send me back there. I swear to you before God I'll be a good woman. I'll give all this up."

She burst into a torrent of confused supplication and the tears coursed down her painted cheeks. He leaned over her and, lifting her face, forced her to look at him.

"Is that it, the penitentiary?"

"I beat it before they could get me," she gasped. "If the bulls grab me it's three years for mine."

He let go his hold of her and she fell in a heap on the floor, sobbing bitterly. Dr Macphail stood up.

"This alters the whole thing," he said. "You can't make her go back when you know this. Give her another chance. She wants to turn over a new leaf."

"I'm going to give her the finest chance she's ever had. If she repents let her accept her punishment."

She misunderstood the words and looked up. There was a gleam of hope in her heavy eyes.

"You'll let me go?"

"No. You shall sail for San Francisco on Tuesday."

She gave a groan of horror and then burst into low, hoarse shrieks which sounded hardly human, and she beat her head passionately on the ground. Dr Macphail sprang to her and lifted her up.

"Come on, you mustn't do that. You'd better go to your room and lie down. I'll get you something."

He raised her to her feet and partly dragging her, partly carrying her, got her downstairs. He was furious with Mrs Davidson and with his wife because they made no effort to help. The half-caste was standing on the landing and with his assistance he managed to get her on the bed. She was moaning and crying. She was almost insensible. He gave her a hypodermic injection. He was hot and exhausted when he went upstairs again.

"I've got her to lie down."

The two women and Davidson were in the same positions as when he had left them. They could not have moved or spoken since he went.

"I was waiting for you," said Davidson, in a strange, distant voice. "I want you all to pray with me for the soul of our erring sister."

He took the Bible off a shelf, and sat down at the table at which they had supped. It had not been cleared, and he pushed the tea-pot out of the way. In a powerful voice, resonant and deep, he read to them the chapter in which is narrated the meeting of Jesus Christ with the woman taken in adultery.

"Now kneel with me and let us pray for the soul of our dear sister, Sadie Thompson."

He burst into a long, passionate prayer in which he implored God to have mercy on the sinful woman. Mrs Macphail and Mrs Davidson knelt with covered eyes. The doctor, taken by surprise, awkward and sheepish, knelt too. The missionary's prayer had a savage eloquence. He was extraordinarily moved, and as he spoke the tears ran down his cheeks. Outside, the pitiless rain fell, fell steadily, with a fierce malignity that was all too human.

At last he stopped. He paused for a moment and said:

"We will now repeat the Lord's prayer."

They said it and then; following him, they rose from their knees. Mrs Davidson's face was pale and restful. She was comforted and at peace, but the Macphails felt suddenly bashful. They did not know which way to look.

"I'll just go down and see how she is now," said Dr Macphail.

When he knocked at her door it was opened for him by Horn. Miss Thompson was in a rocking-chair, sobbing quietly.

"What are you doing there?" exclaimed Macphail. "I told you to lie down."

"I can't lie down. I want to see Mr Davidson."

"My poor child, what do you think is the good of it? You'll never move him."

"He said he'd come if I sent for him."

Macphail motioned to the trader.

"Go and fetch him."

He waited with her in silence while the trader went upstairs. Davidson came in.

"Excuse me for asking you to come here," she said, looking at him sombrely.

"I was expecting you to send for me. I knew the Lord would answer my prayer."

They stared at one another for a moment and then she looked away. She kept her eyes averted when she spoke.

"I've been a bad woman. I want to repent."

"Thank God! thank God! He has heard our prayers."

He turned to the two men.

"Leave me alone with her. Tell Mrs Davidson that our prayers have been answered."

They went out and closed the door behind them.

"Gee whizz," said the trader.

That night Dr Macphail could not get to sleep till late, and when he heard the missionary come upstairs he looked at his watch. It was two o'clock. But even then he did not go to bed at once, for through the wooden partition that separated their rooms he heard him praying aloud, till he himself, exhausted, fell asleep.

When he saw him next morning he was surprised at his appearance. He was paler than ever, tired, but his eyes shone with an inhuman fire. It looked as though he were filled with an overwhelming joy.

"I want you to go down presently and see Sadie," he said. "I can't hope that her body is better, but her soul—her soul is transformed."

The doctor was feeling wan and nervous.

"You were with her very late last night," he said.

"Yes, she couldn't bear to have me leave her."

"You look as pleased as Punch," the doctor said irritably.

Davidson's eyes shone with ecstasy.

"A great mercy has been vouchsafed me. Last night I was privileged to bring a lost soul to the loving arms of Jesus."

Miss Thompson was again in the rocking-chair. The bed had not been made. The room was in disorder. She had not troubled to dress herself, but wore a dirty dressing-gown, and her hair was tied in a sluttish knot. She had given her face a dab with a wet towel, but it was all swollen and creased with crying. She looked a drab.

She raised her eyes dully when the doctor came in. She was cowed and broken.

"Where's Mr Davidson?" she asked.

"He'll come presently if you want him," answered Macphail acidly. "I came here to see how you were."

"Oh, I guess I'm O. K. You needn't worry about that."

"Have you had anything to eat?"

"Horn brought me some coffee."

She looked anxiously at the door.

"D'you think he'll come down soon? I feel as if it wasn't so terrible when he's with me."

"Are you still going on Tuesday?"

"Yes, he says I've got to go. Please tell him to come right along. You can't do me any good. He's the only one as can help me now."

"Very well," said Dr Macphail.

During the next three days the missionary spent almost all his time with Sadie Thompson. He joined the others only to have his meals. Dr Macphail noticed that he hardly ate.

"He's wearing himself out," said Mrs Davidson pitifully. "He'll have a breakdown if he doesn't take care, but he won't spare himself."

She herself was white and pale. She told Mrs Macphail that she had no sleep. When the missionary came upstairs from Miss Thompson he prayed till he was exhausted, but even then he did not sleep for long. After an hour or two he got up and dressed himself, and went for a tramp along the bay. He had strange dreams.

"This morning he told me that he'd been dreaming about the mountains of Nebraska," said Mrs Davidson.

"That's curious," said Dr Macphail.

He remembered seeing them from the windows of the train when he crossed America. They were like huge mole-hills, rounded and smooth, and they rose from the plain abruptly. Dr Macphail remembered how it struck him that they were like a woman's breasts.

Davidson's restlessness was intolerable even to himself. But he was buoyed up by a wonderful exhilaration. He was tearing out by the roots the last vestiges of sin that lurked in the hidden corners of that poor woman's heart. He read with her and prayed with her.

"It's wonderful," he said to them one day at supper. "It's a true rebirth. Her soul, which was black as night, is now pure and white like the new-fallen snow. I am humble and afraid. Her remorse for all her sins is beautiful. I am not worthy to touch the hem of her garment."

"Have you the heart to send her back to San Francisco?" said the doctor. "Three years in an American prison. I should have thought you might have saved her from that."

"Ah, but don't you see? It's necessary. Do you think my heart doesn't bleed for her? I love her as I love my wife and my sister. All the time that she is in prison I shall suffer all the pain that she suffers."

"Bunkum," cried the doctor impatiently.

"You don't understand because you're blind. She's sinned, and she must suffer. I know what she'll endure. She'll be starved and tortured and humiliated. I want her to accept the punishment of man as a sacrifice to God. I want her to accept it joyfully. She has an opportunity which is offered to very few of us. God is very good and very merciful."

Davidson's voice trembled with excitement. He could hardly articulate the words that tumbled passionately from his lips.

"All day I pray with her and when I leave her I pray again, I pray with all my might and main, so that Jesus may grant her this great mercy. I want to put in her heart the passionate desire to be punished so that at the end, even if I offered to let her go, she would refuse. I want her to feel that the bitter punishment of prison is the thank-offering that she places at the feet of our Blessed Lord, who gave his life for her."

The days passed slowly. The whole household, intent on the wretched, tortured woman downstairs, lived in a state of unnatural excitement. She was like a victim that was being prepared for the savage rites of a bloody idolatry. Her terror numbed her. She could not bear to let Davidson out of her sight; it was only when he was with her that she had courage, and she hung upon him with a slavish dependence. She cried a great deal, and she read the Bible, and prayed. Sometimes she was exhausted and apathetic. Then she did indeed look forward to her ordeal, for it seemed to offer an escape, direct and concrete, from the anguish she was enduring. She could not bear much longer the vague terrors which now assailed her. With her sins she had put aside all personal vanity, and she slopped about her room, unkempt and dishevelled, in her tawdry dressing-gown. She had not taken off her night-dress for four days, nor put on stockings. Her room was littered and untidy. Meanwhile the rain fell with a cruel persistence. You felt that the heavens must at last be empty of water, but still it poured down, straight and heavy, with a maddening iteration, on the iron roof. Everything was damp and clammy. There was mildew on the walls and on the boots that stood on the floor. Through the sleepless nights the mosquitoes droned their angry chant.

"If it would only stop raining for a single day it wouldn't be so bad," said Dr Macphail.

They all looked forward to the Tuesday when the boat for San Francisco was to arrive from Sydney. The strain was intolerable. So far as Dr Macphail was concerned, his pity and his resentment were alike extinguished by his desire to be rid of the unfortunate woman. The inevitable must be accepted. He felt he would breathe more freely when the ship had sailed. Sadie Thompson was to be escorted on board by a clerk in the governor's office. This person called on the Monday evening and told Miss Thompson to be prepared at eleven in the morning. Davidson was with her.

"I'll see that everything is ready. I mean to come on board with her myself."

Miss Thompson did not speak.

When Dr Macphail blew out his candle and crawled cautiously under his mosquito curtains, he gave a sigh of relief.

"Well, thank God that's over. By this time to-morrow she'll be gone."

"Mrs Davidson will be glad too. She says he's wearing himself to a shadow," said Mrs Macphail. "She's a different woman."

"Who?"

"Sadie. I should never have thought it possible. It makes one humble."

Dr Macphail did not answer, and presently he fell asleep. He was tired out, and he slept more soundly than usual.

He was awakened in the morning by a hand placed on his arm, and, starting up, saw Horn by the side of his bed. The trader put his finger on his mouth to prevent any exclamation from Dr Macphail and beckoned to him to come. As a rule he wore shabby ducks, but now he was barefoot and wore only the lava-lava of the natives. He looked suddenly savage, and Dr Macphail, getting out of bed, saw that he was heavily tattooed. Horn made him a sign to come on to the verandah. Dr Macphail got out of bed and followed the trader out.

"Don't make a noise," he whispered. "You're wanted. Put on a coat and some shoes. Quick."

Dr Macphail's first thought was that something had happened to Miss Thompson.

"What is it? Shall I bring my instruments?"

"Hurry, please, hurry."

Dr Macphail crept back into the bedroom, put on a waterproof over his pyjamas, and a pair of rubber-soled shoes. He rejoined the trader, and together they tiptoed down the stairs. The door leading out to the road was open and at it were standing half a dozen natives.

"What is it?" repeated the doctor.

"Come along with me," said Horn.

He walked out and the doctor followed him. The natives came after them in a little bunch. They crossed the road and came on to the beach. The doctor saw a group of natives standing round some object at the water's edge. They hurried along, a couple of dozen yards perhaps, and the natives opened out as the doctor came up. The trader pushed him forwards. Then he saw, lying half in the water and half out, a dreadful object, the body of Davidson. Dr Macphail bent down—he was not a man to lose his head in an emergency—and turned the body over. The throat was cut from ear to ear, and in the right hand was still the razor with which the deed was done.

"He's quite cold," said the doctor. "He must have been dead some time."

"One of the boys saw him lying there on his way to work just now and came and told me. Do you think he did it himself?"

"Yes. Someone ought to go for the police."

Horn said something in the native tongue, and two youths started off.

"We must leave him here till they come," said the doctor.

"They mustn't take him into my house. I won't have him in my house."

"You'll do what the authorities say," replied the doctor sharply. "In point of fact I expect they'll take him to the mortuary."

They stood waiting where they were. The trader took a cigarette from a fold in his lava-lava and gave one to Dr Macphail. They smoked while they stared at the corpse. Dr Macphail could not understand.

"Why do you think he did it?" asked Horn.

The doctor shrugged his shoulders. In a little while native police came along, under the charge of a marine, with a stretcher, and immediately afterwards a couple of naval officers and a naval doctor. They managed everything in a businesslike manner.

"What about the wife?" said one of the officers.

"Now that you've come I'll go back to the house and get some

things on. I'll see that it's broken to her. She'd better not see him till
he's been fixed up a little."

"I guess that's right," said the naval doctor.

When Dr Macphail went back he found his wife nearly dressed.

"Mrs Davidson's in a dreadful state about her husband," she said
to him as soon as he appeared. "He hasn't been to bed all night. She
heard him leave Miss Thompson's room at two, but he went out. If
he's been walking about since then he'll be absolutely dead."

Dr Macphail told her what had happened and asked her to break
the news to Mrs Davidson.

"But why did he do it?" she asked, horror-stricken.

"I don't know."

"But I can't. I can't."

"You must."

She gave him a frightened look and went out. He heard her go
into Mrs Davidson's room. He waited a minute to gather himself
together and then began to shave and wash. When he was dressed he
sat down on the bed and waited for his wife. At last she came.

"She wants to see him," she said.

"They've taken him to the mortuary. We'd better go down with
her. How did she take it?"

"I think she's stunned. She didn't cry. But she's trembling like a
leaf."

"We'd better go at once."

When they knocked at her door Mrs Davidson came out. She
was very pale, but dry-eyed. To the doctor she seemed unnaturally
composed. No word was exchanged, and they set out in silence down
the road. When they arrived at the mortuary Mrs Davidson spoke.

"Let me go in and see him alone."

They stood aside. A native opened a door for her and closed it
behind her. They sat down and waited. One or two white men came
and talked to them in undertones. Dr Macphail told them again what
he knew of the tragedy. At last the door was quietly opened and Mrs
Davidson came out. Silence fell upon them.

"I'm ready to go back now," she said.

Her voice was hard and steady. Dr Macphail could not understand the look in her eyes. Her pale face was very stern. They walked back slowly, never saying a word, and at last they came round the bend on the other side of which stood their house. Mrs Davidson gave a gasp, and for a moment they stopped still. An incredible sound assaulted their ears. The gramophone which had been silent for so long was playing, playing ragtime loud and harsh.

"What's that?" cried Mrs Macphail with horror.

"Let's go on," said Mrs Davidson.

They walked up the steps and entered the hall. Miss Thompson was standing at her door, chatting with a sailor. A sudden change had taken place in her. She was no longer the cowed drudge of the last days. She was dressed in all her finery, in her white dress, with the high shiny boots over which her fat legs bulged in their cotton stockings; her hair was elaborately arranged; and she wore that enormous hat covered with gaudy flowers. Her face was painted, her eyebrows were boldly black, and her lips were scarlet. She held herself erect. She was the flaunting quean that they had known at first. As they came in she broke into a loud, jeering laugh; and then, when Mrs Davidson involuntarily stopped, she collected the spittle in her mouth and spat. Mrs Davidson cowered back, and two red spots rose suddenly to her cheeks. Then, covering her face with her hands, she broke away and ran quickly up the stairs. Dr Macphail was outraged. He pushed past the woman into her room.

"What the devil are you doing?" he cried. "Stop that damned machine."

He went up to it and tore the record off. She turned on him.

"Say, doc, you can that stuff with me. What the hell are you doin' in my room?"

"What do you mean?" he cried. "What d'you mean?"

She gathered herself together. No one could describe the scorn of her expression or the contemptuous hatred she put into her answer.

"You men! You filthy, dirty pigs! You're all the same, all of you. Pigs! Pigs!"

Dr Macphail gasped. He understood.

The Pool

WHEN I WAS introduced to Lawson by Chaplin, the owner of the Hotel Metropole at Apia, I paid no particular attention to him. We were sitting in the lounge over an early cocktail and I was listening with amusement to the gossip of the island.

Chaplin entertained me. He was by profession a mining engineer and perhaps it was characteristic of him that he had settled in a place where his professional attainments were of no possible value. It was, however, generally reported that he was an extremely clever mining engineer. He was a small man, neither fat nor thin, with black hair, scanty on the crown, turning grey, and a small, untidy moustache; his face, partly from the sun and partly from liquor, was very red. He was but a figurehead, for the hotel, though so grandly named but a frame building of two storeys, was managed by his wife, a tall, gaunt Australian of five and forty, with an imposing presence and a determined air. The little man, excitable and often tipsy, was terrified of her, and the stranger soon heard of domestic quarrels in which she used her fist and her foot in order to keep him in subjection. She had been known after a night of drunkenness to confine him for twenty-four hours to his own room, and then he could be seen, afraid to leave his prison, talking somewhat pathetically from his verandah to people in the street below.

He was a character, and his reminiscences of a varied life, whether true or not, made him worth listening to, so that when Lawson strolled in I was inclined to resent the interruption. Although not midday, it was clear that he had had enough to drink, and it was without enthusiasm that I yielded to his persistence and accepted his offer of another cocktail. I knew already that Chaplin's head was weak. The next round which in common politeness I should be forced to order would be enough to make him lively, and then Mrs Chaplin would give me black looks.

Nor was there anything attractive in Lawson's appearance. He was a little thin man, with a long, sallow face and a narrow, weak chin, a prominent nose, large and bony, and great shaggy black eyebrows. They gave him a peculiar look. His eyes, very large and very dark, were magnificent. He was jolly, but his jollity did not seem to me sincere; it was on the surface, a mask which he wore to deceive the world, and I suspected that it concealed a mean nature. He was plainly anxious to be thought a "good sport" and he was hail-fellow-well-met; but, I do not know why, I felt that he was cunning and shifty. He talked a great deal in a raucous voice, and he and Chaplin capped one another's stories of beanos which had become legendary, stories of "wet" nights at the English Club, of shooting expeditions where an incredible amount of whisky had been consumed, and of jaunts to Sydney of which their pride was that they could remember nothing from the time they landed till the time they sailed. A pair of drunken swine. But even in their intoxication, for by now after four cocktails each, neither was sober, there was a great difference between Chaplin, rough and vulgar, and Lawson: Lawson might be drunk, but he was certainly a gentleman.

At last he got out of his chair, a little unsteadily.

"Well, I'll be getting along home," he said. "See you before dinner."

"Missus all right?" said Chaplin.

"Yes."

He went out. There was a peculiar note in the monosyllable of his answer which made me look up.

"Good chap," said Chaplin flatly, as Lawson went out of the door into the sunshine. "One of the best. Pity he drinks."

This from Chaplin was an observation not without humour.

"And when he's drunk he wants to fight people."

"Is he often drunk?"

"Dead drunk, three or four days a week. It's the island done it, and Ethel."

"Who's Ethel?"

"Ethel's his wife. Married a half-caste. Old Brevald's daughter. Took her away from here. Only thing to do. But she couldn't stand it, and now they're back again. He'll hang himself one of these days, if he don't drink himself to death before. Good chap. Nasty when he's drunk."

Chaplin belched loudly.

"I'll go and put my head under the shower. I oughtn't to have had that last cocktail. It's always the last one that does you in."

He looked uncertainly at the staircase as he made up his mind to go to the cubby hole in which was the shower, and then with unnatural seriousness got up.

"Pay you to cultivate Lawson," he said. "A well read chap. You'd be surprised when he's sober. Clever too. Worth talking to."

Chaplin had told me the whole story in these few speeches.

When I came in towards evening from a ride along the seashore Lawson was again in the hotel. He was heavily sunk in one of the cane chairs in the lounge and he looked at me with glassy eyes. It was plain that he had been drinking all the afternoon. He was torpid, and the look on his face was sullen and vindictive. His glance rested on me for a moment, but I could see that he did not recognise me. Two or three other men were sitting there, shaking dice, and they took no notice of him. His condition was evidently too usual to attract attention. I sat down and began to play.

"You're a damned sociable lot," said Lawson suddenly.

He got out of his chair and waddled with bent knees towards the door. I do not know whether the spectacle was more ridiculous than revolting. When he had gone one of the men sniggered.

"Lawson's fairly soused to-day," he said.

"If I couldn't carry my liquor better than that," said another, "I'd climb on the waggon and stay there."

Who would have thought that this wretched object was in his way a romantic figure or that his life had in it those elements of pity and terror which the theorist tells us are necessary to achieve the effect of tragedy?

I did not see him again for two or three days.

I was sitting one evening on the first floor of the hotel on a verandah that overlooked the street when Lawson came up and sank into
a chair beside me. He was quite sober. He made a casual remark and
then, when I had replied somewhat indifferently, added with a laugh
which had in it an apologetic tone:

"I was devilish soused the other day."

I did not answer. There was really nothing to say. I pulled away
at my pipe in the vain hope of keeping the mosquitoes away, and
looked at the natives going home from their work. They walked with
long steps, slowly, with care and dignity, and the soft patter of their
naked feet was strange to hear. Their dark hair, curling or straight,
was often white with lime, and then they had a look of extraordinary
distinction. They were tall and finely built. Then a gang of Solomon
Islanders, indentured labourers, passed by, singing; they were shorter
and slighter than the Samoans, coal black with great heads of fuzzy
hair dyed red. Now and then a white man drove past in his buggy or
rode into the hotel yard. In the lagoon two or three schooners reflected their grace in the tranquil water.

"I don't know what there is to do in a place like this except to get
soused," said Lawson at last.

"Don't you like Samoa?" I asked casually, for something to say.

"It's pretty, isn't it?"

The word he chose seemed so inadequate to describe the unimaginable beauty of the island, that I smiled, and smiling I turned
to look at him. I was startled by the expression in those fine sombre
eyes of his, an expression of intolerable anguish; they betrayed a tragic
depth of emotion of which I should never have thought him capable.
But the expression passed away and he smiled. His smile was simple
and a little naïve. It changed his face so that I wavered in my first
feeling of aversion from him.

"I was all over the place when I first came out," he said.

He was silent for a moment.

"I went away for good about three years ago, but I came back."
He hesitated. "My wife wanted to come back. She was born here, you
know."

"Oh, yes."

He was silent again, and then hazarded a remark about Robert Louis Stevenson. He asked me if I had been up to Vailima. For some reason he was making an effort to be agreeable to me. He began to talk of Stevenson's books, and presently the conversation drifted to London.

"I suppose Covent Garden's still going strong," he said. "I think I miss the opera as much as anything here. Have you seen Tristan and Isolde?"

He asked me the question as though the answer were really important to him, and when I said, a little casually I daresay, that I had, he seemed pleased. He began to speak of Wagner, not as a musician, but as the plain man who received from him an emotional satisfaction that he could not analyse.

"I suppose Bayreuth was the place to go really," he said. "I never had the money, worse luck. But of course one might do worse than Covent Garden, all the lights and the women dressed up to the nines, and the music. The first act of the Walküre's all right, isn't it? And the end of Tristan. Golly!"

His eyes were flashing now and his face was lit up so that he hardly seemed the same man. There was a flush on his sallow, thin cheeks, and I forgot that his voice was harsh and unpleasant. There was even a certain charm about him.

"By George, I'd like to be in London to-night. Do you know the Pall Mall restaurant? I used to go there a lot. Piccadilly Circus with the shops all lit up, and the crowd. I think it's stunning to stand there and watch the buses and taxis streaming along as though they'd never stop. And I like the Strand too. What are those lines about God and Charing Cross?"

I was taken aback.

"Thompson's, d'you mean?" I asked.

I quoted them.

> "And when so sad, thou canst not sadder,
> Cry, and upon thy so sore loss
> Shall shine the traffic of Jacob's ladder
> Pitched between Heaven and Charing Cross."

He gave a faint sigh.

"I've read The Hound of Heaven. It's a bit of all right."

"It's generally thought so," I murmured.

"You don't meet anybody here who's read anything. They think it's swank."

There was a wistful look on his face, and I thought I divined the feeling that made him come to me. I was a link with the world he regretted and a life that he would know no more. Because not so very long before I had been in the London which he loved, he looked upon me with awe and envy. He had not spoken for five minutes perhaps when he broke out with words that startled me by their intensity.

"I'm fed up," he said. "I'm fed up."

"Then why don't you clear out?" I asked.

His face grew sullen.

"My lungs are a bit dicky. I couldn't stand an English winter now."

At that moment another man joined us on the verandah and Lawson sank into a moody silence.

"It's about time for a drain," said the new-comer. "Who'll have a drop of Scotch with me? Lawson?"

Lawson seemed to arise from a distant world. He got up.

"Let's go down to the bar," he said.

When he left me I remained with a more kindly feeling towards him than I should have expected. He puzzled and interested me. And a few days later I met his wife. I knew they had been married for five or six years, and I was surprised to see that she was still extremely young. When he married her she could not have been more than sixteen. She was adorably pretty. She was no darker than a Spaniard, small and very beautifully made, with tiny hands and feet, and a slight, lithe figure. Her features were lovely; but I think what struck me most was the delicacy of her appearance; the half-caste as a rule have a certain coarseness, they seem a little roughly formed, but she had an exquisite daintiness which took your breath away. There was something extremely civilised about her, so that it surprised you to see her in those surroundings, and you thought of those famous beauties who had set all the world talking at the Court of the Emperor Napoleon III. Though she wore but a muslin frock and a straw hat she wore them with an elegance that suggested the woman of fashion. She must have been ravishing when Lawson first saw her.

He had but lately come out from England to manage the local branch of an English bank, and, reaching Samoa at the beginning of the dry season, he had taken a room at the hotel. He quickly made the acquaintance of all and sundry. The life of the island is pleasant and easy. He enjoyed the long idle talks in the lounge of the hotel and the gay evenings at the English Club when a group of fellows would play pool. He liked Apia straggling along the edge of the lagoon, with its stores and bungalows, and its native village. Then there were week-ends when he would ride over to the house of one planter or another and spend a couple of nights on the hills. He had never before known freedom or leisure. And he was intoxicated by the sunshine. When he rode through the bush his head reeled a little at the beauty that surrounded him. The country was indescribably fertile. In parts the forest was still virgin, a tangle of strange trees, luxuriant undergrowth, and vine; it gave an impression that was mysterious and troubling.

But the spot that entranced him was a pool a mile or two away from Apia to which in the evenings he often went to bathe. There was a little river that bubbled over the rocks in a swift stream, and then, after forming the deep pool, ran on, shallow and crystalline, past a ford made by great stones where the natives came sometimes to bathe or to wash their clothes. The coconut trees, with their frivolous elegance, grew thickly on the banks, all clad with trailing plants, and they were reflected in the green water. It was just such a scene as you might see in Devonshire among the hills, and yet with a difference, for it had a tropical richness, a passion, a scented languor which seemed to melt the heart. The water was fresh, but not cold; and it was delicious after the heat of the day. To bathe there refreshed not only the body but the soul.

At the hour when Lawson went, there was not a soul and he lingered for a long time, now floating idly in the water, now drying himself in the evening sun, enjoying the solitude and the friendly silence. He did not regret London then, nor the life that he had abandoned, for life as it was seemed complete and exquisite.

It was here that he first saw Ethel.

Occupied till late by letters which had to be finished for the monthly sailing of the boat next day, he rode down one evening to the pool when the light was almost failing. He tied up his horse and sauntered to the bank. A girl was sitting there. She glanced round as he came and noiselessly slid into the water. She vanished like a naiad startled by the approach of a mortal. He was surprised and amused. He wondered where she had hidden herself. He swam downstream and presently saw her sitting on a rock. She looked at him with uncurious eyes. He called out a greeting in Samoan.

"Talofa."

She answered him, suddenly smiling, and then let herself into the water again. She swam easily and her hair spread out behind her. He watched her cross the pool and climb out on the bank. Like all the natives she bathed in a Mother Hubbard, and the water had made it cling to her slight body. She wrung out her hair, and as she stood there, unconcerned, she looked more than ever like a wild creature of the water or the woods. He saw now that she was half-caste. He swam towards her and, getting out, addressed her in English.

"You're having a late swim."

She shook back her hair and then let it spread over her shoulders in luxuriant curls.

"I like it when I'm alone," she said.

"So do I."

She laughed with the childlike frankness of the native. She slipped a dry Mother Hubbard over her head and, letting down the wet one, stepped out of it. She wrung it out and was ready to go. She paused a moment irresolutely and then sauntered off. The night fell suddenly.

Lawson went back to the hotel and, describing her to the men who were in the lounge shaking dice for drinks, soon discovered who she was. Her father was a Norwegian called Brevald who was often to be seen in the bar of the Hotel Metropole drinking rum and water. He was a little old man, knotted and gnarled like an ancient tree, who had come out to the islands forty years before as mate of a sailing vessel. He had been a blacksmith, a trader, a planter, and at one time fairly well-to-do; but, ruined by the great hurricane of the nineties, he had now nothing to live on but a small plantation of coconut trees. He had had four native wives and, as he told you with a cracked chuckle, more children than he could count. But some had died and some had gone out into the world, so that now the only one left at home was Ethel.

"She's a peach," said Nelson, the supercargo of the Moana. "I've given her the glad eye once or twice, but I guess there's nothing doing."

"Old Brevald's not that sort of a fool, sonny," put in another, a man called Miller. "He wants a son-in-law who's prepared to keep him in comfort for the rest of his life."

It was distasteful to Lawson that they should speak of the girl in that fashion. He made a remark about the departing mail and so distracted their attention. But next evening he went again to the pool. Ethel was there; and the mystery of the sunset, the deep silence of the water, the lithe grace of the coconut trees, added to her beauty, giving it a profundity, a magic, which stirred the heart to unknown emotions. For some reason that time he had the whim not to speak to her. She took no notice of him. She did not even glance in his direction. She swam about the green pool. She dived, she rested on the bank, as though she were quite alone: he had a queer feeling that he was invisible. Scraps of poetry, half forgotten, floated across his memory, and vague recollections of the Greece he had negligently studied in his school days. When she had changed her wet clothes for dry ones and sauntered away he found a scarlet hibiscus where she had been. It was a flower that she had worn in her hair when she came to bathe and, having taken it out on getting into the water, had forgotten or not cared to put in again. He took it in his hands and looked at it with a singular emotion. He had an instinct to keep it, but his sentimentality irritated him, and he flung it away. It gave him quite a little pang to see it float down the stream.

He wondered what strangeness it was in her nature that urged her to go down to this hidden pool when there was no likelihood that anyone should be there. The natives of the islands are devoted to the water. They bathe, somewhere or other, every day, once always, and often twice; but they bathe in bands, laughing and joyous, a whole family together; and you often saw a group of girls, dappled by the sun shining through the trees, with the half-castes among them, splashing about the shallows of the stream. It looked as though there were in this pool some secret which attracted Ethel against her will.

Now the night had fallen, mysterious and silent, and he let himself down in the water softly, in order to make no sound, and swam lazily in the warm darkness. The water seemed fragrant still from her slender body. He rode back to the town under the starry sky. He felt at peace with the world.

Now he went every evening to the pool and every evening he saw Ethel. Presently he overcame her timidity. She became playful and friendly. They sat together on the rocks above the pool, where the water ran fast, and they lay side by side on the ledge that overlooked it, watching the gathering dusk envelop it with mystery. It was inevitable that their meetings should become known—in the South Seas everyone seems to know everyone's business—and he was subjected to much rude chaff by the men at the hotel. He smiled and let them talk. It was not even worth while to deny their coarse suggestions. His feelings were absolutely pure. He loved Ethel as a poet might love the moon. He thought of her not as a woman but as something not of this earth. She was the spirit of the pool.

One day at the hotel, passing through the bar, he saw that old Brevald, as ever in his shabby blue overalls, was standing there. Because he was Ethel's father he had a desire to speak to him, so he went in, nodded and, ordering his own drink, casually turned and invited the old man to have one with him. They chatted for a few minutes of local affairs, and Lawson was uneasily conscious that the Norwegian was scrutinising him with sly blue eyes. His manner was not agreeable. It was sycophantic, and yet behind the cringing air of an old man who had been worsted in his struggle with fate was a shadow of old truculence. Lawson remembered that he had once been captain of a schooner engaged in the slave trade, a blackbirder they call it in the Pacific, and he had a large hernia in the chest which was the result of a wound received in a scrap with Solomon Islanders. The bell rang for luncheon.

"Well, I must be off," said Lawson.

"Why don't you come along to my place one time?" said Brevald, in his wheezy voice. "It's not very grand, but you'll be welcome. You know Ethel."

"I'll come with pleasure."

"Sunday afternoon's the best time."

Brevald's bungalow, shabby and bedraggled, stood among the coconut trees of the plantation, a little away from the main road that ran up to Vailima. Immediately around it grew huge plantains. With their tattered leaves they had the tragic beauty of a lovely woman in rags. Everything was slovenly and neglected. Little black pigs, thin and high-backed, rooted about, and chickens clucked noisily as they picked at the refuse scattered here and there. Three or four natives were lounging about the verandah. When Lawson asked for Brevald the old man's cracked voice called out to him, and he found him in the sitting-room smoking an old briar pipe.

"Sit down and make yerself at home," he said. "Ethel's just titivating."

She came in. She wore a blouse and skirt and her hair was done in the European fashion. Although she had not the wild, timid grace of the girl who came down every evening to the pool, she seemed now more usual and consequently more approachable. She shook hands with Lawson. It was the first time he had touched her hand.

"I hope you'll have a cup of tea with us," she said.

He knew she had been at a mission school, and he was amused, and at the same time touched, by the company manners she was putting on for his benefit. Tea was already set out on the table and in a minute old Brevald's fourth wife brought in the tea-pot. She was a handsome native, no longer very young, and she spoke but a few words of English. She smiled and smiled. Tea was rather a solemn meal, with a great deal of bread and butter and a variety of very sweet cakes, and the conversation was formal. Then a wrinkled old woman came in softly.

"That's Ethel's granny," said old Brevald, noisily spitting on the floor.

She sat on the edge of a chair, uncomfortably, so that you saw it was unusual for her and she would have been more at ease on the ground, and remained silently staring at Lawson with fixed, shining eyes. In the kitchen behind the bungalow someone began to play the concertina and two or three voices were raised in a hymn. But they sang for the pleasure of the sounds rather than from piety.

When Lawson walked back to the hotel he was strangely happy. He was touched by the higgledy-piggledy way in which those people lived; and in the smiling good-nature of Mrs Brevald, in the little Norwegian's fantastic career, and in the shining mysterious eyes of the old grandmother, he found something unusual and fascinating. It was a more natural life than any he had known, it was nearer to the friendly, fertile earth; civilisation repelled him at that moment, and by mere contact with these creatures of a more primitive nature he felt a greater freedom.

He saw himself rid of the hotel which already was beginning to irk him, settled in a little bungalow of his own, trim and white, in front of the sea so that he had before his eyes always the multicoloured variety of the lagoon. He loved the beautiful island. London and England meant nothing to him any more, he was content to spend the rest of his days in that forgotten spot, rich in the best of the world's goods, love and happiness. He made up his mind that whatever the obstacles nothing should prevent him from marrying Ethel.

But there were no obstacles. He was always welcome at the Brevalds' house. The old man was ingratiating and Mrs Brevald smiled without ceasing. He had brief glimpses of natives who seemed somehow to belong to the establishment, and once he found a tall youth in a lava-lava, his body tattooed, his hair white with lime, sitting with Brevald, and was told he was Mrs Brevald's brother's son; but for the most part they kept out of his way. Ethel was delightful with him. The light in her eyes when she saw him filled him with ecstasy. She was charming and naïve. He listened enraptured when she told him of the mission school at which she was educated, and of the sisters. He went with her to the cinema which was given once a fortnight and danced with her at the dance which followed it. They came from all parts of the island for this, since gaieties are few in Upolu; and you saw there all the society of the place, the white ladies keeping a good deal to themselves, the half-castes very elegant in American clothes, the natives, strings of dark girls in white Mother Hubbards and young men in unaccustomed ducks and white shoes. It was all very smart and gay. Ethel was pleased to show her friends the white admirer who did not leave her side. The rumour was soon spread that he meant to marry her and her friends looked at her with envy. It was a great thing for a half-caste to get a white man to marry her, even the less regular relation was better than nothing, but one could never tell what it would lead to; and Lawson's position as manager of the bank made him one of the catches of the island. If he had not been so absorbed in Ethel he would have noticed that many eyes were fixed on him curiously, and he would have seen the glances of the white ladies and noticed how they put their heads together and gossiped.

Afterwards, when the men who lived at the hotel were having a whisky before turning in, Nelson burst out with:

"Say, they say Lawson's going to marry that girl."

"He's a damned fool then," said Miller.

Miller was a German-American who had changed his name from Müller, a big man, fat and bald-headed, with a round, clean-shaven face. He wore large gold-rimmed spectacles, which gave him a benign look, and his ducks were always clean and white. He was a heavy drinker, invariably ready to stay up all night with the "boys," but he never got drunk; he was jolly and affable, but very shrewd. Nothing interfered with his business; he represented a firm in San Francisco, jobbers of the goods sold in the islands, calico, machinery and what not; and his good-fellowship was part of his stock-in-trade.

"He don't know what he's up against," said Nelson. "Someone ought to put him wise."

"If you'll take my advice you won't interfere in what don't concern you," said Miller. "When a man's made up his mind to make a fool of himself, there's nothing like letting him."

"I'm all for having a good time with the girls out here, but when it comes to marrying them—this child ain't taking any, I'll tell the world."

Chaplin was there, and now he had his say.

"I've seen a lot of fellows do it, and it's no good."

"You ought to have a talk with him, Chaplin," said Nelson. "You know him better than anyone else does."

"My advice to Chaplin is to leave it alone," said Miller.

Even in those days Lawson was not popular and really no one took enough interest in him to bother. Mrs Chaplin talked it over with two or three of the white ladies, but they contented themselves with saying that it was a pity; and when he told her definitely that he was going to be married it seemed too late to do anything.

For a year Lawson was happy. He took a bungalow at the point of the bay round which Apia is built, on the borders of a native village. It nestled charmingly among the coconut trees and faced the passionate blue of the Pacific. Ethel was lovely as she went about the little house, lithe and graceful like some young animal of the woods, and she was gay. They laughed a great deal. They talked nonsense. Sometimes one or two of the men at the hotel would come over and spend the evening, and often on a Sunday they would go for a day to some planter who had married a native; now and then one or other of the half-caste traders who had a store in Apia would give a party and they went to it. The half-castes treated Lawson quite differently now. His marriage had made him one of themselves and they called him Bertie. They put their arms through his and smacked him on the back. He liked to see Ethel at these gatherings. Her eyes shone and she laughed. It did him good to see her radiant happiness. Sometimes Ethel's relations would come to the bungalow, old Brevald of course, and her mother, but cousins too, vague native women in Mother Hubbards and men and boys in lava-lavas, with their hair dyed red and their bodies elaborately tattooed. He would find them sitting there when he got back from the bank. He laughed indulgently.

"Don't let them eat us out of hearth and home," he said.

"They're my own family. I can't help doing something for them when they ask me."

He knew that when a white man marries a native or a half-caste he must expect her relations to look upon him as a gold mine. He took Ethel's face in his hands and kissed her red lips. Perhaps he could not expect her to understand that the salary which had amply sufficed for a bachelor must be managed with some care when it had to support a wife and a house. Then Ethel was delivered of a son.

It was when Lawson first held the child in his arms that a sudden pang shot through his heart. He had not expected it to be so dark. After all it had but a fourth part of native blood, and there was no reason really why it should not look just like an English baby; but, huddled together in his arms, sallow, its head covered already with black hair, with huge black eyes, it might have been a native child. Since his marriage he had been ignored by the white ladies of the colony. When he came across men in whose houses he had been accustomed to dine as a bachelor, they were a little self-conscious with him; and they sought to cover their embarrassment by an exaggerated cordiality.

"Mrs Lawson well?" they would say. "You're a lucky fellow. Damned pretty girl."

But if they were with their wives and met him and Ethel they would feel it awkward when their wives gave Ethel a patronising nod. Lawson had laughed.

"They're as dull as ditchwater, the whole gang of them," he said. "It's not going to disturb my night's rest if they don't ask me to their dirty parties."

But now it irked him a little.

The little dark baby screwed up its face. That was his son. He thought of the half-caste children in Apia. They had an unhealthy look, sallow and pale, and they were odiously precocious. He had seen them on the boat going to school in New Zealand, and a school had to be chosen which took children with native blood in them; they were huddled together, brazen and yet timid, with traits which set them apart strangely from white people. They spoke the native language among themselves. And when they grew up the men accepted smaller salaries because of their native blood; girls might marry a white man, but boys had no chance; they must marry a half-caste like themselves or a native. Lawson made up his mind passionately that he would take his son away from the humiliation of such a life. At whatever cost he must get back to Europe. And when he went in to see Ethel, frail and lovely in her bed, surrounded by native women, his determination was strengthened. If he took her away among his own people she would belong more completely to him. He loved her so passionately, he wanted her to be one soul and one body with him;

and he was conscious that here, with those deep roots attaching her to the native life, she would always keep something from him.

He went to work quietly, urged by an obscure instinct of secrecy, and wrote to a cousin who was partner in a shipping firm in Aberdeen, saying that his health (on account of which like so many more he had come out to the islands) was so much better, there seemed no reason why he should not return to Europe. He asked him to use what influence he could to get him a job, no matter how poorly paid, on Deeside, where the climate was particularly suitable to such as suffered from diseases of the lungs. It takes five or six weeks for letters to get from Aberdeen to Samoa, and several had to be exchanged. He had plenty of time to prepare Ethel. She was as delighted as a child. He was amused to see how she boasted to her friends that she was going to England; it was a step up for her; she would be quite English there; and she was excited at the interest the approaching departure gave her. When at length a cable came offering him a post in a bank in Kincardineshire she was beside herself with joy.

When, their long journey over, they were settled in the little Scots town with its granite houses Lawson realised how much it meant to him to live once more among his own people. He looked back on the three years he had spent in Apia as exile, and returned to the life that seemed the only normal one with a sigh of relief. It was good to play golf once more, and to fish—to fish properly, that was poor fun in the Pacific when you just threw in your line and pulled out one big sluggish fish after another from the crowded sea—and it was good to see a paper every day with that day's news, and to meet men and women of your own sort, people you could talk to; and it was good to eat meat that was not frozen and to drink milk that was not canned. They were thrown upon their own resources much more than in the Pacific, and he was glad to have Ethel exclusively to himself. After two years of marriage he loved her more devotedly than ever, he could hardly bear her out of his sight, and the need in him grew urgent for a more intimate communion between them. But it was strange that after the first excitement of arrival she seemed to take less interest in the new life than he had expected. She did not accustom herself to her surroundings. She was a little lethargic. As the fine autumn darkened into winter she complained of the cold. She lay half the morning in bed and the rest of the day on a sofa, reading novels sometimes, but more often doing nothing. She looked pinched.

"Never mind, darling," he said. "You'll get used to it very soon. And wait till the summer comes. It can be almost as hot as in Apia."

He felt better and stronger than he had done for years.

The carelessness with which she managed her house had not mattered in Samoa, but here it was out of place. When anyone came he did not want the place to look untidy; and, laughing, chaffing Ethel a little, he set about putting things in order. Ethel watched him indolently. She spent long hours playing with her son. She talked to him in the baby language of her own country. To distract her, Lawson bestirred himself to make friends among the neighbours, and now and then they went to little parties where the ladies sang drawing-room ballads and the men beamed in silent good nature. Ethel was shy. She seemed to sit apart. Sometimes Lawson, seized with a sudden anxiety, would ask her if she was happy.

"Yes, I'm quite happy," she answered.

But her eyes were veiled by some thought he could not guess. She seemed to withdraw into herself so that he was conscious that he knew no more of her than when he had first seen her bathing in the pool. He had an uneasy feeling that she was concealing something from him, and because he adored her it tortured him.

"You don't regret Apia, do you?" he asked her once.

"Oh, no—I think it's very nice here."

An obscure misgiving drove him to make disparaging remarks about the island and the people there. She smiled and did not answer. Very rarely she received a bundle of letters from Samoa and then she went about for a day or two with a set, pale face.

"Nothing would induce me ever to go back there," he said once. "It's no place for a white man."

But he grew conscious that sometimes, when he was away, Ethel cried. In Apia she had been talkative, chatting volubly about all the little details of their common life, the gossip of the place; but now she gradually became silent, and, though he increased his efforts to amuse her, she remained listless. It seemed to him that her recollections of the old life were drawing her away from him, and he was madly jealous of the island and of the sea, of Brevald, and all the dark-skinned people whom he remembered now with horror. When she spoke of Samoa he was bitter and satirical. One evening late in the spring when the birch trees were bursting into leaf, coming home from a round of golf, he found her not as usual lying on the sofa, but at the window, standing. She had evidently been waiting for his return. She addressed him the moment he came into the room. To his amazement she spoke in Samoan.

"I can't stand it. I can't live here any more. I hate it. I hate it."

"For God's sake speak in a civilised language," he said irritably.

She went up to him and clasped her arms around his body awkwardly, with a gesture that had in it something barbaric.

"Let's go away from here. Let's go back to Samoa. If you make me stay here I shall die. I want to go home."

Her passion broke suddenly and she burst into tears. His anger vanished and he drew her down on his knees. He explained to her that it was impossible for him to throw up his job, which after all meant his bread and butter. His place in Apia was long since filled. He had nothing to go back to there. He tried to put it to her reasonably, the inconveniences of life there, the humiliation to which they must be exposed, and the bitterness it must cause their son.

"Scotland's wonderful for education and that sort of thing. Schools are good and cheap, and he can go to the University at Aberdeen. I'll make a real Scot of him."

They had called him Andrew. Lawson wanted him to become a doctor. He would marry a white woman.

"I'm not ashamed of being half native," Ethel said sullenly.

"Of course not, darling. There's nothing to be ashamed of."

With her soft cheek against his he felt incredibly weak.

"You don't know how much I love you," he said. "I'd give anything in the world to be able to tell you what I've got in my heart."

He sought her lips.

The summer came. The highland valley was green and fragrant, and the hills were gay with the heather. One sunny day followed another in that sheltered spot, and the shade of the birch trees was grateful after the glare of the high road. Ethel spoke no more of Samoa and Lawson grew less nervous. He thought that she was resigned to her surroundings, and he felt that his love for her was so passionate that it could leave no room in her heart for any longing. One day the local doctor stopped him in the street.

"I say, Lawson, your missus ought to be careful how she bathes in our highland streams. It's not like the Pacific, you know."

Lawson was surprised, and had not the presence of mind to conceal the fact.

"I didn't know she was bathing."

The doctor laughed.

"A good many people have seen her. It makes them talk a bit, you know, because it seems a rum place to choose, the pool up above the bridge, and bathing isn't allowed there, but there's no harm in that. I don't know how she can stand the water."

Lawson knew the pool the doctor spoke of, and suddenly it occurred to him that in a way it was just like that pool at Upolu where Ethel had been in the habit of bathing every evening. A clear highland stream ran down a sinuous course, rocky, splashing gaily, and then formed a deep, smooth pool, with a little sandy beach. Trees overshadowed it thickly, not coconut trees, but beeches, and the sun played fitfully through the leaves on the sparkling water. It gave him a shock. With his imagination he saw Ethel go there every day and undress on the bank and slip into the water, cold, colder than that of the pool she loved at home, and for a moment regain the feeling of the past. He saw her once more as the strange, wild spirit of the stream, and it seemed to him fantastically that the running water called her. That afternoon he went along to the river. He made his way cautiously among the trees and the grassy path deadened the sound of his steps. Presently he came to a spot from which he could see the pool. Ethel was sitting on the bank, looking down at the water. She sat quite still. It seemed as though the water drew her irresistibly. He wondered what strange thoughts wandered through her head. At last she got up, and for a minute or two she was hidden from his gaze; then he saw her again, wearing a Mother Hubbard, and with her little bare feet she stepped delicately over the mossy bank. She came to the water's edge, and softly, without a splash, let herself down. She swam about quietly, and there was something not quite of a human being in the way she swam. He did not know why it affected him so queerly. He waited till she clambered out. She stood for a moment with the wet folds of her dress clinging to her body, so that its shape was outlined, and then, passing her hands slowly over her breasts, gave a little sigh of delight. Then she disappeared. Lawson turned away and walked back to the village. He had a bitter pain in his heart, for he knew that she was still a stranger to him and his hungry love was destined ever to remain unsatisfied.

He did not make any mention of what he had seen. He ignored the incident completely, but he looked at her curiously, trying to divine what was in her mind. He redoubled the tenderness with which he used her. He sought to make her forget the deep longing of her soul by the passion of his love.

Then one day, when he came home, he was astonished to find her not in the house.

"Where's Mrs Lawson?" he asked the maid.

"She went into Aberdeen, Sir, with the baby," the maid answered, a little surprised at the question. "She said she would not be back till the last train."

"Oh, all right."

He was vexed that Ethel had said nothing to him about the excursion, but he was not disturbed, since of late she had been in now and again to Aberdeen, and he was glad that she should look at the shops and perhaps visit a cinema. He went to meet the last train, but when she did not come he grew suddenly frightened. He went up to the bedroom and saw at once that her toilet things were no longer in their place. He opened the wardrobe and the drawers. They were half empty. She had bolted.

He was seized with a passion of anger. It was too late that night to telephone to Aberdeen and make enquiries, but he knew already all that his enquiries might have taught him. With fiendish cunning she had chosen a time when they were making up their periodical accounts at the bank and there was no chance that he could follow her. He was imprisoned by his work. He took up a paper and saw that there was a boat sailing for Australia next morning. She must be now well on the way to London. He could not prevent the sobs that were wrung painfully from him.

"I've done everything in the world for her," he cried, "and she had the heart to treat me like this. How cruel, how monstrously cruel!"

After two days of misery he received a letter from her. It was written in her school-girl hand. She had always written with difficulty:

> Dear Bertie
> I couldn't stand it any more. I'm going back home. Good-bye.
> Ethel

She did not say a single word of regret. She did not even ask him to come too. Lawson was prostrated. He found out where the ship made its first stop and, though he knew very well she would not come, sent a cable beseeching her to return. He waited with pitiful anxiety. He wanted her to send him just one word of love; she did not even answer. He passed through one violent phase after another. At one moment he told himself that he was well rid of her, and at the next that he would force her to return by withholding money. He was lonely and wretched. He wanted his boy and he wanted her. He knew that, whatever he pretended to himself, there was only one thing to do and that was to follow her. He could never live without her now. All his plans for the future were like a house of cards and he scattered them with angry impatience. He did not care whether he threw away his chances for the future, for nothing in the world mattered but that he should get Ethel back again. As soon as he could he went into Aberdeen and told the manager of his bank that he meant to leave at once. The manager remonstrated. The short notice was inconvenient. Lawson would not listen to reason. He was determined to be free before the next boat sailed; and it was not until he was on board of her, having sold everything he possessed, that in some measure he regained his calm. Till then to those who had come in contact with him he seemed hardly sane. His last action in England was to cable to Ethel at Apia that he was joining her.

He sent another cable from Sydney, and when at last with the dawn his boat crossed the bar at Apia and he saw once more the white houses straggling along the bay he felt an immense relief. The doctor came on board and the agent. They were both old acquaintances and he felt kindly towards their familiar faces. He had a drink or two with them for old times' sake, and also because he was desperately nervous. He was not sure if Ethel would be glad to see him. When he got into the launch and approached the wharf he scanned anxiously the little crowd that waited. She was not there and his heart sank, but then he saw Brevald, in his old blue clothes, and his heart warmed towards him.

"Where's Ethel?" he said, as he jumped on shore.

"She's down at the bungalow. She's living with us."

Lawson was dismayed, but he put on a jovial air.

"Well, have you got room for me? I daresay it'll take a week or two to fix ourselves up."

"Oh, yes, I guess we can make room for you."

After passing through the custom-house they went to the hotel and there Lawson was greeted by several of his old friends. There were a good many rounds of drinks before it seemed possible to get away and when they did go out at last to Brevald's house they were both rather gay. He clasped Ethel in his arms. He had forgotten all his bitter thoughts in the joy of beholding her once more. His mother-in-law was pleased to see him, and so was the old, wrinkled beldame, her mother; natives and half-castes came in, and they all sat round, beaming on him. Brevald had a bottle of whisky and everyone who came was given a nip. Lawson sat with his little dark-skinned boy on his knees, they had taken his English clothes off him and he was stark, with Ethel by his side in a Mother Hubbard. He felt like a returning prodigal. In the afternoon he went down to the hotel again and when he got back he was more than gay, he was drunk. Ethel and her mother knew that white men got drunk now and then, it was what you expected of them, and they laughed good-naturedly as they helped him to bed.

But in a day or two he set about looking for a job. He knew that he could not hope for such a position as that which he had thrown away to go to England; but with his training he could not fail to be useful to one of the trading firms, and perhaps in the end he would not lose by the change.

"After all, you can't make money in a bank," he said. "Trade's the thing."

He had hopes that he would soon make himself so indispensable that he would get someone to take him into partnership, and there was no reason why in a few years he should not be a rich man.

"As soon as I'm fixed up we'll find ourselves a shack," he told Ethel. "We can't go on living here."

Brevald's bungalow was so small that they were all piled on one another, and there was no chance of ever being alone. There was neither peace nor privacy.

"Well, there's no hurry. We shall be all right here till we find just what we want."

It took him a week to get settled and then he entered the firm of a man called Bain. But when he talked to Ethel about moving she said she wanted to stay where she was till her baby was born, for she was expecting another child. Lawson tried to argue with her.

"If you don't like it," she said, "go and live at the hotel."

He grew suddenly pale.

"Ethel, how can you suggest that!"

She shrugged her shoulders.

"What's the good of having a house of our own when we can live here."

He yielded.

When Lawson, after his work, went back to the bungalow he found it crowded with natives. They lay about smoking, sleeping, drinking kava; and they talked incessantly. The place was grubby and untidy. His child crawled about, playing with native children, and it heard nothing spoken but Samoan. He fell into the habit of dropping into the hotel on his way home to have a few cocktails, for he could only face the evening and the crowd of friendly natives when he was fortified with liquor. And all the time, though he loved her more passionately than ever, he felt that Ethel was slipping away from him. When the baby was born he suggested that they should get into a house of their own, but Ethel refused. Her stay in Scotland seemed to have thrown her back on her own people, now that she was once more among them, with a passionate zest, and she turned to her native ways with abandon. Lawson began to drink more. Every Saturday night he went to the English Club and got blind drunk.

He had the peculiarity that as he grew drunk he grew quarrelsome and once he had a violent dispute with Bain, his employer. Bain dismissed him, and he had to look out for another job. He was idle for two or three weeks and during these, sooner than sit in the bungalow, he lounged about in the hotel or at the English Club, and drank. It was more out of pity than anything else that Miller, the German-American, took him into his office; but he was a business man, and though Lawson's financial skill made him valuable, the circumstances were such that he could hardly refuse a smaller salary than he had had before, and Miller did not hesitate to offer it to him. Ethel and Brevald blamed him for taking it, since Pedersen, the half-caste, offered him more. But he resented bitterly the thought of being under the orders of a half-caste. When Ethel nagged him he burst out furiously:

"I'll see myself dead before I work for a nigger."

"You may have to," she said.

And in six months he found himself forced to this final humiliation. The passion for liquor had been gaining on him, he was often heavy with drink, and he did his work badly. Miller warned him once or twice and Lawson was not the man to accept remonstrance easily. One day in the midst of an altercation he put on his hat and walked out. But by now his reputation was well known and he could find no one to engage him. For a while he idled, and then he had an attack of delirium tremens. When he recovered, shameful and weak, he could no longer resist the constant pressure and he went to Pedersen and asked him for a job. Pedersen was glad to have a white man in his store and Lawson's skill at figures made him useful.

From that time his degeneration was rapid. The white people gave him the cold shoulder. They were only prevented from cutting him completely by disdainful pity and by a certain dread of his angry violence when he was drunk. He became extremely susceptible and was always on the lookout for affront.

He lived entirely among the natives and half-castes, but he had no longer the prestige of the white man. They felt his loathing for them and they resented his attitude of superiority. He was one of themselves now and they did not see why he should put on airs. Brevald, who had been ingratiating and obsequious, now treated him with contempt. Ethel had made a bad bargain. There were disgraceful scenes and once or twice the two men came to blows. When there was a quarrel Ethel took the part of her family. They found he was better drunk than sober, for when he was drunk he would lie on the bed or on the floor, sleeping heavily.

Then he became aware that something was being hidden from him.

When he got back to the bungalow for the wretched, half native supper which was his evening meal, often Ethel was not in. If he asked where she was Brevald told him she had gone to spend the evening with one or other of her friends. Once he followed her to the house Brevald had mentioned and found she was not there. On her return he asked her where she had been and she told him her father had made a mistake; she had been to so-and-so's. But he knew that she was lying. She was in her best clothes; her eyes were shining, and she looked lovely.

"Don't try any monkey tricks on me, my girl," he said, "or I'll break every bone in your body."

"You drunken beast," she said, scornfully.

He fancied that Mrs Brevald and the old grandmother looked at him maliciously and he ascribed Brevald's good-humour with him, so unusual those days, to his satisfaction at having something up his sleeve against his son-in-law. And then, his suspicions aroused, he imagined that the white men gave him curious glances. When he came into the lounge of the hotel the sudden silence which fell upon the company convinced him that he had been the subject of the conversation. Something was going on and everyone knew it but himself. He was seized with furious jealousy. He believed that Ethel was carrying on with one of the white men, and he looked at one after the other with scrutinising eyes; but there was nothing to give him even a hint. He was helpless. Because he could find no one on whom definitely to fix his suspicions, he went about like a raving maniac, looking for someone on whom to vent his wrath. Chance caused him in the end to hit upon the man who of all others least deserved to suffer from his violence. One afternoon, when he was sitting in the hotel by himself, moodily, Chaplin came in and sat down beside him. Perhaps Chaplin was the only man on the island who had any sympathy for him. They ordered drinks and chatted a few minutes about the races that were shortly to be run. Then Chaplain said:

"I guess we shall all have to fork out money for new dresses."

Lawson sniggered. Since Mrs Chaplin held the purse-strings if she wanted a new frock for the occasion she would certainly not ask her husband for the money.

"How is your missus?" asked Chaplin, desiring to be friendly.

"What the hell's that got to do with you?" said Lawson, knitting his dark brows.

"I was only asking a civil question."

"Well, keep your civil questions to yourself."

Chaplin was not a patient man; his long residence in the tropics, the whisky bottle, and his domestic affairs had given him a temper hardly more under control than Lawson's.

"Look here, my boy, when you're in my hotel you behave like a gentleman or you'll find yourself in the street before you can say knife."

Lawson's lowering face grew dark and red.

"Let me just tell you once for all and you can pass it on to the others," he said, panting with rage. "If any of you fellows come messing round with my wife he'd better look out."

"Who do you think wants to mess around with your wife?"

"I'm not such a fool as you think. I can see a stone wall in front of me as well as most men, and I warn you straight, that's all. I'm not going to put up with any hanky-panky, not on your life."

"Look here, you'd better clear out of here, and come back when you're sober."

"I shall clear out when I choose and not a minute before," said Lawson.

It was an unfortunate boast, for Chaplin in the course of his experience as a hotel-keeper had acquired a peculiar skill in dealing with gentlemen whose room he preferred to their company, and the words were hardly out of Lawson's mouth before he found himself caught by the collar and arm and hustled not without force into the street. He stumbled down the steps into the blinding glare of the sun.

It was in consequence of this that he had his first violent scene with Ethel. Smarting with humiliation and unwilling to go back to the hotel, he went home that afternoon earlier than usual. He found Ethel dressing to go out. As a rule she lay about in a Mother Hubbard, barefoot, with a flower in her dark hair; but now, in white silk stockings and high-heeled shoes, she was doing up a pink muslin dress which was the newest she had.

"You're making yourself very smart," he said. "Where are you going?"

"I'm going to the Crossleys."

"I'll come with you."

"Why?" she asked coolly.

"I don't want you to gad about by yourself all the time."

"You're not asked."

"I don't care a damn about that. You're not going without me."

"You'd better lie down till I'm ready."

She thought he was drunk and if he once settled himself on the bed would quickly drop off to sleep. He sat down on a chair and began to smoke a cigarette. She watched him with increasing irritation: When she was ready he got up. It happened by an unusual chance that there was no one in the bungalow. Brevald was working on the plantation and his wife had gone into Apia. Ethel faced him.

"I'm not going with you. You're drunk."

"That's a lie. You're not going without me."

She shrugged her shoulders and tried to pass him, but he caught her by the arm and held her.

"Let me go, you devil," she said, breaking into Samoan.

"Why do you want to go without me? Haven't I told you I'm not going to put up with any monkey tricks?"

She clenched her fist and hit him in the face. He lost all control of himself. All his love, all his hatred, welled up in him and he was beside himself.

"I'll teach you," he shouted. "I'll teach you."

He seized a riding-whip which happened to be under his hand, and struck her with it. She screamed, and the scream maddened him so that he went on striking her, again and again. Her shrieks rang through the bungalow and he cursed her as he hit. Then he flung her on the bed. She lay there sobbing with pain and terror. He threw the whip away from him and rushed out of the room. Ethel heard him go and she stopped crying. She looked round cautiously, then she raised herself. She was sore, but she had not been badly hurt, and she looked at her dress to see if it was damaged. The native women are not unused to blows. What he had done did not outrage her. When she looked at herself in the glass and arranged her hair, her eyes were shining. There was a strange look in them. Perhaps then she was nearer loving him than she had ever been before.

But Lawson, driven forth blindly, stumbled through the plantation and suddenly exhausted, weak as a child, flung himself on the ground at the foot of a tree. He was miserable and ashamed. He thought of Ethel, and in the yielding tenderness of his love all his bones seemed to grow soft within him. He thought of the past, and of his hopes, and he was aghast at what he had done. He wanted her more than ever. He wanted to take her in his arms. He must go to her at once. He got up. He was so weak that he staggered as he walked. He went into the house and she was sitting in their cramped bedroom in front of her looking-glass.

"Oh, Ethel, forgive me. I'm so awfully ashamed of myself. I didn't know what I was doing."

He fell on his knees before her and timidly stroked the skirt of her dress.

"I can't bear to think of what I did. It's awful. I think I was mad. There's no one in the world I love as I love you. I'd do anything to save you from pain and I've hurt you. I can never forgive myself, but for God's sake say you forgive me."

He heard her shrieks still. It was unendurable. She looked at him silently. He tried to take her hands and the tears streamed from his eyes. In his humiliation he hid his face in her lap and his frail body shook with sobs. An expression of utter contempt came over her face.

She had the native woman's disdain of a man who abased himself before a woman. A weak creature! And for a moment she had been on the point of thinking there was something in him. He grovelled at her feet like a cur. She gave him a little scornful kick.

"Get out," she said. "I hate you."

He tried to hold her, but she pushed him aside. She stood up. She began to take off her dress. She kicked off her shoes and slid the stockings off her feet, then she slipped on her old Mother Hubbard.

"Where are you going?"

"What's that got to do with you? I'm going down to the pool."

"Let me come too," he said.

He asked as though he were a child.

"Can't you even leave me that?"

He hid his face in his hands, crying miserably, while she, her eyes hard and cold, stepped past him and went out.

From that time she entirely despised him; and though, herded together in the small bungalow, Lawson and Ethel with her two children, Brevald, his wife and her mother, and the vague relations and hangers-on who were always in and about, they had to live cheek by jowl, Lawson, ceasing to be of any account, was hardly noticed. He left in the morning after breakfast, and came back only to have supper. He gave up the struggle, and when for want of money he could not go to the English Club he spent the evening playing hearts with old Brevald and the natives. Except when he was drunk he was cowed and listless. Ethel treated him like a dog. She submitted at times to his fits of wild passion, and she was frightened by the gusts of hatred with which they were followed; but when, afterwards, he was cringing and lachrymose she had such a contempt for him that she could have spat in his face. Sometimes he was violent, but now she was prepared for him, and when he hit her she kicked and scratched and bit. They had horrible battles in which he had not always the best of it. Very soon it was known all over Apia that they got on badly. There was little sympathy for Lawson, and at the hotel the general surprise was that old Brevald did not kick him out of the place.

"Brevald's a pretty ugly customer," said one of the men. "I shouldn't be surprised if he put a bullet into Lawson's carcass one of these days."

Ethel still went in the evenings to bathe in the silent pool. It seemed to have an attraction for her that was not quite human, just that attraction you might imagine that a mermaid who had won a soul would have for the cool salt waves of the sea; and sometimes Lawson went also. I do not know what urged him to go, for Ethel was obviously irritated by his presence; perhaps it was because in that spot he hoped to regain the clean rapture which had filled his heart when first he saw her; perhaps only, with the madness of those who love them that love them not, from the feeling that his obstinacy could force love. One day he strolled down there with a feeling that was rare with him now. He felt suddenly at peace with the world. The evening was drawing in and the dusk seemed to cling to the leaves of the co-conut trees like a little thin cloud. A faint breeze stirred them noise-lessly. A crescent moon hung just over their tops. He made his way to the bank. He saw Ethel in the water floating on her back. Her hair streamed out all round her, and she was holding in her hand a large hibiscus. He stopped a moment to admire her; she was like Ophelia.

"Hulloa, Ethel," he cried joyfully.

She made a sudden movement and dropped the red flower. It floated idly away. She swam a stroke or two till she knew there was ground within her depth and then stood up.

"Go away," she said. "Go away."

He laughed.

"Don't be selfish. There's plenty of room for both of us."

"Why can't you leave me alone? I want to be by myself."

"Hang it all, I want to bathe," he answered, good-humouredly.

"Go down to the bridge. I don't want you here."

"I'm sorry for that," he said, smiling still.

He was not in the least angry, and he hardly noticed that she was in a passion. He began to take off his coat.

"Go away," she shrieked. "I won't have you here. Can't you even leave me this? Go away."

"Don't be silly, darling."

She bent down and picked up a sharp stone and flung it quickly at him. He had no time to duck. It hit him on the temple. With a cry he put his hand to his head and when he took it away it was wet with blood. Ethel stood still, panting with rage. He turned very pale, and without a word, taking up his coat, went away. Ethel let herself fall back into the water and the stream carried her slowly down to the ford.

The stone had made a jagged wound and for some days Lawson went about with a bandaged head. He had invented a likely story to account for the accident when the fellows at the club asked him about it, but he had no occasion to use it. No one referred to the matter. He saw them cast surreptitious glances at his head, but not a word was said. The silence could only mean that they knew how he came by his wound. He was certain now that Ethel had a lover, and they all knew who it was. But there was not the smallest indication to guide him. He never saw Ethel with anyone; no one showed a wish to be with her, or treated him in a manner that seemed strange. Wild rage seized him, and having no one to vent it on he drank more and more heavily. A little while before I came to the island he had had another attack of delirium tremens.

I met Ethel at the house of a man called Caster, who lived two or three miles from Apia with a native wife. I had been playing tennis with him and when we were tired he suggested a cup of tea. We went into the house and in the untidy living-room found Ethel chatting with Mrs Caster.

"Hulloa, Ethel," he said, "I didn't know you were here."

I could not help looking at her with curiosity. I tried to see what there was in her to have excited in Lawson such a devastating passion. But who can explain these things? It was true that she was lovely; she reminded one of the red hibiscus, the common flower of the hedge-row in Samoa, with its grace and its languor and its passion; but what surprised me most, taking into consideration the story I knew even then a good deal of, was her freshness and simplicity. She was quiet and a little shy. There was nothing coarse or loud about her; she had not the exuberance common to the half-caste; and it was almost impossible to believe that she could be the virago that the horrible scenes between husband and wife, which were now common knowledge, indicated. In her pretty pink frock and high-heeled shoes she looked quite European. You could hardly have guessed at that dark background of native life in which she felt herself so much more at home. I did not imagine that she was at all intelligent, and I should not have been surprised if a man, after living with her for some time, had found the passion which had drawn him to her sink into boredom. It suggested itself to me that in her elusiveness, like a thought that presents itself to consciousness and vanishes before it can be captured by words, lay her peculiar charm; but perhaps that was merely fancy, and if I had known nothing about her I should have seen in her only a pretty little half-caste like another.

She talked to me of the various things which they talk of to the stranger in Samoa, of the journey, and whether I had slid down the water rock at Papaseea, and if I meant to stay in a native village. She talked to me of Scotland, and perhaps I noticed in her a tendency to enlarge on the sumptuousness of her establishment there. She asked me naïvely if I knew Mrs This and Mrs That, with whom she had been acquainted when she lived in the north.

Then Miller, the fat German-American, came in. He shook hands all round very cordially and sat down, asking in his loud, cheerful voice for a whisky and soda. He was very fat and he sweated profusely. He took off his gold-rimmed spectacles and wiped them; you saw then that his little eyes, benevolent behind the large round glasses, were shrewd and cunning; the party had been somewhat dull till he came, but he was a good story-teller and a jovial fellow. Soon he had the two women, Ethel and my friend's wife, laughing delightedly at his sallies. He had a reputation on the island of a lady's man, and you could see how this fat, gross fellow, old and ugly, had yet the possibility of fascination. His humour was on a level with the understanding of his company, an affair of vitality and assurance, and his Western accent gave a peculiar point to what he said. At last he turned to me:

"Well, if we want to get back for dinner we'd better be getting. I'll take you along in my machine if you like."

I thanked him and got up. He shook hands with the others, went out of the room, massive and strong in his walk, and climbed into his car.

"Pretty little thing, Lawson's wife," I said, as we drove along.

"Too bad the way he treats her. Knocks her about. Gets my dander up when I hear of a man hitting a woman."

We went on a little. Then he said:

"He was a darned fool to marry her. I said so at the time. If he hadn't, he'd have had the whip hand over her. He's yaller, that's what he is, yaller."

The year was drawing to its end and the time approached when I was to leave Samoa. My boat was scheduled to sail for Sydney on the fourth of January. Christmas Day had been celebrated at the hotel with suitable ceremonies, but it was looked upon as no more than a rehearsal for New Year, and the men who were accustomed to foregather in the lounge determined on New Year's Eve to make a night of it. There was an uproarious dinner, after which the party sauntered down to the English Club, a simple little frame house, to play pool. There was a great deal of talking, laughing, and betting, but some very poor play, except on the part of Miller, who had drunk as much as any of them, all far younger than he, but had kept unimpaired the keenness of his eye and the sureness of his hand. He pocketed the young men's money with humour and urbanity. After an hour of this I grew tired and went out. I crossed the road and came on to the beach. Three coconut trees grew there, like three moon maidens waiting for their lovers to ride out of the sea, and I sat at the foot of one of them, watching the lagoon and the nightly assemblage of the stars.

I do not know where Lawson had been during the evening, but between ten and eleven he came along to the club. He shambled down the dusty, empty road, feeling dull and bored, and when he reached the club, before going into the billiard-room, went into the bar to have a drink by himself. He had a shyness now about joining the company of white men when there were a lot of them together and needed a stiff dose of whisky to give him confidence. He was standing with the glass in his hand when Miller came in to him. He was in his shirt sleeves and still held his cue. He gave the bar-tender a glance.

"Get out, Jack," he said.

The bar-tender, a native in a white jacket and a red lava-lava, without a word slid out of the small room.

"Look here, I've been wanting to have a few words with you,

Lawson," said the big American.

"Well, that's one of the few things you can have free, gratis, and for nothing on this damned island."

Miller fixed his gold spectacles more firmly on his nose and held Lawson with his cold determined eyes.

"See here, young fellow, I understand you've been knocking Mrs Lawson about again. I'm not going to stand for that. If you don't stop it right now I'll break every bone of your dirty little body."

Then Lawson knew what he had been trying to find out so long. It was Miller. The appearance of the man, fat, bald-headed, with his round bare face and double chin and the gold spectacles, his age, his benign, shrewd look, like that of a renegade priest, and the thought of Ethel, so slim and virginal, filled him with a sudden horror. Whatever his faults Lawson was no coward, and without a word he hit out violently at Miller. Miller quickly warded the blow with the hand that held the cue, and then with a great swing of his right arm brought his fist down on Lawson's ear. Lawson was four inches shorter than the American and he was slightly built, frail and weakened not only by illness and the enervating tropics, but by drink. He fell like a log and lay half dazed at the foot of the bar. Miller took off his spectacles and wiped them with his handkerchief.

"I guess you know what to expect now. You've had your warning and you'd better take it."

He took up his cue and went back into the billiard-room. There was so much noise there that no one knew what had happened. Lawson picked himself up. He put his hand to his ear, which was singing still. Then he slunk out of the club.

I saw a man cross the road, a patch of white against the darkness of the night, but did not know who it was. He came down to the beach, passed me sitting at the foot of the tree, and looked down. I saw then that it was Lawson, but since he was doubtless drunk, did not speak. He went on, walked irresolutely two or three steps, and turned back. He came up to me and bending down stared in my face.

"I thought it was you," he said.

He sat down and took out his pipe.

"It was hot and noisy in the club," I volunteered.

"Why are you sitting here?"

"I was waiting about for the midnight mass at the Cathedral."

"If you like I'll come with you."

Lawson was quite sober. We sat for a while smoking in silence. Now and then in the lagoon was the splash of some big fish, and a little way out towards the opening in the reef was the light of a schooner.

"You're sailing next week, aren't you?" he said.

"Yes."

"It would be jolly to go home once more. But I could never stand it now. The cold, you know."

"It's odd to think that in England now they're shivering round the fire," I said.

There was not even a breath of wind. The balminess of the night was like a spell. I wore nothing but a thin shirt and a suit of ducks. I enjoyed the exquisite languor of the night, and stretched my limbs voluptuously.

"This isn't the sort of New Year's Eve that persuades one to make good resolutions for the future," I smiled.

He made no answer, but I do not know what train of thought my casual remark had suggested in him, for presently he began to speak. He spoke in a low voice, without any expression, but his accents were educated, and it was a relief to hear him after the twang and the vulgar intonations which for some time had wounded my ears.

"I've made an awful hash of things. That's obvious, isn't it? I'm right down at the bottom of the pit and there's no getting out for me. 'Black as the pit from pole to pole.'" I felt him smile as he made the quotation. "And the strange thing is that I don't see how I went wrong."

I held my breath, for to me there is nothing more awe-inspiring than when a man discovers to you the nakedness of his soul. Then you see that no one is so trivial or debased but that in him is a spark of something to excite compassion.

"It wouldn't be so rotten if I could see that it was all my own fault. It's true I drink, but I shouldn't have taken to that if things had gone differently. I wasn't really fond of liquor. I suppose I ought not to have married Ethel. If I'd kept her it would be all right. But I did love her so."

His voice faltered.

"She's not a bad lot, you know, not really. It's just rotten luck. We might have been as happy as lords. When she bolted I suppose I ought to have let her go, but I couldn't do that—I was dead stuck on her then; and there was the kid."

"Are you fond of the kid?" I asked.

"I was. There are two, you know. But they don't mean so much to me now. You'd take them for natives anywhere. I have to talk to them in Samoan."

"Is it too late for you to start fresh? Couldn't you make a dash for it and leave the place?"

"I haven't the strength. I'm done for."

"Are you still in love with your wife?"

"Not now. Not now." He repeated the two words with a kind of horror in his voice. "I haven't even got that now. I'm down and out."

The bells of the Cathedral were ringing.

"If you really want to come to the midnight mass we'd better go along," I said.

"Come on."

We got up and walked along the road. The Cathedral, all white, stood facing the sea not without impressiveness, and beside it the Protestant chapels had the look of meeting-houses. In the road were two or three cars, and a great number of traps, and traps were put up against the walls at the side. People had come from all parts of the island for the service, and through the great open doors we saw that the place was crowded. The high altar was all ablaze with light. There were a few whites and a good many half-castes, but the great majority were natives. All the men wore trousers, for the Church has decided that the lava-lava is indecent. We found chairs at the back, near the open door, and sat down. Presently, following Lawson's eyes, I saw Ethel come in with a party of half-castes. They were all very much dressed up, the men in high, stiff collars and shiny boots, the women in large, gay hats. Ethel nodded and smiled to her friends as she passed up the aisle. The service began.

When it was over Lawson and I stood on one side for a while to watch the crowd stream out, then he held out his hand.

"Good-night," he said. "I hope you'll have a pleasant journey home."

"Oh, but I shall see you before I go."

He sniggered.

"The question is if you'll see me drunk or sober."

He turned and left me. I had a recollection of those very large black eyes, shining wildly under the shaggy brows. I paused irresolutely. I did not feel sleepy and I thought I would at all events go along to the club for an hour before turning in. When I got there I found the billiard-room empty, but half-a-dozen men were sitting round a table in the lounge, playing poker. Miller looked up as I came in.

"Sit down and take a hand," he said.

"All right."

I bought some chips and began to play. Of course it is the most fascinating game in the world and my hour lengthened out to two, and then to three. The native bar-tender, cheery and wide-awake notwithstanding the time, was at our elbow to supply us with drinks and from somewhere or other he produced a ham and a loaf of bread. We played on. Most of the party had drunk more than was good for them and the play was high and reckless. I played modestly, neither wishing to win nor anxious to lose, but I watched Miller with a fascinated interest. He drank glass for glass with the rest of the company, but remained cool and level-headed. His pile of chips increased in size and he had a neat little paper in front of him on which he had marked various sums lent to players in distress. He beamed amiably at the young men whose money he was taking. He kept up interminably his stream of jest and anecdote, but he never missed a draw, he never let an expression of the face pass him. At last the dawn crept into the windows, gently, with a sort of deprecating shyness, as though it had no business there, and then it was day.

"Well," said Miller, "I reckon we've seen the old year out in style. Now let's have a round of jackpots and me for my mosquito net. I'm fifty, remember, I can't keep these late hours."

The morning was beautiful and fresh when we stood on the verandah, and the lagoon was like a sheet of multicoloured glass. Someone suggested a dip before going to bed, but none cared to bathe in the lagoon, sticky and treacherous to the feet. Miller had his car at the door and he offered to take us down to the pool. We jumped in and drove along the deserted road. When we reached the pool it seemed as though the day had hardly risen there yet. Under the trees the water was all in shadow and the night had the effect of lurking still. We were in great spirits. We had no towels or any costume and in my prudence I wondered how we were going to dry ourselves. None of us had much on and it did not take us long to snatch off our clothes. Nelson, the little supercargo, was stripped first.

"I'm going down to the bottom," he said.

He dived and in a moment another man dived too, but shallow, and was out of the water before him. Then Nelson came up and scrambled to the side.

"I say, get me out," he said.

"What's up?"

Something was evidently the matter. His face was terrified. Two fellows gave him their hands and he slithered up.

"I say, there's a man down there."

"Don't be a fool. You're drunk."

"Well, if there isn't I'm in for D. T's. But I tell you there's a man down there. It just scared me out of my wits."

Miller looked at him for a moment. The little man was all white. He was actually trembling.

"Come on, Caster," said Miller to the big Australian, "we'd better go down and see."

"He was standing up," said Nelson, "all dressed. I saw him. He tried to catch hold of me."

"Hold your row," said Miller. "Are you ready?"

They dived in. We waited on the bank, silent. It really seemed as though they were under water longer than any men could breathe. Then Caster came up, and immediately after him, red in the face as though he were going to have a fit, Miller. They were pulling something behind them. Another man jumped in to help them, and the three together dragged their burden to the side. They shoved it up. Then we saw that it was Lawson, with a great stone tied up in his coat and bound to his feet.

"He was set on making a good job of it," said Miller, as he wiped the water from his shortsighted eyes.

Red

THE SKIPPER THRUST his hand into one of his trouser pockets and with difficulty, for they were not at the sides but in front and he was a portly man, pulled out a large silver watch. He looked at it and then looked again at the declining sun. The Kanaka at the wheel gave him a glance, but did not speak. The skipper's eyes rested on the island they were approaching. A white line of foam marked the reef. He knew there was an opening large enough to get his ship through, and when they came a little nearer he counted on seeing it. They had nearly an hour of daylight still before them. In the lagoon the water was deep and they could anchor comfortably. The chief of the village, which he could already see among the coconut trees was a friend of the mate's, and it would be pleasant to go ashore for the night. The mate came forward at that minute and the skipper turned to him.

"We'll take a bottle of booze along with us and get some girls in to dance," he said.

"I don't see the opening," said the mate.

He was a Kanaka, a handsome, swarthy fellow, with somewhat the look of a later Roman emperor, inclined to stoutness; but his face was fine and clean-cut.

"I'm dead sure there's one right here," said the captain, looking through his glasses. "I can't understand why I can't pick it up. Send one of the boys up the mast to have a look."

The mate called one of the crew and gave him the order. The captain watched the Kanaka climb and waited for him to speak. But the Kanaka shouted down that he could see nothing but the unbroken line of foam. The captain spoke Samoan like a native, and he cursed him freely.

"Shall he stay up there?" asked the mate.

"What the hell good does that do." answered the captain. "The blame fool can't see worth a cent. You bet your sweet life I'd find the opening if I was up there."

He looked at the slender mast with anger. It was all very well for a native who had been used to climbing up coconut trees all his life. He was fat and heavy.

"Come down," he shouted. "You're no more use than a dead dog. We'll just have to go along the reef till we find the opening."

It was a seventy-ton schooner with paraffin auxiliary, and it ran, when there was no head wind, between four and five knots an hour. It was a bedraggled object; it had been painted white a very long time ago, but it was now dirty, dingy, and mottled. It smell strongly of paraffin, and of the copra which was its usual cargo. They were within a hundred feet of the reef now and the captain told the steersman to run along it till they came to the opening. But when they had gone a couple of miles he realised that they had missed it. He went about and slowly worked back again. The white foam of the reef continued without interruption and now the sun was setting. With a curse at the stupidity of the crew the skipper resigned himself to waiting till next morning.

"Put her about," he said. "I can't anchor here."

They went out to sea a little and presently it was quite dark. They anchored. When the sail was furled the ship began to roll a good deal. They said at Apia that one day she would roll right over; and the owner, a German-American who managed one of the largest stores, said that no money was big enough to induce him to go out in her. The cook, a Chinese in while trousers, very dirty and ragged, and a thin white tunic, came to say that supper was ready, and when the skipper went into the cabin he found the engineer already seated at table. The engineer was a long, lean man with a scraggy neck. He was dressed in blue overalls and a sleeveless jersey which showed his thin arms tattooed from elbow to wrist.

"Hell, having to spend the night outside," said the skipper.

The engineer did not answer, and they ate their supper in silence. The cabin was lit by a dim oil-lamp. When they had eaten the canned apricots with which the meal finished the Chink brought them a cup of tea. The skipper lit a cigar and went on the upper deck. The island now was only a darker mass against the night. The stars were very bright. The only sound was the ceaseless breaking of the surf. The skipper sank into a deck-chair and smoked idly. Presently three or four members of the crew came up and sat down. One of them had a banjo and another a concertina. They began to play, and one of them sang. The native song sounded strange on these instruments. Then to the singing a couple began to dance. It was a barbaric dance, savage and primeval, rapid, with quick movements of the hands and feet and contortions of the body; it was sensual, sexual even, but sexual without passion. It was very animal, direct, weird without mystery, natural in short, and one might almost say childlike. At last they grew tired. They stretched themselves on the deck and slept, and all was silent. The skipper lifted himself heavily out of his chair and clambered down the companion. He went into his cabin and got out of his clothes. He climbed into his bunk and lay there. He panted a little in the heat of the night. But next morning, when the dawn crept over the tranquil sea, the opening in the reef which had eluded them the night before was seen a little to the east of where they lay. The schooner entered the lagoon. There was not a ripple on the surface of the water. Deep down among the coral rocks you saw little coloured fish swim. When he had anchored his ship the skipper ate his breakfast and went on deck. The sun shone from an unclouded sky, but in the early morning the air was grateful and cool. It was Sunday, and there was a feeling of quietness, a silence as though nature were at rest, which gave him a peculiar sense of comfort. He sat, looking at the wooded coast, and felt lazy and well at case. Presently a slow smile moved his lips and he threw the stump of his cigar into the water.

"I guess I'll go ashore," he said. "Get the boat out."

He climbed stiffly down the ladder and was rowed to a little cove. The coconut trees came down to the water's edge, not in rows, but spaced out with an ordered formality. They were like a ballet of spinsters, elderly but flippant, standing in affected altitudes with the simpering graces of a bygone age. He sauntered idly through them, along a path that could be just seen winding its tortuous way, and it led him presently to a broad creek. There was a bridge across it, but a bridge constructed of single trunks of coconut trees, a dozen of them, placed end to end and supported where they met by a forked branch driven into the bed of the creek. You walked on a smooth, round surface, narrow and slippery, and there was no support for the hand. To cross such a bridge required sure feel and a stout heart. The skipper hesitated. But he saw on the other side, nestling among the trees, a white man's house; he made up his mind and, rather gingerly, began to walk. He watched his feet carefully, and where one, trunk joined on to the next and there was a difference of level, he tottered a little. It was with a gasp of relief that he reached the last tree and finally set his feet on the firm ground of the other side. He had been so intent on the difficult crossing that he never noticed anyone was watching him, and it was with surprise that he heard himself spoken to.

"It lakes a bit of nerve to cross these bridges when you're not used to them."

He looked up and saw a man standing in front of him. He had evidently come out of the house which he had seen.

"I saw you hesitate," the man continued, with a smile on his lips, "and I was watching to see you fall in."

"Not on your life," said the captain, who had now recovered his confidence.

"I've fallen in myself before now. I remember, one evening I came back from shooting, and I fell in, gun and all. Now I get a boy to carry my gun for me."

He was a man no longer young, with a small beard, now somewhat grey, and a thin face. He was dressed in a singlet, without arms, and a pair of duck trousers. He wore neither shoes nor socks. He spoke English with a slight accent.

"Are you Neilson?" asked the skipper.

"I am."

"I've heard about you. I thought you lived somewheres round here."

The skipper followed his host into the little bungalow and sat down heavily in the chair which the other motioned him to take.

While Neilson went out to fetch whisky and glasses he took a look round the room. It filled him with amazement. He had never seen so many books. The shelves reached from floor to ceiling on all four walls, and they were closely packed. There was a grand piano littered with music, and a large table on which books and magazines lay in disorder. The room made him feel embarrassed. He remembered that Neilson was a queer fellow. No one knew very much about him, although he had been in the islands for so many years, but those who knew him agreed that he was queer. He was a Swede.

"You've got one big heap of books here," he said, when Neilson returned.

"They do no harm," answered Neilson with a smile.

"Have you read them all?" asked the skipper.

"Most of them."

"I'm a bit of a reader myself. I have the Saturday Evening Post sent me regler."

Neilson poured his visitor a good stiff glass of whisky and gave him a cigar. The skipper volunteered a little information.

"I got in last night, but I couldn't find the opening, so I had to anchor outside. I never been this run before, but my people had some stuff they wanted to bring over here. Gray, d'you know him?"

"Yes, he's got a store a little way along."

"Well, there was a lot of canned stuff that he wanted over, an' he's got some copra. They thought I might just as well come over as lie idle at Apia. I run between Apia and Pago-Pago molly, but they've got smallpox there just now, and there's nothing stirring."

He took a drink of his whisky and lit a cigar. He was a taciturn man, but there was something in Neilson that made him nervous, and his nervousness made him talk. The Swede was looking at him with large dark eyes in which there was an expression of faint amusement.

"This is a tidy little place you've got here,"

"I've done my best with it."

"You must do pretty well with your trees. They look fine. With copra at the price it is now. I had a bit of a plantation myself once, in Upolu it was, but I had to sell it."

He looked round the room again, where all those books gave him a feeling of something incomprehensible and hostile.

"I guess you must find it a bit lonesome here though," he said.

"I've got used to it. I've been here for twenty-five years."

Now the captain could think of nothing more to say, and he smoked in silence. Neilson had apparently no wish to break it. He looked at his guest with a meditative eye. He was a tall man, more than six feet high, and very stout. His face was red and blotchy, with a network of little purple veins on the checks, and his features were sunk into its fatness. His eyes were bloodshot. His neck was buried in rolls of fat. But for a fringe of long curly hair, nearly while, at the back of his head, he was quite bald; and that immense, shiny surface of forehead, which might have given him a false look of intelligence, on the contrary gave him one of peculiar imbecility. He wore a blue flannel shirt, open at the neck and showing his fat chest covered with a mat of reddish hair, and a very old pair of blueserge trousers. He sat in his chair in a heavy ungainly attitude, his great belly thrust forward and his fat legs uncrossed. All elasticity had gone from his limbs. Neilson wondered idly what sort of man he had been in his youth. It was almost impossible to imagine that this creature of vast bulk had ever been a boy who ran about. The skipper finished his whisky, and Neilson pushed the bottle towards him.

"Help yourself."

The skipper leaned forward and with his great hand seized it.

"And how come you in these parts anyways?" he said.

"Oh, I came out to the islands for my health. My lungs were bad and they said I hadn't a year to live. You see they were wrong."

"I meant, how come you to settle down right here?"

"I am a sentimentalist."

"Oh!"

Neilson knew that the skipper had not an idea what he meant, and he looked at him with an ironical twinkle in his dark eyes. Perhaps just because the skipper was so gross and dull a man the whim seized him to talk further.

"You were too busy keeping your balance to notice, when you crossed the bridge, but this spot is generally considered rather pretty."

"It's a cute little house you've got here."

"Ah, that wasn't here when I first came. There was a native hut, with its beehive roof and its pillars, overshadowed by a great tree with red flowers; and the craton bushes, their leaves yellow and red and golden, made a pied fence around it. And then all about were the coconut trees, as fanciful as women, and as vain. They stood at the water's edge and spent all day looking at their reflections. I was a young man then - good heavens, it's a quarter of a century ago - and I wanted to enjoy all the loveliness of the world in the short time allotted to me before I passed into the darkness. I thought it was the most beautiful spot I had ever seen. The first time I saw it I had a catch at my heart, and I was afraid I was going to cry. I wasn't more than twenty-five, and though I put the best face I could on it, I didn't want to die. And somehow it seemed to me that the very beauty of this place made it easier for me to accept my fate. I felt when I came here that all my past life had fallen away, Stockholm and its University, and then Bonn: it all seemed the life of somebody else, as though now at last I had achieved the reality which our doctors of philosophy - I am one myself, you know - had discussed so much. 'A year,' I cried to myself. 'I have a year. I will spend it here and then I am content to die.'"

"We are foolish and sentimental and melodramatic at twenty-five, but if we weren't perhaps we should be less wise at fifty."

"Now drink, my friend. Don't let the nonsense I talk interfere with you."

He waved his thin hand towards the bottle, and the skipper finished what remained in his glass.

"You ain't drinking nothing," he said, reaching for the whisky.

"I am of sober habit," smiled the Swede. "I intoxicate myself in ways which I fancy are more subtle. But perhaps that is only vanity. Anyhow, the effects are more lasting and the results less deleterious."

"They say there's a deal of cocaine taken in the States now," said the captain.

Neilson chuckled.

"But I do not see a white man often," he continued "and for once I don't think a drop of whisky can do me any harm."

He poured himself out a little, added some soda, and took a sip.

"And presently I found out why the spot had such an unearthly loveliness. Here love had tarried for a moment like a migrant bird that happens on a ship in mid-ocean and for a little while folds its tired wings. The fragrance of a beautiful passion hovered over it like the fragrance of hawthorn in May in the meadows of my home. It seems to me that the places where men have loved or suffered keep about them always some faint aroma of something that has not wholly died. It is as though they had acquired a spiritual significance which mysteriously affects those who pass. I wish I could make myself clear." He smiled a little. "Though I cannot imagine that if I did you would understand."

He paused.

"I think this place was beautiful because here for a period the ecstasy of love had invested it with beauty." And now he shrugged his shoulders. "But perhaps it is only that my aesthetic sense is gratified by the happy conjunction of young love and a suitable setting."

Even a man less thick-witted than the skipper might have been forgiven if he were bewildered by Neilson's words. For he seemed family to laugh at what he said. It was as though he spoke from emotion which his intellect found ridiculous. He had said himself that he was a sentimentalist, and when sentimentality is joined with scepticism there is often the devil to pay.

He was silent for an instant and looked at the captain with eyes in which there was a sudden perplexity.

"You know, I can't help thinking that I've seen you before somewhere or other," he said.

"I couldn't say as I remember you," returned the skipper. "I have a curious feeling as though your face were familiar to me. It's been puzzling me for some time. But I can't situate my recollection in any place or at any time."

The skipper massively shrugged his heavy shoulders.

"It's thirty years since I first come to the islands. A man can't figure on remembering all the folk he meets in awhile like that."

The Swede shook his head.

"You know how one sometimes has the feeling that a place one has never been to before is strangely familiar. That's how I seem to see you." He gave a whimsical smile. "Perhaps I knew you in some past existence. Perhaps, perhaps you were the master of a galley in ancient Rome and I was a slave at the oar. Thirty years have been here?"

"Every bit of thirty years."

"I wonder if you knew a man called Red?"

"Red?"

"That is the only name I've ever known him by. I never knew him personally. I never even set eyes on him. And yet I seem to see him more clearly than many men, my brothers, for instance, with whom I passed my daily life for many years. He lives in my imagination with the distinctness of a Paolo Malatesta or a Romeo. But I dare say you have never read Dante or Shakespeare?"

"I can't say as I have," said the captain.

Neilson, smoking a cigar, leaned back in his chair and looked vacantly at the ring of smoke which floated in the still air. A smile played on his lips, but his eyes were grave. Then he looked at the captain. There was in his gross obesity something extraordinarily repellent. He had the plethoric self-satisfaction of the very fat. It was an outrage. It set Neilson's nerves on edge. But the contrast between the man before him and the man he had in mind was pleasant.

"It appears that Red was the most comely thing you ever saw. I've talked to quite a number of people who knew him in those days, white men, and they all agree that the first lime you saw him his beauty just look your breath away. They called him Red on account of his flaming hair. It had a natural wave and he wore it long. It must have been of that wonderful colour that the pre-Raphaelilcs raved over. I don't think he was vain of it, he was much too ingenuous for that, but no one could have blamed him if he had been. He was tall, six feet and an inch or two - in the native house that used to stand here was the mark of his height cut with a knife on the central trunk that supported the roof - and he was made like a Greek god, broad in the shoulders and thin in the flanks; he was like Apollo, with just that soft roundness which Praxiteles gave him, and that suave, feminine grace which has in it something troubling and mysterious. His skin was dazzling while, milky, like satin; his skin was like a woman's."

"I had kind of a white skin myself when I was a kiddie," said the skipper, with a twinkle in his bloodshot eyes.

But Neilson paid no attention to him. He was telling his story now and interruption made him impatient.

"And his face was just as beautiful as his body. He had large blue eyes, very dark, so that some say they were black, and unlike most red-haired people he had dark eyebrows and long dark lashes. His features were perfectly regular and his mouth was like a scarlet wound. He was twenty."

On these words the Swede slopped with a certain sense of the dramatic. He took a sip of whisky.

"He was unique. There never was anyone more beautiful. There was no more reason for him than for a wonderful blossom to flower on a wild plant. He was a happy accident of nature.

"One day he landed at that cove into which you must have put this morning. He was an American sailor, and he had descried from a man-of-war in Apia. He had induced some good-humoured native to give him a passage on a cutter that happened to be sailing from Apia to Safolo, and he had been put ashore here in a dug-out. I do not know why he deserted. Perhaps life on a man-of-war with its restrictions irked him, perhaps he was in trouble, and perhaps it was the South Seas and these romantic islands that got into his bones. Every now and then they take a man strangely, and he finds himself like a fly in a spider's web. It may be that there was a softness of fibre in him, and these green hills with their soft airs, hills blue sea, took the northern strength from him as Delilah' look the Nazarite's. Anyhow, he wanted to hide himself, and he thought he would be safe in this secluded nook till his ship had sailed from Samoa.

"There was a native hut at the cove and as he stood there, wondering where exactly he should turn his steps, a young girl came out and invited him to enter. He knew scarcely two words of the native tongue and she as little English. But he understood well enough what her smiles meant, and her pretty gestures, and he followed her. He sat down on a mat and she gave him slices of pineapple to eat. I can speak of Red only from hearsay, but I saw the girl three years after he first met her, and she was scarcely nineteen then. You cannot imagine how exquisite she was. She had the passionate grace of the hibiscus and the rich colour. She was rather tall, slim, with the delicate features of her race, and large eyes like pools of still water under the palm trees; her hair, black and curling, fell down her back, and she wore a wreath of scented flowers. Her hands were lovely. They were so small, so exquisitely formed, they gave your heart-strings a wrench. And in those days she laughed easily. Her smile was so delightful that it made your knees shake. Her skin was like a field of ripe corn on a summer day. Good heavens, how can I describe her? She was too beautiful to be real.

And these two young things, she was sixteen and he was twenty, fell in love with one another at first sight. That is the real love, not the love that comes from sympathy, common interests, or intellectual community, but love pure and simple. That is the love that Adam felt for Eve when he awoke and found her in the garden gazing at him with dewy eyes. That is the love that draws the beasts to one another, and the Gods. That is the love that makes the world a miracle. That is the love which gives life its pregnant meaning. You have never heard of the wise, cynical French duke who said that with two lovers there is always one who loves and one who lets himself be loved; it is bitter truth to which most of us have to resign ourselves; but now and then there are two who love and two who let themselves be loved. Then one might fancy that the sun stands still as it stood when Joshua prayed to the God of Israel.

"And even now after all these years, when I think of these two, so young, so fair, so simple, and of their love, I feel a pang. It tears my heart just as my heart is torn when on certain nights I watch the full moon shining on the lagoon from an unclouded sky. There is always pain in the contemplation of perfect beauty.

"They were children. She was good and sweet and kind. I know nothing of him, and I like to think that then at all events he was ingenuous and frank. I like to think that his soul was as comely as his body. But I dare say he had no more soul than the creatures of the woods and forests who made pipes from reeds and bathed in the mountain streams when the world was young, and you might catch sight of little fauns galloping through the glade on the back of a bearded centaur. A soul is a troublesome possession and when man developed it he lost the Garden of Eden.

"Well, when Red came to the island it had recently been visited by one of those epidemics which the white man brought to the South Seas, and one third of the inhabitants had died. It seems that the girl had lost all her near kin and she lived now in the house of distant cousins. The household consisted of two ancient crones, bowed and wrinkled, two younger women, and a man and a boy. For a few days he stayed there. But perhaps he felt himself too near the shore, with the possibility that he might fall in with white men who would reveal his hiding-place; perhaps the lovers could not bear that the company of others should rob them for an instant of the delight of being together. One morning (hey set out, the pair of them, with the few things that belonged to the girl, and walked along a grassy path under the coconuts, till they came to the creek you see. They had to cross the bridge you crossed, and the girl laughed gleefully because he was afraid. She held his hand till they came to the end of the first tree, and then his courage failed him and he had to go back. He was obliged to take off all his clothes before he could risk it, and she carried them over for him on her head. They settled down in the empty hut that stood there. Whether she had any rights over it (land tenure is a complicated business in the islands), or whether the owner had died during the epidemic, I do not know, but anyhow no one questioned them, and they took possession. Their furniture consisted of a couple of grass mats on which they slept, a fragment of looking-glass, and a bowl or two. In this pleasant land that is enough to start housekeeping on.

They say that happy people have no history, and certainly a happy love has none. They did nothing all day long and yet the days seemed all too short. The girl had a native name, but Red called her Sally. He picked up the easy language very quickly, and he used to lie on the mat for hours while she chattered gaily to him. He was a silent fellow, and perhaps his mind was lethargic. He smoked incessantly the cigarettes which she made him out of the native tobacco and pandanus leaf, and he watched her while with deft fingers she made grass mats. Often natives would come in and tell long stories of the old days when the island was disturbed by tribal wars. Sometimes he would go fishing on the reef, and bring home a basket full of coloured fish. Sometimes at night he would go out with a lantern to catch lobster. There were plantains round the hut and Sally would roast them for their frugal meal. She knew how to make delicious messes from coconuts, and the breadfruit tree by the side of the creek gave them its fruit. On feast-days they killed a little pig and cooked it on hot stones. They bathed together in the creek; and in the evening they went down to the lagoon and paddled about in a dug-out, with its great outrigger. The sea was deep blue, wine-coloured at sundown, like the sea of Homeric Greece; but in the lagoon the colour had an infinite variety, aquamarine and amethyst and emerald; and the setting sun turned it for a short moment to liquid gold. Then there was the colour of the coral, brown, while, pink, red, purple; and the shapes it took were marvellous. It was like a magic garden, and the hurrying fish were like butterflies. It strangely lacked reality. Among the coral were pools with a floor of while sand and here, where the water was dazzling clear, it was very good to bathe. Then, cool and happy, they wandered back in the gleaming over the soft grass road to the creek, walking hand in hand, and now the mynah birds filled the coconut trees with their clamour. And then the night, with that great sky shining with gold, that seemed to stretch more widely than the skies of Europe, and the soft airs that blew gently through the open hut, the long night again was all too short. She was sixteen and he was barely twenty. The dawn crept in among the wooden pillars of the hut and looked al those lovely children sleeping in one another's arms. The sun hid behind the great tattered leaves of the plantains so that it might not disturb them, and then, with playful malice, shot a golden ray, like the outstretched paw of a Persian cat, on their faces. They opened their sleepy eyes and they smiled to welcome another day. The weeks lengthened into months, and a year passed. They seemed to love one another as - I hesitate to say passionately, for passion has in it always a shade of sadness, a touch of bitterness or anguish, but as wholeheartedly, as simply and naturally as on that first day on which, meeting, they had recognised that a god was in them.

If you had asked them I have no doubt that they would have thought it impossible to suppose their love could ever cease. Do we not know that the essential element of love is a belief in its own eternity? And yet perhaps in Red there was already a very little seed, unknown to himself and unsuspected by the girl, which would in time have grown to weariness. For one day one of the natives from the cove told them that some way down the coast al the anchorage was a British whaling-ship.

"Gee," he said, "I wonder if I could make a trade of some nuts and plantains for a pound or two of tobacco."

"The pandanus cigarettes that Sally made him with untiring hands were strong and pleasant enough to smoke, but they left him unsatisfied; and he earned on a sudden for real tobacco, hard, rank, and pungent. He had not smoked a pipe for many months. His mouth watered at the thought of it.

One would have thought some premonition of harm would have made Sally seek to dissuade him, but love possessed her so completely that it never occurred to her any power on earth could take him from her. They went up into the hills together and gathered a great basket of wild oranges, green, but sweet and juicy; and they picked plantains from around the hut, and coconuts from their trees, and breadfruit and mangoes; and they carried them down to the cove. They loaded the unstable canoe with them, and Red and the native boy who had brought them the news of the ship paddled along outside the reef.

"It was the last time she ever saw him.

"Next day the boy came back alone. He was all in tears. This is the story he told. When after their long paddle they reached the ship and Red hailed it, a white man looked over the side and told them to come on board. They took the fruit they had brought with them and Red piled it up on the deck. The while man and he began to talk, and they seemed to come to some agreement. One of them went below and brought up tobacco. Red took some at once and lit a pipe. The boy imitated the zest with which he blew a great cloud of smoke from his mouth. Then they said something to him and he went into the cabin. Through the open door the boy, watching curiously, saw a bottle brought out and glasses. Red drank and smoked. They seemed to ask him something, for he shook his head and laughed. The man, the first man who had spoken to them, laughed too, and he filled Red's glass once more. They went on talking and drinking, and presently, growing tired of watching a sight that meant nothing to him, the boy curled himself up on the deck and slept. He was awakened by a kick; and jumping to his feet, he saw that the ship was slowly sailing out of the lagoon. He caught sight of Red seated at the table, with his head resting heavily on his arms, fast asleep. He made a movement towards him, intending to wake him, but a rough hand seized his arm, and a man, with a scowl and words which he did not understand, pointed to the side. He shouted to Red, but in a moment he was seized and hung overboard. Helpless, he swam round to his canoe, which was drifting a little way off, and pushed it on to the reef. He climbed in and, sobbing all the way, paddled back to shore.

"What had happened was obvious enough. The whaler, by desertion or sickness, was short of hands, and the captain when Red came aboard had asked him to sign on; on his refusal he had made him drunk and kidnapped him.

"Sally was beside herself with grief. For three days she screamed and cried. The natives did what they could to comfort her, but she would not be comforted. She would not eat. And then, exhausted, she sank into a sullen apathy. She spent long days at the cove, watching the lagoon, in the vain hope that Red somehow or other would manage to escape. She sat on the white sand, hour after hour, with the tears running down her checks, and at night dragged herself wearily back across the creek to the little hut where she had been happy. The people with whom she had lived before Red came to the island wished her to return to them, but she would not; she was convinced that Red would come back, and she wanted him to find her where he had left her. Four months later she was delivered of a still-born child, and the old woman who had come to help her through her confinement remained with her in the hut. All joy was taken from her life. If her anguish with time became less intolerable it was replaced by a settled melancholy. You would not have thought that among these people, whose emotions, though so violent, are very transient, a woman could be found capable of so enduring a passion. She never lost the profound conviction that sooner or later Red would come back. She watched for him, and every time someone crossed this slender little bridge of coconut trees she looked. It might at last be he."

Neilson stopped talking and gave a faint sigh.

"And what happened to her in the end." asked the skipper.

Neilson smiled bitterly.

"Oh, three years afterwards she took up with another white man."

The skipper gave a fat, cynical chuckle.

"That's generally what happens to them," he said.

The Swede shot him a look of hatred. He did not know why that gross, obese man excited in him so violent a repulsion. But his thoughts wandered and he found his mind filled with memories of the past. He went back five-and-twenty years. It was when he first came to the island, weary of Apia, with its heavy drinking, its gambling and coarse sensuality, a sick man, trying to resign himself to the loss of the career which had fired his imagination with ambitious thought. He set behind him resolutely all his hopes of making a great name for himself and strove to content himself with the few poor months of careful life which was all that he could count on. He was boarding with a half-caste trader who had a store a couple of miles along the coast at the edge of a native village; and one day, wandering aimlessly along the grassy paths of the coconut groves, he had come upon the hut in which Sally lived. The beauty of the spot had filled him with a rapture so great that it was almost painful, and then he had seen Sally. She was the loveliest creature he had ever seen, and the sadness in those dark, magnificent eyes of hers affected him strangely. The Kanakas were a handsome race, and beauty was not rare among them, but it was the beauty of shapely animals. It was empty. But those tragic eyes were dark with mystery, and you felt in them the bitter complexity of the groping, human soul. The trader told him the story and it moved him.

"Do you think he'll ever come back?" asked Neilson.

"No fear. Why, it'll be a couple of years before the ship is paid off, and by then he'll have forgotten all about her. I bet he was pretty mad when he woke up and found he'd been shanghaied, and I shouldn't wonder but he wanted to fight somebody. But he'd got to grin and bear it, and I guess in a month he was thinking it the best thing that had ever happened to him that he got away from the island."

But Neilson could not get the story out of his head. Perhaps because he was sick and weakly, the radiant health of Red appealed to his imagination. Himself an ugly man, insignificant of appearance, he prized very highly comeliness in others. He had never been passionately in love, and certainly he had never been passionately loved. The mutual attraction of those two young things gave him a singular delight. It had the ineffable beauty of the Absolute. He went again to the little hut by the creek. He had a gift for languages and an energetic mind, accustomed to work, and he had already given much time to the study of the local tongue. Old habit was strong in him and he was gathering together material for a paper on the Samoan speech. The old crone who shared the hut with Sally invited him to come in and sit down. She gave him kava to drink and cigarettes to smoke. She was glad to have someone to chat with and while she talked he looked at Sally. She reminded him of the Psyche in the museum at Naples. Her features had the same clear purity of line, and though she had borne a child she had still a virginal aspect.

It was not till he had seen her two or three times that he induced her to speak. Then it was only to ask him if he had seen in Apia a man called Red. Two years had passed since his disappearance, but it was plain that she still thought of him incessantly.

It did not take Neilson long to discover that he was in love with her. It was only by an effort of will now that he prevented himself from going every day to the creek, and when he was not with Sally his thoughts were. At first, looking upon himself as a dying man, he asked only to look at her, and occasionally hear her speak, and his love gave him a wonderful happiness. He exulted in its purity. He wanted nothing from her but the opportunity to weave around her graceful person a web of beautiful fancies. But the open air, the equable temperature, the rest, the simple fare, began to have an unexpected effect on his health. His temperature did not soar al night to such alarming heights, he coughed less and began to put on weight; six months passed without his having a haemorrhage; and on a sudden he saw the possibility that he might live. He had studied his disease carefully, and the hope dawned upon him that with great care he might arrest its course. It exhilarated him to look forward once more to the future.

He made plans. It was evident that any active life was out of the question, but he could live on the islands, and the small income he had, insufficient elsewhere, would be ample to keep him. He could grow coconuts; that would give him an occupation; and he would send for his books and a piano; but his quick mind saw that in all this he was merely trying to conceal from himself the desire which obsessed him.

He wanted Sally. He loved not only her beauty, but that dim soul which he divined behind her suffering eyes. He would intoxicate her with his passion. In the end he would make her forget. And in an ecstasy of surrender he fancied himself giving her too the happiness which he had thought never to know again, but had now so miraculously achieved. He asked her to live with him. She refused. He had expected that and did not let it depress him, for he was sure that sooner or later she would yield. His love was irresistible, he told the old woman of his wishes, and found somewhat to his surprise that she and the neighbours, long aware of them, were strongly urging Sally to accept his offer. After all, every native was glad to keep house for a white man, and Neilson according to the standards of the island was a rich one. The trader with whom he boarded went to her and told her not to be a fool; such an opportunity would not come again, and after so long she could not still believe that Red would ever return. The girl's resistance only increased Neilson's desire, and what had been a very pure love now became an agonising passion. He was determined that nothing should stand in his way. He gave Sally no peace. At last, worn out by his persistence and the persuasions, by turns pleading and angry, of everyone around her, she consented. But the day after, when exultant he went to see her he found that in the night she had burnt down the hut in which she and Red had lived together. The old crone ran towards him full of angry abuse of Sally, but he waved her aside; it did not mailer; they would build a bungalow on the place where the hut had stood. A European house would really be more convenient if he wanted to bring out a piano and a vast number of books. And so the little wooden house was built in which he had now lived for many years, and Sally became his wife. But after the first few weeks of rapture, during which he was satisfied with what she gave him, he had known little happiness. She had yielded to him, through weariness, but she had only yielded what she set no store on. The soul which he had dimly glimpsed escaped him. He knew that she cared nothing for him. She still loved Red, and all the time she was waiting for his return. At a sign from him, Neilson knew that, notwithstanding his love, his tenderness, his sympathy, his generosity, she would leave him without a moment's hesitation. She would never give a thought to his distress. Anguish seized him and he battered at that impenetrable self of hers which sullenly resisted him. His love became bitter. He tried to melt her heart with kindness, but it remained as hard as before: he feigned indifference, but she did not notice it.

Sometimes he lost his temper and abused her, and then she wept silently. Sometimes he thought she was nothing but a fraud, and that soul simply an invention of his own, and that he could not get into the sanctuary of her heart because there was no sanctuary there. His love became a prison from which he longed to escape, but he had not the strength merely to open the door - that was all it needed - and walk out into the open air. It was torture and at last he became numb and hopeless. In the end the fire burnt itself out and, when he saw her eyes rest for an instant on the slender bridge, it was no longer rage that filled his heart but impatience. For many years now they had lived together bound by the ties of habit and convenience, and it was with a smile that he looked back on his old passion. She was an old woman, for the women on the islands age quickly, and if he had no love for her any more he had tolerance. She left him alone. He was contented with his piano and his books.

His thoughts led him to a desire for words.

"When I look back now and reflect on that brief passionate love of Red and Sally, I think that perhaps they should thank the ruthless fate that separated them when their love seemed still to be at its height. They suffered, but they suffered in beauty. They were spared the real tragedy of love."

"I don't know exactly as I get you," said the skipper.

"The tragedy of love is not death or separation. How long do you think it would have been before one or other of them ceased to care? Oh, it is dreadfully bitter to look at a woman whom you have loved with all your heart and soul, so that you felt you could not bear to let her out of your sight, and realize that you would not mind if you never saw her again. The tragedy of love is indifference."

But while he was speaking a very extraordinary thing happened. Though he had been addressing the skipper he had not been talking to him, he had been putting his thoughts into words for himself, and with his eyes fixed on the man in front of him he had not seen him. But now an image presented itself to them, an image not of the man he saw, but of another man. It was as though he were looking into one of those distorting mirrors that make you extraordinarily squat or outrageously elongate, but here exactly the opposite look place, and in the obese, ugly old man he caught the shadowy glimpse of a stripling. He gave him now a quick, searching scrutiny. Why had a haphazard stroll brought him just to this place? A sudden tremor of his heart made him slightly breathless. And absurd suspicion seized him. What had occurred to him was impossible, and yet it might be a fact.

"What is your name?" he asked abruptly.

The skipper's face puckered and he gave a cunning chuckle. He looked then malicious and horribly vulgar.

"It's such a damned long time since I heard it that I almost forget it myself. But for thirty years now in the islands they've always called me Red."

His huge form shook as he gave a low, almost silent laugh. It was obscene. Neilson shuddered. Red was hugely amused, and from his bloodshot eyes tears ran down his cheeks.

Neilson gave a gasp, for at that moment a woman came in. She was a native, a woman of somewhat commanding presence, stout without being corpulent, dark, for the natives grow darker with age, with very grey hair. She wore a black Mother Hubbard, and its thinness showed her heavy breasts. The moment had come.

She made an observation to Neilson about some household matter and he answered. He wondered if his voice sounded as unnatural to her as it did to himself. She gave the man who was sitting in the chair by the window an indifferent glance, and went out of the room. The moment had come and gone.

Neilson for a moment could not speak. He was strangely shaken. Then he said:

"I'd be very glad if you'd stay and have a bit of dinner with me. Pot luck."

"I don't think I will," said Red. "I must go after this fellow Gray. I'll give him his stuff and then I'll get away. I want to be back in Apia tomorrow."

"I'll send a boy along with you to show you the way."

"That'll be fine."

Red heaved himself out of his chair, while the Swede called one of the boys who worked on the plantation. He told him where the skipper wanted to go, and the boy stepped along the bridge. Red prepared to follow him.

"Don't fall in," said Neilson.

"Not on your life."

Neilson watched him make his way across and when he had disappeared among the coconuts he looked still. Then he sank heavily in his chair. Was that the man who had prevented him from being happy? Was that the man whom Sally had loved all these years and for whom she had waited so desperately? It was grotesque. A sudden fury seized him so that he had an instinct to spring up and smash everything around him. He had been cheated. They had seen each other at last and had not known it. He began to laugh, mirthlessly, and his laughter grew till it became hysterical. The Gods had played him a cruel trick. And he was old now.

At last Sally came in to tell him dinner was ready. He sat down in front of her and tried to eat. He wondered what she would say if he told her now that the fat old man sitting in the chair was the lover whom she remembered still with the passionate abandonment of her youth. Years ago, when he hated her because she made him so unhappy, he would have been glad to tell her. He wanted to hurt her then as she hurt him, because his hatred was only love. But now he did not care. He shrugged his shoulders listlessly.

"What did that man want?" she asked presently.

He did not answer at once. She was too old, a fat old native woman. He wondered why he had ever loved her so madly. He had laid at her feet all the treasures of his soul, and she had cared nothing for them. Waste, what waste! And now, when he looked at her, he felt only contempt. His patience was at last exhausted. He answered her question.

"He's the captain of a schooner. He's come from Apia."

"Yes."

"He brought me news from home. My eldest brother is very ill and I must go back."

"Will you be gone long?"

He shrugged his shoulders.

The Fall of Edward Barnard

⁂

BATEMAN HUNTER SLEPT badly. For a fortnight on the boat that brought him from Tahiti to San Francisco he had been thinking of the story he had to tell, and for three days on the train he had repeated to himself the words in which he meant to tell it. But in a few hours now he would be in Chicago, and doubts assailed him. His conscience, always very sensitive, was not at ease. He was uncertain that he had done all that was possible, it was on his honour to do much more than the possible, and the thought was disturbing that, in a matter which so nearly touched his own interest, he had allowed his interest to prevail over his quixotry. Self-sacrifice appealed so keenly to his imagination that the inability to exercise it gave him a sense of disillusion. He was like the philanthropist who with altruistic motives builds model dwellings for the poor and finds that he has made a lucrative investment. He cannot prevent the satisfaction he feels in the ten per cent which rewards the bread he had cast upon the waters, but he has an awkward feeling that it detracts somewhat from the savour of his virtue. Bateman Hunter knew that his heart was pure, but he was not quite sure how steadfastly, when he told her his story, he would endure the scrutiny of Isabel Longstaffe's cool grey eyes. They were far-seeing and wise. She measured the standards of others by her own meticulous uprightness and there could be no greater censure than the cold silence with which she expressed her disapproval of a conduct that did not satisfy her exacting code. There was no appeal from her judgment, for, having made up her mind, she never changed it. But Bateman would not have had her different. He loved not only the beauty of her person, slim and straight, with the proud carriage of her head, but still more the beauty of her soul. With her truthfulness, her rigid sense of honour, her fearless outlook, she seemed to him to collect in herself all that was most admirable in his countrywomen. But he saw in her something more than the perfect type of the American girl, he felt that her exquisiteness was peculiar in a way to her environment, and he was assured that no city in the world could have produced her but Chicago. A pang seized him when he remembered that he must deal so bitter a blow to her pride, and anger flamed up in his heart when he thought of Edward Barnard.

But at last the train steamed in to Chicago and he exulted when he saw the long streets of grey houses. He could hardly bear his impatience at the thought of State and Wabash with their crowded pavements, their hustling traffic, and their noise. He was at home. And he was glad that he had been born in the most important city in the United States. San Francisco was provincial, New York was effete; the future of America lay in the development of its economic possibilities, and Chicago, by its position and by the energy of its citizens, was destined to become the real capital of the country.

"I guess I shall live long enough to see it the biggest city in the world," Bateman said to himself as he stepped down to the platform.

His father had come to meet him, and after a hearty handshake, the pair of them, tall, slender, and well-made, with the same fine, ascetic features and thin lips, walked out of the station. Mr Hunter's automobile was waiting for them and they got in. Mr Hunter caught his son's proud and happy glance as he looked at the street.

"Glad to be back, son?" he asked.

"I should just think I was," said Bateman.

His eyes devoured the restless scene.

"I guess there's a bit more traffic here than in your South Sea island," laughed Mr Hunter. "Did you like it there?"

"Give me Chicago, dad," answered Bateman.

"You haven't brought Edward Barnard back with you."

"No."

"How was he?"

Bateman was silent for a moment, and his handsome, sensitive face darkened.

"I'd sooner not speak about him, dad," he said at last.

"That's all right, my son. I guess your mother will be a happy woman to-day."

They passed out of the crowded streets in the Loop and drove along the lake till they came to the imposing house, an exact copy of a château on the Loire, which Mr Hunter had built himself some years before. As soon as Bateman was alone in his room he asked for a number on the telephone. His heart leaped when he heard the voice that answered him.

"Good-morning, Isabel," he said gaily.

"Good-morning, Bateman."

"How did you recognise my voice?"

"It is not so long since I heard it last. Besides, I was expecting you."

"When may I see you?"

"Unless you have anything better to do perhaps you'll dine with us to-night."

"You know very well that I couldn't possibly have anything better to do."

"I suppose that you're full of news?"

He thought he detected in her voice a note of apprehension.

"Yes," he answered.

"Well, you must tell me to-night. Good-bye."

She rang off. It was characteristic of her that she should be able to wait so many unnecessary hours to know what so immensely concerned her. To Bateman there was an admirable fortitude in her restraint.

At dinner, at which beside himself and Isabel no one was present but her father and mother, he watched her guide the conversation into the channels of an urbane small-talk, and it occurred to him that in just such a manner would a marquise under the shadow of the guillotine toy with the affairs of a day that would know no morrow. Her delicate features, the aristocratic shortness of her upper lip, and her wealth of fair hair suggested the marquise again, and it must have

been obvious, even if it were not notorious, that in her veins flowed
the best blood in Chicago. The dining-room was a fitting frame to
her fragile beauty, for Isabel had caused the house, a replica of a palace on the Grand Canal at Venice, to be furnished by an English
expert in the style of Louis XV; and the graceful decoration linked
with the name of that amorous monarch enhanced her loveliness and
at the same time acquired from it a more profound significance. For
Isabel's mind was richly stored, and her conversation, however light,
was never flippant. She spoke now of the Musicale to which she
and her mother had been in the afternoon, of the lectures which an
English poet was giving at the Auditorium, of the political situation,
and of the Old Master which her father had recently bought for fifty
thousand dollars in New York. It comforted Bateman to hear her.
He felt that he was once more in the civilised world, at the centre of
culture and distinction; and certain voices, troubling and yet against
his will refusing to still their clamour, were at last silent in his heart.

"Gee, but it's good to be back in Chicago," he said.

At last dinner was over, and when they went out of the dining-room Isabel said to her mother:

"I'm going to take Bateman along to my den. We have various
things to talk about."

"Very well, my dear," said Mrs Longstaffe. "You'll find your father
and me in the Madame du Barry room when you're through."

Isabel led the young man upstairs and showed him into the room
of which he had so many charming memories. Though he knew it so
well he could not repress the exclamation of delight which it always
wrung from him. She looked round with a smile.

"I think it's a success," she said. "The main thing is that it's right.
There's not even an ashtray that isn't of the period."

"I suppose that's what makes it so wonderful. Like all you do it's
so superlatively right."

They sat down in front of a log fire and Isabel looked at him with
calm grave eyes.

"Now what have you to say to me?" she asked.

"I hardly know how to begin."

"Is Edward Barnard coming back?"

"No."

There was a long silence before Bateman spoke again, and with each of them it was filled with many thoughts. It was a difficult story he had to tell, for there were things in it which were so offensive to her sensitive ears that he could not bear to tell them, and yet in justice to her, no less than in justice to himself, he must tell her the whole truth.

It had all begun long ago when he and Edward Barnard, still at college, had met Isabel Longstaffe at the tea-party given to introduce her to society. They had both known her when she was a child and they long-legged boys, but for two years she had been in Europe to finish her education and it was with a surprised delight that they renewed acquaintance with the lovely girl who returned. Both of them fell desperately in love with her, but Bateman saw quickly that she had eyes only for Edward, and, devoted to his friend, he resigned himself to the role of confidant. He passed bitter moments, but he could not deny that Edward was worthy of his good fortune, and, anxious that nothing should impair the friendship he so greatly valued, he took care never by a hint to disclose his own feelings. In six months the young couple were engaged. But they were very young and Isabel's father decided that they should not marry at least till Edward graduated. They had to wait a year. Bateman remembered the winter at the end of which Isabel and Edward were to be married, a winter of dances and theatre-parties and of informal gaieties at which he, the constant third, was always present. He loved her no less because she would shortly be his friend's wife; her smile, a gay word she flung him, the confidence of her affection, never ceased to delight him; and he congratulated himself, somewhat complacently, because he did not envy them their happiness. Then an accident happened. A great bank failed, there was a panic on the exchange, and Edward Barnard's father found himself a ruined man. He came home one night, told his wife that he was penniless, and after dinner, going into his study, shot himself.

A week later, Edward Barnard, with a tired, white face, went to Isabel and asked her to release him. Her only answer was to throw her arms round his neck and burst into tears.

"Don't make it harder for me, sweet," he said.

"Do you think I can let you go now? I love you."

"How can I ask you to marry me? The whole thing's hopeless. Your father would never let you. I haven't a cent."

"What do I care? I love you."

He told her his plans. He had to earn money at once, and George Braunschmidt, an old friend of his family, had offered to take him into his own business. He was a South Sea merchant, and he had agencies in many of the islands of the Pacific. He had suggested that Edward should go to Tahiti for a year or two, where under the best of his managers he could learn the details of that varied trade, and at the end of that time he promised the young man a position in Chicago. It was a wonderful opportunity, and when he had finished his explanations Isabel was once more all smiles.

"You foolish boy, why have you been trying to make me miserable?"

His face lit up at her words and his eyes flashed.

"Isabel, you don't mean to say you'll wait for me?"

"Don't you think you're worth it?" she smiled.

"Ah, don't laugh at me now. I beseech you to be serious. It may be for two years."

"Have no fear. I love you, Edward. When you come back I will marry you."

Edward's employer was a man who did not like delay and he had told him that if he took the post he offered he must sail that day week from San Francisco. Edward spent his last evening with Isabel. It was after dinner that Mr Longstaffe, saying he wanted a word with Edward, took him into the smoking-room. Mr Longstaffe had accepted good-naturedly the arrangement which his daughter had told him of and Edward could not imagine what mysterious communication he had now to make. He was not a little perplexed to see that his host was embarrassed. He faltered. He talked of trivial things. At last he blurted it out.

"I guess you've heard of Arnold Jackson," he said, looking at Edward with a frown.

Edward hesitated. His natural truthfulness obliged him to admit a knowledge he would gladly have been able to deny.

"Yes, I have. But it's a long time ago. I guess I didn't pay very much attention."

"There are not many people in Chicago who haven't heard of Arnold Jackson," said Mr Longstaffe bitterly, "and if there are they'll have no difficulty in finding someone who'll be glad to tell them. Did you know he was Mrs Longstaffe's brother?"

"Yes, I knew that."

"Of course we've had no communication with him for many years. He left the country as soon as he was able to, and I guess the country wasn't sorry to see the last of him. We understand he lives in Tahiti. My advice to you is to give him a wide berth, but if you do hear anything about him Mrs Longstaffe and I would be very glad if you'd let us know."

"Sure."

"That was all I wanted to say to you. Now I daresay you'd like to join the ladies."

There are few families that have not among their members one whom, if their neighbours permitted, they would willingly forget, and they are fortunate when the lapse of a generation or two has invested his vagaries with a romantic glamour. But when he is actually alive, if his peculiarities are not of the kind that can be condoned by the phrase, "he is nobody's enemy but his own," a safe one when the culprit has no worse to answer for than alcoholism or wandering affections, the only possible course is silence. And it was this which the Longstaffes had adopted towards Arnold Jackson. They never talked of him. They would not even pass through the street in which he had lived. Too kind to make his wife and children suffer for his misdeeds, they had supported them for years, but on the understanding that they should live in Europe. They did everything they could to blot out all recollection of Arnold Jackson and yet were conscious that the story was as fresh in the public mind as when first the scandal burst upon a gaping world. Arnold Jackson was as black a sheep as any family could suffer from. A wealthy banker, prominent in his church, a philanthropist, a man respected by all, not only for his connections (in his veins ran the blue blood of Chicago), but also for his upright character, he was arrested one day on a charge of fraud; and the dishonesty which the trial brought to light was not of the sort which could be explained by a sudden temptation; it was deliberate and systematic. Arnold Jackson was a rogue. When he was sent to the penitentiary for seven years there were few who did not think he had escaped lightly.

When at the end of this last evening the lovers separated it was with many protestations of devotion. Isabel, all tears, was consoled a little by her certainty of Edward's passionate love. It was a strange feeling that she had. It made her wretched to part from him and yet she was happy because he adored her.

This was more than two years ago.

He had written to her by every mail since then, twenty-four letters in all, for the mail went but once a month, and his letters had been all that a lover's letters should be. They were intimate and charming, humorous sometimes, especially of late, and tender. At first they suggested that he was homesick, they were full of his desire to get back to Chicago and Isabel; and, a little anxiously, she wrote begging him to persevere. She was afraid that he might throw up his opportunity and come racing back. She did not want her lover to lack endurance and she quoted to him the lines:

"I could not love thee, dear, so much, Loved I not honour more."

But presently he seemed to settle down and it made Isabel very happy to observe his growing enthusiasm to introduce American methods into that forgotten corner of the world. But she knew him, and at the end of the year, which was the shortest time he could possibly stay in Tahiti, she expected to have to use all her influence to dissuade him from coming home. It was much better that he should learn the business thoroughly, and if they had been able to wait a year there seemed no reason why they should not wait another. She talked it over with Bateman Hunter, always the most generous of friends (during those first few days after Edward went she did not know what she would have done without him), and they decided that Edward's future must stand before everything. It was with relief that she found as the time passed that he made no suggestion of returning.

"He's splendid, isn't he?" she exclaimed to Bateman.

"He's white, through and through."

"Reading between the lines of his letter I know he hates it over there, but he's sticking it out because...."

She blushed a little and Bateman, with the grave smile which was so attractive in him, finished the sentence for her.

"Because he loves you."

"It makes me feel so humble," she said.

"You're wonderful, Isabel, you're perfectly wonderful."

But the second year passed and every month Isabel continued to receive a letter from Edward, and presently it began to seem a little strange that he did not speak of coming back. He wrote as though he were settled definitely in Tahiti, and what was more, comfortably settled. She was surprised. Then she read his letters again, all of them, several times; and now, reading between the lines indeed, she was puzzled to notice a change which had escaped her. The later letters were as tender and as delightful as the first, but the tone was different. She was vaguely suspicious of their humour, she had the instinctive mistrust of her sex for that unaccountable quality, and she discerned in them now a flippancy which perplexed her. She was not quite certain that the Edward who wrote to her now was the same Edward that she had known. One afternoon, the day after a mail had arrived from Tahiti, when she was driving with Bateman he said to her:

"Did Edward tell you when he was sailing?"

"No, he didn't mention it. I thought he might have said something to you about it."

"Not a word."

"You know what Edward is," she laughed in reply, "he has no sense of time. If it occurs to you next time you write you might ask him when he's thinking of coming."

Her manner was so unconcerned that only Bateman's acute sensitiveness could have discerned in her request a very urgent desire. He laughed lightly.

"Yes. I'll ask him. I can't imagine what he's thinking about."

A few days later, meeting him again, she noticed that something troubled him. They had been much together since Edward left Chicago; they were both devoted to him and each in his desire to talk of the absent one found a willing listener; the consequence was that Isabel knew every expression of Bateman's face, and his denials now were useless against her keen instinct. Something told her that his harassed look had to do with Edward and she did not rest till she had made him confess.

"The fact is," he said at last, "I heard in a round-about way that Edward was no longer working for Braunschmidt and Co., and yesterday I took the opportunity to ask Mr Braunschmidt himself."

"Well?"

"Edward left his employment with them nearly a year ago."

"How strange he should have said nothing about it!"

Bateman hesitated, but he had gone so far now that he was obliged to tell the rest. It made him feel dreadfully embarrassed.

"He was fired."

"In heaven's name what for?"

"It appears they warned him once or twice, and at last they told him to get out. They say he was lazy and incompetent."

"Edward?"

They were silent for a while, and then he saw that Isabel was crying. Instinctively he seized her hand.

"Oh, my dear, don't, don't," he said. "I can't bear to see it."

She was so unstrung that she let her hand rest in his. He tried to console her.

"It's incomprehensible, isn't it? It's so unlike Edward. I can't help feeling there must be some mistake."

She did not say anything for a while, and when she spoke it was hesitatingly.

"Has it struck you that there was anything queer in his letters lately?" she asked, looking away, her eyes all bright with tears.

He did not quite know how to answer.

"I have noticed a change in them," he admitted. "He seems to have lost that high seriousness which I admired so much in him. One would almost think that the things that matter—well, don't matter."

Isabel did not reply. She was vaguely uneasy.

"Perhaps in his answer to your letter he'll say when he's coming home. All we can do is to wait for that."

Another letter came from Edward for each of them, and still he made no mention of his return; but when he wrote he could not have received Bateman's enquiry. The next mail would bring them an answer to that. The next mail came, and Bateman brought Isabel the letter he had just received; but the first glance of his face was enough to tell her that he was disconcerted. She read it through carefully and then, with slightly tightened lips, read it again.

"It's a very strange letter," she said. "I don't quite understand it."

"One might almost think that he was joshing me," said Bateman, flushing.

"It reads like that, but it must be unintentional. That's so unlike Edward."

"He says nothing about coming back."

"If I weren't so confident of his love I should think.... I hardly know what I should think."

It was then that Bateman had broached the scheme which during the afternoon had formed itself in his brain. The firm, founded by his father, in which he was now a partner, a firm which manufactured all manner of motor vehicles, was about to establish agencies in Honolulu, Sidney, and Wellington; and Bateman proposed that himself should go instead of the manager who had been suggested. He could return by Tahiti; in fact, travelling from Wellington, it was inevitable to do so; and he could see Edward.

"There's some mystery and I'm going to clear it up. That's the only way to do it."

"Oh, Bateman, how can you be so good and kind?" she exclaimed.

"You know there's nothing in the world I want more than your happiness, Isabel."

She looked at him and she gave him her hands.

"You're wonderful, Bateman. I didn't know there was anyone in the world like you. How can I ever thank you?"

"I don't want your thanks. I only want to be allowed to help you."

She dropped her eyes and flushed a little. She was so used to him that she had forgotten how handsome he was. He was as tall as Edward and as well made, but he was dark and pale of face, while Edward was ruddy. Of course she knew he loved her. It touched her.

She felt very tenderly towards him.

It was from this journey that Bateman Hunter was now returned.

The business part of it took him somewhat longer than he expected and he had much time to think of his two friends. He had come to the conclusion that it could be nothing serious that prevented Edward from coming home, a pride, perhaps, which made him determined to make good before he claimed the bride he adored; but it was a pride that must be reasoned with. Isabel was unhappy. Edward must come back to Chicago with him and marry her at once. A position could be found for him in the works of the Hunter Motor Traction and Automobile Company. Bateman, with a bleeding heart, exulted at the prospect of giving happiness to the two persons he loved best in the world at the cost of his own. He would never marry. He would be godfather to the children of Edward and Isabel, and many years later when they were both dead he would tell Isabel's daughter how long, long ago he had loved her mother. Bateman's eyes were veiled with tears when he pictured this scene to himself.

Meaning to take Edward by surprise he had not cabled to announce his arrival, and when at last he landed at Tahiti he allowed a youth, who said he was the son of the house, to lead him to the Hotel de la Fleur. He chuckled when he thought of his friend's amazement on seeing him, the most unexpected of visitors, walk into his office.

"By the way," he asked, as they went along, "can you tell me where I shall find Mr. Edward Barnard?"

"Barnard?" said the youth. "I seem to know the name."

"He's an American. A tall fellow with light brown hair and blue eyes. He's been here over two years."

"Of course. Now I know who you mean. You mean Mr Jackson's nephew."

"Whose nephew?"

"Mr Arnold Jackson."

"I don't think we're speaking of the same person," answered Bateman, frigidly.

He was startled. It was queer that Arnold Jackson, known apparently to all and sundry, should live here under the disgraceful name in which he had been convicted. But Bateman could not imagine whom it was that he passed off as his nephew. Mrs Longstaffe was his only sister and he had never had a brother. The young man by his side talked volubly in an English that had something in it of the intonation of a foreign tongue, and Bateman, with a sidelong glance, saw, what he had not noticed before, that there was in him a good deal of native blood. A touch of hauteur involuntarily entered into his manner. They reached the hotel. When he had arranged about his room Bateman asked to be directed to the premises of Braunschmidt & Co. They were on the front, facing the lagoon, and, glad to feel the solid earth under his feet after eight days at sea, he sauntered down the sunny road to the water's edge. Having found the place he sought, Bateman sent in his card to the manager and was led through a lofty barn-like room, half store and half warehouse, to an office in which sat a stout, spectacled, bald-headed man.

"Can you tell me where I shall find Mr Edward Barnard? I understand he was in this office for some time."

"That is so. I don't know just where he is."

"But I thought he came here with a particular recommendation from Mr Braunschmidt. I know Mr Braunschmidt very well."

The fat man looked at Bateman with shrewd, suspicious eyes. He called to one of the boys in the warehouse.

"Say, Henry, where's Barnard now, d'you know?"

"He's working at Cameron's, I think," came the answer from someone who did not trouble to move.

The fat man nodded.

"If you turn to your left when you get out of here you'll come to Cameron's in about three minutes."

Bateman hesitated.

"I think I should tell you that Edward Barnard is my greatest friend. I was very much surprised when I heard he'd left Braunschmidt & Co."

The fat man's eyes contracted till they seemed like pin-points, and their scrutiny made Bateman so uncomfortable that he felt himself blushing.

"I guess Braunschmidt & Co. and Edward Barnard didn't see eye to eye on certain matters," he replied.

Bateman did not quite like the fellow's manner, so he got up, not without dignity, and with an apology for troubling him bade him good-day. He left the place with a singular feeling that the man he had just interviewed had much to tell him, but no intention of telling it. He walked in the direction indicated and soon found himself at Cameron's. It was a trader's store, such as he had passed half a dozen of on his way, and when he entered the first person he saw, in his shirt sleeves, measuring out a length of trade cotton, was Edward. It gave him a start to see him engaged in so humble an occupation. But he had scarcely appeared when Edward, looking up, caught sight of him, and gave a joyful cry of surprise.

"Bateman! Who ever thought of seeing you here?"

He stretched his arm across the counter and wrung Bateman's hand. There was no self-consciousness in his manner and the embarrassment was all on Bateman's side.

"Just wait till I've wrapped this package."

With perfect assurance he ran his scissors across the stuff, folded it, made it into a parcel, and handed it to the dark-skinned customer.

"Pay at the desk, please."

Then, smiling, with bright eyes, he turned to Bateman.

"How did you show up here? Gee, I am delighted to see you. Sit down, old man. Make yourself at home."

"We can't talk here. Come along to my hotel. I suppose you can get away?"

This he added with some apprehension.

"Of course I can get away. We're not so businesslike as all that in Tahiti." He called out to a Chinese who was standing behind the opposite counter. "Ah-Ling, when the boss comes tell him a friend of mine's just arrived from America and I've gone out to have a drain with him."

"All-light," said the Chinese, with a grin.

Edward slipped on a coat and, putting on his hat, accompanied Bateman out of the store. Bateman attempted to put the matter facetiously.

"I didn't expect to find you selling three and a half yards of rotten cotton to a greasy nigger," he laughed.

"Braunschmidt fired me, you know, and I thought that would do as well as anything else."

Edward's candour seemed to Bateman very surprising, but he thought it indiscreet to pursue the subject.

"I guess you won't make a fortune where you are," he answered, somewhat dryly.

"I guess not. But I earn enough to keep body and soul together, and I'm quite satisfied with that."

"You wouldn't have been two years ago."

"We grow wiser as we grow older," retorted Edward, gaily.

Bateman took a glance at him. Edward was dressed in a suit of shabby white ducks, none too clean, and a large straw hat of native make. He was thinner than he had been, deeply burned by the sun, and he was certainly better looking than ever. But there was something in his appearance that disconcerted Bateman. He walked with a new jauntiness; there was a carelessness in his demeanour, a gaiety about nothing in particular, which Bateman could not precisely blame, but which exceedingly puzzled him.

"I'm blest if I can see what he's got to be so darned cheerful about," he said to himself.

They arrived at the hotel and sat on the terrace. A Chinese boy brought them cocktails. Edward was most anxious to hear all the news of Chicago and bombarded his friend with eager questions. His interest was natural and sincere. But the odd thing was that it seemed equally divided among a multitude of subjects. He was as eager to know how Bateman's father was as what Isabel was doing. He talked of her without a shade of embarrassment, but she might just as well have been his sister as his promised wife; and before Bateman had done analysing the exact meaning of Edward's remarks he found that the conversation had drifted to his own work and the buildings his father had lately erected. He was determined to bring the conversation back to Isabel and was looking for the occasion when he saw Edward wave his hand cordially. A man was advancing towards them on the terrace, but Bateman's back was turned to him and he could not see him.

"Come and sit down," said Edward gaily.

The new-comer approached. He was a very tall, thin man, in white ducks, with a fine head of curly white hair. His face was thin too, long, with a large, hooked nose and a beautiful, expressive mouth.

"This is my old friend Bateman Hunter. I've told you about him," said Edward, his constant smile breaking on his lips.

"I'm pleased to meet you, Mr Hunter. I used to know your father."

The stranger held out his hand and took the young man's in a strong, friendly grasp. It was not till then that Edward mentioned the other's name.

"Mr Arnold Jackson."

Bateman turned white and he felt his hands grow cold. This was the forger, the convict, this was Isabel's uncle. He did not know what to say. He tried to conceal his confusion. Arnold Jackson looked at him with twinkling eyes.

"I daresay my name is familiar to you."

Bateman did not know whether to say yes or no, and what made it more awkward was that both Jackson and Edward seemed to be amused. It was bad enough to have forced on him the acquaintance of the one man on the island he would rather have avoided, but worse to discern that he was being made a fool of. Perhaps, however, he had reached this conclusion too quickly, for Jackson, without a pause, added:

"I understand you're very friendly with the Longstaffes. Mary Longstaffe is my sister."

Now Bateman asked himself if Arnold Jackson could think him ignorant of the most terrible scandal that Chicago had ever known. But Jackson put his hand on Edward's shoulder.

"I can't sit down, Teddie," he said. "I'm busy. But you two boys had better come up and dine to-night."

"That'll be fine," said Edward.

"It's very kind of you, Mr Jackson," said Bateman, frigidly, "but I'm here for so short a time; my boat sails to-morrow, you know; I think if you'll forgive me, I won't come."

"Oh, nonsense. I'll give you a native dinner. My wife's a wonderful cook. Teddie will show you the way. Come early so as to see the sunset. I can give you both a shake-down if you like."

"Of course we'll come," said Edward. "There's always the devil of a row in the hotel on the night a boat arrives and we can have a good yarn up at the bungalow."

"I can't let you off, Mr Hunter," Jackson continued with the utmost cordiality. "I want to hear all about Chicago and Mary."

He nodded and walked away before Bateman could say another word.

"We don't take refusals in Tahiti," laughed Edward. "Besides, you'll get the best dinner on the island."

"What did he mean by saying his wife was a good cook? I happen to know his wife's in Geneva."

"That's a long way off for a wife, isn't it?" said Edward. "And it's a long time since he saw her. I guess it's another wife he's talking about."

For some time Bateman was silent. His face was set in grave lines. But looking up he caught the amused look in Edward's eyes, and he flushed darkly.

"Arnold Jackson is a despicable rogue," he said.

"I greatly fear he is," answered Edward, smiling.

"I don't see how any decent man can have anything to do with him."

"Perhaps I'm not a decent man."

"Do you see much of him, Edward?"

"Yes, quite a lot. He's adopted me as his nephew."

Bateman leaned forward and fixed Edward with his searching eyes.

"Do you like him?"

"Very much."

"But don't you know, doesn't everyone here know, that he's a forger and that he's been a convict? He ought to be hounded out of civilised society."

Edward watched a ring of smoke that floated from his cigar into the still, scented air.

"I suppose he is a pretty unmitigated rascal," he said at last. "And I can't flatter myself that any repentance for his misdeeds offers one an excuse for condoning them. He was a swindler and a hypocrite. You can't get away from it. I never met a more agreeable companion. He's taught me everything I know."

"What has he taught you?" cried Bateman in amazement.

"How to live."

Bateman broke into ironical laughter.

"A fine master. Is it owing to his lessons that you lost the chance of making a fortune and earn your living now by serving behind a counter in a ten cent store?"

"He has a wonderful personality," said Edward, smiling good-naturedly. "Perhaps you'll see what I mean to-night."

"I'm not going to dine with him if that's what you mean. Nothing would induce me to set foot within that man's house."

"Come to oblige me, Bateman. We've been friends for so many years, you won't refuse me a favour when I ask it."

Edward's tone had in it a quality new to Bateman. Its gentleness was singularly persuasive.

"If you put it like that, Edward, I'm bound to come," he smiled.

Bateman reflected, moreover, that it would be as well to learn what he could about Arnold Jackson. It was plain that he had a great ascendency over Edward, and if it was to be combated it was necessary to discover in what exactly it consisted. The more he talked with Edward the more conscious he became that a change had taken place in him. He had an instinct that it behooved him to walk warily, and he made up his mind not to broach the real purport of his visit till he saw his way more clearly. He began to talk of one thing and another, of his journey and what he had achieved by it, of politics in Chicago, of this common friend and that, of their days together at college.

At last Edward said he must get back to his work and proposed that he should fetch Bateman at five so that they could drive out together to Arnold Jackson's house.

"By the way, I rather thought you'd be living at this hotel," said Bateman, as he strolled out of the garden with Edward. "I understand it's the only decent one here."

"Not I," laughed Edward. "It's a deal too grand for me. I rent a room just outside the town. It's cheap and clean."

"If I remember right those weren't the points that seemed most important to you when you lived in Chicago."

"Chicago!"

"I don't know what you mean by that, Edward. It's the greatest city in the world."

"I know," said Edward.

Bateman glanced at him quickly, but his face was inscrutable.

"When are you coming back to it?"

"I often wonder," smiled Edward.

This answer, and the manner of it, staggered Bateman, but before he could ask for an explanation Edward waved to a half-caste who was driving a passing motor.

"Give us a ride down, Charlie," he said.

He nodded to Bateman, and ran after the machine that had pulled up a few yards in front. Bateman was left to piece together a mass of perplexing impressions.

Edward called for him in a rickety trap drawn by an old mare, and they drove along a road that ran by the sea. On each side of it were plantations, coconut and vanilla; and now and then they saw a great mango, its fruit yellow and red and purple among the massy green of the leaves; now and then they had a glimpse of the lagoon, smooth and blue, with here and there a tiny islet graceful with tall palms. Arnold Jackson's house stood on a little hill and only a path led to it, so they unharnessed the mare and tied her to a tree, leaving the trap by the side of the road. To Bateman it seemed a happy-go-lucky way of doing things. But when they went up to the house they were met by a tall, handsome native woman, no longer young, with whom Edward cordially shook hands. He introduced Bateman to her.

"This is my friend Mr Hunter. We're going to dine with you, Lavina."

"All right," she said, with a quick smile. "Arnold ain't back yet."

"We'll go down and bathe. Let us have a couple of pareos."

The woman nodded and went into the house.

"Who is that?" asked Bateman.

"Oh, that's Lavina. She's Arnold's wife."

Bateman tightened his lips, but said nothing. In a moment the woman returned with a bundle, which she gave to Edward; and the two men, scrambling down a steep path, made their way to a grove of coconut trees on the beach. They undressed and Edward showed his friend how to make the strip of red trade cotton which is called a pareo into a very neat pair of bathing-drawers. Soon they were splashing in the warm, shallow water. Edward was in great spirits. He laughed and shouted and sang. He might have been fifteen. Bateman had never seen him so gay, and afterwards when they lay on the beach, smoking cigarettes, in the limpid air, there was such an irresistible light-heartedness in him that Bateman was taken aback.

"You seem to find life mighty pleasant," said he.

"I do."

They heard a soft movement and looking round saw that Arnold Jackson was coming towards them.

"I thought I'd come down and fetch you two boys back," he said. "Did you enjoy your bath, Mr Hunter?"

"Very much," said Bateman.

Arnold Jackson, no longer in spruce ducks, wore nothing but a pareo round his loins and walked barefoot. His body was deeply browned by the sun. With his long, curling white hair and his ascetic face he made a fantastic figure in the native dress, but he bore himself without a trace of self-consciousness.

"If you're ready we'll go right up," said Jackson.

"I'll just put on my clothes," said Bateman.

"Why, Teddie, didn't you bring a pareo for your friend?"

"I guess he'd rather wear clothes," smiled Edward.

"I certainly would," answered Bateman, grimly, as he saw Edward gird himself in the loincloth and stand ready to start before he himself had got his shirt on.

"Won't you find it rough walking without your shoes?" he asked Edward. "It struck me the path was a trifle rocky."

"Oh, I'm used to it."

"It's a comfort to get into a pareo when one gets back from town," said Jackson. "If you were going to stay here I should strongly recommend you to adopt it. It's one of the most sensible costumes I have ever come across. It's cool, convenient, and inexpensive."

They walked up to the house, and Jackson took them into a large room with white-washed walls and an open ceiling in which a table was laid for dinner. Bateman noticed that it was set for five.

"Eva, come and show yourself to Teddie's friend, and then shake us a cocktail," called Jackson.

Then he led Bateman to a long low window.

"Look at that," he said, with a dramatic gesture. "Look well."

Below them coconut trees tumbled down steeply to the lagoon, and the lagoon in the evening light had the colour, tender and varied, of a dove's breast. On a creek, at a little distance, were the clustered huts of a native village, and towards the reef was a canoe, sharply silhouetted, in which were a couple of natives fishing. Then, beyond, you saw the vast calmness of the Pacific and twenty miles away, airy and unsubstantial like the fabric of a poet's fancy, the unimaginable beauty of the island which is called Murea. It was all so lovely that Bateman stood abashed.

"I've never seen anything like it," he said at last.

Arnold Jackson stood staring in front of him, and in his eyes was a dreamy softness. His thin, thoughtful face was very grave. Bateman, glancing at it, was once more conscious of its intense spirituality.

"Beauty," murmured Arnold Jackson. "You seldom see beauty face to face. Look at it well, Mr Hunter, for what you see now you will never see again, since the moment is transitory, but it will be an imperishable memory in your heart. You touch eternity."

His voice was deep and resonant. He seemed to breathe forth the purest idealism, and Bateman had to urge himself to remember that the man who spoke was a criminal and a cruel cheat. But Edward, as though he heard a sound, turned round quickly.

"Here is my daughter, Mr Hunter."

Bateman shook hands with her. She had dark, splendid eyes and a red mouth tremulous with laughter; but her skin was brown, and her curling hair, rippling down her-shoulders, was coal black. She wore but one garment, a Mother Hubbard of pink cotton, her feet were bare, and she was crowned with a wreath of white scented flowers. She was a lovely creature. She was like a goddess of the Polynesian spring.

She was a little shy, but not more shy than Bateman, to whom the

whole situation was highly embarrassing, and it did not put him at
his ease to see this sylph-like thing take a shaker and with a practised
hand mix three cocktails.

"Let us have a kick in them, child," said Jackson.

She poured them out and smiling delightfully handed one to
each of the men. Bateman flattered himself on his skill in the subtle
art of shaking cocktails and he was not a little astonished, on tasting
this one, to find that it was excellent. Jackson laughed proudly when
he saw his guest's involuntary look of appreciation.

"Not bad, is it? I taught the child myself, and in the old days in
Chicago I considered that there wasn't a bar-tender in the city that
could hold a candle to me. When I had nothing better to do in the
penitentiary I used to amuse myself by thinking out new cocktails,
but when you come down to brass-tacks there's nothing to beat a dry
Martini."

Bateman felt as though someone had given him a violent blow
on the funny-bone and he was conscious that he turned red and
then white. But before he could think of anything to say a native
boy brought in a great bowl of soup and the whole party sat down
to dinner. Arnold Jackson's remark seemed to have aroused in him
a train of recollections, for he began to talk of his prison days. He
talked quite naturally, without malice, as though he were relating his
experiences at a foreign university. He addressed himself to Bateman
and Bateman was confused and then confounded. He saw Edward's
eyes fixed on him and there was in them a flicker of amusement.
He blushed scarlet, for it struck him that Jackson was making a fool
of him, and then because he felt absurd—and knew there was no
reason why he should—he grew angry. Arnold Jackson was impudent—there was no other word for it—and his callousness, whether
assumed or not, was outrageous. The dinner proceeded. Bateman was
asked to eat sundry messes, raw fish and he knew not what, which
only his civility induced him to swallow, but which he was amazed to
find very good eating. Then an incident happened which to Bateman
was the most mortifying experience of the evening. There was a little
circlet of flowers in front of him, and for the sake of conversation he
hazarded a remark about it.

"It's a wreath that Eva made for you," said Jackson, "but I guess she was too shy to give it you."

Bateman took it up in his hand and made a polite little speech of thanks to the girl.

"You must put it on," she said, with a smile and a blush.

"I? I don't think I'll do that."

"It's the charming custom of the country," said Arnold Jackson.

There was one in front of him and he placed it on his hair. Edward did the same.

"I guess I'm not dressed for the part," said Bateman, uneasily.

"Would you like a pareo?" said Eva quickly. "I'll get you one in a minute."

"No, thank you. I'm quite comfortable as I am."

"Show him how to put it on, Eva," said Edward.

At that moment Bateman hated his greatest friend. Eva got up from the table and with much laughter placed the wreath on his black hair.

"It suits you very well," said Mrs Jackson. "Don't it suit him, Arnold?"

"Of course it does."

Bateman sweated at every pore.

"Isn't it a pity it's dark?" said Eva. "We could photograph you all three together."

Bateman thanked his stars it was. He felt that he must look prodigiously foolish in his blue serge suit and high collar—very neat and gentlemanly—with that ridiculous wreath of flowers on his head. He was seething with indignation, and he had never in his life exercised more self-control than now when he presented an affable exterior. He was furious with that old man, sitting at the head of the table, half-naked, with his saintly face and the flowers on his handsome white locks. The whole position was monstrous.

Then dinner came to an end, and Eva and her mother remained to clear away while the three men sat on the verandah. It was very warm and the air was scented with the white flowers of the night. The full moon, sailing across an unclouded sky, made a pathway on the broad sea that led to the boundless realms of Forever. Arnold

Jackson began to talk. His voice was rich and musical. He talked now of the natives and of the old legends of the country. He told strange stories of the past, stories of hazardous expeditions into the unknown, of love and death, of hatred and revenge. He told of the adventurers who had discovered those distant islands, of the sailors who, settling in them, had married the daughters of great chieftains, and of the beach-combers who had led their varied lives on those silvery shores. Bateman, mortified and exasperated, at first listened sullenly, but presently some magic in the words possessed him and he sat entranced. The mirage of romance obscured the light of common day. Had he forgotten that Arnold Jackson had a tongue of silver, a tongue by which he had charmed vast sums out of the credulous public, a tongue which very nearly enabled him to escape the penalty of his crimes? No one had a sweeter eloquence, and no one had a more acute sense of climax. Suddenly he rose.

"Well, you two boys haven't seen one another for a long time. I shall leave you to have a yarn. Teddie will show you your quarters when you want to go to bed."

"Oh, but I wasn't thinking of spending the night, Mr Jackson," said Bateman.

"You'll find it more comfortable. We'll see that you're called in good time."

Then with a courteous shake of the hand, stately as though he were a bishop in canonicals, Arnold Jackson took leave of his guest.

"Of course I'll drive you back to Papeete if you like," said Edward, "but I advise you to stay. It's bully driving in the early morning."

For a few minutes neither of them spoke. Bateman wondered how he should begin on the conversation which all the events of the day made him think more urgent.

"When are you coming back to Chicago?" he asked, suddenly.

For a moment Edward did not answer. Then he turned rather lazily to look at his friend and smiled.

"I don't know. Perhaps never."

"What in heaven's name do you mean?" cried Bateman.

"I'm very happy here. Wouldn't it be folly to make a change?"

"Man alive, you can't live here all your life. This is no life for a man. It's a living death. Oh, Edward, come away at once, before it's too late. I've felt that something was wrong. You're infatuated with the place, you've succumbed to evil influences, but it only requires a wrench, and when you're free from these surroundings you'll thank all the gods there be. You'll be like a dope-fiend when he's broken from his drug. You'll see then that for two years you've been breathing poisoned air. You can't imagine what a relief it will be when you fill your lungs once more with the fresh, pure air of your native country."

He spoke quickly, the words tumbling over one another in his excitement, and there was in his voice sincere and affectionate emotion. Edward was touched.

"It is good of you to care so much, old friend."

"Come with me to-morrow, Edward. It was a mistake that you ever came to this place. This is no life for you."

"You talk of this sort of life and that. How do you think a man gets the best out of life?"

"Why, I should have thought there could be no two answers to that. By doing his duty, by hard work, by meeting all the obligations of his state and station."

"And what is his reward?"

"His reward is the consciousness of having achieved what he set out to do."

"It all sounds a little portentous to me," said Edward, and in the lightness of the night Bateman could see that he was smiling. "I'm afraid you'll think I've degenerated sadly. There are several things I think now which I daresay would have seemed outrageous to me three years ago."

"Have you learnt them from Arnold Jackson?" asked Bateman, scornfully.

"You don't like him? Perhaps you couldn't be expected to. I didn't when I first came. I had just the same prejudice as you. He's a very extraordinary man. You saw for yourself that he makes no secret of the fact that he was in a penitentiary. I do not know that he regrets it or the crimes that led him there. The only complaint he ever made in my hearing was that when he came out his health was impaired. I think he does not know what remorse is. He is completely unmoral.

He accepts everything and he accepts himself as well. He's generous and kind."

"He always was," interrupted Bateman, "on other people's money."

"I've found him a very good friend. Is it unnatural that I should take a man as I find him?"

"The result is that you lose the distinction between right and wrong."

"No, they remain just as clearly divided in my mind as before, but what has become a little confused in me is the distinction between the bad man and the good one. Is Arnold Jackson a bad man who does good things or a good man who does bad things? It's a difficult question to answer. Perhaps we make too much of the difference between one man and another. Perhaps even the best of us are sinners and the worst of us are saints. Who knows?"

"You will never persuade me that white is black and that black is white," said Bateman.

"I'm sure I shan't, Bateman."

Bateman could not understand why the flicker of a smile crossed Edward's lips when he thus agreed with him. Edward was silent for a minute.

"When I saw you this morning, Bateman," he said then, "I seemed to see myself as I was two years ago. The same collar, and the same shoes, the same blue suit, the same energy. The same determination. By God, I was energetic. The sleepy methods of this place made my blood tingle. I went about and everywhere I saw possibilities for development and enterprise. There were fortunes to be made here. It seemed to me absurd that the copra should be taken away from here in sacks and the oil extracted in America. It would be far more economical to do all that on the spot, with cheap labour, and save freight, and I saw already the vast factories springing up on the island. Then the way they extracted it from the coconut seemed to me hopelessly inadequate, and I invented a machine which divided the nut and scooped out the meat at the rate of two hundred and forty an hour. The harbour was not large enough. I made plans to enlarge it, then to form a syndicate to buy land, put up two or three large hotels, and bungalows for occasional residents; I had a scheme for improving the steamer service in order to attract visitors from California. In twenty years, instead of this half French, lazy little town of Papeete I saw a great American city with ten-story buildings and street-cars, a theatre and an opera house, a stock exchange and a mayor."

"But go ahead, Edward," cried Bateman, springing up from the chair in excitement. "You've got the ideas and the capacity. Why, you'll become the richest man between Australia and the States."

Edward chuckled softly.

"But I don't want to," he said.

"Do you mean to say you don't want money, big money, money running into millions? Do you know what you can do with it? Do you know the power it brings? And if you don't care about it for yourself think what you can do, opening new channels for human enterprise, giving occupation to thousands. My brain reels at the visions your words have conjured up."

"Sit down, then, my dear Bateman," laughed Edward. "My machine for cutting the coconuts will always remain unused, and so far as I'm concerned street-cars shall never run in the idle streets of Papeete."

Bateman sank heavily into his chair.

"I don't understand you," he said.

"It came upon me little by little. I came to like the life here, with its ease and its leisure, and the people, with their good-nature and their happy smiling faces. I began to think. I'd never had time to do that before. I began to read."

"You always read."

"I read for examinations. I read in order to be able to hold my own in conversation. I read for instruction. Here I learned to read for pleasure. I learned to talk. Do you know that conversation is one of the greatest pleasures in life? But it wants leisure. I'd always been too busy before. And gradually all the life that had seemed so important to me began to seem rather trivial and vulgar. What is the use of all this hustle and this constant striving? I think of Chicago now and I see a dark, grey city, all stone—it is like a prison—and a ceaseless turmoil. And what does all that activity amount to? Does one get there the best out of life? Is that what we come into the world for, to hurry to an office, and work hour after hour till night, then hurry home and dine and go to a theatre? Is that how I must spend my youth? Youth lasts so short a time, Bateman. And when I am old, what have I to look forward to? To hurry from my home in the morning to my office and work hour after hour till night, and then hurry home again, and dine and go to a theatre? That may be worth while if you make a fortune; I don't know, it depends on your nature; but if you don't, is it worth while then? I want to make more out of my life than that, Bateman."

"What do you value in life then?"

"I'm afraid you'll laugh at me. Beauty, truth, and goodness."

"Don't you think you can have those in Chicago?"

"Some men can, perhaps, but not I." Edward sprang up now. "I tell you when I think of the life I led in the old days I am filled with horror," he cried violently. "I tremble with fear when I think of the danger I have escaped. I never knew I had a soul till I found it here. If I had remained a rich man I might have lost it for good and all."

"I don't know how you can say that," cried Bateman indignantly. "We often used to have discussions about it."

"Yes, I know. They were about as effectual as the discussions of deaf mutes about harmony. I shall never come back to Chicago, Bateman."

"And what about Isabel?"

Edward walked to the edge of the verandah and leaning over looked intently at the blue magic of the night. There was a slight smile on his face when he turned back to Bateman.

"Isabel is infinitely too good for me. I admire her more than any woman I have ever known. She has a wonderful brain and she's as good as she's beautiful. I respect her energy and her ambition. She was born to make a success of life. I am entirely unworthy of her."

"She doesn't think so."

"But you must tell her so, Bateman."

"I?" cried Bateman. "I'm the last person who could ever do that."

Edward had his back to the vivid light of the moon and his face could not be seen. Is it possible that he smiled again?

"It's no good your trying to conceal anything from her, Bateman.

With her quick intelligence she'll turn you inside out in five minutes. You'd better make a clean breast of it right away."

"I don't know what you mean. Of course I shall tell her I've seen you." Bateman spoke in some agitation. "Honestly I don't know what to say to her."

"Tell her that I haven't made good. Tell her that I'm not only poor, but that I'm content to be poor. Tell her I was fired from my job because I was idle and inattentive. Tell her all you've seen to-night and all I've told you."

The idea which on a sudden flashed through Bateman's brain brought him to his feet and in uncontrollable perturbation he faced Edward.

"Man alive, don't you want to marry her?"

Edward looked at him gravely.

"I can never ask her to release me. If she wishes to hold me to my word I will do my best to make her a good and loving husband."

"Do you wish me to give her that message, Edward? Oh, I can't. It's terrible. It's never dawned on her for a moment that you don't want to marry her. She loves you. How can I inflict such a mortification on her?"

Edward smiled again.

"Why don't you marry her yourself, Bateman? You've been in love with her for ages. You're perfectly suited to one another. You'll make her very happy."

"Don't talk to me like that. I can't bear it."

"I resign in your favour, Bateman. You are the better man."

There was something in Edward's tone that made Bateman look up quickly, but Edward's eyes were grave and unsmiling. Bateman did not know what to say. He was disconcerted. He wondered whether Edward could possibly suspect that he had come to Tahiti on a special errand. And though he knew it was horrible he could not prevent the exultation in his heart.

"What will you do if Isabel writes and puts an end to her engagement with you?" he said, slowly.

"Survive," said Edward.

Bateman was so agitated that he did not hear the answer.

"I wish you had ordinary clothes on," he said, somewhat irritably. "It's such a tremendously serious decision you're taking. That fantastic costume of yours makes it seem terribly casual."

"I assure you, I can be just as solemn in a pareo and a wreath of roses, as in a high hat and a cut-away coat."

Then another thought struck Bateman.

"Edward, it's not for my sake you're doing this? I don't know, but perhaps this is going to make a tremendous difference to my future. You're not sacrificing yourself for me? I couldn't stand for that, you know."

"No, Bateman, I have learnt not to be silly and sentimental here. I should like you and Isabel to be happy, but I have not the least wish to be unhappy myself."

The answer somewhat chilled Bateman. It seemed to him a little cynical. He would not have been sorry to act a noble part.

"Do you mean to say you're content to waste your life here? It's nothing less than suicide. When I think of the great hopes you had when we left college it seems terrible that you should be content to be no more than a salesman in a cheap-John store."

"Oh, I'm only doing that for the present, and I'm gaining a great deal of valuable experience. I have another plan in my head. Arnold Jackson has a small island in the Paumotas, about a thousand miles from here, a ring of land round a lagoon. He's planted coconut there. He's offered to give it me."

"Why should he do that?" asked Bateman.

"Because if Isabel releases me I shall marry his daughter."

"You?" Bateman was thunderstruck. "You can't marry a half-caste. You wouldn't be so crazy as that."

"She's a good girl, and she has a sweet and gentle nature. I think she would make me very happy."

"Are you in love with her?"

"I don't know," answered Edward reflectively. "I'm not in love with her as I was in love with Isabel. I worshipped Isabel. I thought she was the most wonderful creature I had ever seen. I was not half good enough for her. I don't feel like that with Eva. She's like a beautiful exotic flower that must be sheltered from bitter winds. I want to protect her. No one ever thought of protecting Isabel. I think she loves me for myself and not for what I may become. Whatever happens to me I shall never disappoint her. She suits me."

Bateman was silent.

"We must turn out early in the morning," said Edward at last. "It's really about time we went to bed."

Then Bateman spoke and his voice had in it a genuine distress.

"I'm so bewildered, I don't know what to say. I came here because I thought something was wrong. I thought you hadn't succeeded in what you set out to do and were ashamed to come back when you'd failed. I never guessed I should be faced with this. I'm so desperately sorry, Edward. I'm so disappointed. I hoped you would do great things. It's almost more than I can bear to think of you wasting your talents and your youth and your chance in this lamentable way."

"Don't be grieved, old friend," said Edward. "I haven't failed. I've succeeded. You can't think with what zest I look forward to life, how full it seems to me and how significant. Sometimes, when you are married to Isabel, you will think of me. I shall build myself a house on my coral island and I shall live there, looking after my trees—getting the fruit out of the nuts in the same old way that they have done for unnumbered years—I shall grow all sorts of things in my garden, and I shall fish. There will be enough work to keep me busy and not enough to make me dull. I shall have my books and Eva, children, I hope, and above all, the infinite variety of the sea and the sky, the freshness of the dawn and the beauty of the sunset, and the rich magnificence of the night. I shall make a garden out of what so short a while ago was a wilderness. I shall have created something. The years will pass insensibly, and when I am an old man I hope that I shall be able to look back on a happy, simple, peaceful life. In my small way I too shall have lived in beauty. Do you think it is so little to have enjoyed contentment? We know that it will profit a man little if he gain the whole world and lose his soul. I think I have won mine."

Edward led him to a room in which there were two beds and he threw himself on one of them. In ten minutes Bateman knew by his regular breathing, peaceful as a child's, that Edward was asleep. But for his part he had no rest, he was disturbed in mind, and it was not till the dawn crept into the room, ghostlike and silent, that he fell asleep.

Bateman finished telling Isabel his long story. He had hidden nothing from her except what he thought would wound her or what made himself ridiculous. He did not tell her that he had been forced to sit at dinner with a wreath of flowers round his head and he did not tell her that Edward was prepared to marry her uncle's half-caste daughter the moment she set him free. But perhaps Isabel had keener intuitions than he knew, for as he went on with his tale her eyes grew colder and her lips closed upon one another more tightly. Now and then she looked at him closely, and if he had been less intent on his narrative he might have wondered at her expression.

"What was this girl like?" she asked when he finished. "Uncle Arnold's daughter. Would you say there was any resemblance between her and me?"

Bateman was surprised at the question.

"It never struck me. You know I've never had eyes for anyone but you and I could never think that anyone was like you. Who could resemble you?"

"Was she pretty?" said Isabel, smiling slightly at his words.

"I suppose so. I daresay some men would say she was very beautiful."

"Well, it's of no consequence. I don't think we need give her any more of our attention."

"What are you going to do, Isabel?" he asked then.

Isabel looked down at the hand which still bore the ring Edward had given her on their betrothal.

"I wouldn't let Edward break our engagement because I thought it would be an incentive to him. I wanted to be an inspiration to him. I thought if anything could enable him to achieve success it was the thought that I loved him. I have done all I could. It's hopeless. It would only be weakness on my part not to recognise the facts. Poor Edward, he's nobody's enemy but his own. He was a dear, nice fellow, but there was something lacking in him, I suppose it was backbone. I hope he'll be happy."

She slipped the ring off her finger and placed it on the table.

Bateman watched her with a heart beating so rapidly that he could hardly breathe.

"You're wonderful, Isabel, you're simply wonderful."

She smiled, and, standing up, held out her hand to him.

"How can I ever thank you for what you've done for me?" she said. "You've done me a great service. I knew I could trust you."

He took her hand and held it. She had never looked more beautiful.

"Oh, Isabel, I would do so much more for you than that. You know that I only ask to be allowed to love and serve you."

"You're so strong, Bateman," she sighed. "It gives me such a delicious feeling of confidence."

"Isabel, I adore you."

He hardly knew how the inspiration had come to him, but suddenly he clasped her in his arms, and she, all unresisting, smiled into his eyes.

"Isabel, you know I wanted to marry you the very first day I saw you," he cried passionately.

"Then why on earth didn't you ask me?" she replied.

She loved him. He could hardly believe it was true. She gave him her lovely lips to kiss. And as he held her in his arms he had a vision of the works of the Hunter Motor Traction and Automobile Company growing in size and importance till they covered a hundred acres, and of the millions of motors they would turn out, and of the great collection of pictures he would form which should beat anything they had in New York. He would wear horn spectacles. And she, with the delicious pressure of his arms about her, sighed with happiness, for she thought of the exquisite house she would have, full of antique furniture, and of the concerts she would give, and of the thés dansants, and the dinners to which only the most cultured people would come. Bateman should wear horn spectacles.

"Poor Edward," she sighed.

NOVELS

The Moon and Sixpence

The Moon and Sixpence

I

I CONFESS THAT when first I made acquaintance with Charles Strickland I never for a moment discerned that there was in him anything out of the ordinary. Yet now few will be found to deny his greatness. I do not speak of that greatness which is achieved by the fortunate politician or the successful soldier; that is a quality which belongs to the place he occupies rather than to the man; and a change of circumstances reduces it to very discreet proportions. The Prime Minister out of office is seen, too often, to have been but a pompous rhetorician, and the General without an army is but the tame hero of a market town. The greatness of Charles Strickland was authentic. It may be that you do not like his art, but at all events you can hardly refuse it the tribute of your interest. He disturbs and arrests. The time has passed when he was an object of ridicule, and it is no longer a mark of eccentricity to defend or of perversity to extol him. His faults are accepted as the necessary complement to his merits. It is still possible to discuss his place in art, and the adulation of his admirers is perhaps no less capricious than the disparagement of his detractors; but one thing can never be doubtful, and that is that he had genius. To my mind the most interesting thing in art is the personality of the artist; and if that is singular, I am willing to excuse a thousand faults. I suppose Velasquez was a better painter than El Greco, but custom stales one's admiration for him: the Cretan, sensual and tragic, proffers the mystery of his soul like a standing sacrifice. The artist, painter, poet, or musician, by his decoration, sublime or beautiful, satisfies the aesthetic sense; but that is akin to the sexual instinct, and shares its barbarity: he lays before you also the greater gift of himself. To pursue his secret has something of the fascination of a detective story. It is a riddle which shares with the universe the merit of having no answer. The most insignificant of Strickland's works suggests a personality which is strange, tormented, and complex; and it is this surely which prevents even those who do not like his pictures from being indifferent to them; it is this which has excited so curious an interest in his life and character.

It was not till four years after Strickland's death that Maurice Huret wrote that article in the *Mercure de France* which rescued the unknown painter from oblivion and blazed the trail which succeeding writers, with more or less docility, have followed. For a long time no critic has enjoyed in France a more incontestable authority, and it was impossible not to be impressed by the claims he made; they seemed extravagant; but later judgments have confirmed his estimate, and the reputation of Charles Strickland is now firmly established on the lines which he laid down. The rise of this reputation is one of the most romantic incidents in the history of art. But I do not propose to deal with Charles Strickland's work except in so far as it touches upon his character. I cannot agree with the painters who claim superciliously that the layman can understand nothing of painting, and that he can best show his appreciation of their works by silence and a cheque-book. It is a grotesque misapprehension which sees in art no more than a craft comprehensible perfectly only to the craftsman: art is a manifestation of emotion, and emotion speaks a language that all may understand. But I will allow that the critic who has not a practical knowledge of technique is seldom able to say anything on the subject of real value, and my ignorance of painting is extreme. Fortunately, there is no need for me to risk the adventure, since my friend, Mr. Edward Leggatt, an able writer as well as an admirable painter, has exhaustively discussed Charles Strickland's work in a little book[1] which is a charming example of a style, for the most part, less happily cultivated in England than in France.

---

1   "A Modern Artist: Notes on the Work of Charles Strickland," by Edward Leggatt, A.R.H.A. Martin Secker, 1917.

Maurice Huret in his famous article gave an outline of Charles Strickland's life which was well calculated to whet the appetites of the inquiring. With his disinterested passion for art, he had a real desire to call the attention of the wise to a talent which was in the highest degree original; but he was too good a journalist to be unaware that the "human interest" would enable him more easily to effect his purpose. And when such as had come in contact with Strickland in the past, writers who had known him in London, painters who had met him in the cafes of Montmartre, discovered to their amazement that where they had seen but an unsuccessful artist, like another, authentic genius had rubbed shoulders with them there began to appear in the magazines of France and America a succession of articles, the reminiscences of one, the appreciation of another, which added to Strickland's notoriety, and fed without satisfying the curiosity of the public. The subject was grateful, and the industrious Weitbrecht-Rotholz in his imposing monograph[2] has been able to give a remarkable list of authorities.

The faculty for myth is innate in the human race. It seizes with avidity upon any incidents, surprising or mysterious, in the career of those who have at all distinguished themselves from their fellows, and invents a legend to which it then attaches a fanatical belief. It is the protest of romance against the commonplace of life. The incidents of the legend become the hero's surest passport to immortality. The ironic philosopher reflects with a smile that Sir Walter Raleigh is more safely inshrined in the memory of mankind because he set his cloak for the Virgin Queen to walk on than because he carried the English name to undiscovered countries. Charles Strickland lived obscurely. He made enemies rather than friends. It is not strange, then, that those who wrote of him should have eked out their scanty recollections with a lively fancy, and it is evident that there was enough in the little that was known of him to give opportunity to the romantic scribe; there was much in his life which was strange and terrible, in his character something outrageous, and in his fate not a little that was pathetic. In due course a legend arose of such circumstantiality

---

2   "Karl Strickland: sein Leben und seine Kunst," by Hugo Weitbrecht-Rotholz, Ph.D. Schwingel und Hanisch. Leipzig, 1914.

that the wise historian would hesitate to attack it.

But a wise historian is precisely what the Rev. Robert Strickland is not. He wrote his biography[3] avowedly to "remove certain misconceptions which had gained currency" in regard to the later part of his father's life, and which had "caused considerable pain to persons still living." It is obvious that there was much in the commonly received account of Strickland's life to embarrass a respectable family. I have read this work with a good deal of amusement, and upon this I congratulate myself, since it is colourless and dull. Mr. Strickland has drawn the portrait of an excellent husband and father, a man of kindly temper, industrious habits, and moral disposition. The modern clergyman has acquired in his study of the science which I believe is called exegesis an astonishing facility for explaining things away, but the subtlety with which the Rev. Robert Strickland has "interpreted" all the facts in his father's life which a dutiful son might find it inconvenient to remember must surely lead him in the fullness of time to the highest dignities of the Church. I see already his muscular calves encased in the gaiters episcopal. It was a hazardous, though maybe a gallant thing to do, since it is probable that the legend commonly received has had no small share in the growth of Strickland's reputation; for there are many who have been attracted to his art by the detestation in which they held his character or the compassion with which they regarded his death; and the son's well-meaning efforts threw a singular chill upon the father's admirers. It is due to no accident that when one of his most important works, *The Woman of Samaria,*[4] was sold at Christie's shortly after the discussion which followed the publication of Mr. Strickland's biography, it fetched £235 less than it had done nine months before when it was bought by the distinguished collector whose sudden death had brought it once more under the hammer. Perhaps Charles Strickland's power and originality would scarcely have sufficed to turn the scale if the remarkable mythopoeic

---

3   "Strickland: The Man and His Work," by his son, Robert Strickland. Wm. Heinemann, 1913.

4   This was described in Christie's catalogue as follows: "A nude woman, a native of the Society Islands, is lying on the ground beside a brook. Behind is a tropical Landscape with palm-trees, bananas, etc. 60 in. x 48 in."

faculty of mankind had not brushed aside with impatience a story which disappointed all its craving for the extraordinary. And presently Dr. Weitbrecht-Rotholz produced the work which finally set at rest the misgivings of all lovers of art.

Dr. Weitbrecht-Rotholz belongs to that school of historians which believes that human nature is not only about as bad as it can be, but a great deal worse; and certainly the reader is safer of entertainment in their hands than in those of the writers who take a malicious pleasure in representing the great figures of romance as patterns of the domestic virtues. For my part, I should be sorry to think that there was nothing between Anthony and Cleopatra but an economic situation; and it will require a great deal more evidence than is ever likely to be available, thank God, to persuade me that Tiberius was as blameless a monarch as King George V. Dr. Weitbrecht-Rotholz has dealt in such terms with the Rev. Robert Strickland's innocent biography that it is difficult to avoid feeling a certain sympathy for the unlucky parson. His decent reticence is branded as hypocrisy, his circumlocutions are roundly called lies, and his silence is vilified as treachery. And on the strength of peccadillos, reprehensible in an author, but excusable in a son, the Anglo-Saxon race is accused of prudishness, humbug, pretentiousness, deceit, cunning, and bad cooking. Personally I think it was rash of Mr. Strickland, in refuting the account which had gained belief of a certain "unpleasantness" between his father and mother, to state that Charles Strickland in a letter written from Paris had described her as "an excellent woman," since Dr. Weitbrecht-Rotholz was able to print the letter in facsimile, and it appears that the passage referred to ran in fact as follows: *God damn my wife. She is an excellent woman. I wish she was in hell.* It is not thus that the Church in its great days dealt with evidence that was unwelcome.

Dr. Weitbrecht-Rotholz was an enthusiastic admirer of Charles Strickland, and there was no danger that he would whitewash him. He had an unerring eye for the despicable motive in actions that had all the appearance of innocence. He was a psycho-pathologist, as well as a student of art, and the subconscious had few secrets from him. No mystic ever saw deeper meaning in common things. The mystic sees the ineffable, and the psycho-pathologist the unspeakable. There is a singular fascination in watching the eagerness with which the learned author ferrets out every circumstance which may throw discredit on his hero. His heart warms to him when he can bring forward some example of cruelty or meanness, and he exults like an inquisitor at the *auto dafé* of an heretic when with some forgotten story he can confound the filial piety of the Rev. Robert Strickland. His industry has been amazing. Nothing has been too small to escape him, and you may be sure that if Charles Strickland left a laundry bill unpaid it will be given you *in extenso*, and if he forebore to return a borrowed half-crown no detail of the transaction will be omitted.

II

WHEN SO MUCH has been written about Charles Strickland, it may seem unnecessary that I should write more. A painter's monument is his work. It is true I knew him more intimately than most: I met him first before ever he became a painter, and I saw him not infrequently during the difficult years he spent in Paris; but I do not suppose I should ever have set down my recollections if the hazards of the war had not taken me to Tahiti. There, as is notorious, he spent the last years of his life; and there I came across persons who were familiar with him. I find myself in a position to throw light on just that part of his tragic career which has remained most obscure. If they who believe in Strickland's greatness are right, the personal narratives of such as knew him in the flesh can hardly be superfluous. What would we not give for the reminiscences of someone who had been as intimately acquainted with El Greco as I was with Strickland?

But I seek refuge in no such excuses. I forget who it was that recommended men for their soul's good to do each day two things they disliked: it was a wise man, and it is a precept that I have followed scrupulously; for every day I have got up and I have gone to bed. But there is in my nature a strain of asceticism, and I have subjected my flesh each week to a more severe mortification. I have never failed to read the Literary Supplement of *The Times*. It is a salutary discipline to consider the vast number of books that are written, the fair hopes with which their authors see them published, and the fate which awaits them. What chance is there that any book will make its way among that multitude? And the successful books are but the successes of a season. Heaven knows what pains the author has been at, what bitter experiences he has endured and what heartache suffered, to give some chance reader a few hours' relaxation or to while away the tedium of a journey. And if I may judge from the reviews, many of these books are well and carefully written; much thought has gone to their composition; to some even has been given the anxious labour of a lifetime. The moral I draw is that the writer should seek his reward in the pleasure of his work and in release from the burden of his thought; and, indifferent to aught else, care nothing for praise or censure, failure or success.

Now the war has come, bringing with it a new attitude. Youth has turned to gods we of an earlier day knew not, and it is possible to see already the direction in which those who come after us will move. The younger generation, conscious of strength and tumultuous, have done with knocking at the door; they have burst in and seated themselves in our seats. The air is noisy with their shouts. Of their elders some, by imitating the antics of youth, strive to persuade themselves that their day is not yet over; they shout with the lustiest, but the war cry sounds hollow in their mouth; they are like poor wantons attempting with pencil, paint and powder, with shrill gaiety, to recover the illusion of their spring. The wiser go their way with a decent grace. In their chastened smile is an indulgent mockery. They remember that they too trod down a sated generation, with just such clamor and with just such scorn, and they foresee that these brave torch-bearers will presently yield their place also. There is no last word. The new evangel was old when Nineveh reared her greatness to the sky. These gallant words which seem so novel to those that speak them were said in accents scarcely changed a hundred times before. The pendulum swings backwards and forwards. The circle is ever travelled anew.

Sometimes a man survives a considerable time from an era in which he had his place into one which is strange to him, and then the curious are offered one of the most singular spectacles in the human comedy. Who now, for example, thinks of George Crabbe? He was a famous poet in his day, and the world recognised his genius with a unanimity which the greater complexity of modern life has rendered infrequent. He had learnt his craft at the school of Alexander Pope, and he wrote moral stories in rhymed couplets. Then came the French Revolution and the Napoleonic Wars, and the poets sang new songs. Mr. Crabbe continued to write moral stories in rhymed couplets. I think he must have read the verse of these young men who were making so great a stir in the world, and I fancy he found it poor stuff. Of course, much of it was. But the odes of Keats and of Wordsworth, a poem or two by Coleridge, a few more by Shelley, discovered vast realms of the spirit that none had explored before. Mr. Crabbe was as dead as mutton, but Mr. Crabbe continued to write moral stories in rhymed couplets. I have read desultorily the writings of the younger generation. It may be that among them a more fervid Keats, a more ethereal Shelley, has already published numbers the world will willingly remember. I cannot tell. I admire their polish—their youth is already so accomplished that it seems absurd to speak of promise—I marvel at the felicity of their style; but with all their copiousness (their vocabulary suggests that they fingered Roget's *Thesaurus* in their cradles) they say nothing to me: to my mind they know too much and feel too obviously; I cannot stomach the heartiness with which they slap me on the back or the emotion with which they hurl themselves on my bosom; their passion seems to me a little anaemic and their dreams a trifle dull. I do not like them. I am on the shelf. I will continue to write moral stories in rhymed couplets. But I should be thrice a fool if I did it for aught but my own entertainment.

III

But all this is by the way.

I was very young when I wrote my first book. By a lucky chance it excited attention, and various persons sought my acquaintance.

It is not without melancholy that I wander among my recollections of the world of letters in London when first, bashful but eager, I was introduced to it. It is long since I frequented it, and if the novels that describe its present singularities are accurate much in it is now changed. The venue is different. Chelsea and Bloomsbury have taken the place of Hampstead, Notting Hill Gate, and High Street, Kensington. Then it was a distinction to be under forty, but now to be more than twenty-five is absurd. I think in those days we were a little shy of our emotions, and the fear of ridicule tempered the more obvious forms of pretentiousness. I do not believe that there was in that genteel Bohemia an intensive culture of chastity, but I do not remember so crude a promiscuity as seems to be practised in the present day. We did not think it hypocritical to draw over our vagaries the curtain of a decent silence. The spade was not invariably called a bloody shovel. Woman had not yet altogether come into her own.

I lived near Victoria Station, and I recall long excursions by bus to the hospitable houses of the literary. In my timidity I wandered up and down the street while I screwed up my courage to ring the bell; and then, sick with apprehension, was ushered into an airless room full of people. I was introduced to this celebrated person after that one, and the kind words they said about my book made me excessively uncomfortable. I felt they expected me to say clever things, and I never could think of any till after the party was over. I tried to conceal my embarrassment by handing round cups of tea and rather ill-cut bread-and-butter. I wanted no one to take notice of me, so that I could observe these famous creatures at my ease and listen to the clever things they said.

I have a recollection of large, unbending women with great noses and rapacious eyes, who wore their clothes as though they were armour; and of little, mouse-like spinsters, with soft voices and a shrewd glance. I never ceased to be fascinated by their persistence in eating buttered toast with their gloves on, and I observed with admiration the unconcern with which they wiped their fingers on their chair when they thought no one was looking. It must have been bad for the furniture, but I suppose the hostess took her revenge on the furniture of her friends when, in turn, she visited them. Some of them were dressed fashionably, and they said they couldn't for the life of them see why you should be dowdy just because you had written a novel; if you had a neat figure you might as well make the most of it, and a smart shoe on a small foot had never prevented an editor from taking your "stuff." But others thought this frivolous, and they wore "art fabrics" and barbaric jewelry. The men were seldom eccentric in appearance. They tried to look as little like authors as possible. They wished to be taken for men of the world, and could have passed anywhere for the managing clerks of a city firm. They always seemed a little tired. I had never known writers before, and I found them very strange, but I do not think they ever seemed to me quite real.

I remember that I thought their conversation brilliant, and I used to listen with astonishment to the stinging humour with which they would tear a brother-author to pieces the moment that his back was turned. The artist has this advantage over the rest of the world, that his friends offer not only their appearance and their character to his satire, but also their work. I despaired of ever expressing myself with such aptness or with such fluency. In those days conversation was still cultivated as an art; a neat repartee was more highly valued than the crackling of thorns under a pot; and the epigram, not yet a mechanical appliance by which the dull may achieve a semblance of wit, gave sprightliness to the small talk of the urbane. It is sad that I can remember nothing of all this scintillation. But I think the conversation never settled down so comfortably as when it turned to the details of the trade which was the other side of the art we practised. When we had done discussing the merits of the latest book, it was natural to wonder how many copies had been sold, what advance the author had received, and how much he was likely to make out of it. Then we would speak of this publisher and of that, comparing the generosity of one with the meanness of another; we would argue whether it was better to go to one who gave handsome royalties or to another who "pushed" a book for all it was worth. Some advertised badly and some well. Some were modern and some were old-fashioned. Then we would talk of agents and the offers they had obtained for us; of editors and the sort of contributions they welcomed, how much they paid a thousand, and whether they paid promptly or otherwise. To me it was all very romantic. It gave me an intimate sense of being a member of some mystic brotherhood.

IV

No ONE WAS kinder to me at that time than Rose Waterford. She combined a masculine intelligence with a feminine perversity, and the novels she wrote were original and disconcerting. It was at her house one day that I met Charles Strickland's wife. Miss Waterford was giving a tea-party, and her small room was more than usually full. Everyone seemed to be talking, and I, sitting in silence, felt awkward; but I was too shy to break into any of the groups that seemed absorbed in their own affairs. Miss Waterford was a good hostess, and seeing my embarrassment came up to me.

"I want you to talk to Mrs. Strickland," she said. "She's raving about your book."

"What does she do?" I asked.

I was conscious of my ignorance, and if Mrs. Strickland was a well-known writer I thought it as well to ascertain the fact before I spoke to her.

Rose Waterford cast down her eyes demurely to give greater effect to her reply.

"She gives luncheon-parties. You've only got to roar a little, and she'll ask you."

Rose Waterford was a cynic. She looked upon life as an opportunity for writing novels and the public as her raw material. Now and then she invited members of it to her house if they showed an appreciation of her talent and entertained with proper lavishness. She held their weakness for lions in good-humoured contempt, but played to them her part of the distinguished woman of letters with decorum.

I was led up to Mrs. Strickland, and for ten minutes we talked together. I noticed nothing about her except that she had a pleasant voice. She had a flat in Westminster, overlooking the unfinished cathedral, and because we lived in the same neighbourhood we felt friendly disposed to one another. The Army and Navy Stores are a bond of union between all who dwell between the river and St. James's Park. Mrs. Strickland asked me for my address, and a few days later I received an invitation to luncheon.

My engagements were few, and I was glad to accept. When I arrived, a little late, because in my fear of being too early I had walked three times round the cathedral, I found the party already complete. Miss Waterford was there and Mrs. Jay, Richard Twining and George Road. We were all writers. It was a fine day, early in spring, and we were in a good humour. We talked about a hundred things. Miss Waterford, torn between the aestheticism of her early youth, when she used to go to parties in sage green, holding a daffodil, and the flippancy of her maturer years, which tended to high heels and Paris frocks, wore a new hat. It put her in high spirits. I had never heard her more malicious about our common friends. Mrs. Jay, aware that impropriety is the soul of wit, made observations in tones hardly above a whisper that might well have tinged the snowy tablecloth with a rosy hue. Richard Twining bubbled over with quaint absurdities, and George Road, conscious that he need not exhibit a brilliancy which was almost a by-word, opened his mouth only to put food into it. Mrs. Strickland did not talk much, but she had a pleasant gift for keeping the conversation general; and when there was a pause she threw in just the right remark to set it going once more. She was a woman of thirty-seven, rather tall and plump, without being fat; she was not pretty, but her face was pleasing, chiefly, perhaps, on account of her kind brown eyes. Her skin was rather sallow. Her dark hair was elaborately dressed. She was the only woman of the three whose face was free of make-up, and by contrast with the others she seemed simple and unaffected.

The dining-room was in the good taste of the period. It was very severe. There was a high dado of white wood and a green paper on which were etchings by Whistler in neat black frames. The green curtains with their peacock design, hung in straight lines, and the green carpet, in the pattern of which pale rabbits frolicked among leafy trees, suggested the influence of William Morris. There was blue delft on the chimney-piece. At that time there must have been five hundred dining-rooms in London decorated in exactly the same manner. It was chaste, artistic, and dull.

When we left I walked away with Miss Waterford, and the fine day and her new hat persuaded us to saunter through the Park.

"That was a very nice party," I said.

"Did you think the food was good? I told her that if she wanted writers she must feed them well."

"Admirable advice," I answered. "But why does she want them?"

Miss Waterford shrugged her shoulders.

"She finds them amusing. She wants to be in the movement. I fancy she's rather simple, poor dear, and she thinks we're all wonderful. After all, it pleases her to ask us to luncheon, and it doesn't hurt us. I like her for it."

Looking back, I think that Mrs. Strickland was the most harmless of all the lion-hunters that pursue their quarry from the rarefied heights of Hampstead to the nethermost studios of Cheyne Walk. She had led a very quiet youth in the country, and the books that came down from Mudie's Library brought with them not only their own romance, but the romance of London. She had a real passion for reading (rare in her kind, who for the most part are more interested in the author than in his book, in the painter than in his pictures), and she invented a world of the imagination in which she lived with a freedom she never acquired in the world of every day. When she came to know writers it was like adventuring upon a stage which till then she had known only from the other side of the footlights. She saw them dramatically, and really seemed herself to live a larger life because she entertained them and visited them in their fastnesses. She accepted the rules with which they played the game of life as valid for them, but never for a moment thought of regulating her own conduct in accordance with them. Their moral eccentricities, like their oddities of dress, their wild theories and paradoxes, were an entertainment which amused her, but had not the slightest influence on her convictions.

"Is there a Mr. Strickland?" I asked

"Oh yes; he's something in the city. I believe he's a stockbroker. He's very dull."

"Are they good friends?"

"They adore one another. You'll meet him if you dine there. But she doesn't often have people to dinner. He's very quiet. He's not in the least interested in literature or the arts."

"Why do nice women marry dull men?"

"Because intelligent men won't marry nice women."

I could not think of any retort to this, so I asked if Mrs. Strickland had children.

"Yes; she has a boy and a girl. They're both at school."

The subject was exhausted, and we began to talk of other things.

V

DURING THE SUMMER I met Mrs. Strickland not infrequently. I went now and then to pleasant little luncheons at her flat, and to rather more formidable tea-parties. We took a fancy to one another. I was very young, and perhaps she liked the idea of guiding my virgin steps on the hard road of letters; while for me it was pleasant to have someone I could go to with my small troubles, certain of an attentive ear and reasonable counsel. Mrs. Strickland had the gift of sympathy. It is a charming faculty, but one often abused by those who are conscious of its possession: for there is something ghoulish in the avidity with which they will pounce upon the misfortune of their friends so that they may exercise their dexterity. It gushes forth like an oil-well, and the sympathetic pour out their sympathy with an abandon that is sometimes embarrassing to their victims. There are bosoms on which so many tears have been shed that I cannot bedew them with mine. Mrs. Strickland used her advantage with tact. You felt that you obliged her by accepting her sympathy. When, in the enthusiasm of my youth, I remarked on this to Rose Waterford, she said:

"Milk is very nice, especially with a drop of brandy in it, but the domestic cow is only too glad to be rid of it. A swollen udder is very uncomfortable."

Rose Waterford had a blistering tongue. No one could say such bitter things; on the other hand, no one could do more charming ones.

There was another thing I liked in Mrs. Strickland. She managed her surroundings with elegance. Her flat was always neat and cheerful, gay with flowers, and the chintzes in the drawing-room, notwithstanding their severe design, were bright and pretty. The meals in the artistic little dining-room were pleasant; the table looked nice, the two maids were trim and comely; the food was well cooked. It was impossible not to see that Mrs. Strickland was an excellent house-keeper. And you felt sure that she was an admirable mother. There were photographs in the drawing-room of her son and daughter. The son—his name was Robert—was a boy of sixteen at Rugby; and you saw him in flannels and a cricket cap, and again in a tail-coat and a stand-up collar. He had his mother's candid brow and fine, reflective eyes. He looked clean, healthy, and normal.

"I don't know that he's very clever," she said one day, when I was looking at the photograph, "but I know he's good. He has a charming character."

The daughter was fourteen. Her hair, thick and dark like her mother's, fell over her shoulders in fine profusion, and she had the same kindly expression and sedate, untroubled eyes.

"They're both of them the image of you," I said.

"Yes; I think they are more like me than their father."

"Why have you never let me meet him?" I asked.

"Would you like to?"

She smiled, her smile was really very sweet, and she blushed a little; it was singular that a woman of that age should flush so readily. Perhaps her naivete was her greatest charm.

"You know, he's not at all literary," she said. "He's a perfect phi-listine."

She said this not disparagingly, but affectionately rather, as though, by acknowledging the worst about him, she wished to protect him from the aspersions of her friends.

"He's on the Stock Exchange, and he's a typical broker. I think he'd bore you to death."

"Does he bore you?" I asked.

"You see, I happen to be his wife. I'm very fond of him."

She smiled to cover her shyness, and I fancied she had a fear that I would make the sort of gibe that such a confession could hardly have failed to elicit from Rose Waterford. She hesitated a little. Her eyes grew tender.

"He doesn't pretend to be a genius. He doesn't even make much money on the Stock Exchange. But he's awfully good and kind."

"I think I should like him very much."

"I'll ask you to dine with us quietly some time, but mind, you come at your own risk; don't blame me if you have a very dull evening."

VI

But when at last I met Charles Strickland, it was under circumstances which allowed me to do no more than just make his acquaintance. One morning Mrs. Strickland sent me round a note to say that she was giving a dinner-party that evening, and one of her guests had failed her. She asked me to stop the gap. She wrote:

> It's only decent to warn you that you will be bored to extinction. It was a thoroughly dull party from the beginning, but if you will come I shall be uncommonly grateful. And you and I can have a little chat by ourselves.

It was only neighbourly to accept.

When Mrs. Strickland introduced me to her husband, he gave me a rather indifferent hand to shake. Turning to him gaily, she attempted a small jest.

"I asked him to show him that I really had a husband. I think he was beginning to doubt it."

Strickland gave the polite little laugh with which people acknowledge a facetiousness in which they see nothing funny, but did not speak. New arrivals claimed my host's attention, and I was left to myself. When at last we were all assembled, waiting for dinner to be announced, I reflected, while I chatted with the woman I had been asked to "take in," that civilised man practises a strange ingenuity in wasting on tedious exercises the brief span of his life. It was the kind of party which makes you wonder why the hostess has troubled to bid her guests, and why the guests have troubled to come. There were ten people. They met with indifference, and would part with relief. It was, of course, a purely social function. The Stricklands "owed" dinners to a number of persons, whom they took no interest in, and so had asked them; these persons had accepted. Why? To avoid the tedium of dining *tête-à-tête*, to give their servants a rest, because there was no reason to refuse, because they were "owed" a dinner.

The dining-room was inconveniently crowded. There was a K.C. and his wife, a Government official and his wife, Mrs. Strickland's sister and her husband, Colonel MacAndrew, and the wife of a Member of Parliament. It was because the Member of Parliament found that he could not leave the House that I had been invited. The respectability of the party was portentous. The women were too nice to be well dressed, and too sure of their position to be amusing. The men were solid. There was about all of them an air of well-satisfied prosperity.

Everyone talked a little louder than natural in an instinctive desire to make the party go, and there was a great deal of noise in the room. But there was no general conversation. Each one talked to his neighbour; to his neighbour on the right during the soup, fish, and entree; to his neighbour on the left during the roast, sweet, and savoury. They talked of the political situation and of golf, of their children and the latest play, of the pictures at the Royal Academy, of the weather and their plans for the holidays. There was never a pause, and the noise grew louder. Mrs. Strickland might congratulate herself that her party was a success. Her husband played his part with decorum. Perhaps he did not talk very much, and I fancied there was towards the end a look of fatigue in the faces of the women on either side of him. They were finding him heavy. Once or twice Mrs. Strickland's eyes rested on him somewhat anxiously.

At last she rose and shepherded the ladies out of one room. Strickland shut the door behind her, and, moving to the other end of the table, took his place between the K.C. and the Government official. He passed round the port again and handed us cigars. The K.C. remarked on the excellence of the wine, and Strickland told us where he got it. We began to chat about vintages and tobacco. The K.C. told us of a case he was engaged in, and the Colonel talked about polo. I had nothing to say and so sat silent, trying politely to show interest in the conversation; and because I thought no one was in the least concerned with me, examined Strickland at my ease. He was bigger than I expected: I do not know why I had imagined him slender and of insignificant appearance; in point of fact he was broad and heavy, with large hands and feet, and he wore his evening clothes clumsily. He gave you somewhat the idea of a coachman dressed up for the occasion. He was a man of forty, not good-looking, and yet not ugly, for his features were rather good; but they were all a little larger than life-size, and the effect was ungainly. He was clean shaven, and his large face looked uncomfortably naked. His hair was reddish, cut very short, and his eyes were small, blue or grey. He looked commonplace. I no longer wondered that Mrs. Strickland felt a certain embarrassment about him; he was scarcely a credit to a woman who wanted to make herself a position in the world of art and letters. It was obvious that he had no social gifts, but these a man can do without; he had no eccentricity even, to take him out of the common run; he was just a good, dull, honest, plain man. One would admire his excellent qualities, but avoid his company. He was null. He was probably a worthy member of society, a good husband and father, an honest broker; but there was no reason to waste one's time over him.

VII

THE SEASON WAS drawing to its dusty end, and everyone I knew was arranging to go away. Mrs. Strickland was taking her family to the coast of Norfolk, so that the children might have the sea and her husband golf. We said good-bye to one another, and arranged to meet in the autumn. But on my last day in town, coming out of the Stores, I met her with her son and daughter; like myself, she had been making her final purchases before leaving London, and we were both hot and tired. I proposed that we should all go and eat ices in the park.

I think Mrs. Strickland was glad to show me her children, and she accepted my invitation with alacrity. They were even more attractive than their photographs had suggested, and she was right to be proud of them. I was young enough for them not to feel shy, and they chattered merrily about one thing and another. They were extraordinarily nice, healthy young children. It was very agreeable under the trees.

When in an hour they crowded into a cab to go home, I strolled idly to my club. I was perhaps a little lonely, and it was with a touch of envy that I thought of the pleasant family life of which I had had a glimpse. They seemed devoted to one another. They had little private jokes of their own which, unintelligible to the outsider, amused them enormously. Perhaps Charles Strickland was dull judged by a standard that demanded above all things verbal scintillation; but his intelligence was adequate to his surroundings, and that is a passport, not only to reasonable success, but still more to happiness. Mrs. Strickland was a charming woman, and she loved him. I pictured their lives, troubled by no untoward adventure, honest, decent, and, by reason of those two upstanding, pleasant children, so obviously destined to carry on the normal traditions of their race and station, not without significance. They would grow old insensibly; they would see their son and daughter come to years of reason, marry in due course—the one a pretty girl, future mother of healthy children; the other a handsome, manly fellow, obviously a soldier; and at last, prosperous in their dignified retirement, beloved by their descendants, after a happy, not unuseful life, in the fullness of their age they would sink into the grave.

That must be the story of innumerable couples, and the pattern of life it offers has a homely grace. It reminds you of a placid rivulet, meandering smoothly through green pastures and shaded by pleasant trees, till at last it falls into the vasty sea; but the sea is so calm, so silent, so indifferent, that you are troubled suddenly by a vague uneasiness. Perhaps it is only by a kink in my nature, strong in me even in those days, that I felt in such an existence, the share of the great majority, something amiss. I recognised its social values, I saw its ordered happiness, but a fever in my blood asked for a wilder course. There seemed to me something alarming in such easy delights. In my heart was a desire to live more dangerously. I was not unprepared for jagged rocks and treacherous shoals if I could only have change—change and the excitement of the unforeseen.

VIII

ON READING OVER what I have written of the Stricklands, I am conscious that they must seem shadowy. I have been able to invest them with none of those characteristics which make the persons of a book exist with a real life of their own; and, wondering if the fault is mine, I rack my brains to remember idiosyncrasies which might lend them vividness. I feel that by dwelling on some trick of speech or some queer habit I should be able to give them a significance peculiar to themselves. As they stand they are like the figures in an old tapestry; they do not separate themselves from the background, and at a distance seem to lose their pattern, so that you have little but a pleasing piece of colour. My only excuse is that the impression they made on me was no other. There was just that shadowiness about them which you find in people whose lives are part of the social organism, so that they exist in it and by it only. They are like cells in the body, essential, but, so long as they remain healthy, engulfed in the momentous whole. The Stricklands were an average family in the middle class. A pleasant, hospitable woman, with a harmless craze for the small lions of literary society; a rather dull man, doing his duty in that state of life in which a merciful Providence had placed him; two nice-looking, healthy children. Nothing could be more ordinary. I do not know that there was anything about them to excite the attention of the curious. When I reflect on all that happened later, I ask myself if I was thick-witted not to see that there was in Charles Strickland at least something out of the common. Perhaps. I think that I have gathered in the years that intervene between then and now a fair knowledge of mankind, but even if when I first met the Stricklands I had the experience which I have now, I do not believe that I should have judged them differently. But because I have learnt that man is incalculable, I should not at this time of day be so surprised by the news that reached me when in the early autumn I returned to London.

I had not been back twenty-four hours before I ran across Rose Waterford in Jermyn Street.

"You look very gay and sprightly," I said. "What's the matter with you?"

She smiled, and her eyes shone with a malice I knew already. It meant that she had heard some scandal about one of her friends, and the instinct of the literary woman was all alert.

"You did meet Charles Strickland, didn't you?"

Not only her face, but her whole body, gave a sense of alacrity. I nodded. I wondered if the poor devil had been hammered on the Stock Exchange or run over by an omnibus.

"Isn't it dreadful? He's run away from his wife."

Miss Waterford certainly felt that she could not do her subject justice on the curb of Jermyn Street, and so, like an artist, flung the bare fact at me and declared that she knew no details. I could not do her the injustice of supposing that so trifling a circumstance would have prevented her from giving them, but she was obstinate.

"I tell you I know nothing," she said, in reply to my agitated questions, and then, with an airy shrug of the shoulders: "I believe that a young person in a city tea-shop has left her situation."

She flashed a smile at me, and, protesting an engagement with her dentist, jauntily walked on. I was more interested than distressed. In those days my experience of life at first hand was small, and it excited me to come upon an incident among people I knew of the same sort as I had read in books. I confess that time has now accustomed me to incidents of this character among my acquaintance. But I was a little shocked. Strickland was certainly forty, and I thought it disgusting that a man of his age should concern himself with affairs of the heart. With the superciliousness of extreme youth, I put thirty-five as the utmost limit at which a man might fall in love without making a fool of himself. And this news was slightly disconcerting to me personally, because I had written from the country to Mrs. Strickland, announcing my return, and had added that unless I heard from her to the contrary, I would come on a certain day to drink a dish of tea with her. This was the very day, and I had received no word from Mrs. Strickland. Did she want to see me or did she not? It was likely enough that in the agitation of the moment my note had escaped her memory. Perhaps I should be wiser not to go. On the other hand, she might wish to keep the affair quiet, and it might be highly indiscreet on my part to give any sign that this strange news had reached me. I was torn between the fear of hurting a nice woman's feelings and the fear of being in the way. I felt she must be suffering, and I did not want to see a pain which I could not help; but in my heart was a desire, that I felt a little ashamed of, to see how she was taking it. I did not know what to do.

Finally it occurred to me that I would call as though nothing had happened, and send a message in by the maid asking Mrs. Strickland if it was convenient for her to see me. This would give her the opportunity to send me away. But I was overwhelmed with embarrassment when I said to the maid the phrase I had prepared, and while I waited for the answer in a dark passage I had to call up all my strength of mind not to bolt. The maid came back. Her manner suggested to my excited fancy a complete knowledge of the domestic calamity.

"Will you come this way, sir?" she said.

I followed her into the drawing-room. The blinds were partly drawn to darken the room, and Mrs. Strickland was sitting with her back to the light. Her brother-in-law, Colonel MacAndrew, stood in front of the fireplace, warming his back at an unlit fire. To myself my entrance seemed excessively awkward. I imagined that my arrival had taken them by surprise, and Mrs. Strickland had let me come in only because she had forgotten to put me off. I fancied that the Colonel resented the interruption.

"I wasn't quite sure if you expected me," I said, trying to seem unconcerned.

"Of course I did. Anne will bring the tea in a minute."

Even in the darkened room, I could not help seeing that Mrs. Strickland's face was all swollen with tears. Her skin, never very good, was earthy.

"You remember my brother-in-law, don't you? You met at dinner, just before the holidays."

We shook hands. I felt so shy that I could think of nothing to say, but Mrs. Strickland came to my rescue. She asked me what I had been doing with myself during the summer, and with this help I managed to make some conversation till tea was brought in. The Colonel asked for a whisky-and-soda.

"You'd better have one too, Amy," he said.

"No; I prefer tea."

This was the first suggestion that anything untoward had happened. I took no notice, and did my best to engage Mrs. Strickland in talk. The Colonel, still standing in front of the fireplace, uttered no word. I wondered how soon I could decently take my leave, and I asked myself why on earth Mrs. Strickland had allowed me to come. There were no flowers, and various knick-knacks, put away during the summer, had not been replaced; there was something cheerless and stiff about the room which had always seemed so friendly; it gave you an odd feeling, as though someone were lying dead on the other side of the wall. I finished tea.

"Will you have a cigarette?" asked Mrs. Strickland.

She looked about for the box, but it was not to be seen.

"I'm afraid there are none."

Suddenly she burst into tears, and hurried from the room.

I was startled. I suppose now that the lack of cigarettes, brought as a rule by her husband, forced him back upon her recollection, and the new feeling that the small comforts she was used to were missing gave her a sudden pang. She realised that the old life was gone and done with. It was impossible to keep up our social pretences any longer.

"I dare say you'd like me to go," I said to the Colonel, getting up.

"I suppose you've heard that blackguard has deserted her," he cried explosively.

I hesitated.

"You know how people gossip," I answered. "I was vaguely told that something was wrong."

"He's bolted. He's gone off to Paris with a woman. He's left Amy without a penny."

"I'm awfully sorry," I said, not knowing what else to say.

The Colonel gulped down his whisky. He was a tall, lean man of fifty, with a drooping moustache and grey hair. He had pale blue eyes and a weak mouth. I remembered from my previous meeting with him that he had a foolish face, and was proud of the fact that for the ten years before he left the army he had played polo three days a week.

"I don't suppose Mrs. Strickland wants to be bothered with me just now," I said. "Will you tell her how sorry I am? If there's anything I can do. I shall be delighted to do it."

He took no notice of me.

"I don't know what's to become of her. And then there are the children. Are they going to live on air? Seventeen years."

"What about seventeen years?"

"They've been married," he snapped. "I never liked him. Of course he was my brother-in-law, and I made the best of it. Did you think him a gentleman? She ought never to have married him."

"Is it absolutely final?"

"There's only one thing for her to do, and that's to divorce him. That's what I was telling her when you came in. 'Fire in with your petition, my dear Amy,' I said. 'You owe it to yourself and you owe it to the children.' He'd better not let me catch sight of him. I'd thrash him within an inch of his life."

I could not help thinking that Colonel MacAndrew might have some difficulty in doing this, since Strickland had struck me as a hefty fellow, but I did not say anything. It is always distressing when outraged morality does not possess the strength of arm to administer direct chastisement on the sinner. I was making up my mind to another attempt at going when Mrs. Strickland came back. She had dried her eyes and powdered her nose.

"I'm sorry I broke down," she said. "I'm glad you didn't go away."

She sat down. I did not at all know what to say. I felt a certain shyness at referring to matters which were no concern of mine. I did not then know the besetting sin of woman, the passion to discuss her private affairs with anyone who is willing to listen. Mrs. Strickland seemed to make an effort over herself.

"Are people talking about it?" she asked.

I was taken aback by her assumption that I knew all about her domestic misfortune.

"I've only just come back. The only person I've seen is Rose Waterford."

Mrs. Strickland clasped her hands.

"Tell me exactly what she said." And when I hesitated, she insisted. "I particularly want to know."

"You know the way people talk. She's not very reliable, is she? She said your husband had left you."

"Is that all?"

I did not choose to repeat Rose Waterford's parting reference to a girl from a tea-shop. I lied.

"She didn't say anything about his going with anyone?"

"No."

"That's all I wanted to know."

I was a little puzzled, but at all events I understood that I might now take my leave. When I shook hands with Mrs. Strickland I told her that if I could be of any use to her I should be very glad. She smiled wanly.

"Thank you so much. I don't know that anybody can do anything for me."

Too shy to express my sympathy, I turned to say good-bye to the Colonel. He did not take my hand.

"I'm just coming. If you're walking up Victoria Street, I'll come along with you."

"All right," I said. "Come on."

IX

"THIS IS A terrible thing," he said, the moment we got out into the street.

I realised that he had come away with me in order to discuss once more what he had been already discussing for hours with his sister-in-law.

"We don't know who the woman is, you know," he said. "All we know is that the blackguard's gone to Paris."

"I thought they got on so well."

"So they did. Why, just before you came in Amy said they'd never had a quarrel in the whole of their married life. You know Amy. There never was a better woman in the world."

Since these confidences were thrust on me, I saw no harm in asking a few questions.

"But do you mean to say she suspected nothing?"

"Nothing. He spent August with her and the children in Norfolk. He was just the same as he'd always been. We went down for two or three days, my wife and I, and I played golf with him. He came back to town in September to let his partner go away, and Amy stayed on in the country. They'd taken a house for six weeks, and at the end of her tenancy she wrote to tell him on which day she was arriving in London. He answered from Paris. He said he'd made up his mind not to live with her any more."

"What explanation did he give?"

"My dear fellow, he gave no explanation. I've seen the letter. It wasn't more than ten lines."

"But that's extraordinary."

We happened then to cross the street, and the traffic prevented us from speaking. What Colonel MacAndrew had told me seemed very improbable, and I suspected that Mrs. Strickland, for reasons of her own, had concealed from him some part of the facts. It was clear that a man after seventeen years of wedlock did not leave his wife without certain occurrences which must have led her to suspect that all was not well with their married life. The Colonel caught me up.

"Of course, there was no explanation he could give except that he'd gone off with a woman. I suppose he thought she could find that out for herself. That's the sort of chap he was."

"What is Mrs. Strickland going to do?"

"Well, the first thing is to get our proofs. I'm going over to Paris myself."

"And what about his business?"

"That's where he's been so artful. He's been drawing in his horns for the last year."

"Did he tell his partner he was leaving?"

"Not a word."

Colonel MacAndrew had a very sketchy knowledge of business matters, and I had none at all, so I did not quite understand under what conditions Strickland had left his affairs. I gathered that the deserted partner was very angry and threatened proceedings. It appeared that when everything was settled he would be four or five hundred pounds out of pocket.

"It's lucky the furniture in the flat is in Amy's name. She'll have that at all events."

"Did you mean it when you said she wouldn't have a bob?"

"Of course I did. She's got two or three hundred pounds and the furniture."

"But how is she going to live?"

"God knows."

The affair seemed to grow more complicated, and the Colonel, with his expletives and his indignation, confused rather than informed me. I was glad that, catching sight of the clock at the Army and Navy Stores, he remembered an engagement to play cards at his club, and so left me to cut across St. James Park.

X

A DAY OR two later Mrs. Strickland sent me round a note asking if I could go and see her that evening after dinner. I found her alone. Her black dress, simple to austerity, suggested her bereaved condition, and I was innocently astonished that notwithstanding a real emotion she was able to dress the part she had to play according to her notions of seemliness.

"You said that if I wanted you to do anything you wouldn't mind doing it," she remarked.

"It was quite true."

"Will you go over to Paris and see Charlie?"

"I?"

I was taken aback. I reflected that I had only seen him once. I did not know what she wanted me to do.

"Fred is set on going." Fred was Colonel MacAndrew. "But I'm sure he's not the man to go. He'll only make things worse. I don't know who else to ask."

Her voice trembled a little, and I felt a brute even to hesitate.

"But I've not spoken ten words to your husband. He doesn't know me. He'll probably just tell me to go to the devil."

"That wouldn't hurt you," said Mrs. Strickland, smiling.

"What is it exactly you want me to do?"

She did not answer directly.

"I think it's rather an advantage that he doesn't know you. You see, he never really liked Fred; he thought him a fool; he didn't understand soldiers. Fred would fly into a passion, and there'd be a quarrel, and things would be worse instead of better. If you said you came on my behalf, he couldn't refuse to listen to you."

"I haven't known you very long," I answered. "I don't see how any-one can be expected to tackle a case like this unless he knows all the details. I don't want to pry into what doesn't concern me. Why don't you go and see him yourself?"

"You forget he isn't alone."

I held my tongue. I saw myself calling on Charles Strickland and sending in my card; I saw him come into the room, holding it be-tween finger and thumb:

"To what do I owe this honour?"

"I've come to see you about your wife."

"Really. When you are a little older you will doubtless learn the advantage of minding your own business. If you will be so good as to turn your head slightly to the left, you will see the door. I wish you good-afternoon."

I foresaw that it would be difficult to make my exit with digni-ty, and I wished to goodness that I had not returned to London till Mrs. Strickland had composed her difficulties. I stole a glance at her. She was immersed in thought. Presently she looked up at me, sighed deeply, and smiled.

"It was all so unexpected," she said. "We'd been married seventeen years. I sever dreamed that Charlie was the sort of man to get infat-uated with anyone. We always got on very well together. Of course, I had a great many interests that he didn't share."

"Have you found out who"—I did not quite know how to express myself—"who the person, who it is he's gone away with?"

"No. No one seems to have an idea. It's so strange. Generally when a man falls in love with someone people see them about togeth-er, lunching or something, and her friends always come and tell the wife. I had no warning—nothing. His letter came like a thunderbolt. I thought he was perfectly happy."

She began to cry, poor thing, and I felt very sorry for her. But in a little while she grew calmer.

"It's no good making a fool of myself," she said, drying her eyes. "The only thing is to decide what is the best thing to do."

She went on, talking somewhat at random, now of the recent

past, then of their first meeting and their marriage; but presently I
began to form a fairly coherent picture of their lives; and it seemed to
me that my surmises had not been incorrect. Mrs. Strickland was the
daughter of an Indian civilian, who on his retirement had settled in
the depths of the country, but it was his habit every August to take his
family to Eastbourne for change of air; and it was here, when she was
twenty, that she met Charles Strickland. He was twenty-three. They
played together, walked on the front together, listened together to the
nigger minstrels; and she had made up her mind to accept him a week
before he proposed to her. They lived in London, first in Hampstead,
and then, as he grew more prosperous, in town. Two children were
born to them.

"He always seemed very fond of them. Even if he was tired of me,
I wonder that he had the hear`t to leave them. It's all so incredible.
Even now I can hardly believe it's true."

At last she showed me the letter he had written. I was curious to
see it, but had not ventured to ask for it.

> *My Dear Amy,*
>
> *I think you will find everything all right in the flat. I have
> given Anne your instructions, and dinner will be ready for you and
> the children when you come. I shall not be there to meet you. I have
> made up my mind to live apart from you, and I am going to Paris
> in the morning. I shall post this letter on my arrival. I shall not come
> back. My decision is irrevocable.*
>
> *Yours always,*
>
> CHARLES STRICKLAND.

"Not a word of explanation or regret. Don't you think it's inhuman?"

"It's a very strange letter under the circumstances," I replied.

"There's only one explanation, and that is that he's not himself. I
don't know who this woman is who's got hold of him, but she's made
him into another man. It's evidently been going on a long time."

"What makes you think that?"

"Fred found that out. My husband said he went to the club three or four nights a week to play bridge. Fred knows one of the members, and said something about Charles being a great bridge-player. The man was surprised. He said he'd never even seen Charles in the card-room. It's quite clear now that when I thought Charles was at his club he was with her."

I was silent for a moment. Then I thought of the children.

"It must have been difficult to explain to Robert," I said.

"Oh, I never said a word to either of them. You see, we only came up to town the day before they had to go back to school. I had the presence of mind to say that their father had been called away on business."

It could not have been very easy to be bright and careless with that sudden secret in her heart, nor to give her attention to all the things that needed doing to get her children comfortably packed off. Mrs. Strickland's voice broke again.

"And what is to happen to them, poor darlings? How are we going to live?"

She struggled for self-control, and I saw her hands clench and unclench spasmodically. It was dreadfully painful.

"Of course I'll go over to Paris if you think I can do any good, but you must tell me exactly what you want me to do."

"I want him to come back."

"I understood from Colonel MacAndrew that you'd made up your mind to divorce him."

"I'll never divorce him," she answered with a sudden violence. "Tell him that from me. He'll never be able to marry that woman. I'm as obstinate as he is, and I'll never divorce him. I have to think of my children."

I think she added this to explain her attitude to me, but I thought it was due to a very natural jealousy rather than to maternal solicitude.

"Are you in love with him still?"

"I don't know. I want him to come back. If he'll do that we'll let bygones be bygones. After all, we've been married for seventeen years. I'm a broadminded woman. I wouldn't have minded what he did as long as I knew nothing about it. He must know that his infatuation won't last. If he'll come back now everything can be smoothed over, and no one will know anything about it."

It chilled me a little that Mrs. Strickland should be concerned with gossip, for I did not know then how great a part is played in women's life by the opinion of others. It throws a shadow of insincerity over their most deeply felt emotions.

It was known where Strickland was staying. His partner, in a violent letter, sent to his bank, had taunted him with hiding his whereabouts: and Strickland, in a cynical and humourous reply, had told his partner exactly where to find him. He was apparently living in an Hotel.

"I've never heard of it," said Mrs. Strickland. "But Fred knows it well. He says it's very expensive."

She flushed darkly. I imagined that she saw her husband installed in a luxurious suite of rooms, dining at one smart restaurant after another, and she pictured his days spent at race-meetings and his evenings at the play.

"It can't go on at his age," she said. "After all, he's forty. I could understand it in a young man, but I think it's horrible in a man of his years, with children who are nearly grown up. His health will never stand it."

Anger struggled in her breast with misery.

"Tell him that our home cries out for him. Everything is just the same, and yet everything is different. I can't live without him. I'd sooner kill myself. Talk to him about the past, and all we've gone through together. What am I to say to the children when they ask for him? His room is exactly as it was when he left it. It's waiting for him. We're all waiting for him."

Now she told me exactly what I should say. She gave me elaborate answers to every possible observation of his.

"You will do everything you can for me?" she said pitifully. "Tell him what a state I'm in."

I saw that she wished me to appeal to his sympathies by every means in my power. She was weeping freely. I was extraordinarily touched. I felt indignant at Strickland's cold cruelty, and I promised to do all I could to bring him back. I agreed to go over on the next day but one, and to stay in Paris till I had achieved something. Then, as it was growing late and we were both exhausted by so much emotion, I left her.

XI

DURING THE JOURNEY I thought over my errand with misgiving. Now that I was free from the spectacle of Mrs. Strickland's distress I could consider the matter more calmly. I was puzzled by the contradictions that I saw in her behaviour. She was very unhappy, but to excite my sympathy she was able to make a show of her unhappiness. It was evident that she had been prepared to weep, for she had provided herself with a sufficiency of handkerchiefs; I admired her forethought, but in retrospect it made her tears perhaps less moving. I could not decide whether she desired the return of her husband because she loved him, or because she dreaded the tongue of scandal; and I was perturbed by the suspicion that the anguish of love contemned was alloyed in her broken heart with the pangs, sordid to my young mind, of wounded vanity. I had not yet learnt how contradictory is human nature; I did not know how much pose there is in the sincere, how much baseness in the noble, nor how much goodness in the reprobate.

But there was something of an adventure in my trip, and my spirits rose as I approached Paris. I saw myself, too, from the dramatic standpoint, and I was pleased with my role of the trusted friend bringing back the errant husband to his forgiving wife. I made up my mind to see Strickland the following evening, for I felt instinctively that the hour must be chosen with delicacy. An appeal to the emotions is little likely to be effectual before luncheon. My own thoughts were then constantly occupied with love, but I never could imagine connubial bliss till after tea.

I enquired at my hotel for that in which Charles Strickland was living. It was called the Hotel des Belges. But the concierge, somewhat to my surprise, had never heard of it. I had understood from Mrs. Strickland that it was a large and sumptuous place at the back of the Rue de Rivoli. We looked it out in the directory. The only hotel of that name was in the Rue des Moines. The quarter was not fashionable; it was not even respectable. I shook my head.

"I'm sure that's not it," I said.

The concierge shrugged his shoulders. There was no other hotel of that name in Paris. It occurred to me that Strickland had concealed his address, after all. In giving his partner the one I knew he was perhaps playing a trick on him. I do not know why I had an inkling that it would appeal to Strickland's sense of humour to bring a furious stockbroker over to Paris on a fool's errand to an ill-famed house in a mean street. Still, I thought I had better go and see. Next day about six o'clock I took a cab to the Rue des Moines, but dismissed it at the corner, since I preferred to walk to the hotel and look at it before I went in. It was a street of small shops subservient to the needs of poor people, and about the middle of it, on the left as I walked down, was the Hotel des Belges. My own hotel was modest enough, but it was magnificent in comparison with this. It was a tall, shabby building, that cannot have been painted for years, and it had so bedraggled an air that the houses on each side of it looked neat and clean. The dirty windows were all shut. It was not here that Charles Strickland lived in guilty splendour with the unknown charmer for whose sake he had abandoned honour and duty. I was vexed, for I felt that I had been made a fool of, and I nearly turned away without making an enquiry. I went in only to be able to tell Mrs. Strickland that I had done my best.

The door was at the side of a shop. It stood open, and just within was a sign: *Bureau au premier.* I walked up narrow stairs, and on the landing found a sort of box, glassed in, within which were a desk and a couple of chairs. There was a bench outside, on which it might be presumed the night porter passed uneasy nights. There was no one about, but under an electric bell was written *Garçon.* I rang, and presently a waiter appeared. He was a young man with furtive eyes and a sullen look. He was in shirt-sleeves and carpet slippers.

I do not know why I made my enquiry as casual as possible.

"Does Mr. Strickland live here by any chance?" I asked.

"Number thirty-two. On the sixth floor."

I was so surprised that for a moment I did not answer.

"Is he in?"

The waiter looked at a board in the *bureau.*

"He hasn't left his key. Go up and you'll see."

I thought it as well to put one more question.

"Madame est là?"

"Monsieur est seul."

The waiter looked at me suspiciously as I made my way upstairs.
They were dark and airless. There was a foul and musty smell. Three
flights up a Woman in a dressing-gown, with touzled hair, opened a
door and looked at me silently as I passed. At length I reached the
sixth floor, and knocked at the door numbered thirty-two. There was
a sound within, and the door was partly opened. Charles Strickland
stood before me. He uttered not a word. He evidently did not know
me.

I told him my name. I tried my best to assume an airy manner.

"You don't remember me. I had the pleasure of dining with you
last July."

"Come in," he said cheerily. "I'm delighted to see you. Take a pew."

I entered. It was a very small room, overcrowded with furniture
of the style which the French know as Louis Philippe. There was a
large wooden bedstead on which was a billowing red eiderdown, and
there was a large wardrobe, a round table, a very small washstand,
and two stuffed chairs covered with red rep. Everything was dirty
and shabby. There was no sign of the abandoned luxury that Colonel
MacAndrew had so confidently described. Strickland threw on the
floor the clothes that burdened one of the chairs, and I sat down on it.

"What can I do for you?" he asked.

In that small room he seemed even bigger than I remembered
him. He wore an old Norfolk jacket, and he had not shaved for several days. When last I saw him he was spruce enough, but he looked ill
at ease: now, untidy and ill-kempt, he looked perfectly at home. I did
not know how he would take the remark I had prepared.

"I've come to see you on behalf of your wife."

"I was just going out to have a drink before dinner. You'd better
come too. Do you like absinthe?"

"I can drink it."

"Come on, then."

He put on a bowler hat much in need of brushing.

"We might dine together. You owe me a dinner, you know."

"Certainly. Are you alone?"

I flattered myself that I had got in that important question very naturally.

"Oh yes. In point of fact I've not spoken to a soul for three days. My French isn't exactly brilliant."

I wondered as I preceded him downstairs what had happened to the little lady in the tea-shop. Had they quarrelled already, or was his infatuation passed? It seemed hardly likely if, as appeared, he had been taking steps for a year to make his desperate plunge. We walked to the Avenue de Clichy, and sat down at one of the tables on the pavement of a large cafe.

XII

THE AVENUE DE CLICHY was crowded at that hour, and a lively fancy might see in the passers-by the personages of many a sordid romance. There were clerks and shopgirls; old fellows who might have stepped out of the pages of Honore de Balzac; members, male and female, of the professions which make their profit of the frailties of mankind. There is in the streets of the poorer quarters of Paris a thronging vitality which excites the blood and prepares the soul for the unexpected.

"Do you know Paris well?" I asked.

"No. We came on our honeymoon. I haven't been since."

"How on earth did you find out your hotel?"

"It was recommended to me. I wanted something cheap."

The absinthe came, and with due solemnity we dropped water over the melting sugar.

"I thought I'd better tell you at once why I had come to see you," I said, not without embarrassment.

His eyes twinkled. "I thought somebody would come along sooner or later. I've had a lot of letters from Amy."

"Then you know pretty well what I've got to say."

"I've not read them."

I lit a cigarette to give myself a moment's time. I did not quite know now how to set about my mission. The eloquent phrases I had arranged, pathetic or indignant, seemed out of place on the Avenue de Clichy. Suddenly he gave a chuckle.

"Beastly job for you this, isn't it?"

"Oh, I don't know," I answered.

"Well, look here, you get it over, and then we'll have a jolly evening."

I hesitated.

"Has it occurred to you that your wife is frightfully unhappy?"

"She'll get over it."

I cannot describe the extraordinary callousness with which he made this reply. It disconcerted me, but I did my best not to show it. I adopted the tone used by my Uncle Henry, a clergyman, when he was asking one of his relatives for a subscription to the Additional Curates Society.

"You don't mind my talking to you frankly?"

He shook his head, smiling.

"Has she deserved that you should treat her like this?"

"No."

"Have you any complaint to make against her?"

"None."

"Then, isn't it monstrous to leave her in this fashion, after seventeen years of married life, without a fault to find with her?"

"Monstrous."

I glanced at him with surprise. His cordial agreement with all I said cut the ground from under my feet. It made my position complicated, not to say ludicrous. I was prepared to be persuasive, touching, and hortatory, admonitory and expostulating, if need be vituperative even, indignant and sarcastic; but what the devil does a mentor do when the sinner makes no bones about confessing his sin? I had no experience, since my own practice has always been to deny everything.

"What, then?" asked Strickland.

I tried to curl my lip.

"Well, if you acknowledge that, there doesn't seem much more to be said."

"I don't think there is."

I felt that I was not carrying out my embassy with any great skill. I was distinctly nettled.

"Hang it all, one can't leave a woman without a bob."

"Why not?"

"How is she going to live?"

"I've supported her for seventeen years. Why shouldn't she support herself for a change?"

"She can't."

"Let her try."

Of course there were many things I might have answered to this. I might have spoken of the economic position of woman, of the contract, tacit and overt, which a man accepts by his marriage, and of much else; but I felt that there was only one point which really signified.

"Don't you care for her any more?"

"Not a bit," he replied.

The matter was immensely serious for all the parties concerned, but there was in the manner of his answer such a cheerful effrontery that I had to bite my lips in order not to laugh. I reminded myself that his behaviour was abominable. I worked myself up into a state of moral indignation.

"Damn it all, there are your children to think of. They've never done you any harm. They didn't ask to be brought into the world. If you chuck everything like this, they'll be thrown on the streets.

"They've had a good many years of comfort. It's much more than the majority of children have. Besides, somebody will look after them. When it comes to the point, the MacAndrews will pay for their schooling."

"But aren't you fond of them? They're such awfully nice kids. Do you mean to say you don't want to have anything more to do with them?"

"I liked them all right when they were kids, but now they're growing up I haven't got any particular feeling for them."

"It's just inhuman."

"I dare say."

"You don't seem in the least ashamed."

"I'm not."

I tried another tack.

"Everyone will think you a perfect swine."

"Let them."

"Won't it mean anything to you to know that people loathe and despise you?"

"No."

His brief answer was so scornful that it made my question, natural though it was, seem absurd. I reflected for a minute or two.

"I wonder if one can live quite comfortably when one's conscious of the disapproval of one's fellows? Are you sure it won't begin to worry you? Everyone has some sort of a conscience, and sooner or later it will find you out. Supposing your wife died, wouldn't you be tortured by remorse?"

He did not answer, and I waited for some time for him to speak. At last I had to break the silence myself.

"What have you to say to that?"

"Only that you're a damned fool."

"At all events, you can be forced to support your wife and children," I retorted, somewhat piqued. "I suppose the law has some protection to offer them."

"Can the law get blood out of a stone? I haven't any money. I've got about a hundred pounds."

I began to be more puzzled than before. It was true that his hotel pointed to the most straitened circumstances.

"What are you going to do when you've spent that?"

"Earn some."

He was perfectly cool, and his eyes kept that mocking smile which made all I said seem rather foolish. I paused for a little while to consider what I had better say next. But it was he who spoke first.

"Why doesn't Amy marry again? She's comparatively young, and she's not unattractive. I can recommend her as an excellent wife. If she wants to divorce me I don't mind giving her the necessary grounds."

Now it was my turn to smile. He was very cunning, but it was evidently this that he was aiming at. He had some reason to conceal the fact that he had run away with a woman, and he was using every precaution to hide her whereabouts. I answered with decision.

"Your wife says that nothing you can do will ever induce her to divorce you. She's quite made up her mind. You can put any possibility of that definitely out of your head."

He looked at me with an astonishment that was certainly not feigned. The smile abandoned his lips, and he spoke quite seriously.

"But, my dear fellow, I don't care. It doesn't matter a twopenny damn to me one way or the other."

I laughed.

"Oh, come now; you mustn't think us such fools as all that. We happen to know that you came away with a woman."

He gave a little start, and then suddenly burst into a shout of laughter. He laughed so uproariously that people sitting near us looked round, and some of them began to laugh too.

"I don't see anything very amusing in that."

"Poor Amy," he grinned.

Then his face grew bitterly scornful.

"What poor minds women have got! Love. It's always love. They think a man leaves only because he wants others. Do you think I should be such a fool as to do what I've done for a woman?"

"Do you mean to say you didn't leave your wife for another woman?"

"Of course not."

"On your word of honour?"

I don't know why I asked for that. It was very ingenuous of me.

"On my word of honour."

"Then, what in God's name have you left her for?"

"I want to paint."

I looked at him for quite a long time. I did not understand. I thought he was mad. It must be remembered that I was very young, and I looked upon him as a middle-aged man. I forgot everything but my own amazement.

"But you're forty."

"That's what made me think it was high time to begin."

"Have you ever painted?"

"I rather wanted to be a painter when I was a boy, but my father made me go into business because he said there was no money in art. I began to paint a bit a year ago. For the last year I've been going to some classes at night."

"Was that where you went when Mrs. Strickland thought you were playing bridge at your club?"

"That's it."

"Why didn't you tell her?"

"I preferred to keep it to myself."

"Can you paint?"

"Not yet. But I shall. That's why I've come over here. I couldn't get what I wanted in London. Perhaps I can here."

"Do you think it's likely that a man will do any good when he starts at your age? Most men begin painting at eighteen."

"I can learn quicker than I could when I was eighteen."

"What makes you think you have any talent?"

He did not answer for a minute. His gaze rested on the passing throng, but I do not think he saw it. His answer was no answer.

"I've got to paint."

"Aren't you taking an awful chance?"

He looked at me. His eyes had something strange in them, so that I felt rather uncomfortable.

"How old are you? Twenty-three?"

It seemed to me that the question was beside the point. It was natural that I should take chances; but he was a man whose youth was past, a stockbroker with a position of respectability, a wife and two children. A course that would have been natural for me was absurd for him. I wished to be quite fair.

"Of course a miracle may happen, and you may be a great painter, but you must confess the chances are a million to one against it. It'll be an awful sell if at the end you have to acknowledge you've made a hash of it."

"I've got to paint," he repeated.

"Supposing you're never anything more than third-rate, do you think it will have been worth while to give up everything? After all, in any other walk in life it doesn't matter if you're not very good; you can get along quite comfortably if you're just adequate; but it's different with an artist."

"You blasted fool," he said.

"I don't see why, unless it's folly to say the obvious."

"I tell you I've got to paint. I can't help myself. When a man falls into the water it doesn't matter how he swims, well or badly: he's got to get out or else he'll drown."

There was real passion in his voice, and in spite of myself I was impressed. I seemed to feel in him some vehement power that was struggling within him; it gave me the sensation of something very strong, overmastering, that held him, as it were, against his will. I could not understand. He seemed really to be possessed of a devil, and I felt that it might suddenly turn and rend him. Yet he looked ordinary enough. My eyes, resting on him curiously, caused him no embarrassment. I wondered what a stranger would have taken him to be, sitting there in his old Norfolk jacket and his unbrushed bowler; his trousers were baggy, his hands were not clean; and his face, with the red stubble of the unshaved chin, the little eyes, and the large, aggressive nose, was uncouth and coarse. His mouth was large, his lips were heavy and sensual. No; I could not have placed him.

"You won't go back to your wife?" I said at last.

"Never."

"She's willing to forget everything that's happened and start afresh. She'll never make you a single reproach."

"She can go to hell."

"You don't care if people think you an utter blackguard? You don't care if she and your children have to beg their bread?"

"Not a damn."

I was silent for a moment in order to give greater force to my next remark. I spoke as deliberately as I could.

"You are a most unmitigated cad."

"Now that you've got that off your chest, let's go and have dinner."

XIII

I DARE SAY it would have been more seemly to decline this proposal. I think perhaps I should have made a show of the indignation I really felt, and I am sure that Colonel MacAndrew at least would have thought well of me if I had been able to report my stout refusal to sit at the same table with a man of such character. But the fear of not being able to carry it through effectively has always made me shy of assuming the moral attitude; and in this case the certainty that my sentiments would be lost on Strickland made it peculiarly embarrassing to utter them. Only the poet or the saint can water an asphalt pavement in the confident anticipation that lilies will reward his labour.

I paid for what we had drunk, and we made our way to a cheap restaurant, crowded and gay, where we dined with pleasure. I had the appetite of youth and he of a hardened conscience. Then we went to a tavern to have coffee and liqueurs.

I had said all I had to say on the subject that had brought me to Paris, and though I felt it in a manner treacherous to Mrs. Strickland not to pursue it, I could not struggle against his indifference. It requires the feminine temperament to repeat the same thing three times with unabated zest. I solaced myself by thinking that it would be useful for me to find out what I could about Strickland's state of mind. It also interested me much more. But this was not an easy thing to do, for Strickland was not a fluent talker. He seemed to express himself with difficulty, as though words were not the medium with which his mind worked; and you had to guess the intentions of his soul by hackneyed phrases, slang, and vague, unfinished gestures. But though he said nothing of any consequence, there was something in his personality which prevented him from being dull. Perhaps it was sincerity. He did not seem to care much about the Paris he was now seeing for the first time (I did not count the visit with his wife), and he accepted sights which must have been strange to him without any sense of astonishment. I have been to Paris a hundred times, and it never fails to give me a thrill of excitement; I can never walk its streets without feeling myself on the verge of adventure. Strickland remained placid. Looking back, I think now that he was blind to everything but to some disturbing vision in his soul.

One rather absurd incident took place. There were a number of harlots in the tavern: some were sitting with men, others by themselves; and presently I noticed that one of these was looking at us. When she caught Strickland's eye she smiled. I do not think he saw her. In a little while she went out, but in a minute returned and, passing our table, very politely asked us to buy her something to drink. She sat down and I began to chat with her; but, it was plain that her interest was in Strickland. I explained that he knew no more than two words of French. She tried to talk to him, partly by signs, partly in pidgin French, which, for some reason, she thought would be more comprehensible to him, and she had half a dozen phrases of English. She made me translate what she could only express in her own tongue, and eagerly asked for the meaning of his replies. He was quite good-tempered, a little amused, but his indifference was obvious.

"I think you've made a conquest," I laughed.

"I'm not flattered."

In his place I should have been more embarrassed and less calm. She had laughing eyes and a most charming mouth. She was young. I wondered what she found so attractive in Strickland. She made no secret of her desires, and I was bidden to translate.

"She wants you to go home with her."

"I'm not taking any," he replied.

I put his answer as pleasantly as I could. It seemed to me a little ungracious to decline an invitation of that sort, and I ascribed his refusal to lack of money.

"But I like him," she said. "Tell him it's for love."

When I translated this, Strickland shrugged his shoulders impatiently.

"Tell her to go to hell," he said.

His manner made his answer quite plain, and the girl threw back her head with a sudden gesture. Perhaps she reddened under her paint. She rose to her feet.

"*Monsieur n'est pas poli,*" she said.

She walked out of the inn. I was slightly vexed.

"There wasn't any need to insult her that I can see," I said. "After all, it was rather a compliment she was paying you."

"That sort of thing makes me sick," he said roughly.

I looked at him curiously. There was a real distaste in his face, and yet it was the face of a coarse and sensual man. I suppose the girl had been attracted by a certain brutality in it.

"I could have got all the women I wanted in London. I didn't come here for that."

XIV

DURING THE JOURNEY back to England I thought much of Strickland. I tried to set in order what I had to tell his wife. It was unsatisfactory, and I could not imagine that she would be content with me; I was not content with myself. Strickland perplexed me. I could not understand his motives. When I had asked him what first gave him the idea of being a painter, he was unable or unwilling to tell me. I could make nothing of it. I tried to persuade myself than an obscure feeling of revolt had been gradually coming to a head in his slow mind, but to challenge this was the undoubted fact that he had never shown any impatience with the monotony of his life. If, seized by an intolerable boredom, he had determined to be a painter merely to break with irksome ties, it would have been comprehensible, and commonplace; but commonplace is precisely what I felt he was not. At last, because I was romantic, I devised an explanation which I acknowledged to be far-fetched, but which was the only one that in any way satisfied me. It was this: I asked myself whether there was not in his soul some deep-rooted instinct of creation, which the circumstances of his life had obscured, but which grew relentlessly, as a cancer may grow in the living tissues, till at last it took possession of his whole being and forced him irresistibly to action. The cuckoo lays its egg in the strange bird's nest, and when the young one is hatched it shoulders its foster-brothers out and breaks at last the nest that has sheltered it.

But how strange it was that the creative instinct should seize upon this dull stockbroker, to his own ruin, perhaps, and to the misfortune of such as were dependent on him; and yet no stranger than the way in which the spirit of God has seized men, powerful and rich, pursuing them with stubborn vigilance till at last, conquered, they have abandoned the joy of the world and the love of women for the painful austerities of the cloister. Conversion may come under many shapes, and it may be brought about in many ways. With some men it needs a cataclysm, as a stone may be broken to fragments by the fury of a torrent; but with some it comes gradually, as a stone may be worn away by the ceaseless fall of a drop of water. Strickland had the directness of the fanatic and the ferocity of the apostle.

But to my practical mind it remained to be seen whether the passion which obsessed him would be justified of its works. When I asked him what his brother-students at the night classes he had attended in London thought of his painting, he answered with a grin:

"They thought it a joke."

"Have you begun to go to a studio here?"

"Yes. The blighter came round this morning—the master, you know; when he saw my drawing he just raised his eyebrows and walked on."

Strickland chuckled. He did not seem discouraged. He was independent of the opinion of his fellows.

And it was just that which had most disconcerted me in my dealings with him. When people say they do not care what others think of them, for the most part they deceive themselves. Generally they mean only that they will do as they choose, in the confidence that no one will know their vagaries; and at the utmost only that they are willing to act contrary to the opinion of the majority because they are supported by the approval of their neighbours. It is not difficult to be unconventional in the eyes of the world when your unconventionality is but the convention of your set. It affords you then an inordinate amount of self-esteem. You have the self-satisfaction of courage without the inconvenience of danger. But the desire for approbation is perhaps the most deeply seated instinct of civilised man. No one runs so hurriedly to the cover of respectability as the unconventional woman who has exposed herself to the slings and arrows of outraged propriety. I do not believe the people who tell me they do not care a row of pins for the opinion of their fellows. It is the bravado of ignorance. They mean only that they do not fear reproaches for peccadillos which they are convinced none will discover.

But here was a man who sincerely did not mind what people thought of him, and so convention had no hold on him; he was like a wrestler whose body is oiled; you could not get a grip on him; it gave him a freedom which was an outrage. I remember saying to him:

"Look here, if everyone acted like you, the world couldn't go on."

"That's a damned silly thing to say. Everyone doesn't want to act like me. The great majority are perfectly content to do the ordinary thing."

And once I sought to be satirical.

"You evidently don't believe in the maxim: Act so that every one of your actions is capable of being made into a universal rule."

"I never heard it before, but it's rotten nonsense."

"Well, it was Kant who said it."

"I don't care; it's rotten nonsense."

Nor with such a man could you expect the appeal to conscience to be effective. You might as well ask for a reflection without a mirror. I take it that conscience is the guardian in the individual of the rules which the community has evolved for its own preservation. It is the policeman in all our hearts, set there to watch that we do not break its laws. It is the spy seated in the central stronghold of the ego. Man's desire for the approval of his fellows is so strong, his dread of their censure so violent, that he himself has brought his enemy within his gates; and it keeps watch over him, vigilant always in the interests of its master to crush any half-formed desire to break away from the herd. It will force him to place the good of society before his own. It is the very strong link that attaches the individual to the whole. And man, subservient to interests he has persuaded himself are greater than his own, makes himself a slave to his taskmaster. He sits him in a seat of honour. At last, like a courtier fawning on the royal stick that is laid about his shoulders, he prides himself on the sensitiveness of his conscience. Then he has no words hard enough for the man who does not recognise its sway; for, a member of society now, he realises accurately enough that against him he is powerless. When I saw that Strickland was really indifferent to the blame his conduct must excite, I could only draw back in horror as from a monster of hardly human shape.

The last words he said to me when I bade him good-night were:

"Tell Amy it's no good coming after me. Anyhow, I shall change my hotel, so she wouldn't be able to find me."

"My own impression is that she's well rid of you," I said.

"My dear fellow, I only hope you'll be able to make her see it. But women are very unintelligent."

XV

WHEN I REACHED London I found waiting for me an urgent request that I should go to Mrs. Strickland's as soon after dinner as I could. I found her with Colonel MacAndrew and his wife. Mrs. Strickland's sister was older than she, not unlike her, but more faded; and she had the efficient air, as though she carried the British Empire in her pocket, which the wives of senior officers acquire from the consciousness of belonging to a superior caste. Her manner was brisk, and her good-breeding scarcely concealed her conviction that if you were not a soldier you might as well be a counter-jumper. She hated the Guards, whom she thought conceited, and she could not trust herself to speak of their ladies, who were so remiss in calling. Her gown was dowdy and expensive.

Mrs. Strickland was plainly nervous.

"Well, tell us your news," she said.

"I saw your husband. I'm afraid he's quite made up his mind not to return." I paused a little. "He wants to paint."

"What do you mean?" cried Mrs. Strickland, with the utmost astonishment.

"Did you never know that he was keen on that sort of thing."

"He must be as mad as a hatter," exclaimed the Colonel.

Mrs. Strickland frowned a little. She was searching among her recollections.

"I remember before we were married he used to potter about with a paint-box. But you never saw such daubs. We used to chaff him. He had absolutely no gift for anything like that."

"Of course it's only an excuse," said Mrs. MacAndrew.

Mrs. Strickland pondered deeply for some time. It was quite clear that she could not make head or tail of my announcement. She had put some order into the drawing-room by now, her housewifely instincts having got the better of her dismay; and it no longer bore that deserted look, like a furnished house long to let, which I had noticed on my first visit after the catastrophe. But now that I had seen Strickland in Paris it was difficult to imagine him in those surroundings. I thought it could hardly have failed to strike them that there was something incongruous in him.

"But if he wanted to be an artist, why didn't he say so?" asked Mrs. Strickland at last. "I should have thought I was the last person to be unsympathetic to—to aspirations of that kind."

Mrs. MacAndrew tightened her lips. I imagine that she had never looked with approval on her sister's leaning towards persons who cultivated the arts. She spoke of "culchaw" derisively.

Mrs. Strickland continued:

"After all, if he had any talent I should be the first to encourage it. I wouldn't have minded sacrifices. I'd much rather be married to a painter than to a stockbroker. If it weren't for the children, I wouldn't mind anything. I could be just as happy in a shabby studio in Chelsea as in this flat."

"My dear, I have no patience with you," cried Mrs. MacAndrew. "You don't mean to say you believe a word of this nonsense?"

"But I think it's true," I put in mildly.

She looked at me with good-humoured contempt.

"A man doesn't throw up his business and leave his wife and children at the age of forty to become a painter unless there's a woman in it. I suppose he met one of your—artistic friends, and she's turned his head."

A spot of colour rose suddenly to Mrs. Strickland's pale cheeks.

"What is she like?"

I hesitated a little. I knew that I had a bombshell.

"There isn't a woman."

Colonel MacAndrew and his wife uttered expressions of incredulity, and Mrs. Strickland sprang to her feet.

"Do you mean to say you never saw her?"

"There's no one to see. He's quite alone."

"That's preposterous," cried Mrs. MacAndrew.

"I knew I ought to have gone over myself," said the Colonel. "You can bet your boots I'd have routed her out fast enough."

"I wish you had gone over," I replied, somewhat tartly. "You'd have seen that every one of your suppositions was wrong. He's not at a smart hotel. He's living in one tiny room in the most squalid way.

If he's left his home, it's not to live a gay life. He's got hardly any money."

"Do you think he's done something that we don't know about, and is lying doggo on account of the police?"

The suggestion sent a ray of hope in all their breasts, but I would have nothing to do with it.

"If that were so, he would hardly have been such a fool as to give his partner his address," I retorted acidly. "Anyhow, there's one thing I'm positive of, he didn't go away with anyone. He's not in love. Nothing is farther from his thoughts."

There was a pause while they reflected over my words.

"Well, if what you say is true," said Mrs. MacAndrew at last, "things aren't so bad as I thought."

Mrs. Strickland glanced at her, but said nothing.

She was very pale now, and her fine brow was dark and lowering. I could not understand the expression of her face. Mrs. MacAndrew continued:

"If it's just a whim, he'll get over it."

"Why don't you go over to him, Amy?" hazarded the Colonel. "There's no reason why you shouldn't live with him in Paris for a year. We'll look after the children. I dare say he'd got stale. Sooner or later he'll be quite ready to come back to London, and no great harm will have been done."

"I wouldn't do that," said Mrs. MacAndrew. "I'd give him all the rope he wants. He'll come back with his tail between his legs and settle down again quite comfortably." Mrs. MacAndrew looked at her sister coolly. "Perhaps you weren't very wise with him sometimes. Men are queer creatures, and one has to know how to manage them."

Mrs. MacAndrew shared the common opinion of her sex that a man is always a brute to leave a woman who is attached to him, but that a woman is much to blame if he does. *Le coeur a ses raisons que la raison ne connait pas.*

Mrs. Strickland looked slowly from one to another of us.

"He'll never come back," she said.

"Oh, my dear, remember what we've just heard. He's been used to comfort and to having someone to look after him. How long do you think it'll be before he gets tired of a scrubby room in a scrubby hotel? Besides, he hasn't any money. He must come back."

"As long as I thought he'd run away with some woman I thought there was a chance. I don't believe that sort of thing ever answers. He'd have got sick to death of her in three months. But if he hasn't gone because he's in love, then it's finished."

"Oh, I think that's awfully subtle," said the Colonel, putting into the word all the contempt he felt for a quality so alien to the traditions of his calling. "Don't you believe it. He'll come back, and, as Dorothy says, I dare say he'll be none the worse for having had a bit of a fling."

"But I don't want him back," she said.

"Amy!"

It was anger that had seized Mrs. Strickland, and her pallor was the pallor of a cold and sudden rage. She spoke quickly now, with little gasps.

"I could have forgiven it if he'd fallen desperately in love with someone and gone off with her. I should have thought that natural. I shouldn't really have blamed him. I should have thought he was led away. Men are so weak, and women are so unscrupulous. But this is different. I hate him. I'll never forgive him now."

Colonel MacAndrew and his wife began to talk to her together. They were astonished. They told her she was mad. They could not understand. Mrs. Strickland turned desperately to me.

"Don't *you* see?" she cried.

"I'm not sure. Do you mean that you could have forgiven him if he'd left you for a woman, but not if he's left you for an idea? You think you're a match for the one, but against the other you're helpless?"

Mrs. Strickland gave me a look in which I read no great friendliness, but did not answer. Perhaps I had struck home. She went on in a low and trembling voice:

"I never knew it was possible to hate anyone as much as I hate him. Do you know, I've been comforting myself by thinking that however long it lasted he'd want me at the end? I knew when he was dying he'd send for me, and I was ready to go; I'd have nursed him like a mother, and at the last I'd have told him that it didn't matter, I'd loved him always, and I forgave him everything."

I have always been a little disconcerted by the passion women have for behaving beautifully at the death-bed of those they love. Sometimes it seems as if they grudge the longevity which postpones their chance of an effective scene.

"But now—now it's finished. I'm as indifferent to him as if he were a stranger. I should like him to die miserable, poor, and starving, without a friend. I hope he'll rot with some loathsome disease. I've done with him."

I thought it as well then to say what Strickland had suggested.

"If you want to divorce him, he's quite willing to do whatever is necessary to make it possible."

"Why should I give him his freedom?"

"I don't think he wants it. He merely thought it might be more convenient to you."

Mrs. Strickland shrugged her shoulders impatiently. I think I was a little disappointed in her. I expected then people to be more of a piece than I do now, and I was distressed to find so much vindictiveness in so charming a creature. I did not realise how motley are the qualities that go to make up a human being. Now I am well aware that pettiness and grandeur, malice and charity, hatred and love, can find place side by side in the same human heart.

I wondered if there was anything I could say that would ease the sense of bitter humiliation which at present tormented Mrs. Strickland. I thought I would try.

"You know, I'm not sure that your husband is quite responsible for his actions. I do not think he is himself. He seems to me to be possessed by some power which is using him for its own ends, and in whose hold he is as helpless as a fly in a spider's web. It's as though someone had cast a spell over him. I'm reminded of those strange stories one sometimes hears of another personality entering into a man and driving out the old one. The soul lives unstably in the body, and is capable of mysterious transformations. In the old days they would say Charles Strickland had a devil."

Mrs. MacAndrew smoothed down the lap of her gown, and gold bangles fell over her wrists.

"All that seems to me very far-fetched," she said acidly. "I don't deny that perhaps Amy took her husband a little too much for granted. If she hadn't been so busy with her own affairs, I can't believe that she wouldn't have suspected something was the matter. I don't think that Alec could have something on his mind for a year or more without my having a pretty shrewd idea of it."

The Colonel stared into vacancy, and I wondered whether anyone could be quite so innocent of guile as he looked.

"But that doesn't prevent the fact that Charles Strickland is a heartless beast." She looked at me severely. "I can tell you why he left his wife—from pure selfishness and nothing else whatever."

"That is certainly the simplest explanation," I said. But I thought it explained nothing. When, saying I was tired, I rose to go, Mrs. Strickland made no attempt to detain me.

XVI

WHAT FOLLOWED SHOWED that Mrs. Strickland was a woman of character. Whatever anguish she suffered she concealed. She saw shrewdly that the world is quickly bored by the recital of misfortune, and willingly avoids the sight of distress. Whenever she went out—and compassion for her misadventure made her friends eager to entertain her—she bore a demeanour that was perfect. She was brave, but not too obviously; cheerful, but not brazenly; and she seemed more anxious to listen to the troubles of others than to discuss her own. Whenever she spoke of her husband it was with pity. Her attitude towards him at first perplexed me. One day she said to me:

"You know, I'm convinced you were mistaken about Charles being alone. From what I've been able to gather from certain sources that I can't tell you, I know that he didn't leave England by himself."

"In that case he has a positive genius for covering up his tracks."

She looked away and slightly coloured.

"What I mean is, if anyone talks to you about it, please don't contradict it if they say he eloped with somebody."

"Of course not."

She changed the conversation as though it were a matter to which she attached no importance. I discovered presently that a peculiar story was circulating among her friends. They said that Charles Strickland had become infatuated with a French dancer, whom he had first seen in the ballet at the Empire, and had accompanied her to Paris. I could not find out how this had arisen, but, singularly enough, it created much sympathy for Mrs. Strickland, and at the same time gave her not a little prestige. This was not without its use in the calling which she had decided to follow. Colonel MacAndrew had not exaggerated when he said she would be penniless, and it was necessary for her to earn her own living as quickly as she could. She made up her mind to profit by her acquaintance with so many writers, and without loss of time began to learn shorthand and typewriting. Her education made it likely that she would be a typist more efficient than the average, and her story made her claims appealing. Her friends promised to send her work, and took care to recommend her to all theirs.

The MacAndrews, who were childless and in easy circumstances, arranged to undertake the care of the children, and Mrs. Strickland had only herself to provide for. She let her flat and sold her furniture. She settled in two tiny rooms in Westminster, and faced the world anew. She was so efficient that it was certain she would make a success of the adventure.

XVII

IT WAS ABOUT five years after this that I decided to live in Paris for a while. I was growing stale in London. I was tired of doing much the same thing every day. My friends pursued their course with uneventfulness; they had no longer any surprises for me, and when I met them I knew pretty well what they would say; even their love-affairs had a tedious banality. We were like tram-cars running on their lines from terminus to terminus, and it was possible to calculate within small limits the number of passengers they would carry. Life was ordered too pleasantly. I was seized with panic. I gave up my small apartment, sold my few belongings, and resolved to start afresh.

I called on Mrs. Strickland before I left. I had not seen her for some time, and I noticed changes in her; it was not only that she was older, thinner, and more lined; I think her character had altered. She had made a success of her business, and now had an office in Chancery Lane; she did little typing herself, but spent her time correcting the work of the four girls she employed. She had had the idea of giving it a certain daintiness, and she made much use of blue and red inks; she bound the copy in coarse paper, that looked vaguely like watered silk, in various pale colours; and she had acquired a reputation for neatness and accuracy. She was making money. But she could not get over the idea that to earn her living was somewhat undignified, and she was inclined to remind you that she was a lady by birth. She could not help bringing into her conversation the names of people she knew which would satisfy you that she had not sunk in the social scale. She was a little ashamed of her courage and business capacity, but delighted that she was going to dine the next night with a K.C. who lived in South Kensington. She was pleased to be able to tell you that her son was at Cambridge, and it was with a little laugh that she spoke of the rush of dances to which her daughter, just out, was invited. I suppose I said a very stupid thing.

"Is she going into your business?" I asked.

"Oh no; I wouldn't let her do that," Mrs. Strickland answered. "She's so pretty. I'm sure she'll marry well."

"I should have thought it would be a help to you."

"Several people have suggested that she should go on the stage, but of course I couldn't consent to that, I know all the chief dramatists, and I could get her a part to-morrow, but I shouldn't like her to mix with all sorts of people."

I was a little chilled by Mrs. Strickland's exclusiveness.

"Do you ever hear of your husband?"

"No; I haven't heard a word. He may be dead for all I know."

"I may run across him in Paris. Would you like me to let you know about him?"

She hesitated a minute.

"If he's in any real want I'm prepared to help him a little. I'd send you a certain sum of money, and you could give it him gradually, as he needed it."

"That's very good of you," I said.

But I knew it was not kindness that prompted the offer. It is not true that suffering ennobles the character; happiness does that sometimes, but suffering, for the most part, makes men petty and vindictive.

XVIII

IN POINT OF fact, I met Strickland before I had been a fortnight in Paris.

I quickly found myself a tiny apartment on the fifth floor of a house in the Rue des Dames, and for a couple of hundred francs bought at a second-hand dealer's enough furniture to make it habitable. I arranged with the concierge to make my coffee in the morning and to keep the place clean. Then I went to see my friend Dirk Stroeve.

Dirk Stroeve was one of those persons whom, according to your character, you cannot think of without derisive laughter or an embarrassed shrug of the shoulders. Nature had made him a buffoon. He was a painter, but a very bad one, whom I had met in Rome, and I still remembered his pictures. He had a genuine enthusiasm for the commonplace. His soul palpitating with love of art, he painted the models who hung about the stairway of Bernini in the Piazza de Spagna, undaunted by their obvious picturesqueness; and his studio was full of canvases on which were portrayed moustachioed, large-eyed peasants in peaked hats, urchins in becoming rags, and women in bright petticoats. Sometimes they lounged at the steps of a church, and sometimes dallied among cypresses against a cloudless sky; sometimes they made love by a Renaissance well-head, and sometimes they wandered through the Campagna by the side of an ox-waggon. They were carefully drawn and carefully painted. A photograph could not have been more exact. One of the painters at the Villa Medici had called him *Le Maître de la Boîte à Chocolats*. To look at his pictures you would have thought that Monet, Manet, and the rest of the Impressionists had never been.

"I don't pretend to be a great painter," he said, "I'm not a Michael Angelo, no, but I have something. I sell. I bring romance into the homes of all sorts of people. Do you know, they buy my pictures not only in Holland, but in Norway and Sweden and Denmark? It's mostly merchants who buy them, and rich tradesmen. You can't imagine what the winters are like in those countries, so long and dark and cold. They like to think that Italy is like my pictures. That's what they expect. That's what I expected Italy to be before I came here."

And I think that was the vision that had remained with him always, dazzling his eyes so that he could not see the truth; and notwithstanding the brutality of fact, he continued to see with the eyes of the spirit an Italy of romantic brigands and picturesque ruins. It was an ideal that he painted—a poor one, common and shop-soiled, but still it was an ideal; and it gave his character a peculiar charm.

It was because I felt this that Dirk Stroeve was not to me, as to others, merely an object of ridicule. His fellow-painters made no secret of their contempt for his work, but he earned a fair amount of money, and they did not hesitate to make free use of his purse. He was generous, and the needy, laughing at him because he believed so naively their stories of distress, borrowed from him with effrontery. He was very emotional, yet his feeling, so easily aroused, had in it something absurd, so that you accepted his kindness, but felt no gratitude. To take money from him was like robbing a child, and you despised him because he was so foolish. I imagine that a pickpocket, proud of his light fingers, must feel a sort of indignation with the careless woman who leaves in a cab a vanity-bag with all her jewels in it. Nature had made him a butt, but had denied him insensibility. He writhed under the jokes, practical and otherwise, which were perpetually made at his expense, and yet never ceased, it seemed wilfully, to expose himself to them. He was constantly wounded, and yet his good-nature was such that he could not bear malice: the viper might sting him, but he never learned by experience, and had no sooner recovered from his pain than he tenderly placed it once more in his bosom. His life was a tragedy written in the terms of knockabout farce. Because I did not laugh at him he was grateful to me, and he used to pour into my sympathetic ear the long list of his troubles. The saddest thing about them was that they were grotesque, and the more pathetic they were, the more you wanted to laugh.

But though so bad a painter, he had a very delicate feeling for art, and to go with him to picture-galleries was a rare treat. His enthusiasm was sincere and his criticism acute. He was catholic. He had not only a true appreciation of the old masters, but sympathy with the moderns. He was quick to discover talent, and his praise was generous. I think I have never known a man whose judgment was surer. And he was better educated than most painters. He was not, like most of them, ignorant of kindred arts, and his taste for music and literature gave depth and variety to his comprehension of painting. To a young man like myself his advice and guidance were of incomparable value.

When I left Rome I corresponded with him, and about once in two months received from him long letters in queer English, which brought before me vividly his spluttering, enthusiastic, gesticulating conversation. Some time before I went to Paris he had married an Englishwoman, and was now settled in a studio in Montmartre. I had not seen him for four years, and had never met his wife.

XIX

I HAD NOT announced my arrival to Stroeve, and when I rang the bell of his studio, on opening the door himself, for a moment he did not know me. Then he gave a cry of delighted surprise and drew me in. It was charming to be welcomed with so much eagerness. His wife was seated near the stove at her sewing, and she rose as I came in. He introduced me.

"Don't you remember?" he said to her. "I've talked to you about him often." And then to me: "But why didn't you let me know you were coming? How long have you been here? How long are you going to stay? Why didn't you come an hour earlier, and we would have dined together?"

He bombarded me with questions. He sat me down in a chair, patting me as though I were a cushion, pressed cigars upon me, cakes, wine. He could not let me alone. He was heart-broken because he had no whisky, wanted to make coffee for me, racked his brain for something he could possibly do for me, and beamed and laughed, and in the exuberance of his delight sweated at every pore.

"You haven't changed," I said, smiling, as I looked at him.

He had the same absurd appearance that I remembered. He was a fat little man, with short legs, young still—he could not have been more than thirty—but prematurely bald. His face was perfectly round, and he had a very high colour, a white skin, red cheeks, and red lips. His eyes were blue and round too, he wore large gold-rimmed spectacles, and his eyebrows were so fair that you could not see them. He reminded you of those jolly, fat merchants that Rubens painted.

When I told him that I meant to live in Paris for a while, and had taken an apartment, he reproached me bitterly for not having let him know. He would have found me an apartment himself, and lent me furniture—did I really mean that I had gone to the expense of buying it?—and he would have helped me to move in. He really looked upon it as unfriendly that I had not given him the opportunity of making himself useful to me. Meanwhile, Mrs. Stroeve sat quietly mending her stockings, without talking, and she listened to all he said with a quiet smile on her lips.

"So, you see, I'm married," he said suddenly; "what do you think of my wife?"

He beamed at her, and settled his spectacles on the bridge of his nose. The sweat made them constantly slip down.

"What on earth do you expect me to say to that?" I laughed.

"Really, Dirk," put in Mrs. Stroeve, smiling.

"But isn't she wonderful? I tell you, my boy, lose no time; get married as soon as ever you can. I'm the happiest man alive. Look at her sitting there. Doesn't she make a picture? Chardin, eh? I've seen all the most beautiful women in the world; I've never seen anyone more beautiful than Madame Dirk Stroeve."

"If you don't be quiet, Dirk, I shall go away."

"*Mon petit chou*", he said.

She flushed a little, embarrassed by the passion in his tone. His letters had told me that he was very much in love with his wife, and I saw that he could hardly take his eyes off her. I could not tell if she loved him. Poor pantaloon, he was not an object to excite love, but the smile in her eyes was affectionate, and it was possible that her reserve concealed a very deep feeling. She was not the ravishing creature that his love-sick fancy saw, but she had a grave comeliness. She was rather tall, and her gray dress, simple and quite well-cut, did not hide the fact that her figure was beautiful. It was a figure that might have appealed more to the sculptor than to the costumier. Her hair, brown and abundant, was plainly done, her face was very pale, and her features were good without being distinguished. She had quiet gray eyes. She just missed being beautiful, and in missing it was not even pretty. But when Stroeve spoke of Chardin it was not without reason, and she reminded me curiously of that pleasant housewife in her mob-cap and apron whom the great painter has immortalised. I could imagine her sedately busy among her pots and pans, making a ritual of her household duties, so that they acquired a moral significance; I did not suppose that she was clever or could ever be amusing, but there was something in her grave intentness which excited my interest. Her reserve was not without mystery. I wondered why she had married Dirk Stroeve. Though she was English, I could not exactly place her, and it was not obvious from what rank in society she sprang, what had been her upbringing, or how she had lived before her marriage. She was very silent, but when she spoke it was with a pleasant voice, and her manners were natural.

I asked Stroeve if he was working.

"Working? I'm painting better than I've ever painted before."

We sat in the studio, and he waved his hand to an unfinished picture on an easel. I gave a little start. He was painting a group of Italian peasants, in the costume of the Campagna, lounging on the steps of a Roman church.

"Is that what you're doing now?" I asked.

"Yes. I can get my models here just as well as in Rome."

"Don't you think it's very beautiful?" said Mrs. Stroeve.

"This foolish wife of mine thinks I'm a great artist," said he.

His apologetic laugh did not disguise the pleasure that he felt. His eyes lingered on his picture. It was strange that his critical sense, so accurate and unconventional when he dealt with the work of others, should be satisfied in himself with what was hackneyed and vulgar beyond belief.

"Show him some more of your pictures," she said.

"Shall I?"

Though he had suffered so much from the ridicule of his friends, Dirk Stroeve, eager for praise and naively self-satisfied, could never resist displaying his work. He brought out a picture of two curly-headed Italian urchins playing marbles.

"Aren't they sweet?" said Mrs. Stroeve.

And then he showed me more. I discovered that in Paris he had been painting just the same stale, obviously picturesque things that he had painted for years in Rome. It was all false, insincere, shoddy; and yet no one was more honest, sincere, and frank than Dirk Stroeve. Who could resolve the contradiction?

I do not know what put it into my head to ask:

"I say, have you by any chance run across a painter called Charles Strickland?"

"You don't mean to say you know him?" cried Stroeve.

"Beast," said his wife.

Stroeve laughed.

"Ma pauvre cherie." He went over to her and kissed both her hands. "She doesn't like him. How strange that you should know Strickland!"

"I don't like bad manners," said Mrs. Stroeve.

Dirk, laughing still, turned to me to explain.

"You see, I asked him to come here one day and look at my pictures. Well, he came, and I showed him everything I had." Stroeve hesitated a moment with embarrassment. I do not know why he had begun the story against himself; he felt an awkwardness at finishing it. "He looked at—at my pictures, and he didn't say anything. I thought he was reserving his judgment till the end. And at last I said: 'There, that's the lot!' He said: 'I came to ask you to lend me twenty francs.'"

"And Dirk actually gave it him," said his wife indignantly.

"I was so taken aback. I didn't like to refuse. He put the money in his pocket, just nodded, said 'Thanks,' and walked out."

Dirk Stroeve, telling the story, had such a look of blank astonishment on his round, foolish face that it was almost impossible not to laugh.

"I shouldn't have minded if he'd said my pictures were bad, but he said nothing—nothing."

"And you *will* tell the story, Dirk," Said his wife.

It was lamentable that one was more amused by the ridiculous figure cut by the Dutchman than outraged by Strickland's brutal treatment of him.

"I hope I shall never see him again," said Mrs. Stroeve.

Stroeve smiled and shrugged his shoulders. He had already re-covered his good-humour.

"The fact remains that he's a great artist, a very great artist."

"Strickland?" I exclaimed. "It can't be the same man."

"A big fellow with a red beard. Charles Strickland. An Englishman."

"He had no beard when I knew him, but if he has grown one it might well be red. The man I'm thinking of only began painting five years ago."

"That's it. He's a great artist."

"Impossible."

"Have I ever been mistaken?" Dirk asked me. "I tell you he has genius. I'm convinced of it. In a hundred years, if you and I are re-membered at all, it will be because we knew Charles Strickland."

I was astonished, and at the same time I was very much excited. I remembered suddenly my last talk with him.

"Where can one see his work?" I asked. "Is he having any success? Where is he living?"

"No; he has no success. I don't think he's ever sold a picture. When you speak to men about him they only laugh. But I *know* he's a great artist. After all, they laughed at Manet. Corot never sold a picture. I don't know where he lives, but I can take you to see him. He goes to a cafe in the Avenue de Clichy at seven o'clock every evening. If you like we'll go there to-morrow."

"I'm not sure if he'll wish to see me. I think I may remind him of a time he prefers to forget. But I'll come all the same. Is there any chance of seeing any of his pictures?"

"Not from him. He won't show you a thing. There's a little dealer

I know who has two or three. But you mustn't go without me; you wouldn't understand. I must show them to you myself."

"Dirk, you make me impatient," said Mrs. Stroeve. "How can you talk like that about his pictures when he treated you as he did?" She turned to me. "Do you know, when some Dutch people came here to buy Dirk's pictures he tried to persuade them to buy Strickland's? He insisted on bringing them here to show."

"What did *you* think of them?" I asked her, smiling.

"They were awful."

"Ah, sweetheart, you don't understand."

"Well, your Dutch people were furious with you. They thought you were having a joke with them."

Dirk Stroeve took off his spectacles and wiped them. His flushed face was shining with excitement.

"Why should you think that beauty, which is the most precious thing in the world, lies like a stone on the beach for the careless passer-by to pick up idly? Beauty is something wonderful and strange that the artist fashions out of the chaos of the world in the torment of his soul. And when he has made it, it is not given to all to know it. To recognize it you must repeat the adventure of the artist. It is a melody that he sings to you, and to hear it again in your own heart you want knowledge and sensitiveness and imagination."

"Why did I always think your pictures beautiful, Dirk? I admired them the very first time I saw them."

Stroeve's lips trembled a little.

"Go to bed, my precious. I will walk a few steps with our friend, and then I will come back."

XX

DIRK STROEVE agreed to fetch me on the following evening and take me to the cafe at which Strickland was most likely to be found. I was interested to learn that it was the same as that at which Strickland and I had drunk absinthe when I had gone over to Paris to see him. The fact that he had never changed suggested a sluggishness of habit which seemed to me characteristic.

"There he is," said Stroeve, as we reached the cafe.

Though it was October, the evening was warm, and the tables on the pavement were crowded. I ran my eyes over them, but did not see Strickland.

"Look. Over there, in the corner. He's playing chess."

I noticed a man bending over a chess-board, but could see only a large felt hat and a red beard. We threaded our way among the tables till we came to him.

"Strickland."

He looked up.

"Hulloa, fatty. What do you want?"

"I've brought an old friend to see you."

Strickland gave me a glance, and evidently did not recognise me. He resumed his scrutiny of the chess-board.

"Sit down, and don't make a noise," he said.

He moved a piece and straightway became absorbed in the game. Poor Stroeve gave me a troubled look, but I was not disconcerted by so little. I ordered something to drink, and waited quietly till Strickland had finished. I welcomed the opportunity to examine him at my ease. I certainly should never have known him. In the first place his red beard, ragged and untrimmed, hid much of his face, and his hair was long; but the most surprising change in him was his extreme thinness. It made his great nose protrude more arrogantly; it emphasized his cheekbones; it made his eyes seem larger. There were deep hollows at his temples. His body was cadaverous. He wore the same suit that I had seen him in five years before; it was torn and stained, threadbare, and it hung upon him loosely, as though it had been made for someone else. I noticed his hands, dirty, with long nails; they were merely bone and sinew, large and strong; but I had forgotten that they were so shapely. He gave me an extraordinary impression as he sat there, his attention riveted on his game—an impression of great strength; and I could not understand why it was that his emaciation somehow made it more striking.

Presently, after moving, he leaned back and gazed with a curious abstraction at his antagonist. This was a fat, bearded Frenchman. The Frenchman considered the position, then broke suddenly into jovial expletives, and with an impatient gesture, gathering up the pieces, flung them into their box. He cursed Strickland freely, then, calling for the waiter, paid for the drinks, and left. Stroeve drew his chair closer to the table.

"Now I suppose we can talk," he said.

Strickland's eyes rested on him, and there was in them a malicious expression. I felt sure he was seeking for some gibe, could think of none, and so was forced to silence.

"I've brought an old friend to see you," repeated Stroeve, beaming cheerfully.

Strickland looked at me thoughtfully for nearly a minute. I did not speak.

"I've never seen him in my life," he said.

I do not know why he said this, for I felt certain I had caught a gleam of recognition in his eyes. I was not so easily abashed as I had been some years earlier.

"I saw your wife the other day," I said. "I felt sure you'd like to have the latest news of her."

He gave a short laugh. His eyes twinkled.

"We had a jolly evening together," he said. "How long ago is it?"

"Five years."

He called for another absinthe. Stroeve, with voluble tongue, explained how he and I had met, and by what an accident we discovered that we both knew Strickland. I do not know if Strickland listened. He glanced at me once or twice reflectively, but for the most part seemed occupied with his own thoughts; and certainly without Stroeve's babble the conversation would have been difficult. In half an hour the Dutchman, looking at his watch, announced that he must go. He asked whether I would come too. I thought, alone, I might get something out of Strickland, and so answered that I would stay.

When the fat man had left I said:

"Dirk Stroeve thinks you're a great artist."

"What the hell do you suppose I care?"

"Will you let me see your pictures?"

"Why should I?"

"I might feel inclined to buy one."

"I might not feel inclined to sell one."

"Are you making a good living?" I asked, smiling.

He chuckled.

"Do I look it?"

"You look half starved."

"I am half starved."

"Then come and let's have a bit of dinner."

"Why do you ask me?"

"Not out of charity," I answered coolly. "I don't really care a two-penny damn if you starve or not."

His eyes lit up again.

"Come on, then," he said, getting up. "I'd like a decent meal."

XXI

I LET HIM take me to a restaurant of his choice, but on the way I bought a paper. When we had ordered our dinner, I propped it against a bottle of St. Galmier and began to read. We ate in silence. I felt him looking at me now and again, but I took no notice. I meant to force him to conversation.

"Is there anything in the paper?" he said, as we approached the end of our silent meal.

I fancied there was in his tone a slight note of exasperation.

"I always like to read the *feuilleton* on the drama," I said.

I folded the paper and put it down beside me.

"I've enjoyed my dinner," he remarked.

"I think we might have our coffee here, don't you?"

"Yes."

We lit our cigars. I smoked in silence. I noticed that now and then his eyes rested on me with a faint smile of amusement. I waited patiently.

"What have you been up to since I saw you last?" he asked at length.

I had not very much to say. It was a record of hard work and of little adventure; of experiments in this direction and in that; of the gradual acquisition of the knowledge of books and of men. I took care to ask Strickland nothing about his own doings. I showed not the least interest in him, and at last I was rewarded. He began to talk of himself. But with his poor gift of expression he gave but indications of what he had gone through, and I had to fill up the gaps with my own imagination. It was tantalising to get no more than hints into a character that interested me so much. It was like making one's way through a mutilated manuscript. I received the impression of a life which was a bitter struggle against every sort of difficulty; but I realised that much which would have seemed horrible to most people did not in the least affect him. Strickland was distinguished from most Englishmen by his perfect indifference to comfort; it did not irk him to live always in one shabby room; he had no need to be surrounded by beautiful things. I do not suppose he had ever noticed how dingy was the paper on the wall of the room in which on my first visit I found him. He did not want arm-chairs to sit in; he really felt more at his ease on a kitchen chair. He ate with appetite, but was indifferent to what he ate; to him it was only food that he devoured to still the pangs of hunger; and when no food was to be had he seemed capable of doing without. I learned that for six months he had lived on a loaf of bread and a bottle of milk a day. He was a sensual man, and yet was indifferent to sensual things. He looked upon privation as no hardship. There was something impressive in the manner in which he lived a life wholly of the spirit.

When the small sum of money which he brought with him from London came to an end he suffered from no dismay. He sold no pictures; I think he made little attempt to sell any; he set about finding some way to make a bit of money. He told me with grim humour of the time he had spent acting as guide to Cockneys who wanted to see the night side of life in Paris; it was an occupation that appealed to his sardonic temper and somehow or other he had acquired a wide acquaintance with the more disreputable quarters of the city. He told me of the long hours he spent walking about the Boulevard de la Madeleine on the look-out for Englishmen, preferably the worse for liquor, who desired to see things which the law forbade. When in luck he was able to make a tidy sum; but the shabbiness of his clothes at last frightened the sight-seers, and he could not find people adventurous enough to trust themselves to him. Then he happened on a job to translate the advertisements of patent medicines which were sent broadcast to the medical profession in England. During a strike he had been employed as a house-painter.

Meanwhile he had never ceased to work at his art; but, soon tiring of the studios, entirely by himself. He had never been so poor that he could not buy canvas and paint, and really he needed nothing else. So far as I could make out, he painted with great difficulty, and in his unwillingness to accept help from anyone lost much time in finding out for himself the solution of technical problems which preceding generations had already worked out one by one. He was aiming at something, I knew not what, and perhaps he hardly knew himself; and I got again more strongly the impression of a man possessed. He did not seem quite sane. It seemed to me that he would not show his pictures because he was really not interested in them. He lived in a dream, and the reality meant nothing to him. I had the feeling that he worked on a canvas with all the force of his violent personality, oblivious of everything in his effort to get what he saw with the mind's eye; and then, having finished, not the picture perhaps, for I had an idea that he seldom brought anything to completion, but the passion that fired him, he lost all care for it. He was never satisfied with what he had done; it seemed to him of no consequence compared with the vision that obsessed his mind.

"Why don't you ever send your work to exhibitions?" I asked. "I should have thought you'd like to know what people thought about it."

"Would you?"

I cannot describe the unmeasurable contempt he put into the two words.

"Don't you want fame? It's something that most artists haven't been indifferent to."

"Children. How can you care for the opinion of the crowd, when you don't care twopence for the opinion of the individual?"

"We're not all reasonable beings," I laughed.

"Who makes fame? Critics, writers, stockbrokers, women."

"Wouldn't it give you a rather pleasing sensation to think of people you didn't know and had never seen receiving emotions, subtle and passionate, from the work of your hands? Everyone likes power. I can't imagine a more wonderful exercise of it than to move the souls of men to pity or terror."

"Melodrama."

"Why do you mind if you paint well or badly?"

"I don't. I only want to paint what I see."

"I wonder if I could write on a desert island, with the certainty that no eyes but mine would ever see what I had written."

Strickland did not speak for a long time, but his eyes shone strangely, as though he saw something that kindled his soul to ecstasy.

"Sometimes I've thought of an island lost in a boundless sea, where I could live in some hidden valley, among strange trees, in silence. There I think I could find what I want."

He did not express himself quite like this. He used gestures instead of adjectives, and he halted. I have put into my own words what I think he wanted to say.

"Looking back on the last five years, do you think it was worth it?" I asked.

He looked at me, and I saw that he did not know what I meant. I explained.

"You gave up a comfortable home and a life as happy as the average. You were fairly prosperous. You seem to have had a rotten time in Paris. If you had your time over again would you do what you did?"

"Rather."

"Do you know that you haven't asked anything about your wife and children? Do you never think of them?"

"No."

"I wish you weren't so damned monosyllabic. Have you never had a moment's regret for all the unhappiness you caused them?"

His lips broke into a smile, and he shook his head.

"I should have thought sometimes you couldn't help thinking of the past. I don't mean the past of seven or eight years ago, but further back still, when you first met your wife, and loved her, and married her. Don't you remember the joy with which you first took her in your arms?"

"I don't think of the past. The only thing that matters is the everlasting present."

I thought for a moment over this reply. It was obscure, perhaps, but I thought that I saw dimly his meaning.

"Are you happy?" I asked.

"Yes."

I was silent. I looked at him reflectively. He held my stare, and presently a sardonic twinkle lit up his eyes.

"I'm afraid you disapprove of me?"

"Nonsense," I answered promptly; "I don't disapprove of the boa-constrictor; on the contrary, I'm interested in his mental processes."

"It's a purely professional interest you take in me?"

"Purely."

"It's only right that you shouldn't disapprove of me. You have a despicable character."

"Perhaps that's why you feel at home with me," I retorted.

He smiled dryly, but said nothing. I wish I knew how to describe his smile. I do not know that it was attractive, but it lit up his face, changing the expression, which was generally sombre, and gave it a look of not ill-natured malice. It was a slow smile, starting and sometimes ending in the eyes; it was very sensual, neither cruel nor kindly, but suggested rather the inhuman glee of the satyr. It was his smile that made me ask him:

"Haven't you been in love since you came to Paris?"

"I haven't got time for that sort of nonsense. Life isn't long enough for love and art."

"Your appearance doesn't suggest the anchorite."

"All that business fills me with disgust."

"Human nature is a nuisance, isn't it?" I said.

"Why are you sniggering at me?"

"Because I don't believe you."

"Then you're a damned fool."

I paused, and I looked at him searchingly.

"What's the good of trying to humbug me?" I said.

"I don't know what you mean."

I smiled.

"Let me tell you. I imagine that for months the matter never comes into your head, and you're able to persuade yourself that you've finished with it for good and all. You rejoice in your freedom, and you feel that at last you can call your soul your own. You seem to walk with your head among the stars. And then, all of a sudden you can't stand it any more, and you notice that all the time your feet have been walking in the mud. And you want to roll yourself in it. And you find some woman, coarse and low and vulgar, some beastly creature in whom all the horror of sex is blatant, and you fall upon her like a wild animal. You drink till you're blind with rage."

He stared at me without the slightest movement. I held his eyes with mine. I spoke very slowly.

"I'll tell you what must seem strange, that when it's over you feel so extraordinarily pure. You feel like a disembodied spirit, immaterial; and you seem to be able to touch beauty as though it were a palpable thing; and you feel an intimate communion with the breeze, and with the trees breaking into leaf, and with the iridescence of the river. You feel like God. Can you explain that to me?"

He kept his eyes fixed on mine till I had finished, and then he turned away. There was on his face a strange look, and I thought that so might a man look when he had died under the torture. He was silent. I knew that our conversation was ended.

XXII

I SETTLED DOWN in Paris and began to write a play. I led a very regular life, working in the morning, and in the afternoon lounging about the gardens of the Luxembourg or sauntering through the streets. I spent long hours in the Louvre, the most friendly of all galleries and the most convenient for meditation; or idled on the quays, fingering second-hand books that I never meant to buy. I read a page here and there, and made acquaintance with a great many authors whom I was content to know thus desultorily. In the evenings I went to see my friends. I looked in often on the Stroeves, and sometimes shared their modest fare. Dirk Stroeve flattered himself on his skill in cooking Italian dishes, and I confess that his *spaghetti* were very much better than his pictures. It was a dinner for a King when he brought in a huge dish of it, succulent with tomatoes, and we ate it together with the good household bread and a bottle of red wine. I grew more intimate with Blanche Stroeve, and I think, because I was English and she knew few English people, she was glad to see me. She was pleasant and simple, but she remained always rather silent, and I knew not why, gave me the impression that she was concealing something. But I thought that was perhaps no more than a natural reserve accentuated by the verbose frankness of her husband. Dirk never concealed anything. He discussed the most intimate matters with a complete lack of self-consciousness. Sometimes he embarrassed his wife, and the only time I saw her put out of countenance was when he insisted on telling me that he had taken a purge, and went into somewhat realistic details on the subject. The perfect seriousness with which he narrated his misfortunes convulsed me with laughter, and this added to Mrs. Stroeve's irritation.

"You seem to like making a fool of yourself," she said.

His round eyes grew rounder still, and his brow puckered in dismay as he saw that she was angry.

"Sweetheart, have I vexed you? I'll never take another. It was only because I was bilious. I lead a sedentary life. I don't take enough exercise. For three days I hadn't . . ."

"For goodness sake, hold your tongue," she interrupted, tears of annoyance in her eyes.

His face fell, and he pouted his lips like a scolded child. He gave me a look of appeal, so that I might put things right, but, unable to control myself, I shook with helpless laughter.

We went one day to the picture-dealer in whose shop Stroeve thought he could show me at least two or three of Strickland's pictures, but when we arrived were told that Strickland himself had taken them away. The dealer did not know why.

"But don't imagine to yourself that I make myself bad blood on that account. I took them to oblige Monsieur Stroeve, and I said I would sell them if I could. But really—" He shrugged his shoulders. "I'm interested in the young men, but *voyons*, you yourself, Monsieur Stroeve, you don't think there's any talent there."

"I give you my word of honour, there's no one painting to-day in

whose talent I am more convinced. Take my word for it, you are missing a good affair. Some day those pictures will be worth more than all
you have in your shop. Remember Monet, who could not get anyone
to buy his pictures for a hundred francs. What are they worth now?"

"True. But there were a hundred as good painters as Monet who
couldn't sell their pictures at that time, and their pictures are worth
nothing still. How can one tell? Is merit enough to bring success?
Don't believe it. Du reste, it has still to be proved that this friend of
yours has merit. No one claims it for him but Monsieur Stroeve."

"And how, then, will you recognise merit?" asked Dirk, red in the
face with anger.

"There is only one way—by success."

"Philistine," cried Dirk.

"But think of the great artists of the past—Raphael, Michael
Angelo, Ingres, Delacroix—they were all successful."

"Let us go," said Stroeve to me, "or I shall kill this man."

XXIII

I saw Strickland not infrequently, and now and then played chess
with him. He was of uncertain temper. Sometimes he would sit silent
and abstracted, taking no notice of anyone; and at others, when he
was in a good humour, he would talk in his own halting way. He never
said a clever thing, but he had a vein of brutal sarcasm which was not
ineffective, and he always said exactly what he thought. He was indifferent to the susceptibilities of others, and when he wounded them
was amused. He was constantly offending Dirk Stroeve so bitterly
that he flung away, vowing he would never speak to him again; but
there was a solid force in Strickland that attracted the fat Dutchman
against his will, so that he came back, fawning like a clumsy dog,
though he knew that his only greeting would be the blow he dreaded.

I do not know why Strickland put up with me. Our relations were
peculiar. One day he asked me to lend him fifty francs.

"I wouldn't dream of it," I replied.

"Why not?"

"It wouldn't amuse me."

"I'm frightfully hard up, you know."

"I don't care."

"You don't care if I starve?"

"Why on earth should I?" I asked in my turn.

He looked at me for a minute or two, pulling his untidy beard. I smiled at him.

"What are you amused at?" he said, with a gleam of anger in his eyes.

"You're so simple. You recognise no obligations. No one is under any obligation to you."

"Wouldn't it make you uncomfortable if I went and hanged myself because I'd been turned out of my room as I couldn't pay the rent?"

"Not a bit."

He chuckled.

"You're bragging. If I really did you'd be overwhelmed with remorse."

"Try it, and we'll see," I retorted.

A smile flickered in his eyes, and he stirred his absinthe in silence.

"Would you like to play chess?" I asked.

"I don't mind."

We set up the pieces, and when the board was ready he considered it with a comfortable eye. There is a sense of satisfaction in looking at your men all ready for the fray.

"Did you really think I'd lend you money?" I asked.

"I didn't see why you shouldn't."

"You surprise me."

"Why?"

"It's disappointing to find that at heart you are sentimental. I should have liked you better if you hadn't made that ingenuous appeal to my sympathies."

"I should have despised you if you'd been moved by it," he answered.

"That's better," I laughed.

We began to play. We were both absorbed in the game. When it was finished I said to him:

"Look here, if you're hard up, let me see your pictures. If there's anything I like I'll buy it."

"Go to hell," he answered.

He got up and was about to go away. I stopped him.

"You haven't paid for your absinthe," I said, smiling.

He cursed me, flung down the money and left.

I did not see him for several days after that, but one evening, when I was sitting in the cafe, reading a paper, he came up and sat beside me.

"You haven't hanged yourself after all," I remarked.

"No. I've got a commission. I'm painting the portrait of a retired plumber for two hundred francs."[5]

"How did you manage that?"

"The woman where I get my bread recommended me. He'd told her he was looking out for someone to paint him. I've got to give her twenty francs."

"What's he like?"

"Splendid. He's got a great red face like a leg of mutton, and on his right cheek there's an enormous mole with long hairs growing out of it."

Strickland was in a good humour, and when Dirk Stroeve came up and sat down with us he attacked him with ferocious banter. He showed a skill I should never have credited him with in finding the places where the unhappy Dutchman was most sensitive. Strickland employed not the rapier of sarcasm but the bludgeon of invective. The attack was so unprovoked that Stroeve, taken unawares, was defenceless. He reminded you of a frightened sheep running aimlessly hither and thither. He was startled and amazed. At last the tears ran from his eyes. And the worst of it was that, though you hated Strickland, and the exhibition was horrible, it was impossible not to laugh. Dirk Stroeve was one of those unlucky persons whose most sincere emotions are ridiculous.

But after all when I look back upon that winter in Paris, my

---

5   This picture, formerly in the possession of a wealthy manufacturer at Lille, who fled from that city on the approach of the Germans, is now in the National Gallery at Stockholm. The Swede is adept at the gentle pastime of fishing in troubled waters.

pleasantest recollection is of Dirk Stroeve. There was something very charming in his little household. He and his wife made a picture which the imagination gratefully dwelt upon, and the simplicity of his love for her had a deliberate grace. He remained absurd, but the sincerity of his passion excited one's sympathy. I could understand how his wife must feel for him, and I was glad that her affection was so tender. If she had any sense of humour, it must amuse her that he should place her on a pedestal and worship her with such an honest idolatry, but even while she laughed she must have been pleased and touched. He was the constant lover, and though she grew old, losing her rounded lines and her fair comeliness, to him she would certainly never alter. To him she would always be the loveliest woman in the world. There was a pleasing grace in the orderliness of their lives. They had but the studio, a bedroom, and a tiny kitchen. Mrs. Stroeve did all the housework herself; and while Dirk painted bad pictures, she went marketing, cooked the luncheon, sewed, occupied herself like a busy ant all the day; and in the evening sat in the studio, sewing again, while Dirk played music which I am sure was far beyond her comprehension. He played with taste, but with more feeling than was always justified, and into his music poured all his honest, sentimental, exuberant soul.

Their life in its own way was an idyl, and it managed to achieve a singular beauty. The absurdity that clung to everything connected with Dirk Stroeve gave it a curious note, like an unresolved discord, but made it somehow more modern, more human; like a rough joke thrown into a serious scene, it heightened the poignancy which all beauty has.

XXIV

SHORTLY BEFORE CHRISTMAS Dirk Stroeve came to ask me to spend the holiday with him. He had a characteristic sentimentality about the day and wanted to pass it among his friends with suitable ceremonies. Neither of us had seen Strickland for two or three weeks—I because I had been busy with friends who were spending a little while in Paris, and Stroeve because, having quarreled with him more violently than usual, he had made up his mind to have nothing more to do with him. Strickland was impossible, and he swore never to speak to him again. But the season touched him with gentle feeling, and he hated the thought of Strickland spending Christmas Day by himself; he ascribed his own emotions to him, and could not bear that on an occasion given up to good-fellowship the lonely painter should be abandoned to his own melancholy. Stroeve had set up a Christmas-tree in his studio, and I suspected that we should both find absurd little presents hanging on its festive branches; but he was shy about seeing Strickland again; it was a little humiliating to forgive so easily insults so outrageous, and he wished me to be present at the reconciliation on which he was determined.

We walked together down the Avenue de Clichy, but Strickland was not in the cafe. It was too cold to sit outside, and we took our places on leather benches within. It was hot and stuffy, and the air was gray with smoke. Strickland did not come, but presently we saw the French painter who occasionally played chess with him. I had formed a casual acquaintance with him, and he sat down at our table. Stroeve asked him if he had seen Strickland.

"He's ill," he said. "Didn't you know?"

"Seriously?"

"Very, I understand."

Stroeve's face grew white.

"Why didn't he write and tell me? How stupid of me to quarrel with him. We must go to him at once. He can have no one to look after him. Where does he live?"

"I have no idea," said the Frenchman.

We discovered that none of us knew how to find him. Stroeve grew more and more distressed.

"He might die, and not a soul would know anything about it. It's dreadful. I can't bear the thought. We must find him at once."

I tried to make Stroeve understand that it was absurd to hunt vaguely about Paris. We must first think of some plan.

"Yes; but all this time he may be dying, and when we get there it may be too late to do anything."

"Sit still and let us think," I said impatiently.

The only address I knew was the Hotel des Belges, but Strickland had long left that, and they would have no recollection of him. With that queer idea of his to keep his whereabouts secret, it was unlikely that, on leaving, he had said where he was going. Besides, it was more than five years ago. I felt pretty sure that he had not moved far. If he continued to frequent the same cafe as when he had stayed at the hotel, it was probably because it was the most convenient. Suddenly I remembered that he had got his commission to paint a portrait through the baker from whom he bought his bread, and it struck me that there one might find his address. I called for a directory and looked out the bakers. There were five in the immediate neighbourhood, and the only thing was to go to all of them. Stroeve accompanied me unwillingly. His own plan was to run up and down the streets that led out of the Avenue de Clichy and ask at every house if Strickland lived there. My commonplace scheme was, after all, effective, for in the second shop we asked at the woman behind the counter acknowledged that she knew him. She was not certain where he lived, but it was in one of the three houses opposite. Luck favoured us, and in the first we tried the concierge told us that we should find him on the top floor.

"It appears that he's ill," said Stroeve.

"It may be," answered the concierge indifferently. "*En effet*, I have not seen him for several days."

Stroeve ran up the stairs ahead of me, and when I reached the top floor I found him talking to a workman in his shirt-sleeves who had opened a door at which Stroeve had knocked. He pointed to another door. He believed that the person who lived there was a painter. He had not seen him for a week. Stroeve made as though he were about to knock, and then turned to me with a gesture of helplessness. I saw that he was panic-stricken.

"Supposing he's dead?"

"Not he," I said.

I knocked. There was no answer. I tried the handle, and found the door unlocked. I walked in, and Stroeve followed me. The room was in darkness. I could only see that it was an attic, with a sloping roof; and a faint glimmer, no more than a less profound obscurity, came from a skylight.

"Strickland," I called.

There was no answer. It was really rather mysterious, and it seemed to me that Stroeve, standing just behind, was trembling in his shoes. For a moment I hesitated to strike a light. I dimly perceived a bed in the corner, and I wondered whether the light would disclose lying on it a dead body.

"Haven't you got a match, you fool?"

Strickland's voice, coming out of the darkness, harshly, made me start.

Stroeve cried out.

"Oh, my God, I thought you were dead."

I struck a match, and looked about for a candle. I had a rapid glimpse of a tiny apartment, half room, half studio, in which was nothing but a bed, canvases with their faces to the wall, an easel, a table, and a chair. There was no carpet on the floor. There was no fireplace. On the table, crowded with paints, palette-knives, and litter of all kinds, was the end of a candle. I lit it. Strickland was lying in the bed, uncomfortably because it was too small for him, and he had put all his clothes over him for warmth. It was obvious at a glance that he was in a high fever. Stroeve, his voice cracking with emotion, went up to him.

"Oh, my poor friend, what is the matter with you? I had no idea you were ill. Why didn't you let me know? You must know I'd have done anything in the world for you. Were you thinking of what I said? I didn't mean it. I was wrong. It was stupid of me to take offence."

"Go to hell," said Strickland.

"Now, be reasonable. Let me make you comfortable. Haven't you anyone to look after you?"

He looked round the squalid attic in dismay. He tried to arrange the bed-clothes. Strickland, breathing laboriously, kept an angry silence. He gave me a resentful glance. I stood quite quietly, looking at him.

"If you want to do something for me, you can get me some milk," he said at last. "I haven't been able to get out for two days." There was an empty bottle by the side of the bed, which had contained milk, and in a piece of newspaper a few crumbs.

"What have you been having?" I asked.

"Nothing."

"For how long?" cried Stroeve. "Do you mean to say you've had nothing to eat or drink for two days? It's horrible."

"I've had water."

His eyes dwelt for a moment on a large can within reach of an outstretched arm.

"I'll go immediately," said Stroeve. "Is there anything you fancy?"

I suggested that he should get a thermometer, and a few grapes, and some bread. Stroeve, glad to make himself useful, clattered down the stairs.

"Damned fool," muttered Strickland.

I felt his pulse. It was beating quickly and feebly. I asked him one or two questions, but he would not answer, and when I pressed him he turned his face irritably to the wall. The only thing was to wait in silence. In ten minutes Stroeve, panting, came back. Besides what I had suggested, he brought candles, and meat-juice, and a spirit-lamp. He was a practical little fellow, and without delay set about making bread-and-milk. I took Strickland's temperature. It was a hundred and four. He was obviously very ill.

XXV

PRESENTLY WE LEFT him. Dirk was going home to dinner, and I proposed to find a doctor and bring him to see Strickland; but when we got down into the street, fresh after the stuffy attic, the Dutchman begged me to go immediately to his studio. He had something in mind which he would not tell me, but he insisted that it was very necessary for me to accompany him. Since I did not think a doctor could at the moment do any more than we had done, I consented. We found Blanche Stroeve laying the table for dinner. Dirk went up to her, and took both her hands.

"Dear one, I want you to do something for me," he said.

She looked at him with the grave cheerfulness which was one of her charms. His red face was shining with sweat, and he had a look of comic agitation, but there was in his round, surprised eyes an eager light.

"Strickland is very ill. He may be dying. He is alone in a filthy attic, and there is not a soul to look after him. I want you to let me bring him here."

She withdrew her hands quickly, I had never seen her make so rapid a movement; and her cheeks flushed.

"Oh no."

"Oh, my dear one, don't refuse. I couldn't bear to leave him where he is. I shouldn't sleep a wink for thinking of him."

"I have no objection to your nursing him."

Her voice was cold and distant.

"But he'll die."

"Let him."

Stroeve gave a little gasp. He wiped his face. He turned to me for support, but I did not know what to say.

"He's a great artist."

"What do I care? I hate him."

"Oh, my love, my precious, you don't mean that. I beseech you to let me bring him here. We can make him comfortable. Perhaps we can save him. He shall be no trouble to you. I will do everything. We'll make him up a bed in the studio. We can't let him die like a dog. It would be inhuman."

"Why can't he go to a hospital?"

"A hospital! He needs the care of loving hands. He must be treated with infinite tact."

I was surprised to see how moved she was. She went on laying the table, but her hands trembled.

"I have no patience with you. Do you think if you were ill he would stir a finger to help you?"

"But what does that matter? I should have you to nurse me. It wouldn't be necessary. And besides, I'm different; I'm not of any importance."

"You have no more spirit than a mongrel cur. You lie down on the ground and ask people to trample on you."

Stroeve gave a little laugh. He thought he understood the reason of his wife's attitude.

"Oh, my poor dear, you're thinking of that day he came here to look at my pictures. What does it matter if he didn't think them any good? It was stupid of me to show them to him. I dare say they're not very good."

He looked round the studio ruefully. On the easel was a half-finished picture of a smiling Italian peasant, holding a bunch of grapes over the head of a dark-eyed girl.

"Even if he didn't like them he should have been civil. He needn't have insulted you. He showed that he despised you, and you lick his hand. Oh, I hate him."

"Dear child, he has genius. You don't think I believe that I have it. I wish I had; but I know it when I see it, and I honour it with all my heart. It's the most wonderful thing in the world. It's a great burden to its possessors. We should be very tolerant with them, and very patient."

I stood apart, somewhat embarrassed by the domestic scene, and wondered why Stroeve had insisted on my coming with him. I saw that his wife was on the verge of tears.

"But it's not only because he's a genius that I ask you to let me bring him here; it's because he's a human being, and he is ill and poor."

"I will never have him in my house—never."

Stroeve turned to me.

"Tell her that it's a matter of life and death. It's impossible to leave him in that wretched hole."

"It's quite obvious that it would be much easier to nurse him here," I said, "but of course it would be very inconvenient. I have an idea that someone will have to be with him day and night."

"My love, it's not you who would shirk a little trouble."

"If he comes here, I shall go," said Mrs. Stroeve violently.

"I don't recognize you. You're so good and kind."

"Oh, for goodness sake, let me be. You drive me to distraction."

Then at last the tears came. She sank into a chair, and buried her face in her hands. Her shoulders shook convulsively. In a moment Dirk was on his knees beside her, with his arms round her, kissing her, calling her all sorts of pet names, and the facile tears ran down his own cheeks. Presently she released herself and dried her eyes.

"Leave me alone," she said, not unkindly; and then to me, trying to smile: "What must you think of me?"

Stroeve, looking at her with perplexity, hesitated. His forehead was all puckered, and his red mouth set in a pout. He reminded me oddly of an agitated guinea-pig.

"Then it's No, darling?" he said at last.

She gave a gesture of lassitude. She was exhausted.

"The studio is yours. Everything belongs to you. If you want to bring him here, how can I prevent you?"

A sudden smile flashed across his round face.

"Then you consent? I knew you would. Oh, my precious."

Suddenly she pulled herself together. She looked at him with haggard eyes. She clasped her hands over her heart as though its beating were intolerable.

"Oh, Dirk, I've never since we met asked you to do anything for me."

"You know there's nothing in the world that I wouldn't do for you."

"I beg you not to let Strickland come here. Anyone else you like. Bring a thief, a drunkard, any outcast off the streets, and I promise you I'll do everything I can for them gladly. But I beseech you not to bring Strickland here."

"But why?"

"I'm frightened of him. I don't know why, but there's something in him that terrifies me. He'll do us some great harm. I know it. I feel it. If you bring him here it can only end badly."

"But how unreasonable!"

"No, no. I know I'm right. Something terrible will happen to us."

"Because we do a good action?"

She was panting now, and in her face was a terror which was inexplicable. I do not know what she thought. I felt that she was possessed by some shapeless dread which robbed her of all self-control. As a rule she was so calm; her agitation now was amazing. Stroeve looked at her for a while with puzzled consternation.

"You are my wife; you are dearer to me than anyone in the world. No one shall come here without your entire consent."

She closed her eyes for a moment, and I thought she was going to faint. I was a little impatient with her; I had not suspected that she was so neurotic a woman. Then I heard Stroeve's voice again. It seemed to break oddly on the silence.

"Haven't you been in bitter distress once when a helping hand was held out to you? You know how much it means. Couldn't you like to do someone a good turn when you have the chance?"

The words were ordinary enough, and to my mind there was in them something so hortatory that I almost smiled. I was astonished at the effect they had on Blanche Stroeve. She started a little, and gave her husband a long look. His eyes were fixed on the ground. I did not know why he seemed embarrassed. A faint colour came into her cheeks, and then her face became white—more than white, ghastly; you felt that the blood had shrunk away from the whole surface of her body; and even her hands were pale. A shiver passed through her. The silence of the studio seemed to gather body, so that it became an almost palpable presence. I was bewildered.

"Bring Strickland here, Dirk. I'll do my best for him."

"My precious," he smiled.

He wanted to take her in his arms, but she avoided him.

"Don't be affectionate before strangers, Dirk," she said. "It makes me feel such a fool."

Her manner was quite normal again, and no one could have told that so shortly before she had been shaken by such a great emotion.

XXVI

Next day we moved Strickland. It needed a good deal of firmness and still more patience to induce him to come, but he was really too ill to offer any effective resistance to Stroeve's entreaties and to my determination. We dressed him, while he feebly cursed us, got him downstairs, into a cab, and eventually to Stroeve's studio. He was so exhausted by the time we arrived that he allowed us to put him to bed without a word. He was ill for six weeks. At one time it looked as though he could not live more than a few hours, and I am convinced that it was only through the Dutchman's doggedness that he pulled

through. I have never known a more difficult patient. It was not that
he was exacting and querulous; on the contrary, he never complained,
he asked for nothing, he was perfectly silent; but he seemed to resent the care that was taken of him; he received all inquiries about
his feelings or his needs with a jibe, a sneer, or an oath. I found him
detestable, and as soon as he was out of danger I had no hesitation in
telling him so.

"Go to hell," he answered briefly.

Dirk Stroeve, giving up his work entirely, nursed Strickland
with tenderness and sympathy. He was dexterous to make him comfortable, and he exercised a cunning of which I should never have
thought him capable to induce him to take the medicines prescribed
by the doctor. Nothing was too much trouble for him. Though his
means were adequate to the needs of himself and his wife, he certainly had no money to waste; but now he was wantonly extravagant
in the purchase of delicacies, out of season and dear, which might
tempt Strickland's capricious appetite. I shall never forget the tactful patience with which he persuaded him to take nourishment. He
was never put out by Strickland's rudeness; if it was merely sullen,
he appeared not to notice it; if it was aggressive, he only chuckled.
When Strickland, recovering somewhat, was in a good humour and
amused himself by laughing at him, he deliberately did absurd things
to excite his ridicule. Then he would give me little happy glances, so
that I might notice in how much better form the patient was. Stroeve
was sublime.

But it was Blanche who most surprised me. She proved herself
not only a capable, but a devoted nurse. There was nothing in her to
remind you that she had so vehemently struggled against her husband's wish to bring Strickland to the studio. She insisted on doing
her share of the offices needful to the sick. She arranged his bed so
that it was possible to change the sheet without disturbing him. She
washed him. When I remarked on her competence, she told me with
that pleasant little smile of hers that for a while she had worked in a
hospital. She gave no sign that she hated Strickland so desperately.
She did not speak to him much, but she was quick to forestall his
wants. For a fortnight it was necessary that someone should stay with

him all night, and she took turns at watching with her husband. I wondered what she thought during the long darkness as she sat by the bedside. Strickland was a weird figure as he lay there, thinner than ever, with his ragged red beard and his eyes staring feverishly into vacancy; his illness seemed to have made them larger, and they had an unnatural brightness.

"Does he ever talk to you in the night?" I asked her once.

"Never."

"Do you dislike him as much as you did?"

"More, if anything."

She looked at me with her calm gray eyes. Her expression was so placid, it was hard to believe that she was capable of the violent emotion I had witnessed.

"Has he ever thanked you for what you do for him?"

"No," she smiled.

"He's inhuman."

"He's abominable."

Stroeve was, of course, delighted with her. He could not do enough to show his gratitude for the whole-hearted devotion with which she had accepted the burden he laid on her. But he was a little puzzled by the behaviour of Blanche and Strickland towards one another.

"Do you know, I've seen them sit there for hours together without saying a word?"

On one occasion, when Strickland was so much better that in a day or two he was to get up, I sat with them in the studio. Dirk and I were talking. Mrs. Stroeve sewed, and I thought I recognised the shirt she was mending as Strickland's. He lay on his back; he did not speak. Once I saw that his eyes were fixed on Blanche Stroeve, and there was in them a curious irony. Feeling their gaze, she raised her own, and for a moment they stared at one another. I could not quite understand her expression. Her eyes had in them a strange perplexity, and perhaps—but why?—alarm. In a moment Strickland looked away and idly surveyed the ceiling, but she continued to stare at him, and now her look was quite inexplicable.

In a few days Strickland began to get up. He was nothing but skin and bone. His clothes hung upon him like rags on a scarecrow. With his untidy beard and long hair, his features, always a little larger than life, now emphasised by illness, he had an extraordinary aspect; but it was so odd that it was not quite ugly. There was something monumental in his ungainliness. I do not know how to express precisely the impression he made upon me. It was not exactly spirituality that was obvious, though the screen of the flesh seemed almost transparent, because there was in his face an outrageous sensuality; but, though it sounds nonsense, it seemed as though his sensuality were curiously spiritual. There was in him something primitive. He seemed to partake of those obscure forces of nature which the Greeks personified in shapes part human and part beast, the satyr and the faun. I thought of Marsyas, whom the god flayed because he had dared to rival him in song. Strickland seemed to bear in his heart strange harmonies and unadventured patterns, and I foresaw for him an end of torture and despair. I had again the feeling that he was possessed of a devil; but you could not say that it was a devil of evil, for it was a primitive force that existed before good and ill.

He was still too weak to paint, and he sat in the studio, silent, occupied with God knows what dreams, or reading. The books he liked were queer; sometimes I would find him poring over the poems of Mallarme, and he read them as a child reads, forming the words with his lips, and I wondered what strange emotion he got from those subtle cadences and obscure phrases; and again I found him absorbed in the detective novels of Gaboriau. I amused myself by thinking that in his choice of books he showed pleasantly the irreconcilable sides of his fantastic nature. It was singular to notice that even in the weak state of his body he had no thought for its comfort. Stroeve liked his ease, and in his studio were a couple of heavily upholstered arm-chairs and a large divan. Strickland would not go near them, not from any affectation of stoicism, for I found him seated on a three-legged stool when I went into the studio one day and he was alone, but because he did not like them. For choice he sat on a kitchen chair without arms. It often exasperated me to see him. I never knew a man so entirely indifferent to his surroundings.

XXVII

TWO OR THREE weeks passed. One morning, having come to a pause in my work, I thought I would give myself a holiday, and I went to the Louvre. I wandered about looking at the pictures I knew so well, and let my fancy play idly with the emotions they suggested. I sauntered into the long gallery, and there suddenly saw Stroeve. I smiled, for his appearance, so rotund and yet so startled, could never fail to excite a smile, and then as I came nearer I noticed that he seemed singularly disconsolate. He looked woebegone and yet ridiculous, like a man who has fallen into the water with all his clothes on, and, being rescued from death, frightened still, feels that he only looks a fool. Turning round, he stared at me, but I perceived that he did not see me. His round blue eyes looked harassed behind his glasses.

"Stroeve," I said.

He gave a little start, and then smiled, but his smile was rueful.

"Why are you idling in this disgraceful fashion?" I asked gaily.

"It's a long time since I was at the Louvre. I thought I'd come and see if they had anything new."

"But you told me you had to get a picture finished this week."

"Strickland's painting in my studio."

"Well?"

"I suggested it myself. He's not strong enough to go back to his own place yet. I thought we could both paint there. Lots of fellows in the Quarter share a studio. I thought it would be fun. I've always thought it would be jolly to have someone to talk to when one was tired of work."

He said all this slowly, detaching statement from statement with a little awkward silence, and he kept his kind, foolish eyes fixed on mine. They were full of tears.

"I don't think I understand," I said.

"Strickland can't work with anyone else in the studio."

"Damn it all, it's your studio. That's his lookout."

He looked at me pitifully. His lips were trembling.

"What happened?" I asked, rather sharply.

He hesitated and flushed. He glanced unhappily at one of the pictures on the wall.

"He wouldn't let me go on painting. He told me to get out."

"But why didn't you tell him to go to hell?"

"He turned me out. I couldn't very well struggle with him. He threw my hat after me, and locked the door."

I was furious with Strickland, and was indignant with myself, because Dirk Stroeve cut such an absurd figure that I felt inclined to laugh.

"But what did your wife say?"

"She'd gone out to do the marketing."

"Is he going to let her in?"

"I don't know."

I gazed at Stroeve with perplexity. He stood like a schoolboy with whom a master is finding fault.

"Shall I get rid of Strickland for you?" I asked.

He gave a little start, and his shining face grew very red.

"No. You'd better not do anything."

He nodded to me and walked away. It was clear that for some reason he did not want to discuss the matter. I did not understand.

XXVIII

THE EXPLANATION CAME a week later. It was about ten o' clock at night; I had been dining by myself at a restaurant, and having returned to my small apartment, was sitting in my parlour, reading I heard the cracked tinkling of the bell, and, going into the corridor, opened the door. Stroeve stood before me.

"Can I come in?" he asked.

In the dimness of the landing I could not see him very well, but there was something in his voice that surprised me. I knew he was of abstemious habit or I should have thought he had been drinking. I led the way into my sitting room and asked him to sit down.

"Thank God I've found you," he said.

"What's the matter?" I asked in astonishment at his vehemence.

I was able now to see him well. As a rule he was neat in his person, but now his clothes were in disorder. He looked suddenly bedraggled. I was convinced he had been drinking, and I smiled. I was on the point of chaffing him on his state.

"I didn't know where to go," he burst out. "I came here earlier, but you weren't in."

"I dined late," I said.

I changed my mind: it was not liquor that had driven him to this obvious desperation. His face, usually so rosy, was now strangely mottled. His hands trembled.

"Has anything happened?" I asked.

"My wife has left me."

He could hardly get the words out. He gave a little gasp, and the tears began to trickle down his round cheeks. I did not know what to say. My first thought was that she had come to the end of her forbearance with his infatuation for Strickland, and, goaded by the latter's cynical behaviour, had insisted that he should be turned out. I knew her capable of temper, for all the calmness of her manner; and if Stroeve still refused, she might easily have flung out of the studio with vows never to return. But the little man was so distressed that I could not smile.

"My dear fellow, don't be unhappy. She'll come back. You mustn't take very seriously what women say when they're in a passion."

"You don't understand. She's in love with Strickland."

"What!" I was startled at this, but the idea had no sooner taken possession of me than I saw it was absurd. "How can you be so silly? You don't mean to say you're jealous of Strickland?" I almost laughed. "You know very well that she can't bear the sight of him."

"You don't understand," he moaned.

"You're an hysterical ass," I said a little impatiently. "Let me give you a whisky-and-soda, and you'll feel better."

I supposed that for some reason or other—and Heaven knows what ingenuity men exercise to torment themselves—Dirk had got it into his head that his wife cared for Strickland, and with his genius for blundering he might quite well have offended her so that, to anger him, perhaps, she had taken pains to foster his suspicion.

"Look here," I said, "let's go back to your studio. If you've made a fool of yourself you must eat humble pie. Your wife doesn't strike me as the sort of woman to bear malice."

"How can I go back to the studio?" he said wearily. "They're there. I've left it to them."

"Then it's not your wife who's left you; it's you who've left your wife."

"For God's sake don't talk to me like that."

Still I could not take him seriously. I did not for a moment believe what he had told me. But he was in very real distress.

"Well, you've come here to talk to me about it. You'd better tell me the whole story."

"This afternoon I couldn't stand it any more. I went to Strickland and told him I thought he was quite well enough to go back to his own place. I wanted the studio myself."

"No one but Strickland would have needed telling," I said. "What did he say?"

"He laughed a little; you know how he laughs, not as though he were amused, but as though you were a damned fool, and said he'd go at once. He began to put his things together. You remember I fetched from his room what I thought he needed, and he asked Blanche for a piece of paper and some string to make a parcel."

Stroeve stopped, gasping, and I thought he was going to faint. This was not at all the story I had expected him to tell me.

"She was very pale, but she brought the paper and the string. He didn't say anything. He made the parcel and he whistled a tune. He took no notice of either of us. His eyes had an ironic smile in them. My heart was like lead. I was afraid something was going to happen, and I wished I hadn't spoken. He looked round for his hat. Then she spoke:

"'I'm going with Strickland, Dirk,' she said. 'I can't live with you any more.'

"I tried to speak, but the words wouldn't come. Strickland didn't say anything. He went on whistling as though it had nothing to do with him."

Stroeve stopped again and mopped his face. I kept quite still. I believed him now, and I was astounded. But all the same I could not understand.

Then he told me, in a trembling voice, with the tears pouring down his cheeks, how he had gone up to her, trying to take her in his arms, but she had drawn away and begged him not to touch her. He implored her not to leave him. He told her how passionately he loved her, and reminded her of all the devotion he had lavished upon her. He spoke to her of the happiness of their life. He was not angry with her. He did not reproach her.

"Please let me go quietly, Dirk," she said at last. "Don't you understand that I love Strickland? Where he goes I shall go."

"But you must know that he'll never make you happy. For your own sake don't go. You don't know what you've got to look forward to."

"It's your fault. You insisted on his coming here."

He turned to Strickland.

"Have mercy on her," he implored him. "You can't let her do anything so mad."

"She can do as she chooses," said Strickland. "She's not forced to come."

"My choice is made," she said, in a dull voice.

Strickland's injurious calm robbed Stroeve of the rest of his self-control. Blind rage seized him, and without knowing what he was doing he flung himself on Strickland. Strickland was taken by surprise and he staggered, but he was very strong, even after his illness, and in a moment, he did not exactly know how, Stroeve found himself on the floor.

"You funny little man," said Strickland.

Stroeve picked himself up. He noticed that his wife had remained perfectly still, and to be made ridiculous before her increased his humiliation. His spectacles had tumbled off in the struggle, and he could not immediately see them. She picked them up and silently handed them to him. He seemed suddenly to realise his unhappiness, and though he knew he was making himself still more absurd, he began to cry. He hid his face in his hands. The others watched him without a word. They did not move from where they stood.

"Oh, my dear," he groaned at last, "how can you be so cruel?"

"I can't help myself, Dirk," she answered.

"I've worshipped you as no woman was ever worshipped before.

If in anything I did I displeased you, why didn't you tell me, and I'd have changed. I've done everything I could for you."

She did not answer. Her face was set, and he saw that he was only boring her. She put on a coat and her hat. She moved towards the door, and he saw that in a moment she would be gone. He went up to her quickly and fell on his knees before her, seizing her hands: he abandoned all self-respect.

"Oh, don't go, my darling. I can't live without you; I shall kill myself. If I've done anything to offend you I beg you to forgive me. Give me another chance. I'll try harder still to make you happy."

"Get up, Dirk. You're making yourself a perfect fool."

He staggered to his feet, but still he would not let her go.

"Where are you going?" he said hastily. "You don't know what Strickland's place is like. You can't live there. It would be awful."

"If I don't care, I don't see why you should."

"Stay a minute longer. I must speak. After all, you can't grudge me that."

"What is the good? I've made up my mind. Nothing that you can say will make me alter it."

He gulped, and put his hand to his heart to ease its painful beating.

"I'm not going to ask you to change your mind, but I want you to listen to me for a minute. It's the last thing I shall ever ask you. Don't refuse me that."

She paused, looking at him with those reflective eyes of hers, which now were so different to him. She came back into the studio and leaned against the table.

"Well?"

Stroeve made a great effort to collect himself.

"You must be a little reasonable. You can't live on air, you know. Strickland hasn't got a penny."

"I know."

"You'll suffer the most awful privations. You know why he took so long to get well. He was half starved."

"I can earn money for him."

"How?"

"I don't know. I shall find a way."

A horrible thought passed through the Dutchman's mind, and he shuddered.

"I think you must be mad. I don't know what has come over you."

She shrugged her shoulders.

"Now may I go?"

"Wait one second longer."

He looked round his studio wearily; he had loved it because her presence had made it gay and homelike; he shut his eyes for an instant; then he gave her a long look as though to impress on his mind the picture of her. He got up and took his hat.

"No; I'll go."

"You?"

She was startled. She did not know what he meant.

"I can't bear to think of you living in that horrible, filthy attic. After all, this is your home just as much as mine. You'll be comfortable here. You'll be spared at least the worst privations."

He went to the drawer in which he kept his money and took out several bank-notes.

"I would like to give you half what I've got here."

He put them on the table. Neither Strickland nor his wife spoke. Then he recollected something else.

"Will you pack up my clothes and leave them with the concierge? I'll come and fetch them to-morrow." He tried to smile. "Good-bye, my dear. I'm grateful for all the happiness you gave me in the past."

He walked out and closed the door behind him. With my mind's eye I saw Strickland throw his hat on a table, and, sitting down, begin to smoke a cigarette.

XXIX

I KEPT SILENCE for a little while, thinking of what Stroeve had told me. I could not stomach his weakness, and he saw my disapproval. "You know as well as I do how Strickland lived," he said tremulously. "I couldn't let her live in those circumstances—I simply couldn't."

"That's your business," I answered.

"What would *you* have done?" he asked.

"She went with her eyes open. If she had to put up with certain inconveniences it was her own lookout."

"Yes; but, you see, you don't love her."

"Do you love her still?"

"Oh, more than ever. Strickland isn't the man to make a woman happy. It can't last. I want her to know that I shall never fail her."

"Does that mean that you're prepared to take her back?"

"I shouldn't hesitate. Why, she'll want me more than ever then. When she's alone and humiliated and broken it would be dreadful if she had nowhere to go."

He seemed to bear no resentment. I suppose it was commonplace in me that I felt slightly outraged at his lack of spirit. Perhaps he guessed what was in my mind, for he said:

"I couldn't expect her to love me as I loved her. I'm a buffoon. I'm not the sort of man that women love. I've always known that. I can't blame her if she's fallen in love with Strickland."

"You certainly have less vanity than any man I've ever known," I said.

"I love her so much better than myself. It seems to me that when vanity comes into love it can only be because really you love yourself best. After all, it constantly happens that a man when he's married falls in love with somebody else; when he gets over it he returns to his wife, and she takes him back, and everyone thinks it very natural. Why should it be different with women?"

"I dare say that's logical," I smiled, "but most men are made differently, and they can't."

But while I talked to Stroeve I was puzzling over the suddenness of the whole affair. I could not imagine that he had had no warning. I remembered the curious look I had seen in Blanche Stroeve's eyes; perhaps its explanation was that she was growing dimly conscious of a feeling in her heart that surprised and alarmed her.

"Did you have no suspicion before to-day that there was anything between them?" I asked.

He did not answer for a while. There was a pencil on the table, and unconsciously he drew a head on the blotting-paper.

"Please say so, if you hate my asking you questions," I said.

"It eases me to talk. Oh, if you knew the frightful anguish in my heart." He threw the pencil down. "Yes, I've known it for a fortnight. I knew it before she did."

"Why on earth didn't you send Strickland packing?"

"I couldn't believe it. It seemed so improbable. She couldn't bear the sight of him. It was more than improbable; it was incredible. I thought it was merely jealousy. You see, I've always been jealous, but I trained myself never to show it; I was jealous of every man she knew; I was jealous of you. I knew she didn't love me as I loved her. That was only natural, wasn't it? But she allowed me to love her, and that was enough to make me happy. I forced myself to go out for hours together in order to leave them by themselves; I wanted to punish myself for suspicions which were unworthy of me; and when I came back I found they didn't want me—not Strickland, he didn't care if I was there or not, but Blanche. She shuddered when I went to kiss her. When at last I was certain I didn't know what to do; I knew they'd only laugh at me if I made a scene. I thought if I held my tongue and pretended not to see, everything would come right. I made up my mind to get him away quietly, without quarrelling. Oh, if you only knew what I've suffered!"

Then he told me again of his asking Strickland to go. He chose his moment carefully, and tried to make his request sound casual; but he could not master the trembling of his voice; and he felt himself that into words that he wished to seem jovial and friendly there crept the bitterness of his jealousy. He had not expected Strickland to take him up on the spot and make his preparations to go there and then; above all, he had not expected his wife's decision to go with him. I saw that now he wished with all his heart that he had held his tongue. He preferred the anguish of jealousy to the anguish of separation.

"I wanted to kill him, and I only made a fool of myself."

He was silent for a long time, and then he said what I knew was in his mind.

"If I'd only waited, perhaps it would have gone all right. I shouldn't have been so impatient. Oh, poor child, what have I driven her to?"

I shrugged my shoulders, but did not speak. I had no sympathy for Blanche Stroeve, but knew that it would only pain poor Dirk if I told him exactly what I thought of her.

He had reached that stage of exhaustion when he could not stop talking. He went over again every word of the scene. Now something occurred to him that he had not told me before; now he discussed what he ought to have said instead of what he did say; then he lamented his blindness. He regretted that he had done this, and blamed himself that he had omitted the other. It grew later and later, and at last I was as tired as he.

"What are you going to do now?" I said finally.

"What can I do? I shall wait till she sends for me."

"Why don't you go away for a bit?"

"No, no; I must be at hand when she wants me."

For the present he seemed quite lost. He had made no plans. When I suggested that he should go to bed he said he could not sleep; he wanted to go out and walk about the streets till day. He was evidently in no state to be left alone. I persuaded him to stay the night with me, and I put him into my own bed. I had a divan in my sitting-room, and could very well sleep on that. He was by now so worn out that he could not resist my firmness. I gave him a sufficient dose of veronal to insure his unconsciousness for several hours. I thought that was the best service I could render him.

XXX

BUT THE BED I made up for myself was sufficiently uncomfortable to give me a wakeful night, and I thought a good deal of what the unlucky Dutchman had told me. I was not so much puzzled by Blanche Stroeve's action, for I saw in that merely the result of a physical appeal. I do not suppose she had ever really cared for her husband, and what I had taken for love was no more than the feminine response to caresses and comfort which in the minds of most women passes for it. It is a passive feeling capable of being roused for any object, as the vine can grow on any tree; and the wisdom of the world recognises its strength when it urges a girl to marry the man who wants her with the assurance that love will follow. It is an emotion made up of the satisfaction in security, pride of property, the pleasure of being desired, the gratification of a household, and it is only by an amiable vanity that women ascribe to it spiritual value. It is an emotion which is defenceless against passion. I suspected that Blanche Stroeve's violent dislike of Strickland had in it from the beginning a vague element of sexual attraction. Who am I that I should seek to unravel the mysterious intricacies of sex? Perhaps Stroeve's passion excited without satisfying that part of her nature, and she hated Strickland because she felt in him the power to give her what she needed. I think she was quite sincere when she struggled against her husband's desire to bring him into the studio; I think she was frightened of him, though she knew not why; and I remembered how she had foreseen disaster. I think in some curious way the horror which she felt for him was a transference of the horror which she felt for herself because he so strangely troubled her. His appearance was wild and uncouth; there was aloofness in his eyes and sensuality in his mouth; he was big and strong; he gave the impression of untamed passion; and perhaps she felt in him, too, that sinister element which had made me think of those wild beings of the world's early history when matter, retaining its early connection with the earth, seemed to possess yet a spirit of its own. If he affected her at all, it was inevitable that she should love or hate him. She hated him.

And then I fancy that the daily intimacy with the sick man moved her strangely. She raised his head to give him food, and it was heavy against her hand; when she had fed him she wiped his sensual mouth and his red beard. She washed his limbs; they were covered with thick hair; and when she dried his hands, even in his weakness they were strong and sinewy. His fingers were long; they were the capable, fashioning fingers of the artist; and I know not what troubling thoughts they excited in her. He slept very quietly, without a movement, so that he might have been dead, and he was like some wild creature of the woods, resting after a long chase; and she wondered what fancies passed through his dreams. Did he dream of the nymph flying through the woods of Greece with the satyr in hot pursuit? She fled, swift of foot and desperate, but he gained on her step by step, till she felt his hot breath on her neck; and still she fled silently, and silently he pursued, and when at last he seized her was it terror that thrilled her heart or was it ecstasy?

Blanche Stroeve was in the cruel grip of appetite. Perhaps she hated Strickland still, but she hungered for him, and everything that had made up her life till then became of no account. She ceased to be a woman, complex, kind and petulant, considerate and thoughtless; she was a Maenad. She was desire.

But perhaps this is very fanciful; and it may be that she was merely bored with her husband and went to Strickland out of a callous curiosity. She may have had no particular feeling for him, but succumbed to his wish from propinquity or idleness, to find then that she was powerless in a snare of her own contriving. How did I know what were the thoughts and emotions behind that placid brow and those cool gray eyes?

But if one could be certain of nothing in dealing with creatures so incalculable as human beings, there were explanations of Blanche Stroeve's behaviour which were at all events plausible. On the other hand, I did not understand Strickland at all. I racked my brain, but could in no way account for an action so contrary to my conception of him. It was not strange that he should so heartlessly have betrayed his friends' confidence, nor that he hesitated not at all to gratify a whim at the cost of another's misery. That was in his character. He was a man without any conception of gratitude. He had no compassion. The emotions common to most of us simply did not exist in him, and it was as absurd to blame him for not feeling them as for blaming the tiger because he is fierce and cruel. But it was the whim I could not understand.

I could not believe that Strickland had fallen in love with Blanche Stroeve. I did not believe him capable of love. That is an emotion in which tenderness is an essential part, but Strickland had no tenderness either for himself or for others; there is in love a sense of weakness, a desire to protect, an eagerness to do good and to give pleasure—if not unselfishness, at all events a selfishness which marvellously conceals itself; it has in it a certain diffidence. These were not traits which I could imagine in Strickland. Love is absorbing; it takes the lover out of himself; the most clear-sighted, though he may know, cannot realise that his love will cease; it gives body to what he knows is illusion, and, knowing it is nothing else, he loves it better than reality. It makes a man a little more than himself, and at the same time a little less. He ceases to be himself. He is no longer an individual, but a thing, an instrument to some purpose foreign to his ego. Love is never quite devoid of sentimentality, and Strickland was the least inclined to that infirmity of any man I have known. I could not believe that he would ever suffer that possession of himself which love is; he could never endure a foreign yoke. I believed him capable of uprooting from his heart, though it might be with agony, so that he was left battered and ensanguined, anything that came between himself and that uncomprehended craving that urged him constantly to he knew not what. If I have succeeded at all in giving the complicated impression that Strickland made on me, it will not seem outrageous to say that I felt he was at once too great and too small for love.

But I suppose that everyone's conception of the passion is formed on his own idiosyncrasies, and it is different with every different person. A man like Strickland would love in a manner peculiar to himself. It was vain to seek the analysis of his emotion.

XXXI

NEXT DAY, THOUGH I pressed him to remain, Stroeve left me. I offered to fetch his things from the studio, but he insisted on going himself; I think he hoped they had not thought of getting them together, so that he would have an opportunity of seeing his wife again and perhaps inducing her to come back to him. But he found his traps waiting for him in the porter's lodge, and the concierge told him that Blanche had gone out. I do not think he resisted the temptation of giving her an account of his troubles. I found that he was telling them to everyone he knew; he expected sympathy, but only excited ridicule.

He bore himself most unbecomingly. Knowing at what time his wife did her shopping, one day, unable any longer to bear not seeing her, he waylaid her in the street. She would not speak to him, but he insisted on speaking to her. He spluttered out words of apology for any wrong he had committed towards her; he told her he loved her devotedly and begged her to return to him. She would not answer; she walked hurriedly, with averted face. I imagined him with his fat little legs trying to keep up with her. Panting a little in his haste, he told her how miserable he was; he besought her to have mercy on him; he promised, if she would forgive him, to do everything she wanted. He offered to take her for a journey. He told her that Strickland would soon tire of her. When he repeated to me the whole sordid little scene I was outraged. He had shown neither sense nor dignity. He had omitted nothing that could make his wife despise him. There is no cruelty greater than a woman's to a man who loves her and whom she does not love; she has no kindness then, no tolerance even, she has only an insane irritation. Blanche Stroeve stopped suddenly, and as hard as she could slapped her husband's face. She took advantage of his confusion to escape, and ran up the stairs to the studio. No word had passed her lips.

When he told me this he put his hand to his cheek as though he still felt the smart of the blow, and in his eyes was a pain that was heartrending and an amazement that was ludicrous. He looked like an overblown schoolboy, and though I felt so sorry for him, I could hardly help laughing.

Then he took to walking along the street which she must pass through to get to the shops, and he would stand at the corner, on the other side, as she went along. He dared not speak to her again, but sought to put into his round eyes the appeal that was in his heart. I suppose he had some idea that the sight of his misery would touch her. She never made the smallest sign that she saw him. She never even changed the hour of her errands or sought an alternative route. I have an idea that there was some cruelty in her indifference. Perhaps she got enjoyment out of the torture she inflicted. I wondered why she hated him so much.

I begged Stroeve to behave more wisely. His want of spirit was exasperating.

"You're doing no good at all by going on like this," I said. "I think you'd have been wiser if you'd hit her over the head with a stick. She wouldn't have despised you as she does now."

I suggested that he should go home for a while. He had often spoken to me of the silent town, somewhere up in the north of Holland, where his parents still lived. They were poor people. His father was a carpenter, and they dwelt in a little old red-brick house, neat and clean, by the side of a sluggish canal. The streets were wide and empty; for two hundred years the place had been dying, but the houses had the homely stateliness of their time. Rich merchants, sending their wares to the distant Indies, had lived in them calm and prosperous lives, and in their decent decay they kept still an aroma of their splendid past. You could wander along the canal till you came to broad green fields, with windmills here and there, in which cattle, black and white, grazed lazily. I thought that among those surroundings, with their recollections of his boyhood, Dirk Stroeve would forget his unhappiness. But he would not go.

"I must be here when she needs me," he repeated. "It would be dreadful if something terrible happened and I were not at hand."

"What do you think is going to happen?" I asked.

"I don't know. But I'm afraid."

I shrugged my shoulders.

For all his pain, Dirk Stroeve remained a ridiculous object. He might have excited sympathy if he had grown worn and thin. He did nothing of the kind. He remained fat, and his round, red cheeks shone like ripe apples. He had great neatness of person, and he continued to wear his spruce black coat and his bowler hat, always a little too small for him, in a dapper, jaunty manner. He was getting something of a paunch, and sorrow had no effect on it. He looked more than ever like a prosperous bagman. It is hard that a man's exterior should tally so little sometimes with his soul. Dirk Stroeve had the passion of Romeo in the body of Sir Toby Belch. He had a sweet and generous nature, and yet was always blundering; a real feeling for what was beautiful and the capacity to create only what was commonplace; a peculiar delicacy of sentiment and gross manners. He could exercise tact when dealing with the affairs of others, but none when dealing with his own. What a cruel practical joke old Nature played when she flung so many contradictory elements together, and left the man face to face with the perplexing callousness of the universe.

XXXII

I DID NOT see Strickland for several weeks. I was disgusted with him, and if I had had an opportunity should have been glad to tell him so, but I saw no object in seeking him out for the purpose. I am a little shy of any assumption of moral indignation; there is always in it an element of self-satisfaction which makes it awkward to anyone who has a sense of humour. It requires a very lively passion to steel me to my own ridicule. There was a sardonic sincerity in Strickland which made me sensitive to anything that might suggest a pose.

But one evening when I was passing along the Avenue de Clichy in front of the cafe which Strickland frequented and which I now avoided, I ran straight into him. He was accompanied by Blanche Stroeve, and they were just going to Strickland's favourite corner.

"Where the devil have you been all this time?" said he. "I thought you must be away."

His cordiality was proof that he knew I had no wish to speak to him. He was not a man with whom it was worth while wasting politeness.

"No," I said; "I haven't been away."

"Why haven't you been here?"

"There are more cafes in Paris than one, at which to trifle away an idle hour."

Blanche then held out her hand and bade me good-evening. I do not know why I had expected her to be somehow changed; she wore the same gray dress that she wore so often, neat and becoming, and her brow was as candid, her eyes as untroubled, as when I had been used to see her occupied with her household duties in the studio.

"Come and have a game of chess," said Strickland.

I do not know why at the moment I could think of no excuse. I followed them rather sulkily to the table at which Strickland always sat, and he called for the board and the chessmen. They both took the situation so much as a matter of course that I felt it absurd to do otherwise. Mrs. Stroeve watched the game with inscrutable face. She was silent, but she had always been silent. I looked at her mouth for an expression that could give me a clue to what she felt; I watched her eyes for some tell-tale flash, some hint of dismay or bitterness; I scanned her brow for any passing line that might indicate a settling emotion. Her face was a mask that told nothing. Her hands lay on her lap motionless, one in the other loosely clasped. I knew from what I had heard that she was a woman of violent passions; and that injurious blow that she had given Dirk, the man who had loved her so devotedly, betrayed a sudden temper and a horrid cruelty. She had abandoned the safe shelter of her husband's protection and the comfortable ease of a well-provided establishment for what she could not but see was an extreme hazard. It showed an eagerness for adventure, a readiness for the hand-to-mouth, which the care she took of her home and her love of good housewifery made not a little remarkable. She must be a woman of complicated character, and there was something dramatic in the contrast of that with her demure appearance.

I was excited by the encounter, and my fancy worked busily while I sought to concentrate myself on the game I was playing. I always tried my best to beat Strickland, because he was a player who despised the opponent he vanquished; his exultation in victory made defeat more difficult to bear. On the other hand, if he was beaten he took it with complete good-humour. He was a bad winner and a good loser. Those who think that a man betrays his character nowhere more clearly than when he is playing a game might on this draw subtle inferences.

When he had finished I called the waiter to pay for the drinks, and left them. The meeting had been devoid of incident. No word had been said to give me anything to think about, and any surmises I might make were unwarranted. I was intrigued. I could not tell how they were getting on. I would have given much to be a disembodied spirit so that I could see them in the privacy of the studio and hear what they talked about. I had not the smallest indication on which to let my imagination work.

XXXIII

Two or three days later Dirk Stroeve called on me.

"I hear you've seen Blanche," he said.

"How on earth did you find out?"

"I was told by someone who saw you sitting with them. Why didn't you tell me?"

"I thought it would only pain you."

"What do I care if it does? You must know that I want to hear the smallest thing about her."

I waited for him to ask me questions.

"What does she look like?" he said.

"Absolutely unchanged."

"Does she seem happy?"

I shrugged my shoulders.

"How can I tell? We were in a cafe; we were playing chess; I had no opportunity to speak to her."

"Oh, but couldn't you tell by her face?"

I shook my head. I could only repeat that by no word, by no hinted gesture, had she given an indication of her feelings. He must know better than I how great were her powers of self-control. He clasped his hands emotionally.

"Oh, I'm so frightened. I know something is going to happen, something terrible, and I can do nothing to stop it."

"What sort of thing?" I asked.

"Oh, I don't know," he moaned, seizing his head with his hands. "I foresee some terrible catastrophe."

Stroeve had always been excitable, but now he was beside himself; there was no reasoning with him. I thought it probable enough that Blanche Stroeve would not continue to find life with Strickland tolerable, but one of the falsest of proverbs is that you must lie on the bed that you have made. The experience of life shows that people are constantly doing things which must lead to disaster, and yet by some chance manage to evade the result of their folly. When Blanche quarrelled with Strickland she had only to leave him, and her husband was waiting humbly to forgive and forget. I was not prepared to feel any great sympathy for her.

"You see, you don't love her," said Stroeve.

"After all, there's nothing to prove that she is unhappy. For all we know they may have settled down into a most domestic couple."

Stroeve gave me a look with his woeful eyes.

"Of course it doesn't much matter to you, but to me it's so serious, so intensely serious."

I was sorry if I had seemed impatient or flippant.

"Will you do something for me?" asked Stroeve.

"Willingly."

"Will you write to Blanche for me?"

"Why can't you write yourself?"

"I've written over and over again. I didn't expect her to answer. I don't think she reads the letters."

"You make no account of feminine curiosity. Do you think she could resist?"

"She could—mine."

I looked at him quickly. He lowered his eyes. That answer of his seemed to me strangely humiliating. He was conscious that she regarded him with an indifference so profound that the sight of his handwriting would have not the slightest effect on her.

"Do you really believe that she'll ever come back to you?" I asked.

"I want her to know that if the worst comes to the worst she can count on me. That's what I want you to tell her."

I took a sheet of paper.

"What is it exactly you wish me to say?"

This is what I wrote:

Dear Mrs. Stroeve,

> *Dirk wishes me to tell you that if at any time you want him he will be grateful for the opportunity of being of service to you. He has no ill-feeling towards you on account of anything that has happened. His love for you is unaltered. You will always find him at the following address:*

XXXIV

BUT THOUGH I was no less convinced than Stroeve that the connection between Strickland and Blanche would end disastrously, I did not expect the issue to take the tragic form it did. The summer came, breathless and sultry, and even at night there was no coolness to rest one's jaded nerves. The sun-baked streets seemed to give back the heat that had beat down on them during the day, and the passers-by dragged their feet along them wearily. I had not seen Strickland for weeks. Occupied with other things, I had ceased to think of him and his affairs. Dirk, with his vain lamentations, had begun to bore me, and I avoided his society. It was a sordid business, and I was not inclined to trouble myself with it further.

One morning I was working. I sat in my Pyjamas. My thoughts wandered, and I thought of the sunny beaches of Brittany and the freshness of the sea. By my side was the empty bowl in which the concierge had brought me my *cafe au lait* and the fragment of croissant which I had not had appetite enough to eat. I heard the concierge in the next room emptying my bath. There was a tinkle at my bell, and I left her to open the door. In a moment I heard Stroeve's voice asking if I was in. Without moving, I shouted to him to come. He entered the room quickly, and came up to the table at which I sat.

"She's killed herself," he said hoarsely.

"What do you mean?" I cried, startled.

He made movements with his lips as though he were speaking, but no sound issued from them. He gibbered like an idiot. My heart thumped against my ribs, and, I do not know why, I flew into a temper.

"For God's sake, collect yourself, man," I said. "What on earth are you talking about?"

He made despairing gestures with his hands, but still no words came from his mouth. He might have been struck dumb. I do not know what came over me; I took him by the shoulders and shook him. Looking back, I am vexed that I made such a fool of myself; I suppose the last restless nights had shaken my nerves more than I knew.

"Let me sit down," he gasped at length.

I filled a glass with St. Galmier, and gave it to him to drink. I held it to his mouth as though he were a child. He gulped down a mouthful, and some of it was spilt on his shirt-front.

"Who's killed herself?"

I do not know why I asked, for I knew whom he meant. He made an effort to collect himself.

"They had a row last night. He went away."

"Is she dead?"

"No; they've taken her to the hospital."

"Then what are you talking about?" I cried impatiently. "Why did you say she'd killed herself?"

"Don't be cross with me. I can't tell you anything if you talk to me like that."

I clenched my hands, seeking to control my irritation. I attempted a smile.

"I'm sorry. Take your time. Don't hurry, there's a good fellow."

His round blue eyes behind the spectacles were ghastly with terror. The magnifying-glasses he wore distorted them.

"When the concierge went up this morning to take a letter she could get no answer to her ring. She heard someone groaning. The door wasn't locked, and she went in. Blanche was lying on the bed. She'd been frightfully sick. There was a bottle of oxalic acid on the table."

Stroeve hid his face in his hands and swayed backwards and forwards, groaning.

"Was she conscious?"

"Yes. Oh, if you knew how she's suffering! I can't bear it. I can't bear it."

His voice rose to a shriek.

"Damn it all, you haven't got to bear it," I cried impatiently. "She's got to bear it."

"How can you be so cruel?"

"What have you done?"

"They sent for a doctor and for me, and they told the police. I'd given the concierge twenty francs, and told her to send for me if anything happened."

He paused a minute, and I saw that what he had to tell me was very hard to say.

"When I went she wouldn't speak to me. She told them to send me away. I swore that I forgave her everything, but she wouldn't listen. She tried to beat her head against the wall. The doctor told me that I mustn't remain with her. She kept on saying, 'Send him away!' I went, and waited in the studio. And when the ambulance came and they put her on a stretcher, they made me go in the kitchen so that she shouldn't know I was there."

While I dressed—for Stroeve wished me to go at once with him to the hospital—he told me that he had arranged for his wife to have a private room, so that she might at least be spared the sordid promiscuity of a ward. On our way he explained to me why he desired my presence; if she still refused to see him, perhaps she would see me. He begged me to repeat to her that he loved her still; he would reproach her for nothing, but desired only to help her; he made no claim on her, and on her recovery would not seek to induce her to return to him; she would be perfectly free.

But when we arrived at the hospital, a gaunt, cheerless building, the mere sight of which was enough to make one's heart sick, and after being directed from this official to that, up endless stairs and through long, bare corridors, found the doctor in charge of the case, we were told that the patient was too ill to see anyone that day. The doctor was a little bearded man in white, with an offhand manner. He evidently looked upon a case as a case, and anxious relatives as a nuisance which must be treated with firmness. Moreover, to him the affair was commonplace; it was just an hysterical woman who had quarrelled with her lover and taken poison; it was constantly happening. At first he thought that Dirk was the cause of the disaster, and he was needlessly brusque with him. When I explained that he was the husband, anxious to forgive, the doctor looked at him suddenly, with curious, searching eyes. I seemed to see in them a hint of mockery; it was true that Stroeve had the head of the husband who is deceived. The doctor faintly shrugged his shoulders.

"There is no immediate danger," he said, in answer to our questioning. "One doesn't know how much she took. It may be that she will get off with a fright. Women are constantly trying to commit suicide for love, but generally they take care not to succeed. It's generally a gesture to arouse pity or terror in their lover."

There was in his tone a frigid contempt. It was obvious that to him Blanche Stroeve was only a unit to be added to the statistical list of attempted suicides in the city of Paris during the current year. He was busy, and could waste no more time on us. He told us that if we came at a certain hour next day, should Blanche be better, it might be possible for her husband to see her.

XXXV

I SCARCELY KNOW how we got through that day. Stroeve could not bear to be alone, and I exhausted myself in efforts to distract him. I took him to the Louvre, and he pretended to look at pictures, but I saw that his thoughts were constantly with his wife. I forced him to eat, and after luncheon I induced him to lie down, but he could not sleep. He accepted willingly my invitation to remain for a few days in my apartment. I gave him books to read, but after a page or two he would put the book down and stare miserably into space. During the evening we played innumerable games of piquet, and bravely, not to disappoint my efforts, he tried to appear interested. Finally I gave him a draught, and he sank into uneasy slumber.

When we went again to the hospital we saw a nursing sister. She told us that Blanche seemed a little better, and she went in to ask if she would see her husband. We heard voices in the room in which she lay, and presently the nurse returned to say that the patient refused to see anyone. We had told her that if she refused to see Dirk the nurse was to ask if she would see me, but this she refused also. Dirk's lips trembled.

"I dare not insist," said the nurse. "She is too ill. Perhaps in a day or two she may change her mind."

"Is there anyone else she wants to see?" asked Dirk, in a voice so low it was almost a whisper.

"She says she only wants to be left in peace."

Dirk's hands moved strangely, as though they had nothing to do with his body, with a movement of their own.

"Will you tell her that if there is anyone else she wishes to see I will bring him? I only want her to be happy."

The nurse looked at him with her calm, kind eyes, which had seen all the horror and pain of the world, and yet, filled with the vision of a world without sin, remained serene.

"I will tell her when she is a little calmer."

Dirk, filled with compassion, begged her to take the message at once.

"It may cure her. I beseech you to ask her now."

With a faint smile of pity, the nurse went back into the room. We heard her low voice, and then, in a voice I did not recognise the answer:

"No. No. No."

The nurse came out again and shook her head.

"Was that she who spoke then?" I asked. "Her voice sounded so strange."

"It appears that her vocal cords have been burnt by the acid."

Dirk gave a low cry of distress. I asked him to go on and wait for me at the entrance, for I wanted to say something to the nurse. He did not ask what it was, but went silently. He seemed to have lost all power of will; he was like an obedient child.

"Has she told you why she did it?" I asked.

"No. She won't speak. She lies on her back quite quietly. She doesn't move for hours at a time. But she cries always. Her pillow is all wet. She's too weak to use a handkerchief, and the tears just run down her face."

It gave me a sudden wrench of the heart-strings. I could have killed Strickland then, and I knew that my voice was trembling when I bade the nurse good-bye.

I found Dirk waiting for me on the steps. He seemed to see nothing, and did not notice that I had joined him till I touched him on the arm. We walked along in silence. I tried to imagine what had happened to drive the poor creature to that dreadful step. I presumed that Strickland knew what had happened, for someone must have been to see him from the police, and he must have made his statement. I did not know where he was. I supposed he had gone back to the shabby attic which served him as a studio. It was curious that she should not wish to see him. Perhaps she refused to have him sent for because she knew he would refuse to come. I wondered what an abyss of cruelty she must have looked into that in horror she refused to live.

XXXVI

THE NEXT WEEK was dreadful. Stroeve went twice a day to the hospital to enquire after his wife, who still declined to see him; and came away at first relieved and hopeful because he was told that she seemed to be growing better, and then in despair because, the complication which the doctor had feared having ensued, recovery was impossible. The nurse was pitiful to his distress, but she had little to say that could console him. The poor woman lay quite still, refusing to speak, with her eyes intent, as though she watched for the coming of death. It could now be only the question of a day or two; and when, late one evening, Stroeve came to see me I knew it was to tell me she was dead. He was absolutely exhausted. His volubility had left him at last, and he sank down wearily on my sofa. I felt that no words of condolence availed, and I let him lie there quietly. I feared he would think it heartless if I read, so I sat by the window, smoking a pipe, till he felt inclined to speak.

"You've been very kind to me," he said at last. "Everyone's been very kind."

"Nonsense," I said, a little embarrassed.

"At the hospital they told me I might wait. They gave me a chair, and I sat outside the door. When she became unconscious they said I might go in. Her mouth and chin were all burnt by the acid. It was awful to see her lovely skin all wounded. She died very peacefully, so that I didn't know she was dead till the sister told me."

He was too tired to weep. He lay on his back limply, as though all the strength had gone out of his limbs, and presently I saw that he had fallen asleep. It was the first natural sleep he had had for a week.

Nature, sometimes so cruel, is sometimes merciful. I covered him and turned down the light. In the morning when I awoke he was still asleep. He had not moved. His gold-rimmed spectacles were still on his nose.

XXXVII

THE CIRCUMSTANCES OF Blanche Stroeve's death necessitated all manner of dreadful formalities, but at last we were allowed to bury her. Dirk and I alone followed the hearse to the cemetery. We went at a foot-pace, but on the way back we trotted, and there was something to my mind singularly horrible in the way the driver of the hearse whipped up his horses. It seemed to dismiss the dead with a shrug of the shoulders. Now and then I caught sight of the swaying hearse in front of us, and our own driver urged his pair so that we might not remain behind. I felt in myself, too, the desire to get the whole thing out of my mind. I was beginning to be bored with a tragedy that did not really concern me, and pretending to myself that I spoke in order to distract Stroeve, I turned with relief to other subjects.

"Don't you think you'd better go away for a bit?" I said. "There can be no object in your staying in Paris now."

He did not answer, but I went on ruthlessly:

"Have you made any plans for the immediate future?"

"No."

"You must try and gather together the threads again. Why don't you go down to Italy and start working?"

Again he made no reply, but the driver of our carriage came to my rescue. Slackening his pace for a moment, he leaned over and spoke. I could not hear what he said, so I put my head out of the window. He wanted to know where we wished to be set down. I told him to wait a minute.

"You'd better come and have lunch with me," I said to Dirk. "I'll tell him to drop us in the Place Pigalle."

"I'd rather not. I want to go to the studio."

I hesitated a moment.

"Would you like me to come with you?" I asked then.

"No; I should prefer to be alone."

"All right."

I gave the driver the necessary direction, and in renewed silence we drove on. Dirk had not been to the studio since the wretched morning on which they had taken Blanche to the hospital. I was glad he did not want me to accompany him, and when I left him at the door I walked away with relief. I took a new pleasure in the streets of Paris, and I looked with smiling eyes at the people who hurried to and fro. The day was fine and sunny, and I felt in myself a more acute delight in life. I could not help it; I put Stroeve and his sorrows out of my mind. I wanted to enjoy.

XXXVIII

I DID NOT see him again for nearly a week. Then he fetched me soon after seven one evening and took me out to dinner. He was dressed in the deepest mourning, and on his bowler was a broad black band. He had even a black border to his handkerchief. His garb of woe suggested that he had lost in one catastrophe every relation he had in the world, even to cousins by marriage twice removed. His plumpness and his red, fat cheeks made his mourning not a little incongruous. It was cruel that his extreme unhappiness should have in it something of buffoonery.

He told me he had made up his mind to go away, though not to Italy, as I had suggested, but to Holland.

"I'm starting to-morrow. This is perhaps the last time we shall ever meet."

I made an appropriate rejoinder, and he smiled wanly.

"I haven't been home for five years. I think I'd forgotten it all; I seemed to have come so far away from my father's house that I was shy at the idea of revisiting it; but now I feel it's my only refuge."

He was sore and bruised, and his thoughts went back to the tenderness of his mother's love. The ridicule he had endured for years seemed now to weigh him down, and the final blow of Blanche's treachery had robbed him of the resiliency which had made him take it so gaily. He could no longer laugh with those who laughed at him.

He was an outcast. He told me of his childhood in the tidy brick house, and of his mother's passionate orderliness. Her kitchen was a miracle of clean brightness. Everything was always in its place, and no where could you see a speck of dust. Cleanliness, indeed, was a mania with her. I saw a neat little old woman, with cheeks like apples, toiling away from morning to night, through the long years, to keep her house trim and spruce. His father was a spare old man, his hands gnarled after the work of a lifetime, silent and upright; in the evening he read the paper aloud, while his wife and daughter (now married to the captain of a fishing smack), unwilling to lose a moment, bent over their sewing. Nothing ever happened in that little town, left behind by the advance of civilisation, and one year followed the next till death came, like a friend, to give rest to those who had laboured so diligently.

"My father wished me to become a carpenter like himself. For five generations we've carried on the same trade, from father to son. Perhaps that is the wisdom of life, to tread in your father's steps, and look neither to the right nor to the left. When I was a little boy I said I would marry the daughter of the harness-maker who lived next door. She was a little girl with blue eyes and a flaxen pigtail. She would have kept my house like a new pin, and I should have had a son to carry on the business after me."

Stroeve sighed a little and was silent. His thoughts dwelt among pictures of what might have been, and the safety of the life he had refused filled him with longing.

"The world is hard and cruel. We are here none knows why, and we go none knows whither. We must be very humble. We must see the beauty of quietness. We must go through life so inconspicuously that Fate does not notice us. And let us seek the love of simple, ignorant people. Their ignorance is better than all our knowledge. Let us be silent, content in our little corner, meek and gentle like them. That is the wisdom of life."

To me it was his broken spirit that expressed itself, and I rebelled against his renunciation. But I kept my own counsel.

"What made you think of being a painter?" I asked.

He shrugged his shoulders.

"It happened that I had a knack for drawing. I got prizes for it at school. My poor mother was very proud of my gift, and she gave me a box of water-colours as a present. She showed my sketches to the pastor and the doctor and the judge. And they sent me to Amsterdam to try for a scholarship, and I won it. Poor soul, she was so proud; and though it nearly broke her heart to part from me, she smiled, and would not show me her grief. She was pleased that her son should be an artist. They pinched and saved so that I should have enough to live on, and when my first picture was exhibited they came to Amsterdam to see it, my father and mother and my sister, and my mother cried when she looked at it." His kind eyes glistened. "And now on every wall of the old house there is one of my pictures in a beautiful gold frame."

He glowed with happy pride. I thought of those cold scenes of his, with their picturesque peasants and cypresses and olive-trees. They must look queer in their garish frames on the walls of the peasant house.

"The dear soul thought she was doing a wonderful thing for me when she made me an artist, but perhaps, after all, it would have been better for me if my father's will had prevailed and I were now but an honest carpenter."

"Now that you know what art can offer, would you change your life? Would you have missed all the delight it has given you?"

"Art is the greatest thing in the world," he answered, after a pause.

He looked at me for a minute reflectively; he seemed to hesitate; then he said:

"Did you know that I had been to see Strickland?"

"You?"

I was astonished. I should have thought he could not bear to set eyes on him. Stroeve smiled faintly.

"You know already that I have no proper pride."

"What do you mean by that?"

He told me a singular story.

XXXIX

WHEN I LEFT him, after we had buried poor Blanche, Stroeve walked into the house with a heavy heart. Something impelled him to go to the studio, some obscure desire for self-torture, and yet he dreaded the anguish that he foresaw. He dragged himself up the stairs; his feet seemed unwilling to carry him; and outside the door he lingered for a long time, trying to summon up courage to go in. He felt horribly sick. He had an impulse to run down the stairs after me and beg me to go in with him; he had a feeling that there was somebody in the studio. He remembered how often he had waited for a minute or two on the landing to get his breath after the ascent, and how absurdly his impatience to see Blanche had taken it away again. To see her was a delight that never staled, and even though he had not been out an hour he was as excited at the prospect as if they had been parted for a month. Suddenly he could not believe that she was dead. What had happened could only be a dream, a frightful dream; and when he turned the key and opened the door, he would see her bending slightly over the table in the gracious attitude of the woman in Chardin's *Benedicite*, which always seemed to him so exquisite. Hurriedly he took the key out of his pocket, opened, and walked in.

The apartment had no look of desertion. His wife's tidiness was one of the traits which had so much pleased him; his own upbringing had given him a tender sympathy for the delight in orderliness; and when he had seen her instinctive desire to put each thing in its appointed place it had given him a little warm feeling in his heart. The bedroom looked as though she had just left it: the brushes were neatly placed on the toilet-table, one on each side of the comb; someone had smoothed down the bed on which she had spent her last night in the studio; and her nightdress in a little case lay on the pillow. It was impossible to believe that she would never come into that room again.

But he felt thirsty, and went into the kitchen to get himself some water. Here, too, was order. On a rack were the plates that she had used for dinner on the night of her quarrel with Strickland, and they had been carefully washed. The knives and forks were put away in a drawer. Under a cover were the remains of a piece of cheese, and in a tin box was a crust of bread. She had done her marketing from day to day, buying only what was strictly needful, so that nothing was left over from one day to the next. Stroeve knew from the enquiries made by the police that Strickland had walked out of the house immediately after dinner, and the fact that Blanche had washed up the things as usual gave him a little thrill of horror. Her methodicalness made her suicide more deliberate. Her self-possession was frightening. A sudden pang seized him, and his knees felt so weak that he almost fell. He went back into the bedroom and threw himself on the bed. He cried out her name.

"Blanche. Blanche."

The thought of her suffering was intolerable. He had a sudden vision of her standing in the kitchen—it was hardly larger than a cupboard—washing the plates and glasses, the forks and spoons, giving the knives a rapid polish on the knife-board; and then putting everything away, giving the sink a scrub, and hanging the dish-cloth up to dry—it was there still, a gray torn rag; then looking round to see that everything was clean and nice. He saw her roll down her sleeves and remove her apron—the apron hung on a peg behind the door—and take the bottle of oxalic acid and go with it into the bedroom.

The agony of it drove him up from the bed and out of the room. He went into the studio. It was dark, for the curtains had been drawn over the great window, and he pulled them quickly back; but a sob broke from him as with a rapid glance he took in the place where he had been so happy. Nothing was changed here, either. Strickland was indifferent to his surroundings, and he had lived in the other's studio without thinking of altering a thing. It was deliberately artistic. It represented Stroeve's idea of the proper environment for an artist. There were bits of old brocade on the walls, and the piano was covered with a piece of silk, beautiful and tarnished; in one corner was a copy of the Venus of Milo, and in another of the Venus of the Medici. Here and there was an Italian cabinet surmounted with Delft, and here and there a bas-relief. In a handsome gold frame was a copy of Velasquez' Innocent X., that Stroeve had made in Rome, and placed so as to make the most of their decorative effect were a number of Stroeve's pictures, all in splendid frames. Stroeve had always been very proud of his taste. He had never lost his appreciation for the romantic atmosphere of a studio, and though now the sight of it was like a stab in his heart, without thinking what he was at, he changed

slightly the position of a Louis XV. table which was one of his treasures. Suddenly he caught sight of a canvas with its face to the wall.
It was a much larger one than he himself was in the habit of using,
and he wondered what it did there. He went over to it and leaned
it towards him so that he could see the painting. It was a nude. His
heart began to beat quickly, for he guessed at once that it was one of
Strickland's pictures. He flung it back against the wall angrily—what
did he mean by leaving it there?—but his movement caused it to
fall, face downwards, on the ground. No mater whose the picture, he
could not leave it there in the dust, and he raised it; but then curiosity
got the better of him. He thought he would like to have a proper look
at it, so he brought it along and set it on the easel. Then he stood back
in order to see it at his ease.

He gave a gasp. It was the picture of a woman lying on a sofa,
with one arm beneath her head and the other along her body; one
knee was raised, and the other leg was stretched out. The pose was
classic. Stroeve's head swam. It was Blanche. Grief and jealousy and
rage seized him, and he cried out hoarsely; he was inarticulate; he
clenched his fists and raised them threateningly at an invisible enemy.
He screamed at the top of his voice. He was beside himself. He could
not bear it. That was too much. He looked round wildly for some instrument; he wanted to hack the picture to pieces; it should not exist
another minute. He could see nothing that would serve his purpose;
he rummaged about his painting things; somehow he could not find
a thing; he was frantic. At last he came upon what he sought, a large
scraper, and he pounced on it with a cry of triumph. He seized it as
though it were a dagger, and ran to the picture.

As Stroeve told me this he became as excited as when the incident occurred, and he took hold of a dinner-knife on the table between us, and brandished it. He lifted his arm as though to strike,
and then, opening his hand, let it fall with a clatter to the ground. He
looked at me with a tremulous smile. He did not speak.

"Fire away," I said.

"I don't know what happened to me. I was just going to make a
great hole in the picture, I had my arm all ready for the blow, when
suddenly I seemed to see it."

"See what?"

"The picture. It was a work of art. I couldn't touch it. I was afraid."

Stroeve was silent again, and he stared at me with his mouth open and his round blue eyes starting out of his head.

"It was a great, a wonderful picture. I was seized with awe. I had nearly committed a dreadful crime. I moved a little to see it better, and my foot knocked against the scraper. I shuddered."

I really felt something of the emotion that had caught him. I was strangely impressed. It was as though I were suddenly transported into a world in which the values were changed. I stood by, at a loss, like a stranger in a land where the reactions of man to familiar things are all different from those he has known. Stroeve tried to talk to me about the picture, but he was incoherent, and I had to guess at what he meant. Strickland had burst the bonds that hitherto had held him. He had found, not himself, as the phrase goes, but a new soul with unsuspected powers. It was not only the bold simplification of the drawing which showed so rich and so singular a personality; it was not only the painting, though the flesh was painted with a passionate sensuality which had in it something miraculous; it was not only the solidity, so that you felt extraordinarily the weight of the body; there was also a spirituality, troubling and new, which led the imagination along unsuspected ways, and suggested dim empty spaces, lit only by the eternal stars, where the soul, all naked, adventured fearful to the discovery of new mysteries.

If I am rhetorical it is because Stroeve was rhetorical. (Do we not know that man in moments of emotion expresses himself naturally in the terms of a novelette?) Stroeve was trying to express a feeling which he had never known before, and he did not know how to put it into common terms. He was like the mystic seeking to describe the ineffable. But one fact he made clear to me; people talk of beauty lightly, and having no feeling for words, they use that one carelessly, so that it loses its force; and the thing it stands for, sharing its name with a hundred trivial objects, is deprived of dignity. They call beautiful a dress, a dog, a sermon; and when they are face to face with Beauty cannot recognise it. The false emphasis with which they try to deck their worthless thoughts blunts their susceptibilities. Like the charlatan who counterfeits a spiritual force he has sometimes felt, they lose the power they have abused. But Stroeve, the unconquerable buffoon, had a love and an understanding of beauty which were as honest and sincere as was his own sincere and honest soul. It meant to him what God means to the believer, and when he saw it he was afraid.

"What did you say to Strickland when you saw him?"

"I asked him to come with me to Holland."

I was dumbfounded. I could only look at Stroeve in stupid amazement.

"We both loved Blanche. There would have been room for him in my mother's house. I think the company of poor, simple people would have done his soul a great good. I think he might have learnt from them something that would be very useful to him."

"What did he say?"

"He smiled a little. I suppose he thought me very silly. He said he had other fish to fry."

I could have wished that Strickland had used some other phrase to indicate his refusal.

"He gave me the picture of Blanche."

I wondered why Strickland had done that. But I made no remark, and for some time we kept silence.

"What have you done with all your things?" I said at last.

"I got a Jew in, and he gave me a round sum for the lot. I'm taking my pictures home with me. Beside them I own nothing in the world now but a box of clothes and a few books."

"I'm glad you're going home," I said.

I felt that his chance was to put all the past behind him. I hoped that the grief which now seemed intolerable would be softened by the lapse of time, and a merciful forgetfulness would help him to take up once more the burden of life. He was young still, and in a few years he would look back on all his misery with a sadness in which there would be something not unpleasurable. Sooner or later he would marry some honest soul in Holland, and I felt sure he would be happy. I smiled at the thought of the vast number of bad pictures he would paint before he died.

Next day I saw him off for Amsterdam.

XL

FOR THE NEXT month, occupied with my own affairs, I saw no one connected with this lamentable business, and my mind ceased to be occupied with it. But one day, when I was walking along, bent on some errand, I passed Charles Strickland. The sight of him brought back to me all the horror which I was not unwilling to forget, and I felt in me a sudden repulsion for the cause of it. Nodding, for it would have been childish to cut him, I walked on quickly; but in a minute I felt a hand on my shoulder.

"You're in a great hurry," he said cordially.

It was characteristic of him to display geniality with anyone who showed a disinclination to meet him, and the coolness of my greeting can have left him in little doubt of that.

"I am," I answered briefly.

"I'll walk along with you," he said.

"Why?" I asked.

"For the pleasure of your society."

I did not answer, and he walked by my side silently. We continued thus for perhaps a quarter of a mile. I began to feel a little ridiculous. At last we passed a stationer's, and it occurred to me that I might as well buy some paper. It would be an excuse to be rid of him.

"I'm going in here," I said. "Good-bye."

"I'll wait for you."

I shrugged my shoulders, and went into the shop. I reflected that French paper was bad, and that, foiled of my purpose, I need not burden myself with a purchase that I did not need. I asked for something I knew could not be provided, and in a minute came out into the street.

"Did you get what you wanted?" he asked.

"No."

We walked on in silence, and then came to a place where several streets met. I stopped at the curb.

"Which way do you go?" I enquired.

"Your way," he smiled.

"I'm going home."

"I'll come along with you and smoke a pipe."

"You might wait for an invitation," I retorted frigidly.

"I would if I thought there was any chance of getting one."

"Do you see that wall in front of you?" I said, pointing.

"Yes."

"In that case I should have thought you could see also that I don't want your company."

"I vaguely suspected it, I confess."

I could not help a chuckle. It is one of the defects of my character that I cannot altogether dislike anyone who makes me laugh. But I pulled myself together.

"I think you're detestable. You're the most loathsome beast that it's ever been my misfortune to meet. Why do you seek the society of someone who hates and despises you?"

"My dear fellow, what the hell do you suppose I care what you think of me?"

"Damn it all," I said, more violently because I had an inkling my motive was none too creditable, "I don't want to know you."

"Are you afraid I shall corrupt you?"

His tone made me feel not a little ridiculous. I knew that he was looking at me sideways, with a sardonic smile.

"I suppose you are hard up," I remarked insolently.

"I should be a damned fool if I thought I had any chance of borrowing money from you."

"You've come down in the world if you can bring yourself to flatter." He grinned.

"You'll never really dislike me so long as I give you the opportunity to get off a good thing now and then."

I had to bite my lip to prevent myself from laughing. What he said had a hateful truth in it, and another defect of my character is that I enjoy the company of those, however depraved, who can give me a Roland for my Oliver. I began to feel that my abhorrence for Strickland could only be sustained by an effort on my part. I recognised my moral weakness, but saw that my disapprobation had in it already something of a pose; and I knew that if I felt it, his own keen instinct had discovered it, too. He was certainly laughing at me up his sleeve. I left him the last word, and sought refuge in a shrug of the shoulders and taciturnity.

XLI

WE ARRIVED AT the house in which I lived. I would not ask him to come in with me, but walked up the stairs without a word. He followed me, and entered the apartment on my heels. He had not been in it before, but he never gave a glance at the room I had been at pains to make pleasing to the eye. There was a tin of tobacco on the table, and, taking out his pipe, he filled it. He sat down on the only chair that had no arms and tilted himself on the back legs.

"If you're going to make yourself at home, why don't you sit in an arm-chair?" I asked irritably.

"Why are you concerned about my comfort?"

"I'm not," I retorted, "but only about my own. It makes me uncomfortable to see someone sit on an uncomfortable chair."

He chuckled, but did not move. He smoked on in silence, taking no further notice of me, and apparently was absorbed in thought. I wondered why he had come.

Until long habit has blunted the sensibility, there is something disconcerting to the writer in the instinct which causes him to take an interest in the singularities of human nature so absorbing that his moral sense is powerless against it. He recognises in himself an artistic satisfaction in the contemplation of evil which a little startles him; but sincerity forces him to confess that the disapproval he feels for certain actions is not nearly so strong as his curiosity in their reasons. The character of a scoundrel, logical and complete, has a fascination for his creator which is an outrage to law and order. I expect that Shakespeare devised Iago with a gusto which he never knew when, weaving moonbeams with his fancy, he imagined Desdemona. It may be that in his rogues the writer gratifies instincts deep-rooted in him, which the manners and customs of a civilised world have forced back to the mysterious recesses of the subconscious. In giving to the character of his invention flesh and bones he is giving life to that part of himself which finds no other means of expression. His satisfaction is a sense of liberation.

The writer is more concerned to know than to judge.

There was in my soul a perfectly genuine horror of Strickland, and side by side with it a cold curiosity to discover his motives. I was puzzled by him, and I was eager to see how he regarded the tragedy he had caused in the lives of people who had used him with so much kindness. I applied the scalpel boldly.

"Stroeve told me that picture you painted of his wife was the best thing you've ever done."

Strickland took his pipe out of his mouth, and a smile lit up his eyes.

"It was great fun to do."

"Why did you give it him?"

"I'd finished it. It wasn't any good to me."

"Do you know that Stroeve nearly destroyed it?"

"It wasn't altogether satisfactory."

He was quiet for a moment or two, then he took his pipe out of his mouth again, and chuckled.

"Do you know that the little man came to see me?"

"Weren't you rather touched by what he had to say?"

"No; I thought it damned silly and sentimental."

"I suppose it escaped your memory that you'd ruined his life?" I remarked.

He rubbed his bearded chin reflectively.

"He's a very bad painter."

"But a very good man."

"And an excellent cook," Strickland added derisively.

His callousness was inhuman, and in my indignation I was not inclined to mince my words.

"As a mere matter of curiosity I wish you'd tell me, have you felt the smallest twinge of remorse for Blanche Stroeve's death?"

I watched his face for some change of expression, but it remained impassive.

"Why should I?" he asked.

"Let me put the facts before you. You were dying, and Dirk Stroeve took you into his own house. He nursed you like a mother. He sacrificed his time and his comfort and his money for you. He snatched you from the jaws of death."

Strickland shrugged his shoulders.

"The absurd little man enjoys doing things for other people. That's his life."

"Granting that you owed him no gratitude, were you obliged to go out of your way to take his wife from him? Until you came on the scene they were happy. Why couldn't you leave them alone?"

"What makes you think they were happy?"

"It was evident."

"You are a discerning fellow. Do you think she could ever have forgiven him for what he did for her?"

"What do you mean by that?"

"Don't you know why he married her?"

I shook my head.

"She was a governess in the family of some Roman prince, and the son of the house seduced her. She thought he was going to marry her. They turned her out into the street neck and crop. She was going to have a baby, and she tried to commit suicide. Stroeve found her and married her."

"It was just like him. I never knew anyone with so compassionate a heart."

I had often wondered why that ill-assorted pair had married, but just that explanation had never occurred to me. That was perhaps the cause of the peculiar quality of Dirk's love for his wife. I had noticed in it something more than passion. I remembered also how I had always fancied that her reserve concealed I knew not what; but now I saw in it more than the desire to hide a shameful secret. Her tranquillity was like the sullen calm that broods over an island which has been swept by a hurricane. Her cheerfulness was the cheerfulness of despair. Strickland interrupted my reflections with an observation the profound cynicism of which startled me.

"A woman can forgive a man for the harm he does her," he said, "but she can never forgive him for the sacrifices he makes on her account."

"It must be reassuring to you to know that you certainly run no risk of incurring the resentment of the women you come in contact with," I retorted.

A slight smile broke on his lips.

"You are always prepared to sacrifice your principles for a repartee," he answered.

"What happened to the child?"

"Oh, it was still-born, three or four months after they were married."

Then I came to the question which had seemed to me most puzzling.

"Will you tell me why you bothered about Blanche Stroeve at all?"

He did not answer for so long that I nearly repeated it.

"How do I know?" he said at last. "She couldn't bear the sight of me. It amused me."

"I see."

He gave a sudden flash of anger.

"Damn it all, I wanted her."

But he recovered his temper immediately, and looked at me with a smile.

"At first she was horrified."

"Did you tell her?"

"There wasn't any need. She knew. I never said a word. She was frightened. At last I took her."

I do not know what there was in the way he told me this that extraordinarily suggested the violence of his desire. It was disconcerting and rather horrible. His life was strangely divorced from material things, and it was as though his body at times wreaked a fearful revenge on his spirit. The satyr in him suddenly took possession, and he was powerless in the grip of an instinct which had all the strength of the primitive forces of nature. It was an obsession so complete that there was no room in his soul for prudence or gratitude.

"But why did you want to take her away with you?" I asked.

"I didn't," he answered, frowning. "When she said she was coming I was nearly as surprised as Stroeve. I told her that when I'd had enough of her she'd have to go, and she said she'd risk that." He paused a little. "She had a wonderful body, and I wanted to paint a nude. When I'd finished my picture I took no more interest in her."

"And she loved you with all her heart."

He sprang to his feet and walked up and down the small room.

"I don't want love. I haven't time for it. It's weakness. I am a man, and sometimes I want a woman. When I've satisfied my passion I'm ready for other things. I can't overcome my desire, but I hate it; it imprisons my spirit; I look forward to the time when I shall be free from all desire and can give myself without hindrance to my work. Because women can do nothing except love, they've given it a ridiculous importance. They want to persuade us that it's the whole of life. It's an insignificant part. I know lust. That's normal and healthy. Love is a disease. Women are the instruments of my pleasure; I have no patience with their claim to be helpmates, partners, companions."

I had never heard Strickland speak so much at one time. He spoke with a passion of indignation. But neither here nor elsewhere do I pretend to give his exact words; his vocabulary was small, and he had no gift for framing sentences, so that one had to piece his meaning together out of interjections, the expression of his face, gestures and hackneyed phrases.

"You should have lived at a time when women were chattels and men the masters of slaves," I said.

"It just happens that I am a completely normal man."

I could not help laughing at this remark, made in all seriousness; but he went on, walking up and down the room like a caged beast, intent on expressing what he felt, but found such difficulty in putting coherently.

"When a woman loves you she's not satisfied until she possesses your soul. Because she's weak, she has a rage for domination, and nothing less will satisfy her. She has a small mind, and she resents the abstract which she is unable to grasp. She is occupied with material things, and she is jealous of the ideal. The soul of man wanders through the uttermost regions of the universe, and she seeks to imprison it in the circle of her account-book. Do you remember my wife? I saw Blanche little by little trying all her tricks. With infinite patience she prepared to snare me and bind me. She wanted to bring me down to her level; she cared nothing for me, she only wanted me to be hers. She was willing to do everything in the world for me except the one thing I wanted: to leave me alone."

I was silent for a while.

"What did you expect her to do when you left her?"

"She could have gone back to Stroeve," he said irritably. "He was ready to take her."

"You're inhuman," I answered. "It's as useless to talk to you about these things as to describe colours to a man who was born blind."

He stopped in front of my chair, and stood looking down at me with an expression in which I read a contemptuous amazement.

"Do you really care a twopenny damn if Blanche Stroeve is alive or dead?"

I thought over his question, for I wanted to answer it truthfully, at all events to my soul.

"It may be a lack of sympathy in myself if it does not make any great difference to me that she is dead. Life had a great deal to offer her. I think it's terrible that she should have been deprived of it in that cruel way, and I am ashamed because I do not really care."

"You have not the courage of your convictions. Life has no value. Blanche Stroeve didn't commit suicide because I left her, but because she was a foolish and unbalanced woman. But we've talked about her quite enough; she was an entirely unimportant person. Come, and I'll show you my pictures."

He spoke as though I were a child that needed to be distracted. I was sore, but not with him so much as with myself. I thought of the happy life that pair had led in the cosy studio in Montmartre, Stroeve and his wife, their simplicity, kindness, and hospitality; it seemed to me cruel that it should have been broken to pieces by a ruthless chance; but the cruellest thing of all was that in fact it made no great difference. The world went on, and no one was a penny the worse for all that wretchedness. I had an idea that Dirk, a man of greater emotional reactions than depth of feeling, would soon forget; and Blanche's life, begun with who knows what bright hopes and what dreams, might just as well have never been lived. It all seemed useless and inane.

Strickland had found his hat, and stood looking at me.

"Are you coming?"

"Why do you seek my acquaintance?" I asked him. "You know that I hate and despise you."

He chuckled good-humouredly.

"Your only quarrel with me really is that I don't care a twopenny damn what you think about me."

I felt my cheeks grow red with sudden anger. It was impossible to make him understand that one might be outraged by his callous selfishness. I longed to pierce his armour of complete indifference. I knew also that in the end there was truth in what he said. Unconsciously, perhaps, we treasure the power we have over people by their regard for our opinion of them, and we hate those upon whom we have no such influence. I suppose it is the bitterest wound to human pride. But I would not let him see that I was put out.

"Is it possible for any man to disregard others entirely?" I said, though more to myself than to him. "You're dependent on others for everything in existence. It's a preposterous attempt to try to live only for yourself and by yourself. Sooner or later you'll be ill and tired and old, and then you'll crawl back into the herd. Won't you be ashamed when you feel in your heart the desire for comfort and sympathy? You're trying an impossible thing. Sooner or later the human being in you will yearn for the common bonds of humanity."

"Come and look at my pictures."

"Have you ever thought of death?"

"Why should I? It doesn't matter."

I stared at him. He stood before me, motionless, with a mocking smile in his eyes; but for all that, for a moment I had an inkling of a fiery, tortured spirit, aiming at something greater than could be conceived by anything that was bound up with the flesh. I had a fleeting glimpse of a pursuit of the ineffable. I looked at the man before me in his shabby clothes, with his great nose and shining eyes, his red beard and untidy hair; and I had a strange sensation that it was only an envelope, and I was in the presence of a disembodied spirit.

"Let us go and look at your pictures," I said.

XLII

I DID NOT know why Strickland had suddenly offered to show them to me. I welcomed the opportunity. A man's work reveals him. In social intercourse he gives you the surface that he wishes the world to accept, and you can only gain a true knowledge of him by inferences from little actions, of which he is unconscious, and from fleeting expressions, which cross his face unknown to him. Sometimes people carry to such perfection the mask they have assumed that in due course they actually become the person they seem. But in his book or his picture the real man delivers himself defenceless. His pretentiousness will only expose his vacuity. The lathe painted to look like iron is seen to be but a lathe. No affectation of peculiarity can conceal a commonplace mind. To the acute observer no one can produce the most casual work without disclosing the innermost secrets of his soul.

As I walked up the endless stairs of the house in which Strickland lived, I confess that I was a little excited. It seemed to me that I was on the threshold of a surprising adventure. I looked about the room with curiosity. It was even smaller and more bare than I remembered it. I wondered what those friends of mine would say who demanded vast studios, and vowed they could not work unless all the conditions were to their liking.

"You'd better stand there," he said, pointing to a spot from which, presumably, he fancied I could see to best advantage what he had to show me.

"You don't want me to talk, I suppose," I said.

"No, blast you; I want you to hold your tongue."

He placed a picture on the easel, and let me look at it for a minute or two; then took it down and put another in its place. I think he showed me about thirty canvases. It was the result of the six years during which he had been painting. He had never sold a picture. The canvases were of different sizes. The smaller were pictures of still-life and the largest were landscapes. There were about half a dozen portraits.

"That is the lot," he said at last.

I wish I could say that I recognised at once their beauty and their great originality. Now that I have seen many of them again and the rest are familiar to me in reproductions, I am astonished that at first sight I was bitterly disappointed. I felt nothing of the peculiar thrill which it is the property of art to give. The impression that Strickland's pictures gave me was disconcerting; and the fact remains, always to reproach me, that I never even thought of buying any. I missed a wonderful chance. Most of them have found their way into museums, and the rest are the treasured possessions of wealthy amateurs. I try to find excuses for myself. I think that my taste is good, but I am conscious that it has no originality. I know very little about painting, and I wander along trails that others have blazed for me. At that time I had the greatest admiration for the impressionists. I longed to possess a Sisley and a Degas, and I worshipped Manet. His *Olympia* seemed to me the greatest picture of modern times, and *Le Dejeuner sur l'Herbe* moved me profoundly. These works seemed to me the last word in painting.

I will not describe the pictures that Strickland showed me. Descriptions of pictures are always dull, and these, besides, are familiar to all who take an interest in such things. Now that his influence has so enormously affected modern painting, now that others have charted the country which he was among the first to explore, Strickland's pictures, seen for the first time, would find the mind more prepared for them; but it must be remembered that I had never seen anything of the sort. First of all I was taken aback by what seemed to me the clumsiness of his technique. Accustomed to the drawing of the old masters, and convinced that Ingres was the greatest draughtsman of recent times, I thought that Strickland drew very badly. I knew nothing of the simplification at which he aimed. I remember a still-life of oranges on a plate, and I was bothered because the plate was not round and the oranges were lop-sided. The portraits were a little larger than life-size, and this gave them an ungainly look. To my eyes the faces looked like caricatures. They were painted in a way that was entirely new to me. The landscapes puzzled me even more. There were two or three pictures of the forest at Fontainebleau and several of

streets in Paris: my first feeling was that they might have been painted by a drunken cabdriver. I was perfectly bewildered. The colour
seemed to me extraordinarily crude. It passed through my mind that
the whole thing was a stupendous, incomprehensible farce. Now that
I look back I am more than ever impressed by Stroeve's acuteness. He
saw from the first that here was a revolution in art, and he recognised
in its beginnings the genius which now all the world allows.

But if I was puzzled and disconcerted, I was not unimpressed.
Even I, in my colossal ignorance, could not but feel that here, trying
to express itself, was real power. I was excited and interested. I felt
that these pictures had something to say to me that was very important for me to know, but I could not tell what it was. They seemed to
me ugly, but they suggested without disclosing a secret of momentous
significance. They were strangely tantalising. They gave me an emotion that I could not analyse. They said something that words were
powerless to utter. I fancy that Strickland saw vaguely some spiritual
meaning in material things that was so strange that he could only
suggest it with halting symbols. It was as though he found in the
chaos of the universe a new pattern, and were attempting clumsily,
with anguish of soul, to set it down. I saw a tormented spirit striving
for the release of expression.

I turned to him.

"I wonder if you haven't mistaken your medium," I said.

"What the hell do you mean?"

"I think you're trying to say something, I don't quite know what
it is, but I'm not sure that the best way of saying it is by means of
painting."

When I imagined that on seeing his pictures I should get a clue
to the understanding of his strange character I was mistaken. They
merely increased the astonishment with which he filled me. I was
more at sea than ever. The only thing that seemed clear to me—and
perhaps even this was fanciful—was that he was passionately striving
for liberation from some power that held him. But what the power
was and what line the liberation would take remained obscure. Each
one of us is alone in the world. He is shut in a tower of brass, and can
communicate with his fellows only by signs, and the signs have no

common value, so that their sense is vague and uncertain. We seek pitifully to convey to others the treasures of our heart, but they have not the power to accept them, and so we go lonely, side by side but not together, unable to know our fellows and unknown by them. We are like people living in a country whose language they know so little that, with all manner of beautiful and profound things to say, they are condemned to the banalities of the conversation manual. Their brain is seething with ideas, and they can only tell you that the umbrella of the gardener's aunt is in the house.

The final impression I received was of a prodigious effort to express some state of the soul, and in this effort, I fancied, must be sought the explanation of what so utterly perplexed me. It was evident that colours and forms had a significance for Strickland that was peculiar to himself. He was under an intolerable necessity to convey something that he felt, and he created them with that intention alone. He did not hesitate to simplify or to distort if he could get nearer to that unknown thing he sought. Facts were nothing to him, for beneath the mass of irrelevant incidents he looked for something significant to himself. It was as though he had become aware of the soul of the universe and were compelled to express it.

Though these pictures confused and puzzled me, I could not be unmoved by the emotion that was patent in them; and, I knew not why, I felt in myself a feeling that with regard to Strickland was the last I had ever expected to experience. I felt an overwhelming compassion.

"I think I know now why you surrendered to your feeling for Blanche Stroeve," I said to him.

"Why?"

"I think your courage failed. The weakness of your body communicated itself to your soul. I do not know what infinite yearning possesses you, so that you are driven to a perilous, lonely search for some goal where you expect to find a final release from the spirit that torments you. I see you as the eternal pilgrim to some shrine that perhaps does not exist. I do not know to what inscrutable Nirvana you aim. Do you know yourself? Perhaps it is Truth and Freedom that you seek, and for a moment you thought that you might find release in Love. I think your tired soul sought rest in a woman's arms, and when you found no rest there you hated her. You had no pity for her, because you have no pity for yourself. And you killed her out of fear, because you trembled still at the danger you had barely escaped."

He smiled dryly and pulled his beard.

"You are a dreadful sentimentalist, my poor friend."

A week later I heard by chance that Strickland had gone to Marseilles. I never saw him again.

XLIII

LOOKING BACK, I realise that what I have written about Charles Strickland must seem very unsatisfactory. I have given incidents that came to my knowledge, but they remain obscure because I do not know the reasons that led to them. The strangest, Strickland's determination to become a painter, seems to be arbitrary; and though it must have had causes in the circumstances of his life, I am ignorant of them. From his own conversation I was able to glean nothing. If I were writing a novel, rather than narrating such facts as I know of a curious personality, I should have invented much to account for this change of heart. I think I should have shown a strong vocation in boyhood, crushed by the will of his father or sacrificed to the necessity of earning a living; I should have pictured him impatient of the restraints of life; and in the struggle between his passion for art and the duties of his station I could have aroused sympathy for him. I should so have made him a more imposing figure. Perhaps it would have been possible to see in him a new Prometheus. There was here, maybe, the opportunity for a modern version of the hero who for the good of mankind exposes himself to the agonies of the damned. It is always a moving subject.

On the other hand, I might have found his motives in the influence of the married relation. There are a dozen ways in which this might be managed. A latent gift might reveal itself on acquaintance with the painters and writers whose society his wife sought; or domestic incompatability might turn him upon himself; a love affair might fan into bright flame a fire which I could have shown smouldering dimly in his heart. I think then I should have drawn Mrs. Strickland quite differently. I should have abandoned the facts and made her a nagging, tiresome woman, or else a bigoted one with no sympathy for the claims of the spirit. I should have made Strickland's marriage a long torment from which escape was the only possible issue. I think I should have emphasised his patience with the unsuitable mate, and the compassion which made him unwilling to throw off the yoke that oppressed him. I should certainly have eliminated the children.

An effective story might also have been made by bringing him into contact with some old painter whom the pressure of want or the desire for commercial success had made false to the genius of his youth, and who, seeing in Strickland the possibilities which himself had wasted, influenced him to forsake all and follow the divine tyranny of art. I think there would have been something ironic in the picture of the successful old man, rich and honoured, living in another the life which he, though knowing it was the better part, had not had the strength to pursue.

The facts are much duller. Strickland, a boy fresh from school, went into a broker's office without any feeling of distaste. Until he married he led the ordinary life of his fellows, gambling mildly on the Exchange, interested to the extent of a sovereign or two on the result of the Derby or the Oxford and Cambridge Race. I think he boxed a little in his spare time. On his chimney-piece he had photographs of Mrs. Langtry and Mary Anderson. He read *Punch* and the *Sporting Times*. He went to dances in Hampstead.

It matters less that for so long I should have lost sight of him. The years during which he was struggling to acquire proficiency in a difficult art were monotonous, and I do not know that there was anything significant in the shifts to which he was put to earn enough money to keep him. An account of them would be an account of the things he had seen happen to other people. I do not think they had any effect on his own character. He must have acquired experiences which would form abundant material for a picaresque novel of modern Paris, but he remained aloof, and judging from his conversation there was nothing in those years that had made a particular impression on him. Perhaps when he went to Paris he was too old to fall a victim to the glamour of his environment. Strange as it may seem, he always appeared to me not only practical, but immensely matter-of-fact. I suppose his life during this period was romantic, but he certainly saw no romance in it. It may be that in order to realise the romance of life you must have something of the actor in you; and, capable of standing outside yourself, you must be able to watch your actions with an interest at once detached and absorbed. But no one was more single-minded than Strickland. I never knew anyone who was less self-conscious. But it is unfortunate that I can give no description of the arduous steps by which he reached such mastery over his art as he ever acquired; for if I could show him undaunted by failure, by an unceasing effort of courage holding despair at bay, doggedly persistent in the face of self-doubt, which is the artist's bitterest enemy, I might excite some sympathy for a personality which, I am all too conscious, must appear singularly devoid of charm. But I have nothing to go on. I never once saw Strickland at work, nor do I know that anyone else did. He kept the secret of his struggles to himself. If in the loneliness of his studio he wrestled desperately with the Angel of the Lord he never allowed a soul to divine his anguish.

When I come to his connection with Blanche Stroeve I am exasperated by the fragmentariness of the facts at my disposal. To give my story coherence I should describe the progress of their tragic union, but I know nothing of the three months during which they lived together. I do not know how they got on or what they talked about. After all, there are twenty-four hours in the day, and the summits of emotion can only be reached at rare intervals. I can only imagine how they passed the rest of the time. While the light lasted and so long as Blanche's strength endured, I suppose that Strickland painted, and it must have irritated her when she saw him absorbed in his work. As a mistress she did not then exist for him, but only as a model; and then there were long hours in which they lived side by side in silence. It must have frightened her. When Strickland suggested that in her surrender to him there was a sense of triumph over Dirk Stroeve, because he had come to her help in her extremity, he opened the door to many a dark conjecture. I hope it was not true. It seems to me rather horrible. But who can fathom the subtleties of the human heart? Certainly not those who expect from it only decorous sentiments and normal emotions. When Blanche saw that, notwithstanding his moments of passion, Strickland remained aloof, she must have been filled with dismay, and even in those moments I surmise that she realised that to him she was not an individual, but an instrument of pleasure; he was a stranger still, and she tried to bind him to herself with pathetic arts. She strove to ensnare him with comfort and would not see that comfort meant nothing to him. She was at pains to get him the things to eat that he liked, and would not see that he was indifferent to food. She was afraid to leave him alone. She pursued him with attentions, and when his passion was dormant sought to excite it, for then at least she had the illusion of holding him. Perhaps she knew with her intelligence that the chains she forged only aroused his instinct of destruction, as the plate-glass window makes your fingers itch for half a brick; but her heart, incapable of reason, made her continue on a course she knew was fatal. She must have been very unhappy. But the blindness of love led her to believe what she wanted to be true, and her love was so great that it seemed impossible to her that it should not in return awake an equal love.

But my study of Strickland's character suffers from a greater defect than my ignorance of many facts. Because they were obvious and striking, I have written of his relations to women; and yet they were but an insignificant part of his life. It is an irony that they should so tragically have affected others. His real life consisted of dreams and of tremendously hard work.

Here lies the unreality of fiction. For in men, as a rule, love is but an episode which takes its place among the other affairs of the day, and the emphasis laid on it in novels gives it an importance which is untrue to life. There are few men to whom it is the most important thing in the world, and they are not very interesting ones; even women, with whom the subject is of paramount interest, have a contempt for them. They are flattered and excited by them, but have an uneasy feeling that they are poor creatures. But even during the brief intervals in which they are in love, men do other things which distract their mind; the trades by which they earn their living engage their attention; they are absorbed in sport; they can interest themselves in art. For the most part, they keep their various activities in various compartments, and they can pursue one to the temporary exclusion of the other. They have a faculty of concentration on that which occupies them at the moment, and it irks them if one encroaches on the other. As lovers, the difference between men and women is that women can love all day long, but men only at times.

With Strickland the sexual appetite took a very small place. It was unimportant. It was irksome. His soul aimed elsewhither. He had violent passions, and on occasion desire seized his body so that he was driven to an orgy of lust, but he hated the instincts that robbed him of his self-possession. I think, even, he hated the inevitable partner in his debauchery. When he had regained command over himself, he shuddered at the sight of the woman he had enjoyed. His thoughts floated then serenely in the empyrean, and he felt towards her the horror that perhaps the painted butterfly, hovering about the flowers, feels to the filthy chrysalis from which it has triumphantly emerged. I suppose that art is a manifestation of the sexual instinct. It is the same emotion which is excited in the human heart by the sight of a lovely woman, the Bay of Naples under the yellow moon, and the *Entombment* of Titian. It is possible that Strickland hated the normal release of sex because it seemed to him brutal by comparison with the satisfaction of artistic creation. It seems strange even to myself, when I have described a man who was cruel, selfish, brutal and sensual, to say that he was a great idealist. The fact remains.

He lived more poorly than an artisan. He worked harder. He cared nothing for those things which with most people make life gracious and beautiful. He was indifferent to money. He cared nothing about fame. You cannot praise him because he resisted the temptation to make any of those compromises with the world which most of us yield to. He had no such temptation. It never entered his head that compromise was possible. He lived in Paris more lonely than an anchorite in the deserts of Thebes. He asked nothing his fellows except that they should leave him alone. He was single-hearted in his aim, and to pursue it he was willing to sacrifice not only himself—many can do that—but others. He had a vision.

Strickland was an odious man, but I still think he was a great one.

XLIV

A CERTAIN IMPORTANCE attaches to the views on art of painters, and this is the natural place for me to set down what I know of Strickland's opinions of the great artists of the past. I am afraid I have very little worth noting. Strickland was not a conversationalist, and he had no gift for putting what he had to say in the striking phrase that the listener remembers. He had no wit. His humour, as will be seen if I have in any way succeeded in reproducing the manner of his conversation, was sardonic. His repartee was rude. He made one laugh sometimes by speaking the truth, but this is a form of humour which gains its force only by its unusualness; it would cease to amuse if it were commonly practised.

Strickland was not, I should say, a man of great intelligence, and his views on painting were by no means out of the ordinary. I never heard him speak of those whose work had a certain analogy with his own—of Cezanne, for instance, or of Van Gogh; and I doubt very much if he had ever seen their pictures. He was not greatly interested in the Impressionists. Their technique impressed him, but I fancy that he thought their attitude commonplace. When Stroeve was holding forth at length on the excellence of Monet, he said: "I prefer Winterhalter." But I dare say he said it to annoy, and if he did he certainly succeeded.

I am disappointed that I cannot report any extravagances in his opinions on the old masters. There is so much in his character which is strange that I feel it would complete the picture if his views were outrageous. I feel the need to ascribe to him fantastic theories about his predecessors, and it is with a certain sense of disillusion that I confess he thought about them pretty much as does everybody else. I do not believe he knew El Greco. He had a great but somewhat impatient admiration for Velasquez. Chardin delighted him, and Rembrandt moved him to ecstasy. He described the impression that Rembrandt made on him with a coarseness I cannot repeat. The only painter that interested him who was at all unexpected was Brueghel the Elder. I knew very little about him at that time, and Strickland had no power to explain himself. I remember what he said about him because it was so unsatisfactory.

"He's all right," said Strickland. "I bet he found it hell to paint."

When later, in Vienna, I saw several of Peter Brueghel's pictures, I thought I understood why he had attracted Strickland's attention. Here, too, was a man with a vision of the world peculiar to himself. I made somewhat copious notes at the time, intending to write something about him, but I have lost them, and have now only the recollection of an emotion. He seemed to see his fellow-creatures grotesquely, and he was angry with them because they were grotesque; life was a confusion of ridiculous, sordid happenings, a fit subject for laughter, and yet it made him sorrowful to laugh. Brueghel gave me the impression of a man striving to express in one medium feelings more appropriate to expression in another, and it may be that it was the obscure consciousness of this that excited Strickland's sympathy. Perhaps both were trying to put down in paint ideas which were more suitable to literature.

Strickland at this time must have been nearly forty-seven.

XLV

I HAVE SAID already that but for the hazard of a journey to Tahiti I should doubtless never have written this book. It is thither that after many wanderings Charles Strickland came, and it is there that he painted the pictures on which his fame most securely rests. I suppose no artist achieves completely the realisation of the dream that obsesses him, and Strickland, harassed incessantly by his struggle with technique, managed, perhaps, less than others to express the vision that he saw with his mind's eye; but in Tahiti the circumstances were favourable to him; he found in his surroundings the accidents necessary for his inspiration to become effective, and his later pictures give at least a suggestion of what he sought. They offer the imagination something new and strange. It is as though in this far country his spirit, that had wandered disembodied, seeking a tenement, at last was able to clothe itself in flesh. To use the hackneyed phrase, here he found himself.

It would seem that my visit to this remote island should immediately revive my interest in Strickland, but the work I was engaged
in occupied my attention to the exclusion of something that was irrelevant, and it was not till I had been there some days that I even
remembered his connection with it. After all, I had not seen him for
fifteen years, and it was nine since he died. But I think my arrival at
Tahiti would have driven out of my head matters of much more immediate importance to me, and even after a week I found it not easy
to order myself soberly. I remember that on my first morning I awoke
early, and when I came on to the terrace of the hotel no one was
stirring. I wandered round to the kitchen, but it was locked, and on a
bench outside it a native boy was sleeping. There seemed no chance
of breakfast for some time, so I sauntered down to the water-front.
The Chinamen were already busy in their shops. The sky had still the
pallor of dawn, and there was a ghostly silence on the lagoon. Ten
miles away the island of Murea, like some high fastness of the Holy
Grail, guarded its mystery.

I did not altogether believe my eyes. The days that had passed
since I left Wellington seemed extraordinary and unusual. Wellington
is trim and neat and English; it reminds you of a seaport town on the
South Coast. And for three days afterwards the sea was stormy. Gray
clouds chased one another across the sky. Then the wind dropped,
and the sea was calm and blue. The Pacific is more desolate than
other seas; its spaces seem more vast, and the most ordinary journey
upon it has somehow the feeling of an adventure. The air you breathe
is an elixir which prepares you for the unexpected. Nor is it vouchsafed to man in the flesh to know aught that more nearly suggests the
approach to the golden realms of fancy than the approach to Tahiti.
Murea, the sister isle, comes into view in rocky splendour, rising from
the desert sea mysteriously, like the unsubstantial fabric of a magic
wand. With its jagged outline it is like a Monseratt of the Pacific, and
you may imagine that there Polynesian knights guard with strange
rites mysteries unholy for men to know. The beauty of the island is
unveiled as diminishing distance shows you in distincter shape its
lovely peaks, but it keeps its secret as you sail by, and, darkly inviolable, seems to fold itself together in a stony, inaccessible grimness. It

would not surprise you if, as you came near seeking for an opening in the reef, it vanished suddenly from your view, and nothing met your gaze but the blue loneliness of the Pacific.

Tahiti is a lofty green island, with deep folds of a darker green, in which you divine silent valleys; there is mystery in their sombre depths, down which murmur and plash cool streams, and you feel that in those umbrageous places life from immemorial times has been led according to immemorial ways. Even here is something sad and terrible. But the impression is fleeting, and serves only to give a greater acuteness to the enjoyment of the moment. It is like the sadness which you may see in the jester's eyes when a merry company is laughing at his sallies; his lips smile and his jokes are gayer because in the communion of laughter he finds himself more intolerably alone. For Tahiti is smiling and friendly; it is like a lovely woman graciously prodigal of her charm and beauty; and nothing can be more conciliatory than the entrance into the harbour at Papeete. The schooners moored to the quay are trim and neat, the little town along the bay is white and urbane, and the flamboyants, scarlet against the blue sky, flaunt their colour like a cry of passion. They are sensual with an unashamed violence that leaves you breathless. And the crowd that throngs the wharf as the steamer draws alongside is gay and debonair; it is a noisy, cheerful, gesticulating crowd. It is a sea of brown faces. You have an impression of coloured movement against the flaming blue of the sky. Everything is done with a great deal of bustle, the unloading of the baggage, the examination of the customs; and everyone seems to smile at you. It is very hot. The colour dazzles you.

XLVI

HAD NOT BEEN in Tahiti long before I met Captain Nichols. He came in one morning when I was having breakfast on the terrace of the hotel and introduced himself. He had heard that I was interested in Charles Strickland, and announced that he was come to have a talk about him. They are as fond of gossip in Tahiti as in an English village, and one or two enquiries I had made for pictures by Strickland had been quickly spread. I asked the stranger if he had breakfasted.

"Yes; I have my coffee early," he answered, "but I don't mind having a drop of whisky."

I called the Chinese boy.

"You don't think it's too early?" said the Captain.

"You and your liver must decide that between you," I replied.

"I'm practically a teetotaller," he said, as he poured himself out a good half-tumbler of Canadian Club.

When he smiled he showed broken and discoloured teeth. He was a very lean man, of no more than average height, with gray hair cut short and a stubbly gray moustache. He had not shaved for a couple of days. His face was deeply lined, burned brown by long exposure to the sun, and he had a pair of small blue eyes which were astonishingly shifty. They moved quickly, following my smallest gesture, and they gave him the look of a very thorough rogue. But at the moment he was all heartiness and good-fellowship. He was dressed in a bedraggled suit of khaki, and his hands would have been all the better for a wash.

"I knew Strickland well," he said, as he leaned back in his chair and lit the cigar I had offered him. "It's through me he came out to the islands."

"Where did you meet him?" I asked.

"In Marseilles."

"What were you doing there?"

He gave me an ingratiating smile.

"Well, I guess I was on the beach."

My friend's appearance suggested that he was now in the same predicament, and I prepared myself to cultivate an agreeable acquaintance. The society of beach-combers always repays the small pains you need be at to enjoy it. They are easy of approach and affable in conversation. They seldom put on airs, and the offer of a drink is a sure way to their hearts. You need no laborious steps to enter upon familiarity with them, and you can earn not only their confidence, but their gratitude, by turning an attentive ear to their discourse. They look upon conversation as the great pleasure of life, thereby proving the excellence of their civilisation, and for the most part they are entertaining talkers. The extent of their experience is pleasantly balanced by the fertility of their imagination. It cannot be said that they are without guile, but they have a tolerant respect for the law, when the law is supported by strength. It is hazardous to play poker with them, but their ingenuity adds a peculiar excitement to the best game in the world. I came to know Captain Nichols very well before I left Tahiti, and I am the richer for his acquaintance. I do not consider that the cigars and whisky he consumed at my expense (he always refused cocktails, since he was practically a teetotaller), and the few dollars, borrowed with a civil air of conferring a favour upon me, that passed from my pocket to his, were in any way equivalent to the entertainment he afforded me. I remained his debtor. I should be sorry if my conscience, insisting on a rigid attention to the matter in hand, forced me to dismiss him in a couple of lines.

I do not know why Captain Nichols first left England. It was a matter upon which he was reticent, and with persons of his kind a direct question is never very discreet. He hinted at undeserved misfortune, and there is no doubt that he looked upon himself as the victim of injustice. My fancy played with the various forms of fraud and violence, and I agreed with him sympathetically when he remarked that the authorities in the old country were so damned technical. But it was nice to see that any unpleasantness he had endured in his native land had not impaired his ardent patriotism. He frequently declared that England was the finest country in the world, sir, and he felt a lively superiority over Americans, Colonials, Dagos, Dutchmen, and Kanakas.

But I do not think he was a happy man. He suffered from dyspepsia, and he might often be seen sucking a tablet of pepsin; in the morning his appetite was poor; but this affliction alone would hardly have impaired his spirits. He had a greater cause of discontent with life than this. Eight years before he had rashly married a wife. There are men whom a merciful Providence has undoubtedly ordained to a single life, but who from wilfulness or through circumstances they could not cope with have flown in the face of its decrees. There is no object more deserving of pity than the married bachelor. Of such was Captain Nichols. I met his wife. She was a woman of twenty-eight, I should think, though of a type whose age is always doubtful; for she cannot have looked different when she was twenty, and at forty would look no older. She gave me an impression of extraordinary tightness. Her plain face with its narrow lips was tight, her skin was stretched tightly over her bones, her smile was tight, her hair was tight, her clothes were tight, and the white drill she wore had all the effect of black bombazine. I could not imagine why Captain Nichols had married her, and having married her why he had not deserted her. Perhaps he had, often, and his melancholy arose from the fact that he could never succeed. However far he went and in howsoever secret a place he hid himself, I felt sure that Mrs. Nichols, inexorable as fate and remorseless as conscience, would presently rejoin him. He could as little escape her as the cause can escape the effect.

The rogue, like the artist and perhaps the gentleman, belongs to no class. He is not embarrassed by the *sans gene* of the hobo, nor put out of countenance by the etiquette of the prince. But Mrs. Nichols belonged to the well-defined class, of late become vocal, which is known as the lower-middle. Her father, in fact, was a policeman. I am certain that he was an efficient one. I do not know what her hold was on the Captain, but I do not think it was love. I never heard her speak, but it may be that in private she had a copious conversation. At any rate, Captain Nichols was frightened to death of her. Sometimes, sitting with me on the terrace of the hotel, he would become conscious that she was walking in the road outside. She did not call him; she gave no sign that she was aware of his existence; she merely walked up and down composedly. Then a strange uneasiness would seize the Captain; he would look at his watch and sigh.

"Well, I must be off," he said.

Neither wit nor whisky could detain him then. Yet he was a man who had faced undaunted hurricane and typhoon, and would not have hesitated to fight a dozen unarmed niggers with nothing but a revolver to help him. Sometimes Mrs. Nichols would send her daughter, a pale-faced, sullen child of seven, to the hotel.

"Mother wants you," she said, in a whining tone.

"Very well, my dear," said Captain Nichols.

He rose to his feet at once, and accompanied his daughter along the road. I suppose it was a very pretty example of the triumph of spirit over matter, and so my digression has at least the advantage of a moral.

XLVII

I HAVE TRIED to put some connection into the various things Captain Nichols told me about Strickland, and I here set them down in the best order I can. They made one another's acquaintance during the latter part of the winter following my last meeting with Strickland in Paris. How he had passed the intervening months I do not know, but life must have been very hard, for Captain Nichols saw him first in the Asile de Nuit. There was a strike at Marseilles at the time, and Strickland, having come to the end of his resources, had apparently found it impossible to earn the small sum he needed to keep body and soul together.

The Asile de Nuit is a large stone building where pauper and vagabond may get a bed for a week, provided their papers are in order and they can persuade the friars in charge that they are workingmen. Captain Nichols noticed Strickland for his size and his singular appearance among the crowd that waited for the doors to open; they waited listlessly, some walking to and fro, some leaning against the wall, and others seated on the curb with their feet in the gutter; and when they filed into the office he heard the monk who read his papers address him in English. But he did not have a chance to speak to him, since, as he entered the common-room, a monk came in with a huge Bible in his arms, mounted a pulpit which was at the end of the room, and began the service which the wretched outcasts had to endure as the price of their lodging. He and Strickland were assigned to different rooms, and when, thrown out of bed at five in the morning by a stalwart monk, he had made his bed and washed his face, Strickland had already disappeared. Captain Nichols wandered about the streets for an hour of bitter cold, and then made his way to the Place Victor Gelu, where the sailor-men are wont to congregate. Dozing against the pedestal of a statue, he saw Strickland again. He gave him a kick to awaken him.

"Come and have breakfast, mate," he said.

"Go to hell," answered Strickland.

I recognised my friend's limited vocabulary, and I prepared to regard Captain Nichols as a trustworthy witness.

"Busted?" asked the Captain.

"Blast you," answered Strickland.

"Come along with me. I'll get you some breakfast."

After a moment's hesitation, Strickland scrambled to his feet, and together they went to the Bouchee de Pain, where the hungry are given a wedge of bread, which they must eat there and then, for it is forbidden to take it away; and then to the Cuillere de Soupe, where for a week, at eleven and four, you may get a bowl of thin, salt soup. The two buildings are placed far apart, so that only the starving should be tempted to make use of them. So they had breakfast, and so began the queer companionship of Charles Strickland and Captain Nichols.

They must have spent something like four months at Marseilles in one another's society. Their career was devoid of adventure, if by adventure you mean unexpected or thrilling incident, for their days were occupied in the pursuit of enough money to get a night's lodging and such food as would stay the pangs of hunger. But I wish I could give here the pictures, coloured and racy, which Captain Nichols' vivid narrative offered to the imagination. His account of their discoveries in the low life of a seaport town would have made a charming book, and in the various characters that came their way the student might easily have found matter for a very complete dictionary of rogues. But I must content myself with a few paragraphs. I received the impression of a life intense and brutal, savage, multicoloured, and vivacious. It made the Marseilles that I knew, gesticulating and sunny, with its comfortable hotels and its restaurants crowded with the well-to-do, tame and commonplace. I envied men who had seen with their own eyes the sights that Captain Nichols described.

When the doors of the Asile de Nuit were closed to them, Strickland and Captain Nichols sought the hospitality of Tough Bill. This was the master of a sailors' boarding-house, a huge mulatto with a heavy fist, who gave the stranded mariner food and shelter till he found him a berth. They lived with him a month, sleeping with a dozen others, Swedes, negroes, Brazilians, on the floor of the two bare rooms in his house which he assigned to his charges; and every day they went with him to the Place Victor Gelu, whither came ships' captains in search of a man. He was married to an American woman, obese and slatternly, fallen to this pass by Heaven knows what process of degradation, and every day the boarders took it in turns to help her with the housework. Captain Nichols looked upon it as a smart piece of work on Strickland's part that he had got out of this by painting a portrait of Tough Bill. Tough Bill not only paid for the canvas, colours, and brushes, but gave Strickland a pound of smuggled tobacco into the bargain. For all I know, this picture may still adorn the parlour of the tumbledown little house somewhere near the Quai de la Joliette, and I suppose it could now be sold for fifteen hundred pounds. Strickland's idea was to ship on some vessel bound for Australia or New Zealand, and from there make his way to Samoa or Tahiti. I do not know how he had come upon the notion of going to the South Seas, though I remember that his imagination had long been haunted by an island, all green and sunny, encircled by a sea more blue than is found in Northern latitudes. I suppose that he clung to Captain Nichols because he was acquainted with those parts, and it was Captain Nichols who persuaded him that he would be more comfortable in Tahiti.

"You see, Tahiti's French," he explained to me. "And the French aren't so damned technical."

I thought I saw his point.

Strickland had no papers, but that was not a matter to disconcert Tough Bill when he saw a profit (he took the first month's wages of the sailor for whom he found a berth), and he provided Strickland with those of an English stoker who had providentially died on his hands. But both Captain Nichols and Strickland were bound East, and it chanced that the only opportunities for signing on were with ships sailing West. Twice Strickland refused a berth on tramps sailing for the United States, and once on a collier going to Newcastle. Tough Bill had no patience with an obstinacy which could only result in loss to himself, and on the last occasion he flung both Strickland and Captain Nichols out of his house without more ado. They found themselves once more adrift.

Tough Bill's fare was seldom extravagant, and you rose from his table almost as hungry as you sat down, but for some days they had good reason to regret it. They learned what hunger was. The Cuillere de Soupe and the Asile de Nuit were both closed to them, and their only sustenance was the wedge of bread which the Bouchee de Pain provided. They slept where they could, sometimes in an empty truck on a siding near the station, sometimes in a cart behind a warehouse; but it was bitterly cold, and after an hour or two of uneasy dozing they would tramp the streets again. What they felt the lack of most bitterly was tobacco, and Captain Nichols, for his part, could not do without it; he took to hunting the "Can o' Beer," for cigarette-ends and the butt-end of cigars which the promenaders of the night before had thrown away.

"I've tasted worse smoking mixtures in a pipe," he added, with a philosophic shrug of his shoulders, as he took a couple of cigars from the case I offered him, putting one in his mouth and the other in his pocket.

Now and then they made a bit of money. Sometimes a mail steamer would come in, and Captain Nichols, having scraped acquaintance with the timekeeper, would succeed in getting the pair of them a job as stevedores. When it was an English boat, they would dodge into the forecastle and get a hearty breakfast from the crew. They took the risk of running against one of the ship's officers and being hustled down the gangway with the toe of a boot to speed their going.

"There's no harm in a kick in the hindquarters when your belly's full," said Captain Nichols, "and personally I never take it in bad part. An officer's got to think about discipline."

I had a lively picture of Captain Nichols flying headlong down a narrow gangway before the uplifted foot of an angry mate, and, like a true Englishman, rejoicing in the spirit of the Mercantile Marine.

There were often odd jobs to be got about the fish-market. Once they each of them earned a franc by loading trucks with innumerable boxes of oranges that had been dumped down on the quay. One day they had a stroke of luck: one of the boarding-masters got a contract to paint a tramp that had come in from Madagascar round the Cape of Good Hope, and they spent several days on a plank hanging over the side, covering the rusty hull with paint. It was a situation that must have appealed to Strickland's sardonic humour. I asked Captain Nichols how he bore himself during these hardships.

"Never knew him say a cross word," answered the Captain. "He'd be a bit surly sometimes, but when we hadn't had a bite since morning, and we hadn't even got the price of a lie down at the Chink's, he'd be as lively as a cricket."

I was not surprised at this. Strickland was just the man to rise superior to circumstances, when they were such as to occasion despondency in most; but whether this was due to equanimity of soul or to contradictoriness it would be difficult to say.

The Chink's Head was a name the beach-combers gave to a wretched inn off the Rue Bouterie, kept by a one-eyed Chinaman, where for six sous you could sleep in a cot and for three on the floor. Here they made friends with others in as desperate condition as themselves, and when they were penniless and the night was bitter cold, they were glad to borrow from anyone who had earned a stray franc during the day the price of a roof over their heads. They were not niggardly, these tramps, and he who had money did not hesitate to share it among the rest. They belonged to all the countries in the world, but this was no bar to good-fellowship; for they felt themselves freemen of a country whose frontiers include them all, the great country of Cockaine.

"But I guess Strickland was an ugly customer when he was roused," said Captain Nichols, reflectively. "One day we ran into Tough Bill in the Place, and he asked Charlie for the papers he'd given him."

"'You'd better come and take them if you want them,' says Charlie.

"He was a powerful fellow, Tough Bill, but he didn't quite like the look of Charlie, so he began cursing him. He called him pretty near every name he could lay hands on, and when Tough Bill began cursing it was worth listening to him. Well, Charlie stuck it for a bit, then he stepped forward and he just said: 'Get out, you bloody swine.' It wasn't so much what he said, but the way he said it. Tough Bill never spoke another word; you could see him go yellow, and he walked away as if he'd remembered he had a date."

Strickland, according to Captain Nichols, did not use exactly the words I have given, but since this book is meant for family reading I have thought it better, at the expense of truth, to put into his mouth expressions familiar to the domestic circle.

Now, Tough Bill was not the man to put up with humiliation at the hands of a common sailor. His power depended on his prestige, and first one, then another, of the sailors who lived in his house told them that he had sworn to do Strickland in.

One night Captain Nichols and Strickland were sitting in one of the bars of the Rue Bouterie. The Rue Bouterie is a narrow street of one-storeyed houses, each house consisting of but one room; they are like the booths in a crowded fair or the cages of animals in a circus. At every door you see a woman. Some lean lazily against the side-posts, humming to themselves or calling to the passer-by in a raucous voice, and some listlessly read. They are French. Italian, Spanish, Japanese, coloured; some are fat and some are thin; and under the thick paint on their faces, the heavy smears on their eyebrows, and the scarlet of their lips, you see the lines of age and the scars of dissipation. Some wear black shifts and flesh-coloured stockings; some with curly hair, dyed yellow, are dressed like little girls in short muslin frocks. Through the open door you see a red-tiled floor, a large wooden bed, and on a deal table a ewer and a basin. A motley crowd saunters along the streets—Lascars off a P. and O., blond Northmen from a Swedish barque, Japanese from a man-of-war, English sailors, Spaniards, pleasant-looking fellows from a French cruiser, negroes off an American tramp. By day it is merely sordid, but at night, lit only by the lamps in the little huts, the street has a sinister beauty. The hideous lust that pervades the air is oppressive and horrible, and yet there is something mysterious in the sight which haunts and troubles you. You feel I know not what primitive force which repels and yet fascinates you. Here all the decencies of civilisation are swept away, and you feel that men are face to face with a sombre reality. There is an atmosphere that is at once intense and tragic.

In the bar in which Strickland and Nichols sat a mechanical piano was loudly grinding out dance music. Round the room people were sitting at table, here half a dozen sailors uproariously drunk, there a group of soldiers; and in the middle, crowded together, couples were dancing. Bearded sailors with brown faces and large horny hands clasped their partners in a tight embrace. The women wore nothing but a shift. Now and then two sailors would get up and dance together. The noise was deafening. People were singing, shouting, laughing; and when a man gave a long kiss to the girl sitting on his knees, cat-calls from the English sailors increased the din. The air was heavy with the dust beaten up by the heavy boots of the men, and gray with smoke. It was very hot. Behind the bar was seated a woman nursing her baby. The waiter, an undersized youth with a flat, spotty face, hurried to and fro carrying a tray laden with glasses of beer.

In a little while Tough Bill, accompanied by two huge negroes, came in, and it was easy to see that he was already three parts drunk. He was looking for trouble. He lurched against a table at which three soldiers were sitting and knocked over a glass of beer. There was an angry altercation, and the owner of the bar stepped forward and or-dered Tough Bill to go. He was a hefty fellow, in the habit of standing no nonsense from his customers, and Tough Bill hesitated. The land-lord was not a man he cared to tackle, for the police were on his side, and with an oath he turned on his heel. Suddenly he caught sight of Strickland. He rolled up to him. He did not speak. He gathered the spittle in his mouth and spat full in Strickland's face. Strickland seized his glass and flung it at him. The dancers stopped suddenly still. There was an instant of complete silence, but when Tough Bill threw himself on Strickland the lust of battle seized them all, and in a moment there was a confused scrimmage. Tables were overturned, glasses crashed to the ground. There was a hellish row. The women scattered to the door and behind the bar. Passers-by surged in from the street. You heard curses in every tongue the sound of blows, cries; and in the middle of the room a dozen men were fighting with all their might. On a sudden the police rushed in, and everyone who could made for the door. When the bar was more or less cleared, Tough Bill was lying insensible on the floor with a great gash in his head. Captain Nichols dragged Strickland, bleeding from a wound in his arm, his clothes in rags, into the street. His own face was covered with blood from a blow on the nose.

"I guess you'd better get out of Marseilles before Tough Bill comes out of hospital," he said to Strickland, when they had got back to the Chink's Head and were cleaning themselves.

"This beats cock-fighting," said Strickland.

I could see his sardonic smile.

Captain Nichols was anxious. He knew Tough Bill's vindictiveness. Strickland had downed the mulatto twice, and the mulatto, sober, was a man to be reckoned with. He would bide his time stealthily. He would be in no hurry, but one night Strickland would get a knife-thrust in his back, and in a day or two the corpse of a nameless beach-comber would be fished out of the dirty water of the harbour. Nichols went next evening to Tough Bill's house and made enquiries. He was in hospital still, but his wife, who had been to see him, said he was swearing hard to kill Strickland when they let him out.

A week passed.

"That's what I always say," reflected Captain Nichols, "when you hurt a man, hurt him bad. It gives you a bit of time to look about and think what you'll do next."

Then Strickland had a bit of luck. A ship bound for Australia had sent to the Sailors' Home for a stoker in place of one who had thrown himself overboard off Gibraltar in an attack of delirium tremens.

"You double down to the harbour, my lad," said the Captain to Strickland, "and sign on. You've got your papers."

Strickland set off at once, and that was the last Captain Nichols saw of him. The ship was only in port for six hours, and in the evening Captain Nichols watched the vanishing smoke from her funnels as she ploughed East through the wintry sea.

I have narrated all this as best I could, because I like the contrast of these episodes with the life that I had seen Strickland live in Ashley Gardens when he was occupied with stocks and shares; but I am aware that Captain Nichols was an outrageous liar, and I dare say there is not a word of truth in anything he told me. I should not be surprised to learn that he had never seen Strickland in his life, and owed his knowledge of Marseilles to the pages of a magazine.

XLVIII

IT IS HERE that I purposed to end my book. My first idea was to begin it with the account of Strickland's last years in Tahiti and with his horrible death, and then to go back and relate what I knew of his beginnings. This I meant to do, not from wilfulness, but because I wished to leave Strickland setting out with I know not what fancies in his lonely soul for the unknown islands which fired his imagination. I liked the picture of him starting at the age of forty-seven, when most men have already settled comfortably in a groove, for a new world. I saw him, the sea gray under the mistral and foam-flecked, watching the vanishing coast of France, which he was destined never to see again; and I thought there was something gallant in his bearing and dauntless in his soul. I wished so to end on a note of hope. It seemed to emphasise the unconquerable spirit of man. But I could not manage it. Somehow I could not get into my story, and after trying once or twice I had to give it up; I started from the beginning in the usual way, and made up my mind I could only tell what I knew of Strickland's life in the order in which I learnt the facts.

Those that I have now are fragmentary. I am in the position of a biologist who from a single bone must reconstruct not only the appearance of an extinct animal, but its habits. Strickland made no particular impression on the people who came in contact with him in Tahiti. To them he was no more than a beach-comber in constant need of money, remarkable only for the peculiarity that he painted pictures which seemed to them absurd; and it was not till he had been dead for some years and agents came from the dealers in Paris and Berlin to look for any pictures which might still remain on the island, that they had any idea that among them had dwelt a man of consequence. They remembered then that they could have bought for a song canvases which now were worth large sums, and they could not forgive themselves for the opportunity which had escaped them. There was a Jewish trader called Cohen, who had come by one of Strickland's pictures in a singular way. He was a little old Frenchman, with soft kind eyes and a pleasant smile, half trader and half seaman, who owned a cutter in which he wandered boldly among the Paumotus and the Marquesas, taking out trade goods and bringing back copra, shell, and pearls. I went to see him because I was told he had a large black pearl which he was willing to sell cheaply, and when I discovered that it was beyond my means I began to talk to him about Strickland. He had known him well.

"You see, I was interested in him because he was a painter," he told me. "We don't get many painters in the islands, and I was sorry for him because he was such a bad one. I gave him his first job. I had a plantation on the peninsula, and I wanted a white overseer. You never get any work out of the natives unless you have a white man over them. I said to him: 'You'll have plenty of time for painting, and you can earn a bit of money.' I knew he was starving, but I offered him good wages."

"I can't imagine that he was a very satisfactory overseer," I said, smiling.

"I made allowances. I have always had a sympathy for artists. It is in our blood, you know. But he only remained a few months. When he had enough money to buy paints and canvases he left me. The place had got hold of him by then, and he wanted to get away into the bush. But I continued to see him now and then. He would turn up in Papeete every few months and stay a little while; he'd get money out of someone or other and then disappear again. It was on one of these visits that he came to me and asked for the loan of two hundred francs. He looked as if he hadn't had a meal for a week, and I hadn't the heart to refuse him. Of course, I never expected to see my money again. Well, a year later he came to see me once more, and he brought a picture with him. He did not mention the money he owed me, but he said: 'Here is a picture of your plantation that I've painted for you.' I looked at it. I did not know what to say, but of course I thanked him, and when he had gone away I showed it to my wife."

"What was it like?" I asked.

"Do not ask me. I could not make head or tail of it. I never saw such a thing in my life. 'What shall we do with it?' I said to my wife. 'We can never hang it up,' she said. 'People would laugh at us.' So she took it into an attic and put it away with all sorts of rubbish, for my wife can never throw anything away. It is her mania. Then, imagine to yourself, just before the war my brother wrote to me from Paris, and said: 'Do you know anything about an English painter who lived in Tahiti? It appears that he was a genius, and his pictures fetch large prices. See if you can lay your hands on anything and send it to me. There's money to be made.' So I said to my wife. 'What about that picture that Strickland gave me?' Is it possible that it is still in the attic?' 'Without doubt,' she answered, 'for you know that I never throw anything away. It is my mania.' We went up to the attic, and there, among I know not what rubbish that had been gathered during the thirty years we have inhabited that house, was the picture. I looked at it again, and I said: 'Who would have thought that the overseer of my plantation on the peninsula, to whom I lent two hundred francs, had genius? Do you see anything in the picture?' 'No,' she said, 'it does not resemble the plantation and I have never seen cocoa-nuts with blue leaves; but they are mad in Paris, and it may be that your brother will be able to sell it for the two hundred francs you lent Strickland.' Well, we packed it up and we sent it to my brother. And at last I received a letter from him. What do you think he said? 'I received your picture,' he said, 'and I confess I thought it was a joke that you had played on me. I would not have given the cost of postage for the picture. I was half afraid to show it to the gentleman who had spoken to me about it. Imagine my surprise when he said it was a masterpiece, and offered me thirty thousand francs. I dare say he would have paid more, but frankly I was so taken aback that I lost my head; I accepted the offer before I was able to collect myself.'"

Then Monsieur Cohen said an admirable thing.

"I wish that poor Strickland had been still alive. I wonder what he would have said when I gave him twenty-nine thousand eight hundred francs for his picture."

XLIX

I LIVED AT the Hotel de la Fleur, and Mrs. Johnson, the proprietress, had a sad story to tell of lost opportunity. After Strickland's death certain of his effects were sold by auction in the market-place at Papeete, and she went to it herself because there was among the truck an American stove she wanted. She paid twenty-seven francs for it.

"There were a dozen pictures," she told me, "but they were unframed, and nobody wanted them. Some of them sold for as much as ten francs, but mostly they went for five or six. Just think, if I had bought them I should be a rich woman now."

But Tiaré Johnson would never under any circumstances have been rich. She could not keep money. The daughter of a native and an English sea-captain settled in Tahiti, when I knew her she was a woman of fifty, who looked older, and of enormous proportions. Tall and extremely stout, she would have been of imposing presence if the great good-nature of her face had not made it impossible for her to express anything but kindliness. Her arms were like legs of mutton, her breasts like giant cabbages; her face, broad and fleshy, gave you an impression of almost indecent nakedness, and vast chin succeeded to vast chin. I do not know how many of them there were. They fell away voluminously into the capaciousness of her bosom. She was dressed usually in a pink Mother Hubbard, and she wore all day long a large straw hat. But when she let down her hair, which she did now and then, for she was vain of it, you saw that it was long and dark and curly; and her eyes had remained young and vivacious. Her laughter was the most catching I ever heard; it would begin, a low peal in her throat, and would grow louder and louder till her whole vast body shook. She loved three things—a joke, a glass of wine, and a handsome man. To have known her is a privilege.

She was the best cook on the island, and she adored good food. From morning till night you saw her sitting on a low chair in the kitchen, surrounded by a Chinese cook and two or three native girls, giving her orders, chatting sociably with all and sundry, and tasting the savoury messes she devised. When she wished to do honour to a friend she cooked the dinner with her own hands. Hospitality was a passion with her, and there was no one on the island who need go without a dinner when there was anything to eat at the Hotel de la Fleur. She never turned her customers out of her house because they did not pay their bills. She always hoped they would pay when they could. There was one man there who had fallen on adversity, and to him she had given board and lodging for several months. When the Chinese laundry-man refused to wash for him without payment she had sent his things to be washed with hers. She could not allow the poor fellow to go about in a dirty shirt, she said, and since he was a man, and men must smoke, she gave him a franc a day for cigarettes. She used him with the same affability as those of her clients who paid their bills once a week.

Age and obesity had made her inapt for love, but she took a keen interest in the amatory affairs of the young. She looked upon venery as the natural occupation for men and women, and was ever ready with precept and example from her own wide experience.

"I was not fifteen when my father found that I had a lover," she said. "He was third mate on the *Tropic Bird*. A good-looking boy."

She sighed a little. They say a woman always remembers her first lover with affection; but perhaps she does not always remember him.

"My father was a sensible man."

"What did he do?" I asked.

"He thrashed me within an inch of my life, and then he made me marry Captain Johnson. I did not mind. He was older, of course, but he was good-looking too."

Tiare—her father had called her by the name of the white, scented flower which, they tell you, if you have once smelt, will always draw you back to Tahiti in the end, however far you may have roamed—Tiaré remembered Strickland very well.

"He used to come here sometimes, and I used to see him walking about Papeete. I was sorry for him, he was so thin, and he never had any money. When I heard he was in town, I used to send a boy to find him and make him come to dinner with me. I got him a job once or twice, but he couldn't stick to anything. After a little while he wanted to get back to the bush, and one morning he would be gone."

Strickland reached Tahiti about six months after he left Marseilles. He worked his passage on a sailing vessel that was making the trip from Auckland to San Francisco, and he arrived with a box of paints, an easel, and a dozen canvases. He had a few pounds in his pocket, for he had found work in Sydney, and he took a small room in a native house outside the town. I think the moment he reached Tahiti he felt himself at home. Tiaré told me that he said to her once:

"I'd been scrubbing the deck, and all at once a chap said to me: 'Why, there it is.' And I looked up and I saw the outline of the island. I knew right away that there was the place I'd been looking for all my life. Then we came near, and I seemed to recognise it. Sometimes when I walk about it all seems familiar. I could swear I've lived here before."

"Sometimes it takes them like that," said Tiare. "I've known men come on shore for a few hours while their ship was taking in cargo, and never go back. And I've known men who came here to be in an office for a year, and they cursed the place, and when they went away they took their dying oath they'd hang themselves before they came back again, and in six months you'd see them land once more, and they'd tell you they couldn't live anywhere else."

L

I HAVE AN idea that some men are born out of their due place. Accident has cast them amid certain surroundings, but they have always a nostalgia for a home they know not. They are strangers in their birthplace, and the leafy lanes they have known from childhood or the populous streets in which they have played, remain but a place of passage. They may spend their whole lives aliens among their kindred and remain aloof among the only scenes they have ever known. Perhaps it is this sense of strangeness that sends men far and wide in the search for something permanent, to which they may attach themselves. Perhaps some deep-rooted atavism urges the wanderer back to lands which his ancestors left in the dim beginnings of history. Sometimes a man hits upon a place to which he mysteriously feels that he belongs. Here is the home he sought, and he will settle amid scenes that he has never seen before, among men he has never known, as though they were familiar to him from his birth. Here at last he finds rest.

I told Tiaré the story of a man I had known at St. Thomas's Hospital. He was a Jew named Abraham, a blond, rather stout young man, shy and very unassuming; but he had remarkable gifts. He entered the hospital with a scholarship, and during the five years of the curriculum gained every prize that was open to him. He was made house-physician and house-surgeon. His brilliance was allowed by all. Finally he was elected to a position on the staff, and his career was assured. So far as human things can be predicted, it was certain that he would rise to the greatest heights of his profession. Honours and wealth awaited him. Before he entered upon his new duties he wished to take a holiday, and, having no private means, he went as surgeon on a tramp steamer to the Levant. It did not generally carry a doctor, but one of the senior surgeons at the hospital knew a director of the line, and Abraham was taken as a favour.

In a few weeks the authorities received his resignation of the coveted position on the staff. It created profound astonishment, and wild rumours were current. Whenever a man does anything unexpected, his fellows ascribe it to the most discreditable motives. But there was a man ready to step into Abraham's shoes, and Abraham was forgotten. Nothing more was heard of him. He vanished.

It was perhaps ten years later that one morning on board ship, about to land at Alexandria, I was bidden to line up with the other passengers for the doctor's examination. The doctor was a stout man in shabby clothes, and when he took off his hat I noticed that he was very bald. I had an idea that I had seen him before. Suddenly I remembered.

"Abraham," I said.

He turned to me with a puzzled look, and then, recognizing me, seized my hand. After expressions of surprise on either side, hearing that I meant to spend the night in Alexandria, he asked me to dine with him at the English Club. When we met again I declared my astonishment at finding him there. It was a very modest position that he occupied, and there was about him an air of straitened circumstance. Then he told me his story. When he set out on his holiday in the Mediterranean he had every intention of returning to London and his appointment at St. Thomas's. One morning the tramp docked at Alexandria, and from the deck he looked at the city, white in the sunlight, and the crowd on the wharf; he saw the natives in their shabby gabardines, the blacks from the Soudan, the noisy throng of Greeks and Italians, the grave Turks in tarbooshes, the sunshine and the blue sky; and something happened to him. He could not describe it. It was like a thunder-clap, he said, and then, dissatisfied with this, he said it was like a revelation. Something seemed to twist his heart, and suddenly he felt an exultation, a sense of wonderful freedom. He felt himself at home, and he made up his mind there and then, in a minute, that he would live the rest of his life in Alexandria. He had no great difficulty in leaving the ship, and in twenty-four hours, with all his belongings, he was on shore.

"The Captain must have thought you as mad as a hatter," I smiled.

"I didn't care what anybody thought. It wasn't I that acted, but something stronger within me. I thought I would go to a little Greek hotel, while I looked about, and I felt I knew where to find one. And do you know, I walked straight there, and when I saw it, I recognised it at once."

"Had you been to Alexandria before?"

"No; I'd never been out of England in my life."

Presently he entered the Government service, and there he had been ever since.

"Have you never regretted it?"

"Never, not for a minute. I earn just enough to live upon, and I'm satisfied. I ask nothing more than to remain as I am till I die. I've had a wonderful life."

I left Alexandria next day, and I forgot about Abraham till a little while ago, when I was dining with another old friend in the profession, Alec Carmichael, who was in England on short leave. I ran across him in the street and congratulated him on the knighthood with which his eminent services during the war had been rewarded. We arranged to spend an evening together for old time's sake, and when I agreed to dine with him, he proposed that he should ask nobody else, so that we could chat without interruption. He had a beautiful old house in Queen Anne Street, and being a man of taste he had furnished it admirably. On the walls of the dining-room I saw a charming Bellotto, and there was a pair of Zoffanys that I envied. When his wife, a tall, lovely creature in cloth of gold, had left us, I remarked laughingly on the change in his present circumstances from those when we had both been medical students. We had looked upon it then as an extravagance to dine in a shabby Italian restaurant in the Westminster Bridge Road. Now Alec Carmichael was on the staff of half a dozen hospitals. I should think he earned ten thousand a year, and his knighthood was but the first of the honours which must inevitably fall to his lot.

"I've done pretty well," he said, "but the strange thing is that I owe it all to one piece of luck."

"What do you mean by that?"

"Well, do you remember Abraham? He was the man who had the future. When we were students he beat me all along the line. He got the prizes and the scholarships that I went in for. I always played second fiddle to him. If he'd kept on he'd be in the position I'm in now. That man had a genius for surgery. No one had a look in with him. When he was appointed Registrar at Thomas's I hadn't a chance of getting on the staff. I should have had to become a G.P., and you know what likelihood there is for a G.P. ever to get out of the common rut. But Abraham fell out, and I got the job. That gave me my opportunity."

"I dare say that's true."

"It was just luck. I suppose there was some kink in Abraham. Poor devil, he's gone to the dogs altogether. He's got some twopenny-halfpenny job in the medical at Alexandria—sanitary officer or something like that. I'm told he lives with an ugly old Greek woman and has half a dozen scrofulous kids. The fact is, I suppose, that it's not enough to have brains. The thing that counts is character. Abraham hadn't got character."

Character? I should have thought it needed a good deal of character to throw up a career after half an hour's meditation, because you saw in another way of living a more intense significance. And it required still more character never to regret the sudden step. But I said nothing, and Alec Carmichael proceeded reflectively:

"Of course it would be hypocritical for me to pretend that I regret what Abraham did. After all, I've scored by it." He puffed luxuriously at the long Corona he was smoking. "But if I weren't personally concerned I should be sorry at the waste. It seems a rotten thing that a man should make such a hash of life."

I wondered if Abraham really had made a hash of life. Is to do what you most want, to live under the conditions that please you, in peace with yourself, to make a hash of life; and is it success to be an eminent surgeon with ten thousand a year and a beautiful wife? I suppose it depends on what meaning you attach to life, the claim which you acknowledge to society, and the claim of the individual. But again I held my tongue, for who am I to argue with a knight?

LI

Tiare, when I told her this story, praised my prudence, and for a few minutes we worked in silence, for we were shelling peas. Then her eyes, always alert for the affairs of her kitchen, fell on some action of the Chinese cook which aroused her violent disapproval. She turned on him with a torrent of abuse. The Chink was not backward to defend himself, and a very lively quarrel ensued. They spoke in the native language, of which I had learnt but half a dozen words, and it sounded as though the world would shortly come to an end; but presently peace was restored and Tiaré gave the cook a cigarette. They both smoked comfortably.

"Do you know, it was I who found him his wife?" said Tiaré suddenly, with a smile that spread all over her immense face.

"The cook?"

"No, Strickland."

"But he had one already."

"That is what he said, but I told him she was in England, and England is at the other end of the world."

"True," I replied.

"He would come to Papeete every two or three months, when he wanted paints or tobacco or money, and then he would wander about like a lost dog. I was sorry for him. I had a girl here then called Ata to do the rooms; she was some sort of a relation of mine, and her father and mother were dead, so I had her to live with me. Strickland used to come here now and then to have a square meal or to play chess with one of the boys. I noticed that she looked at him when he came, and I asked her if she liked him. She said she liked him well enough. You know what these girls are; they're always pleased to go with a white man."

"Was she a native?" I asked.

"Yes; she hadn't a drop of white blood in her. Well, after I'd talked to her I sent for Strickland, and I said to him: 'Strickland, it's time for you to settle down. A man of your age shouldn't go playing about with the girls down at the front. They're bad lots, and you'll come to no good with them. You've got no money, and you can never keep a job for more than a month or two. No one will employ you now. You say you can always live in the bush with one or other of the natives, and they're glad to have you because you're a white man, but it's not decent for a white man. Now, listen to me, Strickland.'"

Tiaré mingled French with English in her conversation, for she used both languages with equal facility. She spoke them with a singing accent which was not unpleasing. You felt that a bird would speak in these tones if it could speak English.

"'Now, what do you say to marrying Ata? She's a good girl and she's only seventeen. She's never been promiscuous like some of these girls—a captain or a first mate, yes, but she's never been touched by a native. *Elle se respecte, vois-tu*. The purser of the *Oahu* told me last journey that he hadn't met a nicer girl in the islands. It's time she settled down too, and besides, the captains and the first mates like a change now and then. I don't keep my girls too long. She has a bit of property down by Taravao, just before you come to the peninsula, and with copra at the price it is now you could live quite comfortably. There's a house, and you'd have all the time you wanted for your painting. What do you say to it?"

Tiaré paused to take breath.

"It was then he told me of his wife in England. 'My poor Strickland,' I said to him, 'they've all got a wife somewhere; that is generally why they come to the islands. Ata is a sensible girl, and she doesn't expect any ceremony before the Mayor. She's a Protestant, and you know they don't look upon these things like the Catholics.'

"Then he said: 'But what does Ata say to it?' 'It appears that she has a *beguin* for you,' I said. 'She's willing if you are. Shall I call her?' He chuckled in a funny, dry way he had, and I called her. She knew what I was talking about, the hussy, and I saw her out of the corner of my eyes listening with all her ears, while she pretended to iron a blouse that she had been washing for me. She came. She was laughing, but I could see that she was a little shy, and Strickland looked at her without speaking."

"Was she pretty?" I asked.

"Not bad. But you must have seen pictures of her. He painted her over and over again, sometimes with a *pareo* on and sometimes with nothing at all. Yes, she was pretty enough. And she knew how to cook. I taught her myself. I saw Strickland was thinking of it, so I said to him: 'I've given her good wages and she's saved them, and the captains and the first mates she's known have given her a little something now and then. She's saved several hundred francs.'

"He pulled his great red beard and smiled.

"'Well, Ata,' he said, 'do you fancy me for a husband.'

"She did not say anything, but just giggled.

"'But I tell you, my poor Strickland, the girl has a *beguin* for you,' I said.

"'I shall beat you,' he said, looking at her.

"'How else should I know you loved me,' she answered."

Tiaré broke off her narrative and addressed herself to me reflectively.

"My first husband, Captain Johnson, used to thrash me regularly. He was a man. He was handsome, six foot three, and when he was drunk there was no holding him. I would be black and blue all over for days at a time. Oh, I cried when he died. I thought I should never get over it. But it wasn't till I married George Rainey that I knew what I'd lost. You can never tell what a man is like till you live with him. I've never been so deceived in a man as I was in George Rainey. He was a fine, upstanding fellow too. He was nearly as tall as Captain Johnson, and he looked strong enough. But it was all on the surface. He never drank. He never raised his hand to me. He might have been a missionary. I made love with the officers of every ship that touched the island, and George Rainey never saw anything. At last I was disgusted with him, and I got a divorce. What was the good of a husband like that? It's a terrible thing the way some men treat women."

I condoled with Tiare, and remarked feelingly that men were deceivers ever, then asked her to go on with her story of Strickland.

"'Well,' I said to him, 'there's no hurry about it. Take your time and think it over. Ata has a very nice room in the annexe. Live with her for a month, and see how you like her. You can have your meals here. And at the end of a month, if you decide you want to marry her, you can just go and settle down on her property.'

"Well, he agreed to that. Ata continued to do the housework, and I gave him his meals as I said I would. I taught Ata to make one or two dishes I knew he was fond of. He did not paint much. He wandered about the hills and bathed in the stream. And he sat about the front looking at the lagoon, and at sunset he would go down and look at Murea. He used to go fishing on the reef. He loved to moon about the harbour talking to the natives. He was a nice, quiet fellow. And every evening after dinner he would go down to the annexe with Ata. I saw he was longing to get away to the bush, and at the end of the month I asked him what he intended to do. He said if Ata was willing to go, he was willing to go with her. So I gave them a wedding dinner. I cooked it with my own hands. I gave them a pea soup and lobster *a la portugaise*, and a curry, and a cocoa-nut salad—you've never had one of my cocoa-nut salads, have you? I must make you one before you go—and then I made them an ice. We had all the champagne we could drink and liqueurs to follow. Oh, I'd made up my mind to do things well. And afterwards we danced in the drawing-room. I was not so fat, then, and I always loved dancing."

The drawing-room at the Hotel de la Fleur was a small room, with a cottage piano, and a suite of mahogany furniture, covered in stamped velvet, neatly arranged around the walls. On round tables were photograph albums, and on the walls enlarged photographs of Tiaré and her first husband, Captain Johnson. Still, though Tiaré was old and fat, on occasion we rolled back the Brussels carpet, brought in the maids and one or two friends of Tiare's, and danced, though now to the wheezy music of a gramaphone. On the verandah the air was scented with the heavy perfume of the tiaré, and overhead the Southern Cross shone in a cloudless sky.

Tiaré smiled indulgently as she remembered the gaiety of a time long passed.

"We kept it up till three, and when we went to bed I don't think anyone was very sober. I had told them they could have my trap to take them as far as the road went, because after that they had a long walk. Ata's property was right away in a fold of the mountain. They started at dawn, and the boy I sent with them didn't come back till next day.

"Yes, that's how Strickland was married."

LII

I SUPPOSE THE next three years were the happiest of Strickland's life. Ata's house stood about eight kilometres from the road that runs round the island, and you went to it along a winding pathway shaded by the luxuriant trees of the tropics. It was a bungalow of unpainted wood, consisting of two small rooms, and outside was a small shed that served as a kitchen. There was no furniture except the mats they used as beds, and a rocking-chair, which stood on the verandah. Bananas with their great ragged leaves, like the tattered habiliments of an empress in adversity, grew close up to the house. There was a tree just behind which bore alligator pears, and all about were the cocoa-nuts which gave the land its revenue. Ata's father had planted crotons round his property, and they grew in coloured profusion, gay and brilliant; they fenced the land with flame. A mango grew in front of the house, and at the edge of the clearing were two flamboyants, twin trees, that challenged the gold of the cocoa-nuts with their scarlet flowers.

Here Strickland lived, coming seldom to Papeete, on the produce of the land. There was a little stream that ran not far away, in which he bathed, and down this on occasion would come a shoal of fish. Then the natives would assemble with spears, and with much shouting would transfix the great startled things as they hurried down to the sea. Sometimes Strickland would go down to the reef, and come back with a basket of small, coloured fish that Ata would fry in cocoa-nut oil, or with a lobster; and sometimes she would make a savoury dish of the great land-crabs that scuttled away under your feet. Up the mountain were wild-orange trees, and now and then Ata would go with two or three women from the village and return laden with the green, sweet, luscious fruit. Then the cocoa-nuts would be ripe for picking, and her cousins (like all the natives, Ata had a host of relatives) would swarm up the trees and throw down the big ripe nuts. They split them open and put them in the sun to dry. Then they cut out the copra and put it into sacks, and the women would carry it down to the trader at the village by the lagoon, and he would give in exchange for it rice and soap and tinned meat and a little money. Sometimes there would be a feast in the neighbourhood, and a pig would be killed. Then they would go and eat themselves sick, and dance, and sing hymns.

But the house was a long way from the village, and the Tahitians are lazy. They love to travel and they love to gossip, but they do not care to walk, and for weeks at a time Strickland and Ata lived alone. He painted and he read, and in the evening, when it was dark, they sat together on the verandah, smoking and looking at the night. Then Ata had a baby, and the old woman who came up to help her through her trouble stayed on. Presently the granddaughter of the old woman came to stay with her, and then a youth appeared—no one quite knew where from or to whom he belonged—but he settled down with them in a happy-go-lucky way, and they all lived together.

LIII

"*TENEZ, VOILA LE Capitaine Brunot*," said Tiare, one day when I was fitting together what she could tell me of Strickland. "He knew Strickland well; he visited him at his house."

I saw a middle-aged Frenchman with a big black beard, streaked with gray, a sunburned face, and large, shining eyes. He was dressed in a neat suit of ducks. I had noticed him at luncheon, and Ah Lin, the Chinese boy, told me he had come from the Paumotus on the boat that had that day arrived. Tiaré introduced me to him, and he handed me his card, a large card on which was printed *Rene Brunot*, and underneath, *Capitaine au Long Cours*. We were sitting on a little verandah outside the kitchen, and Tiaré was cutting out a dress that she was making for one of the girls about the house. He sat down with us.

"Yes; I knew Strickland well," he said. "I am very fond of chess, and he was always glad of a game. I come to Tahiti three or four times a year for my business, and when he was at Papeete he would come here and we would play. When he married"—Captain Brunot smiled and shrugged his shoulders— "*enfin*, when he went to live with the girl that Tiaré gave him, he asked me to go and see him. I was one of the guests at the wedding feast." He looked at Tiare, and they both laughed. "He did not come much to Papeete after that, and about a year later it chanced that I had to go to that part of the island for I forgot what business, and when I had finished it I said to myself: '*Voyons*, why should I not go and see that poor Strickland?' I asked one or two natives if they knew anything about him, and I discovered that he lived not more than five kilometres from where I was. So I went. I shall never forget the impression my visit made on me. I live on an atoll, a low island, it is a strip of land surrounding a lagoon, and its beauty is the beauty of the sea and sky and the varied colour of the lagoon and the grace of the cocoa-nut trees; but the place where Strickland lived had the beauty of the Garden of Eden. Ah, I wish I could make you see the enchantment of that spot, a corner hidden away from all the world, with the blue sky overhead and the rich, luxuriant trees. It was a feast of colour. And it was fragrant and cool. Words cannot describe that paradise. And here he lived, unmindful of the world and by the world forgotten. I suppose to European eyes it would have seemed astonishingly sordid. The house was dilapidated and none too clean. Three or four natives were lying on the verandah. You know how natives love to herd together. There was a young man lying full length, smoking a cigarette, and he wore nothing but a *pareo*."

The *pareo* is a long strip of trade cotton, red or blue, stamped with a white pattern. It is worn round the waist and hangs to the knees.

"A girl of fifteen, perhaps, was plaiting pandanus-leaf to make a hat, and an old woman was sitting on her haunches smoking a pipe. Then I saw Ata. She was suckling a new-born child, and another child, stark naked, was playing at her feet. When she saw me she called out to Strickland, and he came to the door. He, too, wore nothing but a *pareo*. He was an extraordinary figure, with his red beard and matted hair, and his great hairy chest. His feet were horny and scarred, so that I knew he went always bare foot. He had gone native with a vengeance. He seemed pleased to see me, and told Ata to kill a chicken for our dinner. He took me into the house to show me the picture he was at work on when I came in. In one corner of the room was the bed, and in the middle was an easel with the canvas upon it. Because I was sorry for him, I had bought a couple of his pictures for small sums, and I had sent others to friends of mine in France. And though I had bought them out of compassion, after living with them I began to like them. Indeed, I found a strange beauty in them. Everyone thought I was mad, but it turns out that I was right. I was his first admirer in the islands."

He smiled maliciously at Tiare, and with lamentations she told us again the story of how at the sale of Strickland's effects she had neglected the pictures, but bought an American stove for twenty-seven francs.

"Have you the pictures still?" I asked.

"Yes; I am keeping them till my daughter is of marriageable age, and then I shall sell them. They will be her *dot*." Then he went on with the account of his visit to Strickland.

"I shall never forget the evening I spent with him. I had not intended to stay more than an hour, but he insisted that I should spend the night. I hesitated, for I confess I did not much like the look of the mats on which he proposed that I should sleep; but I shrugged my shoulders. When I was building my house in the Paumotus I had slept out for weeks on a harder bed than that, with nothing to shelter me but wild shrubs; and as for vermin, my tough skin should be proof against their malice.

"We went down to the stream to bathe while Ata was preparing the dinner, and after we had eaten it we sat on the verandah. We smoked and chatted. The young man had a concertina, and he played the tunes popular on the music-halls a dozen years before. They sounded strangely in the tropical night thousands of miles from civilisation. I asked Strickland if it did not irk him to live in that promiscuity. No, he said; he liked to have his models under his hand. Presently, after loud yawning, the natives went away to sleep, and Strickland and I were left alone. I cannot describe to you the intense silence of the night. On my island in the Paumotus there is never at night the complete stillness that there was here. There is the rustle of the myriad animals on the beach, all the little shelled things that crawl about ceaselessly, and there is the noisy scurrying of the land-crabs. Now and then in the lagoon you hear the leaping of a fish, and sometimes a hurried noisy splashing as a brown shark sends all the other fish scampering for their lives. And above all, ceaseless like time, is the dull roar of the breakers on the reef. But here there was not a sound, and the air was scented with the white flowers of the night. It was a night so beautiful that your soul seemed hardly able to bear the prison of the body. You felt that it was ready to be wafted away on the immaterial air, and death bore all the aspect of a beloved friend."

Tiaré sighed.

"Ah, I wish I were fifteen again."

Then she caught sight of a cat trying to get at a dish of prawns on the kitchen table, and with a dexterous gesture and a lively volley of abuse flung a book at its scampering tail.

"I asked him if he was happy with Ata.

"'She leaves me alone,' he said. 'She cooks my food and looks after her babies. She does what I tell her. She gives me what I want from a woman.'

"'And do you never regret Europe? Do you not yearn sometimes for the light of the streets in Paris or London, the companionship of your friends, and equals, *que sais-je?* for theatres and newspapers, and the rumble of omnibuses on the cobbled pavements?'

"For a long time he was silent. Then he said:

"'I shall stay here till I die.'

"'But are you never bored or lonely?' I asked.

"He chuckled.

"'*Mon pauvre ami,*' he said. 'It is evident that you do not know what it is to be an artist.'"

Capitaine Brunot turned to me with a gentle smile, and there was a wonderful look in his dark, kind eyes.

"He did me an injustice, for I too know what it is to have dreams. I have my visions too. In my way I also am an artist."

We were all silent for a while, and Tiaré fished out of her capacious pocket a handful of cigarettes. She handed one to each of us, and we all three smoked. At last she said:

"Since *ce monsieur* is interested in Strickland, why do you not take him to see Dr. Coutras? He can tell him something about his illness and death."

"*Volontiers*," said the Captain, looking at me.

I thanked him, and he looked at his watch.

"It is past six o'clock. We should find him at home if you care to come now."

I got up without further ado, and we walked along the road that led to the doctor's house. He lived out of the town, but the Hotel de la Fleur was on the edge of it, and we were quickly in the country. The broad road was shaded by pepper-trees, and on each side were the plantations, cocoa-nut and vanilla. The pirate birds were screeching among the leaves of the palms. We came to a stone bridge over a shallow river, and we stopped for a few minutes to see the native boys bathing. They chased one another with shrill cries and laughter, and their bodies, brown and wet, gleamed in the sunlight.

LIV

As WE WALKED along I reflected on a circumstance which all that I had lately heard about Strickland forced on my attention. Here, on this remote island, he seemed to have aroused none of the detestation with which he was regarded at home, but compassion rather; and his vagaries were accepted with tolerance. To these people, native and European, he was a queer fish, but they were used to queer fish, and they took him for granted; the world was full of odd persons, who did odd things; and perhaps they knew that a man is not what he wants to be, but what he must be. In England and France he was the square peg in the round hole, but here the holes were any sort of shape, and no sort of peg was quite amiss. I do not think he was any gentler here, less selfish or less brutal, but the circumstances were more favourable. If he had spent his life amid these surroundings he might have passed for no worse a man than another. He received here what he neither expected nor wanted among his own people—sympathy.

I tried to tell Captain Brunot something of the astonishment with which this filled me, and for a little while he did not answer.

"It is not strange that I, at all events, should have had sympathy for him," he said at last, "for, though perhaps neither of us knew it, we were both aiming at the same thing."

"What on earth can it be that two people so dissimilar as you and Strickland could aim at?" I asked, smiling.

"Beauty."

"A large order," I murmured.

"Do you know how men can be so obsessed by love that they are deaf and blind to everything else in the world? They are as little their own masters as the slaves chained to the benches of a galley. The passion that held Strickland in bondage was no less tyrannical than love."

"How strange that you should say that!" I answered. "For long ago I had the idea that he was possessed of a devil."

"And the passion that held Strickland was a passion to create beauty. It gave him no peace. It urged him hither and thither. He was eternally a pilgrim, haunted by a divine nostalgia, and the demon within him was ruthless. There are men whose desire for truth is so great that to attain it they will shatter the very foundation of their world. Of such was Strickland, only beauty with him took the place of truth. I could only feel for him a profound compassion."

"That is strange also. A man whom he had deeply wronged told me that he felt a great pity for him." I was silent for a moment. "I wonder if there you have found the explanation of a character which has always seemed to me inexplicable. How did you hit on it?"

He turned to me with a smile.

"Did I not tell you that I, too, in my way was an artist? I realised in myself the same desire as animated him. But whereas his medium was paint, mine has been life."

Then Captain Brunot told me a story which I must repeat, since, if only by way of contrast, it adds something to my impression of Strickland. It has also to my mind a beauty of its own.

Captain Brunot was a Breton, and had been in the French Navy. He left it on his marriage, and settled down on a small property he had near Quimper to live for the rest of his days in peace; but the failure of an attorney left him suddenly penniless, and neither he nor his wife was willing to live in penury where they had enjoyed consideration. During his sea faring days he had cruised the South Seas, and he determined now to seek his fortune there. He spent some months in Papeete to make his plans and gain experience; then, on money borrowed from a friend in France, he bought an island in the Paumotus. It was a ring of land round a deep lagoon, uninhabited, and covered only with scrub and wild guava. With the intrepid woman who was his wife, and a few natives, he landed there, and set about building a house, and clearing the scrub so that he could plant cocoa-nuts. That was twenty years before, and now what had been a barren island was a garden.

"It was hard and anxious work at first, and we worked strenuously, both of us. Every day I was up at dawn, clearing, planting, working on my house, and at night when I threw myself on my bed it was to sleep like a log till morning. My wife worked as hard as I did. Then children were born to us, first a son and then a daughter. My wife and I have taught them all they know. We had a piano sent out from France, and she has taught them to play and to speak English, and I have taught them Latin and mathematics, and we read history together. They can sail a boat. They can swim as well as the natives. There is nothing about the land of which they are ignorant. Our trees have prospered, and there is shell on my reef. I have come to Tahiti now to buy a schooner. I can get enough shell to make it worth while to fish for it, and, who knows? I may find pearls. I have made something where there was nothing. I too have made beauty. Ah, you do not know what it is to look at those tall, healthy trees and think that every one I planted myself."

"Let me ask you the question that you asked Strickland. Do you never regret France and your old home in Brittany?"

"Some day, when my daughter is married and my son has a wife and is able to take my place on the island, we shall go back and finish our days in the old house in which I was born."

"You will look back on a happy life," I said.

"*Evidemment*, it is not exciting on my island, and we are very far from the world—imagine, it takes me four days to come to Tahiti—but we are happy there. It is given to few men to attempt a work and to achieve it. Our life is simple and innocent. We are untouched by ambition, and what pride we have is due only to our contemplation of the work of our hands. Malice cannot touch us, nor envy attack. Ah, *mon cher monsieur*, they talk of the blessedness of labour, and it is a meaningless phrase, but to me it has the most intense significance. I am a happy man."

"I am sure you deserve to be," I smiled.

"I wish I could think so. I do not know how I have deserved to have a wife who was the perfect friend and helpmate, the perfect mistress and the perfect mother."

I reflected for a while on the life that the Captain suggested to my imagination.

"It is obvious that to lead such an existence and make so great a success of it, you must both have needed a strong will and a determined character."

"Perhaps; but without one other factor we could have achieved nothing."

"And what was that?"

He stopped, somewhat dramatically, and stretched out his arm.

"Belief in God. Without that we should have been lost."

Then we arrived at the house of Dr. Coutras.

LV

MR. COUTRAS WAS an old Frenchman of great stature and exceeding bulk. His body was shaped like a huge duck's egg; and his eyes, sharp, blue, and good-natured, rested now and then with self-satisfaction on his enormous paunch. His complexion was florid and his hair white. He was a man to attract immediate sympathy. He received us in a room that might have been in a house in a provincial town in France, and the one or two Polynesian curios had an odd look. He took my hand in both of his—they were huge—and gave me a hearty look, in which, however, was great shrewdness. When he shook hands with Capitaine Brunot he enquired politely after *Madame et les enfants*. For some minutes there was an exchange of courtesies and some local gossip about the island, the prospects of copra and the vanilla crop; then we came to the object of my visit.

I shall not tell what Dr. Coutras related to me in his words, but in my own, for I cannot hope to give at second hand any impression of his vivacious delivery. He had a deep, resonant voice, fitted to his massive frame, and a keen sense of the dramatic. To listen to him was, as the phrase goes, as good as a play; and much better than most.

It appears that Dr. Coutras had gone one day to Taravao in order to see an old chiefess who was ill, and he gave a vivid picture of the obese old lady, lying in a huge bed, smoking cigarettes, and surrounded by a crowd of dark-skinned retainers. When he had seen her he was taken into another room and given dinner—raw fish, fried bananas, and chicken—*que sais-je*, the typical dinner of the *indigene*—and while he was eating it he saw a young girl being driven away from the door in tears. He thought nothing of it, but when he went out to get into his trap and drive home, he saw her again, standing a little way off; she looked at him with a woebegone air, and tears streamed down her cheeks. He asked someone what was wrong with her, and was told that she had come down from the hills to ask him to visit a white man who was sick. They had told her that the doctor could not be disturbed. He called her, and himself asked what she wanted. She told him that Ata had sent her, she who used to be at the Hotel de la Fleur, and that the Red One was ill. She thrust into his hand a crumpled piece of newspaper, and when he opened it he found in it a hundred-franc note.

"Who is the Red One?" he asked of one of the bystanders.

He was told that that was what they called the Englishman, a painter, who lived with Ata up in the valley seven kilometres from where they were. He recognised Strickland by the description. But it was necessary to walk. It was impossible for him to go; that was why they had sent the girl away.

"I confess," said the doctor, turning to me, "that I hesitated. I did not relish fourteen kilometres over a bad pathway, and there was no chance that I could get back to Papeete that night. Besides, Strickland was not sympathetic to me. He was an idle, useless scoundrel, who preferred to live with a native woman rather than work for his living like the rest of us. *Mon Dieu*, how was I to know that one day the world would come to the conclusion that he had genius? I asked the girl if he was not well enough to have come down to see me. I asked her what she thought was the matter with him. She would not answer. I pressed her, angrily perhaps, but she looked down on the ground and began to cry. Then I shrugged my shoulders; after all, perhaps it was my duty to go, and in a very bad temper I bade her lead the way."

His temper was certainly no better when he arrived, perspiring freely and thirsty. Ata was on the look-out for him, and came a little way along the path to meet him.

"Before I see anyone give me something to drink or I shall die of thirst," he cried out. "*Pour l'amour de Dieu*, get me a cocoa-nut."

She called out, and a boy came running along. He swarmed up a tree, and presently threw down a ripe nut. Ata pierced a hole in it, and the doctor took a long, refreshing draught. Then he rolled himself a cigarette and felt in a better humour.

"Now, where is the Red One?" he asked.

"He is in the house, painting. I have not told him you were coming. Go in and see him."

"But what does he complain of? If he is well enough to paint, he is well enough to have come down to Taravao and save me this confounded walk. I presume my time is no less valuable than his."

Ata did not speak, but with the boy followed him to the house. The girl who had brought him was by this time sitting on the verandah, and here was lying an old woman, with her back to the wall, making native cigarettes. Ata pointed to the door. The doctor, wondering irritably why they behaved so strangely, entered, and there found Strickland cleaning his palette. There was a picture on the easel. Strickland, clad only in a *pareo*, was standing with his back to the door, but he turned round when he heard the sound of boots. He gave the doctor a look of vexation. He was surprised to see him, and resented the intrusion. But the doctor gave a gasp, he was rooted to the floor, and he stared with all his eyes. This was not what he expected. He was seized with horror.

"You enter without ceremony," said Strickland. "What can I do for you?"

The doctor recovered himself, but it required quite an effort for him to find his voice. All his irritation was gone, and he felt—*eh bien, oui, je ne le nie pas*—he felt an overwhelming pity.

"I am Dr. Coutras. I was down at Taravao to see the chiefess, and

Ata sent for me to see you."

"She's a damned fool. I have had a few aches and pains lately and a little fever, but that's nothing; it will pass off. Next time anyone went to Papeete I was going to send for some quinine."

"Look at yourself in the glass."

Strickland gave him a glance, smiled, and went over to a cheap mirror in a little wooden frame, that hung on the wall.

"Well?"

"Do you not see a strange change in your face? Do you not see the thickening of your features and a look—how shall I describe it?—the books call it lion-faced. *Mon pauvre ami*, must I tell you that you have a terrible disease?"

"I?"

"When you look at yourself in the glass you see the typical appearance of the leper."

"You are jesting," said Strickland.

"I wish to God I were."

"Do you intend to tell me that I have leprosy?"

"Unfortunately, there can be no doubt of it."

Dr. Coutras had delivered sentence of death on many men, and he could never overcome the horror with which it filled him. He felt always the furious hatred that must seize a man condemned when he compared himself with the doctor, sane and healthy, who had the inestimable privilege of life. Strickland looked at him in silence. Nothing of emotion could be seen on his face, disfigured already by the loathsome disease.

"Do they know?" he asked at last, pointing to the persons on the verandah, now sitting in unusual, unaccountable silence.

"These natives know the signs so well," said the doctor. "They were afraid to tell you."

Strickland stepped to the door and looked out. There must have been something terrible in his face, for suddenly they all burst out into loud cries and lamentation. They lifted up their voices and they wept. Strickland did not speak. After looking at them for a moment, he came back into the room.

"How long do you think I can last?"

"Who knows? Sometimes the disease continues for twenty years. It is a mercy when it runs its course quickly."

Strickland went to his easel and looked reflectively at the picture that stood on it.

"You have had a long journey. It is fitting that the bearer of important tidings should be rewarded. Take this picture. It means nothing to you now, but it may be that one day you will be glad to have it."

Dr. Coutras protested that he needed no payment for his journey; he had already given back to Ata the hundred-franc note, but Strickland insisted that he should take the picture. Then together they went out on the verandah. The natives were sobbing violently. "Be quiet, woman. Dry thy tears," said Strickland, addressing Ata. "There is no great harm. I shall leave thee very soon."

"They are not going to take thee away?" she cried.

At that time there was no rigid sequestration on the islands, and lepers, if they chose, were allowed to go free.

"I shall go up into the mountain," said Strickland.

Then Ata stood up and faced him.

"Let the others go if they choose, but I will not leave thee. Thou art my man and I am thy woman. If thou leavest me I shall hang myself on the tree that is behind the house. I swear it by God."

There was something immensely forcible in the way she spoke. She was no longer the meek, soft native girl, but a determined woman. She was extraordinarily transformed.

"Why shouldst thou stay with me? Thou canst go back to Papeete, and thou wilt soon find another white man. The old woman can take care of thy children, and Tiaré will be glad to have thee back."

"Thou art my man and I am thy woman. Whither thou goest I will go, too."

For a moment Strickland's fortitude was shaken, and a tear filled each of his eyes and trickled slowly down his cheeks. Then he gave the sardonic smile which was usual with him.

"Women are strange little beasts," he said to Dr. Coutras. "You can treat them like dogs, you can beat them till your arm aches, and still they love you." He shrugged his shoulders. "Of course, it is one of the most absurd illusions of Christianity that they have souls."

"What is it that thou art saying to the doctor?" asked Ata suspiciously. "Thou wilt not go?"

"If it please thee I will stay, poor child."

Ata flung herself on her knees before him, and clasped his legs with her arms and kissed them. Strickland looked at Dr. Coutras with a faint smile.

"In the end they get you, and you are helpless in their hands. White or brown, they are all the same."

Dr. Coutras felt that it was absurd to offer expressions of regret in so terrible a disaster, and he took his leave. Strickland told Tane, the boy, to lead him to the village. Dr. Coutras paused for a moment, and then he addressed himself to me.

"I did not like him, I have told you he was not sympathetic to me, but as I walked slowly down to Taravao I could not prevent an unwilling admiration for the stoical courage which enabled him to bear perhaps the most dreadful of human afflictions. When Tane left me I told him I would send some medicine that might be of service; but my hope was small that Strickland would consent to take it, and even smaller that, if he did, it would do him good. I gave the boy a message for Ata that I would come whenever she sent for me. Life is hard, and Nature takes sometimes a terrible delight in torturing her children. It was with a heavy heart that I drove back to my comfortable home in Papeete."

For a long time none of us spoke.

"But Ata did not send for me," the doctor went on, at last, "and it chanced that I did not go to that part of the island for a long time. I had no news of Strickland. Once or twice I heard that Ata had been to Papeete to buy painting materials, but I did not happen to see her. More than two years passed before I went to Taravao again, and then it was once more to see the old chiefess. I asked them whether they had heard anything of Strickland. By now it was known everywhere that he had leprosy. First Tane, the boy, had left the house, and then, a little time afterwards, the old woman and her grandchild. Strickland and Ata were left alone with their babies. No one went near the plantation, for, as you know, the natives have a very lively horror of the disease, and in the old days when it was discovered the sufferer was killed; but sometimes, when the village boys were scrambling about the hills, they would catch sight of the white man, with his great red beard, wandering about. They fled in terror. Sometimes Ata would come down to the village at night and arouse the trader, so that he might sell her various things of which she stood in need. She knew that the natives looked upon her with the same horrified aversion as they looked upon Strickland, and she kept out of their way. Once some women, venturing nearer than usual to the plantation, saw her washing clothes in the brook, and they threw stones at her. After that the trader was told to give her the message that if she used the brook again men would come and burn down her house."

"Brutes," I said.

"*Mais non, mon cher monsieur*, men are always the same. Fear makes them cruel.... I decided to see Strickland, and when I had finished with the chiefess asked for a boy to show me the way. But none would accompany me, and I was forced to find it alone."

When Dr. Coutras arrived at the plantation he was seized with a feeling of uneasiness. Though he was hot from walking, he shivered. There was something hostile in the air which made him hesitate, and he felt that invisible forces barred his way. Unseen hands seemed to draw him back. No one would go near now to gather the cocoa-nuts, and they lay rotting on the ground. Everywhere was desolation. The bush was encroaching, and it looked as though very soon the primeval forest would regain possession of that strip of land which had been snatched from it at the cost of so much labour. He had the sensation that here was the abode of pain. As he approached the house he was struck by the unearthly silence, and at first he thought it was deserted. Then he saw Ata. She was sitting on her haunches in the lean-to that served her as kitchen, watching some mess cooking in a pot. Near her a small boy was playing silently in the dirt. She did not smile when she saw him.

"I have come to see Strickland," he said.

"I will go and tell him."

She went to the house, ascended the few steps that led to the verandah, and entered. Dr. Coutras followed her, but waited outside in obedience to her gesture. As she opened the door he smelt the sickly sweet smell which makes the neighbourhood of the leper nauseous. He heard her speak, and then he heard Strickland's answer, but he did not recognise the voice. It had become hoarse and indistinct. Dr. Coutras raised his eyebrows. He judged that the disease had already attacked the vocal chords. Then Ata came out again.

"He will not see you. You must go away."

Dr. Coutras insisted, but she would not let him pass. Dr. Coutras shrugged his shoulders, and after a moment's rejection turned away. She walked with him. He felt that she too wanted to be rid of him.

"Is there nothing I can do at all?" he asked.

"You can send him some paints," she said. "There is nothing else he wants."

"Can he paint still?"

"He is painting the walls of the house."

"This is a terrible life for you, my poor child."

Then at last she smiled, and there was in her eyes a look of super-human love. Dr. Coutras was startled by it, and amazed. And he was awed. He found nothing to say.

"He is my man," she said.

"Where is your other child?" he asked. "When I was here last you had two."

"Yes; it died. We buried it under the mango."

When Ata had gone with him a little way she said she must turn back. Dr. Coutras surmised she was afraid to go farther in case she met any of the people from the village. He told her again that if she wanted him she had only to send and he would come at once.

LVI

THEN TWO YEARS more went by, or perhaps three, for time passes imperceptibly in Tahiti, and it is hard to keep count of it; but at last a message was brought to Dr. Coutras that Strickland was dying. Ata had waylaid the cart that took the mail into Papeete, and besought the man who drove it to go at once to the doctor. But the doctor was out when the summons came, and it was evening when he received it. It was impossible to start at so late an hour, and so it was not till next day soon after dawn that he set out. He arrived at Taravao, and for the last time tramped the seven kilometres that led to Ata's house. The path was overgrown, and it was clear that for years now it had remained all but untrodden. It was not easy to find the way. Sometimes he had to stumble along the bed of the stream, and sometimes he had to push through shrubs, dense and thorny; often he was obliged to climb over rocks in order to avoid the hornet-nests that hung on the trees over his head. The silence was intense.

It was with a sigh of relief that at last he came upon the little unpainted house, extraordinarily bedraggled now, and unkempt; but here too was the same intolerable silence. He walked up, and a little boy, playing unconcernedly in the sunshine, started at his approach and fled quickly away: to him the stranger was the enemy. Dr. Coutras had a sense that the child was stealthily watching him from behind a tree. The door was wide open. He called out, but no one answered. He stepped in. He knocked at a door, but again there was no answer. He turned the handle and entered. The stench that assailed him turned him horribly sick. He put his handkerchief to his nose and forced himself to go in. The light was dim, and after the brilliant sunshine for a while he could see nothing. Then he gave a start. He could not make out where he was. He seemed on a sudden to have entered a magic world. He had a vague impression of a great primeval forest and of naked people walking beneath the trees. Then he saw that there were paintings on the walls.

"*Mon Dieu*, I hope the sun hasn't affected me," he muttered.

A slight movement attracted his attention, and he saw that Ata was lying on the floor, sobbing quietly.

"Ata," he called. "Ata."

She took no notice. Again the beastly stench almost made him faint, and he lit a cheroot. His eyes grew accustomed to the darkness, and now he was seized by an overwhelming sensation as he stared at the painted walls. He knew nothing of pictures, but there was something about these that extraordinarily affected him. From floor to ceiling the walls were covered with a strange and elaborate composition. It was indescribably wonderful and mysterious. It took his breath away. It filled him with an emotion which he could not understand or analyse. He felt the awe and the delight which a man might feel who watched the beginning of a world. It was tremendous, sensual, passionate; and yet there was something horrible there, too, something which made him afraid. It was the work of a man who had delved into the hidden depths of nature and had discovered secrets which were beautiful and fearful too. It was the work of a man who knew things which it is unholy for men to know. There was something primeval there and terrible. It was not human. It brought to his mind vague recollections of black magic. It was beautiful and obscene.

"*Mon Dieu*, this is genius."

The words were wrung from him, and he did not know he had spoken.

Then his eyes fell on the bed of mats in the corner, and he went up, and he saw the dreadful, mutilated, ghastly object which had been Strickland. He was dead. Dr. Coutras made an effort of will and bent over that battered horror. Then he started violently, and terror blazed in his heart, for he felt that someone was behind him. It was Ata. He had not heard her get up. She was standing at his elbow, looking at what he looked at.

"Good Heavens, my nerves are all distraught," he said. "You nearly frightened me out of my wits."

He looked again at the poor dead thing that had been man, and then he started back in dismay.

"But he was blind."

"Yes; he had been blind for nearly a year."

LVII

AT THAT MOMENT we were interrupted by the appearance of Madame Coutras, who had been paying visits. She came in, like a ship in full sail, an imposing creature, tall and stout, with an ample bust and an obesity girthed in alarmingly by straight-fronted corsets. She had a bold hooked nose and three chins. She held herself upright. She had not yielded for an instant to the enervating charm of the tropics, but contrariwise was more active, more worldly, more decided than anyone in a temperate clime would have thought it possible to be. She was evidently a copious talker, and now poured forth a breathless stream of anecdote and comment. She made the conversation we had just had seem far away and unreal.

Presently Dr. Coutras turned to me.

"I still have in my *bureau* the picture that Strickland gave me," he said. "Would you like to see it?"

"Willingly."

We got up, and he led me on to the verandah which surrounded his house. We paused to look at the gay flowers that rioted in his garden.

"For a long time I could not get out of my head the recollection of the extraordinary decoration with which Strickland had covered the walls of his house," he said reflectively.

I had been thinking of it, too. It seemed to me that here Strickland had finally put the whole expression of himself. Working silently, knowing that it was his last chance, I fancied that here he must have said all that he knew of life and all that he divined. And I fancied that perhaps here he had at last found peace. The demon which possessed him was exorcised at last, and with the completion of the work, for which all his life had been a painful preparation, rest descended on his remote and tortured soul. He was willing to die, for he had fulfilled his purpose.

"What was the subject?" I asked.

"I scarcely know. It was strange and fantastic. It was a vision of the beginnings of the world, the Garden of Eden, with Adam and Eve—*que sais-je?*—it was a hymn to the beauty of the human form, male and female, and the praise of Nature, sublime, indifferent, lovely, and cruel. It gave you an awful sense of the infinity of space and of the endlessness of time. Because he painted the trees I see about me every day, the cocoa-nuts, the banyans, the flamboyants, the alligator-pears, I have seen them ever since differently, as though there were in them a spirit and a mystery which I am ever on the point of seizing and which forever escapes me. The colours were the colours familiar to me, and yet they were different. They had a significance which was all their own. And those nude men and women. They were of the earth, and yet apart from it. They seemed to possess something of the clay of which they were created, and at the same time something divine. You saw man in the nakedness of his primeval instincts, and you were afraid, for you saw yourself."

Dr. Coutras shrugged his shoulders and smiled.

"You will laugh at me. I am a materialist, and I am a gross, fat man—Falstaff, eh?—the lyrical mode does not become me. I make myself ridiculous. But I have never seen painting which made so deep an impression upon me. *Tenez*, I had just the same feeling as when I went to the Sistine Chapel in Rome. There too I was awed by the greatness of the man who had painted that ceiling. It was genius, and it was stupendous and overwhelming. I felt small and insignificant. But you are prepared for the greatness of Michael Angelo. Nothing had prepared me for the immense surprise of these pictures in a native hut, far away from civilisation, in a fold of the mountain above Taravao. And Michael Angelo is sane and healthy. Those great works of his have the calm of the sublime; but here, notwithstanding beauty, was something troubling. I do not know what it was. It made me uneasy. It gave me the impression you get when you are sitting next door to a room that you know is empty, but in which, you know not why, you have a dreadful consciousness that notwithstanding there is someone. You scold yourself; you know it is only your nerves—and yet, and yet... In a little while it is impossible to resist the terror that seizes you, and you are helpless in the clutch of an unseen horror. Yes; I confess I was not altogether sorry when I heard that those strange masterpieces had been destroyed."

"Destroyed?" I cried.

"*Mais oui*; did you not know?"

"How should I know? It is true I had never heard of this work; but I thought perhaps it had fallen into the hands of a private owner. Even now there is no certain list of Strickland's paintings."

"When he grew blind he would sit hour after hour in those two rooms that he had painted, looking at his works with sightless eyes, and seeing, perhaps, more than he had ever seen in his life before. Ata told me that he never complained of his fate, he never lost courage. To the end his mind remained serene and undisturbed. But he made her promise that when she had buried him—did I tell you that I dug his grave with my own hands, for none of the natives would approach the infected house, and we buried him, she and I, sewn up in three *pareos* joined together, under the mango-tree—he made her promise that she would set fire to the house and not leave it till it was burned to the ground and not a stick remained."

I did not speak for a while, for I was thinking. Then I said:

"He remained the same to the end, then."

"Do you understand? I must tell you that I thought it my duty to dissuade her."

"Even after what you have just said?"

"Yes; for I knew that here was a work of genius, and I did not think we had the right to deprive the world of it. But Ata would not listen to me. She had promised. I would not stay to witness the barbarous deed, and it was only afterwards that I heard what she had done. She poured paraffin on the dry floors and on the pandanus-mats, and then she set fire. In a little while nothing remained but smouldering embers, and a great masterpiece existed no longer.

"I think Strickland knew it was a masterpiece. He had achieved what he wanted. His life was complete. He had made a world and saw that it was good. Then, in pride and contempt, he destroyed it."

"But I must show you my picture," said Dr. Coutras, moving on.

"What happened to Ata and the child?"

"They went to the Marquesas. She had relations there. I have heard that the boy works on one of Cameron's schooners. They say he is very like his father in appearance."

At the door that led from the verandah to the doctor's consulting-room, he paused and smiled.

"It is a fruit-piece. You would think it not a very suitable picture for a doctor's consulting-room, but my wife will not have it in the drawing-room. She says it is frankly obscene."

"A fruit-piece!" I exclaimed in surprise.

We entered the room, and my eyes fell at once on the picture. I looked at it for a long time.

It was a pile of mangoes, bananas, oranges, and I know not what and at first sight it was an innocent picture enough. It would have been passed in an exhibition of the Post-Impressionists by a careless person as an excellent but not very remarkable example of the school; but perhaps afterwards it would come back to his recollection, and he would wonder why. I do not think then he could ever entirely forget it.

The colours were so strange that words can hardly tell what a troubling emotion they gave. They were sombre blues, opaque like a delicately carved bowl in lapis lazuli, and yet with a quivering lustre that suggested the palpitation of mysterious life; there were purples, horrible like raw and putrid flesh, and yet with a glowing, sensual passion that called up vague memories of the Roman Empire of Heliogabalus; there were reds, shrill like the berries of holly—one thought of Christmas in England, and the snow, the good cheer, and the pleasure of children—and yet by some magic softened till they had the swooning tenderness of a dove's breast; there were deep yellows that died with an unnatural passion into a green as fragrant as the spring and as pure as the sparkling water of a mountain brook. Who can tell what anguished fancy made these fruits? They belonged to a Polynesian garden of the Hesperides. There was something strangely alive in them, as though they were created in a stage of the earth's dark history when things were not irrevocably fixed to their forms. They were extravagantly luxurious. They were heavy with tropical odours. They seemed to possess a sombre passion of their own. It was enchanted fruit, to taste which might open the gateway to God knows what secrets of the soul and to mysterious palaces of the imagination. They were sullen with unawaited dangers, and to eat them might turn a man to beast or god. All that was healthy and natural, all that clung to happy relationships and the simple joys of simple men, shrunk from them in dismay; and yet a fearful attraction was in them, and, like the fruit on the Tree of the Knowledge of Good and Evil they were terrible with the possibilities of the Unknown.

At last I turned away. I felt that Strickland had kept his secret to the grave.

"*Voyons, Rene, mon ami,*" came the loud, cheerful voice of Madame Coutras, "what are you doing all this time? Here are the *aperitifs*. Ask *Monsieur* if he will not drink a little glass of Quinquina Dubonnet."

"*Volontiers*, Madame," I said, going out on to the verandah.

The spell was broken.

LVIII

THE TIME CAME for my departure from Tahiti. According to the gracious custom of the island, presents were given me by the persons with whom I had been thrown in contact—baskets made of the leaves of the cocoa-nut tree, mats of pandanus, fans; and Tiaré gave me three little pearls and three jars of guava-jelly made with her own plump hands. When the mail-boat, stopping for twenty-four hours on its way from Wellington to San Francisco, blew the whistle that warned the passengers to get on board, Tiaré clasped me to her vast bosom, so that I seemed to sink into a billowy sea, and pressed her red lips to mine. Tears glistened in her eyes. And when we steamed slowly out of the lagoon, making our way gingerly through the opening in the reef, and then steered for the open sea, a certain melancholy fell upon me. The breeze was laden still with the pleasant odours of the land. Tahiti is very far away, and I knew that I should never see it again. A chapter of my life was closed, and I felt a little nearer to inevitable death.

Not much more than a month later I was in London; and after I had arranged certain matters which claimed my immediate attention, thinking Mrs. Strickland might like to hear what I knew of her husband's last years, I wrote to her. I had not seen her since long before the war, and I had to look out her address in the telephone-book. She made an appointment, and I went to the trim little house on Campden Hill which she now inhabited. She was by this time a woman of hard on sixty, but she bore her years well, and no one would have taken her for more than fifty. Her face, thin and not much lined, was of the sort that ages gracefully, so that you thought in youth she must have been a much handsomer woman than in fact she was. Her hair, not yet very gray, was becomingly arranged, and her black gown was modish. I remembered having heard that her sister, Mrs. MacAndrew, outliving her husband but a couple of years, had left money to Mrs. Strickland; and by the look of the house and the trim maid who opened the door I judged that it was a sum adequate to keep the widow in modest comfort.

When I was ushered into the drawing-room I found that Mrs. Strickland had a visitor, and when I discovered who he was, I guessed that I had been asked to come at just that time not without intention. The caller was Mr. Van Busche Taylor, an American, and Mrs. Strickland gave me particulars with a charming smile of apology to him.

"You know, we English are so dreadfully ignorant. You must forgive me if it's necessary to explain." Then she turned to me. "Mr. Van Busche Taylor is the distinguished American critic. If you haven't read his book your education has been shamefully neglected, and you must repair the omission at once. He's writing something about dear Charlie, and he's come to ask me if I can help him."

Mr. Van Busche Taylor was a very thin man with a large, bald head, bony and shining; and under the great dome of his skull his face, yellow, with deep lines in it, looked very small. He was quiet and exceedingly polite. He spoke with the accent of New England, and there was about his demeanour a bloodless frigidity which made me ask myself why on earth he was busying himself with Charles Strickland. I had been slightly tickled at the gentleness which Mrs. Strickland put into her mention of her husband's name, and while the pair conversed I took stock of the room in which we sat. Mrs. Strickland had moved with the times. Gone were the Morris papers and gone the severe cretonnes, gone were the Arundel prints that had adorned the walls of her drawing-room in Ashley Gardens; the room blazed with fantastic colour, and I wondered if she knew that those varied hues, which fashion had imposed upon her, were due to the dreams of a poor painter in a South Sea island. She gave me the answer herself.

"What wonderful cushions you have," said Mr. Van Busche Taylor.

"Do you like them?" she said, smiling. "Bakst, you know."

And yet on the walls were coloured reproductions of several of Strickland's best pictures, due to the enterprise of a publisher in Berlin.

"You're looking at my pictures," she said, following my eyes. "Of course, the originals are out of my reach, but it's a comfort to have these. The publisher sent them to me himself. They're a great consolation to me."

"They must be very pleasant to live with," said Mr. Van Busche Taylor.

"Yes; they're so essentially decorative."

"That is one of my profoundest convictions," said Mr. Van Busche Taylor. "Great art is always decorative."

Their eyes rested on a nude woman suckling a baby, while a girl was kneeling by their side holding out a flower to the indifferent child. Looking over them was a wrinkled, scraggy hag. It was Strickland's version of the Holy Family. I suspected that for the figures had sat his household above Taravao, and the woman and the baby were Ata and his first son. I asked myself if Mrs. Strickland had any inkling of the facts.

The conversation proceeded, and I marvelled at the tact with which Mr. Van Busche Taylor avoided all subjects that might have been in the least embarrassing, and at the ingenuity with which Mrs. Strickland, without saying a word that was untrue, insinuated that her relations with her husband had always been perfect. At last Mr. Van Busche Taylor rose to go. Holding his hostess' hand, he made her a graceful, though perhaps too elaborate, speech of thanks, and left us.

"I hope he didn't bore you," she said, when the door closed behind him. "Of course it's a nuisance sometimes, but I feel it's only right to give people any information I can about Charlie. There's a certain responsibility about having been the wife of a genius."

She looked at me with those pleasant eyes of hers, which had remained as candid and as sympathetic as they had been more than twenty years before. I wondered if she was making a fool of me.

"Of course you've given up your business," I said.

"Oh, yes," she answered airily. "I ran it more by way of a hobby than for any other reason, and my children persuaded me to sell it. They thought I was overtaxing my strength."

I saw that Mrs. Strickland had forgotten that she had ever done anything so disgraceful as to work for her living. She had the true instinct of the nice woman that it is only really decent for her to live on other people's money.

"They're here now," she said. "I thought they'd, like to hear what you had to say about their father. You remember Robert, don't you?

I'm glad to say he's been recommended for the Military Cross."

She went to the door and called them. There entered a tall man in khaki, with the parson's collar, handsome in a somewhat heavy fashion, but with the frank eyes that I remembered in him as a boy. He was followed by his sister. She must have been the same age as was her mother when first I knew her, and she was very like her. She too gave one the impression that as a girl she must have been prettier than indeed she was.

"I suppose you don't remember them in the least," said Mrs. Strickland, proud and smiling. "My daughter is now Mrs. Ronaldson. Her husband's a Major in the Gunners."

"He's by way of being a pukka soldier, you know," said Mrs. Ronaldson gaily. "That's why he's only a Major."

I remembered my anticipation long ago that she would marry a soldier. It was inevitable. She had all the graces of the soldier's wife. She was civil and affable, but she could hardly conceal her intimate conviction that she was not quite as others were. Robert was breezy.

"It's a bit of luck that I should be in London when you turned up," he said. "I've only got three days' leave."

"He's dying to get back," said his mother.

"Well, I don't mind confessing it, I have a rattling good time at the front. I've made a lot of good pals. It's a first-rate life. Of course war's terrible, and all that sort of thing; but it does bring out the best qualities in a man, there's no denying that."

Then I told them what I had learned about Charles Strickland in Tahiti. I thought it unnecessary to say anything of Ata and her boy, but for the rest I was as accurate as I could be. When I had narrated his lamentable death I ceased. For a minute or two we were all silent. Then Robert Strickland struck a match and lit a cigarette.

"The mills of God grind slowly, but they grind exceeding small," he said, somewhat impressively.

Mrs. Strickland and Mrs. Ronaldson looked down with a slightly pious expression which indicated, I felt sure, that they thought the quotation was from Holy Writ. Indeed, I was unconvinced that Robert Strickland did not share their illusion. I do not know why I suddenly thought of Strickland's son by Ata. They had told me he was a merry, light-hearted youth. I saw him, with my mind's eye, on the schooner on which he worked, wearing nothing but a pair of dungarees; and at night, when the boat sailed along easily before a light breeze, and the sailors were gathered on the upper deck, while the captain and the supercargo lolled in deck-chairs, smoking their pipes, I saw him dance with another lad, dance wildly, to the wheezy music of the concertina. Above was the blue sky, and the stars, and all about the desert of the Pacific Ocean.

A quotation from the Bible came to my lips, but I held my tongue, for I know that clergymen think it a little blasphemous when the laity poach upon their preserves. My Uncle Henry, for twenty-seven years Vicar of Whitstable, was on these occasions in the habit of saying that the devil could always quote scripture to his purpose. He remembered the days when you could get thirteen Royal Natives for a shilling.

The Magician

A Fragment of
Autobiography

❦

IN 1897, AFTER spending five years at St Thomas's Hospital I passed the examinations which enabled me to practise medicine. While still a medical student I had published a novel called *Liza of Lambeth* which caused a mild sensation, and on the strength of that I rashly decided to abandon doctoring and earn my living as a writer; so, as soon as I was 'qualified', I set out for Spain and spent the best part of a year in Seville. I amused myself hugely and wrote a bad novel. Then I returned to London and, with a friend of my own age, took and furnished a small flat near Victoria Station. A maid of all work cooked for us and kept the flat neat and tidy. My friend was at the Bar, and so I had the day (and the flat) to myself and my work. During the next six years I wrote several novels and a number of plays. Only one of these novels had any success, but even that failed to make the stir that my first one had made. I could get no manager to take my plays. At last, in desperation, I sent one, which I called *A Man of Honour*, to the Stage Society, which gave two performances, one on Sunday night, another on Monday afternoon, of plays which, unsuitable for the commercial theatre, were considered of sufficient merit to please an intellectual audience. As everyone knows, it was the Stage Society that produced the early plays of Bernard Shaw. The committee accepted *A Man of Honour*, and W. L. Courtney, who was a member of it, thought well enough of my crude play to publish it in *The Fortnightly Review*, of which he was then editor. It was a feather in my cap.

Though these efforts of mine brought me very little money, they attracted not a little attention, and I made friends. I was looked upon as a promising young writer and, I think I may say it without vanity, was accepted as a member of the intelligentsia, an honourable condition which, some years later, when I became a popular writer of light comedies, I lost; and have never since regained. I was invited to literary parties and to parties given by women of rank and fashion who thought it behoved them to patronise the arts. An unattached and fairly presentable young man is always in demand. I lunched out and dined out. Since I could not afford to take cabs, when I dined out, in tails and a white tie, as was then the custom, I went and came back by bus. I was asked to spend week-ends in the country. They were something of a trial on account of the tips you had to give to the butler and to the footman who brought you your morning tea. He unpacked your gladstone bag, and you were uneasily aware that your well-worn pyjamas and modest toilet articles had made an unfavourable impression upon him. For all that, I found life pleasant and I enjoyed myself. There seemed no reason why I should not go on indefinitely in the same way, bringing out a novel once a year (which seldom earned more than the small advance the publisher had given me but which was on the whole respectably reviewed), going to more and more parties, making more and more friends. It was all very nice, but I couldn't see that it was leading me anywhere. I was thirty. I was in a rut. I felt I must get out of it. It did not take me long to make up my mind. I told the friend with whom I shared the flat that I wanted to be rid of it and go abroad. He could not keep it by himself, but we luckily found a middle-aged gentleman who wished to install his mistress in it, and was prepared to take it off our hands. We sold the furniture for what it could fetch, and within a month I was on my way to Paris. I took a room in a cheap hotel on the Left Bank.

A few months before this, I had been fortunate enough to make friends with a young painter who had a studio in the Rue Campagne Première. His name was Gerald Kelly. He had had an upbringing unusual for a painter, for he had been to Eton and to Cambridge. He was highly talented, abundantly loquacious, and immensely enthusiastic. It was he who first made me acquainted with the Impressionists, whose pictures had recently been accepted by the Luxembourg. To my shame, I must admit that I could not make head or tail of them. Without much searching, I found an apartment on the fifth floor of a house near the Lion de Belfort. It had two rooms and a kitchen, and cost seven hundred francs a year, which was then twenty-eight pounds. I bought, second-hand, such furniture and household utensils as were essential, and the *concierge* told me of a woman who would come in for half a day and make my *café au lait* in the morning and my luncheon at noon. I settled down and set to work on still another novel. Soon after my arrival, Gerald Kelly took me to a restaurant called Le Chat Blanc in the Rue d'Odessa, near the Gare Montparnasse, where a number of artists were in the habit of dining; and from then on I dined there every night. I have described the place elsewhere, and in some detail in the novel to which these pages are meant to serve as a preface, so that I need not here say more about it. As a rule, the same people came in every night, but now and then others came, perhaps only once, perhaps two or three times. We were apt to look upon them as interlopers, and I don't think we made them particularly welcome. It was thus that I first met Arnold Bennet and Clive Bell. One of these casual visitors was Aleister Crowley. He was spending the winter in Paris. I took an immediate dislike to him, but he interested and amused me. He was a great talker and he talked uncommonly well. In early youth, I was told, he was extremely handsome, but when I knew him he had put on weight, and his hair was thinning. He had fine eyes and a way, whether natural or acquired I do not know, of so focusing them that, when he looked at you, he seemed to look behind you. He was a fake, but not entirely a fake. At Cambridge he had won his chess blue and was esteemed the best whist player of his time. He was a liar and unbecomingly boastful, but the odd thing was that he had actually done some of the things he boasted of. As a mountaineer, he had made an ascent of K.2 in the Hindu Kush, the second highest mountain in India, and he made it without the elaborate equipment, the cylinders of oxygen and so forth, which render the endeavours of the mountaineers of the present day more likely to succeed. He did not reach the top, but got nearer to it than anyone had done before.

Crowley was a voluminous writer of verse, which he published sumptuously at his own expense. He had a gift for rhyming, and his verse was not entirely without merit. He had been greatly influenced by Swinburne and Robert Browning. He was grossly, but not unintelligently, imitative. As you flip through the pages you may well read a stanza which, if you came across it in a volume of Swinburne's, you would accept without question as the work of the master. *It's rather hard, isn't it, Sir, to make sense of it?'* If you were shown this line and asked what poet had written it, I think you would be inclined to say, Robert Browning. You would be wrong. It was written by Aleister Crowley.

At the time I knew him he was dabbling in Satanism, magic and the occult. There was just then something of a vogue in Paris for that sort of thing, occasioned, I surmise, by the interest that was still taken in a book of Huysman's, *Là Bas.* Crowley told fantastic stories of his experiences, but it was hard to say whether he was telling the truth or merely pulling your leg. During that winter I saw him several times, but never after I left Paris to return to London. Once, long afterwards, I received a telegram from him which ran as follows: 'Please send twenty-five pounds at once. Mother of God and I starving. Aleister Crowley.' I did not do so, and he lived on for many disgraceful years.

I was glad to get back to London. My old friend had by then rooms in Pall Mall, and I was able to take a bedroom in the same building and use his sitting-room to work in. *The Magician* was published in 1908, so I suppose it was written during the first six months of 1907. I do not remember how I came to think that Aleister Crowley might serve as the model for the character whom I called Oliver Haddo; nor, indeed, how I came to think of writing that particular novel at all. When, a little while ago, my publisher expressed a wish to reissue it, I felt that, before consenting to this, I really should read it again. Nearly fifty years had passed since I had done so, and I had completely forgotten it. Some authors enjoy reading their old works; some cannot bear to. Of these I am. When I have corrected the proofs of a book, I have finished with it for good and all. I am impatient when people insist on talking to me about it; I am glad if they like it, but do not much care if they don't. I am no more interested in it than in a worn-out suit of clothes that I have given away.

It was thus with disinclination that I began to read *The Magician*. It held my interest, as two of my early novels, which for the same reason I have been obliged to read, did not. One, indeed, I simply could not get through. Another had to my mind some good dramatic scenes, but the humour filled me with mortification, and I should have been ashamed to see it republished. As I read *The Magician*, I wondered how on earth I could have come by all the material concerning the black arts which I wrote of. I must have spent days and days reading in the library of the British Museum. The style is lush and turgid, not at all the sort of style I approve of now, but perhaps not unsuited to the subject; and there are a great many more adverbs and adjectives than I should use today. I fancy I must have been impressed by the *écriture artiste* which the French writers of the time had not yet entirely abandoned, and unwisely sought to imitate them.

Though Aleister Crowley served, as I have said, as the model for Oliver Haddo, it is by no means a portrait of him. I made my character more striking in appearance, more sinister and more ruthless than Crowley ever was. I gave him magical powers that Crowley, though he claimed them, certainly ever possessed. Crowley, however, recognized himself in the creature of my invention, for such it was, and wrote a full-page review of the novel in *Vanity Fair*, which he signed 'Oliver Haddo'. I did not read it, and wish now that I had. I daresay it was a pretty piece of vituperation, but probably, like his poems, intolerably verbose.

I do not remember what success, if any, my novel had when it was published, and I did not bother about it much, for by then a great change had come into my life. The manager of the Court Theatre, one Otho Stuart, had brought out a play which failed to please, and he could not immediately get the cast he wanted for the next play he had in mind to produce. He had read one of mine, and formed a very poor opinion of it; but he was in a quandary, and it occurred to him that it might just serve to keep his theatre open for a few weeks, by the end of which the actors he wanted for the play he had been obliged to postpone would be at liberty. He put mine on. It was an immediate success. The result of this was that in a very little while other managers accepted the plays they had consistently refused, and

I had four running in London at the same time. I, who for ten years had earned an average of one hundred pounds a year, found myself earning several hundred pounds a week. I made up my mind to abandon the writing of novels for the rest of my life. I did not know that this was something out of my control and that when the urge to write a novel seized me, I should be able to do nothing but submit. Five years later, the urge came and, refusing to write any more plays for the time, I started upon the longest of all my novels. I called it *Of Human Bondage.*

W.S.M.

The Magician

ARTHUR BURDON AND Dr Porhoët walked in silence. They had
lunched at a restaurant in the Boulevard Saint Michel, and were
sauntering now in the gardens of the Luxembourg. Dr Porhoët
walked with stooping shoulders, his hands behind him. He beheld
the scene with the eyes of the many painters who have sought by
means of the most charming garden in Paris to express their sense
of beauty. The grass was scattered with the fallen leaves, but their
wan decay little served to give a touch of nature to the artifice of all
besides. The trees were neatly surrounded by bushes, and the bushes
by trim beds of flowers. But the trees grew without abandonment,
as though conscious of the decorative scheme they helped to form.
It was autumn, and some were leafless already. Many of the flowers
were withered. The formal garden reminded one of a light woman, no
longer young, who sought, with faded finery, with powder and paint,
to make a brave show of despair. It had those false, difficult smiles of
uneasy gaiety, and the pitiful graces which attempt a fascination that
the hurrying years have rendered vain.

Dr Porhoët drew more closely round his fragile body the heavy
cloak which even in summer he could not persuade himself to dis-
card. The best part of his life had been spent in Egypt, in the practice
of medicine, and the frigid summers of Europe scarcely warmed his
blood. His memory flashed for an instant upon those multi-coloured
streets of Alexandria; and then, like a homing bird, it flew to the
green woods and the storm-beaten coasts of his native Brittany. His

brown eyes were veiled with sudden melancholy.

'Let us wait here for a moment,' he said.

They took two straw-bottomed chairs and sat near the octagonal water which completes with its fountain of Cupids the enchanting artificiality of the Luxembourg. The sun shone more kindly now, and the trees which framed the scene were golden and lovely. A balustrade of stone gracefully enclosed the space, and the flowers, freshly bedded, were very gay. In one corner they could see the squat, quaint towers of Saint Sulpice, and on the other side the uneven roofs of the Boulevard Saint Michel.

The palace was grey and solid. Nurses, some in the white caps of their native province, others with the satin streamers of the *nounou*, marched sedately two by two, wheeling perambulators and talking. Brightly dressed children trundled hoops or whipped a stubborn top. As he watched them, Dr Porhoët's lips broke into a smile, and it was so tender that his thin face, sallow from long exposure to subtropical suns, was transfigured. He no longer struck you merely as an insignificant little man with hollow cheeks and a thin grey beard; for the weariness of expression which was habitual to him vanished before the charming sympathy of his smile. His sunken eyes glittered with a kindly but ironic good-humour. Now passed a guard in the romantic cloak of a brigand in comic opera and a peaked cap like that of an *alguacil*. A group of telegraph boys in blue stood round a painter, who was making a sketch—notwithstanding half-frozen fingers. Here and there, in baggy corduroys, tight jackets, and wide-brimmed hats, strolled students who might have stepped from the page of Murger's immortal romance. But the students now are uneasy with the fear of ridicule, and more often they walk in bowler hats and the neat coats of the *boulevardier*.

Dr Porhoët spoke English fluently, with scarcely a trace of foreign accent, but with an elaboration which suggested that he had learned the language as much from study of the English classics as from conversation.

'And how is Miss Dauncey?' he asked, turning to his friend.

Arthur Burdon smiled.

'Oh, I expect she's all right. I've not seen her today, but I'm going to tea at the studio this afternoon, and we want you to dine with us at the Chien Noir.'

'I shall be much pleased. But do you not wish to be by yourselves?'

'She met me at the station yesterday, and we dined together. We talked steadily from half past six till midnight.'

'Or, rather, she talked and you listened with the delighted attention of a happy lover.'

Arthur Burdon had just arrived in Paris. He was a surgeon on the staff of St Luke's, and had come ostensibly to study the methods of the French operators; but his real object was certainly to see Margaret Dauncey. He was furnished with introductions from London surgeons of repute, and had already spent a morning at the Hôtel Dieu, where the operator, warned that his visitor was a bold and skilful surgeon, whose reputation in England was already considerable, had sought to dazzle him by feats that savoured almost of legerdemain. Though the hint of charlatanry in the Frenchman's methods had not escaped Arthur Burdon's shrewd eyes, the audacious sureness of his hand had excited his enthusiasm. During luncheon he talked of nothing else, and Dr Porhoët, drawing upon his memory, recounted the more extraordinary operations that he had witnessed in Egypt.

He had known Arthur Burdon ever since he was born, and indeed had missed being present at his birth only because the Khedive Ismaïl had summoned him unexpectedly to Cairo. But the Levantine merchant who was Arthur's father had been his most intimate friend, and it was with singular pleasure that Dr Porhoët saw the young man, on his advice, enter his own profession and achieve a distinction which himself had never won.

Though too much interested in the characters of the persons whom chance threw in his path to have much ambition on his own behalf, it pleased him to see it in others. He observed with satisfaction the pride which Arthur took in his calling and the determination, backed by his confidence and talent, to become a master of his art. Dr Porhoët knew that a diversity of interests, though it adds charm to a man's personality, tends to weaken him. To excel one's fellows it is needful to be circumscribed. He did not regret, therefore, that Arthur in many ways was narrow. Letters and the arts meant little to him. Nor would he trouble himself with the graceful trivialities which make a man a good talker. In mixed company he was content to listen silently to others, and only something very definite to say could tempt him to join in the general conversation. He worked very hard, operating, dissecting, or lecturing at his hospital, and took pains to read every word, not only in English, but in French and German, which was published concerning his profession. Whenever he could snatch a free day he spent it on the golf-links of Sunningdale, for he was an eager and a fine player.

But at the operating-table Arthur was different. He was no longer the awkward man of social intercourse, who was sufficiently conscious of his limitations not to talk of what he did not understand, and sincere enough not to express admiration for what he did not like. Then, on the other hand, a singular exhilaration filled him; he was conscious of his power, and he rejoiced in it. No unforeseen accident was able to confuse him. He seemed to have a positive instinct for operating, and his hand and his brain worked in a manner that appeared almost automatic. He never hesitated, and he had no fear of failure. His success had been no less than his courage, and it was plain that soon his reputation with the public would equal that which he had already won with the profession.

Dr Porhoët had been making listless patterns with his stick upon the gravel, and now, with that charming smile of his, turned to Arthur.

'I never cease to be astonished at the unexpectedness of human nature,' he remarked. 'It is really very surprising that a man like you should fall so deeply in love with a girl like Margaret Dauncey.'

Arthur made no reply, and Dr Porhoët, fearing that his words might offend, hastened to explain.

'You know as well as I do that I think her a very charming young person. She has beauty and grace and sympathy. But your characters are more different than chalk and cheese. Notwithstanding your birth in the East and your boyhood spent amid the very scenes of the *Thousand and One Nights*, you are the most matter-of-fact creature I have ever come across.'

'I see no harm in your saying insular,' smiled Arthur. 'I confess that I have no imagination and no sense of humour. I am a plain, practical man, but I can see to the end of my nose with extreme clearness. Fortunately it is rather a long one.'

'One of my cherished ideas is that it is impossible to love without imagination.'

Again Arthur Burdon made no reply, but a curious look came into his eyes as he gazed in front of him. It was the look which might fill the passionate eyes of a mystic when he saw in ecstasy the Divine Lady of his constant prayers.

'But Miss Dauncey has none of that narrowness of outlook which, if you forgive my saying so, is perhaps the secret of your strength. She has a delightful enthusiasm for every form of art. Beauty really means as much to her as bread and butter to the more soberly-minded. And she takes a passionate interest in the variety of life.'

'It is right that Margaret should care for beauty, since there is beauty in every inch of her,' answered Arthur.

He was too reticent to proceed to any analysis of his feelings; but he knew that he had cared for her first on account of the physical perfection which contrasted so astonishingly with the countless deformities in the study of which his life was spent. But one phrase escaped him almost against his will.

'The first time I saw her I felt as though a new world had opened to my ken.'

The divine music of Keats's lines rang through Arthur's remark, and to the Frenchman's mind gave his passion a romantic note that foreboded future tragedy. He sought to dispel the cloud which his fancy had cast upon the most satisfactory of love affairs.

'You are very lucky, my friend. Miss Margaret admires you as much as you adore her. She is never tired of listening to my prosy stories of your childhood in Alexandria, and I'm quite sure that she will make you the most admirable of wives.'

'You can't be more sure than I am,' laughed Arthur.

He looked upon himself as a happy man. He loved Margaret with all his heart, and he was confident in her great affection for him. It was impossible that anything should arise to disturb the pleasant life which they had planned together. His love cast a glamour upon his work, and his work, by contrast, made love the more entrancing.

'We're going to fix the date of our marriage now,' he said. 'I'm buying furniture already.'

'I think only English people could have behaved so oddly as you, in postponing your marriage without reason for two mortal years.'

'You see, Margaret was ten when I first saw her, and only seventeen when I asked her to marry me. She thought she had reason to be grateful to me and would have married me there and then. But I knew she hankered after these two years in Paris, and I didn't feel it was fair to bind her to me till she had seen at least something of the world. And she seemed hardly ready for marriage, she was growing still.'

'Did I not say that you were a matter-of-fact young man?' smiled Dr Porhoët.

'And it's not as if there had been any doubt about our knowing our minds. We both cared, and we had a long time before us. We could afford to wait.'

At that moment a man strolled past them, a big stout fellow, showily dressed in a check suit; and he gravely took off his hat to Dr Porhoët. The doctor smiled and returned the salute.

'Who is your fat friend?' asked Arthur.

'That is a compatriot of yours. His name is Oliver Haddo.'

'Art-student?' inquired Arthur, with the scornful tone he used when referring to those whose walk in life was not so practical as his own.

'Not exactly. I met him a little while ago by chance. When I was getting together the material for my little book on the old alchemists I read a great deal at the library of the Arsenal, which, you may have heard, is singularly rich in all works dealing with the occult sciences.'

Burden's face assumed an expression of amused disdain. He could not understand why Dr Porhoët occupied his leisure with studies so profitless. He had read his book, recently published, on the more famous of the alchemists; and, though forced to admire the profound knowledge upon which it was based, he could not forgive the waste of time which his friend might have expended more usefully on topics of pressing moment.

'Not many people study in that library,' pursued the doctor, 'and I soon knew by sight those who were frequently there. I saw this gentleman every day. He was immersed in strange old books when I arrived early in the morning, and he was reading them still when I left, exhausted. Sometimes it happened that he had the volumes I asked for, and I discovered that he was studying the same subjects as myself. His appearance was extraordinary, but scarcely sympathetic; so, though I fancied that he gave me opportunities to address him, I did not avail myself of them. One day, however, curiously enough, I was looking up some point upon which it seemed impossible to find authorities. The librarian could not help me, and I had given up the search, when this person brought me the very book I needed. I surmised that the librarian had told him of my difficulty. I was very grateful to the stranger. We left together that afternoon, and our kindred studies gave us a common topic of conversation. I found that his reading was extraordinarily wide, and he was able to give me information about works which I had never even heard of. He had the advantage over me that he could apparently read, Hebrew as well as Arabic, and he had studied the Kabbalah in the original.'

'And much good it did him, I have no doubt,' said Arthur. 'And what is he by profession?'

Dr Porhoët gave a deprecating smile.

'My dear fellow, I hardly like to tell you. I tremble in every limb at the thought of your unmitigated scorn.'

'Well?'

'You know, Paris is full of queer people. It is the chosen home of every kind of eccentricity. It sounds incredible in this year of grace, but my friend Oliver Haddo claims to be a magician. I think he is quite serious.'

'Silly ass!' answered Arthur with emphasis.

II

MARGARET DAUNCEY SHARED a flat near the Boulevard du Montparnasse with Susie Boyd; and it was to meet her that Arthur had arranged to come to tea that afternoon. The young women waited for him in the studio. The kettle was boiling on the stove; cups and *petits fours* stood in readiness on a model stand. Susie looked forward to the meeting with interest. She had heard a good deal of the young man, and knew that the connexion between him and Margaret was not lacking in romance. For years Susie had led the monotonous life of a mistress in a school for young ladies, and had resigned herself to its dreariness for the rest of her life, when a legacy from a distant relation gave her sufficient income to live modestly upon her means. When Margaret, who had been her pupil, came, soon after this, to announce her intention of spending a couple of years in Paris to study art, Susie willingly agreed to accompany her. Since then she had worked industriously at Colarossi's Academy, by no means under the delusion that she had talent, but merely to amuse herself. She refused to surrender the pleasing notion that her environment was slightly wicked. After the toil of many years it relieved her to be earnest in nothing; and she found infinite satisfaction in watching the lives of those around her.

She had a great affection for Margaret, and though her own stock of enthusiasms was run low, she could enjoy thoroughly Margaret's young enchantment in all that was exquisite. She was a plain woman; but there was no envy in her, and she took the keenest pleasure in Margaret's comeliness. It was almost with maternal pride that she watched each year add a new grace to that exceeding beauty. But her common sense was sound, and she took care by good-natured banter to temper the praises which extravagant admirers at the drawing-class lavished upon the handsome girl both for her looks and for her talent. She was proud to think that she would hand over to Arthur Burdon a woman whose character she had helped to form, and whose loveliness she had cultivated with a delicate care.

Susie knew, partly from fragments of letters which Margaret read to her, partly from her conversation, how passionately he adored his bride; and it pleased her to see that Margaret loved him in return with a grateful devotion. The story of this visit to Paris touched her imagination. Margaret was the daughter of a country barrister, with whom Arthur had been in the habit of staying; and when he died, many years after his wife, Arthur found himself the girl's guardian and executor. He sent her to school; saw that she had everything she could possibly want; and when, at seventeen, she told him of her wish to go to Paris and learn drawing, he at once consented. But though he never sought to assume authority over her, he suggested that she should not live alone, and it was on this account that she went to Susie. The preparations for the journey were scarcely made when Margaret discovered by chance that her father had died penniless and she had lived ever since at Arthur's entire expense. When she went to see him with tears in her eyes, and told him what she knew, Arthur was so embarrassed that it was quite absurd.

'But why did you do it?' she asked him. 'Why didn't you tell me?'

'I didn't think it fair to put you under any obligation to me, and I wanted you to feel quite free.'

She cried. She couldn't help it.

'Don't be so silly,' he laughed. 'You own me nothing at all. I've done very little for you, and what I have done has given me a great deal of pleasure.'

'I don't know how I can ever repay you.'

'Oh, don't say that,' he cried. 'It makes it so much harder for me to say what I want to.'

She looked at him quickly and reddened. Her deep blue eyes were veiled with tears.

'Don't you know that I'd do anything in the world for you?' she cried.

'I don't want you to be grateful to me, because I was hoping—I might ask you to marry me some day.'

Margaret laughed charmingly as she held out her hands.

'You must know that I've been wanting you to do that ever since I was ten.'

She was quite willing to give up her idea of Paris and be married without delay, but Arthur pressed her not to change her plans. At first Margaret vowed it was impossible to go, for she knew now that she had no money, and she could not let her lover pay.

'But what does it matter?' he said. 'It'll give me such pleasure to go on with the small allowance I've been making you. After all, I'm pretty well-to-do. My father left me a moderate income, and I'm making a good deal already by operating.'

'Yes, but it's different now. I didn't know before. I thought I was spending my own money.'

'If I died tomorrow, every penny I have would be yours. We shall be married in two years, and we've known one another much too long to change our minds. I think that our lives are quite irrevocably united.'

Margaret wished very much to spend this time in Paris, and Arthur had made up his mind that in fairness to her they could not marry till she was nineteen. She consulted Susie Boyd, whose common sense prevented her from paying much heed to romantic notions of false delicacy.

'My dear, you'd take his money without scruple if you'd signed your names in a church vestry, and as there's not the least doubt that you'll marry, I don't see why you shouldn't now. Besides, you've got nothing whatever to live on, and you're equally unfitted to be a governess or a typewriter. So it's Hobson's choice, and you'd better put your exquisite sentiments in your pocket.'

Miss Boyd, by one accident after another, had never seen Arthur, but she had heard so much that she looked upon him already as an old friend. She admired him for his talent and strength of character as much as for his loving tenderness to Margaret. She had seen portraits of him, but Margaret said he did not photograph well. She had asked if he was good-looking.

'No, I don't think he is,' answered Margaret, 'but he's very paintable.'

'That is an answer which has the advantage of sounding well and meaning nothing,' smiled Susie.

She believed privately that Margaret's passion for the arts was a not unamiable pose which would disappear when she was happily married. To have half a dozen children was in her mind much more important than to paint pictures. Margaret's gift was by no means despicable, but Susie was not convinced that callous masters would have been so enthusiastic if Margaret had been as plain and old as herself.

Miss Boyd was thirty. Her busy life had not caused the years to pass easily, and she looked older. But she was one of those plain women whose plainness does not matter. A gallant Frenchman had to her face called her a *belle laide*, and, far from denying the justness of his observation, she had been almost flattered. Her mouth was large, and she had little round bright eyes. Her skin was colourless and much disfigured by freckles. Her nose was long and thin. But her face was so kindly, her vivacity so attractive, that no one after ten minutes thought of her ugliness. You noticed then that her hair, though sprinkled with white, was pretty, and that her figure was exceedingly neat. She had good hands, very white and admirably formed, which she waved continually in the fervour of her gesticulation. Now that her means were adequate she took great pains with her dress, and her clothes, though they cost much more than she could afford, were always beautiful. Her taste was so great, her tact so sure, that she was able to make the most of herself. She was determined that if people called her ugly they should be forced in the same breath to confess that she was perfectly gowned. Susie's talent for dress was remarkable, and it was due to her influence that Margaret was arrayed always in the latest mode. The girl's taste inclined to be artistic, and her sense of colour was apt to run away with her discretion. Except for the display of Susie's firmness, she would scarcely have resisted her desire to wear nondescript garments of violent hue. But the older woman expressed herself with decision.

'My dear, you won't draw any the worse for wearing a well-made corset, and to surround your body with bands of grey flannel will certainly not increase your talent.'

'But the fashion is so hideous,' smiled Margaret.

'Fiddlesticks! The fashion is always beautiful. Last year it was beautiful to wear a hat like a pork-pie tipped over your nose; and next year, for all I know, it will be beautiful to wear a bonnet like a sitz-bath at the back of your head. Art has nothing to do with a smart frock, and whether a high-heeled pointed shoe commends itself or not to the painters in the quarter, it's the only thing in which a woman's foot looks really nice.'

Susie Boyd vowed that she would not live with Margaret at all unless she let her see to the buying of her things.

'And when you're married, for heaven's sake ask me to stay with you four times a year, so that I can see after your clothes. You'll never keep your husband's affection if you trust to your own judgment.'

Miss Boyd's reward had come the night before, when Margaret, coming home from dinner with Arthur, had repeated an observation of his.

'How beautifully you're dressed!' he had said. 'I was rather afraid you'd be wearing art-serges.'

'Of course you didn't tell him that I insisted on buying every stitch you'd got on,' cried Susie.

'Yes, I did,' answered Margaret simply. 'I told him I had no taste at all, but that you were responsible for everything.'

'That was the least you could do,' answered Miss Boyd.

But her heart went out to Margaret, for the trivial incident showed once more how frank the girl was. She knew quite well that few of her friends, though many took advantage of her matchless taste, would have made such an admission to the lover who congratulated them on the success of their costume.

There was a knock at the door, and Arthur came in.

'This is the fairy prince,' said Margaret, bringing him to her friend.

'I'm glad to see you in order to thank you for all you've done for Margaret,' he smiled, taking the proffered hand.

Susie remarked that he looked upon her with friendliness, but with a certain vacancy, as though too much engrossed in his beloved really to notice anyone else; and she wondered how to make conversation with a man who was so manifestly absorbed. While Margaret busied herself with the preparations for tea, his eyes followed her movements with a doglike, touching devotion. They travelled from her smiling mouth to her deft hands. It seemed that he had never seen anything so ravishing as the way in which she bent over the kettle. Margaret felt that he was looking at her, and turned round. Their eyes met, and they stood for an appreciable time gazing at one another silently.

'Don't be a pair of perfect idiots,' cried Susie gaily. 'I'm dying for my tea.'

The lovers laughed and reddened. It struck Arthur that he should say something polite.

'I hope you'll show me your sketches afterwards, Miss Boyd. Margaret says they're awfully good.'

'You really needn't think it in the least necessary to show any interest in me,' she replied bluntly.

'She draws the most delightful caricatures,' said Margaret. 'I'll bring you a horror of yourself, which she'll do the moment you leave us.'

'Don't be so spiteful, Margaret.'

Miss Boyd could not help thinking all the same that Arthur Burdon would caricature very well. Margaret was right when she said that he was not handsome, but his clean-shaven face was full of interest to so passionate an observer of her kind. The lovers were silent, and Susie had the conversation to herself. She chattered without pause and had the satisfaction presently of capturing their attention. Arthur seemed to become aware of her presence, and laughed heartily at her burlesque account of their fellow-students at Colarossi's. Meanwhile Susie examined him. He was very tall and very thin. His frame had a Yorkshireman's solidity, and his bones were massive. He missed being ungainly only through the serenity of his self-reliance. He had high cheek-bones and a long, lean face. His nose and mouth were large, and his skin was sallow. But there were two characteristics which fascinated her, an imposing strength of purpose and a singular capacity for suffering. This was a man who knew his mind and was determined to achieve his desire; it refreshed her vastly after the extreme weakness of the young painters with whom of late she had mostly consorted. But those quick dark eyes were able to express an anguish that was hardly tolerable, and the mobile mouth had a nervous intensity which suggested that he might easily suffer the very agonies of woe.

Tea was ready, and Arthur stood up to receive his cup.

'Sit down,' said Margaret. 'I'll bring you everything you want, and I know exactly how much sugar to put in. It pleases me to wait on you.'

With the grace that marked all her movements she walked cross the studio, the filled cup in one hand and the plate of cakes in the other. To Susie it seemed that he was overwhelmed with gratitude by Margaret's condescension. His eyes were soft with indescribable tenderness as he took the sweetmeats she gave him. Margaret smiled with happy pride. For all her good-nature, Susie could not prevent the pang that wrung her heart; for she too was capable of love. There was in her a wealth of passionate affection that none had sought to find. None had ever whispered in her ears the charming nonsense that she read in books. She recognised that she had no beauty to help her, but once she had at least the charm of vivacious youth. That was gone now, and the freedom to go into the world had come too late; yet her instinct told her that she was made to be a decent man's wife and the mother of children. She stopped in the middle of her bright chatter, fearing to trust her voice, but Margaret and Arthur were too much occupied to notice that she had ceased to speak. They sat side by side and enjoyed the happiness of one another's company.

'What a fool I am!' thought Susie.

She had learnt long ago that common sense, intelligence, good-nature, and strength of character were unimportant in comparison with a pretty face. She shrugged her shoulders.

'I don't know if you young things realise that it's growing late. If you want us to dine at the Chien Noir, you must leave us now, so that we can make ourselves tidy.'

'Very well,' said Arthur, getting up. 'I'll go back to my hotel and have a wash. We'll meet at half-past seven.'

When Margaret had closed the door on him, she turned to her friend.

'Well, what do you think?' she asked, smiling.

'You can't expect me to form a definite opinion of a man whom I've seen for so short a time.'

'Nonsense!' said Margaret.

Susie hesitated for a moment.

'I think he has an extraordinarily good face,' she said at last gravely. 'I've never seen a man whose honesty of purpose was so transparent.'

Susie Boyd was so lazy that she could never be induced to occupy herself with household matters and, while Margaret put the tea things away, she began to draw the caricature which every new face suggested to her. She made a little sketch of Arthur, abnormally lanky, with a colossal nose, with the wings and the bow and arrow of the God of Love, but it was not half done before she thought it silly. She tore it up with impatience. When Margaret came back, she turned round and looked at her steadily.

'Well?' said the girl, smiling under the scrutiny.

She stood in the middle of the lofty studio. Half-finished canvases leaned with their faces against the wall; pieces of stuff were hung here and there, and photographs of well-known pictures. She had fallen unconsciously into a wonderful pose, and her beauty gave her, notwithstanding her youth, a rare dignity. Susie smiled mockingly.

'You look like a Greek goddess in a Paris frock,' she said.

'What have you to say to me?' asked Margaret, divining from the searching look that something was in her friend's mind.

Susie stood up and went to her.

'You know, before I'd seen him I hoped with all my heart that he'd make you happy. Notwithstanding all you'd told me of him, I was afraid. I knew he was much older than you. He was the first man you'd ever known. I could scarcely bear to entrust you to him in case you were miserable.'

'I don't think you need have any fear.'

'But now I hope with all my heart that you'll make him happy. It's not you I'm frightened for now, but him.'

Margaret did not answer; she could not understand what Susie meant.

'I've never seen anyone with such a capacity for wretchedness as that man has. I don't think you can conceive how desperately he might suffer. Be very careful, Margaret, and be very good to him, for you have the power to make him more unhappy than any human being should be.'

'Oh, but I want him to be happy,' cried Margaret vehemently. 'You know that I owe everything to him. I'd do all I could to make him happy, even if I had to sacrifice myself. But I can't sacrifice myself, because I love him so much that all I do is pure delight.'

Her eyes filled with tears and her voice broke. Susie, with a little laugh that was half hysterical, kissed her.

'My dear, for heaven's sake don't cry! You know I can't bear people who weep, and if he sees your eyes red, he'll never forgive me.'

III

THE CHIEN NOIR, where Susie Boyd and Margaret generally dined, was the most charming restaurant in the quarter. Downstairs was a public room, where all and sundry devoured their food, for the little

place had a reputation for good cooking combined with cheapness;
and the *patron*, a retired horse-dealer who had taken to victualling
in order to build up a business for his son, was a cheery soul whose
loud-voiced friendliness attracted custom. But on the first floor was
a narrow room, with three tables arranged in a horse-shoe, which
was reserved for a small party of English or American painters and a
few Frenchmen with their wives. At least, they were so nearly wives,
and their manner had such a matrimonial respectability, that Susie,
when first she and Margaret were introduced into this society, judged
it would be vulgar to turn up her nose. She held that it was prudish
to insist upon the conventions of Notting Hill in the Boulevard de
Montparnasse. The young women who had thrown in their lives with
these painters were modest in demeanour and quiet in dress. They
were model housewives, who had preserved their self-respect notwithstanding a difficult position, and did not look upon their relation
with less seriousness because they had not muttered a few words before *Monsieur le Maire*.

The room was full when Arthur Burdon entered, but Margaret
had kept him an empty seat between herself and Miss Boyd. Everyone
was speaking at once, in French, at the top of his voice, and a furious
argument was proceeding on the merit of the later Impressionists.
Arthur sat down, and was hurriedly introduced to a lanky youth, who
sat on the other side of Margaret. He was very tall, very thin, very fair.
He wore a very high collar and very long hair, and held himself like
an exhausted lily.

'He always reminds me of an Aubrey Beardsley that's been dreadfully smudged,' said Susie in an undertone. 'He's a nice, kind creature,
but his name is Jagson. He has virtue and industry. I haven't seen any
of his work, but he has absolutely *no* talent.'

'How do you know, if you've not seen his pictures?' asked Arthur.

'Oh, it's one of our conventions here that nobody has talent,'
laughed Susie. 'We suffer one another personally, but we have no illusions about the value of our neighbour's work.'

'Tell me who everyone is.'

'Well, look at that little bald man in the corner. That is Warren.'

Arthur looked at the man she pointed out. He was a small person, with a pate as shining as a billiard-ball, and a pointed beard. He had protruding, brilliant eyes.

'Hasn't he had too much to drink?' asked Arthur frigidly.

'Much,' answered Susie promptly, 'but he's always in that condition, and the further he gets from sobriety the more charming he is. He's the only man in this room of whom you'll never hear a word of evil. The strange thing is that he's very nearly a great painter. He has the most fascinating sense of colour in the world, and the more intoxicated he is, the more delicate and beautiful is his painting. Sometimes, after more than the usual number of *apéritifs*, he will sit down in a café to do a sketch, with his hand so shaky that he can hardly hold a brush; he has to wait for a favourable moment, and then he makes a jab at the panel. And the immoral thing is that each of these little jabs is lovely. He's the most delightful interpreter of Paris I know, and when you've seen his sketches—he's done hundreds, of unimaginable grace and feeling and distinction—you can never see Paris in the same way again.'

The little maid who looked busily after the varied wants of the customers stood in front of them to receive Arthur's order. She was a hard-visaged creature of mature age, but she looked neat in her black dress and white cap; and she had a motherly way of attending to these people, with a capacious smile of her large mouth which was full of charm.

'I don't mind what I eat,' said Arthur. 'Let Margaret order my dinner for me.'

'It would have been just as good if I had ordered it,' laughed Susie.

They began a lively discussion with Marie as to the merits of the various dishes, and it was only interrupted by Warren's hilarious expostulations.

'Marie, I precipitate myself at your feet, and beg you to bring me a *poule au riz*.'

'Oh, but give me one moment, *monsieur*,' said the maid.

'Do not pay any attention to that gentleman. His morals are detestable, and he only seeks to lead you from the narrow path of virtue.'

Arthur protested that on the contrary the passion of hunger occupied at that moment his heart to the exclusion of all others.

'Marie, you no longer love me,' cried Warren. 'There was a time when you did not look so coldly upon me when I ordered a bottle of white wine.'

The rest of the party took up his complaint, and all besought her not to show too hard a heart to the bald and rubicund painter.

'*Mais si, je vous aime, Monsieur Warren,*' she cried, laughing, '*Je vous aime tous, tous.*'

She ran downstairs, amid the shouts of men and women, to give her orders.

'The other day the Chien Noir was the scene of a tragedy,' said Susie. 'Marie broke off relations with her lover, who is a waiter at Lavenue's, and would have no reconciliation. He waited till he had a free evening, and then came to the room downstairs and ordered dinner. Of course, she was obliged to wait on him, and as she brought him each dish he expostulated with her, and they mingled their tears.'

'She wept in floods,' interrupted a youth with neatly brushed hair and fat nose. 'She wept all over our food, and we ate it salt with tears. We besought her not to yield; except for our encouragement she would have gone back to him; and he beats her.'

Marie appeared again, with no signs now that so short a while ago romance had played a game with her, and brought the dishes that had been ordered. Susie seized once more upon Arthur Burdon's attention.

'Now please look at the man who is sitting next to Mr Warren.'

Arthur saw a tall, dark fellow with strongly-marked features, untidy hair, and a ragged black moustache.

'That is Mr O'Brien, who is an example of the fact that strength of will and an earnest purpose cannot make a painter. He's a failure, and he knows it, and the bitterness has warped his soul. If you listen to him, you'll hear every painter of eminence come under his lash. He can forgive nobody who's successful, and he never acknowledges merit in anyone till he's safely dead and buried.'

'He must be a cheerful companion,' answered Arthur. 'And who is the stout old lady by his side, with the flaunting hat?'

'That is the mother of Madame Rouge, the little palefaced woman sitting next to her. She is the mistress of Rouge, who does all the illustrations for *La Semaine*. At first it rather tickled me that the old lady should call him *mon gendre*, my son-in-law, and take the irregular union of her daughter with such a noble unconcern for propriety; but now it seems quite natural.'

The mother of Madame Rouge had the remains of beauty, and she sat bolt upright, picking the leg of a chicken with a dignified gesture. Arthur looked away quickly, for, catching his eye, she gave him an amorous glance. Rouge had more the appearance of a prosperous tradesman than of an artist; but he carried on with O'Brien, whose French was perfect, an argument on the merits of Cézanne. To one he was a great master and to the other an impudent charlatan. Each hotly repeated his opinion, as though the mere fact of saying the same thing several times made it more convincing.

'Next to me is Madame Meyer,' proceeded Susie. 'She was a governess in Poland, but she was much too pretty to remain one, and now she lives with the landscape painter who is by her side.'

Arthur's eyes followed her words and rested on a cleanshaven man with a large quantity of grey, curling hair. He had a handsome face of a deliberately aesthetic type and was very elegantly dressed. His manner and his conversation had the flamboyance of the romantic thirties. He talked in flowing periods with an air of finality, and what he said was no less just than obvious. The gay little lady who shared his fortunes listened to his wisdom with an admiration that plainly flattered him.

Miss Boyd had described everyone to Arthur except young Raggles, who painted still life with a certain amount of skill, and Clayson, the American sculptor. Raggles stood for rank and fashion at the Chien Noir. He was very smartly dressed in a horsey way, and he walked with bowlegs, as though he spent most of his time in the saddle. He alone used scented pomade upon his neat smooth hair. His chief distinction was a greatcoat he wore, with a scarlet lining; and Warren, whose memory for names was defective, could only recall him by that peculiarity. But it was understood that he knew duchesses in fashionable streets, and occasionally dined with them in solemn splendour.

Clayson had a vinous nose and a tedious habit of saying brilliant things. With his twinkling eyes, red cheeks, and fair, pointed beard, he looked exactly like a Franz Hals; but he was dressed like the caricature of a Frenchman in a comic paper. He spoke English with a Parisian accent.

Miss Boyd was beginning to tear him gaily limb from limb, when the door was flung open, and a large person entered. He threw off his cloak with a dramatic gesture.

'Marie, disembarrass me of this coat of frieze. Hang my sombrero upon a convenient peg.'

He spoke execrable French, but there was a grandiloquence about his vocabulary which set everyone laughing.

'Here is somebody I don't know,' said Susie.

'But I do, at least, by sight,' answered Burdon. He leaned over to Dr Porhoët who was sitting opposite, quietly eating his dinner and enjoying the nonsense which everyone talked. 'Is not that your magician?'

'Oliver Haddo,' said Dr Porhoët, with a little nod of amusement.

The new arrival stood at the end of the room with all eyes upon him. He threw himself into an attitude of command and remained for a moment perfectly still.

'You look as if you were posing, Haddo,' said Warren huskily.

'He couldn't help doing that if he tried,' laughed Clayson.

Oliver Haddo slowly turned his glance to the painter.

'I grieve to see, O most excellent Warren, that the ripe juice of the *aperitif* has glazed your sparkling eye.'

'Do you mean to say I'm drunk, sir?'

'In one gross, but expressive, word, drunk.'

The painter grotesquely flung himself back in his chair as though he had been struck a blow, and Haddo looked steadily at Clayson.

'How often have I explained to you, O Clayson, that your deplorable lack of education precludes you from the brilliancy to which you aspire?'

For an instant Oliver Haddo resumed his effective pose; and Susie, smiling, looked at him. He was a man of great size, two or three inches more than six feet high; but the most noticeable thing about him was a vast obesity. His paunch was of imposing dimensions. His face was large and fleshy. He had thrown himself into the arrogant attitude of Velasquez's portrait of Del Borro in the Museum of Berlin; and his countenance bore of set purpose the same contemptuous smile. He advanced and shook hands with Dr Porhoët.

'Hail, brother wizard! I greet in you, if not a master, at least a student not unworthy my esteem.'

Susie was convulsed with laughter at his pompousness, and he turned to her with the utmost gravity.

'Madam, your laughter is more soft in mine ears than the singing of Bulbul in a Persian garden.'

Dr Porhoët interposed with introductions. The magician bowed solemnly as he was in turn made known to Susie Boyd, and Margaret, and Arthur Burdon. He held out his hand to the grim Irish painter.

'Well, my O'Brien, have you been mixing as usual the waters of bitterness with the thin claret of Bordeaux?'

'Why don't you sit down and eat your dinner?' returned the other, gruffly.

'Ah, my dear fellow, I wish I could drive the fact into this head of yours that rudeness is not synonymous with wit. I shall not have lived in vain if I teach you in time to realize that the rapier of irony is more effective an instrument than the bludgeon of insolence.'

O'Brien reddened with anger, but could not at once find a retort, and Haddo passed on to that faded, harmless youth who sat next to Margaret.

'Do my eyes deceive me, or is this the Jagson whose name in its inanity is so appropriate to the bearer? I am eager to know if you still devote upon the ungrateful arts talents which were more profitably employed upon haberdashery.'

The unlucky creature, thus brutally attacked, blushed feebly without answering, and Haddo went on to the Frenchman, Meyer as more worthy of his mocking.

'I'm afraid my entrance interrupted you in a discourse. Was it the celebrated harangue on the greatness of Michelangelo, or was it the searching analysis of the art of Wagner?'

'We were just going,' said Meyer, getting up with a frown.

'I am desolated to lose the pearls of wisdom that habitually fall from your cultivated lips,' returned Haddo, as he politely withdrew

Madame Meyer's chair.

He sat down with a smile.

'I saw the place was crowded, and with Napoleonic instinct decided that I could only make room by insulting somebody. It is cause for congratulation that my gibes, which Raggles, a foolish youth, mistakes for wit, have caused the disappearance of a person who lives in open sin; thereby vacating two seats, and allowing me to eat a humble meal with ample room for my elbows.'

Marie brought him the bill of fare, and he looked at it gravely.

'I will have a vanilla ice, O well-beloved, and a wing of a tender chicken, a fried sole, and some excellent pea-soup.'

'*Bien, un potage, une sole,* one chicken, and an ice.'

'But why should you serve them in that order rather than in the order I gave you?'

Marie and the two Frenchwomen who were still in the room broke into exclamations at this extravagance, but Oliver Haddo waved his fat hand.

'I shall start with the ice, O Marie, to cool the passion with which your eyes inflame me, and then without hesitation I will devour the wing of a chicken in order to sustain myself against your smile. I shall then proceed to a fresh sole, and with the pea-soup I will finish a not unsustaining meal.'

Having succeeded in capturing the attention of everyone in the room, Oliver Haddo proceeded to eat these dishes in the order he had named. Margaret and Burdon watched him with scornful eyes, but Susie, who was not revolted by the vanity which sought to attract notice, looked at him curiously. He was clearly not old, though his corpulence added to his apparent age. His features were good, his ears small, and his nose delicately shaped. He had big teeth, but they were white and even. His mouth was large, with heavy moist lips. He had the neck of a bullock. His dark, curling hair had retreated from the forehead and temples in such a way as to give his clean-shaven face a disconcerting nudity. The baldness of his crown was vaguely like a tonsure. He had the look of a very wicked, sensual priest. Margaret, stealing a glance at him as he ate, on a sudden violently shuddered; he affected her with an uncontrollable dislike. He lifted his eyes slowly, and she looked away, blushing as though she had been taken in some indiscretion. These eyes were the most curious thing about him. They were not large, but an exceedingly pale blue, and they looked at you in a way that was singularly embarrassing. At first Susie could not discover in what precisely their peculiarity lay, but in a moment she found out: the eyes of most persons converge when they look at you, but Oliver Haddo's, naturally or by a habit he had acquired for effect, remained parallel. It gave the impression that he looked straight through you and saw the wall beyond. It was uncanny. But another strange thing about him was the impossibility of telling whether he was serious. There was a mockery in that queer glance, a sardonic smile upon the mouth, which made you hesitate how to take his outrageous utterances. It was irritating to be uncertain whether, while you were laughing at him, he was not really enjoying an elaborate joke at your expense.

His presence cast an unusual chill upon the party. The French members got up and left. Warren reeled out with O'Brien, whose uncouth sarcasms were no match for Haddo's bitter gibes. Raggles put on his coat with the scarlet lining and went out with the tall Jagson, who smarted still under Haddo's insolence. The American sculptor paid his bill silently. When he was at the door, Haddo stopped him.

'You have modelled lions at the Jardin des Plantes, my dear Clayson. Have you ever hunted them on their native plains?'

'No, I haven't.'

Clayson did not know why Haddo asked the question, but he bristled with incipient wrath.

'Then you have not seen the jackal, gnawing at a dead antelope, scamper away in terror when the King of Beasts stalked down to make his meal.'

Clayson slammed the door behind him. Haddo was left with Margaret, and Arthur Burdon, Dr Porhoët, and Susie. He smiled quietly.

'By the way, are *you* a lion-hunter?' asked Susie flippantly.

He turned on her his straight uncanny glance.

'I have no equal with big game. I have shot more lions than any man alive. I think Jules Gérard, whom the French of the nineteenth century called *Le Tueur de Lions*, may have been fit to compare with me, but I can call to mind no other.'

This statement, made with the greatest calm, caused a moment of silence. Margaret stared at him with amazement.

'You suffer from no false modesty,' said Arthur Burdon.

'False modesty is a sign of ill-breeding, from which my birth amply protects me.'

Dr Porhoët looked up with a smile of irony.

'I wish Mr Haddo would take this opportunity to disclose to us the mystery of his birth and family. I have a suspicion that, like the immortal Cagliostro, he was born of unknown but noble parents, and educated secretly in Eastern palaces.'

'In my origin I am more to be compared with Denis Zachaire or with Raymond Lully. My ancestor, George Haddo, came to Scotland in the suite of Anne of Denmark, and when James I, her consort, ascended the English throne, he was granted the estates in Staffordshire which I still possess. My family has formed alliances with the most noble blood of England, and the Merestons, the Parnabys, the Hollingtons, have been proud to give their daughters to my house.'

'Those are facts which can be verified in works of reference,' said Arthur dryly.

'They can,' said Oliver.

'And the Eastern palaces in which your youth was spent, and the black slaves who waited on you, and the bearded sheikhs who imparted to you secret knowledge?' cried Dr Porhoët.

'I was educated at Eton, and I left Oxford in 1896.'

'Would you mind telling me at what college you were?' said Arthur.

'I was at the House.'

'Then you must have been there with Frank Hurrell.'

'Now assistant physician at St Luke's Hospital. He was one of my most intimate friends.'

'I'll write and ask him about you.'

'I'm dying to know what you did with all the lions you slaughtered,' said Susie Boyd.

The man's effrontery did not exasperate her as it obviously exasperated Margaret and Arthur. He amused her, and she was anxious to make him talk.

'They decorate the floors of Skene, which is the name of my place in Staffordshire.' He paused for a moment to light a cigar. 'I am the only man alive who has killed three lions with three successive shots.'

'I should have thought you could have demolished them by the effects of your oratory,' said Arthur.

Oliver leaned back and placed his two large hands on the table.

'Burkhardt, a German with whom I was shooting, was down with fever and could not stir from his bed. I was awakened one night by the uneasiness of my oxen, and I heard the roaring of lions close at hand. I took my carbine and came out of my tent. There was only the meagre light of the moon. I walked alone, for I knew natives could be of no use to me. Presently I came upon the carcass of an antelope, half-consumed, and I made up my mind to wait for the return of the lions. I hid myself among the boulders twenty paces from the prey. All about me was the immensity of Africa and the silence. I waited, motionless, hour after hour, till the dawn was nearly at hand. At last three lions appeared over a rock. I had noticed, the day before, spoor of a lion and two females.'

'May I ask how you could distinguish the sex?' asked Arthur, incredulously.

'The prints of a lion's fore feet are disproportionately larger than those of the hind feet. The fore feet and hind feet of the lioness are nearly the same size.'

'Pray go on,' said Susie.

'They came into full view, and in the dim light, as they stood chest on, they appeared as huge as the strange beasts of the Arabian tales. I aimed at the lioness which stood nearest to me and fired. Without a sound, like a bullock felled at one blow, she dropped. The lion gave vent to a sonorous roar. Hastily I slipped another cartridge in my rifle. Then I became conscious that he had seen me. He lowered his head, and his crest was erect. His lifted tail was twitching, his lips were drawn back from the red gums, and I saw his great white fangs. Living fire flashed from his eyes, and he growled incessantly. Then he advanced a few steps, his head held low; and his eyes were fixed on mine with a look of rage. Suddenly he jerked up his tail, and when a lion does this he charges. I got a quick sight on his chest and fired. He reared up on his hind legs, roaring loudly and clawing at the air, and fell back dead. One lioness remained, and through the smoke I saw her spring to her feet and rush towards me. Escape was impossible, for behind me were high boulders that I could not climb. She came on with hoarse, coughing grunts, and with desperate courage I fired my remaining barrel. I missed her clean. I took one step backwards in the hope of getting a cartridge into my rifle, and fell, scarcely two lengths in front of the furious beast. She missed me. I owed my safety to that fall. And then suddenly I found that she had collapsed. I had hit her after all. My bullet went clean through her heart, but the spring had carried her forwards. When I scrambled to my feet I found that she was dying. I walked back to my camp and ate a capital breakfast.'

Oliver Haddo's story was received with astonished silence. No one could assert that it was untrue, but he told it with a grandiloquence that carried no conviction. Arthur would have wagered a considerable sum that there was no word of truth in it. He had never met a person of this kind before, and could not understand what pleasure there might be in the elaborate invention of improbable adventures.

'You are evidently very brave,' he said.

'To follow a wounded lion into thick cover is probably the most dangerous proceeding in the world,' said Haddo calmly. 'It calls for the utmost coolness and for iron nerve.'

The answer had an odd effect on Arthur. He gave Haddo a rapid glance, and was seized suddenly with uncontrollable laughter. He leaned back in his chair and roared. His hilarity affected the others, and they broke into peal upon peal of laughter. Oliver watched them gravely. He seemed neither disconcerted nor surprised. When Arthur recovered himself, he found Haddo's singular eyes fixed on him.

'Your laughter reminds me of the crackling of thorns under a pot,' he said.

Haddo looked round at the others. Though his gaze preserved its fixity, his lips broke into a queer, sardonic smile.

'It must be plain even to the feeblest intelligence that a man can only command the elementary spirits if he is without fear. A capricious mind can never rule the sylphs, nor a fickle disposition the undines.'

Arthur stared at him with amazement. He did not know what on earth the man was talking about. Haddo paid no heed.

'But if the adept is active, pliant, and strong, the whole world will be at his command. He will pass through the storm and no rain shall fall upon his head. The wind will not displace a single fold of his garment. He will go through fire and not be burned.'

Dr Porhoët ventured upon an explanation of these cryptic utterances.

'These ladies are unacquainted with the mysterious beings of whom you speak, *cher ami*. They should know that during the Middle Ages imagination peopled the four elements with intelligences, normally unseen, some of which were friendly to man and others hostile. They were thought to be powerful and conscious of their power, though at the same time they were profoundly aware that they possessed no soul. Their life depended upon the continuance of some natural object, and hence for them there could be no immortality. They must return eventually to the abyss of unending night, and the darkness of death afflicted them always. But it was thought that in the same manner as man by his union with God had won a spark of divinity, so might the sylphs, gnomes, undines, and salamanders by an alliance with man partake of his immortality. And many of their women, whose beauty was more than human, gained a human soul by loving one of the race of men. But the reverse occurred also, and often a love-sick youth lost his immortality because he left the haunts of his kind to dwell with the fair, soulless denizens of the running streams or of the forest airs.'

'I didn't know that you spoke figuratively,' said Arthur to Oliver Haddo.

The other shrugged his shoulders.

'What else is the world than a figure? Life itself is but a symbol. You must be a wise man if you can tell us what is reality.'

'When you begin to talk of magic and mysticism I confess that I am out of my depth.'

'Yet magic is no more than the art of employing consciously invisible means to produce visible effects. Will, love, and imagination are magic powers that everyone possesses; and whoever knows how to develop them to their fullest extent is a magician. Magic has but one dogma, namely, that the seen is the measure of the unseen.'

'Will you tell us what the powers are that the adept possesses?'

'They are enumerated in a Hebrew manuscript of the sixteenth century, which is in my possession. The privileges of him who holds in his right hand the Keys of Solomon and in his left the Branch of the Blossoming Almond are twenty-one. He beholds God face to face without dying, and converses intimately with the Seven Genii who command the celestial army. He is superior to every affliction and to every fear. He reigns with all heaven and is served by all hell. He holds the secret of the resurrection of the dead, and the key of immortality.'

'If you possess even these you have evidently the most varied attainments,' said Arthur ironically.

'Everyone can make game of the unknown,' retorted Haddo, with a shrug of his massive shoulders.

Arthur did not answer. He looked at Haddo curiously. He asked himself whether he believed seriously these preposterous things, or whether he was amusing himself in an elephantine way at their expense. His mariner was earnest, but there was an odd expression about the mouth, a hard twinkle of the eyes, which seemed to belie it. Susie was vastly entertained. It diverted her enormously to hear occult matters discussed with apparent gravity in this prosaic tavern. Dr Porhoët broke the silence.

'Arago, after whom has been named a neighbouring boulevard, declared that doubt was a proof of modesty, which has rarely interfered with the progress of science. But one cannot say the same of incredulity, and he that uses the word impossible outside of pure mathematics is lacking in prudence. It should be remembered that Lactantius proclaimed belief in the existence of antipodes inane, and Saint Augustine of Hippo added that in any case there could be no question of inhabited lands.'

'That sounds as if you were not quite sceptical, dear doctor,' said Miss Boyd.

'In my youth I believed nothing, for science had taught me to distrust even the evidence of my five senses,' he replied, with a shrug of the shoulders. 'But I have seen many things in the East which are inexplicable by the known processes of science. Mr Haddo has given you one definition of magic, and I will give you another. It may be described merely as the intelligent utilization of forces which are unknown, contemned, or misunderstood of the vulgar. The young man who settles in the East sneers at the ideas of magic which surround him, but I know not what there is in the atmosphere that saps his unbelief. When he has sojourned for some years among Orientals, he comes insensibly to share the opinion of many sensible men that perhaps there is something in it after all.'

Arthur Burdon made a gesture of impatience.

'I cannot imagine that, however much I lived in Eastern countries, I could believe anything that had the whole weight of science against it. If there were a word of truth in anything Haddo says, we should be unable to form any reasonable theory of the universe.'

'For a scientific man you argue with singular fatuity,' said Haddo icily, and his manner had an offensiveness which was intensely irritating. 'You should be aware that science, dealing only with the general, leaves out of consideration the individual cases that contradict the enormous majority. Occasionally the heart is on the right side of the body, but you would not on that account ever put your stethoscope in any other than the usual spot. It is possible that under certain conditions the law of gravity does not apply, yet you will conduct your life under the conviction that it does so invariably. Now, there are some of us who choose to deal only with these exceptions to the common run. The dull man who plays at Monte Carlo puts his money on the colours, and generally black or red turns up; but now and then zero appears, and he loses. But we, who have backed zero all the time, win many times our stake. Here and there you will find men whose imagination raises them above the humdrum of mankind. They are willing to lose their all if only they have chance of a great prize. Is it nothing not only to know the future, as did the prophets of old, but by making it to force the very gates of the unknown?'

Suddenly the bantering gravity with which he spoke fell away from him. A singular light came into his eyes, and his voice was hoarse. Now at last they saw that he was serious.

'What should you know of that lust for great secrets which consumes me to the bottom of my soul!'

'Anyhow, I'm perfectly delighted to meet a magician,' cried Susie gaily.

'Ah, call me not that,' he said, with a flourish of his fat hands, regaining immediately his portentous flippancy. 'I would be known rather as the Brother of the Shadow.'

'I should have thought you could be only a very distant relation of anything so unsubstantial,' said Arthur, with a laugh.

Oliver's face turned red with furious anger. His strange blue eyes grew cold with hatred, and he thrust out his scarlet lips till he had the ruthless expression of a Nero. The gibe at his obesity had caught him on the raw. Susie feared that he would make so insulting a reply that a quarrel must ensure.

'Well, really, if we want to go to the fair we must start,' she said quickly. 'And Marie is dying to be rid of us.'

They got up, and clattered down the stairs into the street.

IV

THEY CAME DOWN to the busy, narrow street which led into the Boulevard du Montparnasse. Electric trams passed through it with harsh ringing of bells, and people surged along the pavements.

The fair to which they were going was held at the Lion de Belfort, not more than a mile away, and Arthur hailed a cab. Susie told the driver where they wanted to be set down. She noticed that Haddo, who was waiting for them to start, put his hand on the horse's neck. On a sudden, for no apparent reason, it began to tremble. The trembling passed through the body and down its limbs till it shook from head to foot as though it had the staggers. The coachman jumped off his box and held the wretched creature's head. Margaret and Susie got out. It was a horribly painful sight. The horse seemed not to suffer from actual pain, but from an extraordinary fear. Though she knew not why, an idea came to Susie.

'Take your hand away, Mr Haddo,' she said sharply.

He smiled, and did as she bade him. At the same moment the trembling began to decrease, and in a moment the poor old cab-horse was in its usual state. It seemed a little frightened still, but otherwise recovered.

'I wonder what the deuce was the matter with it,' said Arthur.

Oliver Haddo looked at him with the blue eyes that seemed to see right through people, and then, lifting his hat, walked away. Susie turned suddenly to Dr Porhoët.

'Do you think he could have made the horse do that? It came immediately he put his hand on its neck, and it stopped as soon as he took it away.'

'Nonsense!' said Arthur.

'It occurred to me that he was playing some trick,' said Dr Porhoët gravely. 'An odd thing happened once when he came to see me. I have two Persian cats, which are the most properly conducted of all their tribe. They spend their days in front of my fire, meditating on the problems of metaphysics. But as soon as he came in they started up, and their fur stood right on end. Then they began to run madly round and round the room, as though the victims of uncontrollable terror. I opened the door, and they bolted out. I have never been able to understand exactly what took place.'

Margaret shuddered.

'I've never met a man who filled me with such loathing,' she said. 'I don't know what there is about him that frightens me. Even now I feel his eyes fixed strangely upon me. I hope I shall never see him again.'

Arthur gave a little laugh and pressed her hand. She would not let his go, and he felt that she was trembling. Personally, he had no doubt about the matter. He would have no trifling with credibility. Either Haddo believed things that none but a lunatic could, or else he was a charlatan who sought to attract attention by his extravagances. In any case he was contemptible. It was certain, at all events, that neither he nor anyone else could work miracles.

'I'll tell you what I'll do,' said Arthur. 'If he really knows Frank Hurrell I'll find out all about him. I'll drop a note to Hurrell tonight and ask him to tell me anything he can.'

'I wish you would,' answered Susie, 'because he interests me enormously. There's no place like Paris for meeting queer folk. Sooner or later you run across persons who believe in everything. There's no form of religion, there's no eccentricity or enormity, that hasn't its votaries. Just think what a privilege it is to come upon a man in the twentieth century who honestly believes in the occult.'

'Since I have been occupied with these matters, I have come across strange people,' said Dr Porhoët quietly, 'but I agree with Miss Boyd that Oliver Haddo is the most extraordinary. For one thing, it is impossible to know how much he really believes what he says. Is he an impostor or a madman? Does he deceive himself, or is he laughing up his sleeve at the folly of those who take him seriously? I cannot tell. All I know is that he has travelled widely and is acquainted with many tongues. He has a minute knowledge of alchemical literature, and there is no book I have heard of, dealing with the black arts, which he does not seem to know.' Dr Porhoët shook his head slowly. 'I should not care to dogmatize about this man. I know I shall outrage the feelings of my friend Arthur, but I am bound to confess it would not surprise me to learn that he possessed powers by which he was able to do things seemingly miraculous.'

Arthur was prevented from answering by their arrival at the Lion de Belfort.

The fair was in full swing. The noise was deafening. Steam bands thundered out the popular tunes of the moment, and to their din merry-go-rounds were turning. At the door of booths men vociferously importuned the passers-by to enter. From the shooting saloons came a continual spatter of toy rifles. Linking up these sounds, were the voices of the serried crowd that surged along the central avenue, and the shuffle of their myriad feet. The night was lurid with acetylene torches, which flamed with a dull unceasing roar. It was a curious sight, half gay, half sordid. The throng seemed bent with a kind of savagery upon amusement, as though, resentful of the weary round of daily labour, it sought by a desperate effort to be merry.

The English party with Dr Porhoët, mildly ironic, had scarcely entered before they were joined by Oliver Haddo. He was indifferent to the plain fact that they did not want his company. He attracted attention, for his appearance and his manner were remarkable, and Susie noticed that he was pleased to see people point him out to one another. He wore a Spanish cloak, the *capa*, and he flung the red and green velvet of its lining gaudily over his shoulder. He had a large soft hat. His height was great, though less noticeable on account of his obesity, and he towered over the puny multitude.

They looked idly at the various shows, resisting the melodramas, the circuses, the exhibitions of eccentricity, which loudly clamoured for their custom. Presently they came to a man who was cutting silhouettes in black paper, and Haddo insisted on posing for him. A little crowd collected and did not spare their jokes at his singular appearance. He threw himself into his favourite attitude of proud command. Margaret wished to take the opportunity of leaving him, but Miss Boyd insisted on staying.

'He's the most ridiculous creature I've ever seen in my life,' she whispered. 'I wouldn't let him out of my sight for worlds.'

When the silhouette was done, he presented it with a low bow to Margaret.

'I implore your acceptance of the only portrait now in existence of Oliver Haddo,' he said.

'Thank you,' she answered frigidly.

She was unwilling to take it, but had not the presence of mind to put him off by a jest, and would not be frankly rude. As though certain she set much store on it, he placed it carefully in an envelope. They walked on and suddenly came to a canvas booth on which was an Eastern name. Roughly painted on sail-cloth was a picture of an Arab charming snakes, and above were certain words in Arabic. At the entrance, a native sat cross-legged, listlessly beating a drum. When he saw them stop, he addressed them in bad French.

'Does not this remind you of the turbid Nile, Dr Porhoët?' said Haddo.

'Let us go in and see what the fellow has to show.'

Dr Porhoët stepped forward and addressed the charmer, who brightened on hearing the language of his own country.

'He is an Egyptian from Assiut,' said the doctor.

'I will buy tickets for you all,' said Haddo.

He held up the flap that gave access to the booth, and Susie went in. Margaret and Arthur Burdon, somewhat against their will, were obliged to follow. The native closed the opening behind them. They

found themselves in a dirty little tent, ill-lit by two smoking lamps; a
dozen stools were placed in a circle on the bare ground. In one corner
sat a fellah woman, motionless, in ample robes of dingy black. Her
face was hidden by a long veil, which was held in place by a queer
ornament of brass in the middle of the forehead, between the eyes.
These alone were visible, large and sombre, and the lashes were darkened with kohl: her fingers were brightly stained with henna. She
moved slightly as the visitors entered, and the man gave her his drum.
She began to rub it with her hands, curiously, and made a droning
sound, which was odd and mysterious. There was a peculiar odour in
the place, so that Dr Porhoët was for a moment transported to the
evil-smelling streets of Cairo. It was an acrid mixture of incense, of
attar of roses, with every imaginable putrescence. It choked the two
women, and Susie asked for a cigarette. The native grinned when he
heard the English tongue. He showed a row of sparkling and beautiful teeth.

'My name Mohammed,' he said. 'Me show serpents to Sirdar
Lord Kitchener. Wait and see. Serpents very poisonous.'

He was dressed in a long blue gabardine, more suited to the sunny
banks of the Nile than to a fair in Paris, and its colour could hardly be
seen for dirt. On his head was the national tarboosh.

A rug lay at one side of the tent, and from under it he took a
goatskin sack. He placed it on the ground in the middle of the circle
formed by the seats and crouched down on his haunches. Margaret
shuddered, for the uneven surface of the sack moved strangely. He
opened the mouth of it. The woman in the corner listlessly droned
away on the drum, and occasionally uttered a barbaric cry. With a leer
and a flash of his bright teeth, the Arab thrust his hand into the sack
and rummaged as a man would rummage in a sack of corn. He drew
out a long, writhing snake. He placed it on the ground and for a moment waited, then he passed his hand over it: it became immediately
as rigid as a bar of iron. Except that the eyes, the cruel eyes, were open
still, there might have been no life in it.

'Look,' said Haddo. 'That is the miracle which Moses did before
Pharaoh.'

Then the Arab took a reed instrument, not unlike the pipe which

Pan in the hills of Greece played to the dryads, and he piped a weird, monotonous tune. The stiffness broke away from the snake suddenly, and it lifted its head and raised its long body till it stood almost on the tip of its tail, and it swayed slowly to and fro.

Oliver Haddo seemed extraordinarily fascinated. He leaned forward with eager face, and his unnatural eyes were fixed on the charmer with an indescribable expression. Margaret drew back in terror.

'You need not be frightened,' said Arthur. 'These people only work with animals whose fangs have been extracted.'

Oliver Haddo looked at him before answering. He seemed to consider each time what sort of man this was to whom he spoke.

'A man is only a snake-charmer because, without recourse to medicine, he is proof against the fangs of the most venomous serpents.'

'Do you think so?' said Arthur.

'I saw the most noted charmer of Madras die two hours after he had been bitten by a cobra,' said Haddo. I had heard many tales of his prowess, and one evening asked a friend to take me to him. He was out when we arrived, but we waited, and presently, accompanied by some friends, he came. We told him what we wanted. He had been at a marriage-feast and was drunk. But he sent for his snakes, and forthwith showed us marvels which this man has never heard of. At last he took a great cobra from his sack and began to handle it. Suddenly it darted at his chin and bit him. It made two marks like pin-points. The juggler started back.

'"I am a dead man," he said.

'Those about him would have killed the cobra, but he prevented them.

'"Let the creature live," he said. "It may be of service to others of my trade. To me it can be of no other use. Nothing can save me."

'His friends and the jugglers, his fellows, gathered round him and placed him in a chair. In two hours he was dead. In his drunkenness he had forgotten a portion of the spell which protected him, and so he died.'

'You have a marvellous collection of tall stories,' said Arthur. 'I'm afraid I should want better proof that these particular snakes are poisonous.'

Oliver turned to the charmer and spoke to him in Arabic. Then he answered Arthur.

'The man has a horned viper, *cerastes* is the name under which you gentlemen of science know it, and it is the most deadly of all Egyptian snakes. It is commonly known as Cleopatra's Asp, for that is the serpent which was brought in a basket of figs to the paramour of Caesar in order that she might not endure the triumph of Augustus.'

'What are you going to do?' asked Susie.

He smiled but did not answer. He stepped forward to the centre of the tent and fell on his knees. He uttered Arabic words, which Dr. Porhoët translated to the others.

'O viper, I adjure you, by the great God who is all-powerful, to come forth. You are but a snake, and God is greater than all snakes. Obey my call and come.'

A tremor went through the goatskin bag, and in a moment a head was protruded. A lithe body wriggled out. It was a snake of light grey colour, and over each eye was a horn. It lay slightly curled.

'Do you recognize it?' said Oliver in a low voice to the doctor.

'I do.'

The charmer sat motionless, and the woman in the dim background ceased her weird rubbing of the drum. Haddo seized the snake and opened its mouth. Immediately it fastened on his hand, and the reptile teeth went deep into his flesh. Arthur watched him for signs of pain, but he did not wince. The writhing snake dangled from his hand. He repeated a sentence in Arabic, and, with the peculiar suddenness of a drop of water falling from a roof, the snake fell to the ground. The blood flowed freely. Haddo spat upon the bleeding place three times, muttering words they could not hear, and three times he rubbed the wound with his fingers. The bleeding stopped. He stretched out his hand for Arthur to look at.

'That surely is what a surgeon would call healing by first intention,' he said.

Burdon was astonished, but he was irritated, too, and would not allow that there was anything strange in the cessation of the flowing blood.

'You haven't yet shown that the snake was poisonous.'

'I have not finished yet,' smiled Haddo.

He spoke again to the Egyptian, who gave an order to his wife. Without a word she rose to her feet and from a box took a white rabbit. She lifted it up by the ears, and it struggled with its four quaint legs. Haddo put it in front of the horned viper. Before anyone could have moved, the snake darted forward, and like a flash of lightning struck the rabbit. The wretched little beast gave a slight scream, a shudder went through it, and it fell dead.

Margaret sprang up with a cry.

'Oh, how cruel! How hatefully cruel!'

'Are you convinced now?' asked Haddo coolly.

The two women hurried to the doorway. They were frightened and disgusted.

Oliver Haddo was left alone with the snake-charmer.

V

DR PORHOËT HAD asked Arthur to bring Margaret and Miss Boyd to see him on Sunday at his apartment in the Île Saint Louis; and the lovers arranged to spend an hour on their way at the Louvre. Susie, invited to accompany them, preferred independence and her own reflections.

To avoid the crowd which throngs the picture galleries on holidays, they went to that part of the museum where ancient sculpture is kept. It was comparatively empty, and the long halls had the singular restfulness of places where works of art are gathered together. Margaret was filled with a genuine emotion; and though she could not analyse it, as Susie, who loved to dissect her state of mind, would have done, it strangely exhilarated her. Her heart was uplifted from the sordidness of earth, and she had a sensation of freedom which was as delightful as it was indescribable. Arthur had never troubled himself with art till Margaret's enthusiasm taught him that there was a side of life he did not realize. Though beauty meant little to his practical nature, he sought, in his great love for Margaret, to appreciate the works which excited her to such charming ecstasy. He walked by her side with docility and listened, not without deference, to her outbursts. He admired the correctness of Greek anatomy, and there was one statue of an athlete which attracted his prolonged attention, because the muscles were indicated with the precision of a plate in a surgical textbook. When Margaret talked of the Greeks' divine repose and of their blitheness, he thought it very clever because she said it; but in a man it would have aroused his impatience.

Yet there was one piece, the charming statue known as *La Diane de Gabies*, which moved him differently, and to this presently he insisted on going. With a laugh Margaret remonstrated, but secretly she was not displeased. She was aware that his passion for this figure was due, not to its intrinsic beauty, but to a likeness he had discovered in it to herself.

It stood in that fair wide gallery where is the mocking faun, with his inhuman savour of fellowship with the earth which is divine, and the sightless Homer. The goddess had not the arrogance of the huntress who loved Endymion, nor the majesty of the cold mistress of the skies. She was in the likeness of a young girl, and with collected gesture fastened her cloak. There was nothing divine in her save a sweet strange spirit of virginity. A lover in ancient Greece, who offered sacrifice before this fair image, might forget easily that it was a goddess to whom he knelt, and see only an earthly maid fresh with youth and chastity and loveliness. In Arthur's eyes Margaret had all the exquisite grace of the statue, and the same unconscious composure; and in her also breathed the spring odours of ineffable purity. Her features were chiselled with the clear and divine perfection of this Greek girl's; her ears were as delicate and as finely wrought. The colour of her skin was so tender that it reminded you vaguely of all beautiful soft things, the radiance of sunset and the darkness of the night, the heart of roses and the depth of running water. The goddess's hand was raised to her right shoulder, and Margaret's hand was as small, as dainty, and as white.

'Don't be so foolish,' said she, as Arthur looked silently at the statue.

He turned his eyes slowly, and they rested upon her. She saw that they were veiled with tears.

'What on earth's the matter?'

'I wish you weren't so beautiful,' he answered, awkwardly, as though he could scarcely bring himself to say such foolish things. 'I'm so afraid that something will happen to prevent us from being happy. It seems too much to expect that I should enjoy such extraordinarily good luck.'

She had the imagination to see that it meant much for the practical man so to express himself. Love of her drew him out of his character, and, though he could not resist, he resented the effect it had on him. She found nothing to reply, but she took his hand.

'Everything has gone pretty well with me so far,' he said, speaking almost to himself. 'Whenever I've really wanted anything, I've managed to get it. I don't see why things should go against me now.'

He was trying to reassure himself against an instinctive suspicion of the malice of circumstances. But he shook himself and straightened his back.

'It's stupid to be so morbid as that,' he muttered.

Margaret laughed. They walked out of the gallery and turned to the quay. By crossing the bridge and following the river, they must come eventually to Dr. Porhoët's house.

Meanwhile Susie wandered down the Boulevard Saint Michel, alert with the Sunday crowd, to that part of Paris which was dearest to her heart. L'Île Saint Louis to her mind offered a synthesis of the French spirit, and it pleased her far more than the garish boulevards in which the English as a rule seek for the country's fascination. Its position on an island in the Seine gave it a compact charm. The narrow streets, with their array of dainty comestibles, had the look of streets in a provincial town. They had a quaintness which appealed to the fancy, and they were very restful. The names of the streets recalled the monarchy that passed away in bloodshed, and in *poudre de riz*. The very plane trees had a greater sobriety than elsewhere, as though conscious they stood in a Paris where progress was not. In front was the turbid Seine, and below, the twin towers of Notre Dame. Susie could have kissed the hard paving stones of the quay. Her good-natured, plain face lit up as she realized the delight of the scene upon

which her eyes rested; and it was with a little pang, her mind aglow
with characters and events from history and from fiction, that she
turned away to enter Dr Porhoët's house.

She was pleased that the approach did not clash with her fantasies. She mounted a broad staircase, dark but roomy, and, at the
command of the *concierge*, rang a tinkling bell at one of the doorways
that faced her. Dr Porhoët opened in person.

'Arthur and Mademoiselle are already here,' he said, as he led
her in.

They went through a prim French dining-room, with much
woodwork and heavy scarlet hangings, to the library. This was a large
room, but the bookcases that lined the walls, and a large writing-table
heaped up with books, much diminished its size. There were books
everywhere. They were stacked on the floor and piled on every chair.
There was hardly space to move. Susie gave a cry of delight.

'Now you mustn't talk to me. I want to look at all your books.'

'You could not please me more,' said Dr Porhoët, 'but I am afraid
they will disappoint you. They are of many sorts, but I fear there are
few that will interest an English young lady.'

He looked about his writing-table till he found a packet of cigarettes. He gravely offered one to each of his guests. Susie was enchanted with the strange musty smell of the old books, and she took
a first glance at them in general. For the most part they were in paper
bindings, some of them neat enough, but more with broken backs and
dingy edges; they were set along the shelves in serried rows, untidily,
without method or plan. There were many older ones also in bindings of calf and pigskin, treasure from half the bookshops in Europe;
and there were huge folios like Prussian grenadiers; and tiny Elzevirs,
which had been read by patrician ladies in Venice. Just as Arthur was
a different man in the operating theatre, Dr Porhoët was changed
among his books. Though he preserved the amiable serenity which
made him always so attractive, he had there a diverting brusqueness
of demeanour which contrasted quaintly with his usual calm.

'I was telling these young people, when you came in, of an ancient
Korân which I was given in Alexandria by a learned man whom I op-
erated upon for cataract.' He showed her a beautifully-written Arabic

work, with wonderful capitals and headlines in gold. 'You know that it is almost impossible for an infidel to acquire the holy book, and this is a particularly rare copy, for it was written by Kaït Bey, the greatest of the Mameluke Sultans.'

He handled the delicate pages as a lover of flowers would handle rose-leaves.

'And have you much literature on the occult sciences?' asked Susie.

Dr Porhoët smiled.

'I venture to think that no private library contains so complete a collection, but I dare not show it to you in the presence of our friend Arthur. He is too polite to accuse me of foolishness, but his sarcastic smile would betray him.'

Susie went to the shelves to which he vaguely waved, and looked with a peculiar excitement at the mysterious array. She ran her eyes along the names. It seemed to her that she was entering upon an unknown region of romance. She felt like an adventurous princess who rode on her palfrey into a forest of great bare trees and mystic silences, where wan, unearthly shapes pressed upon her way.

'I thought once of writing a life of that fantastic and grandiloquent creature, Philippus Aureolus Theophrastus Paracelsus Bombast von Hohenheim,' said Dr Porhoët, 'and I have collected many of his books.'

He took down a slim volume in duodecimo, printed in the seventeenth century, with queer plates, on which were all manner of cabbalistic signs. The pages had a peculiar, musty odour. They were stained with iron-mould.

'Here is one of the most interesting works concerning the black art. It is the *Grimoire of Honorius*, and is the principal text-book of all those who deal in the darkest ways of the science.'

Then he pointed out the *Hexameron* of Torquemada and the *Tableau de l'Inconstance des Démons*, by Delancre; he drew his finger down the leather back of Delrio's *Disquisitiones Magicae* and set upright the *Pseudomonarchia Daemonorum* of Wierus; his eyes rested for an instant on Hauber's *Acta et Scripta Magica*, and he blew the dust carefully off the most famous, the most infamous, of them all, Sprenger's *Malleus Malefikorum*.

'Here is one of my greatest treasures. It is the *Clavicula Salomonis*;

and I have much reason to believe that it is the identical copy which belonged to the greatest adventurer of the eighteenth century, Jacques Casanova. You will see that the owner's name had been cut out, but enough remains to indicate the bottom of the letters; and these correspond exactly with the signature of Casanova which I have found at the Bibliothéque Nationale. He relates in his memoirs that a copy of this book was seized among his effects when he was arrested in Venice for traffic in the black arts; and it was there, on one of my journeys from Alexandria, that I picked it up.'

He replaced the precious work, and his eye fell on a stout volume bound in vellum.

'I had almost forgotten the most wonderful, the most mysterious, of all the books that treat of occult science. You have heard of the Kabbalah, but I doubt if it is more than a name to you.'

'I know nothing about it at all,' laughed Susie, 'except that it's all very romantic and extraordinary and ridiculous.'

'This, then, is its history. Moses, who was learned in all the wisdom of Egypt, was first initiated into the Kabbalah in the land of his birth; but became most proficient in it during his wanderings in the wilderness. Here he not only devoted the leisure hours of forty years to this mysterious science, but received lessons in it from an obliging angel. By aid of it he was able to solve the difficulties which arose during his management of the Israelites, notwithstanding the pilgrimages, wars, and miseries of that most unruly nation. He covertly laid down the principles of the doctrine in the first four books of the Pentateuch, but withheld them from Deuteronomy. Moses also initiated the Seventy Elders into these secrets, and they in turn transmitted them from hand to hand. Of all who formed the unbroken line of tradition, David and Solomon were the most deeply learned in the Kabbalah. No one, however, dared to write it down till Schimeon ben Jochai, who lived in the time of the destruction of Jerusalem; and after his death the Rabbi Eleazar, his son, and the Rabbi Abba, his secretary, collected his manuscripts and from them composed the celebrated treatise called *Zohar*.'

'And how much do you believe of this marvellous story?' asked Arthur Burdon.

'Not a word,' answered Dr Porhoët, with a smile. 'Criticism has shown that *Zohar* is of modern origin. With singular effrontery, it cites an author who is known to have lived during the eleventh century, mentions the Crusades, and records events which occurred in the year of Our Lord 1264. It was some time before 1291 that copies of *Zohar* began to be circulated by a Spanish Jew named Moses de Leon, who claimed to possess an autograph manuscript by the reputed author Schimeon ben Jochai. But when Moses de Leon was gathered to the bosom of his father Abraham, a wealthy Hebrew, Joseph de Avila, promised the scribe's widow, who had been left destitute, that his son should marry her daughter, to whom he would pay a handsome dowry, if she would give him the original manuscript from which these copies were made. But the widow (one can imagine with what gnashing of teeth) was obliged to confess that she had no such manuscript, for Moses de Leon had composed *Zohar* out of his own head, and written it with his own right hand.'

Arthur got up to stretch his legs. He gave a laugh.

'I never know how much you really believe of all these things you tell us. You speak with such gravity that we are all taken in, and then it turns out that you've been laughing at us.'

'My dear friend, I never know myself how much I believe,' returned Dr Porhoët.

'I wonder if it is for the same reason that Mr Haddo puzzles us so much,' said Susie.

'Ah, there you have a case that is really interesting,' replied the doctor. 'I assure you that, though I know him fairly intimately, I have never been able to make up my mind whether he is an elaborate practical joker, or whether he is really convinced he has the wonderful powers to which he lays claim.'

'We certainly saw things last night that were not quite normal,' said Susie. 'Why had that serpent no effect on him though it was able to kill the rabbit instantaneously? And how are you going to explain the violent trembling of that horse, Mr. Burdon?'

'I can't explain it,' answered Arthur, irritably, 'but I'm not inclined to attribute to the supernatural everything that I can't immediately understand.'

'I don't know what there is about him that excites in me a sort of horror,' said Margaret. 'I've never taken such a sudden dislike to anyone.'

She was too reticent to say all she felt, but she had been strangely affected last night by the recollection of Haddo's words and of his acts. She had awakened more than once from a nightmare in which he assumed fantastic and ghastly shapes. His mocking voice rang in her ears, and she seemed still to see that vast bulk and the savage, sensual face. It was like a spirit of evil in her path, and she was curiously alarmed. Only her reliance on Arthur's common sense prevented her from giving way to ridiculous terrors.

'I've written to Frank Hurrell and asked him to tell me all he knows about him,' said Arthur. 'I should get an answer very soon.'

'I wish we'd never come across him,' cried Margaret vehemently. 'I feel that he will bring us misfortune.'

'You're all of you absurdly prejudiced,' answered Susie gaily. 'He interests me enormously, and I mean to ask him to tea at the studio.'

'I'm sure I shall be delighted to come.'

Margaret cried out, for she recognized Oliver Haddo's deep bantering tones; and she turned round quickly. They were all so taken aback that for a moment no one spoke. They were gathered round the window and had not heard him come in. They wondered guiltily how long he had been there and how much he had heard.

'How on earth did you get here?' cried Susie lightly, recovering herself first.

'No well-bred sorcerer is so dead to the finer feelings as to enter a room by the door,' he answered, with his puzzling smile. 'You were standing round the window, and I thought it would startle you if I chose that mode of ingress, so I descended with incredible skill down the chimney.'

'I see a little soot on your left elbow,' returned Susie. 'I hope you weren't at all burned.'

'Not at all, thanks,' he answered, gravely brushing his coat.

'In whatever way you came, you are very welcome,' said Dr Porhoët, genially holding out his hand.

But Arthur impatiently turned to his host.

'I wish I knew what made you engage upon these studies,' he said.

'I should have thought your medical profession protected you from any tenderness towards superstition.'

Dr Porhoët shrugged his shoulders.

'I have always been interested in the oddities of mankind. At one time I read a good deal of philosophy and a good deal of science, and I learned in that way that nothing was certain. Some people, by the pursuit of science, are impressed with the dignity of man, but I was only made conscious of his insignificance. The greatest questions of all have been threshed out since he acquired the beginnings of civilization and he is as far from a solution as ever. Man can know nothing, for his senses are his only means of knowledge, and they can give no certainty. There is only one subject upon which the individual can speak with authority, and that is his own mind, but even here he is surrounded with darkness. I believe that we shall always be ignorant of the matters which it most behoves us to know, and therefore I cannot occupy myself with them. I prefer to set them all aside, and, since knowledge is unattainable, to occupy myself only with folly.'

'It is a point of view I do not sympathize with,' said Arthur.

'Yet I cannot be sure that it is all folly,' pursued the Frenchman reflectively. He looked at Arthur with a certain ironic gravity. 'Do you believe that I should lie to you when I promised to speak the truth?'

'Certainly not.'

'I should like to tell you of an experience that I once had in Alexandria. So far as I can see, it can be explained by none of the principles known to science. I ask you only to believe that I am not consciously deceiving you.'

He spoke with a seriousness which gave authority to his words. It was plain, even to Arthur, that he narrated the event exactly as it occurred.

'I had heard frequently of a certain shiekh who was able by means of a magic mirror to show the inquirer persons who were absent or dead, and a native friend of mine had often begged me to see him. I had never thought it worth while, but at last a time came when I was greatly troubled in my mind. My poor mother was an old woman, a widow, and I had received no news of her for many weeks. Though I wrote repeatedly, no answer reached me. I was very anxious and very unhappy. I thought no harm could come if I sent for the sorcerer, and perhaps after all he had the power which was attributed to him. My friend, who was interpreter to the French Consulate, brought him to me one evening. He was a fine man, tall and stout, of a fair complexion, but with a dark brown beard. He was shabbily dressed, and, being a descendant of the Prophet, wore a green turban. In his conversation he was affable and unaffected. I asked him what persons could see in the magic mirror, and he said they were a boy not arrived at puberty, a virgin, a black female slave, and a pregnant woman. In order to make sure that there was no collusion, I despatched my servant to an intimate friend and asked him to send me his son. While we waited, I prepared by the magician's direction frankincense and coriander-seed, and a chafing-dish with live charcoal. Meanwhile, he wrote forms of invocation on six strips of paper. When the boy arrived, the sorcerer threw incense and one of the paper strips into the chafing-dish, then took the boy's right hand and drew a square and certain mystical marks on the palm. In the centre of the square he poured a little ink. This formed the magic mirror. He desired the boy to look steadily into it without raising his head. The fumes of the incense filled the room with smoke. The sorcerer muttered Arabic words, indistinctly, and this he continued to do all the time except when he asked the boy a question.

'"Do you see anything in the ink?" he said.

'"No," the boy answered.

'But a minute later, he began to tremble and seemed very much frightened.

'"I see a man sweeping the ground," he said.

'"When he has done sweeping, tell me," said the sheikh.

'"He has done," said the boy.

'The sorcerer turned to me and asked who it was that I wished the boy should see.

'"I desire to see the widow Jeanne-Marie Porhoët."

'The magician put the second and third of the small strips of paper into the chafing-dish, and fresh frankincense was added. The fumes were painful to my eyes. The boy began to speak.

'"I see an old woman lying on a bed. She has a black dress, and on her head is a little white cap. She has a wrinkled face and her eyes are closed. There is a band tied round her chin. The bed is in a sort of hole, in the wall, and there are shutters to it."

The boy was describing a Breton bed, and the white cap was the *coiffe* that my mother wore. And if she lay there in her black dress, with a band about her chin, I knew that it could mean but one thing.

"'What else does he see?" I asked the sorcerer.

'He repeated my question, and presently the boy spoke again.

"'I see four men come in with a long box. And there are women crying. They all wear little white caps and black dresses. And I see a man in a white surplice, with a large cross in his hands, and a little boy in a long red gown. And the men take off their hats. And now everyone is kneeling down."

"'I will hear no more," I said. "It is enough."

'I knew that my mother was dead.

'In a little while, I received a letter from the priest of the village in which she lived. They had buried her on the very day upon which the boy had seen this sight in the mirror of ink.'

Dr Porhoët passed his hand across his eyes, and for a little while there was silence.

'What have you to say to that?' asked Oliver Haddo, at last.

'Nothing,' answered Arthur.

Haddo looked at him for a minute with those queer eyes of his which seemed to stare at the wall behind.

'Have you ever heard of Eliphas Levi?' he inquired. 'He is the most celebrated occultist of recent years. He is thought to have known more of the mysteries than any adept since the divine Paracelsus.'

'I met him once,' interrupted Dr Porhoët. 'You never saw a man who looked less like a magician. His face beamed with good-nature, and he wore a long grey beard, which covered nearly the whole of his breast. He was of a short and very corpulent figure.'

'The practice of black arts evidently disposes to obesity,' said Arthur, icily.

Susie noticed that this time Oliver Haddo made no sign that the taunt moved him. His unwinking, straight eyes remained upon Arthur without expression.

'Levi's real name was Alphonse-Louis Constant, but he adopted that under which he is generally known for reasons that are plain to the romantic mind. His father was a bootmaker. He was destined for the priesthood, but fell in love with a damsel fair and married her. The union was unhappy. A fate befell him which has been the lot of greater men than he, and his wife presently abandoned the marital roof with her lover. To console himself he began to make serious re-searches in the occult, and in due course published a vast number of mystical works dealing with magic in all its branches.'

'I'm sure Mr Haddo was going to tell us something very interest-ing about him,' said Susie.

'I wished merely to give you his account of how he raised the spirit of Apollonius of Tyana in London.'

Susie settled herself more comfortably in her chair and lit a cigarette.

'He went there in the spring of 1856 to escape from internal disquietude and to devote himself without distraction to his studies. He had letters of introduction to various persons of distinction who concerned themselves with the supernatural, but, finding them trivial and indifferent, he immersed himself in the study of the supreme Kabbalah. One day, on returning to his hotel, he found a note in his room. It contained half a card, transversely divided, on which he at once recognized the character of Solomon's Seal, and a tiny slip of paper on which was written in pencil: *The other half of this card will be given you at three o'clock tomorrow in front of Westminster Abbey.* Next day, going to the appointed spot, with his portion of the card in his hand, he found a baronial equipage waiting for him. A footman approached, and, making a sign to him, opened the carriage door. Within was a lady in black satin, whose face was concealed by a thick veil. She motioned him to a seat beside her, and at the same time dis-played the other part of the card he had received. The door was shut, and the carriage rolled away. When the lady raised her veil, Eliphas Levi saw that she was of mature age; and beneath her grey eyebrows were bright black eyes of preternatural fixity.'

Susie Boyd clapped her hands with delight.

'I think it's delicious, and I'm sure every word of it is true,' she cried. 'I'm enchanted with the mysterious meeting at Westminster Abbey in the Mid-Victorian era. Can't you see the elderly lady in a huge crinoline and a black poke bonnet, and the wizard in a ridiculous hat, a bottle-green frock-coat, and a flowing tie of black silk?'

'Eliphas remarks that the lady spoke French with a marked English accent,' pursued Haddo imperturbably. 'She addressed him as follows: "Sir, I am aware that the law of secrecy is rigorous among adepts; and I know that you have been asked for phenomena, but have declined to gratify a frivolous curiosity. It is possible that you do not possess the necessary materials. I can show you a complete magical cabinet, but I must require of you first the most inviolable silence. If you do not guarantee this on your honour, I will give the order for you to be driven home."'

Oliver Haddo told his story not ineffectively, but with a comic gravity that prevented one from knowing exactly how to take it.

'Having given the required promise Eliphas Levi was shown a collection of vestments and of magical instruments. The lady lent him certain books of which he was in need; and at last, as a result of many conversations, determined him to attempt at her house the experience of a complete evocation. He prepared himself for twenty-one days, scrupulously observing the rules laid down by the Ritual. At length everything was ready. It was proposed to call forth the phantom of the divine Apollonius, and to question it upon two matters, one of which concerned Eliphas Levi and the other, the lady of the crinoline. She had at first counted on assisting at the evocation with a trustworthy person, but at the last moment her friend drew back; and as the triad or unity is rigorously prescribed in magical rites, Eliphas was left alone. The cabinet prepared for the experiment was situated in a turret. Four concave mirrors were hung within it, and there was an altar of white marble, surrounded by a chain of magnetic iron. On it was engraved the sign of the Pentagram, and this symbol was drawn on the new, white sheepskin which was stretched beneath. A copper brazier stood on the altar, with charcoal of alder and of laurel wood, and in front a second brazier was placed upon a tripod. Eliphas Levi was clothed in a white robe, longer and more ample than the surplice of a priest, and he wore upon his head a chaplet of vervain leaves entwined about a golden chain. In one hand he held a new sword and in the other the Ritual.'

Susie's passion for caricature at once asserted itself, and she laughed as she saw in fancy the portly little Frenchman, with his round, red face, thus wonderfully attired.

'He set alight the two fires with the prepared materials, and began, at first in a low voice, but rising by degrees, the invocations of the Ritual. The flames invested every object with a wavering light. Presently they went out. He set more twigs and perfumes on the brazier, and when the flame started up once more, he saw distinctly before the altar a human figure larger than life, which dissolved and disappeared. He began the invocations again and placed himself in a circle, which he had already traced between the altar and the tripod. Then the depth of the mirror which was in front of him grew brighter by degrees, and a pale form arose, and it seemed gradually to approach. He closed his eyes, and called three times upon Apollonius. When he opened them, a man stood before him, wholly enveloped in a winding sheet, which seemed more grey than black. His form was lean, melancholy, and beardless. Eliphas felt an intense cold, and when he sought to ask his questions found it impossible to speak. Thereupon, he placed his hand on the Pentagram, and directed the point of his sword toward the figure, adjuring it mentally by that sign not to terrify, but to obey him. The form suddenly grew indistinct and soon it strangely vanished. He commanded it to return, and then felt, as it were, an air pass by him; and, something having touched the hand which held the sword, his arm was immediately benumbed as far as the shoulder. He supposed that the weapon displeased the spirit, and set it down within the circle. The human figure at once reappeared, but Eliphas experienced such a sudden exhaustion in all his limbs that he was obliged to sit down. He fell into a deep coma, and dreamed strange dreams. But of these, when he recovered, only a vague memory remained to him. His arm continued for several days to be numb and painful. The figure had not spoken, but it seemed to Eliphas Levi that the questions were answered in his own mind. For to each an inner voice replied with one grim word: dead.'

'Your friend seems to have had as little fear of spooks as you have of lions,' said Burdon. 'To my thinking it is plain that all these preparations, and the perfumes, the mirrors, the pentagrams, must have the greatest effect on the imagination. My only surprise is that your magician saw no more.'

'Eliphas Levi talked to me himself of this evocation,' said Dr Porhoët. 'He told me that its influence on him was very great. He was no longer the same man, for it seemed to him that something from the world beyond had passed into his soul.'

'I am astonished that you should never have tried such an interesting experiment yourself,' said Arthur to Oliver Haddo.

'I have,' answered the other calmly. 'My father lost his power of speech shortly before he died, and it was plain that he sought with all his might to tell me something. A year after his death, I called up his phantom from the grave so that I might learn what I took to be a dying wish. The circumstances of the apparition are so similar to those I have just told you that it would only bore you if I repeated them. The only difference was that my father actually spoke.'

'What did he say?' asked Susie.

'He said solemnly: "*Buy Ashantis, they are bound to go up.*"

'I did as he told me; but my father was always unlucky in speculation, and they went down steadily. I sold out at considerable loss, and concluded that in the world beyond they are as ignorant of the tendency of the Stock Exchange as we are in this vale of sorrow.'

Susie could not help laughing. But Arthur shrugged his shoulders impatiently. It disturbed his practical mind never to be certain if Haddo was serious, or if, as now, he was plainly making game of them.

VI

TWO DAYS LATER, Arthur received Frank Hurrell's answer to his letter. It was characteristic of Frank that he should take such pains to reply at length to the inquiry, and it was clear that he had lost none of his old interest in odd personalities. He analysed Oliver Haddo's character with the patience of a scientific man studying a new species in which he is passionately concerned.

My dear Burdon:

It is singular that you should write just now to ask what I know of Oliver Haddo, since by chance I met the other night at dinner at Queen Anne's Gate a man who had much to tell me of him. I am curious to know why he excites your interest, for I am sure his peculiarities make him repugnant to a person of your robust common sense. I can with difficulty imagine two men less capable of getting on together. Though I have not seen Haddo now for years, I can tell you, in one way and another, a good deal about him. He erred when he described me as his intimate friend. It is true that at one time I saw much of him, but I never ceased cordially to dislike him. He came up to Oxford from Eton with a reputation for athletics and eccentricity. But you know that there is nothing that arouses the ill-will of boys more than the latter, and he achieved an unpopularity which was remarkable. It turned out that he played football admirably, and except for his rather scornful indolence he might easily have got his blue. He sneered at the popular enthusiasm for games, and was used to say that cricket was all very well for boys but not fit for the pastime of men. (He was then eighteen!) He talked grandiloquently of big-game shooting and of mountain climbing as sports which demanded courage and self-reliance. He seemed, indeed, to like football, but he played it with a brutal savagery which the other persons concerned naturally resented. It became current opinion in other pursuits that he did not play the game. He did nothing that was manifestly unfair, but was capable of taking advantages which most people would have thought mean; and he made defeat more hard to bear because he exulted over the vanquished with the coarse banter that youths find so difficult to endure.

What you would hardly believe is that, when he first came up, he was a person of great physical attractions. He is now grown fat, but in those days was extremely handsome. He reminded one of those colossal statues of Apollo in which the god is represented with a feminine roundness and delicacy. He was very tall and had a magnificent figure. It was so well-formed for his age that one might have foretold his precious corpulence. He held himself with a dashing erectness. Many called it an insolent swagger. His features were regular and fine. He had a great quantity of curling hair, which was worn long, with a sort of poetic grace: I am told that now he is very bald; and I can imagine that this must be a great blow to him, for he was always exceedingly vain. I remember a peculiarity of his eyes, which could scarcely have been natural, but how it was acquired I do not know. The eyes of most people converge upon the object at which they look, but his remained parallel. It gave them a singular expression, as though he were scrutinising the inmost thought of the person with whom he talked. He was notorious also for the extravagance of his costume, but, unlike the aesthetes of that day, who clothed themselves with artistic carelessness, he had a taste for outrageous colours. Sometimes, by a queer freak, he dressed himself at unseasonable moments with excessive formality. He is the only undergraduate I have ever seen walk down the High in a tall hat and a closely-buttoned frock-coat.

I have told you he was very unpopular, but it was not an unpopularity of the sort which ignores a man and leaves him chiefly to his own society. Haddo knew everybody and was to be found in the most unlikely places. Though people disliked him, they showed a curious pleasure in his company, and he was probably entertained more than any man in Oxford. I never saw him but he was surrounded by a little crowd, who abused him behind his back, but could not resist his fascination.

I often tried to analyse this, for I felt it as much as anyone, and though I honestly could not bear him, I could never resist going to see him whenever opportunity arose. I suppose he offered the charm of the unexpected to that mass of undergraduates who, for all their matter-of-fact breeziness, are curiously alive to the romantic. It was impossible to tell what he would do or say next, and you were kept perpetually on the alert. He was certainly not witty, but he had a coarse humour which excited the rather gross sense of the ludicrous possessed by the young.

He had a gift for caricature which was really diverting, and an imperturbable assurance. He had also an ingenious talent for profanity, and his inventiveness in this particular was a power among youths whose imaginations stopped at the commoner sorts of bad language. I have heard him preach a sermon of the most blasphemous sort in the very accents of the late Dean of Christ Church, which outraged and at the same time irresistibly amused everyone who heard it. He had a more varied knowledge than the greater part of undergraduates, and, having at the same time a retentive memory and considerable quickness, he was able to assume an attitude of omniscience which was as impressive as it was irritating. I have never heard him confess that he had not read a book. Often, when I tried to catch him, he confounded me by quoting the identical words of a passage in some work which I could have sworn he had never set eyes on. I daresay it was due only to some juggling, like the conjuror's sleight of hand that apparently lets you choose a card, but in fact forces one on you; and he brought the conversation round cleverly to a point when it was obvious I should mention a definite book. He talked very well, with an entertaining flow of rather pompous language which made the amusing things he said particularly funny. His passion for euphuism contrasted strikingly with the simple speech of those with whom he consorted. It certainly added authority to what he said. He was proud of his family and never hesitated to tell the curious of his distinguished descent. Unless he has much altered, you will already have heard of his relationship with various noble houses. He is, in fact, nearly connected with persons of importance, and his ancestry is no less distinguished than he asserts. His father is dead, and he owns a place in Staffordshire which is almost historic. I have seen photographs of it, and it is certainly very fine. His forebears have been noted in the history of England since the days of the courtier who accompanied Anne of Denmark to Scotland, and, if he is proud of his stock, it is not without cause. So he passed his time at Oxford, cordially disliked, at the same time respected and mistrusted; he had the reputation of a liar and a rogue, but it could not be denied that he had considerable influence over others. He amused, angered, irritated, and interested everyone with whom he came in contact. There was always something mysterious about him, and he loved to wrap himself in a romantic impenetrability. Though he knew so many people, no one knew him, and to the end he remained a stranger in our midst. A legend grew up around him, which he fostered sedulously, and it was reported that he had secret vices which could only be whispered with bated breath. He was said to intoxicate himself with Oriental drugs, and to haunt the vilest opium-dens in the East of London. He kept the greatest surprise for the last, since, though he was never seen to work, he managed, to the universal surprise, to get a first. He went down, and to the best of my belief was never seen in Oxford again.

I have heard vaguely that he was travelling over the world, and, when I met in town now and then some of the fellows who had known him at the 'Varsity, weird rumours reached me. One told me that he was tramping across America, earning his living as he went; another asserted that he had been seen in a monastry in India; a third assured me that he had married a ballet-girl in Milan; and someone else was positive that he had taken to drink. One opinion, however, was common to all my informants, and this was that he did something out of the common. It was clear that he was not the man to settle down to the tame life of a country gentleman which his position and fortune indicated. At last I met him one day in Piccadilly, and we dined together at the Savoy. I hardly recognized him, for he was become enormously stout, and his hair had already grown thin. Though he could not have been more than twenty-five, he looked considerably older. I tried to find out what he had been up to, but, with the air of mystery he affects, he would go into no details. He gave me to understand that he had sojourned in lands where the white man had never been before, and had learnt esoteric secrets which overthrew the foundations of modern science. It seemed to me that he had coarsened in mind as well as in appearance. I do not know if it was due to my own development since the old days at Oxford, and to my greater knowledge of the world, but he did not seem to me so brilliant as I remembered. His facile banter was rather stupid. In fact he bored me. The pose which had seemed amusing in a lad fresh from Eton now was intolerable, and I was glad to leave him. It was characteristic that, after asking me to dinner, he left me in a lordly way to pay the bill.

Then I heard nothing of him till the other day, when our friend Miss Ley asked me to meet at dinner the German explorer Burkhardt. I dare say you remember that Burkhardt brought out a book a little while ago on his adventures in Central Asia. I knew that Oliver Haddo was his companion in that journey and had meant to read it on this account, but, having been excessively busy, had omitted to do so. I took the opportunity to ask the German about our common acquaintance, and we had a long talk. Burkhardt had met him by chance at Mombasa in East Africa, where he was arranging an expedition after big game, and they agreed to go together. He told me that Haddo was a marvellous shot and a hunter of exceptional ability. Burkhardt had been rather suspicious of a man who boasted so much of his attainments, but was obliged soon to confess that he boasted of nothing unjustly. Haddo has had an extraordinary experience, the truth of which Burkhardt can vouch for. He went out alone one night on the trail of three lions and killed them all before morning with one shot each. I know nothing of these things, but from the way in which Burkhardt spoke, I judge it must be a unique occurrence. But, characteristically enough, no one was more conscious than Haddo of the singularity of his feat, and he made life almost insufferable for his fellow-traveller in consequence. Burkhardt assures me that Haddo is really remarkable in pursuit of big game. He has a sort of instinct which leads him to the most unlikely places, and a wonderful feeling for country, whereby he can cut across, and head off animals whose spoor he has noticed. His courage is very great. To follow a wounded lion into thick cover is the most dangerous proceeding in the world, and demands the utmost coolness. The animal invariably sees the sportsman before he sees it, and in most cases charges. But Haddo never hesitated on these occasions, and Burkhardt could only express entire admiration for his pluck. It appears that he is not what is called a good sportsman. He kills wantonly, when there can be no possible excuse, for the mere pleasure of it; and to Burkhardt's indignation frequently shot beasts whose skins and horns they did not even trouble to take. When antelope were so far off that it was impossible to kill them, and the approach of night made it useless to follow, he would often shoot, and leave a wretched wounded beast to die by inches. His selfishness was extreme, and he never shared any information with his friend that might rob him of an uninterrupted pursuit of game. But notwithstanding all this, Burkhardt had so high an opinion of Haddo's general capacity and of his resourcefulness that, when he was arranging his journey in Asia, he asked him to come also. Haddo consented, and it appears that Burkhardt's book gives further proof, if it is needed, of the man's extraordinary qualities. The German confessed that on more than one occasion he owed his life to Haddo's rare power of seizing opportunities. But they quarrelled at last through Haddo's over-bearing treatment of the natives. Burkhardt had vaguely suspected him of cruelty, but at length it was clear that he used them in a manner which could not be defended. Finally he had a desperate quarrel with one of the camp servants, as a result of which the man was shot dead. Haddo swore that he fired in self-defence, but his action caused a general desertion, and the travellers found themselves in a very dangerous predicament. Burkhardt thought that Haddo was clearly to blame and refused to have anything more to do with him. They separated. Burkhardt returned to England; and Haddo, pursued by the friends of the murdered man, had great difficulty in escaping with his life. Nothing has been heard of him since till I got your letter.

Altogether, an extraordinary man. I confess that I can make nothing of him. I shall never be surprised to hear anything in connexion with him. I recommend you to avoid him like the plague. He can be no one's friend. As an acquaintance he is treacherous and insincere; as an enemy, I can well imagine that he would be as merciless as he is unscrupulous.

An immensely long letter!

Goodbye, my son. I hope that your studies in French methods of surgery will have added to your wisdom. Your industry edifies me, and I am sure that you will eventually be a baronet and the President of the Royal College of Surgeons; and you shall relieve royal persons of their, vermiform appendix.

Yours ever,

FRANK HURRELL

Arthur, having read this letter twice, put it in an envelope and left it without comment for Miss Boyd. Her answer came within a couple of hours: 'I've asked him to tea on Wednesday, and I can't put him off. You must come and help us; but please be as polite to him as if, like most of us, he had only taken mental liberties with the Ten Commandments.'

VII

ON THE MORNING of the day upon which they had asked him to tea, Oliver Haddo left at Margaret's door vast masses of chrysanthemums. There were so many that the austere studio was changed in aspect. It gained an ephemeral brightness that Margaret, notwithstanding pieces of silk hung here and there on the walls, had never been able to give it. When Arthur arrived, he was dismayed that the thought had not occurred to him.

'I'm so sorry,' he said. 'You must think me very inconsiderate.'

Margaret smiled and held his hand.

'I think I like you because you don't trouble about the common little attentions of lovers.'

'Margaret's a wise girl,' smiled Susie. 'She knows that when a man sends flowers it is a sign that he has admired more women than one.'

'I don't suppose that these were sent particularly to me.'

Arthur Burdon sat down and observed with pleasure the cheerful fire. The drawn curtains and the lamps gave the place a nice cosiness, and there was the peculiar air of romance which is always in a studio. There is a sense of freedom about it that disposes the mind to diverting speculations. In such an atmosphere it is possible to be serious without pompousness and flippant without inanity.

In the few days of their acquaintance Arthur and Susie had arrived at terms of pleasant familiarity. Susie, from her superior standpoint of an unmarried woman no longer young, used him with the good-natured banter which she affected. To her, he was a foolish young thing in love, and she marvelled that even the cleverest man in that condition could behave like a perfect idiot. But Margaret knew that, if her friend chaffed him, it was because she completely approved of him. As their intimacy increased, Susie learnt to appreciate his solid character. She admired his capacity in dealing with matters that were in his province, and the simplicity with which he left alone those of which he was ignorant. There was no pose in him. She was touched also by an ingenuous candour which gave a persuasive charm to his abruptness. And, though she set a plain woman's value on good looks, his appearance, rough hewn like a statue in porphyry, pleased her singularly. It was an index of his character. The look of him gave you the whole man, strong yet gentle, honest and simple, neither very imaginative nor very brilliant, but immensely reliable and trustworthy to the bottom of his soul. He was seated now with Margaret's terrier on his knees, stroking its ears, and Susie, looking at him, wondered with a little pang why no man like that had even cared for her. It was evident that he would make a perfect companion, and his love, once won, was of the sort that did not alter.

Dr Porhoët came in and sat down with the modest quietness which was one of his charms. He was not a great talker and loved most to listen in silence to the chatter of young people. The dog jumped down from Arthur's knee, went up to the doctor, and rubbed itself in friendly fashion against his legs. They began to talk in the soft light and had forgotten almost that another guest was expected. Margaret hoped fervently that he would not come. She had never looked more lovely than on this afternoon, and she busied herself with the preparations for tea with a housewifely grace that added a peculiar delicacy to her comeliness. The dignity which encompassed the perfection of her beauty was delightfully softened, so that you were reminded of those sweet domestic saints who lighten here and there the passionate records of the Golden Book.

'*C'est tellement intime ici,*' smiled Dr Porhoët, breaking into French in the impossibility of expressing in English the exact feeling which that scene gave him.

It might have been a picture by some master of *genre*. It seemed hardly by chance that the colours arranged themselves in such agreeable tones, or that the lines of the wall and the seated persons achieved such a graceful decoration. The atmosphere was extraordinarily peaceful.

There was a knock at the door, and Arthur got up to open. The terrier followed at his heels. Oliver Haddo entered. Susie watched to see what the dog would do and was by this time not surprised to see a change come over it. With its tail between its legs, the friendly little beast slunk along the wall to the furthermost corner. It turned a suspicious, frightened eye upon Haddo and then hid its head. The visitor, intent upon his greetings, had not noticed even that there was an animal in the room. He accepted with a simple courtesy they hardly expected from him the young woman's thanks for his flowers. His behaviour surprised them. He put aside his poses. He seemed genuinely to admire the cosy little studio. He asked Margaret to show him her sketches and looked at them with unassumed interest. His observations were pointed and showed a certain knowledge of what he spoke about. He described himself as an amateur, that object of a painter's derision: the man 'who knows what he likes'; but his criticism, though generous, showed that he was no fool. The two women were impressed. Putting the sketches aside, he began to talk, of the many places he had seen. It was evident that he sought to please. Susie began to understand how it was that, notwithstanding his affectations, he had acquired so great an influence over the undergraduates of Oxford. There was romance and laughter in his conversation; and though, as Frank Hurrell had said, lacking in wit, he made up for it with a diverting pleasantry that might very well have passed for humour. But Susie, though amused, felt that this was not the purpose for which she had asked him to come. Dr Porhoët had lent her his entertaining work on the old alchemists, and this gave her a chance to bring their conversation to matters on which Haddo was expert. She had read the book with delight and, her mind all aflame with those strange histories wherein fact and fancy were so wonderfully mingled, she was eager to know more. The long toil in which so many had engaged, always to lose their fortunes, often to suffer persecution and torture, interested her no less than the accounts, almost authenticated, of those who had succeeded in their extraordinary quest.

She turned to Dr Porhoët.

'You are a bold man to assert that now and then the old alchemists actually did make gold,' she said.

'I have not gone quite so far as that,' he smiled. 'I assert merely that, if evidence as conclusive were offered of any other historical event, it would be credited beyond doubt. We can disbelieve these circumstantial details only by coming to the conclusion beforehand that it is impossible they should be true.'

'I wish you would write that life of Paracelsus which you suggest in your preface.'

Dr Porhoët, smiling shook his head.

'I don't think I shall ever do that now,' he said. 'Yet he is the most interesting of all the alchemists, for he offers the fascinating problem of an immensely complex character. It is impossible to know to what extent he was a charlatan and to what a man of serious science.'

Susie glanced at Oliver Haddo, who sat in silence, his heavy face in shadow, his eyes fixed steadily on the speaker. The immobility of that vast bulk was peculiar.

'His name is not so ridiculous as later associations have made it seem,' proceeded the doctor, 'for he belonged to the celebrated family of Bombast, and they were called Hohenheim after their ancient residence, which was a castle near Stuttgart in Würtemberg. The most interesting part of his life is that which the absence of documents makes it impossible accurately to describe. He travelled in Germany, Italy, France, the Netherlands, in Denmark, Sweden, and Russia. He went even to India. He was taken prisoner by the Tartars, and brought to the Great Khan, whose son he afterwards accompanied to Constantinople. The mind must be dull indeed that is not thrilled by the thought of this wandering genius traversing the lands of the earth at the most eventful date of the world's history. It was at Constantinople that, according to a certain *aureum vellus* printed at Rorschach in the sixteenth century, he received the philosopher's stone from Solomon Trismosinus. This person possessed also the *Universal Panacea*, and it is asserted that he was seen still alive by a French traveller at the end of the seventeenth century. Paracelsus then passed through the countries that border the Danube, and so reached Italy, where he served as a surgeon in the imperial army. I see no reason why he should not have been present at the battle of Pavia. He collected information from physicians, surgeons and alchemists; from executioners, barbers, shepherds, Jews, gipsies, midwives, and fortune-tellers; from high and low, from learned and vulgar. In the sketch I have given of his career in that volume you hold, I have copied out a few words of his upon the acquirement of knowledge which affect me with a singular emotion.'

Dr Porhoët took his book from Miss Boyd and opened it thoughtfully. He read out the fine passage from the preface of the *Paragranum*:

'I went in search of my art, often incurring danger of life. I have not been ashamed to learn that which seemed useful to me even from vagabonds, hangmen, and barbers. We know that a lover will go far to meet the woman he adores; how much more will the lover of Wisdom be tempted to go in search of his divine mistress.'

He turned the page to find a few more lines further on:

'We should look for knowledge where we may expect to find it, and why should a man be despised who goes in search of it? Those who remain at home may grow richer and live more comfortably than those who wander; but I desire neither to live comfortably nor to grow rich.'

'By Jove, those are fine words,' said Arthur, rising to his feet.

Their brave simplicity moved him as no rhetoric could have done, and they made him more eager still to devote his own life to the difficult acquisition of knowledge. Dr Porhoët gave him his ironic smile.

'Yet the man who could write that was in many ways a mere buffoon, who praised his wares with the vulgar glibness of a quack. He was vain and ostentatious, intemperate and boastful. Listen:

'After me, O Avicenna, Galen, Rhases and Montagnana! After me, not I after you, ye men of Paris, Montpellier, Meissen, and Cologne; all you that come from the countries along the Danube and the Rhine, and you that come from the islands of the sea. It is not for me to follow you, because mine is the lordship. The time will come when none of you shall remain in his dark corner who will not be an object of contempt to the world, because I shall be the King, and the Monarchy will be mine.'

Dr Porhoët closed the book.

'Did you ever hear such gibberish in your life? Yet he did a bold thing. He wrote in German instead of in Latin, and so, by weakening the old belief in authority, brought about the beginning of free thought in science. He continued to travel from place to place, followed by a crowd of disciples, some times attracted to a wealthy city by hope of gain, sometimes journeying to a petty court at the invitation of a prince. His folly and the malice of his rivals prevented him from remaining anywhere for long. He wrought many wonderful cures. The physicians of Nuremberg denounced him as a quack, a charlatan, and an impostor. To refute them he asked the city council to put under his care patients that had been pronounced incurable. They sent him several cases of elephantiasis, and he cured them: testimonials to that effect may still be found in the archives of Nuremberg. He died as the result of a tavern brawl and was buried at Salzburg. Tradition says that, his astral body having already during physical existence become self-conscious, he is now a living adept, residing with others of his sort in a certain place in Asia. From there he still influences the minds of his followers and at times even appears to them in visible and tangible substance.'

'But look here,' said Arthur, 'didn't Paracelsus, like most of these old fellows, in the course of his researches make any practical discoveries?'

'I prefer those which were not practical,' confessed the doctor, with a smile. 'Consider for example the *Tinctura Physicorum*, which neither Pope nor Emperor could buy with all his wealth. It was one of the greatest alchemical mysteries, and, though mentioned under the name of *The Red Lion* in many occult works, was actually known to few before Paracelsus, except Hermes Trismegistus and Albertus Magnus. Its preparation was extremely difficult, for the presence was needed of two perfectly harmonious persons whose skill was equal. It was said to be a red ethereal fluid. The least wonderful of its many properties was its power to transmute all inferior metals into gold. There is an old church in the south of Bavaria where the tincture is said to be still buried in the ground. In the year 1698 some of it penetrated through the soil, and the phenomenon was witnessed by many people, who believed it to be a miracle. The church which was thereupon erected is still a well-known place for pilgrimage. Paracelsus concludes his directions for its manufacture with the words: *But if this be incomprehensible to you, remember that only he who desires with his whole heart will find, and to him only who knocks vehemently shall the door be opened.'*

'I shall never try to make it,' smiled Arthur.

'Then there was the *Electrum Magicum*, of which the wise made mirrors wherein they were able to see not only the events of the past and of the present, but the doings of men in daytime and at night. They might see anything that had been written or spoken, and the person who said it, and the causes that made him say it. But I like best the *Primum Ens Melissae*. An elaborate prescription is given for its manufacture. It was a remedy to prolong life, and not only Paracelsus, but his predecessors Galen, Arnold of Villanova, and Raymond Lulli, had laboured studiously to discover it.'

'Will it make me eighteen again?' cried Susie.

'It is guaranteed to do so,' answered Dr Porhoët gravely. 'Lesebren, a physician to Louis XIV, gives an account of certain experiments witnessed by himself. It appears that one of his friends prepared the remedy, and his curiosity would not let him rest until he had seen with his own eyes the effect of it.'

'That is the true scientific attitude,' laughed Arthur.

'He took every morning at sunrise a glass of white wine tinctured with this preparation; and after using it for fourteen days his nails began to fall out, without, however, causing him any pain. His courage failed him at this point, and he gave the same dose to an old female servant. She regained at least one of the characteristics of youth, much to her astonishment, for she did not know that she had been taking a medicine, and, becoming frightened, refused to continue. The experimenter then took some grain, soaked it in the tincture, and gave it to an aged hen. On the sixth day the bird began to lose its feathers, and kept on losing them till it was naked as a newborn babe; but before two weeks had passed other feathers grew, and these were more beautifully coloured than any that fortunate hen had possessed in her youth. Her comb stood up, and she began again to lay eggs.'

Arthur laughed heartily.

'I confess I like that story much better than the others. The *Primum Ens Melissae* at least offers a less puerile benefit than most magical secrets.'

'Do you call the search for gold puerile?' asked Haddo, who had been sitting for a long time in complete silence.

'I venture to call it sordid.'

'You are very superior.'

'Because I think the aims of mystical persons invariably gross or trivial? To my plain mind, it is inane to raise the dead in order to hear from their phantom lips nothing but commonplaces. And I really cannot see that the alchemist who spent his life in the attempted manufacture of gold was a more respectable object than the outside jobber of modern civilization.'

'But if he sought for gold it was for the power it gave him, and it was power he aimed at when he brooded night and day over dim secrets. Power was the subject of all his dreams, but not a paltry, limited dominion over this or that; power over the whole world, power over all created things, power over the very elements, power over God Himself. His lust was so vast that he could not rest till the stars in their courses were obedient to his will.'

For once Haddo lost his enigmatic manner. It was plain now that his words intoxicated him, and his face assumed a new, a strange, expression. A peculiar arrogance flashed in his shining eyes.

'And what else is it that men seek in life but power? If they want money, it is but for the power that attends it, and it is power again that they strive for in all the knowledge they acquire. Fools and sots aim at happiness, but men aim only at power. The magus, the sorcerer, the alchemist, are seized with fascination of the unknown; and they desire a greatness that is inaccessible to mankind. They think by the science they study so patiently, but endurance and strength, by force of will and by imagination, for these are the great weapons of the magician, they may achieve at last a power with which they can face the God of Heaven Himself.'

Oliver Haddo lifted his huge bulk from the low chair in which he had been sitting. He began to walk up and down the studio. It was curious to see this heavy man, whose seriousness was always problematical, caught up by a curious excitement.

'You've been talking of Paracelsus,' he said. 'There is one of his experiments which the doctor has withheld from you. You will find it neither mean nor mercenary, but it is very terrible. I do not know whether the account of it is true, but it would be of extraordinary interest to test it for oneself.'

He looked round at the four persons who watched him intently. There was a singular agitation in his manner, as though the thing of which he spoke was very near his heart.

'The old alchemists believed in the possibility of spontaneous generation. By the combination of psychical powers and of strange essences, they claim to have created forms in which life became manifest. Of these, the most marvellous were those strange beings, male and female, which were called *homunculi*. The old philosophers doubted the possibility of this operation, but Paracelsus asserts positively that it can be done. I picked up once for a song on a barrow at London Bridge a little book in German. It was dirty and thumbed, many of the pages were torn, and the binding scarcely held the leaves together. It was called *Die Sphinx* and was edited by a certain Dr Emil Besetzny. It contained the most extraordinary account I have ever read of certain spirits generated by Johann-Ferdinand, Count von Küffstein, in the Tyrol, in 1775. The sources from which this account is taken consist of masonic manuscripts, but more especially of a diary kept by a certain James Kammerer, who acted in the capacity of butler and famulus to the Count. The evidence is ten times stronger than any upon which men believe the articles of their religion. If it related to less wonderful subjects, you would not hesitate to believe implicitly every word you read. There were ten *homunculi*—James Kammerer calls them prophesying spirits—kept in strong bottles, such as are used to preserve fruit, and these were filled with water. They were made in five weeks, by the Count von Küffstein and an Italian mystic and rosicrucian, the Abbé Geloni. The bottles were closed with a magic seal. The spirits were about a span long, and the Count was anxious that they should grow. They were therefore buried under two cartloads of manure, and the pile daily sprinkled with a certain liquor prepared with great trouble by the adepts. The pile after such sprinklings began to ferment and steam, as if heated by a subterranean fire. When the bottles were removed, it was found that the spirits had grown to about a span and a half each; the *malehomunculi* were come into possession of heavy beards, and the nails of the fingers had grown. In two of the bottles there was nothing to be seen save clear water, but when the Abbé knocked thrice at the seal upon the mouth, uttering at the same time certain Hebrew words, the water turned a mysterious colour, and the spirits showed their faces, very small at first, but growing in size till they attained that of a human countenance. And this countenance was horrible and fiendish.'

Haddo spoke in a low voice that was hardly steady, and it was plain that he was much moved. It appeared as if his story affected him so that he could scarcely preserve his composure. He went on.

'These beings were fed every three days by the Count with a rose-coloured substance which was kept in a silver box. Once a week the bottles were emptied and filled again with pure rain-water. The change had to be made rapidly, because while the *homunculi* were exposed to the air they closed their eyes and seemed to grow weak and unconscious, as though they were about to die. But with the spirits that were invisible, at certain intervals blood was poured into the water; and it disappeared at once, inexplicably, without colouring or troubling it. By some accident one of the bottles fell one day and was broken. The *homunculus* within died after a few painful respirations in spite of all efforts to save him, and the body was buried in the garden. An attempt to generate another, made by the Count without the assistance of the Abbé, who had left, failed; it produced only a small thing like a leech, which had little vitality and soon died.'

Haddo ceased speaking, and Arthur looked at him with amazement. 'But taking for granted that the thing is possible, what on earth is the use of manufacturing these strange beasts?' he exclaimed.

'Use!' cried Haddo passionately. 'What do you think would be man's sensations when he had solved the great mystery of existence, when he saw living before him the substance which was dead? These *homunculi* were seen by historical persons, by Count Max Lemberg, by Count Franz-Josef von Thun, and by many others. I have no doubt that they were actually generated. But with our modern appliances, with our greater skill, what might it not be possible to do now if we had the courage? There are chemists toiling away in their laboratories to create the primitive protoplasm from matter which is dead, the organic from the inorganic. I have studied their experiments. I know all that they know. Why shouldn't one work on a larger scale, joining to the knowledge of the old adepts the scientific discovery of the moderns? I don't know what would be the result. It might be very strange and very wonderful. Sometimes my mind is verily haunted by the desire to see a lifeless substance move under my spells, by the desire to be as God.'

He gave a low weird laugh, half cruel, half voluptuous. It made Margaret shudder with sudden fright. He had thrown himself down in the chair, and he sat in complete shadow. By a singular effect his eyes appeared blood-red, and they stared into space, strangely parallel, with an intensity that was terrifying. Arthur started a little and gave him a searching glance. The laugh and that uncanny glance, the unaccountable emotion, were extraordinarily significant. The whole thing was explained if Oliver Haddo was mad.

There was an uncomfortable silence. Haddo's words were out of tune with the rest of the conversation. Dr Porhoët had spoken of magical things with a sceptical irony that gave a certain humour to the subject, and Susie was resolutely flippant. But Haddo's vehemence put these incredulous people out of countenance. Dr Porhoët got up to go. He shook hands with Susie and with Margaret. Arthur opened the door for him. The kindly scholar looked round for Margaret's terrier...

'I must bid my farewells to your little dog.'

He had been so quiet that they had forgotten his presence.

'Come here, Copper,' said Margaret.

The dog slowly slunk up to them, and with a terrified expression crouched at Margaret's feet.

'What on earth's the matter with you?' she asked.

'He's frightened of me,' said Haddo, with that harsh laugh of his, which gave such an unpleasant impression.

'Nonsense!'

Dr Porhoët bent down, stroked the dog's back, and shook its paw. Margaret lifted it up and set it on a table.

'Now, be good,' she said, with lifted finger.

Dr Porhoët with a smile went out, and Arthur shut the door behind him. Suddenly, as though evil had entered into it, the terrier sprang at Oliver Haddo and fixed its teeth in his hand. Haddo uttered a cry, and, shaking it off, gave it a savage kick. The dog rolled over with a loud bark that was almost a scream of pain, and lay still for a moment as if it were desperately hurt. Margaret cried out with horror and indignation. A fierce rage on a sudden seized Arthur so that he scarcely knew what he was about. The wretched brute's suffering, Margaret's terror, his own instinctive hatred of the man, were joined together in frenzied passion.

'You brute,' he muttered.

He hit Haddo in the face with his clenched fist. The man collapsed bulkily to the floor, and Arthur, furiously seizing his collar, began to kick him with all his might. He shook him as a dog would shake a rat and then violently flung him down. For some reason Haddo made no resistance. He remained where he fell in utter helplessness. Arthur turned to Margaret. She was holding the poor hurt dog in her hands, crying over it, and trying to comfort it in its pain. Very gently he examined it to see if Haddo's brutal kick had broken a bone. They sat down beside the fire. Susie, to steady her nerves, lit a cigarette. She was horribly, acutely conscious of that man who lay in a mass on the floor behind them. She wondered what he would do. She wondered why he did not go. And she was ashamed of his humiliation. Then her heart stood still; for she realized that he was raising himself to his feet, slowly, with the difficulty of a very fat person. He leaned against the wall and stared at them. He remained there quite motionless. His stillness got on her nerves, and she could have screamed as she felt him look at them, look with those unnatural eyes, whose expression now she dared not even imagine.

At last she could no longer resist the temptation to turn round just enough to see him. Haddo's eyes were fixed upon Margaret so intently that he did not see he was himself observed. His face, distorted by passion, was horrible to look upon. That vast mass of flesh had a malignancy that was inhuman, and it was terrible to see the satanic hatred which hideously deformed it. But it changed. The redness gave way to a ghastly pallor. The revengeful scowl disappeared; and a torpid smile spread over the features, a smile that was even more terrifying than the frown of malice. What did it mean? Susie could have cried out, but her tongue cleaved to her throat. The smile passed away, and the face became once more impassive. It seemed that Margaret and Arthur realized at last the power of those inhuman eyes, and they became quite still. The dog ceased its sobbing. The silence was so great that each one heard the beating of his heart. It was intolerable.

Then Oliver Haddo moved. He came forward slowly.

'I want to ask you to forgive me for what I did,' he said.

'The pain of the dog's bite was so keen that I lost my temper. I deeply regret that I kicked it. Mr Burdon was very right to thrash me. I feel that I deserved no less.'

He spoke in a low voice, but with great distinctness. Susie was astounded. An abject apology was the last thing she expected.

He paused for Margaret's answer. But she could not bear to look at him. When she spoke, her words were scarcely audible. She did not know why his request to be forgiven made him seem more detestable.

'I think, if you don't mind, you had better go away.'

Haddo bowed slightly. He looked at Burdon.

'I wish to tell you that I bear no malice for what you did. I recognize the justice of your anger.'

Arthur did not answer at all. Haddo hesitated a moment, while his eyes rested on them quietly. To Susie it seemed that they flickered with the shadow of a smile. She watched him with bewildered astonishment.

He reached for his hat, bowed again, and went.

VIII

SUSIE COULD NOT persuade herself that Haddo's regret was sincere. The humility of it aroused her suspicion. She could not get out of her mind the ugly slyness of that smile which succeeded on his face the first passionate look of deadly hatred. Her fancy suggested various dark means whereby Oliver Haddo might take vengeance on his enemy, and she was at pains to warn Arthur. But he only laughed.

'The man's a funk,' he said. 'Do you think if he'd had anything in him at all he would have let me kick him without trying to defend himself?'

Haddo's cowardice increased the disgust with which Arthur regarded him. He was amused by Susie's trepidation.

'What on earth do you suppose he can do? He can't drop a brickbat on my head. If he shoots me he'll get his head cut off, and he won't be such an ass as to risk that!'

Margaret was glad that the incident had relieved them of Oliver's society. She met him in the street a couple of days later, and since he took off his hat in the French fashion without waiting for her to acknowledge him, she was able to make her cut more pointed.

She began to discuss with Arthur the date of their marriage. It seemed to her that she had got out of Paris all it could give her, and she wished to begin a new life. Her love for Arthur appeared on a sudden more urgent, and she was filled with delight at the thought of the happiness she would give him.

A day or two later Susie received a telegram. It ran as follows:

Please meet me at the Gare du Nord, 2:40.
Nancy Clerk

It was an old friend, who was apparently arriving in Paris that afternoon. A photograph of her, with a bold signature, stood on the chimney-piece, and Susie gave it an inquisitive glance. She had not seen Nancy for so long that it surprised her to receive this urgent message.

'What a bore it is!' she said. 'I suppose I must go.'

They meant to have tea on the other side of the river, but the journey to the station was so long that it would not be worth Susie's while to come back in the interval; and they arranged therefore to meet at the house to which they were invited. Susie started a little before two.

Margaret had a class that afternoon and set out two or three minutes later. As she walked through the courtyard she started nervously, for Oliver Haddo passed slowly by. He did not seem to see her. Suddenly he stopped, put his hand to his heart, and fell heavily to the ground. The *concierge*, the only person at hand, ran forward with a cry. She knelt down and, looking round with terror, caught sight of Margaret.

'*Oh, mademoiselle, venez vite!*' she cried.

Margaret was obliged to go. Her heart beat horribly. She looked down at Oliver, and he seemed to be dead. She forgot that she loathed him. Instinctively she knelt down by his side and loosened his collar. He opened his eyes. An expression of terrible anguish came into his face.

'For the love of God, take me in for one moment,' he sobbed. 'I shall die in the street.'

Her heart was moved towards him. He could not go into the poky den, evil-smelling and airless, of the *concierge*. But with her help Margaret raised him to his feet, and together they brought him to the studio. He sank painfully into a chair.

'Shall I fetch you some water?' asked Margaret.

'Can you get a pastille out of my pocket?'

He swallowed a white tabloid, which she took out of a case attached to his watch-chain.

'I'm very sorry to cause you this trouble,' he gasped. 'I suffer from a disease of the heart, and sometimes I am very near death.'

'I'm glad that I was able to help you,' she said.

He seemed able to breathe more easily. She left him to himself for a while, so that he might regain his strength. She took up a book and began to read. Presently, without moving from his chair, he spoke.

'You must hate me for intruding on you.'

His voice was stronger, and her pity waned as he seemed to recover. She answered with freezing indifference.

'I couldn't do any less for you than I did. I would have brought a dog into my room if it seemed hurt.'

'I see that you wish me to go.'

He got up and moved towards the door, but he staggered and with a groan tumbled to his knees. Margaret sprang forward to help him. She reproached herself bitterly for those scornful words. The man had barely escaped death, and she was merciless.

'Oh, please stay as long as you like,' she cried. 'I'm sorry, I didn't mean to hurt you.'

He dragged himself with difficulty back to the chair, and she, conscience-stricken, stood over him helplessly. She poured out a glass of water, but he motioned it away as though he would not be beholden to her even for that.

'Is there nothing I can do for you at all?' she exclaimed, painfully.

'Nothing, except allow me to sit in this chair,' he gasped.

'I hope you'll remain as long as you choose.'

He did not reply. She sat down again and pretended to read. In a little while he began to speak. His voice reached her as if from a long way off.

'Will you never forgive me for what I did the other day?'

She answered without looking at him, her back still turned.

'Can it matter to you if I forgive or not?'

'You have not pity. I told you then how sorry I was that a sudden uncontrollable pain drove me to do a thing which immediately I bitterly regretted. Don't you think it must have been hard for me, under the actual circumstances, to confess my fault?'

'I wish you not to speak of it. I don't want to think of that horrible scene.'

'If you knew how lonely I was and how unhappy, you would have a little mercy.'

His voice was strangely moved. She could not doubt now that he was sincere.

'You think me a charlatan because I aim at things that are unknown to you. You won't try to understand. You won't give me any credit for striving with all my soul to a very great end.'

She made no reply, and for a time there was silence. His voice was different now and curiously seductive.

'You look upon me with disgust and scorn. You almost persuaded yourself to let me die in the street rather than stretch out to me a helping hand. And if you hadn't been merciful then, almost against your will, I should have died.'

'It can make no difference to you how I regard you,' she whispered.

She did not know why his soft, low tones mysteriously wrung her heartstrings. Her pulse began to beat more quickly.

'It makes all the difference in the world. It is horrible to think of your contempt. I feel your goodness and your purity. I can hardly bear my own unworthiness. You turn your eyes away from me as though I were unclean.'

She turned her chair a little and looked at him. She was astonished at the change in his appearance. His hideous obesity seemed no longer repellent, for his eyes wore a new expression; they were incredibly tender now, and they were moist with tears. His mouth was tortured by a passionate distress. Margaret had never seen so much unhappiness on a man's face, and an overwhelming remorse seized her.

'I don't want to be unkind to you,' she said.

'I will go. That is how I can best repay you for what you have done.'

The words were so bitter, so humiliated, that the colour rose to her cheeks.

'I ask you to stay. But let us talk of other things.'

For a moment he kept silence. He seemed no longer to see Margaret, and she watched him thoughtfully. His eyes rested on a print of *La Gioconda* which hung on the wall. Suddenly he began to speak. He recited the honeyed words with which Walter Pater expressed his admiration for that consummate picture.

'Hers is the head upon which all the ends of the world are come, and the eyelids are a little weary. It is a beauty wrought out from within upon the flesh, the deposit, little cell by cell, of strange thoughts and fantastic reveries and exquisite passions. Set it for a moment beside one of those white Greek goddesses or beautiful women of antiquity, and how would they be troubled by this beauty, into which the soul with all its maladies has passed. All the thoughts and experience of the world have etched and moulded there, in that which they have of power to refine and make expressive the outward form, the animalism of Greece, the lust of Rome, the mysticism of the Middle Ages, with its spiritual ambition and imaginative loves, the return of the Pagan world, the sins of the Borgias.'

His voice, poignant and musical, blended with the suave music of the words so that Margaret felt she had never before known their divine significance. She was intoxicated with their beauty. She wished him to continue, but had not the strength to speak. As if he guessed her thought, he went on, and now his voice had a richness in it as of an organ heard afar off. It was like an overwhelming fragrance and she could hardly bear it.

'She is older than the rocks among which she sits; like the vampire, she has been dead many times, and learned the secrets of the grave; and has been a diver in deep seas, and keeps their fallen day about her; and trafficked for strange evils with Eastern merchants; and, as Leda, was the mother of Helen of Troy, and, as Saint Anne, the mother of Mary; and all this has been to her but as the sound of lyres and flutes, and lives only in the delicacy with which it has moulded the changing lineaments, and tinged the eyelids and the hands.'

Oliver Haddo began then to speak of Leonardo da Vinci, mingling with his own fantasies the perfect words of that essay which, so wonderful was his memory, he seemed to know by heart. He found exotic fancies in the likeness between Saint John the Baptist, with his soft flesh and waving hair, and Bacchus, with his ambiguous smile. Seen through his eyes, the seashore in the Saint Anne had the airless lethargy of some damasked chapel in a Spanish nunnery, and over the landscapes brooded a wan spirit of evil that was very troubling. He loved the mysterious pictures in which the painter had sought to express something beyond the limits of painting, something of unsatisfied desire and of longing for unhuman passions. Oliver Haddo found this quality in unlikely places, and his words gave a new meaning to paintings that Margaret had passed thoughtlessly by. There was the portrait of a statuary by Bronzino in the Long Gallery of the Louvre. The features were rather large, the face rather broad. The expression was sombre, almost surly in the repose of the painted canvas, and the eyes were brown, almond-shaped like those of an Oriental; the red lips were exquisitely modelled, and the sensuality was curiously disturbing; the dark, chestnut hair, cut short, curled over the head with an infinite grace. The skin was like ivory softened with a delicate carmine. There was in that beautiful countenance more than beauty, for what most fascinated the observer was a supreme and disdainful indifference to the passion of others. It was a vicious face, except that beauty could never be quite vicious; it was a cruel face, except that indolence could never be quite cruel. It was a face that haunted you, and yet your admiration was alloyed with an unreasoning terror. The hands were nervous and adroit, with long fashioning fingers; and you felt that at their touch the clay almost moulded itself into gracious forms. With Haddo's subtle words the character of that man rose before her, cruel yet indifferent, indolent and passionate, cold yet sensual; unnatural secrets dwelt in his mind, and mysterious crimes, and a lust for the knowledge that was arcane. Oliver Haddo was attracted by all that was unusual, deformed, and monstrous, by the pictures that represented the hideousness of man or that reminded you of his mortality. He summoned before Margaret the whole array of Ribera's ghoulish dwarfs, with their cunning smile, the insane light of their eyes, and their malice: he dwelt with a horrible fascination upon their malformations, the humped backs, the club feet, the hydrocephalic heads. He described the picture by Valdes Leal, in a certain place at Seville, which represents a priest at the altar; and the altar is sumptuous with gilt and florid carving. He wears a magnificent cope and a surplice of exquisite lace, but he wears them as though their weight was more than he could bear; and in the meagre trembling hands, and in the white, ashen face, in the dark hollowness of the eyes, there is a bodily corruption that is terrifying. He seems to hold together with difficulty the bonds of the flesh, but with no eager yearning of the soul to burst its prison, only with despair; it is as if the Lord Almighty had forsaken him and the high heavens were empty of their solace. All the beauty of life appears forgotten, and there is nothing in the world but decay. A ghastly putrefaction has attacked already the living man; the worms of the grave, the piteous horror of mortality, and the darkness before him offer naught but fear. Beyond, dark night is seen and a turbulent sea, the dark night of the soul of which the mystics write, and the troublous sea of life whereon there is no refuge for the weary and the sick at heart.

Then, as if in pursuance of a definite plan, he analysed with a searching, vehement intensity the curious talent of the modern Frenchman, Gustave Moreau. Margaret had lately visited the Luxembourg, and his pictures were fresh in her memory. She had found in them little save a decorative arrangement marred by faulty drawing; but Oliver Haddo gave them at once a new, esoteric import. Those effects as of a Florentine jewel, the clustered colours, emerald and ruby, the deep blue of sapphires, the atmosphere of scented chambers, the mystic persons who seem ever about secret, religious rites, combined in his cunning phrases to create, as it were, a pattern on her soul of morbid and mysterious intricacy. Those pictures were filled with a strange sense of sin, and the mind that contemplated them was burdened with the decadence of Rome and with the passionate vice of the Renaissance; and it was tortured, too, by all the introspection of this later day.

Margaret listened, rather breathlessly, with the excitement of an explorer before whom is spread the plain of an undiscovered continent. The painters she knew spoke of their art technically, and this imaginative appreciation was new to her. She was horribly fascinated by the personality that imbued these elaborate sentences. Haddo's eyes were fixed upon hers, and she responded to his words like a delicate instrument made for recording the beatings of the heart. She felt an extraordinary languor. At last he stopped. Margaret neither moved nor spoke. She might have been under a spell. It seemed to her that she had no power in her limbs.

'I want to do something for you in return for what you have done for me,' he said.

He stood up and went to the piano.

'Sit in this chair,' he said.

She did not dream of disobeying. He began to play. Margaret was hardly surprised that he played marvellously. Yet it was almost incredible that those fat, large hands should have such a tenderness of touch. His fingers caressed the notes with a peculiar suavity, and he drew out of the piano effects which she had scarcely thought possible. He seemed to put into the notes a troubling, ambiguous passion, and the instrument had the tremulous emotion of a human being. It was strange and terrifying. She was vaguely familiar with the music to which she listened; but there was in it, under his fingers, an exotic savour that made it harmonious with all that he had said that afternoon. His memory was indeed astonishing. He had an infinite tact to know the feeling that occupied Margaret's heart, and what he chose seemed to be exactly that which at the moment she imperatively needed. Then he began to play things she did not know. It was music the like of which she had never heard, barbaric, with a plaintive weirdness that brought to her fancy the moonlit nights of desert places, with palm trees mute in the windless air, and tawny distances. She seemed to know tortuous narrow streets, white houses of silence with strange moon-shadows, and the glow of yellow light within, and the tinkling of uncouth instruments, and the acrid scents of Eastern perfumes. It was like a procession passing through her mind of persons who were not human, yet existed mysteriously, with a life of vampires. Mona Lisa and Saint John the Baptist, Bacchus and the mother of Mary, went with enigmatic motions. But the daughter of Herodias raised her hands as though, engaged for ever in a mystic rite, to invoke outlandish gods. Her face was very pale, and her dark eyes were sleepless; the jewels of her girdle gleamed with sombre fires; and her dress was of colours that have long been lost. The smile, in which was all the sorrow of the world and all its wickedness, beheld the wan head of the Saint, and with a voice that was cold with the coldness of death she murmured the words of the poet:

'I am amorous of thy body, Iokanaan! Thy body is white like the lilies of a field that the mower hath never mowed. Thy body is white like the snows that lie on the mountains of Judea, and come down into the valleys. The roses in the garden of the Queen of Arabia are not so white as thy body. Neither the roses in the garden of the Queen of Arabia, the garden of spices of the Queen of Arabia, nor the feet of the dawn when they light on the leaves, nor the breast of the moon when she lies on the breast of the sea... There is nothing in the world so white as thy body. Suffer me to touch thy body.'

Oliver Haddo ceased to play. Neither of them stirred. At last Margaret sought by an effort to regain her self-control.

'I shall begin to think that you really are a magician,' she said, lightly.

'I could show you strange things if you cared to see them,' he answered, again raising his eyes to hers.

'I don't think you will ever get me to believe in occult philosophy,' she laughed.

'Yet it reigned in Persia with the magi, it endowed India with wonderful traditions, it civilised Greece to the sounds of Orpheus's lyre.'

He stood before Margaret, towering over her in his huge bulk; and there was a singular fascination in his gaze. It seemed that he spoke only to conceal from her that he was putting forth now all the power that was in him.

'It concealed the first principles of science in the calculations of Pythagoras. It established empires by its oracles, and at its voice tyrants grew pale upon their thrones. It governed the minds of some by curiosity, and others it ruled by fear.'

His voice grew very low, and it was so seductive that Margaret's brain reeled. The sound of it was overpowering like too sweet a fragrance.

I tell you that for this art nothing is impossible. It commands the elements, and knows the language of the stars, and directs the planets in their courses. The moon at its bidding falls blood-red from the sky. The dead rise up and form into ominous words the night wind that moans through their skulls. Heaven and Hell are in its province; and all forms, lovely and hideous; and love and hate. With Circe's wand it can change men into beasts of the field, and to them it can give a monstrous humanity. Life and death are in the right hand and in the left of him who knows its secrets. It confers wealth by the transmutation of metals and immortality by its quintessence.'

Margaret could not hear what he said. A gradual lethargy seized her under his baleful glance, and she had not even the strength to wish to free herself. She seemed bound to him already by hidden chains.

'If you have powers, show them,' she whispered, hardly conscious that she spoke.

Suddenly he released the enormous tension with which he held her. Like a man who has exerted all his strength to some end, the victory won, he loosened his muscles, with a faint sigh of exhaustion. Margaret did not speak, but she knew that something horrible was about to happen. Her heart beat like a prisoned bird, with helpless flutterings, but it seemed too late now to draw back. Her words by a mystic influence had settled something beyond possibility of recall.

On the stove was a small bowl of polished brass in which water was kept in order to give a certain moisture to the air. Oliver Haddo put his hand in his pocket and drew out a little silver box. He tapped it, with a smile, as a man taps a snuff-box, and it opened. He took an infinitesimal quantity of a blue powder that it contained and threw it on the water in the brass bowl. Immediately a bright flame sprang up, and Margaret gave a cry of alarm. Oliver looked at her quickly and motioned her to remain still. She saw that the water was on fire. It was burning as brilliantly, as hotly, as if it were common gas; and it burned with the same dry, hoarse roar. Suddenly it was extinguished. She leaned forward and saw that the bowl was empty.

The water had been consumed, as though it were straw, and not a drop remained. She passed her hand absently across her forehead.

'But water cannot burn,' she muttered to herself.

It seemed that Haddo knew what she thought, for he smiled strangely.

'Do you know that nothing more destructive can be invented than this blue powder, and I have enough to burn up all the water in Paris? Who dreamt that water might burn like chaff?'

He paused, seeming to forget her presence. He looked thoughtfully at the little silver box.

'But it can be made only in trivial quantities, at enormous expense and with exceeding labour; it is so volatile that you cannot keep it for three days. I have sometimes thought that with a little ingenuity I might make it more stable, I might so modify it that, like radium, it lost no strength as it burned; and then I should possess the greatest secret that has ever been in the mind of man. For there would be no end of it. It would continue to burn while there was a drop of water on the earth, and the whole world would be consumed. But it would be a frightful thing to have in one's hands; for once it were cast upon the waters, the doom of all that existed would be sealed beyond repeal.'

He took a long breath, and his eyes glittered with a devilish ardour. His voice was hoarse with overwhelming emotion.

'Sometimes I am haunted by the wild desire to have seen the great and final scene when the irrevocable flames poured down the river, hurrying along the streams of the earth, searching out the moisture in all growing things, tearing it even from the eternal rocks; when the flames poured down like the rushing of the wind, and all that lived fled from before them till they came to the sea; and the sea itself was consumed in vehement fire.'

Margaret shuddered, but she did not think the man was mad. She had ceased to judge him. He took one more particle of that atrocious powder and put it in the bowl. Again he thrust his hand in his pocket and brought out a handful of some crumbling substance that might have been dried leaves, leaves of different sorts, broken and powdery. There was a trace of moisture in them still, for a low flame sprang up immediately at the bottom of the dish, and a thick vapour filled the room. It had a singular and pungent odour that Margaret did not know. It was difficult to breathe, and she coughed. She wanted to beg Oliver to stop, but could not. He took the bowl in his hands and brought it to her.

'Look,' he commanded.

She bent forward, and at the bottom saw a blue fire, of a peculiar solidity, as though it consisted of molten metal. It was not still, but writhed strangely, like serpents of fire tortured by their own unearthly ardour.

'Breathe very deeply.'

She did as he told her. A sudden trembling came over her, and darkness fell across her eyes. She tried to cry out, but could utter no sound. Her brain reeled. It seemed to her that Haddo bade her cover her face. She gasped for breath, and it was as if the earth spun under her feet. She appeared to travel at an immeasurable speed. She made a slight movement, and Haddo told her not to look round. An immense terror seized her. She did not know whither she was borne, and still they went quickly, quickly; and the hurricane itself would have lagged behind them. At last their motion ceased; and Oliver was holding her arm.

'Don't be afraid,' he said. 'Open your eyes and stand up.'

The night had fallen; but it was not the comfortable night that soothes the troubled minds of mortal men; it was a night that agitated the soul mysteriously so that each nerve in the body tingled. There was a lurid darkness which displayed and yet distorted the objects that surrounded them. No moon shone in the sky, but small stars appeared to dance on the heather, vague night-fires like spirits of the damned. They stood in a vast and troubled waste, with huge stony boulders and leafless trees, rugged and gnarled like tortured souls in pain. It was as if there had been a devastating storm, and the country reposed after the flood of rain and the tempestuous wind and the lightning. All things about them appeared dumbly to suffer, like a man racked by torments who has not the strength even to realize that his agony has ceased. Margaret heard the flight of monstrous birds, and they seemed to whisper strange things on their passage. Oliver took her hand. He led her steadily to a cross-road, and she did not know if they walked amid rocks or tombs.

She heard the sound of a trumpet, and from all parts, strangely appearing where before was nothing, a turbulent assembly surged about her. That vast empty space was suddenly filled by shadowy forms, and they swept along like the waves of the sea, crowding upon one another's heels. And it seemed that all the mighty dead appeared before her; and she saw grim tyrants, and painted courtesans, and Roman emperors in their purple, and sultans of the East. All those fierce evil women of olden time passed by her side, and now it was Mona Lisa and now the subtle daughter of Herodias. And Jezebel looked out upon her from beneath her painted brows, and Cleopatra turned away a wan, lewd face; and she saw the insatiable mouth and the wanton eyes of Messalina, and Fustine was haggard with the eternal fires of lust. She saw cardinals in their scarlet, and warriors in their steel, gay gentlemen in periwigs, and ladies in powder and patch. And on a sudden, like leaves by the wind, all these were driven before the silent throngs of the oppressed; and they were innumerable as the sands of the sea. Their thin faces were earthy with want and cavernous from disease, and their eyes were dull with despair. They passed in their tattered motley, some in the fantastic rags of the beggars of Albrecht Dürer and some in the grey cerecloths of Le Nain; many wore the blouses and the caps of the rabble in France, and many the dingy, smoke-grimed weeds of English poor. And they surged onward like a riotous crowd in narrow streets flying in terror before the mounted troops. It seemed as though all the world were gathered there in strange confusion.

Then all again was void; and Margaret's gaze was riveted upon a great, ruined tree that stood in that waste place, alone, in ghastly desolation; and though a dead thing, it seemed to suffer a more than human pain. The lightning had torn it asunder, but the wind of centuries had sought in vain to drag up its roots. The tortured branches, bare of any twig, were like a Titan's arms, convulsed with intolerable anguish. And in a moment she grew sick with fear, for a change came into the tree, and the tremulousness of life was in it; the rough bark was changed into brutish flesh and the twisted branches into human arms. It became a monstrous, goat-legged thing, more vast than the creatures of nightmare. She saw the horns and the long beard, the great hairy legs with their hoofs, and the man's rapacious hands. The

face was horrible with lust and cruelty, and yet it was divine. It was
Pan, playing on his pipes, and the lecherous eyes caressed her with a
hideous tenderness. But even while she looked, as the mist of early
day, rising, discloses a fair country, the animal part of that ghoulish
creature seemed to fall away, and she saw a lovely youth, titanic but
sublime, leaning against a massive rock. He was more beautiful than
the Adam of Michelangelo who wakes into life at the call of the
Almighty; and, like him freshly created, he had the adorable languor
of one who feels still in his limbs the soft rain on the loose brown
earth. Naked and full of majesty he lay, the outcast son of the morning; and she dared not look upon his face, for she knew it was impossible to bear the undying pain that darkened it with ruthless shadows.
Impelled by a great curiosity, she sought to come nearer, but the vast
figure seemed strangely to dissolve into a cloud; and immediately she
felt herself again surrounded by a hurrying throng. Then came all legendary monsters and foul beasts of a madman's fancy; in the darkness
she saw enormous toads, with paws pressed to their flanks, and huge
limping scarabs, shelled creatures the like of which she had never
seen, and noisome brutes with horny scales and round crabs' eyes,
uncouth primeval things, and winged serpents, and creeping animals
begotten of the slime. She heard shrill cries and peals of laughter and
the terrifying rattle of men at the point of death. Haggard women,
dishevelled and lewd, carried wine; and when they spilt it there were
stains like the stains of blood. And it seemed to Margaret that a fire
burned in her veins, and her soul fled from her body; but a new soul
came in its place, and suddenly she knew all that was obscene. She
took part in some festival of hideous lust, and the wickedness of the
world was patent to her eyes. She saw things so vile that she screamed
in terror, and she heard Oliver laugh in derision by her side. It was
a scene of indescribable horror, and she put her hands to her eyes so
that she might not see.

She felt Oliver Haddo take her hands. She would not let him
drag them away. Then she heard him speak.

'You need not be afraid.'

His voice was quite natural once more, and she realized with a
start that she was sitting quietly in the studio. She looked around her

with frightened eyes. Everything was exactly as it had been. The early night of autumn was fallen, and the only light in the room came from the fire. There was still that vague, acrid scent of the substance which Haddo had burned.

'Shall I light the candles?' he said.

He struck a match and lit those which were on the piano. They threw a strange light. Then Margaret suddenly remembered all that she had seen, and she remembered that Haddo had stood by her side. Shame seized her, intolerable shame, so that the colour, rising to her cheeks, seemed actually to burn them. She hid her face in her hands and burst into tears.

'Go away,' she said. 'For God's sake, go.'

He looked at her for a moment; and the smile came to his lips which Susie had seen after his tussle with Arthur, when last he was in the studio.

'When you want me you will find me in the Rue de Vaugiraud, number 209,' he said. 'Knock at the second door on the left, on the third floor.'

She did not answer. She could only think of her appalling shame.

'I'll write it down for you in case you forget.'

He scribbled the address on a sheet of paper that he found on the table. Margaret took no notice, but sobbed as though her heart would break. Suddenly, looking up with a start, she saw that he was gone. She had not heard him open the door or close it. She sank down on her knees and prayed desperately, as though some terrible danger threatened her.

But when she heard Susie's key in the door, Margaret sprang to her feet. She stood with her back to the fireplace, her hands behind her, in the attitude of a prisoner protesting his innocence. Susie was too much annoyed to observe this agitation.

'Why on earth didn't you come to tea?' she asked. 'I couldn't make out what had become of you.'

'I had a dreadful headache,' answered Margaret, trying to control herself.

Susie flung herself down wearily in a chair. Margaret forced herself to speak.

'Had Nancy anything particular to say to you?' she asked.

'She never turned up,' answered Susie irritably. 'I can't understand it. I waited till the train came in, but there was no sign of her. Then I thought she might have hit upon that time by chance and was not coming from England, so I walked about the station for half an hour.'

She went to the chimneypiece, on which had been left the telegram that summoned her to the Gare du Nord, and read it again. She gave a little cry of surprise.

'How stupid of me! I never noticed the postmark. It was sent from the Rue Littré.'

This was less than ten minutes' walk from the studio. Susie looked at the message with perplexity.

'I wonder if someone has been playing a silly practical joke on me.' She shrugged her shoulders. 'But it's too foolish. If I were a suspicious woman,' she smiled, 'I should think you had sent it yourself to get me out of the way.'

The idea flashed through Margaret that Oliver Haddo was the author of it. He might easily have seen Nancy's name on the photograph during his first visit to the studio. She had no time to think before she answered lightly.

'If I wanted to get rid of you, I should have no hesitation in saying so.'

'I suppose no one has been here?' asked Susie.

'No one.'

The lie slipped from Margaret's lips before she had made up her mind to tell it. Her heart gave a great beat against her chest. She felt herself redden.

Susie got up to light a cigarette. She wished to rest her nerves. The box was on the table and, as she helped herself, her eyes fell carelessly on the address that Haddo had left. She picked it up and read it aloud.

'Who on earth lives there?' she asked.

'I don't know at all,' answered Margaret.

She braced herself for further questions, but Susie, without interest, put down the sheet of paper and struck a match.

Margaret was ashamed. Her nature was singularly truthful, and it troubled her extraordinarily that she had lied to her greatest friend. Something stronger than herself seemed to impel her. She would have given much to confess her two falsehoods, but had not the courage. She could not bear that Susie's implicit trust in her straightforwardness should be destroyed; and the admission that Oliver Haddo had been there would entail a further acknowledgment of the nameless horrors she had witnessed. Susie would think her mad.

There was a knock at the door; and Margaret, her nerves shattered by all that she had endured, could hardly restrain a cry of terror. She feared that Haddo had returned. But it was Arthur Burdon. She greeted him with a passionate relief that was unusual, for she was by nature a woman of great self-possession. She felt excessively weak, physically exhausted as though she had gone a long journey, and her mind was highly wrought. Margaret remembered that her state had been the same on her first arrival in Paris, when, in her eagerness to get a preliminary glimpse of its marvels, she had hurried till her bones ached from one celebrated monument to another. They began to speak of trivial things. Margaret tried to join calmly in the conversation, but her voice sounded unnatural, and she fancied that more than once Arthur gave her a curious look. At length she could control herself no longer and burst into a sudden flood of tears. In a moment, uncomprehending but affectionate, he caught her in his arms. He asked tenderly what was the matter. He sought to comfort her. She wept ungovernably, clinging to him for protection.

'Oh, it's nothing,' she gasped. 'I don't know what is the matter with me. I'm only nervous and frightened.'

Arthur had an idea that women were often afflicted with what he described by the old-fashioned name of vapours, and was not disposed to pay much attention to this vehement distress. He soothed her as he would have done a child.

'Oh, take care of me, Arthur. I'm so afraid that some dreadful thing will happen to me. I want all your strength. Promise that you'll never forsake me.'

He laughed, as he kissed away her tears, and she tried to smile.

'Why can't we be married at once?' she asked. 'I don't want to wait any longer. I shan't feel safe till I'm actually your wife.'

He reasoned with her very gently. After all, they were to be married in a few weeks. They could not easily hasten matters, for their house was not yet ready, and she needed time to get her clothes. The date had been fixed by her. She listened sullenly to his words. Their wisdom was plain, and she did not see how she could possibly insist. Even if she told him all that had passed he would not believe her; he would think she was suffering from some trick of her morbid fancy.

'If anything happens to me,' she answered, with the dark, anguished eyes of a hunted beast, 'you will be to blame.'

'I promise you that nothing will happen.'

IX

MARGARET'S NIGHT WAS disturbed, and next day she was unable to go about her work with her usual tranquillity. She tried to reason herself into a natural explanation of the events that had happened. The telegram that Susie had received pointed to a definite scheme on Haddo's part, and suggested that his sudden illness was but a device to get into the studio. Once there, he had used her natural sympathy as a means whereby to exercise his hypnotic power, and all she had seen was merely the creation of his own libidinous fancy. But though she sought to persuade herself that, in playing a vile trick on her, he had taken a shameful advantage of her pity, she could not look upon him with anger. Her contempt for him, her utter loathing, were alloyed with a feeling that aroused in her horror and dismay. She could not get the man out of her thoughts. All that he had said, all that she had seen, seemed, as though it possessed a power of material growth, unaccountably to absorb her. It was as if a rank weed were planted in her heart and slid long poisonous tentacles down every artery, so that each part of her body was enmeshed. Work could not distract her, conversation, exercise, art, left her listless; and between her and all the actions of life stood the flamboyant, bulky form of Oliver Haddo. She was terrified of him now as never before, but curiously had no longer the physical repulsion which hitherto had mastered all other feelings. Although she repeated to herself that she wanted never to see him again, Margaret could scarcely resist an overwhelming desire to go to him. Her will had been taken from her, and she was an automaton. She struggled, like a bird in the fowler's net with useless beating of the wings; but at the bottom of her heart she was dimly conscious that she did not want to resist. If he had given her that address, it was because he knew she would use it. She did not know why she wanted to go to him; she had nothing to say to him; she knew only that it was necessary to go. But a few days before she had seen the *Phèdre* of Racine, and she felt on a sudden all the torments that wrung the heart of that unhappy queen; she, too, struggled aimlessly to escape from the poison that the immortal gods poured in her veins. She asked herself frantically whether a spell had been cast over her, for now she was willing to believe that Haddo's power was all-embracing. Margaret knew that if she yielded to the horrible temptation nothing could save her from destruction. She would have cried for help to Arthur or to Susie, but something, she knew not what, prevented her. At length, driven almost to distraction, she thought that Dr Porhoët might do something for her. He, at least, would understand her misery. There seemed not a moment to lose, and she hastened to his house. They told her he was out. Her heart sank, for it seemed that her last hope was gone. She was like a person drowning, who clings to a rock; and the waves dash against him, and beat upon his bleeding hands with a malice all too human, as if to tear them from their refuge.

Instead of going to the sketch-class, which was held at six in the evening, she hurried to the address that Oliver Haddo had given her. She went along the crowded street stealthily, as though afraid that someone would see her, and her heart was in a turmoil. She desired with all her might not to go, and sought vehemently to prevent herself, and yet withal she went. She ran up the stairs and knocked at the door. She remembered his directions distinctly. In a moment Oliver Haddo stood before her. He did not seem astonished that she was there. As she stood on the landing, it occurred to her suddenly that she had no reason to offer for her visit, but his words saved her from any need for explanation.

'I've been waiting for you,' he said.

Haddo led her into a sitting-room. He had an apartment in a *maison meublée*, and heavy hangings, the solid furniture of that sort of house in Paris, was unexpected in connexion with him. The surroundings were so commonplace that they seemed to emphasise his singularity. There was a peculiar lack of comfort, which suggested that he was indifferent to material things. The room was large, but so cumbered that it gave a cramped impression. Haddo dwelt there as if he were apart from any habitation that might be his. He moved cautiously among the heavy furniture, and his great obesity was somehow more remarkable. There was the acrid perfume which Margaret remembered a few days before in her vision of an Eastern city.

Asking her to sit down, he began to talk as if they were old acquaintances between whom nothing of moment had occurred. At last she took her courage in both hands.

'Why did you make me come here?' she asked suddenly,

'You give me credit now for very marvellous powers,' he smiled.

'You knew I should come.'

'I knew.'

'What have I done to you that you should make me so unhappy? I want you to leave me alone.'

'I shall not prevent you from going out if you choose to go. No harm has come to you. The door is open.'

Her heart beat quickly, painfully almost, and she remained silent. She knew that she did not want to go. There was something that drew her strangely to him, and she was ceasing to resist. A strange feeling began to take hold of her, creeping stealthily through her limbs; and she was terrified, but unaccountably elated.

He began to talk with that low voice of his that thrilled her with a curious magic. He spoke not of pictures now, nor of books, but of life. He told her of strange Eastern places where no infidel had been, and her sensitive fancy was aflame with the honeyed fervour of his phrase. He spoke of the dawn upon sleeping desolate cities, and the moonlit nights of the desert, of the sunsets with their splendour, and of the crowded streets at noon. The beauty of the East rose before her. He told her of many-coloured webs and of silken carpets, the glittering steel of armour damascened, and of barbaric, priceless gems. The splendour of the East blinded her eyes. He spoke of frankincense and myrrh and aloes, of heavy perfumes of the scent-merchants, and drowsy odours of the Syrian gardens. The fragrance of the East filled her nostrils. And all these things were transformed by the power of his words till life itself seemed offered to her, a life of infinite vivacity, a life of freedom, a life of supernatural knowledge. It seemed to her that a comparison was drawn for her attention between the narrow round which awaited her as Arthur's wife and this fair, full existence. She shuddered to think of the dull house in Harley Street and the insignificance of its humdrum duties. But it was possible for her also to enjoy the wonder of the world. Her soul yearned for a beauty that the commonalty of men did not know. And what devil suggested, a warp as it were in the woof of Oliver's speech, that her exquisite loveliness gave her the right to devote herself to the great art of living? She felt a sudden desire for perilous adventures. As though fire passed through her, she sprang to her feet and stood with panting bosom, her flashing eyes bright with the multi-coloured pictures that his magic presented.

Oliver Haddo stood too, and they faced one another. Then, on a sudden, she knew what the passion was that consumed her. With a quick movement, his eyes more than ever strangely staring, he took her in his arms, and he kissed her lips. She surrendered herself to him voluptuously. Her whole body burned with the ecstasy of his embrace.

'I think I love you,' she said, hoarsely.

She looked at him. She did not feel ashamed.

'Now you must go,' he said.

He opened the door, and, without another word, she went. She walked through the streets as if nothing at all had happened. She felt neither remorse nor revulsion.

Then Margaret felt every day that uncontrollable desire to go to him; and, though she tried to persuade herself not to yield, she knew that her effort was only a pretence: she did not want anything to prevent her. When it seemed that some accident would do so, she could scarcely control her irritation. There was always that violent hunger of the soul which called her to him, and the only happy hours she had were those spent in his company. Day after day she felt that complete ecstasy when he took her in his huge arms, and kissed her with his heavy, sensual lips. But the ecstasy was extraordinarily mingled with loathing, and her physical attraction was allied with physical abhorrence.

Yet when he looked at her with those pale blue eyes, and threw into his voice those troubling accents, she forgot everything. He spoke of unhallowed things. Sometimes, as it were, he lifted a corner of the veil, and she caught a glimpse of terrible secrets. She understood how men had bartered their souls for infinite knowledge. She seemed to stand upon a pinnacle of the temple, and spiritual kingdoms of darkness, principalities of the unknown, were spread before her eyes to lure her to destruction. But of Haddo himself she learned nothing. She did not know if he loved her. She did not know if he had ever loved. He appeared to stand apart from human kind. Margaret discovered by chance that his mother lived, but he would not speak of her.

'Some day you shall see her,' he said.

'When?'

'Very soon.'

Meanwhile her life proceeded with all outward regularity. She found it easy to deceive her friends, because it occurred to neither that her frequent absence was not due to the plausible reasons she gave. The lies which at first seemed intolerable now tripped glibly off her tongue. But though they were so natural, she was seized often with a panic of fear lest they should be discovered; and sometimes, suffering agonies of remorse, she would lie in bed at night and think with utter shame of the way she was using Arthur. But things had gone too far now, and she must let them take their course. She scarcely knew why her feelings towards him had so completely changed. Oliver Haddo had scarcely mentioned his name and yet had poisoned her mind. The comparison between the two was to Arthur's disadvantage. She thought him a little dull now, and his commonplace way of looking at life contrasted with Haddo's fascinating boldness. She reproached Arthur in her heart because he had never understood what was in her. He narrowed her mind. And gradually she began to hate him because her debt of gratitude was so great. It seemed unfair that he should have done so much for her. He forced her to marry him by his beneficence. Yet Margaret continued to discuss with him the arrangement of their house in Harley Street. It had been her wish to furnish the drawing-room in the style of Louis XV; and together they

made long excursions to buy chairs or old pieces of silk with which
to cover them. Everything should be perfect in its kind. The date
of their marriage was fixed, and all the details were settled. Arthur
was ridiculously happy. Margaret made no sign. She did not think
of the future, and she spoke of it only to ward off suspicion. She was
inwardly convinced now that the marriage would never take place,
but what was to prevent it she did not know. She watched Susie and
Arthur cunningly. But though she watched in order to conceal her
own secret, it was another's that she discovered. Suddenly Margaret
became aware that Susie was deeply in love with Arthur Burdon. The
discovery was so astounding that at first it seemed absurd.

'You've never done that caricature of Arthur for me that you
promised,' she said, suddenly.

'I've tried, but he doesn't lend himself to it,' laughed Susie.

'With that long nose and the gaunt figure I should have thought
you could make something screamingly funny.'

'How oddly you talk of him! Somehow I can only see his beautiful, kind eyes and his tender mouth. I would as soon do a caricature
of him as write a parody on a poem I loved.'

Margaret took the portfolio in which Susie kept her sketches. She
caught the look of alarm that crossed her friend's face, but Susie had
not the courage to prevent her from looking. She turned the drawings
carelessly and presently came to a sheet upon which, in a more or less
finished state, were half a dozen heads of Arthur. Pretending not to
see it, she went on to the end. When she closed the portfolio Susie
gave a sigh of relief.

'I wish you worked harder,' said Margaret, as she put the sketches
down. 'I wonder you don't do a head of Arthur as you can't do a caricature.'

'My dear, you mustn't expect everyone to take such an overpowering interest in that young man as you do.'

The answer added a last certainty to Margaret's suspicion. She
told herself bitterly that Susie was no less a liar than she. Next day,
when the other was out, Margaret looked through the portfolio once
more, but the sketches of Arthur had disappeared. She was seized on
a sudden with anger because Susie dared to love the man who loved

her.

The web in which Oliver Haddo enmeshed her was woven with skilful intricacy. He took each part of her character separately and fortified with consummate art his influence over her. There was something satanic in his deliberation, yet in actual time it was almost incredible that he could have changed the old abhorrence with which she regarded him into that hungry passion. Margaret could not now realize her life apart from his. At length he thought the time was ripe for the final step.

'It may interest you to know that I'm leaving Paris on Thursday,' he said casually, one afternoon.

She started to her feet and stared at him with bewildered eyes.

'But what is to become of me?'

'You will marry the excellent Mr Burdon.'

'You know I cannot live without you. How can you be so cruel?'

'Then the only alternative is that you should accompany me.'

Her blood ran cold, and her heart seemed pressed in an iron vice.

'What do you mean?'

'There is no need to be agitated. I am making you an eminently desirable offer of marriage.'

She sank helplessly into her chair. Because she had refused to think of the future, it had never struck her that the time must come when it would be necessary to leave Haddo or to throw in her lot with his definitely. She was seized with revulsion. Margaret realized that, though an odious attraction bound her to the man, she loathed and feared him. The scales fell from her eyes. She remembered on a sudden Arthur's great love and all that he had done for her sake. She hated herself. Like a bird at its last gasp beating frantically against the bars of a cage, Margaret made a desperate effort to regain her freedom. She sprang up.

'Let me go from here. I wish I'd never seen you. I don't know what you've done with me.'

'Go by all means if you choose,' he answered.

He opened the door, so that she might see he used no compulsion, and stood lazily at the threshold, with a hateful smile on his face. There was something terrible in his excessive bulk. Rolls of fat descended from his chin and concealed his neck. His cheeks were huge, and the lack of beard added to the hideous nakedness of his face. Margaret stopped as she passed him, horribly repelled yet horribly fascinated. She had an immense desire that he should take her again in his arms and press her lips with that red voluptuous mouth. It was as though fiends of hell were taking revenge upon her loveliness by inspiring in her a passion for this monstrous creature. She trembled with the intensity of her desire. His eyes were hard and cruel.

'Go,' he said.

She bent her head and fled from before him. To get home she passed through the gardens of the Luxembourg, but her legs failed her, and in exhaustion she sank upon a bench. The day was sultry. She tried to collect herself. Margaret knew well the part in which she sat, for in the enthusiastic days that seemed so long gone by she was accustomed to come there for the sake of a certain tree upon which her eyes now rested. It had all the slim delicacy of a Japanese print. The leaves were slender and fragile, half gold with autumn, half green, but so tenuous that the dark branches made a pattern of subtle beauty against the sky. The hand of a draughtsman could not have fashioned it with a more excellent skill. But now Margaret could take no pleasure in its grace. She felt a heartrending pang to think that thenceforward the consummate things of art would have no meaning for her. She had seen Arthur the evening before, and remembered with an agony of shame the lies to which she had been forced in order to explain why she could not see him till late that day. He had proposed that they should go to Versailles, and was bitterly disappointed when she told him they could not, as usual on Sundays, spend the whole day together. He accepted her excuse that she had to visit a sick friend. It would not have been so intolerable if he had suspected her of deceit, and his reproaches would have hardened her heart. It was his entire confidence which was so difficult to bear.

'Oh, if I could only make a clean breast of it all,' she cried.

The bell of Saint Sulpice was ringing for vespers. Margaret walked slowly to the church, and sat down in the seats reserved in the transept for the needy. She hoped that the music she must hear there would rest her soul, and perhaps she might be able to pray. Of late she had not dared. There was a pleasant darkness in the place, and its large simplicity was soothing. In her exhaustion, she watched list-lessly the people go to and fro. Behind her was a priest in the confes-sional. A little peasant girl, in a Breton *coiffe*, perhaps a maid-servant lately come from her native village to the great capital, passed in and knelt down. Margaret could hear her muttered words, and at intervals the deep voice of the priest. In three minutes she tripped neatly away. She looked so fresh in her plain black dress, so healthy and innocent, that Margaret could not restrain a sob of envy. The child had so little to confess, a few puny errors which must excite a smile on the lips of the gentle priest, and her candid spirit was like snow. Margaret would have given anything to kneel down and whisper in those passionless ears all that she suffered, but the priest's faith and hers were not the same. They spoke a different tongue, not of the lips only but of the soul, and he would not listen to the words of an heretic.

A long procession of seminarists came in from the college which is under the shadow of that great church, two by two, in black cas-socks and short white surplices. Many were tonsured already. Some were quite young. Margaret watched their faces, wondering if they were tormented by such agony as she. But they had a living faith to sustain them, and if some, as was plain, were narrow and obtuse, they had at least a fixed rule which prevented them from swerving into treacherous byways. One of two had a wan ascetic look, such as the saints may have had when the terror of life was known to them only in the imaginings of the cloister. The canons of the church followed in their more gorgeous vestments, and finally the officiating clergy.

The music was beautiful. There was about it a staid, sad dignity; and it seemed to Margaret fit thus to adore God. But it did not move her. She could not understand the words that the priests chanted; their gestures, their movements to and fro, were strange to her. For her that stately service had no meaning. And with a great cry in her heart she said that God had forsaken her. She was alone in an alien land. Evil was all about her, and in those ceremonies she could find no comfort. What could she expect when the God of her fathers left her to her fate? So that she might not weep in front of all those people, Margaret with down-turned face walked to the door. She felt utterly lost. As she walked along the interminable street that led to her own house, she was shaken with sobs.

'God has forsaken me,' she repeated. 'God has foresaken me.'

Next day, her eyes red with weeping, she dragged herself to Haddo's door. When he opened it, she went in without a word. She sat down, and he watched her in silence.

'I am willing to marry you whenever you choose,' she said at last.

'I have made all the necessary arrangements.'

'You have spoken to me of your mother. Will you take me to her at once.'

The shadow of a smile crossed his lips.

'If you wish it.'

Haddo told her that they could be married before the Consul early enough on the Thursday morning to catch a train for England. She left everything in his hands.

'I'm desperately unhappy,' she said dully.

Oliver laid his hands upon her shoulders and looked into her eyes.

'Go home, and you will forget your tears. I command you to be happy.'

Then it seemed that the bitter struggle between the good and the evil in her was done, and the evil had conquered. She felt on a sudden curiously elated. It seemed no longer to matter that she deceived her faithful friends. She gave a bitter laugh, as she thought how easy it was to hoodwink them.

Wednesday happened to be Arthur's birthday, and he asked her to dine with him alone.

'We'll do ourselves proud, and hang the expense,' he said.

They had arranged to eat at a fashionable restaurant on the other side of the river, and soon after seven he fetched her. Margaret was dressed with exceeding care. She stood in the middle of the room, waiting for Arthur's arrival, and surveyed herself in the glass. Susie thought she had never been more beautiful.

'I think you've grown more pleasing to look upon than you ever were,' she said. 'I don't know what it is that has come over you of late, but there's a depth in your eyes that is quite new. It gives you an odd mysteriousness which is very attractive.'

Knowing Susie's love for Arthur, she wondered whether her friend was not heartbroken as she compared her own plainness with the radiant beauty that was before her. Arthur came in, and Margaret did not move. He stopped at the door to look at her. Their eyes met. His heart beat quickly, and yet he was seized with awe. His good fortune was too great to bear, when he thought that this priceless treasure was his. He could have knelt down and worshipped as though a goddess of old Greece stood before him. And to him also her eyes had changed. They had acquired a burning passion which disturbed and yet enchanted him. It seemed that the lovely girl was changed already into a lovely woman. An enigmatic smile came to her lips.

'Are you pleased?' she asked.

Arthur came forward and Margaret put her hands on his shoulders.

'You have scent on,' he said.

He was surprised, for she had never used it before. It was a faint, almost acrid perfume that he did not know. It reminded him vaguely of those odours which he remembered in his childhood in the East. It was remote and strange. It gave Margaret a new and troubling charm. There had ever been something cold in her statuesque beauty, but this touch somehow curiously emphasized her sex. Arthur's lips twitched, and his gaunt face grew pale with passion. His emotion was so great that it was nearly pain. He was puzzled, for her eyes expressed things that he had never seen in them before.

'Why don't you kiss me?' she said.

She did not see Susie, but knew that a quick look of anguish crossed her face. Margaret drew Arthur towards her. His hands began to tremble. He had never ventured to express the passion that consumed him, and when he kissed her it was with a restraint that was almost brotherly. Now their lips met. Forgetting that anyone else was in the room, he flung his arms around Margaret. She had never kissed him in that way before, and the rapture was intolerable. Her lips were like living fire. He could not take his own away. He forgot everything. All his strength, all his self-control, deserted him. It crossed his mind that at this moment he would willingly die. But the delight of it was so great that he could scarcely withhold a cry of agony. At length

Susie's voice reminded him of the world.

'You'd far better go out to dinner instead of behaving like a pair of complete idiots.'

She tried to make her tone as flippant as the words, but her voice was cut by a pang of agony. With a little laugh, Margaret withdrew from Arthur's embrace and lightly looked at her friend. Susie's brave smile died away as she caught this glance, for there was in it a malicious hatred that startled her. It was so unexpected that she was terrified. What had she done? She was afraid, dreadfully afraid, that Margaret had guessed her secret. Arthur stood as if his senses had left him, quivering still with the extremity of passion.

'Susie says we must go,' smiled Margaret.

He could not speak. He could not regain the conventional manner of polite society. Very pale, like a man suddenly awaked from deep sleep, he went out at Margaret's side. They walked along the passage. Though the door was closed behind them and they were out of earshot, Margaret seemed not withstanding to hear Susie's passionate sobbing. It gave her a horrible delight.

⁂

The tavern to which they went was on the Boulevard des Italiens, and at this date the most frequented in Paris. It was crowded, but Arthur had reserved a table in the middle of the room. Her radiant loveliness made people stare at Margaret as she passed, and her consciousness of the admiration she excited increased her beauty. She was satisfied that amid that throng of the best-dressed women in the world she had cause to envy no one. The gaiety was charming. Shaded lights gave an opulent cosiness to the scene, and there were flowers everywhere. Innumerable mirrors reflected women of the world, admirably gowned, actresses of renown, and fashionable courtesans. The noise was very great. A Hungarian band played in a distant corner, but the music was drowned by the loud talking of excited men and the boisterous laughter of women. It was plain that people had come to spend their money with a lavish hand. The vivacious crowd was given over with all its heart to the pleasure of the fleeting moment. Everyone had put aside grave thoughts and sorrow.

Margaret had never been in better spirits. The champagne went quickly to her head, and she talked all manner of charming nonsense. Arthur was enchanted. He was very proud, very pleased, and very happy. They talked of all the things they would do when they were married. They talked of the places they must go to, of their home and of the beautiful things with which they would fill it. Margaret's animation was extraordinary. Arthur was amused at her delight with the brightness of the place, with the good things they ate, and with the wine. Her laughter was like a rippling brook. Everything tended to take him out of his usual reserve. Life was very pleasing, at that moment, and he felt singularly joyful.

'Let us drink to the happiness of our life,' he said.

They touched glasses. He could not take his eyes away from her.

'You're simply wonderful tonight,' he said. 'I'm almost afraid of my good fortune.'

'What is there to be afraid of?' she cried.

'I should like to lose something I valued in order to propitiate the fates. I am too happy now. Everything goes too well with me.'

She gave a soft, low laugh and stretched out her hand on the table. No sculptor could have modelled its exquisite delicacy. She wore only one ring, a large emerald which Arthur had given her on their engagement. He could not resist taking her hand.

'Would you like to go on anywhere?' he said, when they had finished dinner and were drinking their coffee.

'No, let us stay here. I must go to bed early, as I have a tiring day before me tomorrow.'

'What are you going to do?' he asked.

'Nothing of any importance,' she laughed.

Presently the diners began to go in little groups, and Margaret suggested that they should saunter towards the Madeleine. The night was fine, but rather cold, and the broad avenue was crowded. Margaret watched the people. It was no less amusing than a play. In a little while, they took a cab and drove through the streets, silent already, that led to the quarter of the Montparnasse. They sat in silence, and Margaret nestled close to Arthur. He put his arm around her waist. In the shut cab that faint, oriental odour rose again to his nostrils, and his head reeled as it had before dinner.

'You've made me very happy, Margaret,' he whispered. 'I feel that, however long I live, I shall never have a happier day than this.'

'Do you love me very much?' she asked, lightly.

He did not answer, but took her face in his hands and kissed her passionately. They arrived at Margaret's house, and she tripped up to the door. She held out her hand to him, smiling.

'Goodnight.'

'It's dreadful to think that I must spend a dozen hours without seeing you. When may I come?'

'Not in the morning, because I shall be too busy. Come at twelve.'

She remembered that her train started exactly at that hour. The door was opened, and with a little wave of the hand she disappeared.

X

SUSIE STARED WITHOUT comprehension at the note that announced Margaret's marriage. It was a *petit bleu* sent off from the Gare du Nord, and ran as follows:

When you receive this I shall be on my way to London. I was married to Oliver Haddo this morning. I love him as I never loved Arthur. I have acted in this manner because I thought I had gone too far with Arthur to make an explanation possible. Please tell him.

MARGARET

Susie was filled with dismay. She did not know what to do nor what to think. There was a knock at the door, and she knew it must be Arthur, for he was expected at midday. She decided quickly that it was impossible to break the news to him then and there. It was needful first to find out all manner of things, and besides, it was incredible. Making up her mind, she opened the door.

'Oh, I'm so sorry Margaret isn't here,' she said. 'A friend of hers is ill and sent for her suddenly.'

'What a bore!' answered Arthur. 'Mrs Bloomfield as usual, I suppose?'

'Oh, you know she's been ill?'

'Margaret has spent nearly every afternoon with her for some days.'

Susie did not answer. This was the first she had heard of Mrs Bloomfield's illness, and it was news that Margaret was in the habit of visiting her. But her chief object at this moment was to get rid of Arthur.

'Won't you come back at five o'clock?' she said.

'But, look here, why shouldn't we lunch together, you and I?'

'I'm very sorry, but I'm expecting somebody in.'

'Oh, all right. Then I'll come back at five.'

He nodded and went out. Susie read the brief note once more, and asked herself if it could possibly be true. The callousness of it was appalling. She went to Margaret's room and saw that everything was in its place. It did not look as if the owner had gone on a journey. But then she noticed that a number of letters had been destroyed. She opened a drawer and found that Margaret's trinkets were gone. An idea struck her. Margaret had bought lately a number of clothes, and these she had insisted should be sent to her dressmaker, saying that it was needless to cumber their little apartment with them. They could stay there till she returned to England a few weeks later for her marriage, and it would be simpler to despatch them all from one place. Susie went out. At the door it occurred to her to ask the *concierge* if she knew where Margaret had gone that morning.

'*Parfaitement, Mademoiselle,*' answered the old woman. 'I heard her tell the coachman to go to the British Consulate.'

The last doubt was leaving Susie. She went to the dressmaker and there discovered that by Margaret's order the boxes containing her things had gone on the previous day to the luggage office of the Gare du Nord.

'I hope you didn't let them go till your bill was paid,' said Susie lightly, as though in jest.

The dressmaker laughed.

'Mademoiselle paid for everything two or three days ago.'

With indignation, Susie realised that Margaret had not only taken away the trousseau bought for her marriage with Arthur; but, since she was herself penniless, had paid for it with the money which he had generously given her. Susie drove then to Mrs Bloomfield, who at once reproached her for not coming to see her.

'I'm sorry, but I've been exceedingly busy, and I knew that Margaret was looking after you.'

'I've not seen Margaret for three weeks,' said the invalid.

'Haven't you? I thought she dropped in quite often.'

Susie spoke as though the matter were of no importance. She asked herself now where Margaret could have spent those afternoons. By a great effort she forced herself to speak of casual things with the garrulous old lady long enough to make her visit seem natural. On leaving her, she went to the Consulate, and her last doubt was dissipated. Then nothing remained but to go home and wait for Arthur. Her first impulse had been to see Dr Porhoët and ask for his advice; but, even if he offered to come back with her to the studio, his presence would be useless. She must see Arthur by himself. Her heart was wrung as she thought of the man's agony when he knew the truth. She had confessed to herself long before that she loved him passionately, and it seemed intolerable that she of all persons must bear him this great blow.

She sat in the studio, counting the minutes, and thought with a bitter smile that his eagerness to see Margaret would make him punctual. She had eaten nothing since the *petit déjeuner* of the morning, and she was faint with hunger. But she had not the heart to make herself tea. At last he came. He entered joyfully and looked around.

'Is Margaret not here yet?' he asked, with surprise.

'Won't you sit down?'

He did not notice that her voice was strange, nor that she kept her eyes averted.

'How lazy you are,' he cried. 'You haven't got the tea.'

'Mr Burdon, I have something to say to you. It will cause you very great pain.'

He observed now the hoarseness of her tone. He sprang to his feet, and a thousand fancies flashed across his brain. Something horrible had happened to Margaret. She was ill. His terror was so great that he could not speak. He put out his hands as does a blind man.

Susie had to make an effort to go on. But she could not. Her voice was choked, and she began to cry. Arthur trembled as though he were seized with ague. She gave him the letter.

'What does it mean?'

He looked at her vacantly. Then she told him all that she had done that day and the places to which she had been.

'When you thought she was spending every afternoon with Mrs Bloomfield, she was with that man. She made all the arrangements with the utmost care. It was quite premeditated.'

Arthur sat down and leaned his head on his hand. He turned his back to her, so that she should not see his face. They remained in perfect silence. And it was so terrible that Susie began to cry quietly. She knew that the man she loved was suffering an agony greater than the agony of death, and she could not help him. Rage flared up in her heart, and hatred for Margaret.

'Oh, it's infamous!' she cried suddenly. 'She's lied to you, she's been odiously deceitful. She must be vile and heartless. She must be rotten to the very soul.'

He turned round sharply, and his voice was hard.

'I forbid you to say anything against her.'

Susie gave a little gasp. He had never spoken to her before in anger. She flashed out bitterly.

'Can you love her still, when she's shown herself capable of such vile treachery? For nearly a month this man must have been making love to her, and she's listened to all we said of him. She's pretended to hate the sight of him, I've seen her cut him in the street. She's gone on with all the preparations for your marriage. She must have lived in a world of lies, and you never suspected anything because you had an unalterable belief in her love and truthfulness. She owes everything to you. For four years she's lived on your charity. She was only able to be here because you gave her money to carry out a foolish whim, and the very clothes on her back were paid for by you.'

'I can't help it if she didn't love me,' he cried desperately.

'You know just as well as I do that she pretended to love you. Oh, she's behaved shamefully. There can be no excuse for her.'

He looked at Susie with haggard, miserable eyes.

'How can you be so cruel? For God's sake don't make it harder.'

There was an indescribable agony in his voice. And as if his own words of pain overcame the last barrier of his self-control, he broke down. He hid his face in his hands and sobbed. Susie was horribly conscience-stricken.

'Oh, I'm so sorry,' she said. 'I didn't mean to say such hateful things. I didn't mean to be unkind. I ought to have remembered how passionately you love her.'

It was very painful to see the effort he made to regain his self-command. Susie suffered as much as he did. Her impulse was to throw herself on her knees, and kiss his hands, and comfort him; but she knew that he was interested in her only because she was Margaret's friend. At last he got up and, taking his pipe from his pocket, filled it silently. She was terrified at the look on his face. The first time she had ever seen him, Susie wondered at the possibility of self-torture which was in that rough-hewn countenance; but she had never dreamed that it could express such unutterable suffering. Its lines were suddenly changed, and it was terrible to look upon.

'I can't believe it's true,' he muttered. 'I can't believe it.'

There was a knock at the door, and Arthur gave a startled cry.

'Perhaps she's come back.'

He opened it hurriedly, his face suddenly lit up by expectation; but it was Dr Porhoët.

'How do you do?' said the Frenchman. 'What is happening?'

He looked round and caught the dismay that was on the faces of Arthur and Susie.

'Where is Miss Margaret? I thought you must be giving a party.'

There was something in his manner that made Susie ask why.

'I received a telegram from Mr Haddo this morning.'

He took it from his pocket and handed it to Susie. She read it and passed it to Arthur. It said:

> Come to the studio at five. High jinks.
> OLIVER HADDO

'Margaret was married to Mr Haddo this morning,' said Arthur, quietly. 'I understand they have gone to England.'

Susie quickly told the doctor the few facts they knew. He was as surprised, as distressed, as they.

'But what is the explanation of it all?' he asked.

Arthur shrugged his shoulders wearily.

'She cared for Haddo more than she cared for me, I suppose. It is natural enough that she should go away in this fashion rather than offer explanations. I suppose she wanted to save herself a scene she thought might be rather painful.'

'When did you see her last?'

'We spent yesterday evening together.'

'And did she not show in any way that she contemplated such a step?'

Arthur shook his head.

'You had no quarrel?'

'We've never quarrelled. She was in the best of spirits. I've never seen her more gay. She talked the whole time of our house in London, and of the places we must visit when we were married.'

Another contraction of pain passed over his face as he remembered that she had been more affectionate than she had ever been before. The fire of her kisses still burnt upon his lips. He had spent a night of almost sleepless ecstasy because he had been certain for the first time that the passion which consumed him burnt in her heart too. Words were dragged out of him against his will.

'Oh, I'm sure she loved me.'

Meanwhile Susie's eyes were fixed on Haddo's cruel telegram. She seemed to hear his mocking laughter.

'Margaret loathed Oliver Haddo with a hatred that was almost unnatural. It was a physical repulsion like that which people sometimes have for certain animals. What can have happened to change it into so great a love that it has made her capable of such villainous acts?'

'We mustn't be unfair to him,' said Arthur. 'He put our backs up, and we were probably unjust. He has done some very remarkable things in his day, and he's no fool. It's possible that some people wouldn't mind the eccentricities which irritated us. He's certainly of very good family and he's rich. In many ways it's an excellent match for Margaret.'

He was trying with all his might to find excuses for her. It would not make her treachery so intolerable if he could persuade himself that Haddo had qualities which might explain her infatuation. But as his enemy stood before his fancy, monstrously obese, vulgar, and overbearing, a shudder passed through him. The thought of Margaret in that man's arms tortured him as though his flesh were torn with iron hooks.

'Perhaps it's not true. Perhaps she'll return,' he cried.

'Would you take her back if she came to you?' asked Susie.

'Do you think anything she can do has the power to make me love her less? There must be reasons of which we know nothing that caused her to do all she has done. I daresay it was inevitable from the beginning.'

Dr Porhoët got up and walked across the room.

'If a woman had done me such an injury that I wanted to take some horrible vengeance, I think I could devise nothing more subtly cruel than to let her be married to Oliver Haddo.'

'Ah, poor thing, poor thing!' said Arthur. 'If I could only suppose she would be happy! The future terrifies me.'

'I wonder if she knew that Haddo had sent that telegram,' said Susie.

'What can it matter?'

She turned to Arthur gravely.

'Do you remember that day, in this studio, when he kicked Margaret's dog, and you thrashed him? Well, afterwards, when he thought no one saw him, I happened to catch sight of his face. I never saw in my life such malignant hatred. It was the face of a fiend of wickedness. And when he tried to excuse himself, there was a cruel gleam in his eyes which terrified me. I warned you; I told you that he had made up his mind to revenge himself, but you laughed at me. And then he seemed to go out of our lives and I thought no more about it. I wonder why he sent Dr Porhoët here today. He must have known that the doctor would hear of his humiliation, and he may have wished that he should be present at his triumph. I think that very moment he made up his mind to be even with you, and he devised this odious scheme.'

'How could he know that it was possible to carry out such a horrible thing?' said Arthur.

'I wonder if Miss Boyd is right,' murmured the doctor. 'After all, if you come to think of it, he must have thought that he couldn't hurt you more. The whole thing is fiendish. He took away from you all your happiness. He must have known that you wanted nothing in the world more than to make Margaret your wife, and he has not only prevented that, but he has married her himself. And he can only have done it by poisoning her mind, by warping her very character. Her soul must be horribly besmirched; he must have entirely changed her personality.'

'Ah, I feel that,' cried Arthur. 'If Margaret has broken her word to me, if she's gone to him so callously, it's because it's not the Margaret I know. Some devil must have taken possession of her body.'

'You use a figure of speech. I wonder if it can possibly be a reality.'

Arthur and Dr Porhoët looked at Susie with astonishment.

'I can't believe that Margaret could have done such a thing,' she went on. 'The more I think of it, the more incredible it seems. I've known Margaret for years, and she was incapable of deceit. She was very kind-hearted. She was honest and truthful. In the first moment of horror, I was only indignant, but I don't want to think too badly of her. There is only one way to excuse her, and that is by supposing she acted under some strange compulsion.'

Arthur clenched his hands.

'I'm not sure if that doesn't make it more awful than before. If he's married her, not because he cares, but in order to hurt me, what life will she lead with him? We know how heartless he is, how vindictive, how horribly cruel.'

'Dr Porhoët knows more about these things than we do,' said Susie. 'Is it possible that Haddo can have cast some spell upon her that would make her unable to resist his will? Is it possible that he can have got such an influence over her that her whole character was changed?'

'How can I tell?' cried the doctor helplessly. 'I have heard that such things may happen. I have read of them, but I have no proof. In these matters all is obscurity. The adepts in magic make strange claims. Arthur is a man of science, and he knows what the limits of hypnotism are.'

'We know that Haddo had powers that other men have not,' answered Susie. 'Perhaps there was enough truth in his extravagant pretensions to enable him to do something that we can hardly imagine.'

Arthur passed his hands wearily over his face.

'I'm so broken, so confused, that I cannot think sanely. At this moment everything seems possible. My faith in all the truths that have supported me is tottering.'

For a while they remained silent. Arthur's eyes rested on the chair in which Margaret had so often sat. An unfinished canvas still stood upon the easel. It was Dr Porhoët who spoke at last.

'But even if there were some truth in Miss Boyd's suppositions, I don't see how it can help you. You cannot do anything. You have no remedy, legal or otherwise. Margaret is apparently a free agent, and she has married this man. It is plain that many people will think she has done much better in marrying a country gentleman than in marrying a young surgeon. Her letter is perfectly lucid. There is no trace of compulsion. To all intents and purposes she has married him of her own free-will, and there is nothing to show that she desires to be released from him or from the passion which we may suppose enslaves her.'

What he said was obviously true, and no reply was possible.

'The only thing is to grin and bear it,' said Arthur, rising.

'Where are you going?' said Susie.

'I think I want to get away from Paris. Here everything will remind me of what I have lost. I must get back to my work.'

He had regained command over himself, and except for the hopeless woe of his face, which he could not prevent from being visible, he was as calm as ever. He held out his hand to Susie.

'I can only hope that you'll forget,' she said.

'I don't wish to forget,' he answered, shaking his head. 'It's possible that you will hear from Margaret. She'll want the things that she has left here, and I daresay will write to you. I should like you to tell her that I bear her no ill-will for anything she has done, and I will never venture to reproach her. I don't know if I shall be able to do anything for her, but I wish her to know that in any case and always I will do everything that she wants.'

'If she writes to me, I will see that she is told,' answered Susie gravely.

'And now goodbye.'

'You can't go to London till tomorrow. Shan't I see you in the morning?'

'I think if you don't mind, I won't come here again. The sight of all this rather disturbs me.'

Again a contraction of pain passed across his eyes, and Susie saw that he was using a superhuman effort to preserve the appearance of composure. She hesitated a moment.

'Shall I never see you again?' she said. 'I should be sorry to lose sight of you entirely.'

'I should be sorry, too,' he answered. 'I have learned how good and kind you are, and I shall never forget that you are Margaret's friend. When you come to London, I hope that you will let me know.'

He went out. Dr Porhoët, his hands behind his back, began to walk up and down the room. At last he turned to Susie.

'There is one thing that puzzles me,' he said. 'Why did he marry her?'

'You heard what Arthur said,' answered Susie bitterly. 'Whatever happened, he would have taken her back. The other man knew that he could only bind her to him securely by going through the ceremonies of marriage.'

Dr Porhoët shrugged his shoulders, and presently he left her. When Susie was alone she began to weep broken-heartedly, not for herself, but because Arthur suffered an agony that was hardly endurable.

XI

ARTHUR WENT BACK to London next day.

Susie felt it impossible any longer to stay in the deserted studio, and accepted a friend's invitation to spend the winter in Italy. The good Dr Porhoët remained in Paris with his books and his occult studies.

Susie travelled slowly through Tuscany and Umbria. Margaret had not written to her, and Susie, on leaving Paris, had sent her friend's belongings to an address from which she knew they would eventually be forwarded. She could not bring herself to write. In answer to a note announcing her change of plans, Arthur wrote briefly that he had much work to do and was delivering a new course of lectures at St. Luke's; he had lately been appointed visiting surgeon to another hospital, and his private practice was increasing. He did not mention Margaret. His letter was abrupt, formal, and constrained. Susie, reading it for the tenth time, could make little of it. She saw that he wrote only from civility, without interest; and there was nothing to indicate his state of mind. Susie and her companion had made up their minds to pass some weeks in Rome; and here, to her astonishment, Susie had news of Haddo and his wife. It appeared that they had spent some time there, and the little English circle was talking still of their eccentricities. They travelled in some state, with a courier and a suite of servants; they had taken a carriage and were in the habit of driving every afternoon on the Pincio. Haddo had excited attention by the extravagance of his costume, and Margaret by her beauty; she was to be seen in her box at the opera every night, and her diamonds were the envy of all beholders. Though people had laughed a good deal at Haddo's pretentiousness, and been exasperated by his arrogance, they could not fail to be impressed by his obvious wealth. But finally the pair had disappeared suddenly without saying a word to anybody. A good many bills remained unpaid, but these, Susie learnt, had been settled later. It was reported that they were now in Monte Carlo.

'Did they seem happy?' Susie asked the gossiping friend who gave her this scanty information.

'I think so. After all, Mrs Haddo has almost everything that a woman can want, riches, beauty, nice clothes, jewels. She would be very unreasonable not to be happy.'

Susie had meant to pass the later spring on the Riviera, but when she heard that the Haddos were there, she hesitated. She did not want to run the risk of seeing them, and yet she had a keen desire to find out exactly how things were going. Curiosity and distaste struggled in her mind, but curiosity won; and she persuaded her friend to go to Monte Carlo instead of to Beaulieu. At first Susie did not see the Haddos; but rumour was already much occupied with them, and she had only to keep her ears open. In that strange place, where all that is extravagant and evil, all that is morbid, insane, and fantastic, is gathered together, the Haddos were in fit company. They were notorious for their assiduity at the tables and for their luck, for the dinners and suppers they gave at places frequented by the very opulent, and for their eccentric appearance. It was a complex picture that Susie put together from the scraps of information she collected. After two or three days she saw them at the tables, but they were so absorbed in their game that she felt quite safe from discovery. Margaret was playing, but Haddo stood behind her and directed her movements. Their faces were extraordinarily intent. Susie fixed her attention on Margaret, for in what she had heard of her she had been quite unable to recognize the girl who had been her friend. And what struck her most now was that there was in Margaret's expression a singular likeness to Haddo's. Notwithstanding her exquisite beauty, she had a curiously vicious look, which suggested that somehow she saw literally with Oliver's eyes. They had won great sums that evening, and many persons watched them. It appeared that they played always in this fashion, Margaret putting on the stakes and Haddo telling her what to do and when to stop. Susie heard two Frenchmen talking of them. She listened with all her ears. She flushed as she heard one of them make an observation about Margaret which was more than coarse. The other laughed.

'It is incredible,' he said.

'I assure you it's true. They have been married six months, and she is still only his wife in name. The superstitious through all the ages have believed in the power of virginity, and the Church has made use of the idea for its own ends. The man uses her simply as a mascot.'

The men laughed, and their conversation proceeded so grossly that Susie's cheeks burned. But what she had heard made her look at Margaret more closely still. She was radiant. Susie could not deny that something had come to her that gave a new, enigmatic savour to her beauty. She was dressed more gorgeously than Susie's fastidious taste would have permitted; and her diamonds, splendid in themselves, were too magnificent for the occasion. At last, sweeping up the money, Haddo touched her on the shoulder, and she rose. Behind her was standing a painted woman of notorious disreputability. Susie was astonished to see Margaret smile and nod as she passed her.

Susie learnt that the Haddos had a suite of rooms at the most expensive of the hotels. They lived in a whirl of gaiety. They knew few English except those whose reputations were damaged, but seemed to prefer the society of those foreigners whose wealth and eccentricities made them the cynosure of that little world. Afterwards, she often saw them, in company of Russian Grand-Dukes and their mistresses, of South American women with prodigious diamonds, of noble gamblers and great ladies of doubtful fame, of strange men overdressed and scented. Rumour was increasingly busy with them. Margaret moved among all those queer people with a cold mysteriousness that excited the curiosity of the sated idlers. The suggestion which Susie overheard was repeated more circumstantially. But to this was joined presently the report of orgies that were enacted in the darkened sitting-room of the hotel, when all that was noble and vicious in Monte Carlo was present. Oliver's eccentric imagination invented whimsical festivities. He had a passion for disguise, and he gave a fancy-dress party of which fabulous stories were told. He sought to revive the mystical ceremonies of old religions, and it was reported that horrible rites had been performed in the garden of the villa, under the shining moon, in imitation of those he had seen in Eastern places. It was said that Haddo had magical powers of extraordinary character, and the tired imagination of those pleasure-seekers was tickled by his talk of black art. Some even asserted that the blasphemous ceremonies of the Black Mass had been celebrated in the house of a Polish Prince. People babbled of satanism and of necromancy. Haddo was thought to be immersed in occult studies for the performance of a magical operation; and some said that he was occupied with the Magnum Opus, the greatest and most fantastic of alchemical experiments. Gradually these stories were narrowed down to the monstrous assertion that he was attempting to create living beings. He had explained at length to somebody that magical receipts existed for the manufacture of *homunculi*.

Haddo was known generally by the name he was pleased to give himself. The Brother of the Shadow; but most people used it in derision, for it contrasted absurdly with his astonishing bulk. They were amused or outraged by his vanity, but they could not help talking about him, and Susie knew well enough by now that nothing pleased him more. His exploits as a lion-hunter were well known, and it was reported that human blood was on his hands. It was soon discovered that he had a queer power over animals, so that in his presence they were seized with unaccountable terror. He succeeded in surrounding himself with an atmosphere of the fabulous, and nothing that was told of him was too extravagant for belief. But unpleasant stories were circulated also, and someone related that he had been turned out of a club in Vienna for cheating at cards. He played many games, but here, as at Oxford, it was found that he was an unscrupulous opponent. And those old rumours followed him that he took strange drugs. He was supposed to have odious vices, and people whispered to one another of scandals that had been with difficulty suppressed. No one quite understood on what terms he was with his wife, and it was vaguely asserted that he was at times brutally cruel to her. Susie's heart sank when she heard this; but on the few occasions upon which she caught sight of Margaret, she seemed in the highest spirits. One story inexpressibly shocked her. After lunching at some restaurant, Haddo gave a bad louis among the money with which he paid the bill, and there was a disgraceful altercation with the waiter. He refused to change the coin till a policeman was brought in. His guests were furious, and several took the first opportunity to cut him dead. One of those present narrated the scene to Susie, and she was told that Margaret laughed unconcernedly with her neighbour while the sordid quarrel was proceeding. The man's blood was as good as his fortune was substantial, but it seemed to please him to behave like an adventurer. The incident was soon common property, and gradually the Haddos found themselves cold-shouldered. The persons with whom they mostly consorted had reputations too delicate to stand the glare of publicity which shone upon all who were connected with him, and the suggestion of police had thrown a shudder down many a spine. What had happened in Rome happened here again: they suddenly disappeared.

Susie had not been in London for some time, and as the spring advanced she remembered that her friends would be glad to see her.

It would be charming to spend a few weeks there with an adequate income; for its pleasures had hitherto been closed to her, and she looked forward to her visit as if it were to a foreign city. But though she would not confess it to herself, her desire to see Arthur was the strongest of her motives. Time and absence had deadened a little the intensity of her feelings, and she could afford to acknowledge that she regarded him with very great affection. She knew that he would never care for her, but she was content to be his friend. She could think of him without pain.

Susie stayed in Paris for three weeks to buy some of the clothes which she asserted were now her only pleasure in life, and then went to London.

She wrote to Arthur, and he invited her at once to lunch with him at a restaurant. She was vexed, for she felt they could have spoken more freely in his own house; but as soon as she saw him, she realized that he had chosen their meeting-place deliberately. The crowd of people that surrounded them, the gaiety, the playing of the band, prevented any intimacy of conversation. They were forced to talk of commonplaces. Susie was positively terrified at the change that had taken place in him. He looked ten years older; he had lost flesh, and his hair was sprinkled with white. His face was extraordinarily drawn, and his eyes were weary from lack of sleep. But what most struck her was the change in his expression. The look of pain which she had seen on his face that last evening in the studio was now become settled, so that it altered the lines of his countenance. It was harrowing to look at him. He was more silent than ever, and when he spoke it was in a strange low voice that seemed to come from a long way off. To be with him made Susie curiously uneasy, for there was a strenuousness in him which deprived his manner of all repose. One of the things that had pleased her in him formerly was the tranquillity which gave one the impression that here was a man who could be relied on in difficulties. At first she could not understand exactly what had happened, but in a moment saw that he was making an unceasing effort at self-control. He was never free from suffering and he was constantly on the alert to prevent anyone from seeing it. The strain gave him a peculiar restlessness.

But he was gentler than he had ever been before. He seemed gen-

uinely glad to see her and asked about her travels with interest. Susie
led him to talk of himself, and he spoke willingly enough of his daily
round. He was earning a good deal of money, and his professional
reputation was making steady progress. He worked hard. Besides his
duties at the two hospitals with which he was now connected, his
teaching, and his private practice, he had read of late one or two papers before scientific bodies, and was editing a large work on surgery.

'How on earth can you find time to do so much?' asked Susie.

'I can do with less sleep than I used,' he answered. 'It almost dou-
bles my working-day.'

He stopped abruptly and looked down. His remark had given accidentally some hint at the inner life which he was striving to conceal.
Susie knew that her suspicion was well-founded. She thought of the
long hours he lay awake, trying in vain to drive from his mind the
agony that tortured him, and the short intervals of troubled sleep. She
knew that he delayed as long as possible the fatal moment of going
to bed, and welcomed the first light of day, which gave him an excuse
for getting up. And because he knew that he had divulged the truth
he was embarrassed. They sat in awkward silence. To Susie, the tragic
figure in front of her was singularly impressive amid that lighthearted
throng: all about them happy persons were enjoying the good things
of life, talking, laughing, and making merry. She wondered what re-
finement of self-torture had driven him to choose that place to come
to. He must hate it.

When they finished luncheon, Susie took her courage in both
hands.

'Won't you come back to my rooms for half an hour? We can't
talk here.'

He made an instinctive motion of withdrawal, as though he
sought to escape. He did not answer immediately, and she insisted.

'You have nothing to do for an hour, and there are many things I
want to speak to you about'

'The only way to be strong is never to surrender to one's weakness,' he said, almost in a whisper, as though ashamed to talk so
intimately.

'Then you won't come?'

'No.'

It was not necessary to specify the matter which it was proposed to discuss. Arthur knew perfectly that Susie wished to talk of Margaret, and he was too straightforward to pretend otherwise. Susie paused for one moment.

'I was never able to give Margaret your message. She did not write to me.'

A certain wildness came into his eyes, as if the effort he made was almost too much for him.

'I saw her in Monte Carlo,' said Susie. 'I thought you might like to hear about her.'

'I don't see that it can do any good,' he answered.

Susie made a little hopeless gesture. She was beaten.

'Shall we go?' she said.

'You are not angry with me?' he asked. 'I know you mean to be kind. I'm very grateful to you.'

'I shall never be angry with you,' she smiled.

Arthur paid the bill, and they threaded their way among the tables. At the door she held out her hand.

'I think you do wrong in shutting yourself away from all human comradeship,' she said, with that good-humoured smile of hers. 'You must know that you will only grow absurdly morbid.'

'I go out a great deal,' he answered patiently, as though he reasoned with a child. 'I make a point of offering myself distractions from my work. I go to the opera two or three times a week.'

'I thought you didn't care for music.'

'I don't think I did,' he answered. 'But I find it rests me.'

He spoke with a weariness that was appalling. Susie had never beheld so plainly the torment of a soul in pain.

'Won't you let me come to the opera with you one night?' she asked. 'Or does it bore you to see me?'

'I should like it above all things,' he smiled, quite brightly. 'You're like a wonderful tonic. They're giving Tristan on Thursday. Shall we go together?'

'I should enjoy it enormously.'

She shook hands with him and jumped into a cab.

'Oh, poor thing!' she murmured. 'Poor thing! What can I do for him?'

She clenched, her hands when she thought of Margaret. It was monstrous that she should have caused such havoc in that good, strong man.

'Oh, I hope she'll suffer for it,' she whispered vindictively. 'I hope she'll suffer all the agony that he has suffered.'

Susie dressed herself for Covent Garden as only she could do. Her gown pleased her exceedingly, not only because it was admirably made, but because it had cost far more than she could afford. To dress well was her only extravagance. It was of taffeta silk, in that exquisite green which the learned in such matters call E*au de Nil*; and its beauty was enhanced by the old lace which had formed not the least treasured part of her inheritance. In her hair she wore an ornament of Spanish paste, of exquisite workmanship, and round her neck a chain which had once adorned that of a madonna in an Andalusian church. Her individuality made even her plainness attractive. She smiled at herself in the glass ruefully, because Arthur would never notice that she was perfectly dressed.

When she tripped down the stairs and across the pavement to the cab with which he fetched her, Susie held up her skirt with a grace she flattered herself was quite Parisian. As they drove along, she flirted a little with her Spanish fan and stole a glance at herself in the glass. Her gloves were so long and so new and so expensive that she was really indifferent to Arthur's inattention.

Her joyous temperament expanded like a spring flower when she found herself in the Opera House. She put up her glasses and examined the women as they came into the boxes of the Grand Tier. Arthur pointed out a number of persons whose names were familiar to her, but she felt the effort he was making to be amiable. The weariness of his mouth that evening was more noticeable because of the careless throng. But when the music began he seemed to forget that any eye was upon him; he relaxed the constant tension in which he held himself; and Susie, watching him surreptitiously, saw the emotions chase one another across his face. It was now very mobile. The passionate sounds ate into his soul, mingling with his own love and his own sorrow, till he was taken out of himself; and sometimes he panted strangely. Through the interval he remained absorbed in his emotion. He sat as quietly as before and did not speak a word. Susie understood why Arthur, notwithstanding his old indifference, now showed such eager appreciation of music; it eased the pain he suffered by transferring it to an ideal world, and his own grievous sorrow made the music so real that it gave him an enjoyment of extraordinary vehemence. When it was all over and Isolde had given her last wail of sorrow, Arthur was so exhausted that he could hardly stir.

But they went out with the crowd, and while they were waiting in the vestibule for space to move in, a common friend came up to them. This was Arbuthnot, an eye-specialist, whom Susie had met on the Riviera and who, she presently discovered, was a colleague of Arthur's at St Luke's. He was a prosperous bachelor with grey hair and a red, contented face, well-to-do, for his practice was large, and lavish with his money. He had taken Susie out to luncheon once or twice in Monte Carlo; for he liked women, pretty or plain, and she attracted him by her good-humour. He rushed up to them now and wrung their hands. He spoke in a jovial voice.

'The very people I wanted to see! Why haven't you been to see me, you wicked woman? I'm sure your eyes are in a deplorable condition.'

'Do you think I would let a bold, bad man like you stare into them with an ophthalmoscope?' laughed Susie.

'Now look here, I want you both to do me a great favour. I'm giving a supper party at the Savoy, and two of my people have suddenly failed me. The table is ordered for eight, and you must come and take their places.'

'I'm afraid I must get home,' said Arthur. 'I have a deuce of a lot of work to do.'

'Nonsense,' answered Arbuthnot. 'You work much too hard, and a little relaxation will do you good.' He turned to Susie: 'I know you like curiosities in human nature; I'm having a man and his wife who will positively thrill you, they're so queer, and a lovely actress, and an awfully jolly American girl.'

'I should love to come,' said Susie, with an appealing look at

Arthur, 'if only to show you how much more amusing I am than lovely actresses.'

Arthur, forcing himself to smile, accepted the invitation. The specialist patted him cheerily on the back, and they agreed to meet at the Savoy.

'It's awfully good of you to come,' said Susie, as they drove along. 'Do you know, I've never been there in my life, and I'm palpitating with excitement.'

'What a selfish brute I was to refuse!' he answered.

When Susie came out of the dressing-room, she found Arthur waiting for her. She was in the best of spirits.

'Now you must say you like my frock. I've seen six women turn green with envy at the sight of it. They think I must be French, and they're sure I'm not respectable.'

'That is evidently a great compliment,' he smiled.

At that moment Arbuthnot came up to them in his eager way and seized their arms.

'Come along. We're waiting for you. I'll just introduce you all round, and then we'll go in to supper.'

They walked down the steps into the foyer, and he led them to a group of people. They found themselves face to face with Oliver Haddo and Margaret.

'Mr Arthur Burdon—Mrs Haddo. Mr Burdon is a colleague of mine at St Luke's; and he will cut out your appendix in a shorter time than any man alive.'

Arbuthnot rattled on. He did not notice that Arthur had grown ghastly pale and that Margaret was blank with consternation. Haddo, his heavy face wreathed with smiles, stepped forward heartily. He seemed thoroughly to enjoy the situation.

'Mr Burdon is an old friend of ours,' he said. 'In fact, it was he who introduced me to my wife. And Miss Boyd and I have discussed Art and the Immortality of the Soul with the gravity due to such topics.'

He held out his hand, and Susie took it. She had a horror of scenes, and, though this encounter was as unexpected as it was disagreeable, she felt it needful to behave naturally. She shook hands with Margaret.

'How disappointing!' cried their host. 'I was hoping to give Miss Boyd something quite new in the way of magicians, and behold! she knows all about him.'

'If she did, I'm quite sure she wouldn't speak to me,' said Oliver, with a bantering smile.

They went into the supper-room.

'Now, how shall we sit?' said Arbuthnot, glancing round the table.

Oliver looked at Arthur, and his eyes twinkled.

'You must really let my wife and Mr Burdon be together. They haven't seen one another for so long that I'm sure they have no end of things to talk about.' He chuckled to himself. 'And pray give me Miss Boyd, so that she can abuse me to her heart's content.'

This arrangement thoroughly suited the gay specialist, for he was able to put the beautiful actress on one side of him and the charming American on the other. He rubbed his hands.

'I feel that we're going to have a delightful supper.'

Oliver laughed boisterously. He took, as was his habit, the whole conversation upon himself, and Susie was obliged to confess that he was at his best. There was a grotesque drollery about him that was very diverting, and it was almost impossible to resist him. He ate and drank with tremendous appetite. Susie thanked her stars at that moment that she was a woman who knew by long practice how to conceal her feelings, for Arthur, overcome with dismay at the meeting, sat in stony silence. But she talked gaily. She chaffed Oliver as though he were an old friend, and laughed vivaciously. She noticed meanwhile that Haddo, more extravagantly dressed than usual, had managed to get an odd fantasy into his evening clothes: he wore knee-breeches, which in itself was enough to excite attention; but his frilled shirt, his velvet collar, and oddly-cut satin waistcoat gave him the appearance of a comic Frenchman. Now that she was able to examine him more closely, she saw that in the last six months he was grown much balder; and the shiny whiteness of his naked crown contrasted oddly with the redness of his face. He was stouter, too, and the fat hung in heavy folds under his chin; his paunch was preposterous. The vivacity of his movements made his huge corpulence subtly alarming. He was growing indeed strangely terrible in appearance. His eyes had still that fixed, parallel look, but there was in them now at times a ferocious gleam. Margaret was as beautiful as ever, but Susie noticed that his influence was apparent in her dress; for there could be no doubt that it had crossed the line of individuality and had degenerated into the eccentric. Her gown was much too gorgeous. It told against the classical character of her beauty. Susie shuddered a little, for it reminded her of a courtesan's.

Margaret talked and laughed as much as her husband, but Susie could not tell whether this animation was affected or due to an utter callousness. Her voice seemed natural enough, yet it was inconceivable that she should be so lighthearted. Perhaps she was trying to show that she was happy. The supper proceeded, and the lights, the surrounding gaiety, the champagne, made everyone more lively. Their host was in uproarious spirits. He told a story or two at which everyone laughed. Oliver Haddo had an amusing anecdote handy. It was a little risky, but it was so funnily narrated that everyone roared but Arthur, who remained in perfect silence. Margaret had been drinking glass after glass of wine, and no sooner had her husband finished than she capped his story with another. But whereas his was wittily immoral, hers was simply gross. At first the other women could not understand to what she was tending, but when they saw, they looked down awkwardly at their plates. Arbuthnot, Haddo, and the other man who was there laughed very heartily; but Arthur flushed to the roots of his hair. He felt horribly uncomfortable. He was ashamed. He dared not look at Margaret. It was inconceivable that from her exquisite mouth such indecency should issue. Margaret, apparently quite unconscious of the effect she had produced, went on talking and laughing.

Soon the lights were put out, and Arthur's agony was ended. He wanted to rush away, to hide his face, to forget the sight of her and her gaiety, above all to forget that story. It was horrible, horrible.

She shook hands with him quite lightly.

'You must come and see us one day. We've got rooms at the Carlton.'

He bowed and did not answer. Susie had gone to the dressing-room to get her cloak. She stood at the door when Margaret came out.

'Can we drop you anywhere?' said Margaret. 'You must come and see us when you have nothing better to do.'

Susie threw back her head. Arthur was standing just in front of them looking down at the ground in complete abstraction.

'Do you see him?' she said, in a low voice quivering with indignation. 'That is what you have made him.'

He looked up at that moment and turned upon them his sunken, tormented eyes. They saw his wan, pallid face with its look of hopeless woe.

'Do you know that he's killing himself on your account? He can't sleep at night. He's suffered the tortures of the damned. Oh, I hope you'll suffer as he's suffered!'

'I wonder that you blame me,' said Margaret. 'You ought to be rather grateful.'

'Why?'

'You're not going to deny that you've loved him passionately from the first day you saw him? Do you think I didn't see that you cared for him in Paris? You care for him now more than ever.'

Susie felt suddenly sick at heart. She had never dreamt that her secret was discovered. Margaret gave a bitter little laugh and walked past her.

XII

ARTHUR BURDON SPENT two or three days in a state of utter uncertainty, but at last the idea he had in mind grew so compelling as to overcome all objections. He went to the Carlton and asked for Margaret. He had learnt from the porter that Haddo was gone out and so counted on finding her alone. A simple device enabled him to avoid sending up his name. When he was shown into her private room Margaret was sitting down. She neither read nor worked.

'You told me I might call upon you,' said Arthur.

She stood up without answering, and turned deathly pale.

'May I sit down?' he asked.

She bowed her head. For a moment they looked at one another in silence. Arthur suddenly forgot all he had prepared to say. His intrusion seemed intolerable.

'Why have you come?' she said hoarsely.

They both felt that it was useless to attempt the conventionality of society. It was impossible to deal with the polite commonplaces that ease an awkward situation.

'I thought that I might be able to help you,' he answered gravely.

'I want no help. I'm perfectly happy. I have nothing to say to you.'

She spoke hurriedly, with a certain nervousness, and her eyes were fixed anxiously on the door as though she feared that someone would come in.

'I feel that we have much to say to one another,' he insisted. 'If it is inconvenient for us to talk here, will you not come and see me?'

'He'd know,' she cried suddenly, as if the words were dragged out of her. 'D'you think anything can be hidden from him?'

Arthur glanced at her. He was horrified by the terror that was in her eyes. In the full light of day a change was plain in her expression. Her face was strangely drawn, and pinched, and there was in it a constant look as of a person cowed. Arthur turned away.

'I want you to know that I do not blame you in the least for anything you did. No action of yours can ever lessen my affection for you.'

'Oh, why did you come here? Why do you torture me by saying such things?'

She burst on a sudden into a flood of tears, and walked excitedly up and down the room.

'Oh, if you wanted me to be punished for the pain I've caused you, you can triumph now. Susie said she hoped I'd suffer all the agony that I've made you suffer. If she only knew!'

Margaret gave a hysterical laugh. She flung herself on her knees by Arthur's side and seized his hands.

'Did you think I didn't see? My heart bled when I looked at your poor wan face and your tortured eyes. Oh, you've changed. I could never have believed that a man could change so much in so few months, and it's I who've caused it all. Oh, Arthur, Arthur, you must forgive me. And you must pity me.'

'But there's nothing to forgive, darling,' he cried.

She looked at him steadily. Her eyes now were shining with a hard brightness.

'You say that, but you don't really think it. And yet if you only knew, all that I have endured is on your account.'

She made a great effort to be calm.

'What do you mean?' said Arthur.

'He never loved me, he would never have thought of me if he hadn't wanted to wound you in what you treasured most. He hated you, and he's made me what I am so that you might suffer. It isn't I who did all this, but a devil within me; it isn't I who lied to you and left you and caused you all this unhappiness.'

She rose to her feet and sighed deeply.

'Once, I thought he was dying, and I helped him. I took him into the studio and gave him water. And he gained some dreadful power over me so that I've been like wax in his hands. All my will has disappeared, and I have to do his bidding. And if I try to resist ...'

Her face twitched with pain and fear.

'I've found out everything since. I know that on that day when he seemed to be at the point of death, he was merely playing a trick on me, and he got Susie out of the way by sending a telegram from a girl whose name he had seen on a photograph. I've heard him roar with laughter at his cleverness.'

She stopped suddenly, and a look of frightful agony crossed her face.

'And at this very minute, for all I know, it may be by his influence that I say this to you, so that he may cause you still greater suffering by allowing me to tell you that he never cared for me. You know now that my life is hell, and his vengeance is complete.'

'Vengeance for what?'

'Don't you remember that you hit him once, and kicked him unmercifully? I know him well now. He could have killed you, but he hated you too much. It pleased him a thousand times more to devise this torture for you and me.'

Margaret's agitation was terrible to behold. This was the first time that she had ever spoken to a soul of all these things, and now the long restraint had burst as burst the waters of a dam. Arthur sought to calm her.

'You're ill and overwrought. You must try to compose yourself. After all, Haddo is a human being like the rest of us.'

'Yes, you always laughed at his claims. You wouldn't listen to the things he said. But I know. Oh, I can't explain it; I daresay common sense and probability are all against it, but I've seen things with my own eyes that pass all comprehension. I tell you, he has powers of the most awful kind. That first day when I was alone with him, he seemed to take me to some kind of sabbath. I don't know what it was, but I saw horrors, vile horrors, that rankled for ever after like poison in my mind; and when we went up to his house in Staffordshire, I recognized the scene; I recognized the arid rocks, and the trees, and the lie of the land. I knew I'd been there before on that fatal afternoon. Oh, you must believe me! Sometimes I think I shall go mad with the terror of it all.'

Arthur did not speak. Her words caused a ghastly suspicion to flash through his mind, and he could hardly contain himself. He thought that some dreadful shock had turned her brain. She buried her face in her hands.

'Look here,' he said, 'you must come away at once. You can't continue to live with him. You must never go back to Skene.'

'I can't leave him. We're bound together inseparably.'

'But it's monstrous. There can be nothing to keep you to him. Come back to Susie. She'll be very kind to you; she'll help you to forget all you've endured.'

'It's no use. You can do nothing for me.'

'Why not?'

'Because, notwithstanding, I love him with all my soul.'

'Margaret!'

'I hate him. He fills me with repulsion. And yet I do not know what there is in my blood that draws me to him against my will. My flesh cries out for him.'

Arthur looked away in embarrassment. He could not help a slight, instinctive movement of withdrawal.

'Do I disgust you?' she said.

He flushed slightly, but scarcely knew how to answer. He made a vague gesture of denial.

'If you only knew,' she said.

There was something so extraordinary in her tone that he gave her a quick glance of surprise. He saw that her cheeks were flaming. Her bosom was panting as though she were again on the point of breaking into a passion of tears.

'For God's sake, don't look at me!' she cried.

She turned away and hid her face. The words she uttered were in a shamed, unnatural voice.

'If you'd been at Monte Carlo, you'd have heard them say, God knows how they knew it, that it was only through me he had his luck at the tables. He's contented himself with filling my soul with vice. I have no purity in me. I'm sullied through and through. He has made me into a sink of iniquity, and I loathe myself. I cannot look at myself without a shudder of disgust.'

A cold sweat came over Arthur, and he grew more pale than ever. He realized now he was in the presence of a mystery that he could not unravel. She went on feverishly.

'The other night, at supper, I told a story, and I saw you wince with shame. It wasn't I that told it. The impulse came from him, and I knew it was vile, and yet I told it with gusto. I enjoyed the telling of it; I enjoyed the pain I gave you, and the dismay of those women. There seem to be two persons in me, and my real self, the old one that you knew and loved, is growing weaker day by day, and soon she will be dead entirely. And there will remain only the wanton soul in the virgin body.'

Arthur tried to gather his wits together. He felt it an occasion on which it was essential to hold on to the normal view of things.

'But for God's sake leave him. What you've told me gives you every ground for divorce. It's all monstrous. The man must be so mad that he ought to be put in a lunatic asylum.'

'You can do nothing for me,' she said.

'But if he doesn't love you, what does he want you for?'

'I don't know, but I'm beginning to suspect.'

She looked at Arthur steadily. She was now quite calm.

'I think he wishes to use me for a magical operation. I don't know if he's mad or not. But I think he means to try some horrible experiment, and I am needful for its success. That is my safeguard.'

'Your safeguard?'

'He won't kill me because he needs me for that. Perhaps in the process I shall regain my freedom.'

Arthur was shocked at the callousness with which she spoke. He went up to her and put his hands on her shoulders.

'Look here, you must pull yourself together, Margaret. This isn't sane. If you don't take care, your mind will give way altogether. You must come with me now. When you're out of his hands, you'll soon regain your calmness of mind. You need never see him again. If you're afraid, you shall be hidden from him, and lawyers shall arrange everything between you.'

'I daren't.'

'But I promise you that you can come to no harm. Be reasonable. We're in London now, surrounded by people on every side. How do you think he can touch you while we drive through the crowded streets? I'll take you straight to Susie. In a week you'll laugh at the idle fears you had.'

'How do you know that he is not in the room at this moment, listening to all you say?'

The question was so sudden, so unexpected, that Arthur was startled. He looked round quickly.

'You must be mad. You see that the room is empty.'

'I tell you that you don't know what powers he has. Have you ever heard those old legends with which nurses used to frighten our childhood, of men who could turn themselves into wolves, and who scoured the country at night?' She looked at him with staring eyes. 'Sometimes, when he's come in at Skene in the morning, with bloodshot eyes, exhausted with fatigue and strangely discomposed, I've imagined that he too ...' She stopped and threw back her head. 'You're right, Arthur, I think I shall go mad.'

He watched her helplessly. He did not know what to do. Margaret went on, her voice quivering with anguish.

'When we were married, I reminded him that he'd promised to

take me to his mother. He would never speak of her, but I felt I must see her. And one day, suddenly, he told me to get ready for a journey, and we went a long way, to a place I did not know, and we drove into the country. We seemed to go miles and miles, and we reached at last a large house, surrounded by a high wall, and the windows were heavily barred. We were shown into a great empty room. It was dismal and cold like the waiting-room at a station. A man came in to us, a tall man, in a frock-coat and gold spectacles. He was introduced to me as Dr Taylor, and then, suddenly, I understood.'

Margaret spoke in hurried gasps, and her eyes were staring wide, as though she saw still the scene which at the time had seemed the crowning horror of her experience.

'I knew it was an asylum, and Oliver hadn't told me a word. He took us up a broad flight of stairs, through a large dormitory—oh, if you only knew what I saw there! I was so horribly frightened, I'd never been in such a place before—to a cell. And the walls and the floor were padded.'

Margaret passed her hand across her forehead to chase away the recollection of that awful sight.

'Oh, I see it still. I can never get it out of my mind.'

She remembered with a morbid vividness the vast misshapen mass which she had seen heaped strangely in one corner. There was a slight movement in it as they entered, and she perceived that it was a human being. It was a woman, dressed in shapeless brown flannel; a woman of great stature and of a revolting, excessive corpulence. She turned upon them a huge, impassive face; and its unwrinkled smoothness gave it an appearance of aborted childishness. The hair was dishevelled, grey, and scanty. But what most terrified Margaret was that she saw in this creature an appalling likeness to Oliver.

'He told me it was his mother, and she'd been there for five-and-twenty years.'

Arthur could hardly bear the terror that was in Margaret's eyes. He did not know what to say to her. In a little while she began to speak again, in a low voice and rapidly, as though to herself, and she wrung her hands.

'Oh, you don't know what I've endured! He used to spend long periods away from me, and I remained alone at Skene from morning till night, alone with my abject fear. Sometimes, it seemed that he was seized with a devouring lust for the gutter, and he would go to Liverpool or Manchester and throw himself among the very dregs of the people. He used to pass long days, drinking in filthy pot-houses. While the bout lasted, nothing was too depraved for him. He loved the company of all that was criminal and low. He used to smoke opium in foetid dens—oh, you have no conception of his passion to degrade himself—and at last he would come back, dirty, with torn clothes, begrimed, sodden still with his long debauch; and his mouth was hot with the kisses of the vile women of the docks. Oh, he's so cruel when the fit takes him that I think he has a fiendish pleasure in the sight of suffering!'

It was more than Arthur could stand. His mind was made up to try a bold course. He saw on the table a whisky bottle and glasses. He poured some neat spirit into a tumbler and gave it to Margaret.

'Drink this,' he said.

'What is it?'

'Never mind! Drink it at once.'

Obediently she put it to her lips. He stood over her as she emptied the glass. A sudden glow filled her.

'Now come with me.'

He took her arm and led her down the stairs. He passed through the hall quickly. There was a cab just drawn up at the door, and he told her to get in. One or two persons stared at seeing a woman come out of that hotel in a teagown and without a hat. He directed the driver to the house in which Susie lived and looked round at Margaret. She had fainted immediately she got into the cab.

When they arrived, he carried Margaret upstairs and laid her on a sofa. He told Susie what had happened and what he wanted of her. The dear woman forgot everything except that Margaret was very ill, and promised willingly to do all he wished.

∸

For a week Margaret could not be moved. Arthur hired a little cottage in Hampshire, opposite the Isle of Wight, hoping that amid the most charming, restful scenery in England she would quickly regain her strength; and as soon as it was possible Susie took her down. But she was much altered. Her gaiety had disappeared and with it her determination. Although her illness had been neither long nor serious, she seemed as exhausted, physically and mentally, as if she had been for months at the point of death. She took no interest in her surroundings, and was indifferent to the shady lanes through which they drove and to the gracious trees and the meadows. Her old passion for beauty was gone, and she cared neither for the flowers which filled their little garden nor for the birds that sang continually. But at last it seemed necessary to discuss the future. Margaret acquiesced in all that was suggested to her, and agreed willingly that the needful steps should be taken to procure her release from Oliver Haddo. He made apparently no effort to trace her, and nothing had been heard of him. He did not know where Margaret was, but he might have guessed that Arthur was responsible for her flight, and Arthur was easily to be found. It made Susie vaguely uneasy that there was no sign of his existence. She wished that Arthur were not kept by his work in London.

At last a suit for divorce was instituted.

Two days after this, when Arthur was in his consultingroom, Haddo's card was brought to him. Arthur's jaw set more firmly.

'Show the gentleman in,' he ordered.

When Haddo entered, Arthur, standing with his back to the fireplace, motioned him to sit down.

'What can I do for you?' he asked coldly.

'I have not come to avail myself of your surgical skill, my dear Burdon,' smiled Haddo, as he fell ponderously into an armchair.

'So I imagined.'

'You perspicacity amazes me. I surmise that it is to you I owe this amusing citation which was served on me yesterday.'

'I allowed you to come in so that I might tell you I will have no communication with you except through my solicitors.'

'My dear fellow, why do you treat me with such discourtesy? It is true that you have deprived me of the wife of my bosom, but you might at least so far respect my marital rights as to use me civilly.'

'My patience is not as good as it was,' answered Arthur, 'I venture to remind you that once before I lost my temper with you, and the result you must have found unpleasant.'

'I should have thought you regretted that incident by now, O Burdon,' answered Haddo, entirely unabashed.

'My time is very short,' said Arthur.

'Then I will get to my business without delay. I thought it might interest you to know that I propose to bring a counter-petition against my wife, and I shall make you co-respondent.'

'You infamous blackguard!' cried Arthur furiously. 'You know as well as I do that your wife is above suspicion.'

'I know that she left my hotel in your company, and has been living since under your protection.'

Arthur grew livid with rage. He could hardly restrain himself from knocking the man down. He gave a short laugh.

'You can do what you like. I'm really not frightened.'

'The innocent are so very incautious. I assure you that I can make a good enough story to ruin your career and force you to resign your appointments at the various hospitals you honour with your attention.'

'You forget that the case will not be tried in open court,' said Arthur.

Haddo looked at him steadily. He did not answer for a moment.

'You're quite right,' he said at last, with a little smile. 'I had forgotten that.'

'Then I need not detain you longer.'

Oliver Haddo got up. He passed his hand reflectively over his huge face. Arthur watched him with scornful eyes. He touched a bell, and the servant at once appeared.

'Show this gentleman out.'

Not in the least disconcerted, Haddo strolled calmly to the door.

Arthur gave a sigh of relief, for he concluded that Haddo would not show fight. His solicitor indeed had already assured him that Oliver would not venture to defend the case.

Margaret seemed gradually to take more interest in the proceedings, and she was full of eagerness to be set free. She did not shrink from the unpleasant ordeal of a trial. She could talk of Haddo with composure. Her friends were able to persuade themselves that in a little while she would be her old self again, for she was growing stronger and more cheerful; her charming laughter rang through the little house as it had been used to do in the Paris studio. The case was to come on at the end of July, before the long vacation, and Susie had agreed to take Margaret abroad as soon as it was done.

But presently a change came over her. As the day of the trial drew nearer, Margaret became excited and disturbed; her gaiety deserted her, and she fell into long, moody silences. To some extent this was comprehensible, for she would have to disclose to callous ears the most intimate details of her married life; but at last her nervousness grew so marked that Susie could no longer ascribe it to natural causes. She thought it necessary to write to Arthur about it.

My Dear Arthur:

I don't know what to make of Margaret, and I wish you would come down and see her. The good-humour which I have noticed in her of late has given way to a curious irritability. She is so restless that she cannot keep still for a moment. Even when she is sitting down her body moves in a manner that is almost convulsive. I am beginning to think that the strain from which she suffered is bringing on some nervous disease, and I am really alarmed. She walks about the house in a peculiarly aimless manner, up and down the stairs, in and out of the garden. She has grown suddenly much more silent, and the look has come back to her eyes which they had when first we brought her down here. When I beg her to tell me what is troubling her, she says: 'I'm afraid that something is going to happen.' She will not or cannot explain what she means. The last few weeks have set my own nerves on edge, so that I do not know how much of what I observe is real, and how much is due to my fancy; but I wish you would come and put a little courage into me. The oddness of it all is making me uneasy, and I am seized with preposterous terrors. I don't know what there is in Haddo that inspires me with this unaccountable dread. He is always present to my thoughts. I seem to see his dreadful eyes and his cold, sensual smile. I wake up at night, my heart beating furiously, with the consciousness that something quite awful has happened.

Oh, I wish the trial were over, and that we were happy in Germany.

> Yours ever
> SUSAN BOYD

Susie took a certain pride in her common sense, and it was humiliating to find that her nerves could be so distraught. She was worried and unhappy. It had not been easy to take Margaret back to her bosom as if nothing had happened. Susie was human; and, though she did ten times more than could be expected of her, she could not resist a feeling of irritation that Arthur sacrificed her so calmly. He had no room for other thoughts, and it seemed quite natural to him that she should devote herself entirely to Margaret's welfare.

Susie walked some way along the road to post this letter and then went to her room. It was a wonderful night, starry and calm, and the silence was like balm to her troubles. She sat at the window for a long time, and at last, feeling more tranquil, went to bed. She slept more soundly than she had done for many days. When she awoke the sun was streaming into her room, and she gave a deep sigh of delight. She could see trees from her bed, and blue sky. All her troubles seemed easy to bear when the world was so beautiful, and she was ready to laugh at the fears that had so affected her.

She got up, put on a dressing-gown, and went to Margaret's room. It was empty. The bed had not been slept in. On the pillow was a note.

> It's no good; I can't help myself. I've gone back to him. Don't trouble about me any more. It's quite hopeless and useless.
>
> M

Susie gave a little gasp. Her first thought was for Arthur, and she uttered a wail of sorrow because he must be cast again into the agony of desolation. Once more she had to break the dreadful news. She dressed hurriedly and ate some breakfast. There was no train till nearly eleven, and she had to bear her impatience as best she could. At last it was time to start, and she put on her gloves. At that moment the door was opened, and Arthur came in.

She gave a cry of terror and turned pale.

'I was just coming to London to see you,' she faltered. 'How did you find out?'

'Haddo sent me a box of chocolates early this morning with a card on which was written: *I think the odd trick is mine.*'

This cruel vindictiveness, joined with a schoolboy love of taunting the vanquished foe, was very characteristic. Susie gave Arthur Burdon the note which she had found in Margaret's room. He read it and then thought for a long time.

'I'm afraid she's right,' he said at length. 'It seems quite hopeless. The man has some power over her which we can't counteract.'

Susie wondered whether his strong scepticism was failing at last. She could not withstand her own feeling that there was something preternatural about the hold that Oliver had over Margaret. She had no shadow of a doubt that he was able to affect his wife even at a distance, and was convinced now that the restlessness of the last few days was due to this mysterious power. He had been at work in some strange way, and Margaret had been aware of it. At length she could not resist and had gone to him instinctively: her will was as little concerned as when a chip of steel flies to a magnet.

'I cannot find it in my heart now to blame her for anything she has done,' said Susie. 'I think she is the victim of a most lamentable fate. I can't help it. I must believe that he was able to cast a spell on her; and to that is due all that has happened. I have only pity for her great misfortunes.'

'Has it occurred to you what will happen when she is back in Haddo's hands?' cried Arthur. 'You know as well as I do how revengeful he is and how hatefully cruel. My heart bleeds when I think of the tortures, sheer physical tortures, which she may suffer.'

He walked up and down in desperation.

'And yet there's nothing whatever that one can do. One can't go to the police and say that a man has cast a magic spell on his wife.'

'Then you believe it too?' said Susie.

'I don't know what I believe now,' he cried. 'After all, we can't do anything if she chooses to go back to her husband. She's apparently her own mistress.' He wrung his hands. 'And I'm imprisoned in London! I can't leave it for a day. I ought not to be here now, and I must get back in a couple of hours. I can do nothing, and yet I'm convinced that Margaret is utterly wretched.'

Susie paused for a minute or two. She wondered how he would accept the suggestion that was in her mind.

'Do you know, it seems to me that common methods are useless. The only chance is to fight him with his own weapons. Would you mind if I went over to Paris to consult Dr Porhoët? You know that he is learned in every branch of the occult, and perhaps he might help us.'

But Arthur pulled himself together.

'It's absurd. We mustn't give way to superstition. Haddo is merely a scoundrel and a charlatan. He's worked on our nerves as he's worked on poor Margaret's. It's impossible to suppose that he has any powers greater than the common run of mankind.'

'Even after all you've seen with your own eyes?'

'If my eyes show me what all my training assures me is impossible, I can only conclude that my eyes deceive me.'

'Well, I shall run over to Paris.'

XIII

SOME WEEKS LATER Dr Porhoët was sitting among his books in the quiet, low room that overlooked the Seine. He had given himself over to a pleasing melancholy. The heat beat down upon the noisy streets of Paris, and the din of the great city penetrated even to his fastness in the Île Saint Louis. He remembered the cloud-laden sky of the country where he was born, and the south-west wind that blew with a salt freshness. The long streets of Brest, present to his fancy always in a drizzle of rain, with the lights of cafés reflected on the wet pavements, had a familiar charm. Even in foul weather the sailor-men who trudged along them gave one a curious sense of comfort. There was delight in the smell of the sea and in the freedom of the great

Atlantic. And then he thought of the green lanes and of the waste places with their scented heather, the fair broad roads that led from one old sweet town to another, of the *Pardons* and their gentle, sad crowds. Dr Porhoët gave a sigh.

'It is good to be born in the land of Brittany,' he smiled.

But his *bonne* showed Susie in, and he rose with a smile to greet her. She had been in Paris for some time, and they had seen much of one another. He basked in the gentle sympathy with which she interested herself in all the abstruse, quaint matters on which he spent his time; and, divining her love for Arthur, he admired the courage with which she effaced herself. They had got into the habit of eating many of their meals together in a quiet house opposite the Cluny called La Reine Blanche, and here they had talked of so many things that their acquaintance was grown into a charming friendship.

'I'm ashamed to come here so often,' said Susie, as she entered. 'Matilde is beginning to look at me with a suspicious eye.'

'It is very good of you to entertain a tiresome old man,' he smiled, as he held her hand. 'But I should have been disappointed if you had forgotten your promise to come this afternoon, for I have much to tell you.'

'Tell me at once,' she said, sitting down.

'I have discovered an MS. at the library of the Arsenal this morning that no one knew anything about.'

He said this with an air of triumph, as though the achievement were of national importance. Susie had a tenderness for his innocent mania; and, though she knew the work in question was occult and incomprehensible, congratulated him heartily.

'It is the original version of a book by Paracelsus. I have not read it yet, for the writing is most difficult to decipher, but one point caught my eye on turning over the pages. That is the gruesome fact that Paracelsus fed the *homunculi* he manufactured on human blood. One wonders how he came by it.'

Susie gave a little start, which Dr Porhoët noticed.

'What is the matter with you?'

'Nothing,' she said quickly.

He looked at her for a moment, then proceeded with the subject that strangely fascinated him.

'You must let me take you one day to the library of the Arsenal. There is no richer collection in the world of books dealing with the occult sciences. And of course you know that it was at the Arsenal that the tribunal sat, under the suggestive name of *chambre ardente*, to deal with cases of sorcery and magic?'

'I didn't,' smiled Susie.

'I always think that these manuscripts and queer old books, which are the pride of our library, served in many an old trial. There are volumes there of innocent appearance that have hanged wretched men and sent others to the stake. You would not believe how many persons of fortune, rank, and intelligence, during the great reign of Louis XIV, immersed themselves in these satanic undertakings.'

Susie did not answer. She could not now deal with these matters in an indifferent spirit. Everything she heard might have some bearing on the circumstances which she had discussed with Dr Porhoët times out of number. She had never been able to pin him down to an affirmation of faith. Certain strange things had manifestly happened, but what the explanation of them was, no man could say. He offered analogies from his well-stored memory. He gave her books to read till she was saturated with occult science. At one moment, she was inclined to throw them all aside impatiently, and, at another, was ready to believe that everything was possible.

Dr Porhoët stood up and stretched out a meditative finger. He spoke in that agreeably academic manner which, at the beginning of their acquaintance, had always entertained Susie, because it contrasted so absurdly with his fantastic utterances.

'It was a strange dream that these wizards cherished. They sought to make themselves beloved of those they cared for and to revenge themselves on those they hated; but, above all, they sought to become greater than the common run of men and to wield the power of the gods. They hesitated at nothing to gain their ends. But Nature with difficulty allows her secrets to be wrested from her. In vain they lit their furnaces, and in vain they studied their crabbed books, called up the dead, and conjured ghastly spirits. Their reward was disappointment and wretchedness, poverty, the scorn of men, torture, imprisonment, and shameful death. And yet, perhaps after all, there may be some particle of truth hidden away in these dark places.'

'You never go further than the cautious perhaps,' said Susie. 'You never give me any definite opinion.'

'In these matters it is discreet to have no definite opinion,' he smiled, with a shrug of the shoulders. 'If a wise man studies the science of the occult, his duty is not to laugh at everything, but to seek patiently, slowly, perseveringly, the truth that may be concealed in the night of these illusions.'

The words were hardly spoken when Matilde, the ancient *bonne*, opened the door to let a visitor come in. It was Arthur Burdon. Susie gave a cry of surprise, for she had received a brief note from him two days before, and he had said nothing of crossing the Channel.

'I'm glad to find you both here,' said Arthur, as he shook hands with them.

'Has anything happened?' cried Susie.

His manner was curiously distressing, and there was a nervousness about his movements that was very unexpected in so restrained a person.

'I've seen Margaret again,' he said.

'Well?'

He seemed unable to go on, and yet both knew that he had something important to tell them. He looked at them vacantly, as though all he had to say was suddenly gone out of his mind.

'I've come straight here,' he said, in a dull, bewildered fashion. 'I went to your hotel, Susie, in the hope of finding you; but when they told me you were out, I felt certain you would be here.'

'You seem worn out, *cher ami*,' said Dr Porhoët, looking at him. 'Will you let Matilde make you a cup of coffee?'

'I should like something,' he answered, with a look of utter weariness.

'Sit still for a minute or two, and you shall tell us what you want to when you are a little rested.'

Dr Porhoët had not seen Arthur since that afternoon in the previous year when, in answer to Haddo's telegram, he had gone to the studio in the Rue Campagne Première. He watched him anxiously while Arthur drank his coffee. The change in him was extraordinary; there was a cadaverous exhaustion about his face, and his eyes were sunken in their sockets. But what alarmed the good doctor most was that Arthur's personality seemed thoroughly thrown out of gear. All that he had endured during these nine months had robbed him of the strength of purpose, the matter-of-fact sureness, which had distinguished him. He was now unbalanced and neurotic.

Arthur did not speak. With his eyes fixed moodily on the ground, he wondered how much he could bring himself to tell them. It revolted him to disclose his inmost thoughts, yet he was come to the end of his tether and needed the doctor's advice. He found himself obliged to deal with circumstances that might have existed in a world of nightmare, and he was driven at last to take advantage of his friend's peculiar knowledge.

Returning to London after Margaret's flight, Arthur Burdon had thrown himself again into the work which for so long had been his only solace. It had lost its savour; but he would not take this into account, and he slaved away mechanically, by perpetual toil seeking to deaden his anguish. But as the time passed he was seized on a sudden with a curious feeling of foreboding, which he could in no way resist; it grew in strength till it had all the power of an obsession, and he could not reason himself out of it. He was sure that a great danger threatened Margaret. He could not tell what it was, nor why the fear of it was so persistent, but the idea was there always, night and day; it haunted him like a shadow and pursued him like remorse. His anxiety increased continually, and the vagueness of his terror made it more tormenting. He felt quite certain that Margaret was in imminent peril, but he did not know how to help her. Arthur supposed that Haddo had taken her back to Skene; but, even if he went there, he had no chance of seeing her. What made it more difficult still, was that his chief at St Luke's was away, and he was obliged to be in London in case he should be suddenly called upon to do some operation. But he could think of nothing else. He felt it urgently needful to see Margaret. Night after night he dreamed that she was at the point of death, and heavy fetters prevented him from stretching out a hand to help her. At last he could stand it no more. He told a brother surgeon that private business forced him to leave London, and put the work into his hands. With no plan in his head, merely urged by an obscure impulse, he set out for the village of Venning, which was about three miles from Skene.

It was a tiny place, with one public-house serving as a hotel to the rare travellers who found it needful to stop there, and Arthur felt that some explanation of his presence was necessary. Having seen at the station an advertisement of a large farm to let, he told the inquisitive landlady that he had come to see it. He arrived late at night. Nothing could be done then, so he occupied the time by trying to find out something about the Haddos.

Oliver was the local magnate, and his wealth would have made him an easy topic of conversation even without his eccentricity. The landlady roundly called him insane, and as an instance of his queerness told Arthur, to his great dismay, that Haddo would have no servants to sleep in the house: after dinner everyone was sent away to the various cottages in the park, and he remained alone with his wife. It was an awful thought that Margaret might be in the hands of a raving madman, with not a soul to protect her. But if he learnt no more than this of solid fact, Arthur heard much that was significant. To his amazement the old fear of the wizard had grown up again in that lonely place, and the garrulous woman gravely told him of Haddo's evil influence on the crops and cattle of farmers who had aroused his anger. He had had an altercation with his bailiff, and the man had died within a year. A small freeholder in the neighbourhood had refused to sell the land which would have rounded off the estate of Skene, and a disease had attacked every animal on his farm so that he was ruined. Arthur was impressed because, though she reported these rumours with mock scepticism as the stories of ignorant yokels and old women, the innkeeper had evidently a terrified belief in their truth. No one could deny that Haddo had got possession of the land he wanted; for, when it was put up to auction, no one would bid against him, and he bought it for a song.

As soon as he could do so naturally, Arthur asked after Margaret. The woman shrugged her shoulders. No one knew anything about her. She never came out of the park gates, but sometimes you could see her wandering about inside by herself. She saw no one. Haddo had long since quarrelled with the surrounding gentry; and though one old lady, the mother of a neighbouring landowner, had called when Margaret first came, she had not been admitted, and the visit was never returned.

'She'll come to no good, poor lady,' said the hostess of the inn. 'And they do say she's a perfect picture to look at.'

Arthur went to his room. He longed for the day to come. There was no certain means of seeing Margaret. It was useless to go to the park gates, since even the tradesmen were obliged to leave their goods at the lodge; but it appeared that she walked alone, morning and afternoon, and it might be possible to see her then. He decided to climb into the park and wait till he came upon her in some spot where they were not likely to be observed.

Next day the great heat of the last week was gone, and the melancholy sky was dark with lowering clouds. Arthur inquired for the road which led to Skene, and set out to walk the three miles which separated him from it. The country was grey and barren. There was a broad waste of heath, with gigantic boulders strewn as though in pre-historic times Titans had waged there a mighty battle. Here and there were trees, but they seemed hardly to withstand the fierce winds of winter; they were old and bowed before the storm. One of them attracted his attention. It had been struck by lightning and was riven asunder, leafless; but the maimed branches were curiously set on the trunk so that they gave it the appearance of a human being writhing in the torture of infernal agony. The wind whistled strangely. Arthur's heart sank as he walked on. He had never seen a country so desolate.

He came to the park gates at last and stood for some time in front of them. At the end of a long avenue, among the trees, he could see part of a splendid house. He walked along the wooden palisade that surrounded the park. Suddenly he came to a spot where a board had been broken down. He looked up and down the road. No one was in sight. He climbed up the low, steep bank, wrenched down a piece more of the fence, and slipped in.

He found himself in a dense wood. There was no sign of a path, and he advanced cautiously. The bracken was so thick and high that it easily concealed him. Dead owners had plainly spent much care upon the place, for here alone in the neighbourhood were trees in abundance; but of late it had been utterly neglected. It had run so wild that there were no traces now of its early formal arrangement; and it was so hard to make one's way, the vegetation was so thick, that it might almost have been some remnant of primeval forest. But at last he came to a grassy path and walked along it slowly. He stopped on a sudden, for he heard a sound. But it was only a pheasant that flew heavily through the low trees. He wondered what he should do if he came face to face with Oliver. The innkeeper had assured him that the squire seldom came out, but spent his days locked in the great attics at the top of the house. Smoke came from the chimneys of them, even in the hottest days of summer, and weird tales were told of the devilries there committed.

Arthur went on, hoping in the end to catch sight of Margaret, but he saw no one. In that grey, chilly day the woods, notwithstanding their greenery, were desolate and sad. A sombre mystery seemed to hang over them. At last he came to a stone bench at a cross-way among the trees, and, since it was the only resting-place he had seen, it struck him that Margaret might come there to sit down. He hid himself in the bracken. He had forgotten his watch and did not know how the time passed; he seemed to be there for hours.

But at length his heart gave a great beat against his ribs, for all at once, so silently that he had not heard her approach, Margaret came into view. She sat on the stone bench. For a moment he dared not move in case the sound frightened her. He could not tell how to make his presence known. But it was necessary to do something to attract her attention, and he could only hope that she would not cry out.

'Margaret,' he called softly.

She did not move, and he repeated her name more loudly. But still she made no sign that she had heard. He came forward and stood in front of her.

'Margaret.'

She looked at him quietly. He might have been someone she had never set eyes on, and yet from her composure she might have expected him to be standing there.

'Margaret, don't you know me?'

'What do you want?' she answered placidly.

He was so taken aback that he did not know what to say. She kept gazing at him steadfastly. On a sudden her calmness vanished, and she sprang to her feet.

'Is it you really?' she cried, terribly agitated. 'I thought it was only a shape that mimicked you.'

'Margaret, what do you mean? What has come over you?'

She stretched out her hand and touched him.

'I'm flesh and blood all right,' he said, trying to smile.

She shut her eyes for a moment, as though in an effort to collect herself.

'I've had hallucinations lately,' she muttered. 'I thought it was some trick played upon me.'

Suddenly she shook herself.

'But what are you doing here? You must go. How did you come? Oh, why won't you leave me alone?'

'I've been haunted by a feeling that something horrible was going to happen to you. I was obliged to come.'

'For God's sake, go. You can do me no good. If he finds out you've been here—'

She stopped, and her eyes were dilated with terror. Arthur seized her hands.

'Margaret, I can't go—I can't leave you like this. For Heaven's sake, tell me what is the matter. I'm so dreadfully frightened.'

He was aghast at the difference wrought in her during the two months since he had seen her last. Her colour was gone, and her face had the greyness of the dead. There were strange lines on her forehead, and her eyes had an unnatural glitter. Her youth had suddenly left her. She looked as if she were struck down by mortal illness.

'What is that matter with you?' he asked.

'Nothing.' She looked about her anxiously. 'Oh, why don't you go? How can you be so cruel?'

'I must do something for you,' he insisted.

She shook her head.

'It's too late. Nothing can help me now.' She paused; and when she spoke again it was with a voice so ghastly that it might have come from the lips of a corpse. 'I've found out at last what he's going to do with me He wants me for his great experiment, and the time is growing shorter.'

'What do you mean by saying he wants you?'

'He wants—my life.'

Arthur gave a cry of dismay, but she put up her hand.

'It's no use resisting. It can't do any good—I think I shall be glad when the moment comes. I shall at least cease to suffer.'

'But you must be mad.'

'I don't know. I know that he is.'

'But if your life is in danger, come away for God's sake. After all, you're free. He can't stop you.'

'I should have to go back to him, as I did last time,' she answered, shaking her head. 'I thought I was free then, but gradually I knew that he was calling me. I tried to resist, but I couldn't. I simply had to go to him.'

'But it's awful to think that you are alone with a man who's practically raving mad.'

'I'm safe for today,' she said quietly. 'It can only be done in the very hot weather. If there's no more this year, I shall live till next summer.'

'Oh, Margaret, for God's sake don't talk like that. I love you—I want to have you with me always. Won't you come away with me and let me take care of you? I promise you that no harm shall come to you.'

'You don't love me any more; you're only sorry for me now.'

'It's not true.'

'Oh yes it is. I saw it when we were in the country. Oh, I don't blame you. I'm a different woman from the one you loved. I'm not the Margaret you knew.'

'I can never care for anyone but you.'

She put her hand on his arm.

'If you loved me, I implore you to go. You don't know what you expose me to. And when I'm dead you must marry Susie. She loves you with all your heart, and she deserves your love.'

'Margaret, don't go. Come with me.'

'And take care. He will never forgive you for what you did. If he can, he will kill you.'

She started violently, as though she heard a sound. Her face was convulsed with sudden fear.

'For God's sake go, go!'

She turned from him quickly, and, before he could prevent her, had vanished. With heavy heart he plunged again into the bracken.

When Arthur had given his friends some account of this meeting, he stopped and looked at Dr Porhoët. The doctor went thoughtfully to his bookcase.

'What is it you want me to tell you?' he asked.

'I think the man is mad,' said Arthur. 'I found out at what asylum his mother was, and by good luck was able to see the superintendent on my way through London. He told me that he had grave doubts about Haddo's sanity, but it was impossible at present to take any steps. I came straight here because I wanted your advice. Granting that the man is out of his mind, is it possible that he may be trying some experiment that entails a sacrifice of human life?'

'Nothing is more probable,' said Dr Porhoët gravely.

Susie shuddered. She remembered the rumour that had reached her ears in Monte Carlo.

'They said there that he was attempting to make living creatures by a magical operation.' She glanced at the doctor, but spoke to Arthur. 'Just before you came in, our friend was talking of that book of Paracelsus in which he speaks of feeding the monsters he has made on human blood.'

Arthur gave a horrified cry.

'The most significant thing to my mind is that fact about Margaret which we are certain of,' said Dr Porhoët. 'All works that deal with the Black Arts are unanimous upon the supreme efficacy of the virginal condition.'

'But what is to be done?' asked Arthur is desperation. 'We can't leave her in the hands of a raving madman.' He turned on a sudden deathly white. 'For all we know she may be dead now.'

'Have you ever heard of Gilles de Rais?' said Dr Porhoët, continuing his reflections. 'That is the classic instance of human sacrifice. I know the country in which he lived; and the peasants to this day dare not pass at night in the neighbourhood of the ruined castle which was the scene of his horrible crimes.'

'It's awful to know that this dreadful danger hangs over her, and to be able to do nothing.'

'We can only wait,' said Dr Porhoët.

'And if we wait too long, we may be faced by a terrible catastrophe.'

'Fortunately we live in a civilized age. Haddo has a great care of his neck. I hope we are frightened unduly.'

It seemed to Susie that the chief thing was to distract Arthur, and she turned over in her mind some means of directing his attention to other matters.

'I was thinking of going down to Chartres for two days with Mrs Bloomfield,' she said. 'Won't you come with me? It is the most lovely cathedral in the world, and I think you will find it restful to wander about it for a little while. You can do no good, here or in London. Perhaps when you are calm, you will be able to think of something practical.'

Dr Porhoët saw what her plan was, and joined his entreaties to hers that Arthur should spend a day or two in a place that had no associations for him. Arthur was too exhausted to argue, and from sheer weariness consented. Next day Susie took him to Chartres. Mrs Bloomfield was no trouble to them, and Susie induced him to linger for a week in that pleasant, quiet town. They passed many hours in the stately cathedral, and they wandered about the surrounding country. Arthur was obliged to confess that the change had done him good, and a certain apathy succeeded the agitation from which he had suffered so long. Finally Susie persuaded him to spend three or four weeks in Brittany with Dr Porhoët, who was proposing to revisit the scenes of his childhood. They returned to Paris. When Arthur left her at the station, promising to meet her again in an hour at the restaurant where they were going to dine with Dr Porhoët, he thanked her for all she had done.

'I was in an absurdly hysterical condition,' he said, holding her hand. 'You've been quite angelic. I knew that nothing could be done, and yet I was tormented with the desire to do something. Now I've got myself in hand once more. I think my common sense was deserting me, and I was on the point of believing in the farrago of nonsense which they call magic. After all, it's absurd to think that Haddo is going to do any harm to Margaret. As soon at I get back to London, I'll see my lawyers, and I daresay something can be done. If he's really mad, we'll have to put him under restraint, and Margaret will be free. I shall never forget your kindness.'

Susie smiled and shrugged her shoulders.

She was convinced that he would forget everything if Margaret came back to him. But she chid herself for the bitterness of the thought. She loved him, and she was glad to be able to do anything for him.

She returned to the hotel, changed her frock, and walked slowly to the Chien Noir. It always exhilarated her to come back to Paris; and she looked with happy, affectionate eyes at the plane trees, the yellow trams that rumbled along incessantly, and the lounging people. When she arrived, Dr Porhoët was waiting, and his delight at seeing her again was flattering and pleasant. They talked of Arthur. They wondered why he was late.

In a moment he came in. They saw at once that something quite extraordinary had taken place.

'Thank God, I've found you at last!' he cried.

His face was moving strangely. They had never seen him so discomposed.

'I've been round to your hotel, but I just missed you. Oh, why did you insist on my going away?'

'What on earth's the matter?' cried Susie.

'Something awful has happened to Margaret.'

Susie started to her feet with a sudden cry of dismay.

'How do you know?' she asked quickly.

He looked at them for a moment and flushed. He kept his eyes upon them, as though actually to force his listeners into believing what he was about to say.

'I feel it,' he answered hoarsely.

'What do you mean?'

'It came upon me quite suddenly, I can't explain why or how. I only know that something has happened.'

He began again to walk up and down, prey to an agitation that was frightful to behold. Susie and Dr Porhoët stared at him helplessly. They tried to think of something to say that would calm him.

'Surely if anything had occurred, we should have been informed.'

He turned to Susie angrily.

'How do you suppose we could know anything? She was quite helpless. She was imprisoned like a rat in a trap.'

'But, my dear friend, you mustn't give way in this fashion,' said the doctor. 'What would you say of a patient who came to you with such a story?'

Arthur answered the question with a shrug of the shoulders.

'I should say he was absurdly hysterical.'

'Well?'

'I can't help it, the feeling's there. If you try all night you'll never be able to argue me out of it. I feel it in every bone of my body. I couldn't be more certain if I saw Margaret lying dead in front of me.'

Susie saw that it was indeed useless to reason with him. The only course was to accept his conviction and make the best of it.

'What do you want us to do?' she asked.

'I want you both to come to England with me at once. If we start now we can catch the evening train.'

Susie did not answer, but she got up. She touched the doctor on the arm.

'Please come,' she whispered.

He nodded and untucked the napkin he had already arranged over his waistcoat.

'I've got a cab at the door,' said Arthur.

'And what about clothes for Miss Susie?' said the doctor.

'Oh, we can't wait for that,' cried Arthur. 'For God's sake, come quickly.'

Susie knew that there was plenty of time to fetch a few necessary things before the train started, but Arthur's impatience was too great to be withstood.

'It doesn't matter,' she said. 'I can get all I want in England.'

He hurried them to the door and told the cabman to drive to the station as quickly as ever he could.

'For Heaven's sake, calm down a little,' said Susie. 'You'll be no good to anyone in that state.'

'I feel certain we're too late.'

'Nonsense! I'm convinced that you'll find Margaret safe and sound.'

He did not answer. He gave a sigh of relief as they drove into the courtyard of the station.

XIV

SUSIE NEVER FORGOT the horror of that journey to England. They arrived in London early in the morning and, without stopping, drove to Euston. For three or four days there had been unusual heat, and even at that hour the streets were sultry and airless. The train north was crowded, and it seemed impossible to get a breath of air. Her head ached, but she was obliged to keep a cheerful demeanour in the effort to allay Arthur's increasing anxiety. Dr Porhoët sat in front of her. After the sleepless night his eyes were heavy and his face deeply lined. He was exhausted. At length, after much tiresome changing, they reached Venning. She had expected a greater coolness in that northern country; but there was a hot blight over the place, and, as they walked to the inn from the little station, they could hardly drag their limbs along.

Arthur had telegraphed from London that they must have rooms ready, and the landlady expected them. She recognized Arthur. He passionately desired to ask her whether anything had happened since he went away, but forced himself to be silent for a while. He greeted her with cheerfulness.

'Well, Mrs Smithers, what has been going on since I left you?' he cried.

'Of course you wouldn't have heard, sir,' she answered gravely.

He began to tremble, but with an almost superhuman effort controlled his voice.

'Has the squire hanged himself?' he asked lightly.

'No sir—but the poor lady's dead.'

He did not answer. He seemed turned to stone. He stared with ghastly eyes.

'Poor thing!' said Susie, forcing herself to speak. 'Was it—very sudden?'

The woman turned to Susie, glad to have someone with whom to discuss the event. She took no notice of Arthur's agony.

'Yes, mum; no one expected it. She died quite sudden like. She was only buried this morning.'

'What did she die of?' asked Susie, her eyes on Arthur.

She feared that he would faint. She wanted enormously to get him away, but did not know how to manage it.

'They say it was heart disease,' answered the landlady. 'Poor thing! It's a happy release for her.'

'Won't you get us some tea, Mrs Smithers? We're very tired, and we should like something immediately.'

'Yes, miss. I'll get it at once.'

The good woman bustled away. Susie quickly locked the door. She seized Arthur's arm.

'Arthur, Arthur.'

She expected him to break down. She looked with agony at Dr Porhoët, who stood helplessly by.

'You couldn't have done anything if you'd been here. You heard what the woman said. If Margaret died of heart disease, your suspicions were quite without ground.'

He shook her away, almost violently.

'For God's sake, speak to us,' cried Susie.

His silence terrified her more than would have done any outburst of grief. Dr Porhoët went up to him gently.

'Don't try to be brave, my friend. You will not suffer as much if you allow yourself a little weakness.'

'For Heaven's sake leave me alone!' said Arthur, hoarsely.

They drew back and watched him silently. Susie heard their hostess come along to the sitting-room with tea, and she unlocked the door. The landlady brought in the things. She was on the point of leaving them when Arthur stopped her.

'How do you know that Mrs Haddo died of heart disease?' he asked suddenly.

His voice was hard and stern. He spoke with a peculiar abruptness that made the poor woman look at him in amazement.

'Dr Richardson told me so.'

'Had he been attending her?'

'Yes, sir. Mr Haddo had called him in several times to see his lady.'

'Where does Dr Richardson live?'

'Why, sir, he lives at the white house near the station.'

She could not make out why Arthur asked these questions.

'Did Mr Haddo go to the funeral?'

'Oh yes, sir. I've never seen anyone so upset.'

'That'll do. You can go.'

Susie poured out the tea and handed a cup to Arthur. To her surprise, he drank the tea and ate some bread and butter. She could not understand him. The expression of strain, and the restlessness which had been so painful, were both gone from his face, and it was set now to a look of grim determination. At last he spoke to them.

'I'm going to see this doctor. Margaret's heart was as sound as mine.'

'What are you going to do?'

'Do?'

He turned on her with a peculiar fierceness.

'I'm going to put a rope round that man's neck, and if the law won't help me, by God, I'll kill him myself.'

'*Mais, mon ami, vous êtes fou,*' cried Dr Porhoët, springing up.

Arthur put out his hand angrily, as though to keep him back. The frown on his face grew darker.

'You *must* leave me alone. Good Heavens, the time has gone by for tears and lamentation. After all I've gone through for months, I can't weep because Margaret is dead. My heart is dried up. But I know that she didn't die naturally, and I'll never rest so long as that fellow lives.'

He stretched out his hands and with clenched jaws prayed that one day he might hold the man's neck between them, and see his face turn livid and purple as he died.

'I am going to this fool of a doctor, and then I shall go to Skene.'

'You must let us come with you,' said Susie.

'You need not be frightened,' he answered. 'I shall not take any steps of my own till I find the law is powerless.'

'I want to come with you all the same.'

'As you like.'

Susie went out and ordered a trap to be got ready. But since Arthur would not wait, she arranged that it should be sent for them to the doctor's door. They went there at once, on foot.

Dr Richardson was a little man of five-and-fifty, with a fair beard that was now nearly white, and prominent blue eyes. He spoke with a broad Staffordshire accent. There was in him something of the farmer, something of the well-to-do tradesman, and at the first glance his intelligence did not impress one.

Arthur was shewn with his two friends into the consulting-room, and after a short interval the doctor came in. He was dressed in flannels and had an old-fashioned racket in his hand.

'I'm sorry to have kept you waiting, but Mrs Richardson has got a few lady-friends to tea, and I was just in the middle of a set.'

His effusiveness jarred upon Arthur, whose manner by contrast became more than usually abrupt.

'I have just learnt of the death of Mrs Haddo. I was her guardian and her oldest friend. I came to you in the hope that you would be able to tell me something about it.'

Dr Richardson gave him at once, the suspicious glance of a stupid man.

'I don't know why you come to me instead of to her husband. He will be able to tell you all that you wish to know.'

'I came to you as a fellow-practitioner,' answered Arthur. 'I am at St Luke's Hospital.' He pointed to his card, which Dr Richardson still held. 'And my friend is Dr Porhoët, whose name will be familiar to you with respect to his studies in Malta Fever.'

'I think I read an article of yours in the *B.M.J.*' said the country doctor.

His manner assumed a singular hostility. He had no sympathy with London specialists, whose attitude towards the general practitioner he resented. He was pleased to sneer at their pretensions to omniscience, and quite willing to pit himself against them.

'What can I do for you, Mr Burdon?'

'I should be very much obliged if you would tell me as exactly as possible how Mrs Haddo died.'

'It was a very simple case of endocarditis.'

'May I ask how long before death you were called in?'

The doctor hesitated. He reddened a little.

'I'm not inclined to be cross-examined,' he burst out, suddenly making up his mind to be angry. 'As a surgeon I daresay your knowledge of cardiac diseases is neither extensive nor peculiar. But this was a very simple case, and everything was done that was possible. I don't think there's anything I can tell you.'

Arthur took no notice of the outburst.

'How many times did you see her?'

'Really, sir, I don't understand your attitude. I can't see that you have any right to question me.'

'Did you have a post-mortem?'

'Certainly not. In the first place there was no need, as the cause of death was perfectly clear, and secondly you must know as well as I do that the relatives are very averse to anything of the sort. You gentlemen in Harley Street don't understand the conditions of private practice. We haven't the time to do post-mortems to gratify a needless curiosity.'

Arthur was silent for a moment. The little man was evidently convinced that there was nothing odd about Margaret's death, but his foolishness was as great as his obstinacy. It was clear that several motives would induce him to put every obstacle in Arthur's way, and chief of these was the harm it would do him if it were discovered that he had given a certificate of death carelessly. He would naturally do anything to avoid social scandal. Still Arthur was obliged to speak.

'I think I'd better tell you frankly that I'm not satisfied, Dr Richardson. I can't persuade myself that this lady's death was due to natural causes.'

'Stuff and nonsense!' cried the other angrily. 'I've been in practice for hard upon thirty-five years, and I'm willing to stake my professional reputation on it.'

'I have reason to think you are mistaken.'

'And to what do you ascribe death, pray?' asked the doctor.

'I don't know yet.'

'Upon my soul, I think you must be out of your senses. Really, sir, your behaviour is childish. You tell me that you are a surgeon of some eminence …'

'I surely told you nothing of the sort.'

'Anyhow, you read papers before learned bodies and have them printed. And you come with as silly a story as a Staffordshire peasant who thinks someone has been trying to poison him because he's got a stomach-ache. You may be a very admirable surgeon, but I venture to think I am more capable than you of judging in a case which I attended and you know nothing about.'

'I mean to take the steps necessary to get an order for exhumation, Dr Richardson, and I cannot help thinking it will be worth your while to assist me in every possible way.'

'I shall do nothing of the kind. I think you very impertinent, sir. There is no need for exhumation, and I shall do everything in my power to prevent it. And I tell you as chairman of the board of magistrates, my opinion will have as great value as any specialist's in Harley Street.'

He flounced to the door and held it open. Susie and Dr Porhoët walked out; and Arthur, looking down thoughtfully, followed on their heels. Dr Richardson slammed the street-door angrily.

Dr Porhoët slipped his arm in Arthur's.

'You must be reasonable, my friend,' he said. 'From his own point of view this doctor has all the rights on his side. You have nothing to justify your demands. It is monstrous to expect that for a vague suspicion you will be able to get an order for exhumation.'

Arthur did not answer. The trap was waiting for them.

'Why do you want to see Haddo?' insisted the doctor. 'You will do no more good than you have with Dr Richardson.'

'I have made up my mind to see him,' answered Arthur shortly. 'But there is no need that either of you should accompany me.'

'If you go, we will come with you,' said Susie.

Without a word Arthur jumped into the dog-cart, and Susie took a seat by his side. Dr Porhoët, with a shrug of the shoulders, mounted behind. Arthur whipped up the pony, and at a smart trot they traversed the three miles across the barren heath that lay between Venning and Skene.

When they reached the park gates, the lodgekeeper, as luck would have it, was standing just inside, and she held one of them open for her little boy to come in. He was playing in the road and showed no inclination to do so. Arthur jumped down.

'I want to see Mr Haddo,' he said.

'Mr Haddo's not in,' she answered roughly.

She tried to close the gate, but Arthur quickly put his foot inside.

'Nonsense! I have to see him on a matter of great importance.'

'Mr Haddo's orders are that no one is to be admitted.'

'I can't help that, I'm proposing to come in, all the same.'

Susie and Dr Porhoët came forward. They promised the small boy a shilling to hold their horse.

'Now then, get out of here,' cried the woman. 'You're not coming in, whatever you say.'

She tried to push the gate to, but Arthur's foot prevented her. Paying no heed to her angry expostulations, he forced his way in. He walked quickly up the drive. The lodge-keeper accompanied him, with shrill abuse. The gate was left unguarded, and the others were able to follow without difficulty.

'You can go to the door, but you won't see Mr Haddo,' the woman cried angrily. 'You'll get me sacked for letting you come.'

Susie saw the house. It was a fine old building in the Elizabethan style, but much in need of repair; and it had the desolate look of a place that has been uninhabited. The garden that surrounded it had been allowed to run wild, and the avenue up which they walked was green with rank weeds. Here and there a fallen tree, which none had troubled to remove, marked the owner's negligence. Arthur went to the door and rang a bell. They heard it clang through the house as though not a soul lived there. A man came to the door, and as soon as he opened it, Arthur, expecting to be refused admission, pushed in. The fellow was as angry as the virago, his wife, who explained noisily how the three strangers had got into the park.

'You can't see the squire, so you'd better be off. He's up in the attics, and no one's allowed to go to him.'

The man tried to push Arthur away.

'Be off with you, or I'll send for the police.'

'Don't be a fool,' said Arthur. 'I mean to find Mr Haddo.'

The housekeeper and his wife broke out with abuse, to which Arthur listened in silence. Susie and Dr Porhoët stood by anxiously. They did not know what to do. Suddenly a voice at their elbows made them start, and the two servants were immediately silent.

'What can I do for you?'

Oliver Haddo was standing motionless behind them. It startled Susie that he should have come upon them so suddenly, without a sound. Dr Porhoët, who had not seen him for some time, was astounded at the change which had taken place in him. The corpulence which had been his before was become now a positive disease. He was enormous. His chin was a mass of heavy folds distended with fat, and his cheeks were puffed up so that his eyes were preternaturally small. He peered at you from between the swollen lids. All his features had sunk into that hideous obesity. His ears were horribly bloated, and the lobes were large and swelled. He had apparently a difficulty in breathing, for his large mouth, with its scarlet, shining lips, was constantly open. He had grown much balder and now there was only a crescent of long hair stretching across the back of his head from ear to ear. There was something terrible about that great shining scalp. His paunch was huge; he was a very tall man and held himself erect, so that it protruded like a vast barrel. His hands were infinitely repulsive; they were red and soft and moist. He was sweating freely, and beads of perspiration stood on his forehead and on his shaven lip.

For a moment they all looked at one another in silence. Then Haddo turned to his servants.

'Go,' he said.

As though frightened out of their wits, they made for the door and with a bustling hurry flung themselves out. A torpid smile crossed his face as he watched them go. Then he moved a step nearer his visitors. His manner had still the insolent urbanity which was customary to him.

'And now, my friends, will you tell me how I can be of service to you?'

'I have come about Margaret's death,' said Arthur.

Haddo, as was his habit, did not immediately answer. He looked slowly from Arthur to Dr Porhoët, and from Dr Porhoët to Susie. His eyes rested on her hat, and she felt uncomfortably that he was inventing some gibe about it.

'I should have thought this hardly the moment to intrude upon my sorrow,' he said at last. 'If you have condolences to offer, I venture to suggest that you might conveniently send them by means of the penny post.'

Arthur frowned.

'Why did you not let me know that she was ill?' he asked.

'Strange as it may seem to you, my worthy friend, it never occurred to me that my wife's health could be any business of yours.'

A faint smile flickered once more on Haddo's lips, but his eyes had still the peculiar hardness which was so uncanny. Arthur looked at him steadily.

'I have every reason to believe that you killed her,' he said.

Haddo's face did not for an instant change its expression.

'And have you communicated your suspicions to the police?'

'I propose to.'

'And, if I am not indiscreet, may I inquire upon what you base them?'

'I saw Margaret three weeks ago, and she told me that she went in terror of her life.'

'Poor Margaret! She had always the romantic temperament. I think it was that which first brought us together.'

'You damned scoundrel!' cried Arthur.

'My dear fellow, pray moderate your language. This is surely not an occasion when you should give way to your lamentable taste for abuse. You outrage all Miss Boyd's susceptibilities.' He turned to her with an airy wave of his fat hand. 'You must forgive me if I do not offer you the hospitality of Skene, but the loss I have so lately sustained does not permit me to indulge in the levity of entertaining.'

He gave her an ironical, low bow; then looked once more at Arthur.

'If I can be of no further use to you, perhaps you would leave me to my own reflections. The lodgekeeper will give you the exact address of the village constable.'

Arthur did not answer. He stared into vacancy, as if he were turning over things in his mind. Then he turned sharply on his heel and walked towards the gate. Susie and Dr Porhoët, taken completely aback, did not know what to do; and Haddo's little eyes twinkled as he watched their discomfiture.

'I always thought that your friend had deplorable manners,' he murmured.

Susie, feeling very ridiculous, flushed, and Dr Porhoët awkwardly took off his hat. As they walked away, they felt Haddo's mocking gaze fixed upon them, and they were heartily thankful to reach the gate. They found Arthur waiting for them.

'I beg your pardon,' he said, 'I forgot that I was not alone.'

The three of them drove slowly back to the inn.

'What are you going to do now?' asked Susie.

For a long time Arthur made no reply, and Susie thought he could not have heard her. At last he broke the silence.

'I see that I can do nothing by ordinary methods. I realize that it is useless to make a public outcry. There is only my own conviction that Margaret came to a violent end, and I cannot expect anyone to pay heed to that.'

'After all, it's just possible that she really died of heart disease.'

Arthur gave Susie a long look. He seemed to consider her words deliberately.

'Perhaps there are means to decide that conclusively,' he replied at length, thoughtfully, as though he were talking to himself.

'What are they?'

Arthur did not answer. When they came to the door of the inn, he stopped.

'Will you go in? I wish to take a walk by myself,' he said.

Susie looked at him anxiously.

'You're not going to do anything rash?'

'I will do nothing till I have made quite sure that Margaret was foully murdered.'

He turned on his heel and walked quickly away. It was late now, and they found a frugal meal waiting for them in the little sitting-room. It seemed no use to delay it till Arthur came back, and silently, sorrowfully, they ate. Afterwards, the doctor smoked cigarettes, while Susie sat at the open window and looked at the stars. She thought of Margaret, of her beauty and her charming frankness, of her fall and of her miserable end; and she began to cry quietly. She knew enough of the facts now to be aware that the wretched girl was not to blame for anything that had happened. A cruel fate had fallen upon her, and she had been as powerless as in the old tales Phaedra, the daughter of Minos, or Myrrha of the beautiful hair. The hours passed, and still Arthur did not return. Susie thought now only of him, and she was frightfully anxious.

But at last he came in. The night was far advanced. He put down his hat and sat down. For a long while he looked silently at Dr. Porhoët.

'What is it, my friend?' asked the good doctor at length.

'Do you remember that you told us once of an experiment you made in Alexandria?' he said, after some hesitation.

He spoke in a curious voice.

'You told us that you took a boy, and when he looked in a magic mirror, he saw things which he could not possibly have known.'

'I remember very well,' said the doctor.

'I was much inclined to laugh at you at the time. I was convinced that the boy was a knave who deceived you.'

'Yes?'

'Of late I've thought of that story often. Some hidden recess of my memory has been opened, and I seem to remember strange things. Was I the boy who looked in the ink?'

'Yes,' said the doctor quietly.

Arthur did not say anything. A profound silence fell upon them, while Susie and the doctor watched him intently. They wondered what was in his mind.

'There is a side of my character which I did not know till lately,'

Arthur said at last. 'When first it dawned upon me, I fought against it. I said to myself that deep down in all of us, a relic from the long past, is the remains of the superstition that blinded our fathers; and it is needful for the man of science to fight against it with all his might. And yet it was stronger than I. Perhaps my birth, my early years, in those Eastern lands where everyone believes in the super-natural, affected me although I did not know it. I began to remember vague, mysterious things, which I never knew had been part of my knowledge. And at last one day it seemed that a new window was opened on to my soul, and I saw with extraordinary clearness the incident which you had described. I knew suddenly it was part of my own experience. I saw you take me by the hand and pour the ink on my palm and bid me look at it. I felt again the strange glow that thrilled me, and with an indescribable bitterness I saw things in the mirror which were not there before. I saw people whom I had never seen. I saw them perform certain actions. And some force I knew not, obliged me to speak. And at length everything grew dim, and I was as exhausted as if I had not eaten all day.'

He went over to the open window and looked out. Neither of the others spoke. The look on Arthur's face, curiously outlined by the light of the lamp, was very stern. He seemed to undergo some mental struggle of extraordinary violence. He breath came quickly. At last he turned and faced them. He spoke hoarsely, quickly.

'I must see Margaret again.'

'Arthur, you're mad!' cried Susie.

He went up to Dr Porhoët and, putting his hands on his shoulders, looked fixedly into his eyes.

'You have studied this science. You know all that can be known of it. I want you to show her to me.'

The doctor gave an exclamation of alarm.

'My dear fellow, how can I? I have read many books, but I have never practised anything. I have only studied these matters for my amusement.'

'Do you believe it can be done?'

'I don't understand what you want.'

'I want you to bring her to me so that I may speak with her, so that I may find out the truth.'

'Do you think I am God that I can raise men from the dead?'

Arthur's hands pressed him down in the chair from which he sought to rise. His fingers were clenched on the old man's shoulders so that he could hardly bear the pain.

'You told us how once Eliphas Levi raised a spirit. Do you believe that was true?'

'I don't know. I have always kept an open mind. There was much to be said on both sides.'

'Well, now you must believe. You must do what he did.'

'You must be mad, Arthur.'

'I want you to come to that spot where I saw her last. If her spirit can be brought back anywhere, it must be in that place where she sat and wept. You know all the ceremonies and all the words that are necessary.'

But Susie came forward and laid her hand on his arm. He looked at her with a frown.

'Arthur, you know in your heart that nothing can come of it. You're only increasing your unhappiness. And even if you could bring her from the grave for a moment, why can you not let her troubled soul rest in peace?'

'If she died a natural death we shall have no power over her, but if her death was violent perhaps her spirit is earthbound still. I tell you I must be certain. I want to see her once more, and afterwards I shall know what to do.'

'I cannot, I cannot,' said the doctor.

'Give me the books and I will do it alone.'

'You know that I have nothing here.'

'Then you must help me,' said Arthur. 'After all, why should you mind? We perform a certain operation, and if nothing happens we are no worse off then before. On the other hand, if we succeed.... Oh, for God's sake, help me! If you have any care for my happiness do this one thing for me.'

He stepped back and looked at the doctor. The Frenchman's eyes were fixed upon the ground.

'It's madness,' he muttered.

He was intensely moved by Arthur's appeal. At last he shrugged his shoulders.

'After all, if it is but a foolish mummery it can do no harm.'

'You will help me?' cried Arthur.

'If it can give you any peace or any satisfaction, I am willing to do what I can. But I warn you to be prepared for a great disappointment.'

XV

ARTHUR WISHED TO set about the invocation then and there, but Dr Porhoët said it was impossible. They were all exhausted after the long journey, and it was necessary to get certain things together without which nothing could be done. In his heart he thought that a night's rest would bring Arthur to a more reasonable mind. When the light of day shone upon the earth he would be ashamed of the desire which ran counter to all his prepossessions. But Arthur remembered that on the next day it would be exactly a week since Margaret's death, and it seemed to him that then their spells might have a greater efficacy.

When they came down in the morning and greeted one another, it was plain that none of them had slept.

'Are you still of the same purpose as last night?' asked Dr Porhoët gravely.

'I am.'

The doctor hesitated nervously.

'It will be necessary, if you wish to follow out the rules of the old necromancers, to fast through the whole day.'

'I am ready to do anything.'

'It will be no hardship to me,' said Susie, with a little hysterical laugh. 'I feel I couldn't eat a thing if I tried.'

'I think the whole affair is sheer folly,' said Dr Porhoët.

'You promised me you would try.'

The day, the long summer day, passed slowly. There was a hard brilliancy in the sky that reminded the Frenchman of those Egyptian heavens when the earth seemed crushed beneath a bowl of molten fire. Arthur was too restless to remain indoors and left the others to their own devices. He walked without aim, as fast as he could go; he felt no weariness. The burning sun beat down upon him, but he did not know it. The hours passed with lagging feet. Susie lay on her bed and tried to read. Her nerves were so taut that, when there was a sound in the courtyard of a pail falling on the cobbles, she cried out in terror. The sun rose, and presently her window was flooded with quivering rays of gold. It was midday. The day passed, and it was afternoon. The evening came, but it brought no freshness. Meanwhile Dr Porhoët sat in the little parlour, with his head between his hands, trying by a great mental effort to bring back to his memory all that he had read. His heart began to beat more quickly. Then the night fell, and one by one the stars shone out. There was no wind. The air was heavy. Susie came downstairs and began to talk with Dr Porhoët. But they spoke in a low tone, as if they were afraid that someone would overhear. They were faint now with want of food. The hours went one by one, and the striking of a clock filled them each time with a mysterious apprehension. The lights in the village were put out little by little, and everybody slept. Susie had lighted the lamp, and they watched beside it. A cold shiver passed through her.

'I feel as though someone were lying dead in the room,' she said.

'Why does not Arthur come?'

They spoke inconsequently, and neither heeded what the other said. The window was wide open, but the air was difficult to breathe. And now the silence was so unusual that Susie grew strangely nervous. She tried to think of the noisy streets in Paris, the constant roar of traffic, and the shuffling of the crowds toward evening as the work people returned to their homes. She stood up.

'There's no air tonight. Look at the trees. Not a leaf is moving.'

'Why does not Arthur come?' repeated the doctor.

'There's no moon tonight. It will be very dark at Skene.'

'He's walked all day. He should be here by now.'

Susie felt an extraordinary oppression, and she panted for breath. At last they heard a step on the road outside, and Arthur stood at the window.

'Are you ready to come?' he said.

'We've been waiting for you.'

They joined him, bringing the few things that Dr Porhoët had said were necessary, and they walked along the solitary road that led to Skene. On each side the heather stretched into the dark night, and there was a blackness about it that was ominous. There was no sound save that of their own steps. Dimly, under the stars, they saw the desolation with which they were surrounded. The way seemed very long. They were utterly exhausted, and they could hardly drag one foot after the other.

'You must let me rest for a minute,' said Susie.

They did not answer, but stopped, and she sat on a boulder by the wayside. They stood motionless in front of her, waiting patiently till she was ready. After a little while she forced herself to get up.

'Now I can go,' she said.

Still they did not speak, but walked on. They moved like figures in a dream, with a stealthy directness, as though they acted under the influence of another's will. Suddenly the road stopped, and they found themselves at the gates of Skene.

'Follow me very closely,' said Arthur.

He turned on one side, and they followed a paling. Susie could feel that they walked along a narrow path. She could see hardly two steps in front of her. At last he stood still.

'I came here earlier in the night and made the opening easier to get through.'

He turned back a broken piece of railing and slipped in. Susie followed, and Dr Porhoët entered after her.

'I can see nothing,' said Susie.

'Give my your hand, and I will lead you.'

They walked with difficulty through the tangled bracken, among closely planted trees. They stumbled, and once Dr Porhoët fell. It seemed that they went a long way. Susie's heart beat fast with anxiety. All her weariness was forgotten.

Then Arthur stopped them, and he pointed in front of him. Through an opening in the trees, they saw the house. All the windows were dark except those just under the roof, and from them came bright lights.

'Those are the attics which he uses as a laboratory. You see, he is working now. There is no one else in the house.'

Susie was curiously fascinated by the flaming lights. There was an awful mystery in those unknown labours which absorbed Oliver Haddo night after night till the sun rose. What horrible things were done there, hidden from the eyes of men? By himself in that vast house the madman performed ghastly experiments; and who could tell what dark secrets he trafficked in?

'There is no danger that he will come out,' said Arthur. 'He remains there till the break of day.'

He took her hand again and led her on. Back they went among the trees, and presently they were on a pathway. They walked along with greater safety.

'Are you all right, Porhoët?' asked Arthur.

'Yes.'

But the trees grew thicker and the night more sombre. Now the stars were shut out, and they could hardly see in front of them.

'Here we are,' said Arthur.

They stopped, and found that there was in front of them a green space formed by four cross-ways. In the middle a stone bench gleamed vaguely against the darkness.

'This is where Margaret sat when last I saw her.'

'I can see to do nothing here,' said the doctor.

They had brought two flat bowls of brass to serve as censers, and these Arthur gave to Dr Porhoët. He stood by Susie's side while the doctor busied himself with his preparations. They saw him move to and fro. They saw him bend to the ground. Presently there was a crackling of wood, and from the brazen bowls red flames shot up. They did not know what he burnt, but there were heavy clouds of smoke, and a strong, aromatic odour filled the air. Now and again the doctor was sharply silhouetted against the light. His slight, bowed figure was singularly mysterious. When Susie caught sight of his face, she saw that it was touched with a strong emotion. The work he was at affected him so that his doubts, his fears, had vanished. He looked like some old alchemist busied with unnatural things. Susie's heart began to beat painfully. She was growing desperately frightened and stretched out her hand so that she might touch Arthur. Silently he put his arm through hers. And now the doctor was tracing strange signs upon the ground. The flames died down and only a glow remained, but he seemed to have no difficulty in seeing what he was about. Susie could not discern what figures he drew. Then he put more twigs upon the braziers, and the flames sprang up once more, cutting the darkness sharply as with a sword.

'Now come,' he said.

But, inexplicably, a sudden terror seized Susie. She felt that the hairs of her head stood up, and a cold sweat broke out on her body. Her limbs had grown on an instant inconceivably heavy so that she could not move. A panic such as she had never known came upon her, and, except that her legs would not carry her, she would have fled blindly. She began to tremble. She tried to speak, but her tongue clave to her throat.

'I can't, I'm afraid,' she muttered hoarsely.

'You must. Without you we can do nothing,' said Arthur.

She could not reason with herself. She had forgotten everything except that she was frightened to death. Her heart was beating so quickly that she almost fainted. And now Arthur held her, so firmly that she winced.

'Let me go,' she whispered. 'I won't help you. I'm afraid.'

'You must,' he said. 'You must.'

'No.'

'I tell you, you must come.'

'Why?'

Her deadly fear expressed itself in a passion of sudden anger.

'Because you love me, and it's the only way to give me peace.'

She uttered a low wail of pain, and her terror gave way to shame. She blushed to the roots of her hair because he too knew her secret. And then she was seized again with anger because he had the cruelty to taunt her with it. She had recovered her courage now, and she stepped forward. Dr. Porhoët told her where to stand. Arthur took his place in front of her.

'You must not move till I give you leave. If you go outside the figure I have drawn, I cannot protect you.'

For a moment Dr Porhoët stood in perfect silence. Then he began to recite strange words in Latin. Susie heard him but vaguely. She did not know the sense, and his voice was so low that she could not have distinguished the words. But his intonation had lost that gentle irony which was habitual to him, and he spoke with a trembling gravity that was extraordinarily impressive. Arthur stood immobile as a rock. The flames died away, and they saw one another only by the glow of the ashes, dimly, like persons in a vision of death. There was silence. Then the necromancer spoke again, and now his voice was louder. He seemed to utter weird invocations, but they were in a tongue that the others knew not. And while he spoke the light from the burning cinders on a sudden went out.

It did not die, but was sharply extinguished, as though by invisible hands. And now the darkness was more sombre than that of the blackest night. The trees that surrounded them were hidden from their eyes, and the whiteness of the stone bench was seen no longer. They stood but a little way one from the other, but each might have stood alone. Susie strained her eyes, but she could see nothing. She looked up quickly; the stars were gone out, and she could see no further over her head than round about. The darkness was terrifying. And from it, Dr Porhoët's voice had a ghastly effect. It seemed to come, wonderfully changed, from the void of bottomless chaos. Susie clenched her hands so that she might not faint.

All at once she started, for the old man's voice was cut by a sudden gust of wind. A moment before, the utter silence had been almost intolerable, and now a storm seemed to have fallen upon them. The trees all around them rocked in the wind; they heard the branches creak; and they heard the hissing of the leaves. They were in the midst of a hurricane. And they felt the earth sway as it resisted the straining roots of great trees, which seemed to be dragged up by the force of the furious gale. Whistling and roaring, the wind stormed all about them, and the doctor, raising his voice, tried in vain to command it. But the strangest thing of all was that, where they stood, there was no sign of the raging blast. The air immediately about them was as still as it had been before, and not a hair on Susie's head was moved.

And it was terrible to hear the tumult, and yet to be in a calm that was almost unnatural.

On a sudden, Dr Porhoët raised his voice, and with a sternness they had never heard in it before, cried out in that unknown language. Then he called upon Margaret. He called her name three times. In the uproar Susie could scarcely hear. Terror had seized her again, but in her confusion she remembered his command, and she dared not move.

'Margaret, Margaret, Margaret.'

Without a pause between, as quickly as a stone falls to the ground, the din which was all about them ceased. There was no gradual diminution. But at one moment there was a roaring hurricane and at the next a silence so complete that it might have been the silence of death.

And then, seeming to come out of nothingness, extraordinarily, they heard with a curious distinctness the sound of a woman weeping. Susie's heart stood still. They heard the sound of a woman weeping, and they recognized the voice of Margaret. A groan of anguish burst from Arthur's lips, and he was on the point of starting forward. But quickly Dr Porhoët put out his hand to prevent him. The sound was heartrending, the sobbing of a woman who had lost all hope, the sobbing of a woman terrified. If Susie had been able to stir, she would have put her hands to her ears to shut out the ghastly agony of it.

And in a moment, notwithstanding the heavy darkness of the starless night, Arthur saw her. She was seated on the stone bench as when last he had spoken with her. In her anguish she sought not to hide her face. She looked at the ground, and the tears fell down her cheeks. Her bosom heaved with the pain of her weeping.

Then Arthur knew that all his suspicions were justified.

XVI

ARTHUR WOULD NOT leave the little village of Venning. Neither Susie nor the doctor could get him to make any decision. None of them spoke of the night which they had spent in the woods of Skene; but it coloured all their thoughts, and they were not free for a single moment from the ghastly memory of it. They seemed still to hear the sound of that passionate weeping. Arthur was moody. When he was with them, he spoke little; he opposed a stubborn resistance to their efforts at diverting his mind. He spent long hours by himself, in the country, and they had no idea what he did. Susie was terribly anxious. He had lost his balance so completely that she was prepared for any rashness. She divined that his hatred of Haddo was no longer within the bounds of reason. The desire for vengeance filled him entirely, so that he was capable of any violence.

Several days went by.

At last, in concert with Dr Porhoët, she determined to make one more attempt. It was late at night, and they sat with open windows in the sitting-room of the inn. There was a singular oppressiveness in the air which suggested that a thunderstorm was at hand. Susie prayed for it; for she ascribed to the peculiar heat of the last few days much of Arthur's sullen irritability.

'Arthur, you *must* tell us what you are going to do,' she said. 'It is useless to stay here. We are all so ill and nervous that we cannot consider anything rationally. We want you to come away with us tomorrow.'

'You can go if you choose,' he said. 'I shall remain till that man is dead.'

'It is madness to talk like that. You can do nothing. You are only making yourself worse by staying here.'

'I have quite made up my mind.'

'The law can offer you no help, and what else can you do?'

She asked the question, meaning if possible to get from him some hint of his intentions; but the grimness of his answer, though it only confirmed her vague suspicions, startled her.

'If I can do nothing else, I shall shoot him like a dog.'

She could think of nothing to say, and for a while they remained in silence. Then he got up.

'I think I should prefer it if you went,' he said. 'You can only hamper me.'

'I shall stay here as long as you do.'

'Why?'

'Because if you do anything, I shall be compromised. I may be arrested. I think the fear of that may restrain you.'

He looked at her steadily. She met his eyes with a calmness which showed that she meant exactly what she said, and he turned uneasily away. A silence even greater than before fell upon them. They did not move. It was so still in the room that it might have been empty. The breathlessness of the air increased, so that it was horribly oppressive. Suddenly there was a loud rattle of thunder, and a flash of lightning tore across the heavy clouds. Susie thanked Heaven for the storm which would give presently a welcome freshness. She felt excessively ill at ease, and it was a relief to ascribe her sensation to a state of the atmosphere. Again the thunder rolled. It was so loud that it seemed to be immediately above their heads. And the wind rose suddenly and swept with a long moan through the trees that surrounded the house. It was a sound so human that it might have come from the souls of dead men suffering hopeless torments of regret.

The lamp went out, so suddenly that Susie was vaguely frightened. It gave one flicker, and they were in total darkness. It seemed as though someone had leaned over the chimney and blown it out. The night was very black, and they could not see the window which opened on to the country. The darkness was so peculiar that for a moment no one stirred.

Then Susie heard Dr Porhoët slip his hand across the table to find matches, but it seemed that they were not there. Again a loud peal of thunder startled them, but the rain would not fall. They panted for fresh air. On a sudden Susie's heart gave a bound, and she sprang up.

'There's someone in the room.'

The words were no sooner out of her mouth than she heard Arthur fling himself upon the intruder. She knew at once, with the certainty of an intuition, that it was Haddo. But how had he come in? What did he want? She tried to cry out, but no sound came from her throat. Dr Porhoët seemed bound to his chair. He did not move. He made no sound. She knew that an awful struggle was proceeding. It was a struggle to the death between two men who hated one another, but the most terrible part of it was that nothing was heard. They were perfectly noiseless. She tried to do something, but she could not stir.

And Arthur's heart exulted, for his enemy was in his grasp, under his hands, and he would not let him go while life was in him. He clenched his teeth and tightened his straining muscles. Susie heard his laboured breathing, but she only heard the breathing of one man. She wondered in abject terror what that could mean. They struggled silently, hand to hand, and Arthur knew that his strength was greater. He had made up his mind what to do and directed all his energy to a definite end. His enemy was extraordinarily powerful, but Arthur appeared to create some strength from the sheer force of his will. It seemed for hours that they struggled. He could not bear him down.

Suddenly, he knew that the other was frightened and sought to escape from him. Arthur tightened his grasp; for nothing in the world now would he ever loosen his hold. He took a deep, quick breath, and then put out all his strength in a tremendous effort. They swayed from side to side. Arthur felt as if his muscles were being torn from the bones, he could not continue for more than a moment longer; but the agony that flashed across his mind at the thought of failure braced him to a sudden angry jerk. All at once Haddo collapsed, and they fell heavily to the ground. Arthur was breathing more quickly now. He thought that if he could keep on for one instant longer, he would be safe. He threw all his weight on the form that rolled beneath him, and bore down furiously on the man's arm. He twisted it sharply, with all his might, and felt it give way. He gave a low cry of triumph; the arm was broken. And now his enemy was seized with panic; he struggled madly, he wanted only to get away from those long hands that were killing him. They seemed to be of iron. Arthur seized the huge bullock throat and dug his fingers into it, and they sunk into the heavy rolls of fat; and he flung the whole weight of his body into them. He exulted, for he knew that his enemy was in his power at last; he was strangling him, strangling the life out of him. He wanted light so that he might see the horror of that vast face, and the deadly fear, and the staring eyes. And still he pressed with those iron hands. And now the movements were strangely convulsive. His victim writhed in the agony of death. His struggles were desperate, but the avenging hands held him as in a vice. And then the movements grew spasmodic, and then they grew weaker. Still the hands pressed upon the gigantic throat, and Arthur forgot everything. He was mad with rage and fury and hate and sorrow. He thought of Margaret's anguish and of her fiendish torture, and he wished the man had ten lives so that he might take them one by one. And at last all was still, and that vast mass of flesh was motionless, and he knew that his enemy was dead. He loosened his grasp and slipped one hand over the heart. It would never beat again. The man was stone dead. Arthur got up and straightened himself. The darkness was intense still, and he could see nothing. Susie heard him, and at length she was able to speak.

'Arthur what have you done?'

'I've killed him,' he said hoarsely.

'O God, what shall we do?'

Arthur began to laugh aloud, hysterically, and in the darkness his hilarity was terrifying.

'For God's sake let us have some light.'

'I've found the matches,' said Dr Porhoët.

He seemed to awake suddenly from his long stupor. He struck one, and it would not light. He struck another, and Susie took off the globe and the chimney as he kindled the wick. Then he held up the lamp, and they saw Arthur looking at them. His face was ghastly. The sweat ran off his forehead in great beads, and his eyes were bloodshot. He trembled in every limb. Then Dr Porhoët advanced with the lamp and held it forward. They looked down on the floor for the man who lay there dead. Susie gave a sudden cry of horror.

There was no one there.

Arthur stepped back in terrified surprise. There was no one in the room, living or dead, but the three friends. The ground sank under Susie's feet, she felt horribly ill, and she fainted. When she awoke, seeming difficultly to emerge from an eternal night, Arthur was holding down her head.

'Bend down,' he said. 'Bend down.'

All that had happened came back to her, and she burst into tears. Her self-control deserted her, and, clinging to him for protection, she sobbed as though her heart would break. She was shaking from head to foot. The strangeness of this last horror had overcome her, and she could have shrieked with fright.

'It's all right,' he said. 'You need not be afraid.'

'Oh, what does it mean?'

'You must pluck up courage. We're going now to Skene.'

She sprang to her feet, as though to get away from him; her heart beat wildly.

'No, I can't; I'm frightened.'

'We must see what it means. We have no time to lose, or the morning will be upon us before we get back.'

Then she sought to prevent him.

'Oh, for God's sake, don't go, Arthur. Something awful may await you there. Don't risk your life.'

'There is no danger. I tell you the man is dead.'

'If anything happened to you ...'

She stopped, trying to restrain her sobs; she dared not go on. But he seemed to know what was in her mind.

'I will take no risks, because of you. I know that whether I live or die is not a—matter of indifference to you.'

She looked up and saw that his eyes were fixed upon her gravely. She reddened. A curious feeling came into her heart.

'I will go with you wherever you choose,' she said humbly.

'Come, then.'

They stepped out into the night. And now, without rain, the storm had passed away, and the stars were shining. They walked quickly. Arthur went in front of them. Dr Porhoët and Susie followed him, side by side, and they had to hasten their steps in order not to be left behind. It seemed to them that the horror of the night was passed, and there was a fragrancy in the air which was wonderfully refreshing. The sky was beautiful. And at last they came to Skene. Arthur led them again to the opening in the palisade, and he took Susie's hand. Presently they stood in the place from which a few days before they had seen the house. As then, it stood in massive blackness against the night and, as then, the attic windows shone out with brilliant lights. Susie started, for she had expected that the whole place would be in darkness.

'There is no danger, I promise you,' said Arthur gently. 'We are going to find out the meaning of all this mystery.'

He began to walk towards the house.

'Have you a weapon of some sort?' asked the doctor.

Arthur handed him a revolver.

'Take this. It will reassure you, but you will have no need of it. I bought it the other day when—I had other plans.'

Susie gave a little shudder. They reached the drive and walked to the great portico which adorned the facade of the house. Arthur tried the handle, but it would not open.

'Will you wait here?' he said. 'I can get through one of the windows, and I will let you in.'

He left them. They stood quietly there, with anxious hearts; they could not guess what they would see. They were afraid that something would happen to Arthur, and Susie regretted that she had not insisted on going with him. Suddenly she remembered that awful moment when the light of the lamp had been thrown where all expected to see a body, and there was nothing.

'What do you think it meant?' she cried suddenly. 'What is the explanation?'

'Perhaps we shall see now,' answered the doctor.

Arthur still lingered, and she could not imagine what had become of him. All sorts of horrible fancies passed through her mind, and she dreaded she knew not what. At last they heard a footstep inside the house, and the door was opened.

'I was convinced that nobody slept here, but I was obliged to make sure. I had some difficulty in getting in.'

Susie hesitated to enter. She did not know what horrors awaited her, and the darkness was terrifying.

'I cannot see,' she said.

'I've brought a torch,' said Arthur.

He pressed a button, and a narrow ray of bright light was cast upon the floor. Dr Porhoët and Susie went in. Arthur carefully closed the door, and flashed the light of his torch all round them. They stood in a large hall, the floor of which was scattered with the skins of lions that Haddo on his celebrated expedition had killed in Africa. There were perhaps a dozen, and their number gave a wild, barbaric note. A great oak staircase led to the upper floors.

'We must go through all the rooms,' said Arthur.

He did not expect to find Haddo till they came to the lighted attics, but it seemed needful nevertheless to pass right through the house on their way. A flash of his torch had shown him that the walls of the hall were decorated with all manner of armour, ancient swords of Eastern handiwork, barbaric weapons from central Africa, savage implements of medieval warfare; and an idea came to him. He took down a huge battle-axe and swung it in his hand.

'Now come.'

Silently, holding their breath as though they feared to wake the dead, they went into the first room. They saw it difficultly with their scant light, since the thin shaft of brilliancy, emphasising acutely the surrounding darkness, revealed it only piece by piece. It was a large room, evidently unused, for the furniture was covered with holland, and there was a mustiness about it which suggested that the windows were seldom opened. As in many old houses, the rooms led not from a passage but into one another, and they walked through many till they came back into the hall. They had all a desolate, uninhabited air. Their sombreness was increased by the oak with which they were panelled. There was panelling in the hall too, and on the stairs that led broadly to the top of the house. As they ascended, Arthur stopped for one moment and passed his hand over the polished wood.

'It would burn like tinder,' he said.

They went through the rooms on the first floor, and they were as empty and as cheerless. Presently they came to that which had been Margaret's. In a bowl were dead flowers. Her brushes were still on the toilet table. But it was a gloomy chamber, with its dark oak, and, so comfortless that Susie shuddered. Arthur stood for a time and looked at it, but he said nothing. They found themselves again on the stairs and they went to the second storey. But here they seemed to be at the top of the house.

'How does one get up to the attics?' said Arthur, looking about him with surprise.

He paused for a while to think. Then he nodded his head.

'There must be some steps leading out of one of the rooms.'

They went on. And now the ceilings were much lower, with heavy beams, and there was no furniture at all. The emptiness seemed to make everything more terrifying. They felt that they were on the threshold of a great mystery, and Susie's heart began to beat fast. Arthur conducted his examination with the greatest method; he walked round each room carefully, looking for a door that might lead to a staircase; but there was no sign of one.

'What will you do if you can't find the way up?' asked Susie.

'I shall find the way up,' he answered.

They came to the staircase once more and had discovered nothing. They looked at one another helplessly.

'It's quite clear there is a way,' said Arthur, with impatience. 'There must be something in the nature of a hidden door somewhere or other.'

He leaned against the balustrade and meditated. The light of his lantern threw a narrow ray upon the opposite wall.

'I feel certain it must be in one of the rooms at the end of the house. That seems the most natural place to put a means of ascent to the attics.'

They went back, and again he examined the panelling of a small room that had outside walls on three sides of it. It was the only room that did not lead into another.

'It must be here,' he said.

Presently he gave a little laugh, for he saw that a small door was concealed by the woodwork. He pressed it where he thought there might be a spring, and it flew open. Their torch showed them a narrow wooden staircase. They walked up and found themselves in front of a door. Arthur tried it, but it was locked. He smiled grimly.

'Will you get back a little,' he said.

He lifted his axe and swung it down upon the latch. The handle was shattered, but the lock did not yield. He shook his head. As he paused for a moment, an there was a complete silence, Susie distinctly heard a slight noise. She put her hand on Arthur's arm to call his attention to it, and with strained ears they listened. There was something alive on the other side of the door. They heard its curious sound: it was not that of a human voice, it was not the crying of an animal, it was extraordinary.

It was the sort of gibber, hoarse and rapid, and it filled them with an icy terror because it was so weird and so unnatural.

'Come away, Arthur,' said Susie. 'Come away.'

'There's some living thing in there,' he answered.

He did not know why the sound horrified him. The sweat broke out on his forehead.

'Something awful will happen to us,' whispered Susie, shaking with uncontrollable fear.

'The only thing is to break the door down.'

The horrid gibbering was drowned by the noise he made. Quickly, without pausing, he began to hack at the oak door with all his might. In rapid succession his heavy blows rained down, and the sound echoed through the empty house. There was a crash, and the door swung back. They had been so long in almost total darkness that they were blinded for an instant by the dazzling light. And then instinctively they started back, for, as the door opened, a wave of heat came out upon them so that they could hardly breathe. The place was like an oven.

They entered. It was lit by enormous lamps, the light of which was increased by reflectors, and warmed by a great furnace. They could not understand why so intense a heat was necessary. The narrow windows were closed. Dr Porhoët caught sight of a thermometer and was astounded at the temperature it indicated. The room was used evidently as a laboratory. On broad tables were test-tubes, basins and baths of white porcelain, measuring-glasses, and utensils of all sorts; but the surprising thing was the great scale upon which everything was. Neither Arthur nor Dr Porhoët had ever seen such gigantic measures nor such large test-tubes. There were rows of bottles, like those in the dispensary of a hospital, each containing great quantities of a different chemical. The three friends stood in silence. The emptiness of the room contrasted so oddly with its appearance of being in immediate use that it was uncanny. Susie felt that he who worked there was in the midst of his labours, and might return at any moment; he could have only gone for an instant into another chamber in order to see the progress of some experiment. It was quite silent. Whatever had made those vague, unearthly noises was hushed by their approach.

The door was closed between this room and the next. Arthur

opened it, and they found themselves in a long, low attic, ceiled with great rafters, as brilliantly lit and as hot as the first. Here too were broad tables laden with retorts, instruments for heating, huge test-tubes, and all manner of vessels. The furnace that warmed it gave a steady heat. Arthur's gaze travelled slowly from table to table, and he wondered what Haddo's experiments had really been. The air was heavy with an extraordinary odour: it was not musty, like that of the closed rooms through which they had passed, but singularly pungent, disagreeable and sickly. He asked himself what it could spring from. Then his eyes fell upon a huge receptacle that stood on the table nearest to the furnace. It was covered with a white cloth. He took it off. The vessel was about four feet high, round, and shaped somewhat like a washing tub, but it was made of glass more than an inch thick. In it a spherical mass, a little larger than a football, of a peculiar, livid colour. The surface was smooth, but rather coarsely grained, and over it ran a dense system of blood-vessels. It reminded the two medical men of those huge tumours which are preserved in spirit in hospital museums. Susie looked at it with an incomprehensible disgust. Suddenly she gave a cry.

'Good God, it's moving!'

Arthur put his hand on her arm quickly to quieten her and bent down with irresistible curiosity. They saw that it was a mass of flesh unlike that of any human being; and it pulsated regularly. The movement was quite distinct, up and down, like the delicate heaving of a woman's breast when she is asleep. Arthur touched the thing with one finger and it shrank slightly.

'Its quite warm,' he said.

He turned it over, and it remained in the position in which he had placed it, as if there were neither top nor bottom to it. But they could see now, irregularly placed on one side, a few short hairs. They were just like human hairs.

'Is it alive?' whispered Susie, struck with horror and amazement.

'Yes!'

Arthur seemed fascinated. He could not take his eyes off the loathsome thing. He watched it slowly heave with even motion.

'What can it mean?' he asked.

He looked at Dr Porhoët with pale startled face. A thought was coming to him, but a thought so unnatural, extravagant, and terrible that he pushed it from him with a movement of both hands, as though it were a material thing. Then all three turned around abruptly with a start, for they heard again the wild gibbering which had first shocked their ears. In the wonder of this revolting object they had forgotten all the rest. The sound seemed extraordinarily near, and Susie drew back instinctively, for it appeared to come from her very side.

'There's nothing here,' said Arthur. 'It must be in the next room.'

'Oh, Arthur, let us go,' cried Susie. 'I'm afraid to see what may be in store for us. It is nothing to us; and what we see may poison our sleep for ever.'

She looked appealingly at Dr Porhoët. He was white and anxious. The heat of that place had made the sweat break out on his forehead.

'I have seen enough. I want to see no more,' he said.

'Then you may go, both of you,' answered Arthur. 'I do not wish to force you to see anything. But I shall go on. Whatever it is, I wish to find out.'

'But Haddo? Supposing he is there, waiting? Perhaps you are only walking into a trap that he has set for you.'

'I am convinced that Haddo is dead.'

Again that unintelligible jargon, unhuman and shrill, fell upon their ears, and Arthur stepped forward. Susie did not hesitate. She was prepared to follow him anywhere. He opened the door, and there was a sudden quiet. Whatever made those sounds was there. It was a larger room than any on the others and much higher, for it ran along the whole front of the house. The powerful lamps showed every corner of it at once, but, above, the beams of the open ceiling were dark with shadow. And here the nauseous odour, which had struck them before, was so overpowering that for a while they could not go in. It was indescribably foul. Even Arthur thought it would make him sick, and he looked at the windows to see if it was possible to open them; but it seemed they were hermetically closed. The extreme warmth made the air more overpowering. There were four furnaces here, and they were all alight. In order to give out more heat and to burn slowly, the fronts of them were open, and one could see that they were filled with glowing coke.

The room was furnished no differently from the others, but to the various instruments for chemical operations on a large scale were added all manner of electrical appliances. Several books were lying about, and one had been left open face downwards on the edge of a table. But what immediately attracted their attention was a row of those large glass vessels like that which they had seen in the adjoining room. Each was covered with a white cloth. They hesitated a moment, for they knew that here they were face to face with the great enigma. At last Arthur pulled away the cloth from one. None of them spoke. They stared with astonished eyes. For here, too, was a strange mass of flesh, almost as large as a new-born child, but there was in it the beginnings of something ghastly human. It was shaped vaguely like an infant, but the legs were joined together so that it looked like a mummy rolled up in its coverings. There were neither feet nor knees. The trunk was formless, but there was a curious thickening on each side; it was as if a modeller had meant to make a figure with the arms loosely bent, but had left the work unfinished so that they were still one with the body. There was something that resembled a human head, covered with long golden hair, but it was horrible; it was an uncouth mass, without eyes or nose or mouth. The colour was a kind of sickly pink, and it was almost transparent. There was a very slight movement in it, rhythmical and slow. It was living too.

Then quickly Arthur removed the covering from all the other jars but one; and in a flash of the eyes they saw abominations so awful that Susie had to clench her fists in order not to scream. There was one monstrous thing in which the limbs approached nearly to the human. It was extraordinarily heaped up, with fat tiny arms, little bloated legs, and an absurd squat body, so that it looked like a Chinese mandarin in porcelain. In another the trunk was almost like that of a human child, except that it was patched strangely with red and grey. But the terror of it was that at the neck it branched hideously, and there were two distinct heads, monstrously large, but duly provided with all their features. The features were a caricature of humanity so shameful that one could hardly bear to look. And as the light fell on it, the eyes of each head opened slowly. They had no pigment in them,

but were pink, like the eyes of white rabbits; and they stared for a moment with an odd, unseeing glance. Then they were shut again, and
what was curiously terrifying was that the movements were not quite
simultaneous; the eyelids of one head fell slowly just before those
of the other. And in another place was a ghastly monster in which
it seemed that two bodies had been dreadfully entangled with one
another. It was a creature of nightmare, with four arms and four legs,
and this one actually moved. With a peculiar motion it crawled along
the bottom of the great receptacle in which it was kept, towards the
three persons who looked at it. It seemed to wonder what they did.
Susie started back with fright, as it raised itself on its four legs and
tried to reach up to them.

Susie turned away and hid her face. She could not look at those
ghastly counterfeits of humanity. She was terrified and ashamed.

'Do you understand what this means?' said Dr Porhoët to Arthur,
in an awed voice. 'It means that he has discovered the secret of life.'

'Was it for these vile monstrosities that Margaret was sacrificed
in all her loveliness?'

The two men looked at one another with sad, wondering eyes.

'Don't you remember that he talked of the manufacture of human
beings? It's these misshapen things that he's succeeding in produc-
ing,' said the doctor.

'There is one more that we haven't seen,' said Arthur.

He pointed to the covering which still hid the largest of the vases.
He had a feeling that it contained the most fearful of all these monsters; and it was not without an effort that he drew the cloth away.
But no sooner had he done this than something sprang up, so that
instinctively he started back, and it began to gibber in piercing tones.
These were the unearthly sounds that they had heard. It was not a
voice, it was a kind of raucous crying, hoarse yet shrill, uneven like the
barking of a dog, and appalling. The sounds came forth in rapid succession, angrily, as though the being that uttered them sought to express itself in furious words. It was mad with passion and beat against
the glass walls of its prison with clenched fists. For the hands were
human hands, and the body, though much larger, was of the shape of
a new-born child. The creature must have stood about four feet high.

The head was horribly misshapen. The skull was enormous, smooth and distended like that of a hydrocephalic, and the forehead protruded over the face hideously. The features were almost unformed, preternaturally small under the great, overhanging brow; and they had an expression of fiendish malignity.

The tiny, misshapen countenance writhed with convulsive fury, and from the mouth poured out a foaming spume. It raised its voice higher and higher, shrieking senseless gibberish in its rage. Then it began to hurl its whole body madly against the glass walls and to beat its head. It appeared to have a sudden incomprehensible hatred for the three strangers. It was trying to fly at them. The toothless gums moved spasmodically, and it threw its face into horrible grimaces. That nameless, loathsome abortion was the nearest that Oliver Haddo had come to the human form.

'Come away,' said Arthur. 'We must not look at this.'

He quickly flung the covering over the jar.

'Yes, for God's sake let us go,' said Susie.

'We haven't done yet,' answered Arthur. 'We haven't found the author of all this.'

He looked at the room in which they were, but there was no door except that by which they had entered. Then he uttered a startled cry, and stepping forward fell on his knee.

On the other side of the long tables heaped up with instruments, hidden so that at first they had not seen him, Oliver Haddo lay on the floor, dead. His blue eyes were staring wide, and they seemed larger than they had ever been. They kept still the expression of terror which they had worn in the moment of his agony, and his heavy face was distorted with deadly fear. It was purple and dark, and the eyes were injected with blood.

'He died of suffocation,' whispered Dr Porhoët.

Arthur pointed to the neck. There could be seen on it distinctly the marks of the avenging fingers that had strangled the life out of him. It was impossible to hesitate.

'I told you that I had killed him,' said Arthur.

Then he remembered something more. He took hold of the right arm. He was convinced that it had been broken during that desperate struggle in the darkness. He felt it carefully and listened. He heard plainly the two parts of the bone rub against one another. The dead man's arm was broken just in the place where he had broken it. Arthur stood up. He took one last look at his enemy. That vast mass of flesh lay heaped up on the floor in horrible disorder.

'Now that you have seen, will you come away?' said Susie, interrupting him.

The words seemed to bring him suddenly to himself.

'Yes, we must go quickly.'

They turned away and with hurried steps walked through those bright attics till they came to the stairs.

'Now go down and wait for me at the door,' said Arthur. 'I will follow you immediately.'

'What are you going to do?' asked Susie.

'Never mind. Do as I tell you. I have not finished here yet.'

They went down the great oak staircase and waited in the hall. They wondered what Arthur was about. Presently he came running down.

'Be quick!' he cried. 'We have no time to lose.'

'What have you done, Arthur?'

'There's no time to tell you now.'

He hurried them out and slammed the door behind him. He took Susie's hand.

'Now we must run. Come.'

She did not know what his haste signified, but her heart beat furiously. He dragged her along. Dr Porhoët hurried on behind them. Arthur plunged into the wood. He would not leave them time to breathe.

'You must be quick,' he said.

At last they came to the opening in the fence, and he helped them to get through. Then he carefully replaced the wooden paling and, taking Susie's arm began to walk rapidly towards their inn.

'I'm frightfully tired,' she said. 'I simply can't go so fast.'

'You must. Presently you can rest as long as you like.'

They walked very quickly for a while. Now and then Arthur looked back. The night was still quite dark, and the stars shone out in their myriads. At last he slackened their pace.

'Now you can go more slowly,' he said.

Susie saw the smiling glance that he gave her. His eyes were full of tenderness. He put his arm affectionately round her shoulders to support her.

'I'm afraid you're quite exhausted, poor thing,' he said. 'I'm sorry to have had to hustle you so much.'

'It doesn't matter at all.'

She leaned against him comfortably. With that protecting arm about her, she felt capable of any fatigue. Dr Porhoët stopped.

'You must really let me roll myself a cigarette,' he said.

'You may do whatever you like,' answered Arthur.

There was a different ring in his voice now, and it was soft with a good-humour that they had not heard in it for many months. He appeared singularly relieved. Susie was ready to forget the terrible past and give herself over to the happiness that seemed at last in store for her. They began to saunter slowly on. And now they could take pleasure in the exquisite night. The air was very suave, odorous with the heather that was all about them, and there was an enchanting peace in that scene which wonderfully soothed their weariness. It was dark still, but they knew the dawn was at hand, and Susie rejoiced in the approaching day. In the east the azure of the night began to thin away into pale amethyst, and the trees seemed gradually to stand out from the darkness in a ghostly beauty. Suddenly birds began to sing all around them in a splendid chorus. From their feet a lark sprang up with a rustle of wings and, mounting proudly upon the air, chanted blithe canticles to greet the morning. They stood upon a little hill.

'Let us wait here and see the sun rise,' said Susie.

'As you will.'

They stood all three of them, and Susie took in deep, joyful breaths of the sweet air of dawn. The whole land, spread at her feet, was clothed in the purple dimness that heralds day, and she exulted in its beauty. But she noticed that Arthur, unlike herself and Dr Porhoët, did not look toward the east. His eyes were fixed steadily upon the place from which they had come. What did he look for in the darkness of the west? She turned round, and a cry broke from her lips, for the shadows there were lurid with a deep red glow.

'It looks like a fire,' she said.

'It is. Skene is burning like tinder.'

And as he spoke it seemed that the roof fell in, for suddenly vast flames sprang up, rising high into the still night air; and they saw that the house they had just left was blazing furiously. It was a magnificent sight from the distant hill on which they stood to watch the fire as it soared and sank, as it shot scarlet tongues along like strange Titanic monsters, as it raged from room to room. Skene was burning. It was beyond the reach of human help. In a little while there would be no trace of all those crimes and all those horrors. Now it was one mass of flame. It looked like some primeval furnace, where the gods might work unheard-of miracles.

'Arthur, what have you done?' asked Susie, in a tone that was hardly audible.

He did not answer directly. He put his arm about her shoulder again, so that she was obliged to turn round.

'Look, the sun is rising.'

In the east, a long ray of light climbed up the sky, and the sun, yellow and round, appeared upon the face of the earth.

Liza of Lambeth

Liza of Lambeth

⎯⎯⎯⎯

I

IT WAS THE first Saturday afternoon in August; it had been broiling hot all day, with a cloudless sky, and the sun had been beating down on the houses, so that the top rooms were like ovens; but now with the approach of evening it was cooler, and everyone in Vere Street was out of doors.

Vere street, Lambeth, is a short, straight street leading out of the Westminster Bridge Road; it has forty houses on one side and forty houses on the other, and these eighty houses are very much more like one another than ever peas are like peas, or young ladies like young ladies. They are newish, three-storied buildings of dingy grey brick with slate roofs, and they are perfectly flat, without a bow-window or even a projecting cornice or window-sill to break the straightness of the line from one end of the street to the other.

This Saturday afternoon the street was full of life; no traffic came down Vere Street, and the cemented space between the pavements was given up to children. Several games of cricket were being played by wildly excited boys, using coats for wickets, an old tennis-ball or a bundle of rags tied together for a ball, and, generally, an old broom-stick for bat. The wicket was so large and the bat so small that the man in was always getting bowled, when heated quarrels would arise, the batter absolutely refusing to go out and the bowler absolutely insisting on going in. The girls were more peaceable; they were chiefly employed in skipping, and only abused one another mildly when the rope was not properly turned or the skipper did not jump sufficiently high. Worst off of all were the very young children, for there had been no rain for weeks, and the street was as dry and clean as a covered court, and, in the lack of mud to wallow in, they sat about the road, disconsolate as poets. The number of babies was prodigious; they sprawled about everywhere, on the pavement, round the doors, and about their mothers' skirts. The grown-ups were gathered round the open doors; there were usually two women squatting on the doorstep, and two or three more seated on either side on chairs; they were invariably nursing babies, and most of them showed clear signs that the present object of the maternal care would be soon ousted by a new arrival. Men were less numerous but such as there were leant against the walls, smoking, or sat on the sills of the ground-floor windows. It was the dead season in Vere Street as much as in Belgravia, and really if it had not been for babies just come or just about to come, and an opportune murder in a neighbouring doss-house, there would have been nothing whatever to talk about. As it was, the little groups talked quietly, discussing the atrocity or the merits of the local midwives, comparing the circumstances of their various confinements.

'You'll be 'avin' your little trouble soon, eh, Polly?' asked one good lady of another.

'Oh, I reckon I've got another two months ter go yet,' answered Polly.

'Well,' said a third. 'I wouldn't 'ave thought you'd go so long by the look of yer!'

'I 'ope you'll have it easier this time, my dear,' said a very stout old person, a woman of great importance.

'She said she wasn't goin' to 'ave no more, when the last one come.' This remark came from Polly's husband.

'Ah,' said the stout old lady, who was in the business, and boasted vast experience. 'That's wot they all says; but, Lor' bless yer, they don't mean it.'

'Well, I've got three, and I'm not goin' to 'ave no more bli'me if I will; 'tain't good enough—that's wot I says.'

'You're abaht right there, ole gal,' said Polly, 'My word, 'Arry, if you 'ave any more I'll git a divorce, that I will.'

At that moment an organ-grinder turned the corner and came down the street.

'Good biz; 'ere's an organ!' cried half a dozen people at once.

The organ-man was an Italian, with a shock of black hair and a ferocious moustache. Drawing his organ to a favourable spot, he stopped, released his shoulder from the leather straps by which he dragged it, and cocking his large soft hat on the side of his head, began turning the handle. It was a lively tune, and in less than no time a little crowd had gathered round to listen, chiefly the young men and the maidens, for the married ladies were never in a fit state to dance, and therefore disinclined to trouble themselves to stand round the organ. There was a moment's hesitation at opening the ball; then one girl said to another:

'Come on, Florrie, you and me ain't shy; we'll begin, and bust it!'

The two girls took hold of one another, one acting gentleman, the other lady; three or four more pairs of girls immediately joined them, and they began a waltz. They held themselves very upright; and with an air of grave dignity which was quite impressive, glided slowly about, making their steps with the utmost precision, bearing themselves with sufficient decorum for a court ball. After a while the men began to itch for a turn, and two of them, taking hold of one another in the most approved fashion, waltzed round the circle with the gravity of judges.

All at once there was a cry: 'There's Liza!' And several members of the group turned and called out: 'Oo, look at Liza!'

The dancers stopped to see the sight, and the organ-grinder, having come to the end of his tune, ceased turning the handle and looked to see what was the excitement.

'Oo, Liza!' they called out. 'Look at Liza; oo, I sy!'

It was a young girl of about eighteen, with dark eyes, and an enormous fringe, puffed-out and curled and frizzed, covering her whole forehead from side to side, and coming down to meet her eyebrows. She was dressed in brilliant violet, with great lappets of velvet, and she had on her head an enormous black hat covered with feathers.

'I sy, ain't she got up dossy?' called out the groups at the doors, as she passed.

'Dressed ter death, and kill the fashion; that's wot I calls it.'

Liza saw what a sensation she was creating; she arched her back and lifted her head, and walked down the street, swaying her body from side to side, and swaggering along as though the whole place belonged to her.

''Ave yer bought the street, Bill?' shouted one youth; and then half a dozen burst forth at once, as if by inspiration:

'Knocked 'em in the Old Kent Road!'

It was immediately taken up by a dozen more, and they all yelled it out:

'Knocked 'em in the Old Kent Road. Yah, ah, knocked 'em in the Old Kent Road!'

'Oo, Liza!' they shouted; the whole street joined in, and they gave long, shrill, ear-piercing shrieks and strange calls, that rung down the street and echoed back again.

'Hextra special!' called out a wag.

'Oh, Liza! Oo! Ooo!' yells and whistles, and then it thundered forth again:

'Knocked 'em in the Old Kent Road!'

Liza put on the air of a conquering hero, and sauntered on, enchanted at the uproar. She stuck out her elbows and jerked her head on one side, and said to herself as she passed through the bellowing crowd:

'This is jam!'

'Knocked 'em in the Old Kent Road!'

When she came to the group round the barrel-organ, one of the girls cried out to her:

'Is that yer new dress, Liza?'

'Well, it don't look like my old one, do it?' said Liza.

'Where did yer git it?' asked another friend, rather enviously.

'Picked it up in the street, of course,' scornfully answered Liza.

'I believe it's the same one as I saw in the pawnbroker's dahn the road,' said one of the men, to tease her.

'Thet's it; but wot was you doin' in there? Pledgin' yer shirt, or was it yer trousers?'

'Yah, I wouldn't git a second-'and dress at a pawnbroker's!'

'Garn!' said Liza indignantly. 'I'll swipe yer over the snitch if yer talk ter me. I got the mayterials in the West Hend, didn't I? And I 'ad it mide up by my Court Dressmiker, so you jolly well dry up, old jellybelly.'

'Garn!' was the reply.

Liza had been so intent on her new dress and the comment it was exciting that she had not noticed the organ.

'Oo, I say, let's 'ave some dancin',' she said as soon as she saw it. 'Come on, Sally,' she added, to one of the girls, 'you an' me'll dance togither. Grind away, old cock!'

The man turned on a new tune, and the organ began to play the Intermezzo from the 'Cavalleria'; other couples quickly followed Liza's example, and they began to waltz round with the same solemnity as before; but Liza outdid them all; if the others were as stately as queens, she was as stately as an empress; the gravity and dignity with which she waltzed were something appalling, you felt that the minuet was a frolic in comparison; it would have been a fitting measure to tread round the grave of a *première danseuse*, or at the funeral of a professional humorist. And the graces she put on, the languor of the eyes, the contemptuous curl of the lips, the exquisite turn of the hand, the dainty arching of the foot! You felt there could be no questioning her right to the tyranny of Vere Street.

Suddenly she stopped short, and disengaged herself from her companion.

'Oh, I sy,' she said, 'this is too bloomin' slow; it gives me the sick.'

That is not precisely what she said, but it is impossible always to give the exact unexpurgated words of Liza and the other personages of the story, the reader is therefore entreated with his thoughts to piece out the necessary imperfections of the dialogue.

'It's too bloomin' slow,' she said again; 'it gives me the sick. Let's 'ave somethin' a bit more lively than this 'ere waltz. You stand over there, Sally, an' we'll show 'em 'ow ter skirt dance.'

They all stopped waltzing.

'Talk of the ballet at the Canterbury and South London. You just wite till you see the ballet at Vere Street, Lambeth—we'll knock 'em!'

She went up to the organ-grinder.

'Na then, Italiano,' she said to him, 'you buck up; give us a tune that's got some guts in it! See?'

She caught hold of his big hat and squashed it down over his eyes. The man grinned from ear to ear, and, touching the little catch at the side, began to play a lively tune such as Liza had asked for.

The men had fallen out, but several girls had put themselves in position, in couples, standing face to face; and immediately the music struck up, they began. They held up their skirts on each side, so as to show their feet, and proceeded to go through the difficult steps and motions of the dance. Liza was right; they could not have done it better in a trained ballet. But the best dancer of them all was Liza; she threw her whole soul into it; forgetting the stiff bearing which she had thought proper to the waltz, and casting off its elaborate graces, she gave herself up entirely to the present pleasure. Gradually the other couples stood aside, so that Liza and Sally were left alone. They paced it carefully, watching each other's steps, and as if by instinct performing corresponding movements, so as to make the whole a thing of symmetry.

'I'm abaht done,' said Sally, blowing and puffing. 'I've 'ad enough of it.'

'Go on, Liza!' cried out a dozen voices when Sally stopped.

She gave no sign of having heard them other than calmly to continue her dance. She glided through the steps, and swayed about, and manipulated her skirt, all with the most charming grace imaginable, then, the music altering, she changed the style of her dancing, her feet moved more quickly, and did not keep so strictly to the ground. She was getting excited at the admiration of the onlookers, and her dance grew wilder and more daring. She lifted her skirts higher, brought in new and more difficult movements into her improvisation, kicking up her legs she did the wonderful twist, backwards and forwards, of which the dancer is proud.

'Look at 'er legs!' cried one of the men.

'Look at 'er stockin's!' shouted another; and indeed they were remarkable, for Liza had chosen them of the same brilliant hue as her dress, and was herself most proud of the harmony.

Her dance became gayer: her feet scarcely touched the ground, she whirled round madly.

'Take care yer don't split!' cried out one of the wags, at a very audacious kick.

The words were hardly out of his mouth when Liza, with a gigantic effort, raised her foot and kicked off his hat. The feat was greeted with applause, and she went on, making turns and twists, flourishing her skirts, kicking higher and higher, and finally, among a volley of shouts, fell on her hands and turned head over heels in a magnificent catharine-wheel; then scrambling to her feet again, she tumbled into the arms of a young man standing in the front of the ring.

'That's right, Liza,' he said. 'Give us a kiss, now,' and promptly tried to take one.

'Git aht!' said Liza, pushing him away, not too gently.

'Yus, give us a kiss,' cried another, running up to her.

'I'll smack yer in the fice!' said Liza, elegantly, as she dodged him.

'Ketch 'old on 'er, Bill,' cried out a third, 'an' we'll all kiss her.'

'Na, you won't!' shrieked Liza, beginning to run.

'Come on,' they cried, 'we'll ketch 'er.'

She dodged in and out, between their legs, under their arms, and then, getting clear of the little crowd, caught up her skirts so that they might not hinder her, and took to her heels along the street. A score of men set in chase, whistling, shouting, yelling; the people at the doors looked up to see the fun, and cried out to her as she dashed past; she ran like the wind. Suddenly a man from the side darted into the middle of the road, stood straight in her way, and before she knew where she was, she had jumped shrieking into his arms, and he, lifting her up to him, had imprinted two sounding kisses on her cheeks.

'Oh, you ——!' she said. Her expression was quite unprintable; nor can it be euphemized.

There was a shout of laughter from the bystanders, and the young men in chase of her, and Liza, looking up, saw a big, bearded man whom she had never seen before. She blushed to the very roots of her hair, quickly extricated herself from his arms, and, amid the jeers and laughter of everyone, slid into the door of the nearest house and was lost to view.

II

LIZA AND HER mother were having supper. Mrs. Kemp was an elderly woman, short, and rather stout, with a red face, and grey hair brushed tight back over her forehead. She had been a widow for many years, and since her husband's death had lived with Liza in the ground-floor front room in which they were now sitting. Her husband had been a soldier, and from a grateful country she received a pension large enough to keep her from starvation, and by charring and doing such odd jobs as she could get she earned a little extra to supply herself with liquor. Liza was able to make her own living by working at a factory.

Mrs. Kemp was rather sulky this evening.

'Wot was yer doin' this afternoon, Liza?' she asked.

'I was in the street.'

'You're always in the street when I want yer.'

'I didn't know as 'ow yer wanted me, mother,' answered Liza.

'Well, yer might 'ave come ter see! I might 'ave been dead, for all you knew.'

Liza said nothing.

'My rheumatics was thet bad to-dy, thet I didn't know wot ter do with myself. The doctor said I was to be rubbed with that stuff 'e give me, but yer won't never do nothin' for me.'

'Well, mother,' said Liza, 'your rheumatics was all right yesterday.'

'I know wot you was doin'; you was showin' off thet new dress of yours. Pretty waste of money thet is, instead of givin' it me ter sive up. An' for the matter of thet, I wanted a new dress far worse than you did. But, of course, I don't matter.'

Liza did not answer, and Mrs. Kemp, having nothing more to say, continued her supper in silence.

It was Liza who spoke next.

'There's some new people moved in the street. 'Ave you seen 'em?' she asked.

'No, wot are they?'

'I dunno; I've seen a chap, a big chap with a beard. I think 'e lives up at the other end.'

She felt herself blushing a little.

'No one any good you be sure,' said Mrs. Kemp. 'I can't swaller these new people as are comin' in; the street ain't wot it was when I fust come.'

When they had done, Mrs. Kemp got up, and having finished her half-pint of beer, said to her daughter:

'Put the things away, Liza. I'm just goin' round to see Mrs. Clayton; she's just 'ad twins, and she 'ad nine before these come. It's a pity the Lord don't see fit ter tike some on 'em—thet's wot I say.'

After which pious remark Mrs. Kemp went out of the house and turned into another a few doors up.

Liza did not clear the supper things away as she was told, but opened the window and drew her chair to it. She leant on the sill, looking out into the street. The sun had set, and it was twilight, the sky was growing dark, bringing to view the twinkling stars; there was no breeze, but it was pleasantly and restfully cool. The good folk still sat at their doorsteps, talking as before on the same inexhaustible subjects, but a little subdued with the approach of night. The boys were still playing cricket, but they were mostly at the other end of the street, and their shouts were muffled before they reached Liza's ears.

She sat, leaning her head on her hands, breathing in the fresh air and feeling a certain exquisite sense of peacefulness which she was not used to. It was Saturday evening, and she thankfully remembered that there would be no factory on the morrow; she was glad to rest. Somehow she felt a little tired, perhaps it was through the excitement of the afternoon, and she enjoyed the quietness of the evening. It seemed so tranquil and still; the silence filled her with a strange delight, she felt as if she could sit there all through the night looking out into the cool, dark street, and up heavenwards at the stars. She was very happy, but yet at the same time experienced a strange new sensation of melancholy, and she almost wished to cry.

Suddenly a dark form stepped in front of the open window. She gave a little shriek.

"Oo's thet?' she asked, for it was quite dark, and she did not recognize the man standing in front of her.

'Me, Liza,' was the answer.

'Tom?'

'Yus!'

It was a young man with light yellow hair and a little fair moustache, which made him appear almost boyish; he was light-complexioned and blue-eyed, and had a frank and pleasant look mingled with a curious bashfulness that made him blush when people spoke to him.

'Wot's up?' asked Liza.

'Come aht for a walk, Liza, will yer?'

'No!' she answered decisively.

'You promised ter yesterday, Liza.'

'Yesterday an' ter-day's two different things,' was her wise reply.

'Yus, come on, Liza.'

'Na, I tell yer, I won't.'

'I want ter talk ter yer, Liza.' Her hand was resting on the window-sill, and he put his upon it. She quickly drew it back.

'Well, I don't want yer ter talk ter me.'

But she did, for it was she who broke the silence.

'Say, Tom, 'oo are them new folk as 'as come into the street? It's a big chap with a brown beard.'

'D'you mean the bloke as kissed yer this afternoon?'

Liza blushed again.

'Well, why shouldn't 'e kiss me?' she said, with some inconsequence.

'I never said as 'ow 'e shouldn't; I only arst yer if it was the sime.'

'Yea, thet's 'oo I mean.'

"Is nime is Blakeston—Jim Blakeston. I've only spoke to 'im once; he's took the two top rooms at No. 19 'ouse.'

'Wot's 'e want two top rooms for?'

"Im? Oh, 'e's got a big family—five kids. Ain't yer seen 'is wife abaht the street? She's a big, fat woman, as does 'er 'air funny.'

'I didn't know 'e 'ad a wife.'

There was another silence; Liza sat thinking, and Tom stood at the window, looking at her.

'Won't yer come aht with me, Liza?' he asked, at last.

'Na, Tom,' she said, a little more gently, 'it's too lite.'

'Liza,' he said, blushing to the roots of his hair.

'Well?'

'Liza'—he couldn't go on, and stuttered in his shyness—'Liza, I—I—I loves yer, Liza.'

'Garn awy!'

He was quite brave now, and took hold of her hand.

'Yer know, Liza, I'm earnin' twenty-three shillin's at the works now, an' I've got some furniture as mother left me when she was took.'

The girl said nothing.

'Liza, will you 'ave me? I'll make yer a good 'usband, Liza, swop me bob, I will; an' yer know I'm not a drinkin' sort. Liza, will yer marry me?'

'Na, Tom,' she answered quietly.

'Oh, Liza, won't you 'ave me?'

'Na, Tom, I can't.'

'Why not? You've come aht walkin' with me ever since Whitsun.'

'Ah, things is different now.'

'You're not walkin' aht with anybody else, are you, Liza?' he asked quickly.

'Na, not that.'

'Well, why won't yer, Liza? Oh Liza, I do love yer, I've never loved anybody as I love you!'

'Oh, I can't, Tom!'

'There ain't no one else?'

'Na.'

'Then why not?'

'I'm very sorry, Tom, but I don't love yer so as ter marry yer.'

'Oh, Liza!'

She could not see the look upon his face, but she heard the agony in his voice; and, moved with sudden pity, she bent out, threw her arms round his neck, and kissed him on both cheeks.

'Never mind old chap!' she said. 'I'm not worth troublin' abaht.'

And quickly drawing back, she slammed the window to, and moved into the further part of the room.

III

THE FOLLOWING DAY was Sunday. Liza when she was dressing her-self in the morning, felt the hardness of fate in the impossibility of eating one's cake and having it; she wished she had reserved her new dress, and had still before her the sensation of a first appearance in it. With a sigh she put on her ordinary everyday working dress, and proceeded to get the breakfast ready, for her mother had been out late the previous night, celebrating the new arrivals in the street, and had the 'rheumatics' this morning.

'Oo, my 'ead!' she was saying, as she pressed her hands on each side of her forehead. 'I've got the neuralgy again, wot shall I do? I dunno 'ow it is, but it always comes on Sunday mornings. Oo, an' my rheumatics, they give me sich a doin' in the night!'

'You'd better go to the 'orspital mother.'

'Not I!' answered the worthy lady, with great decision. 'You 'as a dozen young chaps messin' you abaht, and lookin' at yer, and then they tells yer ter leave off beer and spirrits. Well, wot I says, I says I can't do withaht my glass of beer.' She thumped her pillow to emphasize the statement.

'Wot with the work I 'ave ter do, lookin' after you and the cookin' and gettin' everythin' ready and doin' all the 'ouse-work, and goin' aht charring besides—well, I says, if I don't 'ave a drop of beer, I says, ter pull me together, I should be under the turf in no time.'

She munched her bread-and-butter and drank her tea.

'When you've done breakfast, Liza,' she said, 'you can give the grate a cleanin', an' my boots'd do with a bit of polishin'. Mrs. Tike, in the next 'ouse, 'll give yer some blackin'.'

She remained silent for a bit, then said:

'I don't think I shall get up ter-day. Liza. My rheumatics is bad. You can put the room straight and cook the dinner.'

'Arright, mother, you stay where you are, an' I'll do everythin' for yer.'

'Well, it's only wot yer ought to do, considerin' all the trouble you've been ter me when you was young, and considerin' thet when you was born the doctor thought I never should get through it. Wot 'ave you done with your week's money, Liza?'

'Oh, I've put it awy,' answered Liza quietly.

'Where?' asked her mother.

'Where it'll be safe.'

'Where's that?'

Liza was driven into a corner.

'Why d'you want ter know?' she asked.

'Why shouldn't I know; d'you think I want ter steal it from yer?'

'Na, not thet.'

'Well, why won't you tell me?'

'Oh, a thing's sifer when only one person knows where it is.'

This was a very discreet remark, but it set Mrs. Kemp in a whirlwind of passion. She raised herself and sat up in the bed, flourishing her clenched fist at her daughter.

'I know wot yer mean, you —— you!' Her language was emphatic, her epithets picturesque, but too forcible for reproduction. 'You think I'd steal it,' she went on. 'I know yer! D'yer think I'd go an' tike yer dirty money?'

'Well, mother,' said Liza, 'when I've told yer before, the money's perspired like.'

'Wot d'yer mean?'

'It got less.'

'Well, I can't 'elp thet, can I? Anyone can come in 'ere and tike the money.'

'If it's 'idden awy, they can't, can they, mother?' said Liza.

Mrs. Kemp shook her fist.

'You dirty slut, you,' she said, 'yer think I tike yer money! Why, you ought ter give it me every week instead of savin' it up and spendin' it on all sorts of muck, while I 'ave ter grind my very bones down to keep yer.'

'Yer know, mother, if I didn't 'ave a little bit saved up, we should be rather short when you're dahn in yer luck.'

Mrs. Kemp's money always ran out on Tuesday, and Liza had to keep things going till the following Saturday.

'Oh, don't talk ter me!' proceeded Mrs. Kemp. 'When I was a

girl I give all my money ter my mother. She never 'ad ter ask me for nothin'. On Saturday when I come 'ome with my wiges, I give it 'er every farthin'. That's wot a daughter ought ter do. I can say this for myself, I be'aved by my mother like a gal should. None of your prodigal sons for me! She didn't 'ave ter ask me for three 'apence ter get a drop of beer.'

Liza was wise in her generation; she held her tongue, and put on her hat.

'Now, you're goin' aht, and leavin' me; I dunno wot you get up to in the street with all those men. No good, I'll be bound. An' 'ere am I left alone, an' I might die for all you care.'

In her sorrow at herself the old lady began to cry, and Liza slipped out of the room and into the street.

Leaning against the wall of the opposite house was Tom; he came towards her.

''Ulloa!' she said, as she saw him. 'Wot are you doin' 'ere?'

'I was waitin' for you ter come aht, Liza,' he answered.

She looked at him quickly.

'I ain't comin' aht with yer ter-day, if thet's wot yer mean,' she said.

'I never thought of arskin' yer, Liza—after wot you said ter me last night.'

His voice was a little sad, and she felt so sorry for him.

'But yer did want ter speak ter me, didn't yer, Tom?' she said, more gently.

'You've got a day off ter-morrow, ain't yer?'

'Bank 'Oliday. Yus! Why?'

'Why, 'cause they've got a drag startin' from the "Red Lion" that's goin' down ter Chingford for the day—an' I'm goin'.'

'Yus!' she said.

He looked at her doubtfully.

'Will yer come too, Liza? It'll be a regular beeno; there's only goin' ter be people in the street. Eh, Liza?'

'Na, I can't'

'Why not?'

'I ain't got—I ain't got the ooftish.'

'I mean, won't yer come with me?'

'Na, Tom, thank yer; I can't do thet neither.'

'Yer might as well, Liza; it wouldn't 'urt yer.'

'Na, it wouldn't be right like; I can't come aht with yer, and then mean nothin'! It would be doin' yer aht of an outing.'

'I don't see why,' he said, very crestfallen.

'I can't go on keepin' company with you—after what I said last night.'

'I shan't enjoy it a bit without you, Liza.'

'You git somebody else, Tom. You'll do withaht me all right.'

She nodded to him, and walked up the street to the house of her friend Sally. Having arrived in front of it, she put her hands to her mouth in trumpet form, and shouted:

''I! 'I! 'I! Sally!'

A couple of fellows standing by copied her.

''I! 'I! 'I! Sally!'

'Garn!' said Liza, looking round at them.

Sally did not appear and she repeated her call. The men imitated her, and half a dozen took it up, so that there was enough noise to wake the seven sleepers.

''I! 'I! 'I! Sally!'

A head was put out of a top window, and Liza, taking off her hat, waved it, crying:

'Come on dahn, Sally!'

'Arright, old gal!' shouted the other. 'I'm comin'!'

'So's Christmas!' was Liza's repartee.

There was a clatter down the stairs, and Sally, rushing through the passage, threw herself on to her friend. They began fooling, in reminiscence of a melodrama they had lately seen together.

'Oh, my darlin' duck!' said Liza, kissing her and pressing her, with affected rapture, to her bosom.

'My sweetest sweet!' replied Sally, copying her.

'An' 'ow does your lidyship ter-day?'

'Oh!'—with immense languor—''fust class; and is your royal 'igh-ness quite well?'

'I deeply regret,' answered Liza, 'but my royal 'ighness 'as got the collywobbles.'

Sally was a small, thin girl, with sandy hair and blue eyes, and a very freckled complexion. She had an enormous mouth, with terrible, square teeth set wide apart, which looked as if they could masticate an iron bar. She was dressed like Liza, in a shortish black skirt and an old-fashioned bodice, green and grey and yellow with age; her sleeves were tucked up to the elbow, and she wore a singularly dirty apron, that had once been white.

'Wot 'ave you got yer 'air in them things for?' asked Liza, pointing to the curl-papers. 'Goin' aht with yer young man ter-day?'

'No, I'm going ter stay 'ere all day.'

'Wot for, then?'

'Why, 'Arry's going ter tike me ter Chingford ter-morrer.'

'Oh? In the "Red Lion" brake?'

'Yus. Are you goin'?'

'Na!'

'Not! Well, why don't you get round Tom? 'E'll tike yer, and jolly glad 'e'll be, too.'

''E arst me ter go with 'im, but I wouldn't.'

'Swop me bob—why not?'

'I ain't keeping company with 'im.'

'Yer might 'ave gone with 'im all the sime.'

'Na. You're goin' with 'Arry, ain't yer?'

'Yus!'

'An' you're goin' to 'ave 'im?'

'Right again!'

'Well, I couldn't go with Tom, and then throw him over.'

'Well, you are a mug!'

The two girls had strolled down towards the Westminster Bridge Road, and Sally, meeting her young man, had gone to him. Liza walked back, wishing to get home in time to cook the dinner. But she went slowly, for she knew every dweller in the street, and as she passed the groups sitting at their doors, as on the previous evening, but this time mostly engaged in peeling potatoes or shelling peas, she stopped and had a little chat. Everyone liked her, and was glad to have her company. 'Good old Liza,' they would say, as she left them, 'she's a rare good sort, ain't she?'

She asked after the aches and pains of all the old people, and delicately inquired after the babies, past and future; the children hung on to her skirts and asked her to play with them, and she would hold one end of the rope while tiny little ragged girls skipped, invariably entangling themselves after two jumps.

She had nearly reached home, when she heard a voice cry:

'Mornin'!'

She looked round and recognized the man whom Tom had told her was called Jim Blakeston. He was sitting on a stool at the door of one of the houses, playing with two young children, to whom he was giving rides on his knee. She remembered his heavy brown beard from the day before, and she had also an impression of great size; she noticed this morning that he was, in fact, a big man, tall and broad, and she saw besides that he had large, masculine features and pleasant brown eyes. She supposed him to be about forty.

'Mornin'!' he said again, as she stopped and looked at him.

'Well, yer needn't look as if I was goin' ter eat yer up, 'cause I ain't,' he said.

''Oo are you? I'm not afeard of yer.'

'Wot are yer so bloomin' red abaht?' he asked pointedly.

'Well, I'm 'ot.'

'You ain't shirty 'cause I kissed yer last night?'

'I'm not shirty; but it was pretty cool, considerin' like as I didn't know yer.'

'Well, you run into my arms.'

'Thet I didn't; you run aht and caught me.'

'An' kissed yer before you could say "Jack Robinson".' He laughed at the thought. 'Well, Liza,' he went on, 'seein' as 'ow I kissed yer against yer will, the best thing you can do ter make it up is to kiss me not against yer will.'

'Me?' said Liza, looking at him, open-mouthed. 'Well you are a pill!'

The children began to clamour for the riding, which had been discontinued on Liza's approach.

'Are them your kids?' she asked.

'Yus; them's two on 'em.'

"Ow many 'ave yer got?'

'Five; the eldest gal's fifteen, and the next one 'oo's a boy's twelve, and then there are these two and baby.'

'Well, you've got enough for your money.'

'Too many for me—and more comin'.'

'Ah well,' said Liza, laughing, 'thet's your fault, ain't it?'

Then she bade him good morning, and strolled off.

He watched her as she went, and saw half a dozen little boys surround her and beg her to join them in their game of cricket. They caught hold of her arms and skirts, and pulled her to their pitch.

'No, I can't,' she said trying to disengage herself. 'I've got the dinner ter cook.'

'Dinner ter cook?' shouted one small boy. 'Why, they always cooks the cats' meat at the shop.'

'You little so-and-so!' said Liza, somewhat inelegantly, making a dash at him.

He dodged her and gave a whoop; then turning he caught her round the legs, and another boy catching hold of her round the neck they dragged her down, and all three struggled on the ground, rolling over and over; the other boys threw themselves on the top, so that there was a great heap of legs and arms and heads waving and bobbing up and down.

Liza extricated herself with some difficulty, and taking off her hat she began cuffing the boys with it, using all the time the most lively expressions. Then, having cleared the field, she retired victorious into her own house and began cooking the dinner.

IV

BANK HOLIDAY WAS a beautiful day: the cloudless sky threatened a stifling heat for noontide, but early in the morning, when Liza got out of bed and threw open the window, it was fresh and cool. She dressed herself, wondering how she should spend her day; she thought of Sally going off to Chingford with her lover, and of herself remaining alone in the dull street with half the people away. She almost wished it were an ordinary work-day, and that there were no such things as bank holidays. And it seemed to be a little like two Sundays running, but with the second rather worse than the first. Her mother was still sleeping, and she was in no great hurry about getting the breakfast, but stood quietly looking out of the window at the house opposite.

In a little while she saw Sally coming along. She was arrayed in purple and fine linen—a very smart red dress, trimmed with velveteen, and a tremendous hat covered with feathers. She had reaped the benefit of keeping her hair in curl-papers since Saturday, and her sandy fringe stretched from ear to ear. She was in enormous spirits.

'Ulloa, Liza!' she called as soon as she saw her at the window.

Liza looked at her a little enviously.

'Ulloa!' she answered quietly.

'I'm just goin' to the "Red Lion" to meet 'Arry.'

'At what time d'yer start?'

'The brake leaves at 'alf-past eight sharp.'

'Why, it's only eight; it's only just struck at the church. 'Arry won't be there yet, will he?'

'Oh, 'e's sure ter be early. I couldn't wite. I've been witin' abaht since 'alf-past six. I've been up since five this morning.'

'Since five! What 'ave you been doin'?'

'Dressin' myself and doin' my 'air. I woke up so early. I've been dreamin' all the night abaht it. I simply couldn't sleep.'

'Well, you are a caution!' said Liza.

'Bust it, I don't go on the spree every day! Oh, I do 'ope I shall enjoy myself.'

'Why, you simply dunno where you are!' said Liza, a little crossly.

'Don't you wish you was comin', Liza?' asked Sally.

'Na! I could if I liked, but I don't want ter.'

'You are a coughdrop—thet's all I can say. Ketch me refusin' when I 'ave the chanst.'

'Well, it's done now. I ain't got the chanst any more.' Liza said this with just a little regret in her voice.

'Come on dahn to the "Red Lion", Liza, and see us off,' said Sally.

'No, I'm damned if I do!' answered Liza, with some warmth.

'You might as well. P'raps 'Arry won't be there, an' you can keep me company till 'e comes. An' you can see the 'orses.'

Liza was really very anxious to see the brake and the horses and the people going; but she hesitated a little longer. Sally asked her once again. Then she said:

'Arright; I'll come with yer, and wite till the bloomin' old thing starts.'

She did not trouble to put on a hat, but just walked out as she was, and accompanied Sally to the public-house which was getting up the expedition.

Although there was still nearly half an hour to wait, the brake was drawn up before the main entrance; it was large and long, with seats arranged crosswise, so that four people could sit on each; and it was drawn by two powerful horses, whose harness the coachman was now examining. Sally was not the first on the scene, for already half a dozen people had taken their places, but Harry had not yet arrived. The two girls stood by the public-door, looking at the preparations. Huge baskets full of food were brought out and stowed away; cases of beer were hoisted up and put in every possible place—under the seats, under the driver's legs, and even beneath the brake. As more people came up, Sally began to get excited about Harry's non-appearance.

'I say, I wish 'e'd come!' she said. ''E is lite.'

Then she looked up and down the Westminster Bridge Road to see if he was in view.

'Suppose 'e don't turn up! I will give it 'im when 'e comes for keepin' me witin' like this.'

'Why, there's a quarter of an hour yet,' said Liza, who saw nothing at all to get excited about.

At last Sally saw her lover, and rushed off to meet him. Liza was left alone, rather disconsolate at all this bustle and preparation. She was not sorry that she had refused Tom's invitation, but she did wish that she had conscientiously been able to accept it. Sally and her friend came up; attired in his Sunday best, he was a fit match for his lady-love—he wore a shirt and collar, unusual luxuries—and be carried under his arm a concertina to make things merry on the way.

'Ain't you goin', Liza?' he asked in surprise at seeing her without a hat and with her apron on.

'Na,' said Sally, 'ain't she a soft? Tom said 'e'd tike 'er, an' she wouldn't.'

'Well, I'm dashed!'

Then they climbed the ladder and took their seats, so that Liza was left alone again. More people had come along, and the brake was nearly full. Liza knew them all, but they were too busy taking their places to talk to her. At last Tom came. He saw her standing there and went up to her.

'Won't yer change yer mind, Liza, an' come along with us?'

'Na, Tom, I told yer I wouldn't—it's not right like.' She felt she must repeat that to herself often.

'I shan't enjoy it a bit without you,' he said.

'Well, I can't 'elp it!' she answered, somewhat sullenly.

At that moment a man came out of the public-house with a horn in his hand; her heart gave a great jump, for if there was anything she adored it was to drive along to the tootling of a horn. She really felt it was very hard lines that she must stay at home when all these people were going to have such a fine time; and they were all so merry, and she could picture to herself so well the delights of the drive and the picnic. She felt very much inclined to cry. But she mustn't go, and she wouldn't go: she repeated that to herself twice as the trumpeter gave a preliminary tootle.

Two more people hurried along, and when they came near Liza saw that they were Jim Blakeston and a woman whom she supposed to be his wife.

'Are you comin', Liza?' Jim said to her.

'No,' she answered. 'I didn't know you was goin'.'

'I wish you was comin',' he replied, 'we shall 'ave a game.'

She could only just keep back the sobs; she so wished she were going. It did seem hard that she must remain behind; and all because she wasn't going to marry Tom. After all, she didn't see why that should prevent her; there really was no need to refuse for that. She began to think she had acted foolishly: it didn't do anyone any good that she refused to go out with Tom, and no one thought it anything specially fine that she should renounce her pleasure. Sally merely thought her a fool.

Tom was standing by her side, silent, and looking disappointed and rather unhappy. Jim said to her, in a low voice:

'I am sorry you're not comin'!'

It was too much. She did want to go so badly, and she really couldn't resist any longer. If Tom would only ask her once more, and if she could only change her mind reasonably and decently, she would accept; but he stood silent, and she had to speak herself. It was very undignified.

'Yer know, Tom.' she said, 'I don't want ter spoil your day.'

'Well, I don't think I shall go alone; it 'ud be so precious slow.'

Supposing he didn't ask her again! What should she do? She looked up at the clock on the front of the pub, and noticed that it only wanted five minutes to the half-hour. How terrible it would be if the brake started and he didn't ask her! Her heart beat violently against her chest, and in her agitation she fumbled with the corner of her apron.

'Well, what can I do, Tom dear?'

'Why, come with me, of course. Oh. Liza, do say yes.'

She had got the offer again, and it only wanted a little seemly hesitation, and the thing was done.

'I should like ter, Tom,' she said. 'But d'you think it 'ud be arright?'

'Yus, of course it would. Come on, Liza!' In his eagerness he clasped her hand.

'Well,' she remarked, looking down, 'if it'd spoil your 'oliday—.'

'I won't go if you don't—swop me bob, I won't!' he answered.

'Well, if I come, it won't mean that I'm keepin' company with you.'

'Na, it won't mean anythin' you don't like.'

'Arright!' she said.

'You'll come?' he could hardly believe her.

'Yus!' she answered, smiling all over her face.

'You're a good sort, Liza! I say, 'Arry, Liza's comin'!' he shouted.

'Liza? 'Oorray!' shouted Harry.

"S'at right, Liza?' called Sally.

And Liza feeling quite joyful and light of heart called back: 'Yus!'

"Oorray!' shouted Sally in answer.

'Thet's right, Liza,' called Jim; and he smiled pleasantly as she looked at him.

'There's just room for you two 'ere,' said Harry, pointing to the vacant places by his side.

'Arright!' said Tom.

'I must jest go an' get a 'at an' tell mother,' said Liza.

'There's just three minutes. Be quick!' answered Tom, and as she scampered off as hard as she could go, he shouted to the coachman: "Old 'ard; there' another passenger comin' in a minute.'

'Arright, old cock,' answered the coachman: 'no 'urry!'

Liza rushed into the room, and called to her mother, who was still asleep:

'Mother! mother! I'm going to Chingford!'

Then tearing off her old dress she slipped into her gorgeous violet one; she kicked off her old ragged shoes and put on her new boots. She brushed her hair down and rapidly gave her fringe a twirl and a twist—it was luckily still moderately in curl from the previous Saturday—and putting on her black hat with all the feathers, she rushed along the street, and scrambling up the brake steps fell panting on Tom's lap.

The coachman cracked his whip, the trumpeter tootled his horn, and with a cry and a cheer from the occupants, the brake clattered down the road.

V

As SOON AS Liza had recovered herself she started examining the people on the brake; and first of all she took stock of the woman whom Jim Blakeston had with him.

'This is my missus!' said Jim, pointing to her with his thumb.

'You ain't been dahn in the street much, 'ave yer?' said Liza, by way of making the acquaintance.

'Na,' answered Mrs. Blakeston, 'my youngster's been dahn with the measles, an' I've 'ad my work cut out lookin' after 'im.'

'Oh, an' is 'e all right now?'

'Yus, 'e's gettin' on fine, an' Jim wanted ter go ter Chingford terday, an' 'e says ter me, well, 'e says, "You come along ter Chingford, too; it'll do you good." An' 'e says, "You can leave Polly"—she's my eldest, yer know— "you can leave Polly," says 'e, "ter look after the kids." So I says, "Well, I don't mind if I do," says I.'

Meanwhile Liza was looking at her. First she noticed her dress: she wore a black cloak and a funny, old-fashioned black bonnet; then examining the woman herself, she saw a middle-sized, stout person anywhere between thirty and forty years old. She had a large, fat face with a big mouth, and her hair was curiously done, parted in the middle and plastered down on each side of the head in little plaits. One could see that she was a woman of great strength, notwithstanding evident traces of hard work and much child-bearing.

Liza knew all the other passengers, and now that everyone was settled down and had got over the excitement of departure, they had time to greet one another. They were delighted to have Liza among them, for where she was there was no dullness. Her attention was first of all taken up by a young coster who had arrayed himself in the traditional costume—grey suit, tight trousers, and shiny buttons in profusion.

'Wot cheer, Bill!' she cried to him.

'Wot cheer, Liza!' he answered.

'You are got up dossy, you'll knock 'em.'

'Na then, Liza Kemp,' said his companion, turning round with mock indignation, 'you let my Johnny alone. If you come gettin' round 'im I'll give you wot for.'

'Arright, Clary Sharp, I don't want 'im,' answered Liza. 'I've got one of my own, an' thet's a good 'andful—ain't it, Tom?'

Tom was delighted, and, unable to find a repartee, in his pleasure gave Liza a great nudge with his elbow.

"Oo, I say,' said Liza, putting her hand to her side. 'Tike care of my ribs; you'll brike 'em.'

'Them's not yer ribs,' shouted a candid friend—'them's yer whale-bones yer afraid of breakin'.'

'Garn!'

"Ave yer got whale-bones?' said Tom, with affected simplicity, putting his arm round her waist to feel.

'Na, then,' she said, 'keep off the grass!'

'Well, I only wanted ter know if you'd got any.'

'Garn; yer don't git round me like thet.'

He still kept as he was.

'Na then,' she repeated, 'tike yer 'and away. If yer touch me there you'll 'ave ter marry me.'

'Thet's just wot I wants ter do, Liza!'

'Shut it!' she answered cruelly, and drew his arm away from her waist.

The horses scampered on, and the man behind blew his horn with vigour.

'Don't bust yerself, guv'nor!' said one of the passengers to him when he made a particularly discordant sound. They drove along eastwards, and as the hour grew later the streets became more filled and the traffic greater. At last they got on the road to Chingford, and caught up numbers of other vehicles going in the same direction—donkey-shays, pony-carts, tradesmen's carts, dog-carts, drags, brakes, every conceivable kind of wheel thing, all filled with people, the wretched donkey dragging along four solid rate-payers to the pair of stout horses easily managing a couple of score. They exchanged cheers and greetings as they passed, the 'Red Lion' brake being noticeable above all for its uproariousness. As the day wore on the sun became hotter, and the road seemed more dusty and threw up a greater heat.

'I am getting 'ot!' was the common cry, and everyone began to puff and sweat.

The ladies removed their cloaks and capes, and the men, following their example, took off their coats and sat in their shirt-sleeves. Whereupon ensued much banter of a not particularly edifying kind respecting the garments which each person would like to remove—which showed that the innuendo of French farce is not so unknown to the upright, honest Englishman as might be supposed.

At last came in sight the half-way house, where the horses were to have a rest and a sponge down. They had been talking of it for the last quarter of a mile, and when at length it was observed on the top of a hill a cheer broke out, and some thirsty wag began to sing 'Rule Britannia', whilst others burst forth with a different national ditty, 'Beer, Glorious Beer!' They drew up before the pub entrance, and all climbed down as quickly as they could. The bar was besieged, and potmen and barmaids were quickly busy drawing beer and handing it over to the eager folk outside.

THE IDYLL OF CORYDON AND PHYLLIS.

Gallantry ordered that the faithful swain and the amorous shepherdess should drink out of one and the same pot.

"Urry up an' 'ave your whack,' said Corydon, politely handing the foaming bowl for his fair one to drink from.

Phyllis, without replying, raised it to her lips and drank deep. The swain watched anxiously.

"Ere, give us a chanst!' he said, as the pot was raised higher and higher and its contents appeared to be getting less and less.

At this the amorous shepherdess stopped and handed the pot to her lover.

'Well, I'm dashed!' said Corydon, looking into it; and added: 'I guess you know a thing or two.' Then with courtly grace putting his own lips to the place where had been those of his beloved, finished the pint.

'Go' lumme!' remarked the shepherdess, smacking her lips, 'that was somethin' like!' And she put out her tongue and licked her lips, and then breathed deeply.

The faithful swain having finished, gave a long sigh, and said:

'Well, I could do with some more!'

'For the matter of thet, I could do with a gargle!'

Thus encouraged, the gallant returned to the bar, and soon brought out a second pint.

'You 'ave fust pop,' amorously remarked Phyllis, and he took a long drink and handed the pot to her.

She, with maiden modesty, turned it so as to have a different part to drink from; but he remarked as he saw her:

'You are bloomin' particular.'

Then, unwilling to grieve him, she turned it back again and applied her ruby lips to the place where his had been.

'Now we shan't be long!' she remarked, as she handed him back the pot.

The faithful swain took out of his pocket a short clay pipe, blew through it, filled it, and began to smoke, while Phyllis sighed at the thought of the cool liquid gliding down her throat, and with the pleasing recollection gently stroked her stomach. Then Corydon spat, and immediately his love said:

'I can spit farther than thet.'

'I bet yer yer can't.'

She tried, and did. He collected himself and spat again, further than before, she followed him, and in this idyllic contest they remained till the tootling horn warned them to take their places.

At last they reached Chingford, and here the horses were taken out and the drag, on which they were to lunch, drawn up in a sheltered spot. They were all rather hungry, but as it was not yet feeding-time, they scattered to have drinks meanwhile. Liza and Tom, with Sally and her young man, went off together to the nearest public-house, and as they drank beer, Harry, who was a great sportsman, gave them a graphic account of a prize-fight he had seen on the previous Saturday evening, which had been rendered specially memorable by one man being so hurt that he had died from the effects. It had evidently been a very fine affair, and Harry said that several swells from the West End had been present, and he related their ludicrous efforts to get in without being seen by anyone, and their terror when someone to frighten them called out 'Copper!' Then Tom and he entered into a discussion on the subject of boxing, in which Tom, being a shy and undogmatic sort of person, was entirely worsted. After this they strolled back to the brake, and found things being prepared for luncheon; the hampers were brought out and emptied, and the bottles of beer in great profusion made many a thirsty mouth thirstier.

'Come along, lidies an' gentlemen—if you are gentlemen,' shouted the coachman; 'the animals is now goin' ter be fed!'

'Garn awy,' answered somebody, 'we're not hanimals; we don't drink water.'

'You're too clever,' remarked the coachman; 'I can see you've just come from the board school.'

As the former speaker was a lady of quite mature appearance, the remark was not without its little irony. The other man blew his horn by way of grace, at which Liza called out to him:

'Don't do thet, you'll bust, I know you will, an' if you bust you'll quite spoil my dinner!'

Then they all set to. Pork-pies, saveloys, sausages, cold potatoes, hard-boiled eggs, cold bacon, veal, ham, crabs and shrimps, cheese, butter, cold suet-puddings and treacle, gooseberry-tarts, cherry-tarts, butter, bread, more sausages, and yet again pork-pies! They devoured the provisions like ravening beasts, stolidly, silently, earnestly, in large mouthfuls which they shoved down their throats unmasticated. The intelligent foreigner seeing them thus dispose of their food would have understood why England is a great nation. He would have understood why Britons never, never will be slaves. They never stopped except to drink, and then at each gulp they emptied their glass; no heel-taps! And still they ate, and still they drank—but as all things must cease, they stopped at last, and a long sigh of content broke from their two-and-thirty throats.

Then the gathering broke up, and the good folk paired themselves and separated. Harry and his lady strolled off to secluded byways in the forest, so that they might discourse of their loves and digest their dinner. Tom had all the morning been waiting for this happy moment; he had counted on the expansive effect of a full stomach to thaw his Liza's coldness, and he had pictured himself sitting on the grass with his back against the trunk of a spreading chestnut-tree, with his arm round his Liza's waist, and her head resting affectionately on his manly bosom. Liza, too, had foreseen the separation into couples after dinner, and had been racking her brains to find a means of getting out of it.

'I don't want 'im slobberin' abaht me,' she said; 'it gives me the sick, all this kissin' an' cuddlin'!'

She scarcely knew why she objected to his caresses; but they bored her and made her cross. But luckily the blessed institution of marriage came to her rescue, for Jim and his wife naturally had no particular desire to spend the afternoon together, and Liza, seeing a little embarrassment on their part, proposed that they should go for a walk together in the forest.

Jim agreed at once, and with pleasure, but Tom was dreadfully disappointed. He hadn't the courage to say anything, but he glared at Blakeston. Jim smiled benignly at him, and Tom began to sulk. Then they began a funny walk through the woods. Jim tried to go on with Liza, and Liza was not at all disinclined to this, for she had come to the conclusion that Jim, notwithstanding his 'cheek', was not "alf a bad sort'. But Tom kept walking alongside of them, and as Jim slightly quickened his pace so as to get Liza on in front, Tom quickened his, and Mrs. Blakeston, who didn't want to be left behind, had to break into a little trot to keep up with them. Jim tried also to get Liza all to himself in the conversation, and let Tom see that he was out in the cold, but Tom would break in with cross, sulky remarks, just to make the others uncomfortable. Liza at last got rather vexed with him.

'Strikes me you got aht of bed the wrong way this mornin',' she said to him.

'Yer didn't think thet when yer said you'd come aht with me.' He emphasized the 'me'.

Liza shrugged her shoulders.

'You give me the 'ump,' she said. 'If yer wants ter mike a fool of yerself, you can go elsewhere an' do it.'

'I suppose yer want me ter go awy now,' he said angrily.

'I didn't say I did.'

'Arright, Liza, I won't stay where I'm not wanted.' And turning on his heel he marched off, striking through the underwood into the midst of the forest.

He felt extremely unhappy as he wandered on, and there was a choky feeling in his throat as he thought of Liza: she was very unkind and ungrateful, and he wished he had never come to Chingford. She might so easily have come for a walk with him instead of going with that beast of a Blakeston; she wouldn't ever do anything for him, and he hated her—but all the same, he was a poor foolish thing in love, and he began to feel that perhaps he had been a little exacting and a little forward to take offence. And then he wished he had never said anything, and he wanted so much to see her and make it up. He made his way back to Chingford, hoping she would not make him wait too long.

Liza was a little surprised when Tom turned and left them.

'Wot 'as 'e got the needle abaht?' she said.

'Why, 'e's jealous,' answered Jim, with a laugh.

'Tom jealous?'

'Yus; 'e's jealous of me.'

'Well, 'e ain't got no cause ter be jealous of anyone—that 'e ain't!' said Liza, and continued by telling him all about Tom: how he had wanted to marry her and she wouldn't have him, and how she had only agreed to come to Chingford with him on the understanding that she should preserve her entire freedom. Jim listened sympathetically, but his wife paid no attention; she was doubtless engaged in thought respecting her household or her family.

When they got back to Chingford they saw Tom standing in solitude looking at them. Liza was struck by the woebegone expression on his face; she felt she had been cruel to him, and leaving the Blakestons went up to him.

'I say, Tom,' she said, 'don't tike on so; I didn't mean it.'

He was bursting to apologize for his behaviour.

'Yer know, Tom,' she went on, 'I'm rather 'asty, an' I'm sorry I said wot I did.'

'Oh, Liza, you are good! You ain't cross with me?'

'Me? Na; it's you thet oughter be cross.'

'You are a good sort, Liza!'

'You ain't vexed with me?'

'Give me Liza every time; that's wot I say,' he answered, as his face lit up. 'Come along an' 'ave tea, an' then we'll go for a donkey-ride.'

The donkey-ride was a great success. Liza was a little afraid at first, so Tom walked by her side to take care of her, she screamed the moment the beast began to trot, and clutched hold of Tom to save herself from falling, and as he felt her hand on his shoulder, and heard her appealing cry: 'Oh, do 'old me! I'm fallin'!' he felt that he had never in his life been so deliciously happy. The whole party joined in, and it was proposed that they should have races; but in the first heat, when the donkeys broke into a canter, Liza fell off into Tom's arms and the donkeys scampered on without her.

'I know wot I'll do,' she said, when the runaway had been recovered. 'I'll ride 'im straddlewyse.'

'Garn!' said Sally, 'yer can't with petticoats.'

'Yus, I can, an' I will too!'

So another donkey was procured, this time with a man's saddle, and putting her foot in the stirrup, she cocked her leg over and took her seat triumphantly. Neither modesty nor bashfulness was to be reckoned among Liza's faults, and in this position she felt quite at ease.

'I'll git along arright now, Tom,' she said; 'you garn and git yerself a moke, and come an' jine in.'

The next race was perfectly uproarious. Liza kicked and beat her donkey with all her might, shrieking and laughing the white, and finally came in winner by a length. After that they felt rather warm and dry, and repaired to the public-house to restore themselves and talk over the excitements of the racecourse.

When they had drunk several pints of beer Liza and Sally, with their respective adorers and the Blakestons, walked round to find other means of amusing themselves; they were arrested by a coconut-shy.

'Oh, let's 'ave a shy!' said Liza, excitedly, at which the unlucky men had to pull out their coppers, while Sally and Liza made ludicrously bad shots at the coconuts.

'It looks so bloomin' easy,' said Liza, brushing up her hair, 'but I can't 'it the blasted thing. You 'ave a shot, Tom.'

He and Harry were equally unskilful, but Jim got three coconuts running, and the proprietors of the show began to look on him with some concern.

'You are a dab at it,' said Liza, in admiration.

They tried to induce Mrs. Blakeston to try her luck, but she stoutly refused.

'I don't old with such foolishness. It's wiste of money ter me,' she said.

'Na then, don't crack on, old tart,' remarked her husband, 'let's go an' eat the coconuts.'

There was one for each couple, and after the ladies had sucked the juice they divided them and added their respective shares to their dinners and teas. Supper came next. Again they fell to sausage-rolls, boiled eggs, and saveloys, and countless bottles of beer were added to those already drunk.

'I dunno 'ow many bottles of beer I've drunk—I've lost count,' said Liza; whereat there was a general laugh.

They still had an hour before the brake was to start back, and it was then the concertinas came in useful. They sat down on the grass, and the concert was begun by Harry, who played a solo; then there was a call for a song, and Jim stood up and sang that ancient ditty, 'O dem Golden Kippers, O'. There was no shyness in the company, and Liza, almost without being asked, gave another popular comic song. Then there was more concertina playing, and another demand for a song. Liza turned to Tom, who was sitting quietly by her side.

'Give us a song, old cock,' she said.

'I can't,' he answered. 'I'm not a singin' sort.' At which Blakeston got up and offered to sing again.

'Tom is rather a soft,' said Liza to herself, 'not like that cove Blakeston.'

They repaired to the public-house to have a few last drinks before the brake started, and when the horn blew to warn them, rather unsteadily, they proceeded to take their places.

Liza, as she scrambled up the steps, said: 'Well, I believe I'm boozed.'

The coachman had arrived at the melancholy stage of intoxication, and was sitting on his box holding his reins, with his head bent on his chest. He was thinking sadly of the long-lost days of his youth, and wishing he had been a better man.

Liza had no respect for such holy emotions, and she brought down her fist on the crown of his hat, and bashed it over his eyes.

'Na then, old jellybelly,' she said, 'wot's the good of 'avin' a fice as long as a kite?'

He turned round and smote her.

'Jellybelly yerself!' said he.

'Puddin' fice!' she cried.

'Kite fice!'

'Boss eye!'

She was tremendously excited, laughing and singing, keeping the whole company in an uproar. In her jollity she had changed hats with Tom, and he in her big feathers made her shriek with laughter. When they started they began to sing 'For 'e's a jolly good feller', making the night resound with their noisy voices.

Liza and Tom and the Blakestons had got a seat together, Liza being between the two men. Tom was perfectly happy, and only wished that they might go on so for ever. Gradually as they drove along they became quieter, their singing ceased, and they talked in undertones. Some of them slept; Sally and her young man were leaning up against one another, slumbering quite peacefully. The night was beautiful, the sky still blue, very dark, scattered over with countless brilliant stars, and Liza, as she looked up at the heavens, felt a certain emotion, as if she wished to be taken in someone's arms, or feel some strong man's caress; and there was in her heart a strange sensation as though it were growing big. She stopped speaking, and all four were silent. Then slowly she felt Tom's arm steal round her waist, cautiously, as though it were afraid of being there; this time both she and Tom were happy. But suddenly there was a movement on the other side of her, a hand was advanced along her leg, and her hand was grasped and gently pressed. It was Jim Blakeston. She started a little and began trembling so that Tom noticed it, and whispered:

'You're cold, Liza.'

'Na, I'm not, Tom; it's only a sort of shiver thet went through me.'

His arm gave her waist a squeeze, and at the same time the big rough hand pressed her little one. And so she sat between them till they reached the 'Red Lion' in the Westminster Bridge Road, and Tom said to himself: 'I believe she does care for me after all.'

When they got down they all said good night, and Sally and Liza, with their respective slaves and the Blakestons, marched off homewards. At the corner of Vere Street Harry said to Tom and Blakeston:

'I say, you blokes, let's go an' 'ave another drink before closin' time.'

'I don't mind,' said Tom, 'after we've took the gals 'ome.'

'Then we shan't 'ave time, it's just on closin' time now.' answered Harry.

'Well, we can't leave 'em 'ere.'

'Yus, you can,' said Sally. 'No one'll run away with us.'

Tom did not want to part from Liza, but she broke in with:

'Yus, go on, Tom. Sally an' me'll git along arright, an' you ain't got too much time.'

'Yus, good night, 'Arry,' said Sally to settle the matter.

'Good night, old gal,' he answered, 'give us another slobber.'

And she, not at all unwilling, surrendered herself to him, while he imprinted two sounding kisses on her cheeks.

'Good night, Tom,' said Liza, holding out her hand.

'Good night, Liza,' he answered, taking it, but looking very wistfully at her.

She understood, and with a kindly smile lifted up her face to him. He bent down and, taking her in his arms, kissed her passionately.

'You do kiss nice, Liza,' he said, making the others laugh.

'Thanks for tikin' me aht, old man,' she said as they parted.

'Arright, Liza,' he answered, and added, almost to himself: 'God bless yer!'

''Ulloa, Blakeston, ain't you comin'?' said Harry, seeing that Jim was walking off with his wife instead of joining him and Tom.

'Na,' he answered, 'I'm goin''ome. I've got ter be up at five ter-morrer.'

'You are a chap!' said Harry, disgustedly, strolling off with Tom to the pub, while the others made their way down the sleeping street.

The house where Sally lived came first, and she left them; then, walking a few yards more, they came to the Blakestons', and after a little talk at the door Liza bade the couple good night, and was left to walk the rest of the way home. The street was perfectly silent, and the lamp-posts, far apart, threw a dim light which only served to make Lisa realize her solitude. There was such a difference between the street at midday, with its swarms of people, and now, when there was neither sound nor soul besides herself, that even she was struck by it. The regular line of houses on either side, with the even pavements and straight, cemented road, seemed to her like some desert place, as if everyone were dead, or a fire had raged and left it all desolate. Suddenly she heard a footstep, she started and looked back. It was a man hurrying behind her, and in a moment she had recognized Jim. He beckoned to her, and in a low voice called:

'Liza!'

She stopped till he had come up to her.

'Wot 'ave yer come aht again for?' she said.

'I've come aht ter say good night to you, Liza,' he answered.

'But yer said good night a moment ago.'

'I wanted to say it again—properly.'

'Where's yer missus?'

'Oh, she's gone in. I said I was dry and was goin' ter 'ave a drink after all.'

'But she'll know yer didn't go ter the pub.'

'Na, she won't, she's gone straight upstairs to see after the kid. I wanted ter see yer alone, Liza.'

'Why?'

He didn't answer, but tried to take hold of her hand. She drew it away quickly. They walked in silence till they came to Liza's house.

'Good night,' said Liza.

'Won't you come for a little walk, Liza?'

'Tike care no one 'ears you,' she added, in a whisper, though why she whispered she did not know.

'Will yer?' he asked again.

'Na—you've got to get up at five.'

'Oh, I only said thet not ter go inter the pub with them.'

'So as yer might come 'ere with me?' asked Liza.

'Yus!'

'No, I'm not comin'. Good night.'

'Well, say good night nicely.'

'Wot d'yer mean?'

'Tom said you did kiss nice.'

She looked at him without speaking, and in a moment he had clasped his arms round her, almost lifting her off her feet, and kissed her. She turned her face away.

'Give us yer lips, Liza,' he whispered—'give us yer lips.'

He turned her face without resistance and kissed her on the mouth.

At last she tore herself from him, and opening the door slid away into the house.

VI

NEXT MORNING ON her way to the factory Liza came up with Sally. They were both of them rather stale and bedraggled after the day's outing; their fringes were ragged and untidily straying over their foreheads, their back hair, carelessly tied in a loose knot, fell over their necks and threatened completely to come down. Liza had not had time to put her hat on, and was holding it in her hand. Sally's was pinned on sideways, and she had to bash it down on her head every now and then to prevent its coming off. Cinderella herself was not more transformed than they were; but Cinderella even in her rags was virtuously tidy and patched up, while Sally had a great tear in her shabby dress, and Liza's stockings were falling over her boots.

'Wot cheer, Sal!' said Liza, when she caught her up.

'Oh, I 'ave got sich a 'ead on me this mornin'!' she remarked, turning round a pale face: heavily lined under the eyes.

'I don't feel too chirpy neither,' said Liza, sympathetically.

'I wish I 'adn't drunk so much beer,' added Sally, as a pang shot through her head.

'Oh, you'll be arright in a bit,' said Liza. Just then they heard the clock strike eight, and they began to run so that they might not miss getting their tokens and thereby their day's pay; they turned into the street at the end of which was the factory, and saw half a hundred women running like themselves to get in before it was too late.

All the morning Liza worked in a dead-and-alive sort of fashion, her head like a piece of lead with electric shocks going through it when she moved, and her tongue and mouth hot and dry. At last lunch-time came.

'Come on, Sal,' said Liza, 'I'm goin' to 'ave a glass o' bitter. I can't stand this no longer.'

So they entered the public-house opposite, and in one draught finished their pots. Liza gave a long sigh of relief.

'That bucks you up, don't it?'

'I was dry! I ain't told yer yet, Liza, 'ave I? 'E got it aht last night.'

'Who d'yer mean?'

'Why, 'Arry. 'E spit it aht at last.'

'Arst yer ter nime the day?' said Liza, smiling.

'Thet's it.'

'And did yer?'

'Didn't I jest!' answered Sally, with some emphasis. 'I always told yer I'd git off before you.'

'Yus!' said Liza, thinking.

'Yer know, Liza, you'd better tike Tom; 'e ain't a bad sort.' She was quite patronizing.

'I'm goin' ter tike 'oo I like; an' it ain't nobody's business but mine.'

'Arright, Liza, don't get shirty over it; I don't mean no offence.'

'What d'yer say it for then?'

'Well, I thought as seeing as yer'd gone aht with 'im yesterday thet yer meant ter after all.'

''E wanted ter tike me; I didn't arsk 'im.'

'Well, I didn't arsk my 'Arry, either.'

'I never said yer did,' replied Liza.

'Oh, you've got the 'ump, you 'ave!' finished Sally, rather angrily.

The beer had restored Liza: she went back to work without a headache, and, except for a slight languor, feeling no worse for the previous day's debauch. As she worked on she began going over in her mind the events of the preceding day, and she found entwined in all her thoughts the burly person of Jim Blakeston. She saw him walking by her side in the Forest, presiding over the meals, playing the concertina, singing, joking, and finally, on the drive back, she felt the heavy form by her side, and the big, rough hand holding hers, while Tom's arm was round her waist. Tom! That was the first time he had entered her mind, and he sank into a shadow beside the other. Last of all she remembered the walk home from the pub, the good nights, and the rapid footsteps as Jim caught her up, and the kiss. She blushed and looked up quickly to see whether any of the girls were looking at her; she could not help thinking of that moment when he took her in his arms; she still felt the roughness of his beard pressing on her mouth. Her heart seemed to grow larger in her breast, and she caught for breath as she threw back her head as if to receive his lips again. A shudder ran through her from the vividness of the thought.

'Wot are you shiverin' for, Liza?' asked one of the girls. 'You ain't cold.'

'Not much,' answered Liza, blushing awkwardly on her meditations being broken into. 'Why, I'm sweatin' so—I'm drippin' wet.'

'I expect yer caught cold in the Faurest yesterday.'

'I see your mash as I was comin' along this mornin'.'

Liza stared a little.

'I ain't got one, 'oo d'yer mean, ay?'

'Yer only Tom, of course. 'E did look washed aht. Wot was yer doin' with 'im yesterday?'

"E ain't got nothin' ter do with me, 'e ain't.'

'Garn, don't you tell me!'

The bell rang, and, throwing over their work, the girls trooped off, and after chattering in groups outside the factory gates for a while, made their way in different directions to their respective homes. Liza and Sally went along together.

'I sy, we are comin' aht!' cried Sally, seeing the advertisement of a play being acted at the neighbouring theatre.

'I should like ter see thet!' said Liza, as they stood arm-in-arm in front of the flaring poster. It represented two rooms and a passage in between; in one room a dead man was lying on the floor, while two others were standing horror-stricken, listening to a youth who was in the passage, knocking at the door.

'You see, they've 'killed im,' said Sally, excitedly.

'Yus, any fool can see thet! an' the one ahtside, wot's 'e doin' of?'

'Ain't 'e beautiful? I'll git my 'Arry ter tike me, I will. I should like ter see it. 'E said 'e'd tike me to the ply.'

They strolled on again, and Liza, leaving Sally, made her way to her mother's. She knew she must pass Jim's house, and wondered whether she would see him. But as she walked along the street she saw Tom coming the opposite way; with a sudden impulse she turned back so as not to meet him, and began walking the way she had come. Then thinking herself a fool for what she had done, she turned again and walked towards him. She wondered if she had seen her or noticed her movement, but when she looked down the street he was nowhere to be seen; he had not caught sight of her, and had evidently gone in to see a mate in one or other of the houses. She quickened her step, and passing the house where lived Jim, could not help looking up; he was standing at the door watching her, with a smile on his lips.

'I didn't see yer, Mr. Blakeston,' she said, as he came up to her.

'Didn't yer? Well, I knew yer would; an' I was witin' for yer ter look up. I see yer before ter-day.'

'Na, when?'

'I passed be'ind yer as you an' thet other girl was lookin' at the advertisement of thet ply.'

'I never see yer.'

'Na, I know yer didn't. I 'ear yer say, you says: "I should like to see thet."'

'Yus, an' I should too.'

'Well, I'll tike yer.'

'You?'

'Yus; why not?'

'I like thet; wot would yer missus sy?'

'She wouldn't know.'

'But the neighbours would!'

'No they wouldn't, no one 'd see us.'

He was speaking in a low voice so that people could not hear.

'You could meet me ahtside the theatre,' he went on.

'Na, I couldn't go with you; you're a married man.'

'Garn! wot's the matter—jest ter go ter the ply? An' besides, my missus can't come if she wanted, she's got the kids ter look after.'

'I should like ter see it,' said Liza meditatively.

They had reached her house, and Jim said:

'Well, come aht this evenin' and tell me if yer will—eh, Liza?'

'Na, I'm not comin' aht this evening.'

'Thet won't 'urt yer. I shall wite for yer.'

"Tain't a bit of good your witing', 'cause I shan't come.'

'Well, then, look 'ere, Liza; next Saturday night's the last night, an' I shall go to the theatre, any'ow. An' if you'll come, you just come to the door at 'alf-past six, an' you'll find me there. See?'

'Na, I don't,' said Liza, firmly.

'Well, I shall expect yer.'

'I shan't come, so you needn't expect.' And with that she walked into the house and slammed the door behind her.

Her mother had not come in from her day's charing, and Liza set about getting her tea. She thought it would be rather lonely eating it alone, so pouring out a cup of tea and putting a little condensed milk into it, she cut a huge piece of bread-and-butter, and sat herself down outside on the doorstep. Another woman came downstairs, and seeing Liza, sat down by her side and began to talk.

'Why, Mrs. Stanley, wot 'ave yer done to your 'ead?' asked Liza, noticing a bandage round her forehead.

'I 'ad an accident last night,' answered the woman, blushing uneasily.

'Oh, I am sorry! Wot did yer do to yerself?'

'I fell against the coal-scuttle and cut my 'ead open.'

'Well, I never!'

'To tell yer the truth, I 'ad a few words with my old man. But one doesn't like them things to get abaht; yer won't tell anyone, will yer?'

'Not me!' answered Liza. 'I didn't know yer husband was like thet.'

'Oh, 'e's as gentle as a lamb when 'e's sober,' said Mrs. Stanley, apologetically. 'But, Lor' bless yer, when 'e's 'ad a drop too much 'e's a demond, an' there's no two ways abaht it.'

'An' you ain't been married long neither?' said Liza.

'Na, not above eighteen months; ain't it disgriceful? Thet's wot the doctor at the 'orspital says ter me. I 'ad ter go ter the 'orspital. You should have seen 'ow it bled!—it bled all dahn' my fice, and went streamin' like a bust waterpipe. Well, it fair frightened my old man, an' I says ter 'im, "I'll charge yer," an' although I was bleedin' like a bloomin' pig I shook my fist at 'im, an' I says, "I'll charge ye—see if I don't!" An' 'e says, "Na," says 'e, "don't do thet, for God's sike, Kitie, I'll git three months." "An' serve yer damn well right!" says I, an' I went aht an' left 'im. But, Lor' bless yer, I wouldn't charge 'im! I know 'e don't mean it; 'e's as gentle as a lamb when 'e's sober.' She smiled quite affectionately as she said this.

'Wot did yer do, then?' asked Liza.

'Well, as I wos tellin' yer, I went to the 'orspital, an' the doctor 'e says to me, "My good woman," says 'e, "you might have been very seriously injured." An' me not been married eighteen months! An' as I was tellin' the doctor all about it, "Missus," 'e says ter me, lookin' at me straight in the eyeball. "Missus," says 'e, "'ave you been drinkin'?" "Drinkin'?" says I; "no! I've 'ad a little drop, but as for drinkin'! Mind," says I, "I don't say I'm a teetotaller—I'm not, I 'ave my glass of beer, and I like it. I couldn't do withaht it, wot with the work I 'ave, I must 'ave somethin' ter keep me tergether. But as for drinkin' 'eavily! Well! I can say this, there ain't a soberer woman than myself in all London. Why, my first 'usband never touched a drop. Ah, my first 'usband, 'e was a beauty, 'e was.'"

She stopped the repetition of her conversation and addressed herself to Liza.

"E was thet different ter this one. 'E was a man as 'ad seen better days. 'E was a gentleman!' She mouthed the word and emphasized it with an expressive nod.

"E was a gentleman and a Christian. 'E'd been in good circumstances in 'is time; an' 'e was a man of education and a teetotaller, for twenty-two years.'

At that moment Liza's mother appeared on the scene.

'Good evenin', Mrs. Stanley,' she said, politely.

'The sime ter you, Mrs. Kemp.' replied that lady, with equal courtesy.

'An' 'ow is your poor 'ead?' asked Liza's mother, with sympathy.

'Oh, it's been achin' cruel. I've hardly known wot ter do with myself.'

'I'm sure 'e ought ter be ashimed of 'imself for treatin' yer like thet.'

'Oh, it wasn't 'is blows I minded so much, Mrs. Kemp,' replied Mrs. Stanley, 'an' don't you think it. It was wot 'e said ter me. I can stand a blow as well as any woman. I don't mind thet, an' when 'e don't tike a mean advantage of me I can stand up for myself an' give as good as I tike; an' many's the time I give my fust husband a black eye. But the language 'e used, an' the things 'e called me! It made me blush to the roots of my 'air; I'm not used ter bein' spoken ter like thet. I was in good circumstances when my fust 'usband was alive, 'e earned between two an' three pound a week, 'e did. As I said to 'im this mornin', "'Ow a gentleman can use sich language, I dunno."'

"Usbands is cautious, 'owever good they are,' said Mrs. Kemp, aphoristically. 'But I mustn't stay aht 'ere in the night air.'

"As yer rheumatism been troublin' yer litely?' asked Mrs. Stanley.

'Oh, cruel. Liza rubs me with embrocation every night, but it torments me cruel.'

Mrs. Kemp then went into the house, and Liza remained talking to Mrs. Stanley, she, too, had to go in, and Liza was left alone. Some while she spent thinking of nothing, staring vacantly in front of her, enjoying the cool and quiet of the evening. But Liza could not be left alone long, several boys came along with a bat and a ball, and fixed upon the road just in front of her for their pitch. Taking off their coats they piled them up at the two ends, and were ready to begin.

'I say, old gal,' said one of them to Liza, 'come an' have a gime of cricket, will yer?'

'Na, Bob, I'm tired.'

'Come on!'

'Na, I tell you I won't.'

'She was on the booze yesterday, an' she ain't got over it,' cried another boy.

'I'll swipe yer over the snitch!' replied Liza to him, and then on being asked again, said:

'Leave me alone, won't yer?'

'Liza's got the needle ter-night, thet's flat,' commented a third member of the team.

'I wouldn't drink if I was you, Liza,' added another, with mock gravity. 'It's a bad 'abit ter git into,' and he began rolling and swaying about like a drunken man.

If Liza had been 'in form' she would have gone straight away and given the whole lot of them a sample of her strength; but she was only rather bored and vexed that they should disturb her quietness, so she let them talk. They saw she was not to be drawn, and leaving her, set to their game. She watched them for some time, but her thoughts gradually lost themselves, and insensibly her mind was filled with a burly form, and she was again thinking of Jim.

"E is a good sort ter want ter tike me ter the ply,' she said to herself. 'Tom never arst me!'

Jim had said he would come out in the evening; he ought to be here soon, she thought. Of course she wasn't going to the theatre with him, but she didn't mind talking to him; she rather enjoyed being asked to do a thing and refusing, and she would have liked another opportunity of doing so. But he didn't come and he had said he would!

'I say, Bill,' she said at last to one of the boys who was fielding close beside her, 'that there Blakeston—d'you know 'im?'

'Yes, rather; why, he works at the sime plice as me.'

'Wot's 'e do with 'isself in the evening; I never see 'im abaht?'

'I dunno. I see 'im this evenin' go into the "Red Lion". I suppose 'e's there, but I dunno.'

Then he wasn't coming. Of course she had told him she was going to stay indoors, but he might have come all the same—just to see.

'I know Tom 'ud 'ave come,' she said to herself, rather sulkily.

'Liza! Liza!' she heard her mother's voice calling her.

'Arright, I'm comin',' said Liza.

'I've been witin' for you this last 'alf-hour ter rub me.'

'Why didn't yer call?' asked Liza.

'I did call. I've been callin' this last I dunno 'ow long; it's give me quite a sore throat.'

'I never 'eard yer.'

'Na, yer didn't want ter 'ear me, did yer? Yer don't mind if I dies with rheumatics, do yer? I know.'

Liza did not answer, but took the bottle, and, pouring some of the liniment on her hand, began to rub it into Mrs. Kemp's rheumatic joints, while the invalid kept complaining and grumbling at everything Liza did.

'Don't rub so 'ard, Liza, you'll rub all the skin off.'

Then when Liza did it as gently as she could, she grumbled again.

'If yer do it like thet, it won't do no good at all. You want ter sive yerself trouble—I know yer. When I was young girls didn't mind a little bit of 'ard work—but, law bless yer, you don't care abaht my rheumatics, do yer?'

At last she finished, and Liza went to bed by her mother's side.

VII

TWO DAYS PASSED, and it was Friday morning. Liza had got up early and strolled off to her work in good time, but she did not meet her faithful Sally on the way, nor find her at the factory when she herself arrived. The bell rang and all the girls trooped in, but still Sally did not come. Liza could not make it out, and was thinking she would be shut out, when just as the man who gave out the tokens for the day's work was pulling down the shutter in front of his window, Sally arrived, breathless and perspiring.

'Whew! Go' lumme, I am 'ot!' she said, wiping her face with her apron.

'I thought you wasn't comin',' said Liza.

'Well, I only just did it; I overslep' myself. I was aht lite last night.'

'Were yer?'

'Me an' 'Arry went ter see the ply. Oh, Liza, it's simply spiffin'! I've never see sich a good ply in my life. Lor'! Why, it mikes yer blood run cold: they 'ang a man on the stige; oh, it mide me creep all over!'

And then she began telling Liza all about it—the blood and thunder, the shooting, the railway train, the murder, the bomb, the hero, the funny man—jumbling everything up in her excitement, repeating little scraps of dialogue—all wrong—gesticulating, getting excited and red in the face at the recollection. Liza listened rather crossly, feeling bored at the detail into which Sally was going: the piece really didn't much interest her.

'One 'ud think yer'd never been to a theatre in your life before,' she said.

'I never seen anything so good, I can tell yer. You tike my tip, and git Tom ter tike yer.'

'I don't want ter go; an' if I did I'd py for myself an' go alone.'

'Cheese it! That ain't 'alf so good. Me an' 'Arry, we set together, 'im with 'is arm round my wiste and me oldin' 'is 'and. It was jam, I can tell yer!'

'Well, I don't want anyone sprawlin' me abaht, thet ain't my mark!'

'But I do like 'Arry; you dunno the little ways 'e 'as; an' we're goin' ter be married in three weeks now. 'Arry said, well, 'e says, "I'll git a licence." "Na," says I, "'ave the banns read aht in church: it seems more reg'lar like to 'ave banns; so they're goin' ter be read aht next Sunday. You'll come with me 'an 'ear them, won't yer, Liza?"'

'Yus, I don't mind.'

On the way home Sally insisted on stopping in front of the poster and explaining to Liza all about the scene represented.

'Oh, you give me the sick with your "Fital Card", you do! I'm goin' 'ome.' And she left Sally in the midst of her explanation.

'I dunno wot's up with Liza,' remarked Sally to a mutual friend. 'She's always got the needle, some'ow.'

'Oh, she's barmy,' answered the friend.

'Well, I do think she's a bit dotty sometimes—I do really,' rejoined Sally.

Liza walked homewards, thinking of the play; at length she tossed her head impatiently.

'I don't want ter see the blasted thing; an' if I see that there Jim I'll tell 'im so; swop me bob, I will.'

She did see him; he was leaning with his back against the wall of his house, smoking. Liza knew he had seen her, and as she walked by pretended not to have noticed him. To her disgust, he let her pass, and she was thinking he hadn't seen her after all, when she heard him call her name.

'Liza!'

She turned round and started with surprise very well imitated. 'I didn't see you was there!' she said.

'Why did yer pretend not ter notice me, as yer went past—eh, Liza?'

'Why, I didn't see yer.'

'Garn! But you ain't shirty with me?'

'Wot 'ave I got to be shirty abaht?'

He tried to take her hand, but she drew it away quickly. She was getting used to the movement. They went on talking, but Jim did not mention the theatre; Liza was surprised, and wondered whether he had forgotten.

'Er—Sally went to the ply last night,' she said, at last.

'Oh!' he said, and that was all.

She got impatient.

'Well, I'm off!' she said.

'Na, don't go yet; I want ter talk ter yer,' he replied.

'Wot abaht? anythin' in partickler?' She would drag it out of him if she possibly could.

'Not thet I knows on,' he said, smiling.

'Good night!' she said, abruptly, turning away from him.

'Well, I'm damned if 'e ain't forgotten!' she said to herself, sulkily, as she marched home.

The following evening about six o'clock, it suddenly struck her that it was the last night of the 'New and Sensational Drama'.

'I do like thet Jim Blakeston,' she said to herself; 'fancy treatin' me like thet! You wouldn't catch Tom doin' sich a thing. Bli'me if I speak to 'im again, the ——. Now I shan't see it at all. I've a good mind ter go on my own 'ook. Fancy 'is forgettin' all abaht it, like thet!'

She was really quite indignant; though, as she had distinctly refused Jim's offer, it was rather hard to see why.

"E said 'e'd wite for me ahtside the doors; I wonder if 'e's there. I'll go an' see if 'e is, see if I don't—an' then if 'e's there, I'll go in on my own 'ook, jist ter spite 'im!'

She dressed herself in her best, and, so that the neighbours shouldn't see her, went up a passage between some model lodging-house buildings, and in this roundabout way got into the Westminster Bridge Road, and soon found herself in front of the theatre.

'I've been witin' for yer this 'alf-hour.'

She turned round and saw Jim standing just behind her.

"Oo are you talkin' to? I'm not goin' to the ply with you. Wot d'yer tike me for, eh?'

"Oo are yer goin' with, then?'

'I'm goin' alone.'

'Garn! don't be a bloomin' jackass!'

Liza was feeling very injured.

'Thet's 'ow you treat me! I shall go 'ome. Why didn't you come aht the other night?'

'Yer told me not ter.'

She snorted at the ridiculous ineptitude of the reply.

'Why didn't you say nothin' abaht it yesterday?'

'Why, I thought you'd come if I didn't talk on it.'

'Well, I think you're a —— brute!' She felt very much inclined to cry.

'Come on, Liza, don't tike on; I didn't mean no offence.' And be put his arm round her waist and led her to take their places at the gallery door. Two tears escaped from the corners of her eyes and ran down her nose, but she felt very relieved and happy, and let him lead her where he would.

There was a long string of people waiting at the door, and Liza was delighted to see a couple of niggers who were helping them to while away the time of waiting. The niggers sang and danced, and made faces, while the people looked on with appreciative gravity, like royalty listening to de Reské, and they were very generous of applause and halfpence at the end of the performance. Then, when the niggers moved to the pit doors, paper boys came along offering *Tit-Bits* and 'extra specials'; after that three little girls came round and sang sentimental songs and collected more halfpence. At last a movement ran through the serpent-like string of people, sounds were heard behind the door, everyone closed up, the men told the women to keep close and hold tight; there was a great unbarring and unbolting, the doors were thrown open, and, like a bursting river, the people surged in.

Half an hour more and the curtain went up. The play was indeed thrilling. Liza quite forgot her companion, and was intent on the scene; she watched the incidents breathlessly, trembling with excitement, almost beside herself at the celebrated hanging incident. When the curtain fell on the first act she sighed and mopped her face.

'See 'ow 'ot I am.' she said to Jim, giving him her hand.

'Yus, you are!' he remarked, taking it.

'Leave go!' she said, trying to withdraw it from him.

'Not much,' he answered, quite boldly.

'Garn! Leave go!' But he didn't, and she really did not struggle very violently.

The second act came, and she shrieked over the comic man; and her laughter rang higher than anyone else's, so that people turned to look at her, and said:

'She is enjoyin''erself.'

Then when the murder came she bit her nails and the sweat stood on her forehead in great drops; in her excitement she even called out as loud as she could to the victim, 'Look aht!' It caused a laugh and slackened the tension, for the whole house was holding its breath as it looked at the villains listening at the door, creeping silently forward, crawling like tigers to their prey.

Liza trembling all over, and in her terror threw herself against Jim, who put both his arms round her, and said:

'Don't be afride, Liza; it's all right.'

At last the men sprang, there was a scuffle, and the wretch was killed, then came the scene depicted on the posters—the victim's son knocking at the door, on the inside of which were the murderers and the murdered man. At last the curtain came down, and the house in relief burst forth into cheers and cheers; the handsome hero in his top hat was greeted thunderously; the murdered man, with his clothes still all disarranged, was hailed with sympathy; and the villains—the house yelled and hissed and booed, while the poor brutes bowed and tried to look as if they liked it.

'I am enjoyin' myself,' said Liza, pressing herself quite close to Jim; 'you are a good sort ter tike me—Jim.'

He gave her a little hug, and it struck her that she was sitting just as Sally had done, and, like Sally, she found it 'jam'.

The *entr'actes* were short and the curtain was soon up again, and the comic man raised customary laughter by undressing and exposing his nether garments to the public view; then more tragedy, and the final act with its darkened room, its casting lots, and its explosion.

When it was all over and they had got outside Jim smacked his lips and said:

'I could do with a gargle; let's go onto thet pub there.'

'I'm as dry as bone,' said Liza; and so they went.

When they got in they discovered they were hungry, and seeing some appetising sausage-rolls, ate of them, and washed them down with a couple of pots of beer; then Jim lit his pipe and they strolled off. They had got quite near the Westminster Bridge Road when Jim

suggested that they should go and have one more drink before closing time.

'I shall be tight,' said Liza.

'Thet don't matter,' answered Jim, laughing. 'You ain't got ter go
ter work in the mornin' an' you can sleep it aht.'

'Arright, I don't mind if I do then, in for a penny, in for a pound.'

At the pub door she drew back.

'I say, guv'ner,' she said, 'there'll be some of the coves from dahn
our street, and they'll see us.'

'Na, there won't be nobody there, don't yer 'ave no fear.'

'I don't like ter go in for fear of it.'

'Well, we ain't doin' no 'arm if they does see us, an' we can go into
the private bar, an' you bet your boots there won't be no one there.'

She yielded, and they went in.

'Two pints of bitter, please, miss,' ordered Jim.

'I say, 'old 'ard. I can't drink more than 'alf a pint,' said Liza.

'Cheese it,' answered Jim. 'You can do with all you can get, I know.'

At closing time they left and walked down the broad road which
led homewards.

'Let's 'ave a little sit dahn,' said Jim, pointing to an empty bench
between two trees.

'Na, it's gettin' lite; I want ter be 'ome.'

'It's such a fine night, it's a pity ter go in already;' and he drew her
unresisting towards the seat. He put his arm round her waist.

'Un'and me, villin!' she said, in apt misquotation of the melodrama,
but Jim only laughed, and she made no effort to disengage herself.

They sat there for a long while in silence; the beer had got to
Liza's head, and the warm night air filled her with a double intoxication. She felt the arm round her waist, and the big, heavy form
pressing against her side; she experienced again the curious sensation
as if her heart were about to burst, and it choked her—a feeling so
oppressive and painful it almost made her feel sick. Her hands began
to tremble, and her breathing grew rapid, as though she were suffo-
cating. Almost fainting, she swayed over towards the man, and a cold
shiver ran through her from top to toe. Jim bent over her, and, taking
her in both arms, he pressed his lips to hers in a long, passionate kiss.

At last, panting for breath, she turned her head away and groaned.

Then they again sat for a long while in silence, Liza full of a strange happiness, feeling as if she could laugh aloud hysterically, but restrained by the calm and silence of the night. Close behind struck a church clock—one.

'Bless my soul!' said Liza, starting, 'there's one o'clock. I must get 'ome.'

'It's so nice out 'ere; do sty, Liza.' He pressed her closer to him. 'Yer know, Liza, I love yer—fit ter kill.'

'Na, I can't stay; come on.' She got up from the seat, and pulled him up too. 'Come on,' she said.

Without speaking they went along, and there was no one to be seen either in front or behind them. He had not got his arm round her now, and they were walking side by side, slightly separated. It was Liza who spoke first.

'You'd better go dahn the Road and by the church an' git into Vere Street the other end, an' I'll go through the passage, so thet no one shouldn't see us comin' together,' she spoke almost in a whisper.

'Arright, Liza,' he answered, 'I'll do just as you tell me.'

They came to the passage of which Liza spoke; it was a narrow way between blank walls, the backs of factories, and it led into the upper end of Vere Street. The entrance to it was guarded by two iron posts in the middle so that horses or barrows should not be taken through.

They had just got to it when a man came out into the open road. Liza quickly turned her head away.

'I wonder if 'e see us,' she said, when he had passed out of earshot. ''E's lookin' back,' she added.

'Why, 'oo is it?' asked Jim.

'It's a man aht of our street,' she answered. 'I dunno 'im, but I know where 'e lodges. D'yer think 'e sees us?'

'Na, 'e wouldn't know 'oo it was in the dark.'

'But he looked round; all the street'll know it if he see us.'

'Well, we ain't doin' no 'arm.'

She stretched out her hand to say good night.

'I'll come a wy with yer along the passage,' said Jim.

'Na, you mustn't; you go straight round.'

'But it's so dark; p'raps summat'll 'appen to yer.'

'Not it! You go on 'ome an' leave me,' she replied, and entering the passage, stood facing him with one of the iron pillars between them.

'Good night, old cock,' she said, stretching out her hand. He took it, and said:

'I wish yer wasn't goin' ter leave me, Liza.'

'Garn! I must!' She tried to get her hand away from his, but he held it firm, resting it on the top of the pillar.

'Leave go my 'and,' she said. He made no movement, but looked into her eyes steadily, so that it made her uneasy. She repented having come out with him. 'Leave go my 'and.' And she beat down on his with her closed fist.

'Liza!' he said, at last.

'Well, wot is it?' she answered, still thumping down on his hand with her fist.

'Liza,' he said a whisper, 'will yer?'

'Will I wot?' she said, looking down.

'You know, Liza. Sy, will yer?'

'Na,' she said.

He bent over her and repeated—

'Will yer?'

She did not speak, but kept beating down on his hand.

'Liza,' he said again, his voice growing hoarse and thick—'Liza, will yer?'

She still kept silence, looking away and continually bringing down her fist. He looked at her a moment, and she, ceasing to thump his hand, looked up at him with half-opened mouth. Suddenly he shook himself, and closing his fist gave her a violent, swinging blow in the belly.

'Come on,' he said.

And together they slid down into the darkness of the passage.

VIII

Mrs. Kemp was in the habit of slumbering somewhat heavily on Sunday mornings, or Liza would not have been allowed to go on sleeping as she did. When she woke, she rubbed her eyes to gather her senses together and gradually she remembered having gone to the theatre on the previous evening; then suddenly everything came back to her. She stretched out her legs and gave a long sigh of delight. Her heart was full; she thought of Jim, and the delicious sensation of love came over her. Closing her eyes, she imagined his warm kisses, and she lifted up her arms as if to put them round his neck and draw him down to her; she almost felt the rough beard on her face, and the strong heavy arms round her body. She smiled to herself and took a long breath; then, slipping back the sleeves of her nightdress, she looked at her own thin arms, just two pieces of bone with not a muscle on them, but very white and showing distinctly the interlacement of blue veins: she did not notice that her hands were rough, and red and dirty with the nails broken, and bitten to the quick. She got out of bed and looked at herself in the glass over the mantelpiece: with one hand she brushed back her hair and smiled at herself; her face was very small and thin, but the complexion was nice, clear and white, with a delicate tint of red on the cheeks, and her eyes were big and dark like her hair. She felt very happy.

She did not want to dress yet, but rather to sit down and think, so she twisted up her hair into a little knot, slipped a skirt over her nightdress, and sat on a chair near the window and began looking around. The decorations of the room had been centred on the mantelpiece; the chief ornament consisted of a pear and an apple, a pineapple, a bunch of grapes, and several fat plums, all very beautifully done in wax, as was the fashion about the middle of this most glorious reign. They were appropriately coloured—the apple blushing red, the grapes an inky black, emerald green leaves were scattered here and there to lend finish, and the whole was mounted on an ebonised stand covered with black velvet, and protected from dust and dirt by a beautiful glass cover bordered with red plush. Liza's eyes rested on this with approbation, and the pineapple quite made her mouth water. At either end of the mantelpiece were pink jars with blue flowers on the front; round the top in Gothic letters of gold was inscribed: 'A Present from a Friend'—these were products of a later, but not less artistic age. The intervening spaces were taken up with little jars and

cups and saucers—gold inside, with a view of a town outside, and surrounding them, 'A Present from Clacton-on-Sea,' or, alliteratively, 'A
Memento of Margate.' Of these many were broken, but they had been
mended with glue, and it is well known that pottery in the eyes of the
connoisseur loses none of its value by a crack or two. Then there were
portraits innumerable—little yellow cartes-de-visite in velvet frames,
some of which were decorated with shells; they showed strange people with old-fashioned clothes, the women with bodices and sleeves
fitting close to the figure, stern-featured females with hair carefully
parted in the middle and plastered down on each side, firm chins and
mouths, with small, pig-like eyes and wrinkled faces, and the men
were uncomfortably clad in Sunday garments, very stiff and uneasy
in their awkward postures, with large whiskers and shaved chins and
upper lips and a general air of horny-handed toil. Then there were
one or two daguerreotypes, little full-length figures framed in gold
paper. There was one of Mrs. Kemp's father and one of her mother,
and there were several photographs of betrothed or newly-married
couples, the lady sitting down and the man standing behind her with
his hand on the chair, or the man sitting and the woman with her
hand on his shoulder. And from all sides of the room, standing on
the mantelpiece, hanging above it, on the wall and over the bed, they
stared full-face into the room, self-consciously fixed for ever in their
stiff discomfort.

The walls were covered with dingy, antiquated paper, and or-
namented with coloured supplements from Christmas Numbers—
there was a very patriotic picture of a soldier shaking the hand of a
fallen comrade and waving his arm in defiance of a band of advancing
Arabs; there was a 'Cherry Ripe,' almost black with age and dirt; there
were two almanacks several years old, one with a coloured portrait
of the Marquess of Lorne, very handsome and elegantly dressed, the
object of Mrs. Kemp's adoration since her husband's demise; the other a Jubilee portrait of the Queen, somewhat losing in dignity by a
moustache which Liza in an irreverent moment had smeared on with
charcoal.

The furniture consisted of a wash-hand stand and a little deal
chest of drawers, which acted as sideboard to such pots and pans and

crockery as could not find room in the grate; and besides the bed there was nothing but two kitchen chairs and a lamp. Liza looked at it all and felt perfectly satisfied; she put a pin into one corner of the noble Marquess to prevent him from falling, fiddled about with the ornaments a little, and then started washing herself. After putting on her clothes she ate some bread-and-butter, swallowed a dishful of cold tea, and went out into the street.

She saw some boys playing cricket and went up to them.

'Let me ply,' she said.

'Arright, Liza,' cried half a dozen of them in delight; and the captain added: 'You go an' scout over by the lamp-post.'

'Go an' scout my eye!' said Liza, indignantly. 'When I ply cricket I does the battin'.'

'Na, you're not goin' ter bat all the time. 'Oo are you gettin' at?' replied the captain, who had taken advantage of his position to put himself in first, and was still at the wicket.

'Well, then I shan't ply,' answered Liza.

'Garn, Ernie, let 'er go in!' shouted two or three members of the team.

'Well, I'm busted!' remarked the captain, as she took his bat. 'You won't sty in long, I lay,' he said, as he sent the old bowler fielding and took the ball himself. He was a young gentleman who did not suffer from excessive backwardness.

'Aht!' shouted a dozen voices as the ball went past Liza's bat and landed in the pile of coats which formed the wicket. The captain came forward to resume his innings, but Liza held the bat away from him.

'Garn!' she said; 'thet was only a trial.'

'You never said trial,' answered the captain indignantly.

'Yus, I did,' said Liza; 'I said it just as the ball was comin'—under my breath.'

'Well, I am busted!' repeated the captain.

Just then Liza saw Tom among the lookers-on, and as she felt very kindly disposed to the world in general that morning, she called out to him:

"Ulloa, Tom!' she said. 'Come an' give us a ball; this chap can't bowl.'

'Well, I got yer aht, any'ow,' said that person.

'Ah, yer wouldn't 'ave got me aht plyin' square. But a trial ball—well, one don't ever know wot a trial ball's goin' ter do.'

Tom began bowling very slowly and easily, so that Liza could swing her bat round and hit mightily; she ran well, too, and pantingly brought up her score to twenty. Then the fielders interposed.

'I sy, look 'ere, 'e's only givin' 'er lobs; 'e's not tryin' ter git 'er aht.'

'You're spoilin' our gime.'

'I don't care; I've got twenty runs—thet's more than you could do. I'll go aht now of my own accord, so there! Come on, Tom.'

Tom joined her, and as the captain at last resumed his bat and the game went on, they commenced talking, Liza leaning against the wall of a house, while Tom stood in front of her, smiling with pleasure.

'Where 'ave you been idin' yerself, Tom? I ain't seen yer for I dun-no 'ow long.'

'I've been abaht as usual; an' I've seen you when you didn't see me.'

'Well, yer might 'ave come up and said good mornin' when you see me.'

'I didn't want ter force myself on, yer, Liza.'

'Garn! You are a bloomin' cuckoo. I'm blowed!'

'I thought yer didn't like me 'angin' round yer; so I kep' awy.'

'Why, yer talks as if I didn't like yer. Yer don't think I'd 'ave come aht beanfeastin' with yer if I 'adn't liked yer?'

Liza was really very dishonest, but she felt so happy this morning that she loved the whole world, and of course Tom came in with the others. She looked very kindly at him, and he was so affected that a great lump came in his throat and he could not speak.

Liza's eyes turned to Jim's house, and she saw coming out of the door a girl of about her own age; she fancied she saw in her some likeness to Jim.

'Say, Tom,' she asked, 'thet ain't Blakeston's daughter, is it?'

'Yus thet's it.'

'I'll go an' speak to 'er,' said Liza, leaving Tom and going over the road.

'You're Polly Blakeston, ain't yer?' she said.

'Thet's me!' said the girl.

'I thought you was. Your dad, 'e says ter me, "You dunno my daughter, Polly, do yer?" says 'e. "Na," says I, "I don't." "Well," says 'e, "You can't miss 'er when you see 'er." An' right enough I didn't.'

'Mother says I'm all father, an' there ain't nothin' of 'er in me. Dad says it's lucky it ain't the other wy abaht, or e'd 'ave got a divorce.'

They both laughed.

'Where are you goin' now?' asked Liza, looking at the slop-basin she was carrying.

'I was just goin' dahn into the road ter get some ice-cream for dinner. Father 'ad a bit of luck last night, 'e says, and 'e'd stand the lot of us ice-cream for dinner ter-day.'

'I'll come with yer if yer like.'

'Come on!' And, already friends, they walked arm-in-arm to the Westminster Bridge Road. Then they went along till they came to a stall where an Italian was selling the required commodity, and having had a taste apiece to see if they liked it, Polly planked down sixpence and had her basin filled with a poisonous-looking mixture of red and white ice-cream.

On the way back, looking up the street, Polly cried:

'There's father!'

Liza's heart beat rapidly and she turned red; but suddenly a sense of shame came over her, and casting down her head so that she might not see him, she said:

'I think I'll be off 'ome an' see 'ow mother's gettin' on.' And before Polly could say anything she had slipped away and entered her own house.

Mother was not getting on at all well.

'You've come in at last, you ——, you!' snarled Mrs. Kemp, as Liza entered the room.

'Wot's the matter, mother?'

'Matter! I like thet—matter indeed! Go an' matter yerself an' be mattered! Nice way ter treat an old woman like me—an' yer own mother, too!'

'Wot's up now?'

'Don't talk ter me; I don't want ter listen ter you. Leavin' me all alone, me with my rheumatics, an' the neuralgy! I've 'ad the neuralgy all the mornin', and my 'ead's been simply splittin', so thet I thought the bones 'ud come apart and all my brains go streamin' on the floor. An' when I wake up there's no one ter git my tea for me, an' I lay there witin' an' witin', an' at last I 'ad ter git up and mike it myself. And, my 'ead simply cruel! Why, I might 'ave been burnt ter death with the fire alight an' me asleep.'

'Well, I am sorry, mother; but I went aht just for a bit, an' didn't think you'd wike. An' besides, the fire wasn't alight.'

'Garn with yer! I didn't treat my mother like thet. Oh, you've been a bad daughter ter me—an' I 'ad more illness carryin' you than with all the other children put togither. You was a cross at yer birth, an' you've been a cross ever since. An' now in my old age, when I've worked myself ter the bone, yer leaves me to starve and burn to death.' Here she began to cry, and the rest of her utterances was lost in sobs.

⚒

The dusk had darkened into night, and Mrs. Kemp had retired to rest with the dicky-birds. Liza was thinking of many things; she wondered why she had been unwilling to meet Jim in the morning.

'I was a bally fool,' she said to herself.

It really seemed an age since the previous night, and all that had happened seemed very long ago. She had not spoken to Jim all day, and she had so much to say to him. Then, wondering whether he was about, she went to the window and looked out; but there was nobody there. She closed the window again and sat just beside it; the time went on, and she wondered whether he would come, asking herself whether he had been thinking of her as she of him; gradually her thoughts grew vague, and a kind of mist came over them. She nodded. Suddenly she roused herself with a start, fancying she had heard something; she listened again, and in a moment the sound was repeated, three or four gentle taps on the window. She opened it quickly and whispered:

'Jim.'

'Thet's me,' he answered, 'come aht.'

Closing the window, she went into the passage and opened the street door; it was hardly unlocked before Jim had pushed his way in; partly shutting it behind him, he took her in his arms and hugged her to his breast. She kissed him passionately.

'I thought yer'd come ter-night, Jim; summat in my 'eart told me so. But you 'ave been long.'

'I wouldn't come before, 'cause I thought there'd be people abaht. Kiss us!' And again he pressed his lips to hers, and Liza nearly fainted with the delight of it.

'Let's go for a walk, shall we?' he said.

'Arright!' They were speaking in whispers. 'You go into the road through the passage, an' I'll go by the street.'

'Yus, thet's right,' and kissing her once more, he slid out, and she closed the door behind him.

Then going back to get her hat, she came again into the passage, waiting behind the door till it might be safe for her to venture. She had not made up her mind to risk it, when she heard a key put in the lock, and she hardly had time to spring back to prevent herself from being hit by the opening door. It was a man, one of the upstairs lodgers.

"Ulloa!' he said, "oo's there?'

'Mr. 'Odges! Strikes me, you did give me a turn; I was just goin' aht.' She blushed to her hair, but in the darkness he could see nothing.

'Good night,' she said, and went out.

She walked close along the sides of the houses like a thief, and the policeman as she passed him turned round and looked at her, wondering whether she was meditating some illegal deed. She breathed freely on coming into the open road, and seeing Jim skulking behind a tree, ran up to him, and in the shadows they kissed again.

IX

Thus BEGAN A time of love and joy. As soon as her work was over and she had finished tea, Liza would slip out and at some appointed spot meet Jim. Usually it would be at the church, where the Westminster Bridge Road bends down to get to the river, and they would go off, arm-in-arm, till they came to some place where they could sit down and rest. Sometimes they would walk along the Albert Embankment to Battersea Park, and here sit on the benches, watching the children play. The female cyclist had almost abandoned Battersea for the parks on the other side of the river, but often enough one went by, and Liza, with the old-fashioned prejudice of her class, would look after the rider and make some remark about her, not seldom more forcible than ladylike. Both Jim and she liked children, and, tiny, ragged urchins would gather round to have rides on the man's knees or mock fights with Liza.

They thought themselves far away from anyone in Vere Street, but twice, as they were walking along, they were met by people they knew. Once it was two workmen coming home from a job at Vauxhall: Liza did not see them till they were quite near; she immediately dropped Jim's arm, and they both cast their eyes to the ground as the men passed, like ostriches, expecting that if they did not look they would not be seen.

'D'you see 'em, Jim?' asked Liza, in a whisper, when they had gone by. 'I wonder if they see us.' Almost instinctively she turned round, and at the same moment one of the men turned too; then there was no doubt about it.

'Thet did give me a turn,' she said.

'So it did me,' answered Jim; 'I simply went 'ot all over.'

'We was bally fools,' said Liza; 'we oughter 'ave spoken to 'em! D'you think they'll let aht?'

They heard nothing of it, when Jim afterwards met one of the men in a public-house he did not mention a meeting, and they thought that perhaps they had not been recognized. But the second time was worse.

It was on the Albert Embankment again. They were met by a party of four, all of whom lived in the street. Liza's heart sank within her, for there was no chance of escape; she thought of turning quickly and walking in the opposite direction, but there was not time, for the men had already seen them. She whispered to Jim:

'Back us up,' and as they met she said to one of the men:

''Ulloa there! Where are you off to?'

The men stopped, and one of them asked the question back.

'Where are you off to?'

'Me? Oh, I've just been to the 'orspital. One of the gals at our place is queer, an' so I says ter myself, "I'll go an' see 'er.'" She faltered a little as she began, but quickly gathered herself together, lying fluently and without hesitation.

'An' when I come aht,' she went on, ''oo should I see just passin' the 'orspital but this 'ere cove, an' 'e says to me, "Wot cheer," says 'e, "I'm goin' ter Vaux'all, come an' walk a bit of the wy with us."" "Arright," says I, "I don't mind if I do.'"

One man winked, and another said: 'Go it, Liza!'

She fired up with the dignity of outraged innocence.

'Wot d'yer mean by thet?' she said; 'd'yer think I'm kiddin'?'

'Kiddin'? No! You've only just come up from the country, ain't yer?'

'Think I'm kidding? What d'yer think I want ter kid for? Liars never believe anyone, thet's fact.'

'Na then, Liza, don't be saucy.'

'Saucy! I'll smack yer in the eye if yer sy much ter me. Come on,' she said to Jim, who had been standing sheepishly by; and they walked away.

The men shouted: 'Now we shan't be long!' and went off laughing.

After that they decided to go where there was no chance at all of their being seen. They did not meet till they got over Westminster Bridge, and thence they made their way into the park; they would lie down on the grass in one another's arms, and thus spend the long summer evenings. After the heat of the day there would be a gentle breeze in the park, and they would take in long breaths of the air; it seemed far away from London, it was so quiet and cool; and Liza, as she lay by Jim's side, felt her love for him overflowing to the rest of the world and enveloping mankind itself in a kind of grateful happiness. If it could only have lasted! They would stay and see the stars shine out dimly, one by one, from the blue sky, till it grew late and the blue darkened into black, and the stars glittered in thousands all above them. But as the nights grew cooler, they found it cold on the grass, and the time they had there seemed too short for the long journey they had to make; so, crossing the bridge as before, they strolled along the Embankment till they came to a vacant bench, and there they would sit, with Liza nestling close up to her lover and his great arms around her. The rain of September made no difference to them; they went as usual to their seat beneath the trees, and Jim would take Liza on his knee, and, opening his coat, shelter her with it, while she, with her arms round his neck, pressed very close to him, and occasionally gave a little laugh of pleasure and delight. They hardly spoke at all through these evenings, for what had they to say to one another? Often without exchanging a word they would sit for an hour with their faces touching, the one feeling on his cheek the hot breath from the other's mouth; while at the end of the time the only motion was an upraising of Liza's lips, a bending down of Jim's, so that they might meet and kiss. Sometimes Liza fell into a light doze, and Jim would sit very still for fear of waking her, and when she roused herself she would smile, while he bent down again and kissed her. They were very happy. But the hours passed by so quickly, that Big Ben striking twelve came upon them as a surprise, and unwillingly they got up and made their way homewards; their partings were never ending—each evening Jim refused to let her go from his arms, and tears stood in his eyes at the thought of the separation.

'I'd give somethin',' he would say, 'if we could be togither always.'

'Never mind, old chap!' Liza would answer, herself half crying, 'it can't be 'elped, so we must jolly well lump it.'

But notwithstanding all their precautions people in Vere Street appeared to know. First of all Liza noticed that the women did not seem quite so cordial as before, and she often fancied they were talking of her; when she passed by they appeared to look at her, then say something or other, and perhaps burst out laughing; but when she approached they would immediately stop speaking, and keep silence in a rather awkward, constrained manner. For a long time she was unwilling to believe that there was any change in them, and Jim who had observed nothing, persuaded her that it was all fancy. But gradually it became clearer, and Jim had to agree with her that somehow or other people had found out. Once when Liza had been talking to Polly, Jim's daughter, Mrs. Blakeston had called her, and when the girl had come to her mother Liza saw that she spoke angrily, and they both looked across at her. When Liza caught Mrs. Blakeston's eye she saw in her face a surly scowl, which almost frightened her; she wanted to brave it out, and stepped forward a little to go and speak with the woman, but

Mrs. Blakeston, standing still, looked so angrily at her that she was afraid to. When she told Jim his face grew dark, and he said: 'Blast the woman! I'll give 'er wot for if she says anythin' ter you.'

'Don't strike 'er, wotever 'appens, will yer, Jim?' said Liza.

'She'd better tike care then!' he answered, and he told her that lately his wife had been sulking, and not speaking to him. The previous night, on coming home after the day's work and bidding her 'Good evenin',' she had turned her back on him without answering.

'Can't you answer when you're spoke to?' he had said.

'Good evenin',' she had replied sulkily, with her back still turned.

After that Liza noticed that Polly avoided her.

'Wot's up, Polly?' she said to her one day. 'You never speaks now; 'ave you 'ad yer tongue cut aht?'

'Me? I ain't got nothin' ter speak abaht, thet I knows of,' answered Polly, abruptly walking off. Liza grew very red and quickly looked to see if anyone had noticed the incident. A couple of youths, sitting on the pavement, had seen it, and she saw them nudge one another and wink.

Then the fellows about the street began to chaff her.

'You look pale,' said one of a group to her one day.

'You're overworkin' yerself, you are,' said another.

'Married life don't agree with Liza, thet's wot it is,' added a third.

''Oo d'yer think yer gettin' at? I ain't married, an' never like ter be,' she answered.

'Liza 'as all the pleasures of a 'usband an' none of the trouble.'

'Bli'me if I know wot yer mean!' said Liza.

'Na, of course not; you don't know nothin', do yer?'

'Innocent as a bibe. Our Father which art in 'eaven!'

''Aven't been in London long, 'ave yer?'

They spoke in chorus, and Liza stood in front of them, bewildered, not knowing what to answer.

'Don't you mike no mistake abaht it, Liza knows a thing or two.'

'O me darlin', I love yer fit to kill, but tike care your missus ain't round the corner.' This was particularly bold, and they all laughed.

Liza felt very uncomfortable, and fiddled about with her apron, wondering how she should get away.

'Tike care yer don't git into trouble, thet's all,' said one of the men, with burlesque gravity.

'Yer might give us a chanst, Liza, you come aht with me one eve-nin'. You oughter give us all a turn, just ter show there's no ill-feelin'.'

'Bli'me if I know wot yer all talkin' abaht. You're all barmy on the crumpet,' said Liza indignantly, and, turning her back on them, made for home.

Among other things that had happened was Sally's marriage. One Saturday a little procession had started from Vere Street, con-sisting of Sally, in a state of giggling excitement, her fringe magnif-icent after a whole week of curling-papers, clad in a perfectly new velveteen dress of the colour known as electric blue; and Harry, rather nervous and ill at ease in the unaccustomed restraint of a collar; these two walked arm-in-arm, and were followed by Sally's mother and uncle, also arm-in-arm, and the procession was brought up by Harry's brother and a friend. They started with a flourish of trumpets and an old boot, and walked down the middle of Vere Street, accompanied by the neighbours' good wishes; but as they got into the Westminster Bridge Road and nearer to the church, the happy couple grew silent, and Harry began to perspire freely, so that his collar gave him perfect torture. There was a public-house just opposite the church, and it was suggested that they should have a drink before going in. As it was a solemn occasion they went into the private bar, and there Sally's un-cle, who was a man of means, ordered six pots of beer.

'Feel a bit nervous, 'Arry?' asked his friend.

'Na,' said Harry, as if he had been used to getting married every day of his life; 'bit warm, thet's all.'

'Your very good 'ealth, Sally,' said her mother, lifting her mug; 'this is the last time as I shall ever address you as miss.'

'An' may she be as good a wife as you was,' added Sally's uncle.

'Well, I don't think my old man ever 'ad no complaint ter mike abaht me. I did my duty by 'im, although it's me as says it,' answered the good lady.

'Well, mates,' said Harry's brother, 'I reckon it's abaht time to go in. So 'ere's to the 'ealth of Mr. 'Enry Atkins an' 'is future missus.'

'An' God bless 'em!' said Sally's mother.

Then they went into the church, and as they solemnly walked up the aisle a pale-faced young curate came out of the vestry and down to the bottom of the chancel. The beer had had a calming effect on their troubled minds, and both Harry and Sally began to think it rather a good joke. They smiled on each other, and at those parts of the service which they thought suggestive violently nudged one another in the ribs. When the ring had to be produced, Harry fumbled about in different pockets, and his brother whispered:

'Swop me bob, 'e's gone and lorst it!'

However, all went right, and Sally having carefully pocketed the certificate, they went out and had another drink to celebrate the happy event.

In the evening Liza and several friends came into the couple's room, which they had taken in the same house as Sally had lived in before, and drank the health of the bride and bridegroom till they thought fit to retire.

X

IT WAS NOVEMBER. The fine weather had quite gone now, and with it much of the sweet pleasure of Jim and Liza's love. When they came out at night on the Embankment they found it cold and dreary; sometimes a light fog covered the river-banks, and made the lamps glow out dim and large; a light rain would be falling, which sent a chill into their very souls; foot passengers came along at rare intervals, holding up umbrellas, and staring straight in front of them as they hurried along in the damp and cold; a cab would pass rapidly by, splashing up the mud on each side. The benches were deserted, except, perhaps, for some poor homeless wretch who could afford no shelter, and, huddled up in a corner, with his head buried in his breast, was sleeping heavily, like a dead man. The wet mud made Liza's skirts cling about her feet, and the damp would come in and chill her legs and creep up her body, till she shivered, and for warmth pressed herself close against Jim. Sometimes they would go into the third-class waiting-rooms at Waterloo or Charing Cross and sit there, but it was not like the park or the Embankment on summer nights; they had warmth, but the heat made their wet clothes steam and smell, and the gas flared in their eyes, and they hated the people perpetually coming in and out, opening the doors and letting in a blast of cold air; they hated the noise of the guards and porters shouting out the departure of the trains, the shrill whistling of the steam-engine, the hurry and bustle and confusion. About eleven o'clock, when the trains grew less frequent, they got some quietness; but then their minds were troubled, and they felt heavy, sad and miserable.

One evening they had been sitting at Waterloo Station; it was foggy outside—a thick, yellow November fog, which filled the waiting-room, entering the lungs, and making the mouth taste nasty and the eyes smart. It was about half-past eleven, and the station was unusually quiet; a few passengers, in wraps and overcoats, were walking to and fro, waiting for the last train, and one or two porters were standing about yawning. Liza and Jim had remained for an hour in perfect silence, filled with a gloomy unhappiness, as of a great weight on their brains. Liza was sitting forward, with her elbows on her knees, resting her face on her hands.

'I wish I was straight,' she said at last, not looking up.

'Well, why won't yer come along of me altogether, an' you'll be arright then?' he answered.

'Na, that's no go; I can't do thet.' He had often asked her to live with him entirely, but she had always refused.

'You can come along of me, an' I'll tike a room in a lodgin' 'ouse in 'Olloway, an' we can live there as if we was married.'

'Wot abaht yer work?'

'I can get work over the other side as well as I can 'ere. I'm abaht sick of the wy things is goin' on.'

'So am I; but I can't leave mother.'

'She can come, too.'

'Not when I'm not married. I shouldn't like 'er ter know as I'd—as I'd gone wrong.'

'Well, I'll marry yer. Swop me bob, I wants ter badly enough.'

'Yer can't; yer married already.'

'Thet don't matter! If I give the missus so much a week aht of my screw, she'll sign a piper ter give up all clime ter me, an' then we can get spliced. One of the men as I works with done thet, an' it was arright.'

Liza shook her head.

'Na, yer can't do thet now; it's bigamy, an' the cop tikes yer, an' yer gits twelve months' 'ard for it.'

'But swop me bob, Liza, I can't go on like this. Yer knows the missus—well, there ain't no bloomin' doubt abaht it, she knows as you an' me are carryin' on, an' she mikes no bones abaht lettin' me see it.'

'She don't do thet?'

'Well, she don't exactly sy it, but she sulks an' won't speak, an' then when I says anythin' she rounds on me an' calls me all the nimes she can think of. I'd give 'er a good 'idin', but some'ow I don't like ter! She mikes the plice a 'ell ter me, an' I'm not goin' ter stand it no longer!'

'You'll ave ter sit it, then; yer can't chuck it.'

'Yus I can, an' I would if you'd come along of me. I don't believe you like me at all, Liza, or you'd come.'

She turned towards him and put her arms round his neck.

'Yer know I do, old cock,' she said. 'I like yer better than anyone else in the world; but I can't go awy an' leave mother.'

'Bli'me me if I see why; she's never been much ter you. She mikes yer slave awy ter pay the rent, an' all the money she earns she boozes.'

'Thet's true, she ain't been wot yer might call a good mother ter me—but some'ow she's my mother, an' I don't like ter leave 'er on 'er own, now she's so old—an' she can't do much with the rheumatics. An' besides, Jim dear, it ain't only mother, but there's yer own kids, yer can't leave them.'

He thought for a while, and then said:

'You're abaht right there, Liza; I dunno if I could get on without the kids. If I could only tike them an' you too, swop me bob, I should be 'appy.'

Liza smiled sadly.

'So yer see, Jim, we're in a bloomin' 'ole, an' there ain't no way aht of it thet I can see.'

He took her on his knees, and pressing her to him, kissed her very long and very lovingly.

'Well, we must trust ter luck,' she said again, 'p'raps somethin' 'll 'appen soon, an' everythin' 'll come right in the end—when we gets four balls of worsted for a penny.'

It was past twelve, and separating, they went by different ways along the dreary, wet, deserted roads till they came to Vere Street.

The street seemed quite different to Liza from what it had been three months before. Tom, the humble adorer, had quite disappeared from her life. One day, three or four weeks after the August Bank Holiday, she saw him dawdling along the pavement, and it suddenly struck her that she had not seen him for a long time; but she had been so full of her happiness that she had been unable to think of anyone but Jim. She wondered at his absence, since before wherever she had been there was he certain to be also. She passed him, but to her astonishment he did not speak to her. She thought by some wonder he had not seen her, but she felt his gaze resting upon her. She turned back, and suddenly he dropped his eyes and looked down, walking on as if he had not seen her, but blushing furiously.

'Tom,' she said, 'why don't yer speak ter me.'

He started and blushed more than ever.

'I didn't know yer was there,' he stuttered.

'Don't tell me,' she said, 'wot's up?'

'Nothin' as I knows of,' he answered uneasily.

'I ain't offended yer, 'ave I, Tom?'

'Na, not as I knows of,' he replied, looking very unhappy.

'You don't ever come my way now,' she said.

'I didn't know as yer wanted ter see me.'

'Garn! Yer knows I likes you as well as anybody.'

'Yer likes so many people, Liza,' he said, flushing.

'What d'yer mean?' said Liza indignantly, but very red; she was afraid he knew now, and it was from him especially she would have been so glad to hide it.

'Nothin',' he answered.

'One doesn't say things like thet without any meanin', unless one's a blimed fool.'

'You're right there, Liza,' he answered. 'I am a blimed fool.' He looked at her a little reproachfully, she thought, and then he said 'Good-bye,' and turned away.

At first she was horrified that he should know of her love for Jim, but then she did not care. After all, it was nobody's business, and what did anything matter as long as she loved Jim and Jim loved her? Then she grew angry that Tom should suspect her; he could know nothing but that some of the men had seen her with Jim near Vauxhall, and it seemed mean that he should condemn her for that. Thenceforward, when she ran against Tom, she cut him; he never tried to speak to her, but as she passed him, pretending to look in front of her, she could see that he always blushed, and she fancied his eyes were very sorrowful. Then several weeks went by, and as she began to feel more and more lonely in the street she regretted the quarrel; she cried a little as she thought that she had lost his faithful gentle love and she would have much liked to be friends with him again. If he had only made some advance she would have welcomed him so cordially, but she was too proud to go to him herself and beg him to forgive her—and then how could he forgive her?

She had lost Sally too, for on her marriage Harry had made her give up the factory; he was a young man with principles worthy of a Member of Parliament, and he had said:

'A woman's plice is 'er 'ome, an' if 'er old man can't afford ter keep 'er without 'er workin' in a factory—well, all I can say is thet 'e'd better go an' git single.'

'Quite right, too,' agreed his mother-in-law; 'an' wot's more, she'll 'ave a baby ter look after soon, an' thet'll tike 'er all 'er time, an' there's no one as knows thet better than me, for I've 'ad twelve, ter sy nothin' of two stills an' one miss.'

Liza quite envied Sally her happiness, for the bride was brimming over with song and laughter; her happiness overwhelmed her.

'I am 'appy,' she said to Liza one day a few weeks after her marriage. 'You dunno wot a good sort 'Arry is. 'E's just a darlin', an' there's no mistikin' it. I don't care wot other people sy, but wot I says is, there's nothin' like marriage. Never a cross word passes his lips, an' mother 'as all 'er meals with us an' 'e says all the better. Well I'm thet 'appy I simply dunno if I'm standin' on my 'ead or on my 'eels.'

But alas! it did not last too long. Sally was not so full of joy when next Liza met her, and one day her eyes looked very much as if she had been crying.

'Wot's the matter?' asked Liza, looking at her. 'Wot 'ave yer been blubberin' abaht?'

'Me?' said Sally, getting very red. 'Oh, I've got a bit of a toothache, an'—well, I'm rather a fool like, an' it 'urt so much that I couldn't 'elp cryin'.'

Liza was not satisfied, but could get nothing further out of her. Then one day it came out. It was a Saturday night, the time when women in Vere Street weep. Liza went up into Sally's room for a few minutes on her way to the Westminster Bridge Road, where she was to meet Jim. Harry had taken the top back room, and Liza, climbing up the second flight of stairs, called out as usual.

'Wot ho, Sally!'

The door remained shut, although Liza could see that there was a light in the room; but on getting to the door she stood still, for she heard the sound of sobbing. She listened for a minute and then knocked: there was a little flurry inside, and someone called out:

'Oo's there?'

'Only me,' said Liza, opening the door. As she did so she saw Sally rapidly wipe her eyes and put her handkerchief away. Her mother was sitting by her side, evidently comforting her.

'Wot's up, Sal?' asked Liza.

'Nothin',' answered Sally, with a brave little gasp to stop the crying, turning her face downwards so that Liza should not see the tears in her eyes; but they were too strong for her, and, quickly taking out her handkerchief, she hid her face in it and began to sob broken-heartedly. Liza looked at the mother in interrogation.

'Oh, it's thet man again!' said the lady, snorting and tossing her head.

'Not 'Arry?' asked Liza, in surprise.

'Not 'Arry—'oo is it if it ain't 'Arry? The villin!'

'Wot's 'e been doin', then?' asked Liza again.

'Beatin' 'er, that's wot 'e's been doin'! Oh, the villin, 'e oughter be ashimed of 'isself 'e ought!'

'I didn't know 'e was like that!' said Liza.

'Didn't yer? I thought the 'ole street knew it by now,' said Mrs.

Cooper indignantly. 'Oh, 'e's a wrong 'un, 'e is.'

'It wasn't 'is fault,' put in Sally, amidst her sobs; 'it's only because 'e's 'ad a little drop too much. 'E's arright when 'e's sober.'

'A little drop too much! I should just think 'e'd 'ad, the beast! I'd give it 'im if I was a man. They're all like thet—'usbinds is all alike; they're arright when they're sober—sometimes—but when they've got the liquor in 'em, they're beasts, an' no mistike. I 'ad a 'usbind myself for five-an'-twenty years, an' I know 'em.'

'Well, mother,' sobbed Sally, 'it was all my fault. I should 'ave come 'ome earlier.'

'Na, it wasn't your fault at all. Just you look 'ere, Liza: this is wot 'e done an' call 'isself a man. Just because Sally'd gone aht to 'ave a chat with Mrs. McLeod in the next 'ouse, when she come in 'e start bangin' 'er abaht. An' me, too, wot d'yer think of that!' Mrs. Cooper was quite purple with indignation.

'Yus,' she went on, 'thet's a man for yer. Of course, I wasn't goin' ter stand there an' see my daughter bein' knocked abaht; it wasn't like-ly—was it? An' 'e rounds on me, an' 'e 'its me with 'is fist. Look 'ere.' She pulled up her sleeves and showed two red and brawny arms. ''E's bruised my arms; I thought 'e'd broken it at fust. If I 'adn't put my arm up, 'e'd 'ave got me on the 'ead, an' 'e might 'ave killed me. An' I says to 'im, "If you touch me again, I'll go ter the police-station, thet I will!" Well, that frightened 'im a bit, an' then didn't I let 'im 'ave it! "You call yerself a man," says I, "an' you ain't fit ter clean the drains aht." You should 'ave 'eard the language 'e used. "You dirty old woman," says 'e, "you go away; you're always interferin' with me." Well, I don't like ter repeat wot 'e said, and thet's the truth. An' I says ter 'im, "I wish yer'd never married my daughter, an' if I'd known you was like this I'd 'ave died sooner than let yer."'

'Well, I didn't know 'e was like thet!' said Liza.

''E was arright at fust,' said Sally.

'Yus, they're always arright at fust! But ter think it should 'ave come to this now, when they ain't been married three months, an' the first child not born yet! I think it's disgraceful.'

Liza stayed a little while longer, helping to comfort Sally, who kept pathetically taking to herself all the blame of the dispute; and then, bidding her good night and better luck, she slid off to meet Jim.

When she reached the appointed spot he was not to be found. She waited for some time, and at last saw him come out of the neighbouring pub.

'Good night, Jim,' she said as she came up to him.

'So you've turned up, 'ave yer?' he answered roughly, turning round.

'Wot's the matter, Jim?' she asked in a frightened way, for he had never spoken to her in that manner.

'Nice thing ter keep me witin' all night for yer to come aht.'

She saw that he had been drinking, and answered humbly.

'I'm very sorry, Jim, but I went in to Sally, an' 'er bloke 'ad been knockin' 'er abaht, an' so I sat with 'er a bit.'

'Knockin' 'er abaht, 'ad 'e? and serve 'er damn well right too; an' there's many more as could do with a good 'idin'!'

Liza did not answer. He looked at her, and then suddenly said:

'Come in an' 'ave a drink.'

'Na, I'm not thirsty; I don't want a drink,' she answered.

'Come on,' he said angrily.

'Na, Jim, you've had quite enough already.'

"Oo are you talkin' ter?' he said. 'Don't come if yer don't want ter; I'll go an' 'ave one by myself.'

'Na, Jim, don't.' She caught hold of his arm.

'Yus, I shall,' he said, going towards the pub, while she held him back. 'Let me go, can't yer! Let me go!' He roughly pulled his arm away from her. As she tried to catch hold of it again, he pushed her back, and in the little scuffle caught her a blow over the face.

'Oh!' she cried, 'you did 'urt!'

He was sobered at once.

'Liza,' he said. 'I ain't 'urt yer?' She didn't answer, and he took her in his arms. 'Liza, I ain't 'urt you, 'ave I? Say I ain't 'urt yer. I'm so sorry, I beg your pardon, Liza.'

'Arright, old chap,' she said, smiling charmingly on him. 'It wasn't the blow that 'urt me much; it was the wy you was talkin'.'

'I didn't mean it, Liza.' He was so contrite, he could not humble himself enough. 'I 'ad another bloomin' row with the missus ter-night, an' then when I didn't find you 'ere, an' I kept witin' an' witin'—well,

I fair downright lost my 'air. An' I 'ad two or three pints of four 'alf, an'—well, I dunno—'

'Never mind, old cock. I can stand more than thet as long as yer loves me.'

He kissed her and they were quite friends again. But the little quarrel had another effect which was worse for Liza. When she woke up next morning she noticed a slight soreness over the ridge of bone under the left eye, and on looking in the glass saw that it was black and blue and green. She bathed it, but it remained, and seemed to get more marked. She was terrified lest people should see it, and kept indoors all day; but next morning it was blacker than ever. She went to the factory with her hat over her eyes and her head bent down; she escaped observation, but on the way home she was not so lucky. The sharp eyes of some girls noticed it first.

'Wot's the matter with yer eye?' asked one of them.

'Me?' answered Liza, putting her hand up as if in ignorance. 'Nothin' thet I knows of.'

Two or three young men were standing by, and hearing the girl, looked up.

'Why, yer've got a black eye, Liza!'

'Me? I ain't got no black eye!'

'Yus you 'ave; 'ow d'yer get it?'

'I dunno,' said Liza. 'I didn't know I 'ad one.'

'Garn! tell us another!' was the answer. 'One doesn't git a black eye without knowin' 'ow they got it.'

'Well, I did fall against the chest of drawers yesterday; I suppose I must 'ave got it then.'

'Oh yes, we believe thet, don't we?'

'I didn't know 'e was so 'andy with 'is dukes, did you, Ted?' asked one man of another.

Liza felt herself grow red to the tips of her toes.

'Who?' she asked.

'Never you mind; nobody you know.'

At that moment Jim's wife passed and looked at her with a scowl. Liza wished herself a hundred miles away, and blushed more violently than ever.

'Wot are yer blushin' abaht?' ingenuously asked one of the girls.

And they all looked from her to Mrs. Blakeston and back again. Someone said: "Ow abaht our Sunday boots on now?' And a titter went through them. Liza's nerve deserted her; she could think of nothing to say, and a sob burst from her. To hide the tears which were coming from her eyes she turned away and walked homewards. Immediately a great shout of laughter broke from the group, and she heard them positively screaming till she got into her own house.

XI

A FEW DAYS afterwards Liza was talking with Sally, who did not seem very much happier than when Liza had last seen her.

"E ain't wot I thought 'e wos,' she said. 'I don't mind sayin' thet; but 'e 'as a lot ter put up with; I expect I'm rather tryin' sometimes, an' 'e means well. P'raps 'e'll be kinder like when the biby's born.'

'Cheer up, old gal,' answered Liza, who had seen something of the lives of many married couples; 'it won't seem so bad after yer gets used to it; it's a bit disappointin' at fust, but yer gits not ter mind it.'

After a little Sally said she must go and see about her husband's tea. She said good-bye, and then rather awkwardly:

'Say, Liza, tike care of yerself!'

'Tike care of meself—why?' asked Liza, in surprise.

'Yer know wot I mean.'

'Na, I'm darned if I do.'

'Thet there Mrs. Blakeston, she's lookin' aht for you.'

'Mrs. Blakeston!' Liza was startled.

'Yus; she says she's goin' ter give you somethin' if she can git 'old on yer. I should advise yer ter tike care.'

'Me?' said Liza.

Sally looked away, so as not to see the other's face.

'She says as 'ow yer've been messin' abaht with 'er old man.'

Liza didn't say anything, and Sally, repeating her good-bye, slid off.

Liza felt a chill run through her. She had several times noticed a scowl and a look of anger on Mrs. Blakeston's face, and she had avoided her as much as possible; but she had no idea that the woman meant to do anything to her. She was very frightened, a cold sweat broke out over her face. If Mrs. Blakeston got hold of her she would be helpless, she was so small and weak, while the other was strong and muscular. Liza wondered what she would do if she did catch her.

That night she told Jim, and tried to make a joke of it.

'I say, Jim, your missus—she says she's goin' ter give me socks if she catches me.'

'My missus! 'Ow d'yer know?'

'She's been tellin' people in the street.'

'Go' lumme,' said Jim, furious, 'if she dares ter touch a 'air of your 'ead, swop me dicky I'll give 'er sich a 'idin' as she never 'ad before! By God, give me the chanst, an' I would let 'er 'ave it; I'm bloomin' well sick of 'er sulks!' He clenched his fist as he spoke.

Liza was a coward. She could not help thinking of her enemy's threat; it got on her nerves, and she hardly dared go out for fear of meeting her; she would look nervously in front of her, quickly turning round if she saw in the distance anyone resembling Mrs. Blakeston. She dreamed of her at night; she saw the big, powerful form, the heavy, frowning face, and the curiously braided brown hair; and she would wake up with a cry and find herself bathed in sweat.

It was the Saturday afternoon following this, a chill November day, with the roads sloshy, and a grey, comfortless sky that made one's spirits sink. It was about three o'clock, and Liza was coming home from work; she got into Vere Street, and was walking quickly towards her house when she saw Mrs. Blakeston coming towards her. Her heart gave a great jump. Turning, she walked rapidly in the direction she had come; with a screw round of her eyes she saw that she was being followed, and therefore went straight out of Vere Street. She went right round, meaning to get into the street from the other end and, unobserved, slip into her house, which was then quite close; but she dared not risk it immediately for fear Mrs. Blakeston should still be there; so she waited about for half an hour. It seemed an age. Finally, taking her courage in both hands, she turned the corner and entered Vere Street. She nearly ran into the arms of Mrs. Blakeston, who was standing close to the public-house door.

Liza gave a little cry, and the woman said, with a sneer:

'Yer didn't expect ter see me, did yer?'

Liza did not answer, but tried to walk past her. Mrs. Blakeston stepped forward and blocked her way.

'Yer seem ter be in a mighty fine 'urry,' she said.

'Yus, I've got ter git 'ome,' said Liza, again trying to pass.

'But supposin' I don't let yer?' remarked Mrs. Blakeston, preventing her from moving.

'Why don't yer leave me alone?' Liza said. 'I ain't interferin' with you!'

'Not interferin' with me, aren't yer? I like thet!'

'Let me go by,' said Liza. 'I don't want ter talk ter you.'

'Na, I know thet,' said the other; 'but I want ter talk ter you, an' I shan't let yer go until I've said wot I wants ter sy.'

Liza looked round for help. At the beginning of the altercation the loafers about the public-house had looked up with interest, and gradually gathered round in a little circle. Passers-by had joined in, and a number of other people in the street, seeing the crowd, added themselves to it to see what was going on. Liza saw that all eyes were fixed on her, the men amused and excited, the women unsympathetic, rather virtuously indignant. Liza wanted to ask for help, but there were so many people, and they all seemed so much against her, that she had not the courage to. So, having surveyed the crowd, she turned her eyes to Mrs. Blakeston, and stood in front of her, trembling a little, and very white.

'Na, 'e ain't there,' said Mrs. Blakeston, sneeringly, 'so yer needn't look for 'im.'

'I dunno wot yer mean,' answered Liza, 'an' I want ter go away. I ain't done nothin' ter you.'

'Not done nothin' ter me?' furiously repeated the woman. 'I'll tell yer wot yer've done ter me—you've robbed me of my 'usbind, you 'ave. I never 'ad a word with my 'usbind until you took 'im from me. An' now it's all you with 'im. 'E's got no time for 'is wife an' family—it's all you. An' 'is money, too. I never git a penny of it; if it weren't for the little bit I 'ad saved up in the siving-bank, me an' my children 'ud be starvin' now! An' all through you!' She shook her fist at her.

'I never 'ad any money from anyone.'

'Don' talk ter me; I know yer did. Yer dirty bitch! You oughter be ishimed of yourself tikin' a married man from 'is family, an' 'im old enough ter be yer father.'

'She's right there!' said one or two of the onlooking women. 'There can't be no good in 'er if she tikes somebody else's 'usbind.'

'I'll give it yer!' proceeded Mrs. Blakeston, getting more hot and excited, brandishing her fist, and speaking in a loud voice, hoarse with rage. 'Oh, I've been tryin' ter git 'old on yer this four weeks. Why, you're a prostitute—that's wot you are!'

'I'm not!' answered Liza indignantly.

'Yus, you are,' repeated Mrs. Blakeston, advancing menacingly, so that Liza shrank back. 'An' wot's more, 'e treats yer like one. I know 'oo give yer thet black eye; thet shows what 'e thinks of yer! An' serve yer bloomin' well right if 'e'd give yer one in both eyes!'

Mrs. Blakeston stood close in front of her, her heavy jaw protruded and the frown of her eyebrows dark and stern. For a moment she stood silent, contemplating Liza, while the surrounders looked on in breathless interest.

'Yer dirty little bitch, you!' she said at last. 'Tike that!' and with her open hand she gave her a sharp smack on the cheek.

Liza started back with a cry and put her hand up to her face.

'An' tike thet!' added Mrs. Blakeston, repeating the blow. Then, gathering up the spittle in her mouth, she spat in Liza's face.

Liza sprang on her, and with her hands spread out like claws buried her nails in the woman's face and drew them down her cheeks. Mrs. Blakeston caught hold of her hair with both hands and tugged at it as hard as she could. But they were immediately separated.

"Ere, 'old 'ard!' said some of the men. 'Fight it aht fair and square. Don't go scratchin' and maulin' like thet.'

'I'll fight 'er, I don't mind!' shouted Mrs. Blakeston, tucking up her sleeves and savagely glaring at her opponent.

Liza stood in front of her, pale and trembling; as she looked at her enemy, and saw the long red marks of her nails, with blood coming from one or two of them, she shrank back.

'I don't want ter fight,' she said hoarsely.

'Na, I don't suppose yer do,' hissed the other, 'but yer'll damn well 'ave ter!'

'She's ever so much bigger than me; I've got no chanst,' added Liza tearfully.

'You should 'ave thought of thet before. Come on!' and with these words Mrs. Blakeston rushed upon her. She hit her with both fists one after the other. Liza did not try to guard herself, but imitating the woman's motion, hit out with her own fists; and for a minute or two they continued thus, raining blows on one another with the same windmill motion of the arms. But Liza could not stand against the other woman's weight; the blows came down heavy and rapid all over her face and head. She put up her hands to cover her face and turned her head away, while Mrs. Blakeston kept on hitting mercilessly.

'Time!' shouted some of the men—'Time!' and Mrs. Blakeston stopped to rest herself.

'It don't seem 'ardly fair to set them two on tergether. Liza's got no chanst against a big woman like thet,' said a man among the crowd.

'Well, it's er' own fault,' answered a woman; 'she didn't oughter mess about with 'er 'usbind.'

'Well, I don't think it's right,' added another man. 'She's gettin' it too much.'

'An' serve 'er right too!' said one of the women. 'She deserves all she gets an' a damn sight more inter the bargain.'

'Quite right,' put in a third; 'a woman's got no right ter tike someone's 'usbind from 'er. An' if she does she's bloomin' lucky if she gits off with a 'idin'—thet's wot I think.'

'So do I. But I wouldn't 'ave thought it of Liza. I never thought she was a wrong 'un.'

'Pretty specimen she is!' said a little dark woman, who looked like a Jewess. 'If she messed abaht with my old man, I'd stick 'er—I swear I would!'

'Now she's been carryin' on with one, she'll try an' git others—you see if she don't.'

'She'd better not come round my 'ouse; I'll soon give 'er wot for.'

Meanwhile Liza was standing at one corner of the ring, trembling all over and crying bitterly. One of her eyes was bunged up, and her hair, all dishevelled, was hanging down over her face. Two young fellows, who had constituted themselves her seconds, were standing in front of her, offering rather ironical comfort. One of them had taken the bottom corners of her apron and was fanning her with it, while the other was showing her how to stand and hold her arms.

'You stand up to 'er, Liza,' he was saying; 'there ain't no good funkin' it, you'll simply get it all the worse. You 'it 'er back. Give 'er one on the boko, like this—see; yer must show a bit of pluck, yer know.'

Liza tried to check her sobs.

'Yus, 'it 'er 'ard, that's wot yer've got ter do,' said the other. 'An' if yer find she's gettin' the better on yer, you close on 'er and catch 'old of 'er 'air and scratch 'er.'

'You've marked 'er with yer nails, Liza. By gosh, you did fly on her when she spat at yer! thet's the way ter do the job!'

Then turning to his fellow, he said:

'D'yer remember thet fight as old Mother Cregg 'ad with another woman in the street last year?'

'Na,' he answered, 'I never saw thet.'

'It was a cawker; an' the cops come in and took 'em both off ter quod.'

Liza wished the policemen would come and take her off; she would willingly have gone to prison to escape the fiend in front of her; but no help came.

'Time's up!' shouted the referee. 'Fire away!'

'Tike care of the cops!' shouted a man.

'There's no fear abaht them,' answered somebody else. 'They always keeps out of the way when there's anythin' goin' on.'

'Fire away!'

Mrs. Blakeston attacked Liza madly; but the girl stood up bravely, and as well as she could gave back the blows she received. The spectators grew tremendously excited.

'Got 'im again!' they shouted. 'Give it 'er, Liza, thet's a good 'un!— 'it 'er 'ard!'

'Two ter one on the old 'un!' shouted a sporting gentleman; but Liza found no backers.

'Ain't she standin' up well now she's roused?' cried someone.

'Oh, she's got some pluck in 'er, she 'as!'

'Thet's a knock-aht!' they shouted as Mrs. Blakeston brought her fist down on to Liza's nose; the girl staggered back, and blood began to flow. Then, losing all fear, mad with rage, she made a rush on her enemy, and rained down blows all over her nose and eyes and mouth. The woman recoiled at the sudden violence of the onslaught, and the men cried:

'By God, the little 'un's gettin' the best of it!'

But quickly recovering herself the woman closed with Liza, and dug her nails into her flesh. Liza caught hold of her hair and pulled with all her might, and turning her teeth on Mrs. Blakeston tried to bite her. And thus for a minute they swayed about, scratching, tearing, biting, sweat and blood pouring down their faces, and their eyes fixed on one another, bloodshot and full of rage. The audience shouted and cheered and clapped their hands.

'Wot the 'ell's up 'ere?'

'I sy, look there,' said some of the women in a whisper. 'It's the 'usbind!'

He stood on tiptoe and looked over the crowd.

'My Gawd,' he said, 'it's Liza!'

Then roughly pushing the people aside, he made his way through the crowd into the centre, and thrusting himself between the two women, tore them apart. He turned furiously on his wife.

'By Gawd, I'll give yer somethin' for this!'

And for a moment they all three stood silently looking at one another.

Another man had been attracted by the crowd, and he, too, pushed his way through.

'Come 'ome, Liza,' he said.

'Tom!'

He took hold of her arm, and led her through the people, who gave way to let her pass. They walked silently through the street, Tom very grave, Liza weeping bitterly.

'Oh, Tom,' she sobbed after a while, 'I couldn't 'elp it!' Then, when her tears permitted, 'I did love 'im so!'

When they got to the door she plaintively said: 'Come in,' and he followed her to her room. Here she sank on to a chair, and gave herself up to her tears.

Tom wetted the end of a towel and began wiping her face, grimy with blood and tears. She let him do it, just moaning amid her sobs:

'You are good ter me, Tom.'

'Cheer up, old gal,' he said kindly, 'it's all over now.'

After a while the excess of crying brought its cessation. She drank some water, and then taking up a broken handglass she looked at herself, saying:

'I am a sight!' and proceeded to wind up her hair. 'You 'ave been good ter me, Tom,' she repeated, her voice still broken with sobs; and as he sat down beside her she took his hand.

'Na, I ain't,' he answered; 'it's only wot anybody 'ud 'ave done.'

'Yer know, Tom,' she said, after a little silence, 'I'm so sorry I spoke cross like when I met yer in the street; you ain't spoke ter me since.'

'Oh, thet's all over now, old lidy, we needn't think of thet.'

'Oh, but I 'ave treated yer bad. I'm a regular wrong 'un, I am.'

He pressed her hand without speaking.

'I say, Tom,' she began, after another pause. 'Did yer know thet— well, you know—before ter-day?'

He blushed as he answered:

'Yus.'

She spoke very sadly and slowly.

'I thought yer did; yer seemed so cut up like when I used to meet yer. Yer did love me then, Tom, didn't yer?'

'I do now, dearie,' he answered.

'Ah, it's too lite now,' she sighed.

'D'yer know, Liza,' he said, 'I just abaht kicked the life aht of a feller 'cause 'e said you was messin' abaht with—with 'im.'

'An' yer knew I was?'

'Yus—but I wasn't goin' ter 'ave anyone say it before me.'

'They've all rounded on me except you, Tom. I'd 'ave done better if I'd tiken you when you arst me; I shouldn't be where I am now, if I 'ad.'

'Well, won't yer now? Won't yer 'ave me now?'

'Me? After wot's 'appened?'

'Oh, I don't mind abaht thet. Thet don't matter ter me if you'll marry me. I fair can't live without yer, Liza—won't yer?'

She groaned.

'Na, I can't, Tom, it wouldn't be right.'

'Why, not, if I don't mind?'

'Tom,' she said, looking down, almost whispering, 'I'm like that—you know!'

'Wot d'yer mean?'

She could scarcely utter the words—

'I think I'm in the family wy.'

He paused a moment; then spoke again.

'Well—I don't mind, if yer'll only marry me.'

'Na, I can't, Tom,' she said, bursting into tears; 'I can't, but you are so good ter me; I'd do anythin' ter mike it up ter you.'

She put her arms round his neck and slid on to his knees.

'Yer know, Tom, I couldn't marry yer now; but anythin' else—if yer wants me ter do anythin' else, I'll do it if it'll mike you 'appy.'

He did not understand, but only said:

'You're a good gal, Liza,' and bending down he kissed her gravely on the forehead.

Then with a sigh he lifted her down, and getting up left her alone. For a while she sat where he left her, but as she thought of all she had gone through her loneliness and misery overcame her, the tears welled forth, and throwing herself on the bed she buried her face in the pillows.

❦

Jim stood looking at Liza as she went off with Tom, and his wife watched him jealously.

'It's 'er you're thinkin' abaht. Of course you'd 'ave liked ter tike 'er 'ome yerself, I know, an' leave me to shift for myself.'

'Shut up!' said Jim, angrily turning upon her.

'I shan't shut up,' she answered, raising her voice. 'Nice 'usbind you are. Go' lumme, as good as they mike 'em! Nice thing ter go an' leave yer wife and children for a thing like thet! At your age, too! You oughter be ashimed of yerself. Why, it's like messin' abaht with your own daughter!'

'By God!'—he ground his teeth with rage—'if yer don't leave me alone, I'll kick the life aht of yer!'

'There!' she said, turning to the crowd—'there, see 'ow 'e treats me! Listen ter that! I've been 'is wife for twenty years, an' yer couldn't 'ave 'ad a better wife, an' I've bore 'im nine children, yet say nothin' of a miscarriage, an' I've got another comin', an' thet's 'ow 'e treats me! Nice 'usbind, ain't it?' She looked at him scornfully, then again at the surrounders as if for their opinion.

'Well, I ain't goin' ter stay 'ere all night; get aht of the light!' He pushed aside the people who barred his way, and the one or two who growled a little at his roughness, looking at his angry face, were afraid to complain.

'Look at 'im!' said his wife. "E's afraid, 'e is. See 'im slinkin' awy like a bloomin' mongrel with 'is tail between 'is legs. Ugh!' She walked just behind him, shouting and brandishing her arms.

'Yer dirty beast, you,' she yelled, 'ter go foolin' abaht with a little girl! Ugh! I wish yer wasn't my 'usbind; I wouldn't be seen drowned with yer, if I could 'elp it. Yer mike me sick ter look at yer.'

The crowd followed them on both sides of the road, keeping at a discreet distance, but still eagerly listening.

Jim turned on her once or twice and said:

'Shut up!'

But it only made her more angry. 'I tell yer I shan't shut up. I don't care 'oo knows it, you're a ——, you are! I'm ashimed the children should 'ave such a father as you. D'yer think I didn't know wot you was up ter them nights you was awy—courtin', yus, courtin'? You're a nice man, you are!'

Jim did not answer her, but walked on. At last he turned round to the people who were following and said:

'Na then, wot d'you want 'ere? You jolly well clear, or I'll give some of you somethin'!'

They were mostly boys and women, and at his words they shrank back.

"E's afraid ter sy anythin' ter me,' jeered Mrs. Blakeston. "E's a beauty!'

Jim entered his house, and she followed him till they came up into their room. Polly was giving the children their tea. They all started up as they saw their mother with her hair and clothes in disorder, blotches of dried blood on her face, and the long scratch-marks.

'Oh, mother,' said Polly, 'wot is the matter?'

''E's the matter.' she answered, pointing to her husband. 'It's through 'im I've got all this. Look at yer father, children; e's a father to be proud of, leavin' yer ter starve an' spendin' 'is week's money on a dirty little strumper.'

Jim felt easier now he had not got so many strange eyes on him.

'Now, look 'ere,' he said, 'I'm not goin' ter stand this much longer, so just you tike care.'

'I ain't frightened of yer. I know yer'd like ter kill me, but yer'll get strung up if you do.'

'Na, I won't kill yer, but if I 'ave any more of your sauce I'll do the next thing to it.'

'Touch me if yer dare,' she said, 'I'll 'ave the law on you. An' I shouldn't mind 'ow many month's 'ard you got.'

'Be quiet!' he said, and, closing his hand, gave her a heavy blow in the chest that made her stagger.

'Oh, you ——!' she screamed.

She seized the poker, and in a fury of rage rushed at him.

'Would yer?' he said, catching hold of it and wrenching it from her grasp. He threw it to the end of the room and grappled with her. For a moment they swayed about from side to side, then with an effort he lifted her off her feet and threw her to the ground; but she caught hold of him and he came down on the top of her. She screamed as her head thumped down on the floor, and the children, who were standing huddled up in a corner, terrified, screamed too.

Jim caught hold of his wife's head and began beating it against the floor.

She cried out: 'You're killing me! Help! help!'

Polly in terror ran up to her father and tried to pull him off.

'Father, don't 'it 'er! Anythin' but thet—for God's sike!'

'Leave me alone,' he said, 'or I'll give you somethin' too.'

She caught hold of his arm, but Jim, still kneeling on his wife, gave Polly a backhanded blow which sent her staggering back.

'Tike that!'

Polly ran out of the room, downstairs to the first-floor front, where two men and two women were sitting at tea.

'Oh, come an' stop father!' she cried. ''E's killin' mother!'

'Why, wot's 'e doin'?'

'Oh, 'e's got 'er on the floor, an' 'e's bangin' 'er 'ead. 'E's payin' 'er aht for givin' Liza Kemp a 'idin'.'

One of the women started up and said to her husband:

'Come on, John, you go an' stop it.'

'Don't you, John,' said the other man. 'When a man's givin' 'is wife socks it's best not ter interfere.'

'But 'e's killin' 'er,' repeated Polly, trembling with fright.

'Garn!' rejoined the man, 'she'll git over it; an' p'raps she deserves it, for all you know.'

John sat undecided, looking now at Polly, now at his wife, and now at the other man.

'Oh, do be quick—for God's sike!' said Polly.

At that moment a sound as of something smashing was heard upstairs, and a woman's shriek. Mrs. Blakeston, in an effort to tear herself away from her husband, had knocked up against the wash-hand stand, and the whole thing had crashed down.

'Go on, John,' said the wife.

'No, I ain't goin'; I shan't do no good, an' 'e'll only round on me.'

'Well, you are a bloomin' lot of cowards, thet's all I can say,' indignantly answered the wife. 'But I ain't goin' ter see a woman murdered; I'll go an' stop 'im.'

With that she ran upstairs and threw open the door. Jim was still kneeling on his wife, hitting her furiously, while she was trying to protect her head and face with her hands.

'Leave off!' shouted the woman.

Jim looked up. ''Oo the devil are you?' he said.

'Leave off, I tell yer. Aren't yer ashimed of yerself, knockin' a woman abaht like that?' And she sprang at him, seizing his fist.

'Let go,' he said, 'or I'll give you a bit.'

'Yer'd better not touch me,' she said. 'Yer dirty coward! Why, look at 'er, she's almost senseless.'

Jim stopped and gazed at his wife. He got up and gave her a kick.

'Git up!' he said; but she remained huddled up on the floor, moaning feebly. The woman from downstairs went on her knees and took her head in her arms.

'Never mind, Mrs. Blakeston. 'E's not goin' ter touch yer. 'Ere, drink this little drop of water.' Then turning to Jim, with infinite disdain: 'Yer dirty blackguard, you! If I was a man I'd give you something for this.'

Jim put on his hat and went out, slamming the door, while the woman shouted after him: 'Good riddance!'

'Lord love yer,' said Mrs. Kemp, 'wot is the matter?'

She had just come in, and opening the door had started back in surprise at seeing Liza on the bed, all tears. Liza made no answer, but cried as if her heart were breaking. Mrs. Kemp went up to her and tried to look at her face.

'Don't cry, dearie; tell us wot it is.'

Liza sat up and dried her eyes.

'I am so un'appy!'

'Wot 'ave yer been doin' ter yer fice? My!'

'Nothin'.'

'Garn! Yer can't 'ave got a fice like thet all by itself.'

'I 'ad a bit of a scrimmage with a woman dahn the street,' sobbed out Liza.

'She 'as give yer a doin'; an' yer all upset—an' look at yer eye! I brought in a little bit of stike for ter-morrer's dinner; you just cut a bit off an' put it over yer optic, that'll soon put it right. I always used ter do thet myself when me an' your poor father 'ad words.'

'Oh, I'm all over in a tremble, an' my 'ead, oo, my 'ead does feel bad!'

'I know wot yer want,' remarked Mrs. Kemp, nodding her head, 'an' it so 'appens as I've got the very thing with me.' She pulled a medicine bottle out of her pocket, and taking out the cork smelt it. 'Thet's good stuff, none of your firewater or your methylated spirit. I don't often indulge in sich things, but when I do I likes to 'ave the best.'

She handed the bottle to Liza, who took a mouthful and gave it her back; she had a drink herself, and smacked her lips.

'Thet's good stuff. 'Ave a drop more.'

'Na,' said Liza, 'I ain't used ter drinkin' spirits.'

She felt dull and miserable, and a heavy pain throbbed through her head. If she could only forget!

'Na, I know you're not, but, bless your soul, thet won' 'urt yer. It'll do you no end of good. Why, often when I've been feelin' thet done up thet I didn't know wot ter do with myself, I've just 'ad a little drop of whisky or gin—I'm not partic'ler wot spirit it is—an' it's pulled me up wonderful.'

Liza took another sip, a slightly longer one; it burnt as it went down her throat, and sent through her a feeling of comfortable warmth.

'I really do think it's doin' me good,' she said, wiping her eyes and giving a sigh of relief as the crying ceased.

'I knew it would. Tike my word for it, if people took a little drop of spirits in time, there'd be much less sickness abaht.'

They sat for a while in silence, then Mrs. Kemp remarked:

'Yer know, Liza, it strikes me as 'ow we could do with a drop more. You not bein' in the 'abit of tikin' anythin' I only brought just this little drop for me; an' it ain't took us long ter finish thet up. But as you're an invalid like we'll git a little more this time; it's sure ter turn aht useful.'

'But you ain't got nothin' ter put it in.'

'Yus, I 'ave,' answered Mrs. Kemp; 'there's thet bottle as they gives me at the 'orspital. Just empty the medicine aht into the pile, an' wash it aht, an' I'll tike it round to the pub myself.'

Liza, when she was left alone, began to turn things over in her mind. She did not feel so utterly unhappy as before, for the things she had gone through seemed further away.

'After all,' she said, 'it don't so much matter.'

Mrs. Kemp came in.

''Ave a little drop more, Liza.' she said.

'Well, I don't mind if I do. I'll get some tumblers, shall I? There's no mistike abaht it,' she added, when she had taken a little, 'it do buck yer up.'

'You're right, Liza—you're right. An' you wanted it badly. Fancy you 'avin' a fight with a woman! Oh, I've 'ad some in my day, but then I wasn't a little bit of a thing like you is. I wish I'd been there, I wouldn't 'ave stood by an' looked on while my daughter was gettin' the worst of it; although I'm turned sixty-five, an' gettin' on for sixty-six, I'd 'ave said to 'er: "If you touch my daughter you'll 'ave me ter deal with, so just look aht!"'

She brandished her glass, and that reminding her, she refilled it and Liza's.

'Ah, Liza,' she remarked, 'you're a chip of the old block. Ter see you settin' there an' 'avin' your little drop, it mikes me feel as if I was livin' a better life. Yer used ter be rather 'ard on me, Liza, 'cause I took a little drop on Saturday nights. An', mind, I don't sy I didn't tike a little drop too much sometimes—accidents will occur even in the best regulated of families, but wot I say is this—it's good stuff, I say, an' it don't 'urt yer.'

'Buck up, old gal!' said Liza, filling the glasses, 'no 'eel-taps. I feel like a new woman now. I was thet dahn in the dumps—well, I shouldn't 'ave cared if I'd been at the bottom of the river, an' thet's the truth.'

'You don't sy so,' replied her affectionate mother.

'Yus, I do, an' I mean it too, but I don't feel like thet now. You're right, mother, when you're in trouble there's nothin' like a bit of spirits.'

'Well, if I don't know, I dunno 'oo does, for the trouble I've 'ad, it 'ud be enough to kill many women. Well, I've 'ad thirteen children, an' you can think wot thet was; everyone I 'ad I used ter sy I wouldn't 'ave no more—but one does, yer know. You'll 'ave a family some day, Liza, an' I shouldn't wonder if you didn't 'ave as many as me. We come from a very prodigal family, we do, we've all gone in ter double figures, except your Aunt Mary, who only 'ad three—but then she wasn't married, so it didn't count, like.'

They drank each other's health. Everything was getting blurred to Liza, she was losing her head.

'Yus,' went on Mrs. Kemp, 'I've 'ad thirteen children an' I'm proud of it. As your poor dear father used ter sy, it shows as 'ow one's got the blood of a Briton in one. Your poor dear father, 'e was a great 'and at speakin' 'e was: 'e used ter speak at parliamentary meetin's—I really believe 'e'd 'ave been a Member of Parliament if 'e'd been alive now. Well, as I was sayin', your father 'e used ter sy, "None of your small families for me, I don't approve of them," says 'e. 'E was a man of very 'igh principles, an' by politics 'e was a Radical. "No," says 'e, when 'e got talkin', "when a man can 'ave a family risin' into double figures, it shows 'e's got the backbone of a Briton in 'im. That's the stuff as 'as built up England's nime and glory! When one thinks of the mighty British Hempire," says 'e, "on which the sun never sets from mornin' till night, one 'as ter be proud of 'isself, an' one 'as ter do one's duty in thet walk of life in which it 'as pleased Providence ter set one—an' every man's fust duty is ter get as many children as 'e bloomin' well can." Lord love yer—'e could talk, I can tell yer.'

'Drink up, mother,' said Liza. 'You're not 'alf drinkin'.' She flourished the bottle. 'I don't care a twopanny 'ang for all them blokes; I'm quite 'appy, an' I don't want anythin' else.'

'I can see you're my daughter now,' said Mrs. Kemp. 'When yer used ter round on me I used ter think as 'ow if I 'adn't carried yer for nine months, it must 'ave been some mistike, an' yer wasn't my daughter at all. When you come ter think of it, a man 'e don't know if it's 'is child or somebody else's, but yer can't deceive a woman like thet. Yer couldn't palm off somebody else's kid on 'er.'

'I am beginnin' ter feel quite lively,' said Liza. 'I dunno wot it is, but I feel as if I wanted to laugh till I fairly split my sides.'

And she began to sing: 'For 'e's a jolly good feller—for 'e's a jolly good feller!'

Her dress was all disarranged; her face covered with the scars of scratches, and clots of blood had fixed under her nose; her eye had swollen up so that it was nearly closed, and red; her hair was hanging over her face and shoulders, and she laughed stupidly and leered with heavy, sodden ugliness.

'Disy, Disy! I can't afford a kerridge. But you'll look neat, on the seat Of a bicycle mide for two.'

She shouted out the tunes, beating time on the table, and her mother, grinning, with her thin, grey hair hanging dishevelled over her head, joined in with her weak, cracked voice—

'Oh, dem golden kippers, oh!'

Then Liza grew more melancholy and broke into 'Auld Lang Syne'.

> *'Should old acquaintance be forgot. And never brought to mind?*
> *For old lang syne'.*

Finally they both grew silent, and in a little while there came a snore from Mrs. Kemp; her head fell forward to her chest; Liza tumbled from her chair on to the bed, and sprawling across it fell asleep.

> *'Although I am drunk and bad, be you kind, Cast a glance at this*
> *heart which is bewildered and distressed. O God, take away from my*
> *mind my cry and my complaint. Offer wine, and take sorrow from*
> *my remembrance. Offer wine.'*

XII

ABOUT THE MIDDLE of the night Liza woke; her mouth was hot and dry, and a sharp, cutting pain passed through her head as she moved. Her mother had evidently roused herself, for she was lying in bed by her side, partially undressed, with all the bedclothes rolled round her. Liza shivered in the cold night, and taking off some of her things— her boots, her skirt, and jacket—got right into bed; she tried to get some of the blanket from her mother, but as she pulled Mrs. Kemp gave a growl in her sleep and drew the clothes more tightly round her. So Liza put over herself her skirt and a shawl, which was lying over the end of the bed, and tried to go to sleep.

But she could not; her head and hands were broiling hot, and she was terribly thirsty; when she lifted herself up to get a drink of water such a pang went through her head that she fell back on the bed groaning, and lay there with beating heart. And strange pains that she did not know went through her. Then a cold shiver seemed to rise in the very marrow of her bones and run down every artery and vein, freezing the blood; her skin puckered up, and drawing up her legs she lay huddled together in a heap, the shawl wrapped tightly round her, and her teeth chattering. Shivering, she whispered:

'Oh, I'm so cold, so cold. Mother, give me some clothes; I shall die of the cold. Oh, I'm freezing!'

But after awhile the cold seemed to give way, and a sudden heat seized her, flushing her face, making her break out into perspiration, so that she threw everything off and loosened the things about her neck.

'Give us a drink,' she said. 'Oh, I'd give anythin' for a little drop of water!'

There was no one to hear; Mrs. Kemp continued to sleep heavily, occasionally breaking out into a little snore.

Liza remained there, now shivering with cold, now panting for breath, listening to the regular, heavy breathing by her side, and in her pain she sobbed. She pulled at her pillow and said:

'Why can't I go to sleep? Why can't I sleep like 'er?'

And the darkness was awful; it was a heavy, ghastly blackness, that seemed palpable, so that it frightened her and she looked for relief at the faint light glimmering through the window from a distant street-lamp. She thought the night would never end—the minutes seemed like hours, and she wondered how she should live through till morning. And strange pains that she did not know went through her.

Still the night went on, the darkness continued, cold and horrible, and her mother breathed loudly and steadily by her side.

At last with the morning sleep came; but the sleep was almost worse than the wakefulness, for it was accompanied by ugly, disturbing dreams. Liza thought she was going through the fight with her enemy, and Mrs. Blakeston grew enormous in size, and multiplied, so that every way she turned the figure confronted her. And she began running away, and she ran and ran till she found herself reckoning up an account she had puzzled over in the morning, and she did it backwards and forwards, upwards and downwards, starting here, starting there, and the figures got mixed up with other things, and she had to begin over again, and everything jumbled up, and her head whirled, till finally, with a start, she woke.

The darkness had given way to a cold, grey dawn, her uncovered legs were chilled to the bone, and by her side she heard again the regular, nasal breathing of the drunkard.

For a long while she lay where she was, feeling very sick and ill, but better than in the night. At last her mother woke.

'Liza!' she called.

'Yus, mother,' she answered feebly.

'Git us a cup of tea, will yer?'

'I can't, mother, I'm ill.'

'Garn!' said Mrs. Kemp, in surprise. Then looking at her: 'Swop me bob, wot's up with yer? Why, yer cheeks is flushed, an' yer forehead—it is 'ot! Wot's the matter with yer, gal?'

'I dunno,' said Liza. 'I've been thet bad all night, I thought I was goin' ter die.'

'I know wot it is,' said Mrs. Kemp, shaking her head; 'the fact is, you ain't used ter drinkin', an' of course it's upset yer. Now me, why I'm as fresh as a disy. Tike my word, there ain't no good in teetotalism; it finds yer aht in the end, an' it's found you aht.'

Mrs. Kemp considered it a judgment of Providence. She got up and mixed some whisky and water.

"Ere, drink this,' she said. 'When one's 'ad a drop too much at night, there's nothin' like havin' a drop more in the mornin' ter put one right. It just acts like magic.'

'Tike it awy,' said Liza, turning from it in disgust; 'the smell of it gives me the sick. I'll never touch spirits again.'

'Ah, thet's wot we all says sometime in our lives, but we does, an' wot's more we can't do withaht it. Why, me, the 'ard life I've 'ad—' It is unnecessary to repeat Mrs. Kemp's repetitions.

Liza did not get up all day. Tom came to inquire after her, and was told she was very ill. Liza plaintively asked whether anyone else had been, and sighed a little when her mother answered no. But she felt too ill to think much or trouble much about anything. The fever came again as the day wore on, and the pains in her head grew worse. Her mother came to bed, and quickly went off to sleep, leaving Liza to bear her agony alone. She began to have frightful pains all over her, and she held her breath to prevent herself from crying out and waking her mother. She clutched the sheets in her agony, and at last, about six o'clock in the morning, she could bear it no longer, and in the anguish of labour screamed out, and woke her mother.

Mrs. Kemp was frightened out of her wits. Going upstairs she woke the woman who lived on the floor above her. Without hesitating, the good lady put on a skirt and came down.

'She's 'ad a miss,' she said, after looking at Liza. 'Is there anyone you could send to the 'orspital?'

'Na, I dunno 'oo I could get at this hour?'

'Well, I'll git my old man ter go.'

She called her husband, and sent him off. She was a stout, middle-aged woman, rough-visaged and strong-armed. Her name was Mrs. Hodges.

'It's lucky you came ter me,' she said, when she had settled down. 'I go aht nursin', yer know, so I know all abaht it.'

'Well, you surprise me,' said Mrs. Kemp. 'I didn't know as Liza was thet way. She never told me nothin' abaht it.'

'D'yer know 'oo it is 'as done it?'

'Now you ask me somethin' I don't know,' replied Mrs. Kemp. 'But now I come ter think of it, it must be thet there Tom. 'E's been keepin' company with Liza. 'E's a single man, so they'll be able ter get married—thet's somethin'.'

'It ain't Tom,' feebly said Liza.

'Not 'im; 'oo is it, then?'

Liza did not answer.

'Eh?' repeated the mother, ''oo is it?'

Liza lay still without speaking.

'Never mind, Mrs. Kemp,' said Mrs. Hodges, 'don't worry 'er now; you'll be able ter find aht all abaht it when she gits better.'

For a while the two women sat still, waiting the doctor's coming, and Liza lay gazing vacantly at the wall, panting for breath. Sometimes Jim crossed her mind, and she opened her mouth to call for him, but in her despair she restrained herself.

The doctor came.

'D'you think she's bad, doctor?' asked Mrs. Hodges.

'I'm afraid she is rather,' he answered. 'I'll come in again this evening.'

'Oh, doctor,' said Mrs. Kemp, as he was going, 'could yer give me somethin' for my rheumatics? I'm a martyr to rheumatism, an' these cold days I 'ardly knows wot ter do with myself. An', doctor, could you let me 'ave some beef-tea? My 'usbind's dead, an' of course I can't do no work with my daughter ill like this, an' we're very short—'

The day passed, and in the evening Mrs. Hodges, who had been attending to her own domestic duties, came downstairs again. Mrs. Kemp was on the bed sleeping.

'I was just 'avin' a little nap,' she said to Mrs. Hodges, on waking.

''Ow is the girl?' asked that lady.

'Oh,' answered Mrs. Kemp, 'my rheumatics 'as been thet bad I really 'aven't known wot ter do with myself, an' now Liza can't rub me I'm worse than ever. It is unfortunate thet she should get ill just now when I want so much attendin' ter myself, but there, it's just my luck!'

Mrs. Hodges went over and looked at Liza; she was lying just as when she left in the morning, her cheeks flushed, her mouth open for breath, and tiny beads of sweat stood on her forehead.

''Ow are yer, ducky?' asked Mrs. Hodges; but Liza did not answer.

'It's my belief she's unconscious,' said Mrs. Kemp. 'I've been askin' 'er 'oo it was as done it, but she don't seem to 'ear wot I say. It's been a great shock ter me, Mrs. 'Odges.'

'I believe you,' replied that lady, sympathetically.

'Well, when you come in and said wot it was, yer might 'ave knocked me dahn with a feather. I knew no more than the dead wot 'ad 'appened.'

'I saw at once wot it was,' said Mrs. Hodges, nodding her head.

'Yus, of course, you knew. I expect you've 'ad a great deal of practice one way an' another.'

'You're right, Mrs. Kemp, you're right. I've been on the job now for nearly twenty years, an' if I don't know somethin' abaht it I ought.'

'D'yer finds it pays well?'

'Well, Mrs. Kemp, tike it all in all, I ain't got no grounds for complaint. I'm in the 'abit of askin' five shillings, an' I will say this, I don't think it's too much for wot I do.'

The news of Liza's illness had quickly spread, and more than once in the course of the day a neighbour had come to ask after her. There was a knock at the door now, and Mrs. Hodges opened it. Tom stood on the threshold asking to come in.

'Yus, you can come,' said Mrs. Kemp.

He advanced on tiptoe, so as to make no noise, and for a while stood silently looking at Liza. Mrs. Hodges was by his side.

'Can I speak to 'er?' he whispered.

'She can't 'ear you.'

He groaned.

'D'yer think she'll get arright?' he asked.

Mrs. Hodges shrugged her shoulders.

'I shouldn't like ter give an opinion,' she said, cautiously.

Tom bent over Liza, and, blushing, kissed her; then, without speaking further, went out of the room.

'Thet's the young man as was courtin' 'er,' said Mrs. Kemp, pointing over her shoulder with her thumb.

Soon after the Doctor came.

'Wot do yer think of 'er, doctor?' said Mrs. Hodges, bustling forwards authoritatively in her position of midwife and sick-nurse.

'I'm afraid she's very bad.'

'D'yer think she's goin' ter die?' she asked, dropping her voice to a whisper.

'I'm afraid so!'

As the doctor sat down by Liza's side Mrs. Hodges turned round and significantly nodded to Mrs. Kemp, who put her handkerchief to her eyes. Then she went outside to the little group waiting at the door.

'Wot does the doctor sy?' they asked, among them Tom.

''E says just wot I've been sayin' all along; I knew she wouldn't live.'

And Tom burst out: 'Oh, Liza!'

As she retired a woman remarked:

'Mrs. 'Odges is very clever, I think.'

'Yus,' remarked another, 'she got me through my last confinement simply wonderful. If it come to choosin' between 'em I'd back Mrs. 'Odges against forty doctors.'

'Ter tell yer the truth, so would I. I've never known 'er wrong yet.'

Mrs. Hodges sat down beside Mrs. Kemp and proceeded to comfort her.

'Why don't yer tike a little drop of brandy ter calm yer nerves,

Mrs. Kemp?' she said, 'you want it.'

'I was just feelin' rather faint, an' I couldn't 'elp thinkin' as 'ow two-penneth of whisky 'ud do me good.'

'Na, Mrs. Kemp,' said Mrs. Hodges, earnestly, putting her hand on the other's arm. 'You tike my tip—when you're queer there's nothin' like brandy for pullin' yer togither. I don't object to whisky myself, but as a medicine yer can't beat brandy.'

'Well, I won't set up myself as knowin' better than you Mrs. 'Odges; I'll do wot you think right.'

Quite accidentally there was some in the room, and Mrs. Kemp poured it out for herself and her friend.

'I'm not in the 'abit of tikin' anythin' when I'm aht on business,' she apologized, 'but just ter keep you company I don't mind if I do.'

'Your 'ealth. Mrs. 'Odges.'

'Sime ter you, an' thank yer, Mrs. Kemp.'

Liza lay still, breathing very quietly, her eyes closed. The doctor kept his fingers on her pulse.

'I've been very unfortunate of lite,' remarked Mrs. Hodges, as she licked her lips, 'this mikes the second death I've 'ad in the last ten days—women, I mean, of course I don't count bibies.'

'Yer don't sy so.'

'Of course the other one—well, she was only a prostitute, so it didn't so much matter. It ain't like another woman is it?'

'Na, you're right.'

'Still, one don't like 'em ter die, even if they are thet. One mustn't be too 'ard on 'em.'

'Strikes me you've got a very kind 'eart, Mrs. 'Odges,' said Mrs. Kemp.

'I 'ave thet; an' I often says it 'ud be better for my peace of mind an' my business if I 'adn't. I 'ave ter go through a lot, I do; but I can say this for myself, I always gives satisfaction, an' thet's somethin' as all lidies in my line can't say.'

They sipped their brandy for a while.

'It's a great trial ter me that this should 'ave 'appened,' said Mrs. Kemp, coming to the subject that had been disturbing her for some time. 'Mine's always been a very respectable family, an' such a thing as this 'as never 'appened before. No, Mrs. 'Odges, I was lawfully married in church, an' I've got my marriage lines now ter show I was, an' thet one of my daughters should 'ave gone wrong in this way—well, I can't understand it. I give 'er a good education, an' she 'ad all the comforts of a 'ome. She never wanted for nothin'; I worked myself to the bone ter keep 'er in luxury, an' then thet she should go an' disgrace me like this!'

'I understand wot yer mean. Mrs. Kemp.'

'I can tell you my family was very respectable; an' my 'usband, 'e earned twenty-five shillings a week, an' was in the sime plice seventeen years; an' 'is employers sent a beautiful wreath ter put on 'is coffin; an' they tell me they never 'ad such a good workman an' sich an 'onest man before. An' me! Well, I can sy this—I've done my duty by the girl, an' she's never learnt anythin' but good from me. Of course I ain't always been in wot yer might call flourishing circumstances, but I've always set her a good example, as she could tell yer so 'erself if she wasn't speechless.'

Mrs. Kemp paused for a moment's reflection.

'As they sy in the Bible,' she finished, 'it's enough ter mike one's grey 'airs go dahn into the ground in sorrer. I can show yer my marriage certificate. Of course one doesn't like ter say much, because of course she's very bad; but if she got well I should 'ave given 'er a talkin' ter.'

There was another knock.

'Do go an' see 'oo thet is; I can't, on account of my rheumatics.'

Mrs. Hodges opened the door. It was Jim.

He was very white, and the blackness of his hair and beard, contrasting with the deathly pallor of his face, made him look ghastly. Mrs. Hodges stepped back.

"Oo's 'e?' she said, turning to Mrs. Kemp.

Jim pushed her aside and went up to the bed.

'Doctor, is she very bad?' he asked.

The doctor looked at him questioningly.

Jim whispered: 'It was me as done it. She ain't goin' ter die, is she?'

The doctor nodded.

'O God! wot shall I do? It was my fault! I wish I was dead!'

Jim took the girl's head in his hands, and the tears burst from his eyes.

'She ain't dead yet, is she?'

'She's just living,' said the doctor.

Jim bent down.

'Liza, Liza, speak ter me! Liza, say you forgive me! Oh, speak ter me!'

His voice was full of agony. The doctor spoke.

'She can't hear you.'

'Oh, she must hear me! Liza! Liza!'

He sank on his knees by the bedside.

They all remained silent: Liza lying stiller than ever, her breast unmoved by the feeble respiration, Jim looking at her very mournfully; the doctor grave, with his fingers on the pulse. The two women looked at Jim.

'Fancy it bein' 'im!' said Mrs. Kemp. 'Strike me lucky, ain't 'e a sight!'

'You 'ave got 'er insured, Mrs. Kemp?' asked the midwife. She could bear the silence no longer.

'Trust me fur thet!' replied the good lady. 'I've 'ad 'er insured ever since she was born. Why, only the other dy I was sayin' ter myself thet all thet money 'ad been wisted, but you see it wasn't; yer never know yer luck, you see!'

'Quite right, Mrs. Kemp; I'm a rare one for insurin'. It's a great thing. I've always insured all my children.'

'The way I look on it is this,' said Mrs. Kemp—'wotever yer do when they're alive, an' we all know as children is very tryin' sometimes, you should give them a good funeral when they dies. Thet's my motto, an' I've always acted up to it.'

'Do you deal with Mr. Stearman?' asked Mrs. Hodges.

'No, Mrs. 'Odges, for undertikin' give me Mr. Footley every time. In the black line 'e's fust an' the rest nowhere!'

'Well, thet's very strange now—thet's just wot I think. Mr. Footley does 'is work well, an' 'e's very reasonable. I'm a very old customer of 'is, an' 'e lets me 'ave things as cheap as anybody.'

'Does 'e indeed! Well Mrs. 'Odges if it ain't askin' too much of yer,

I should look upon it as very kind if you'd go an' mike the arrangements for Liza.'

'Why, certainly, Mrs. Kemp. I'm always willin' ter do a good turn to anybody, if I can.'

'I want it done very respectable,' said Mrs. Kemp; 'I'm not goin' ter stint for nothin' for my daughter's funeral. I like plumes, you know, although they is a bit extra.'

'Never you fear, Mrs. Kemp, it shall be done as well as if it was for my own 'usbind, an' I can't say more than thet. Mr. Footley thinks a deal of me, 'e does! Why, only the other dy as I was goin' inter 'is shop 'e says "Good mornin', Mrs. 'Odges." "Good mornin', Mr. Footley," says I. "You've jest come in the nick of time," says 'e. "This gentleman an' myself," pointin' to another gentleman as was standin' there, "we was 'avin' a bit of an argument. Now you're a very intelligent woman, Mrs. 'Odges, and a good customer too." "I can say thet for myself," say I, "I gives yer all the work I can." "I believe you," says 'e. "Well," 'e says, "now which do you think? Does hoak look better than helm, or does helm look better than hoak? Hoak *versus* helm, thet's the question." "Well, Mr. Footley," says I, "for my own private opinion, when you've got a nice brass plite in the middle, an' nice brass 'andles each end, there's nothin' like hoak." "Quite right," says 'e, "thet's wot I think; for coffins give me hoak any day, an' I 'ope," says 'e, "when the Lord sees fit ter call me to 'Imself, I shall be put in a hoak coffin myself." "Amen," says I.'

'I like hoak,' said Mrs. Kemp. 'My poor 'usband 'e 'ad a hoak coffin. We did 'ave a job with 'im, I can tell yer. You know 'e 'ad dropsy, an' 'e swell up—oh, 'e did swell; 'is own mother wouldn't 'ave known 'im. Why, 'is leg swell up till it was as big round as 'is body, swop me bob, it did.'

'Did it indeed!' ejaculated Mrs. Hodges.

'Yus, an' when 'e died they sent the coffin up. I didn't 'ave Mr. Footley at thet time; we didn't live 'ere then, we lived in Battersea, an' all our undertikin' was done by Mr. Brownin'; well, 'e sent the coffin up, an' we got my old man in, but we couldn't get the lid down, he was so swell up. Well, Mr. Brownin', 'e was a great big man, thirteen stone if 'e was a ounce. Well, 'e stood on the coffin, an' a young man 'e 'ad